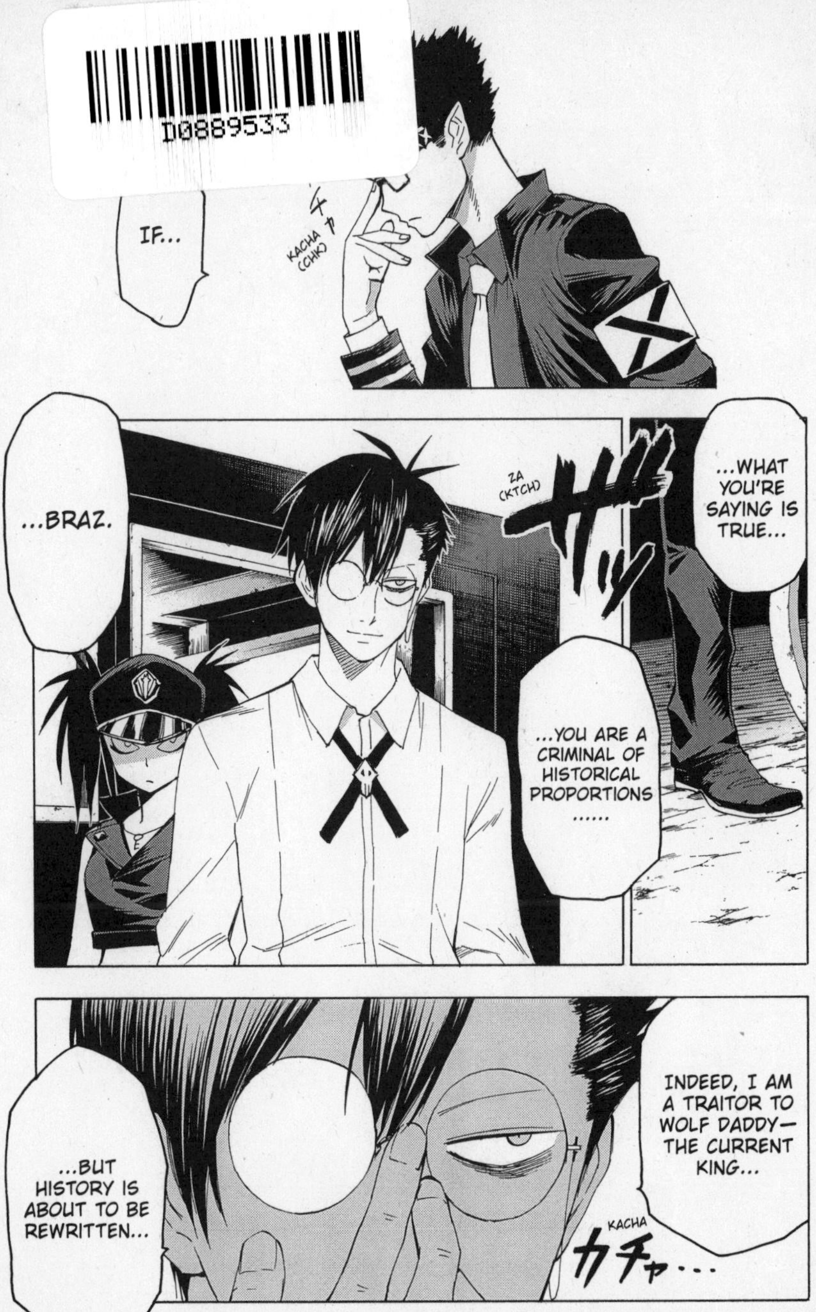
IF...
KACHA (CHK)
ZA (KTCH)
...WHAT YOU'RE SAYING IS TRUE...
...YOU ARE A CRIMINAL OF HISTORICAL PROPORTIONS ......
...BRAZ.
INDEED, I AM A TRAITOR TO WOLF DADDY— THE CURRENT KING...
KACHA
...BUT HISTORY IS ABOUT TO BE REWRITTEN...

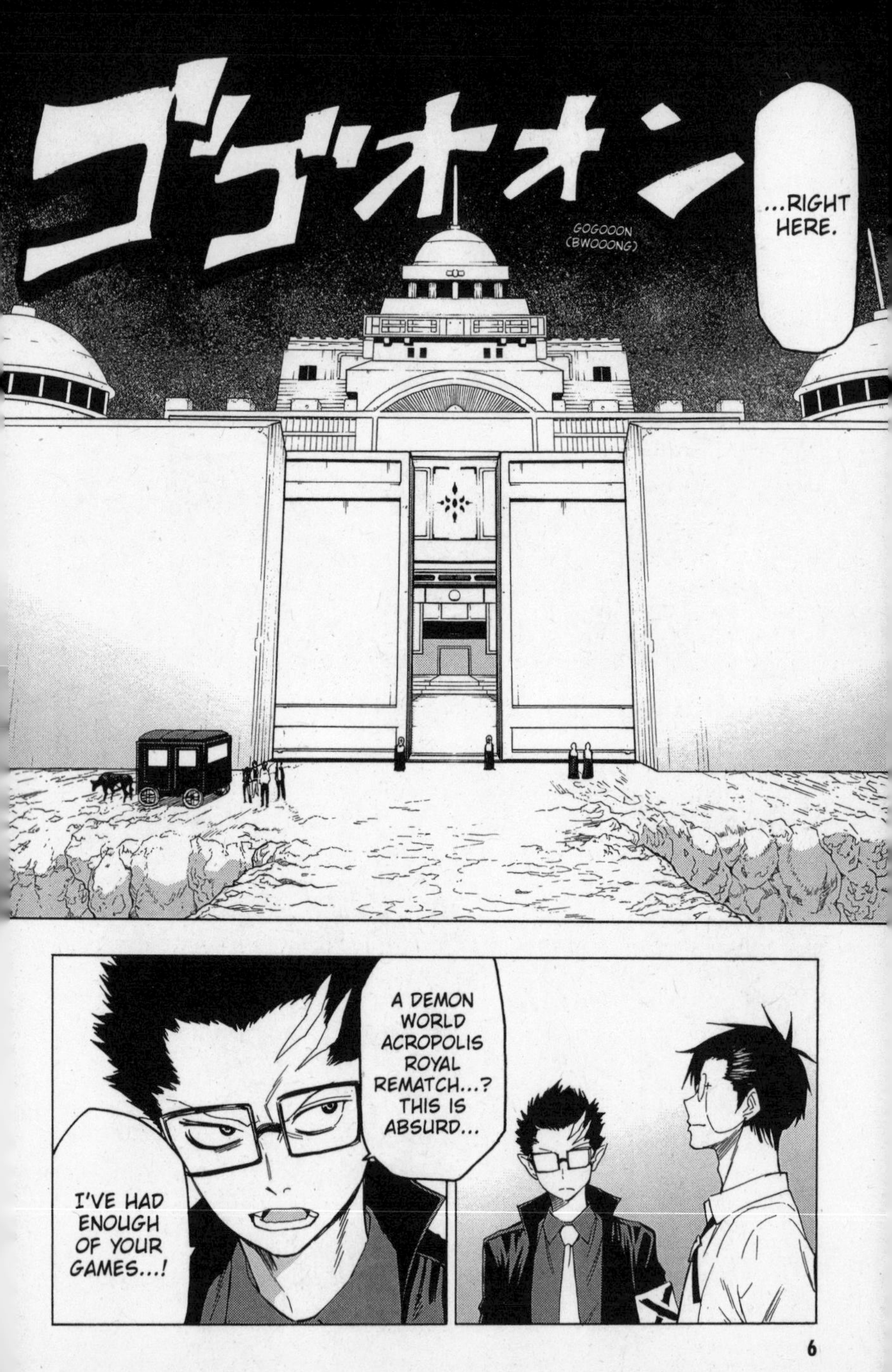
...RIGHT HERE.
ゴゴオオン
GOGOOON (BWOOONG)
A DEMON WORLD ACROPOLIS ROYAL REMATCH...? THIS IS ABSURD...
I'VE HAD ENOUGH OF YOUR GAMES...!

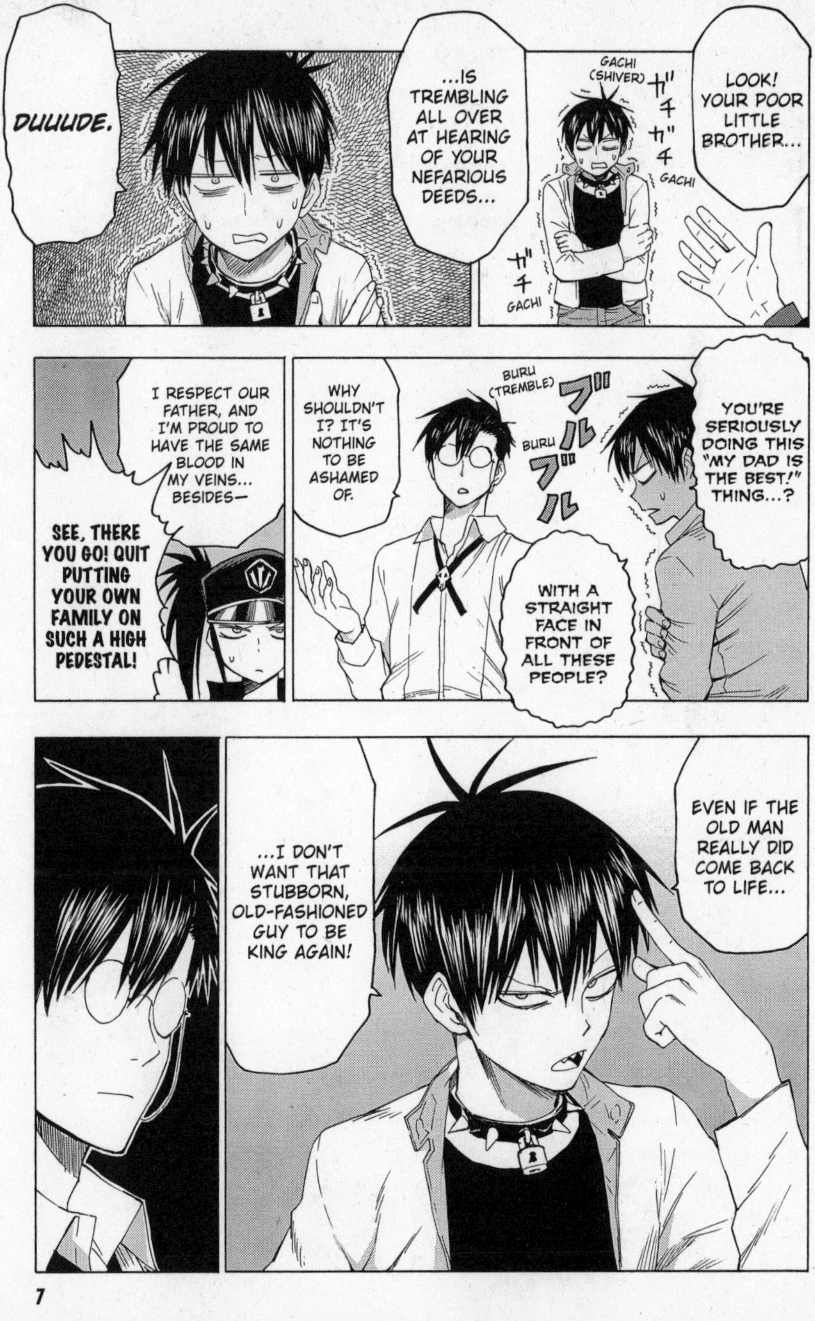
LOOK! YOUR POOR LITTLE BROTHER...
GACHI (SHIVER)
ガチガチ
GACHI
GACHI
ガチ
...IS TREMBLING ALL OVER AT HEARING OF YOUR NEFARIOUS DEEDS...
DUUUDE.
YOU'RE SERIOUSLY DOING THIS "MY DAD IS THE BEST!" THING...?
BURU (TREMBLE)
ブルブル
BURU
WITH A STRAIGHT FACE IN FRONT OF ALL THESE PEOPLE?
WHY SHOULDN'T I? IT'S NOTHING TO BE ASHAMED OF.
I RESPECT OUR FATHER, AND I'M PROUD TO HAVE THE SAME BLOOD IN MY VEINS... BESIDES—
SEE, THERE YOU GO! QUIT PUTTING YOUR OWN FAMILY ON SUCH A HIGH PEDESTAL!
EVEN IF THE OLD MAN REALLY DID COME BACK TO LIFE...
...I DON'T WANT THAT STUBBORN, OLD-FASHIONED GUY TO BE KING AGAIN!

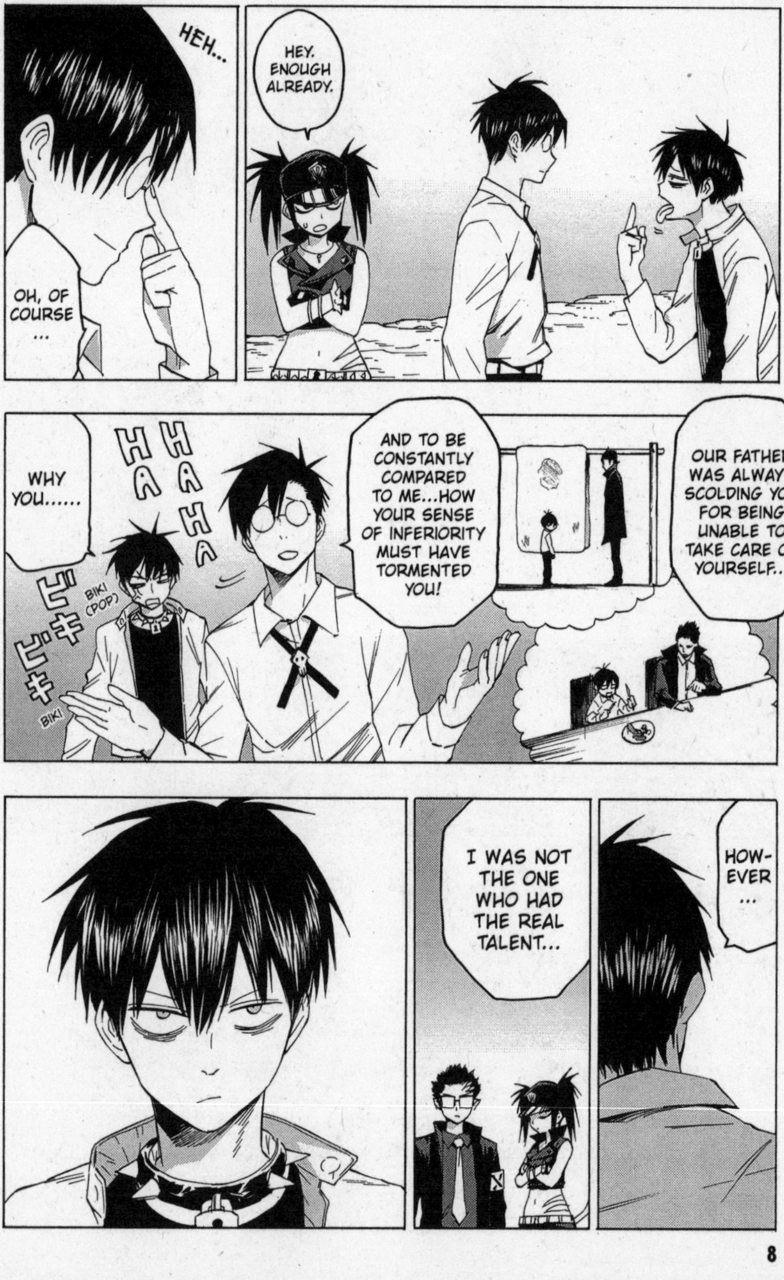
HEY. ENOUGH ALREADY.
HEH...
OH, OF COURSE ...
OUR FATHER WAS ALWAYS SCOLDING YOU FOR BEING UNABLE TO TAKE CARE OF YOURSELF...
AND TO BE CONSTANTLY COMPARED TO ME...HOW YOUR SENSE OF INFERIORITY MUST HAVE TORMENTED YOU!
HAHAHAHA
ビキ
BIKI (POP)
ビキ
BIKI
WHY YOU......
HOW-EVER ...
I WAS NOT THE ONE WHO HAD THE REAL TALENT...

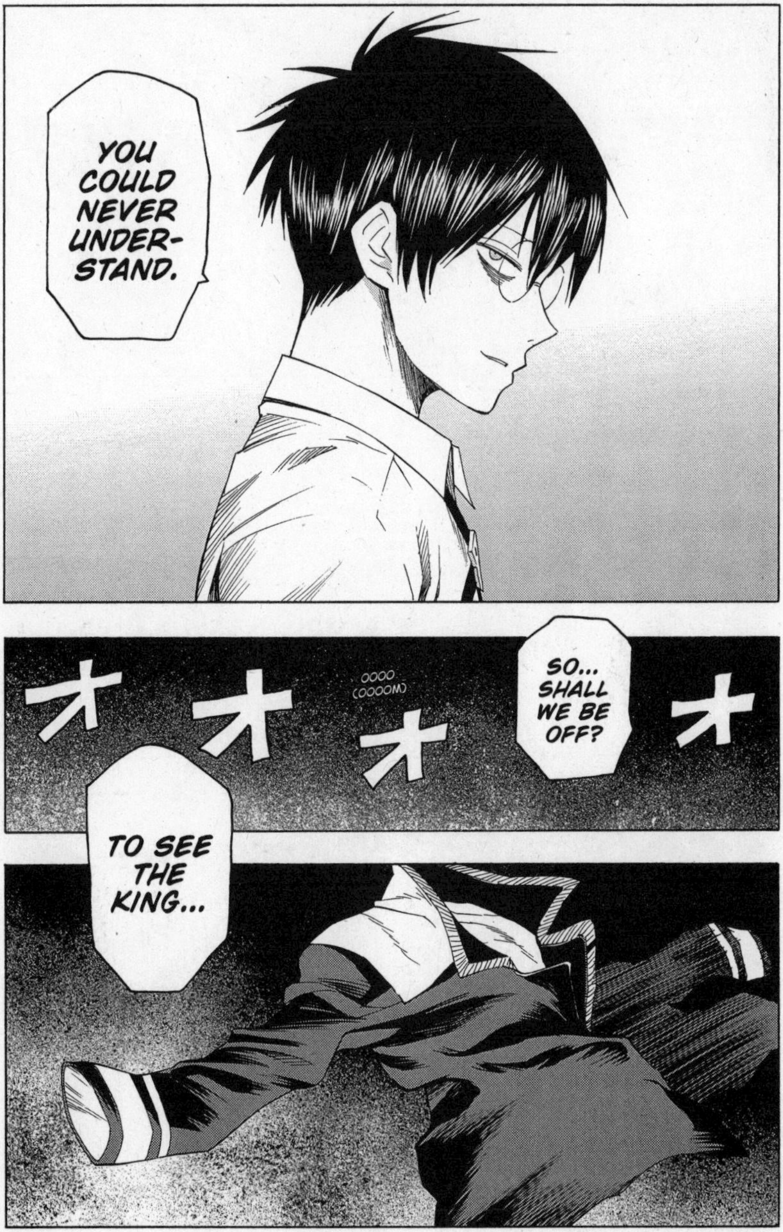
YOU COULD NEVER UNDER-STAND.
オオオオ
OOOO (OOOOM)
SO... SHALL WE BE OFF?
TO SEE THE KING...

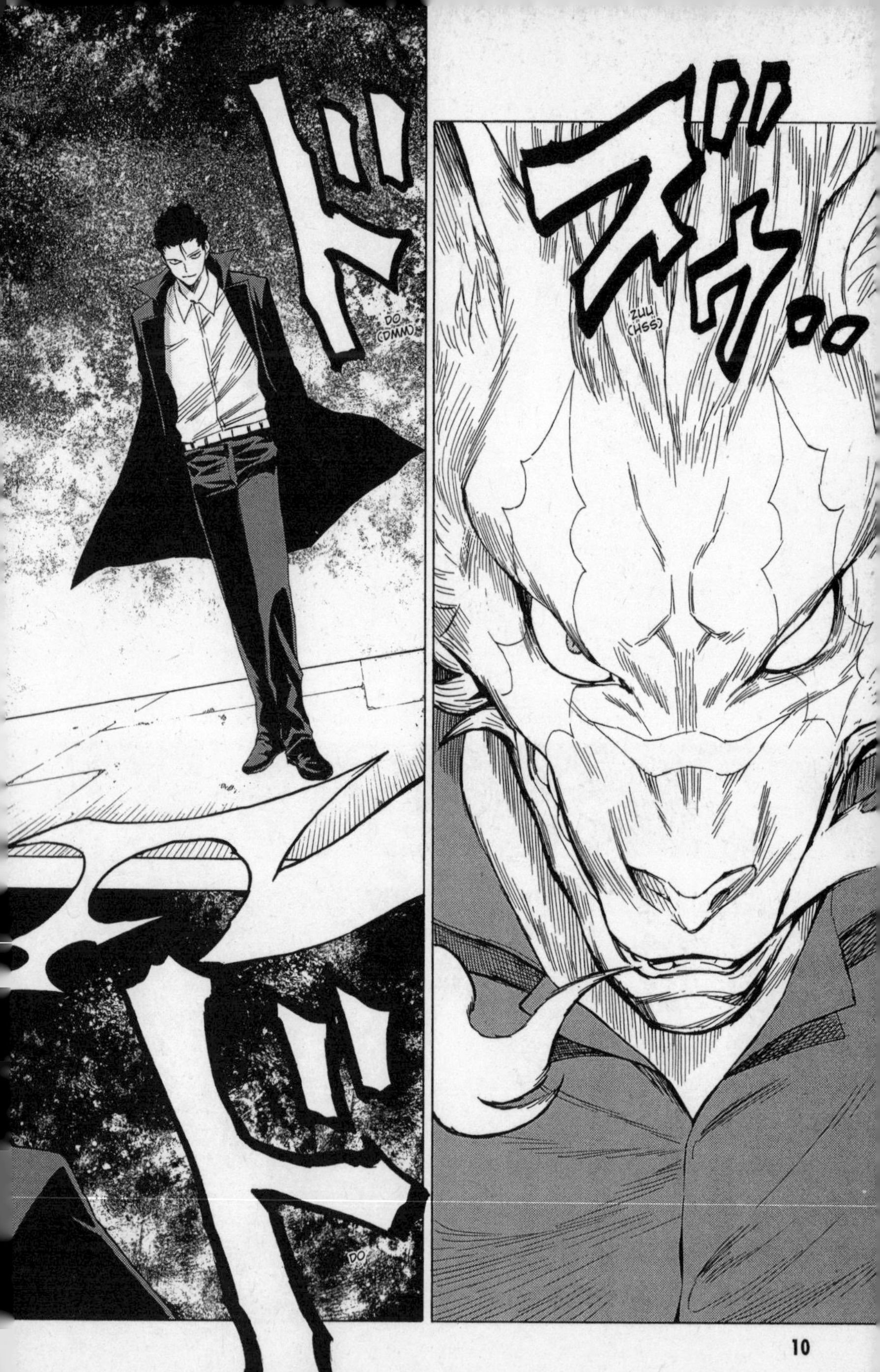
ズゥ..
ZUU (HSS)
ド
DO (DMM)
ド
DO

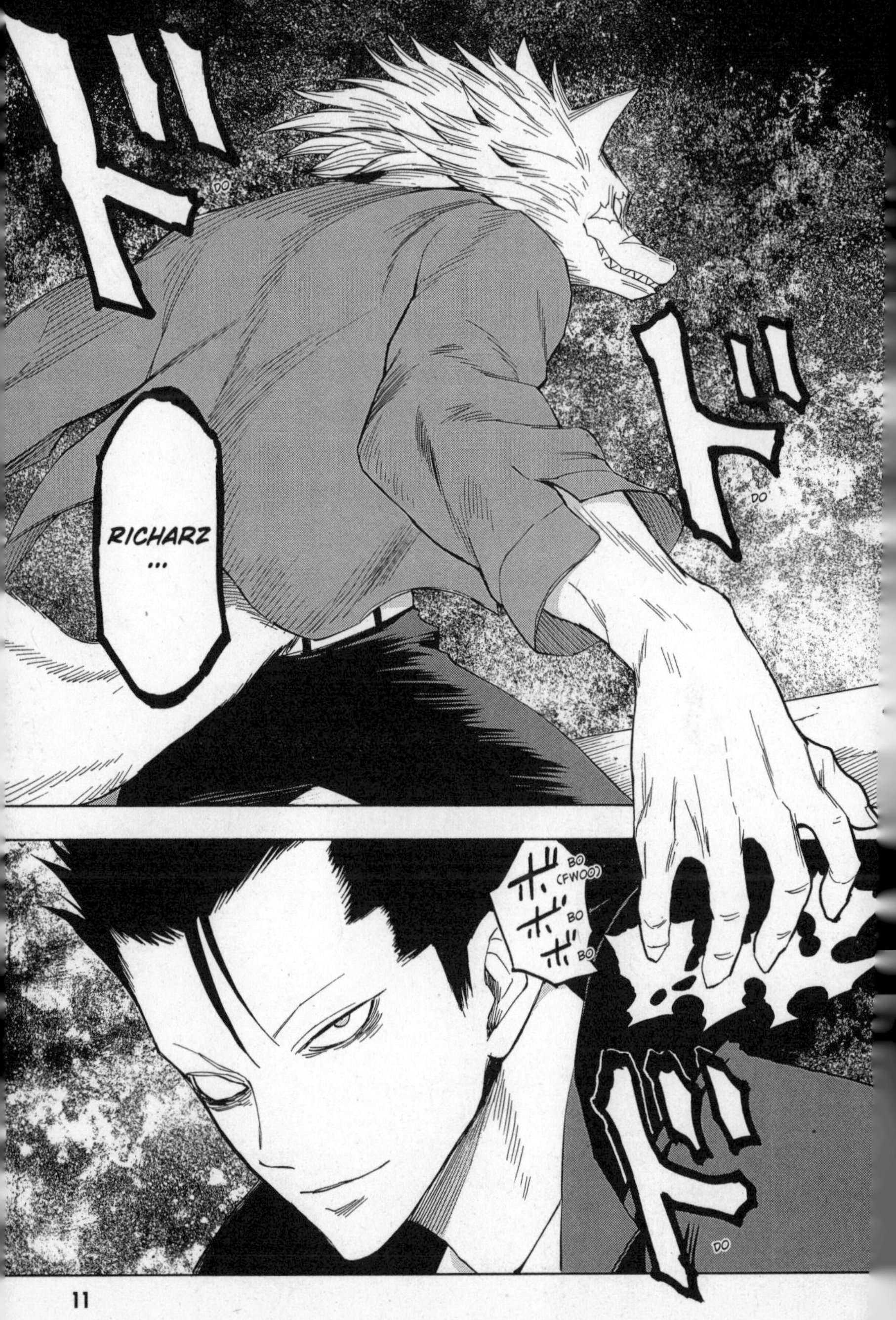
DO
DO
RICHARZ ...
BO (FWOO)
BO
BO
DO

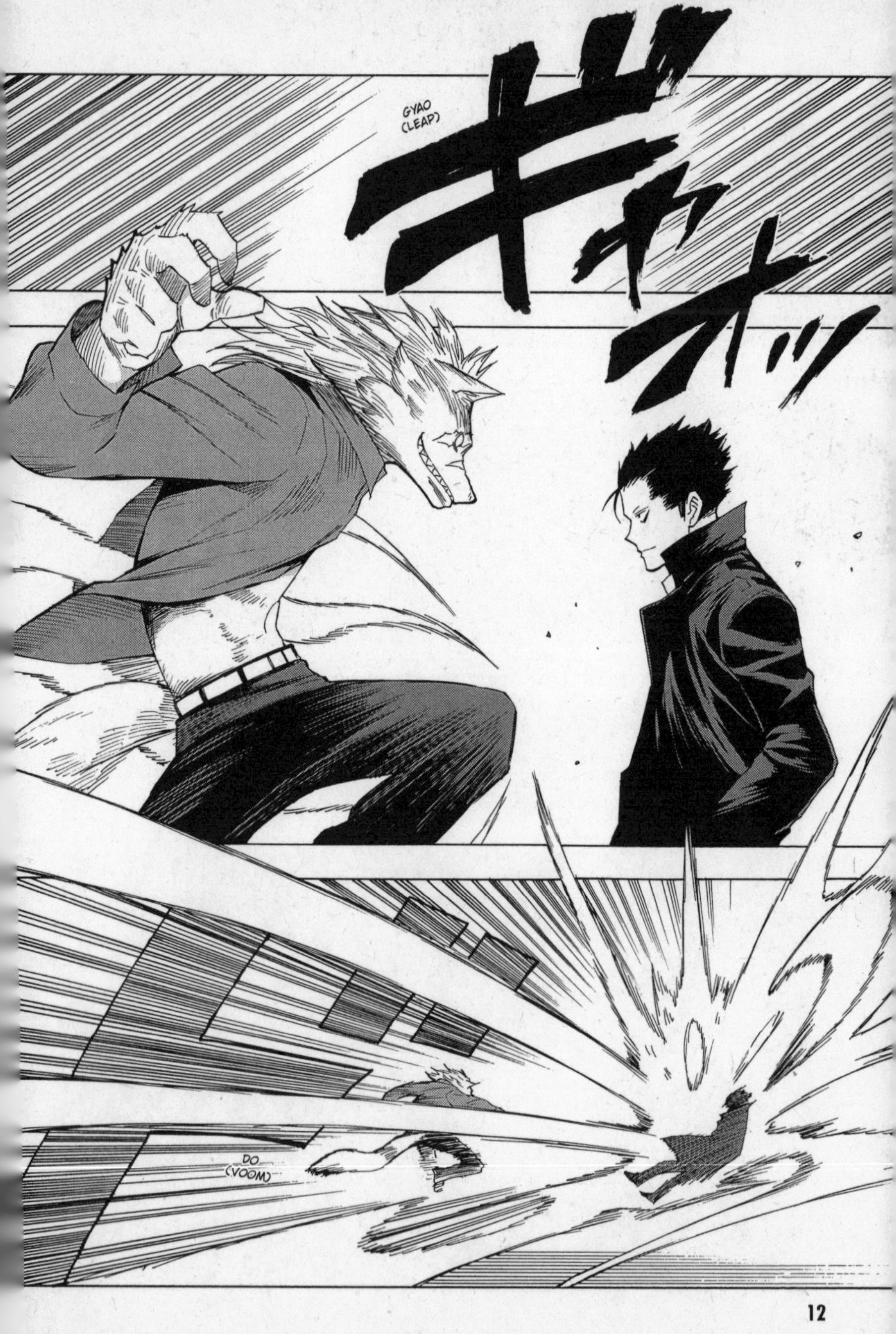
ギャオッ
GYAO (LEAP)
DO (VOOM)

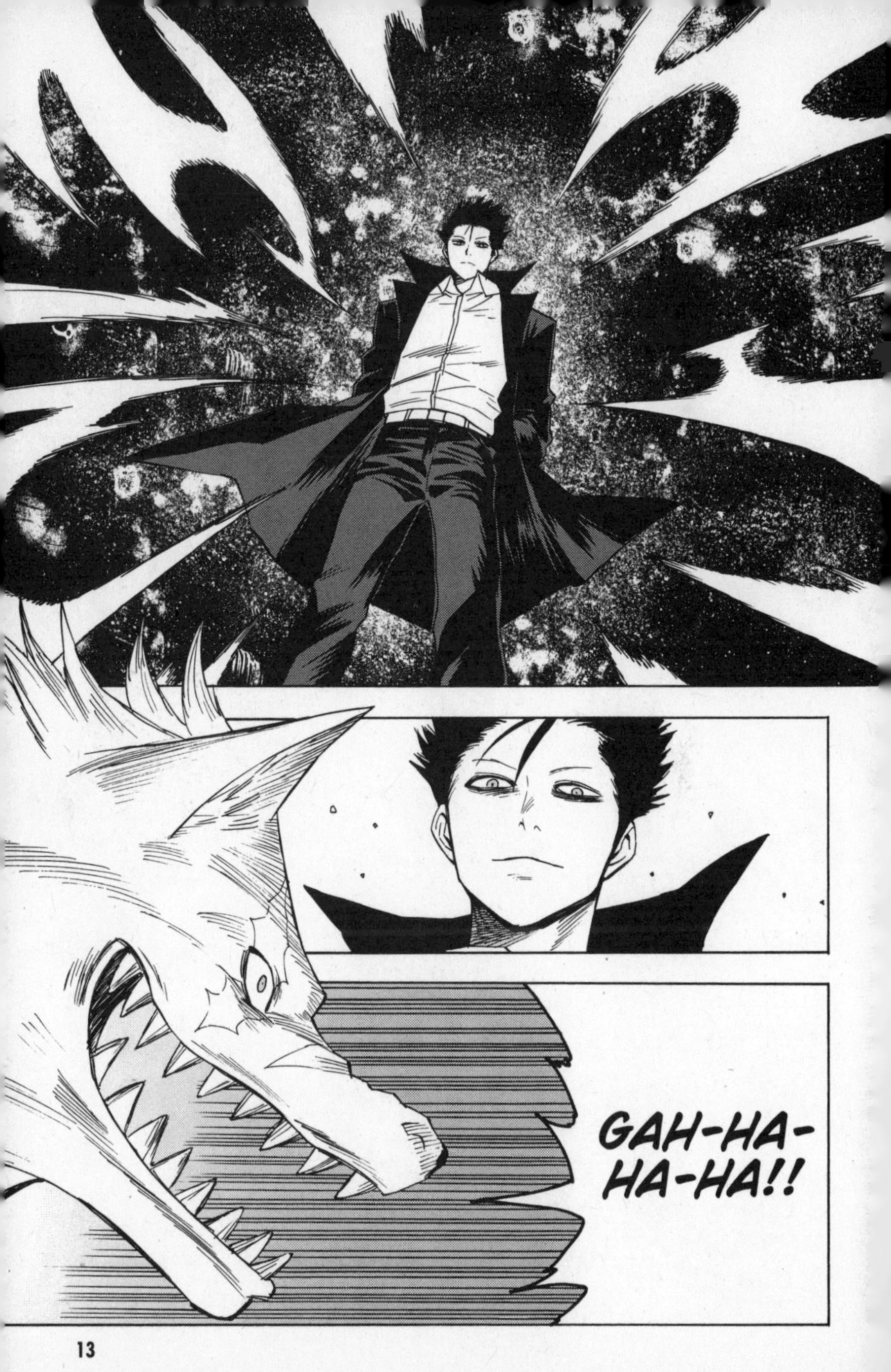
GAH-HA-HA-HA!!

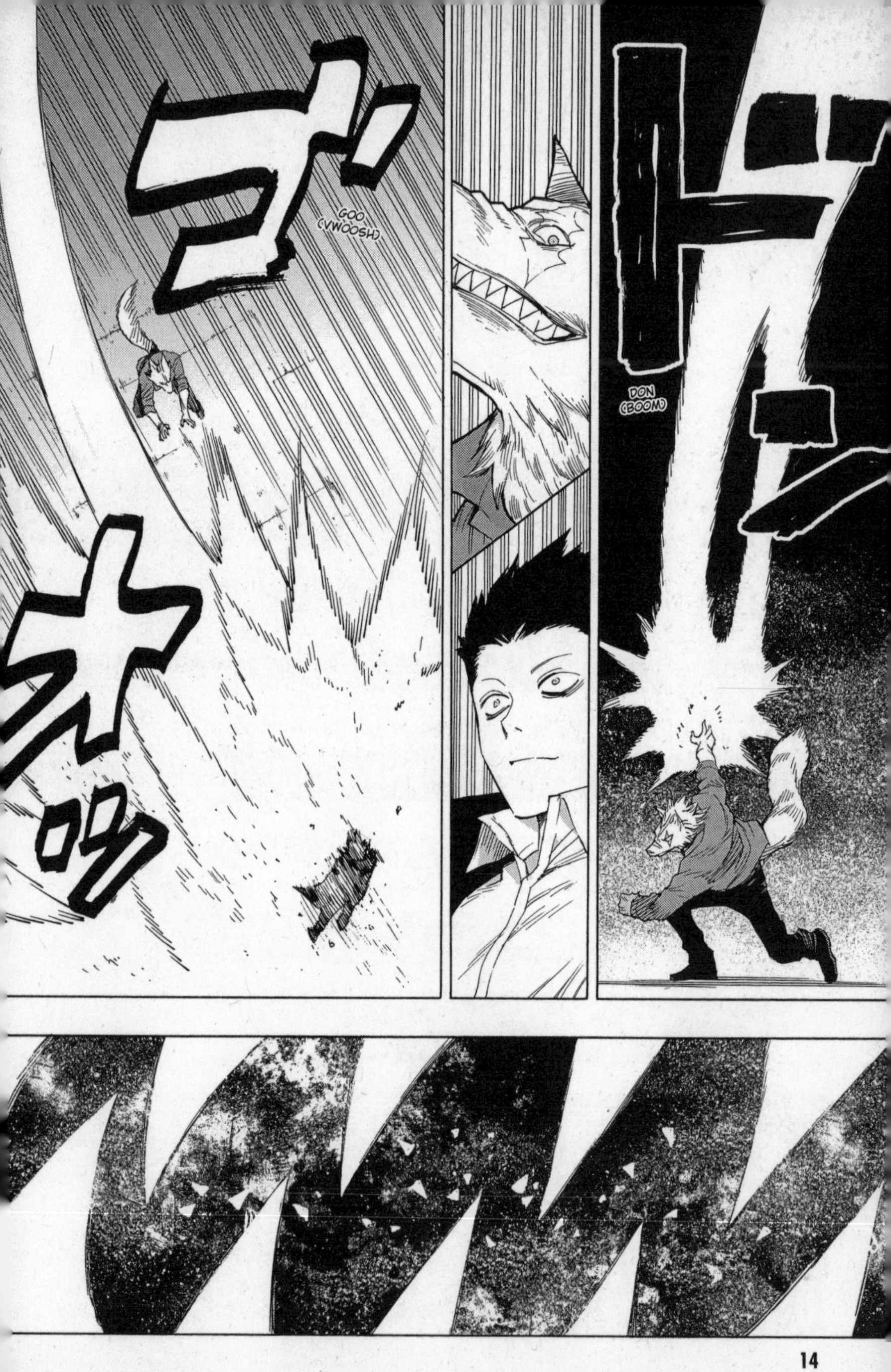
DON
(BOOM)
GOO
(VWOOSH)

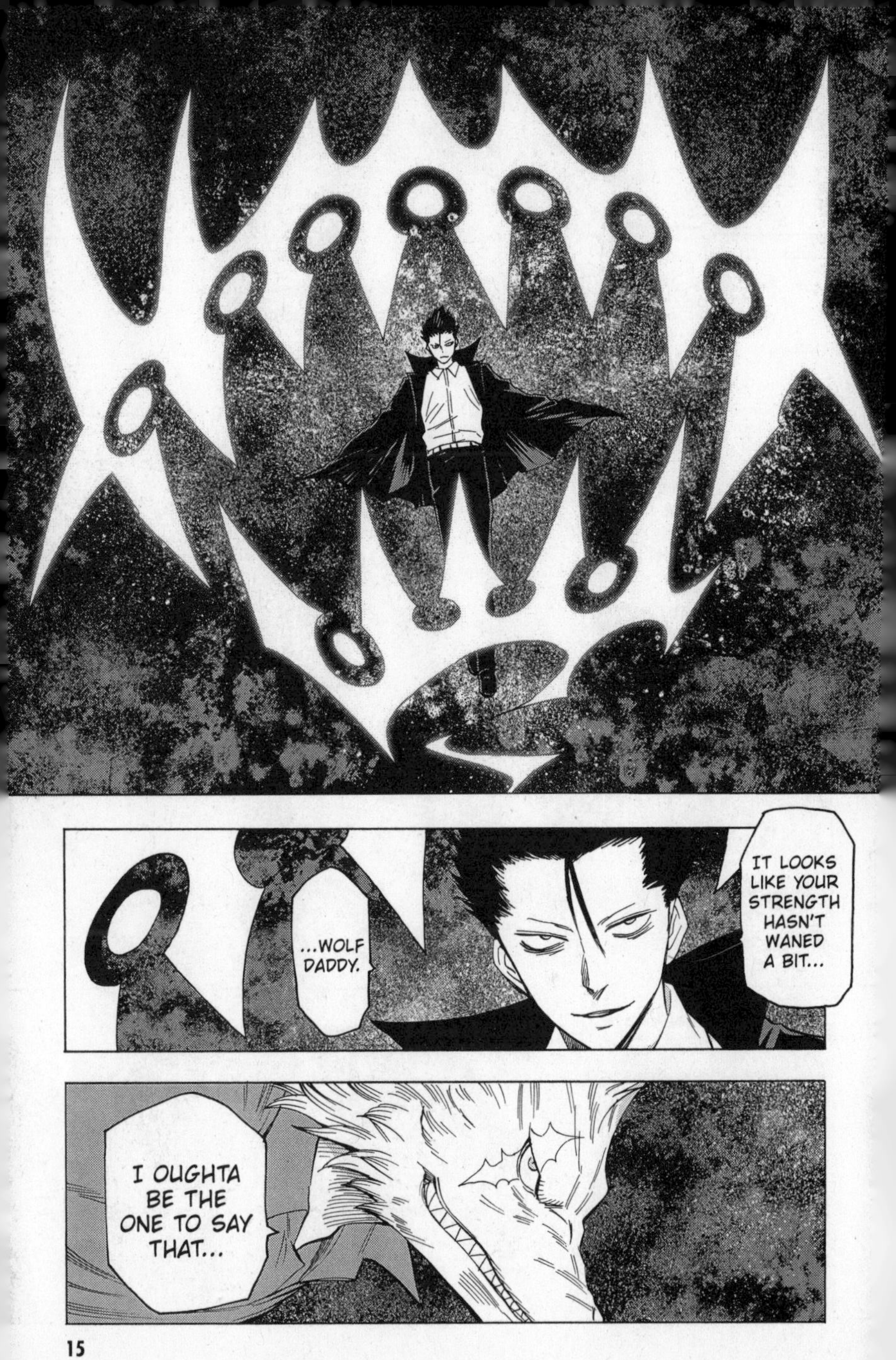
IT LOOKS LIKE YOUR STRENGTH HASN'T WANED A BIT...
...WOLF DADDY.
I OUGHTA BE THE ONE TO SAY THAT...

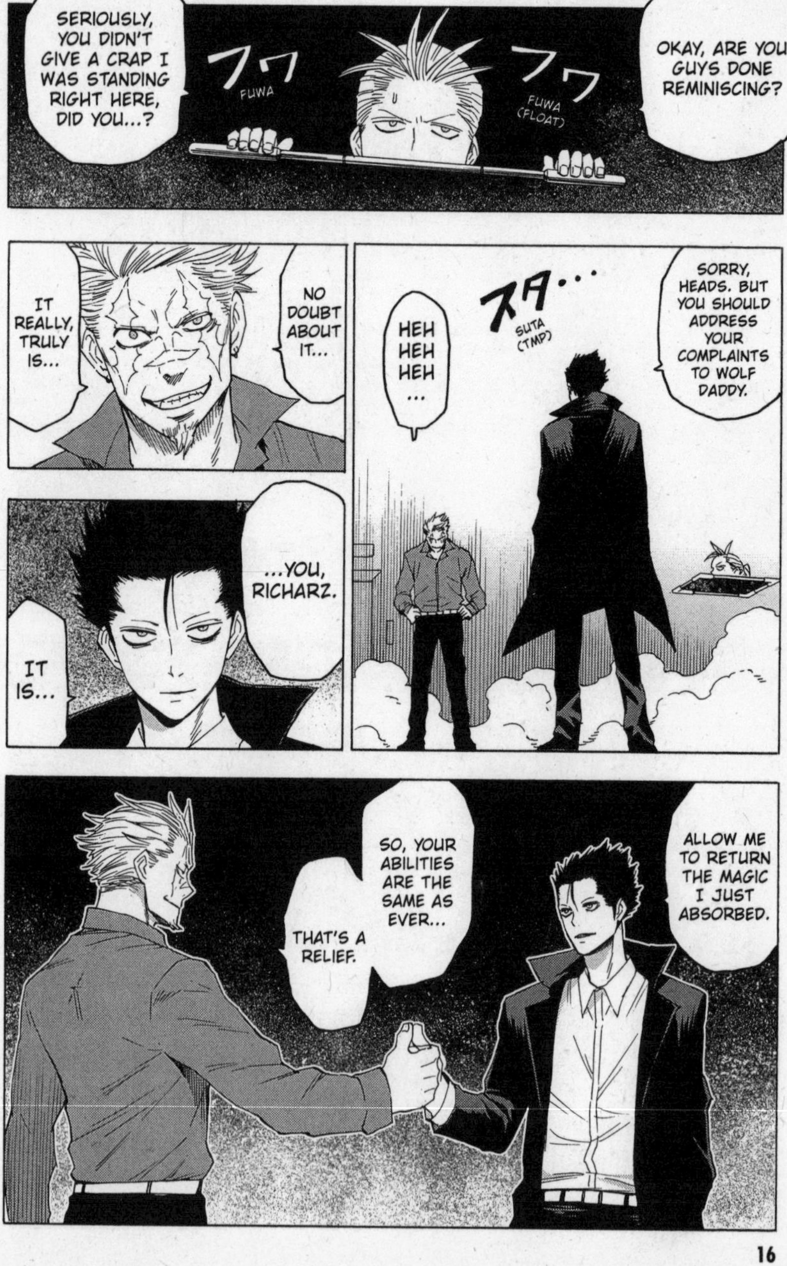
OKAY, ARE YOU GUYS DONE REMINISCING?
フワ
FUWA (FLOAT)
フワ
FUWA
SERIOUSLY, YOU DIDN'T GIVE A CRAP I WAS STANDING RIGHT HERE, DID YOU...?
SORRY, HEADS. BUT YOU SHOULD ADDRESS YOUR COMPLAINTS TO WOLF DADDY.
スタ…
SUTA (TMP)
HEH HEH HEH ...
NO DOUBT ABOUT IT...
IT REALLY, TRULY IS...
...YOU, RICHARZ.
IT IS...
ALLOW ME TO RETURN THE MAGIC I JUST ABSORBED.
SO, YOUR ABILITIES ARE THE SAME AS EVER...
THAT'S A RELIEF.

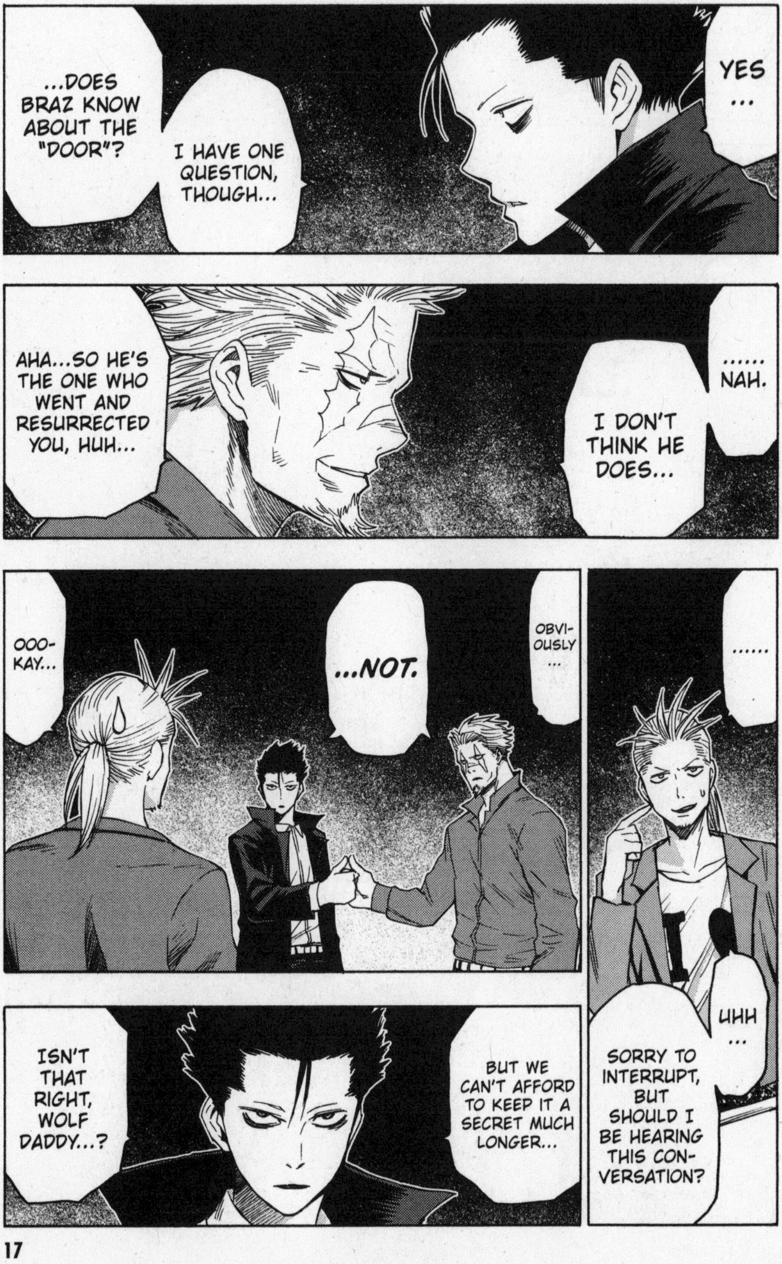
YES ...
I HAVE ONE QUESTION, THOUGH...
...DOES BRAZ KNOW ABOUT THE "DOOR"?
...... NAH.
I DON'T THINK HE DOES...
AHA...SO HE'S THE ONE WHO WENT AND RESURRECTED YOU, HUH...
......
UHH ...
SORRY TO INTERRUPT, BUT SHOULD I BE HEARING THIS CONVERSATION?
OBVI-OUSLY ...
...NOT.
OOO-KAY...
BUT WE CAN'T AFFORD TO KEEP IT A SECRET MUCH LONGER...
ISN'T THAT RIGHT, WOLF DADDY...?

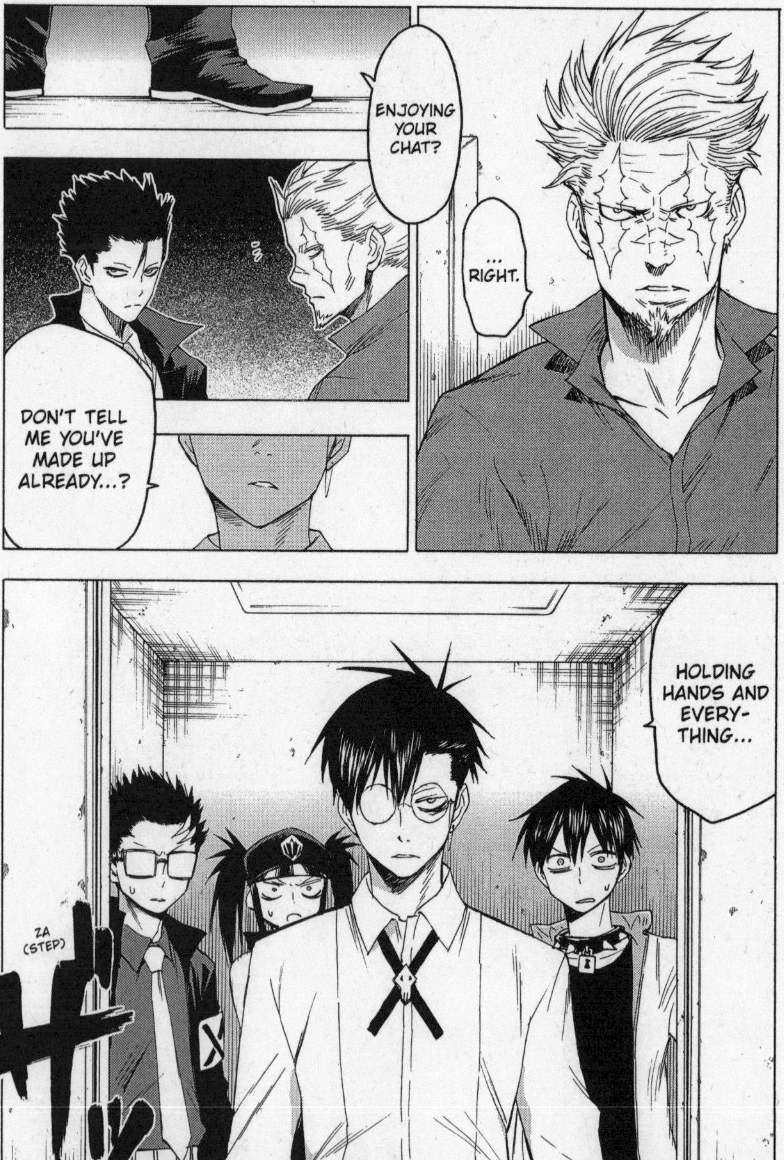
ENJOYING YOUR CHAT?
... RIGHT.
DON'T TELL ME YOU'VE MADE UP ALREADY...?
HOLDING HANDS AND EVERY-THING...
ZA (STEP)

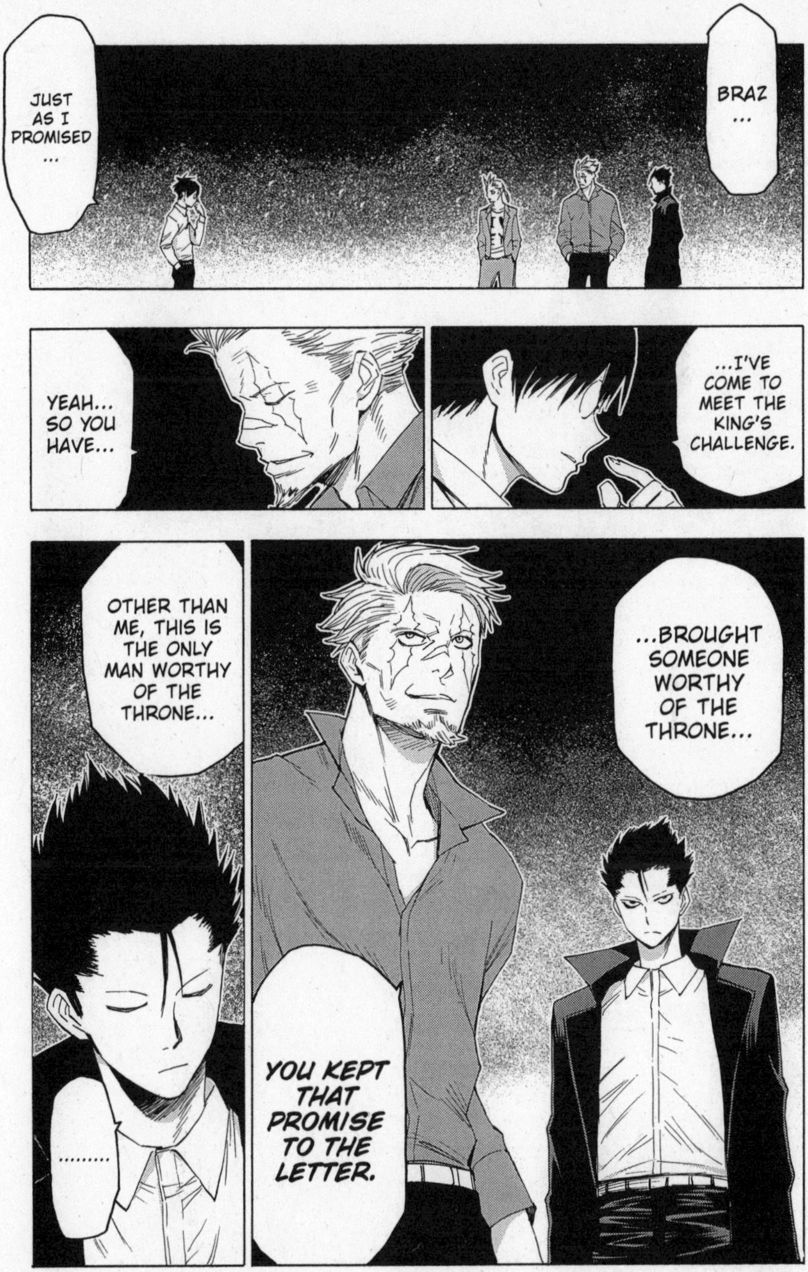
BRAZ ...
JUST AS I PROMISED ...
...I'VE COME TO MEET THE KING'S CHALLENGE.
YEAH... SO YOU HAVE...
...BROUGHT SOMEONE WORTHY OF THE THRONE...
YOU KEPT THAT PROMISE TO THE LETTER.
OTHER THAN ME, THIS IS THE ONLY MAN WORTHY OF THE THRONE...
....

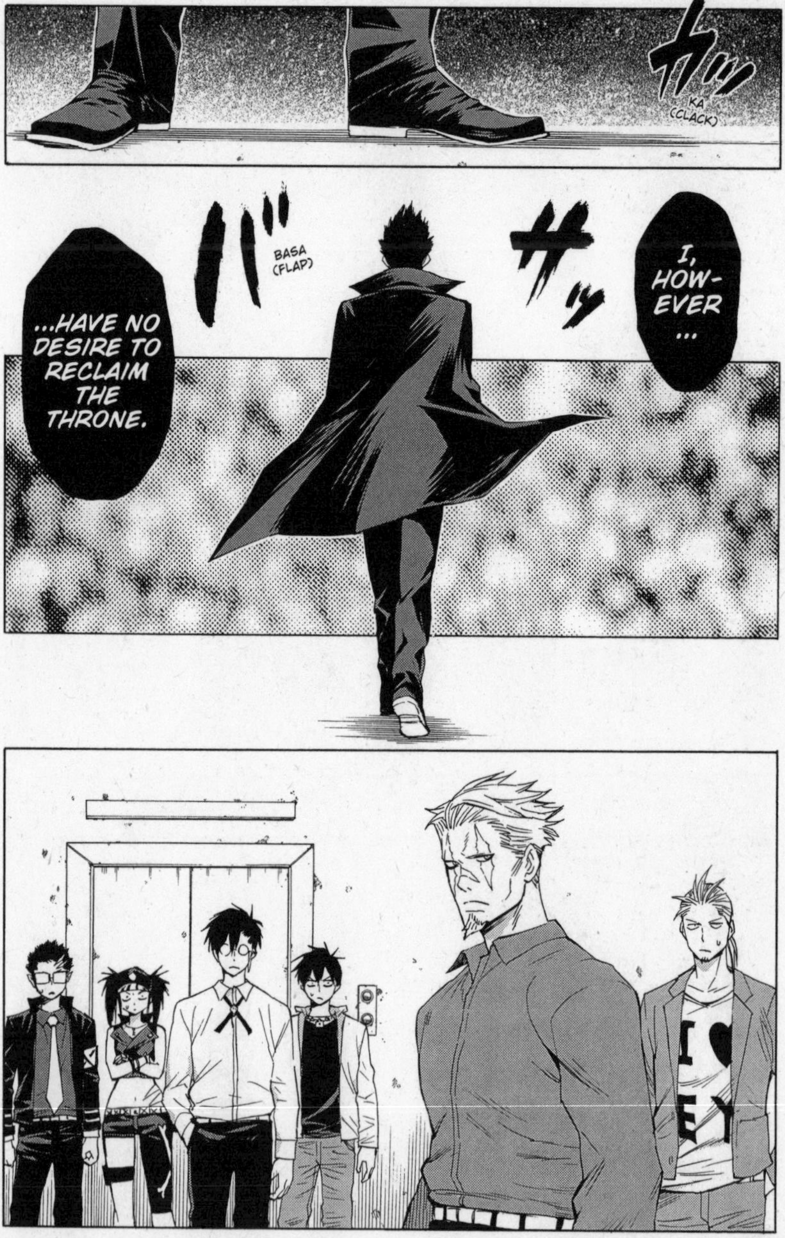
KA
(CLACK)
I, HOW-
EVER
...
BASA
(FLAP)
...HAVE NO
DESIRE TO
RECLAIM
THE
THRONE.

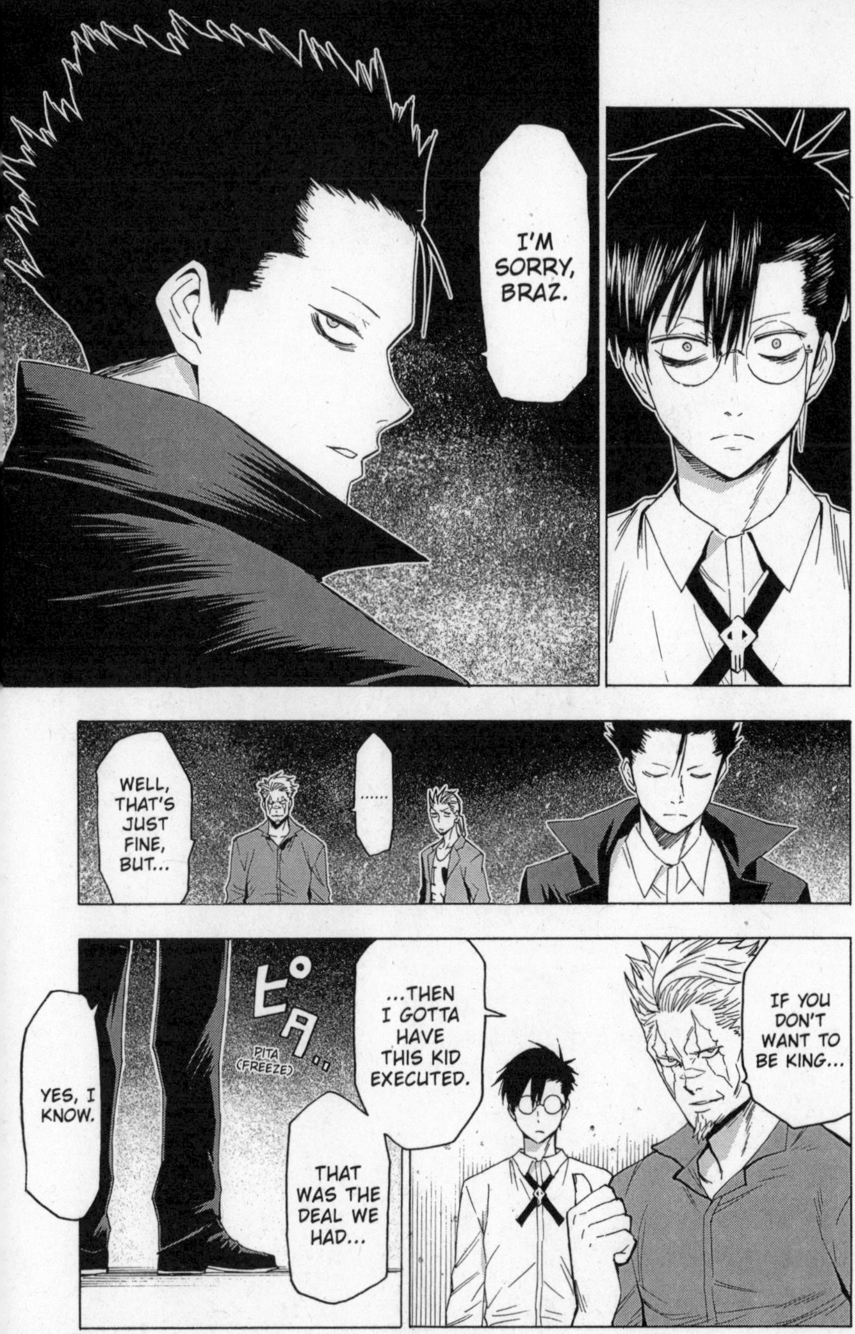
I'M SORRY, BRAZ.
......
WELL, THAT'S JUST FINE, BUT...
IF YOU DON'T WANT TO BE KING...
...THEN I GOTTA HAVE THIS KID EXECUTED.
THAT WAS THE DEAL WE HAD...
ピタ..
PITA (FREEZE)
YES, I KNOW.

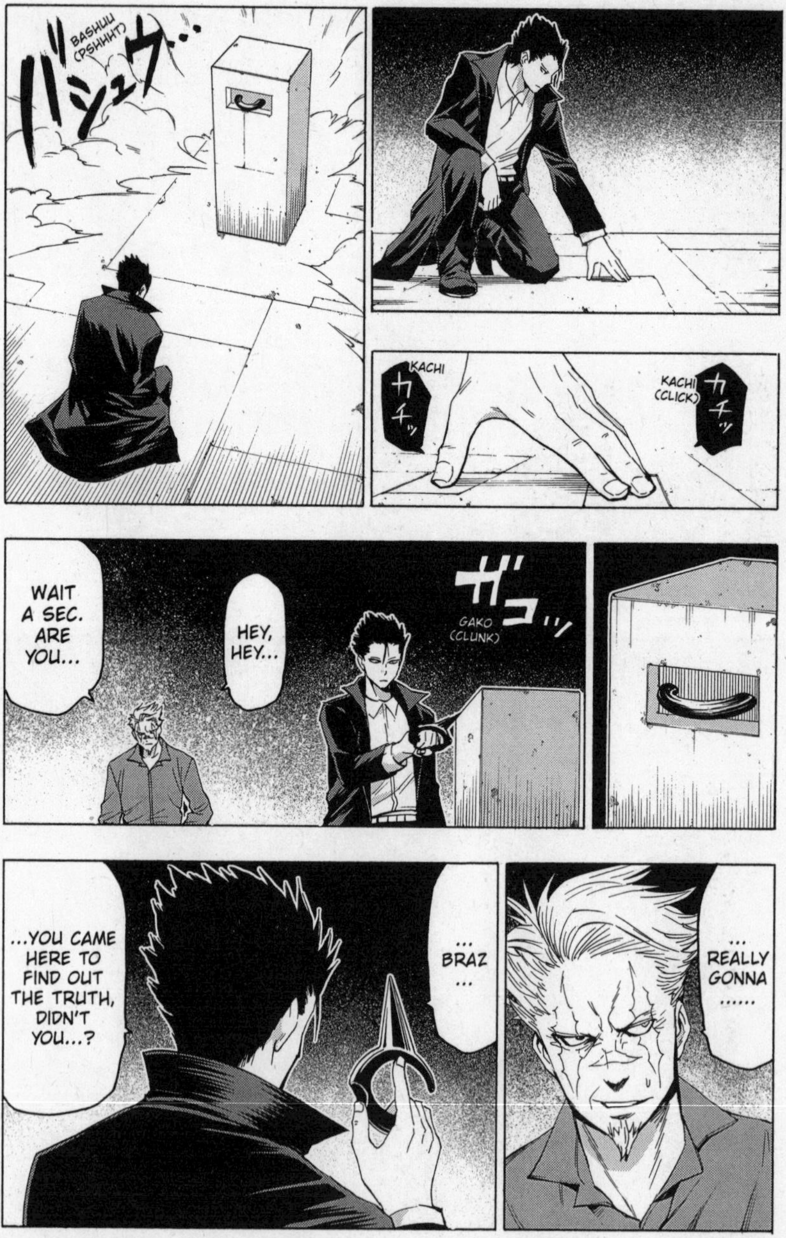
KACHI (CLICK)
カチッ
KACHI
カチッ
BASHUU (PSHHHT)
バシュゥ…
GAKO (CLUNK)
ガコッ
HEY, HEY...
WAIT A SEC. ARE YOU...
... REALLY GONNA ......
... BRAZ ...
...YOU CAME HERE TO FIND OUT THE TRUTH, DIDN'T YOU...?

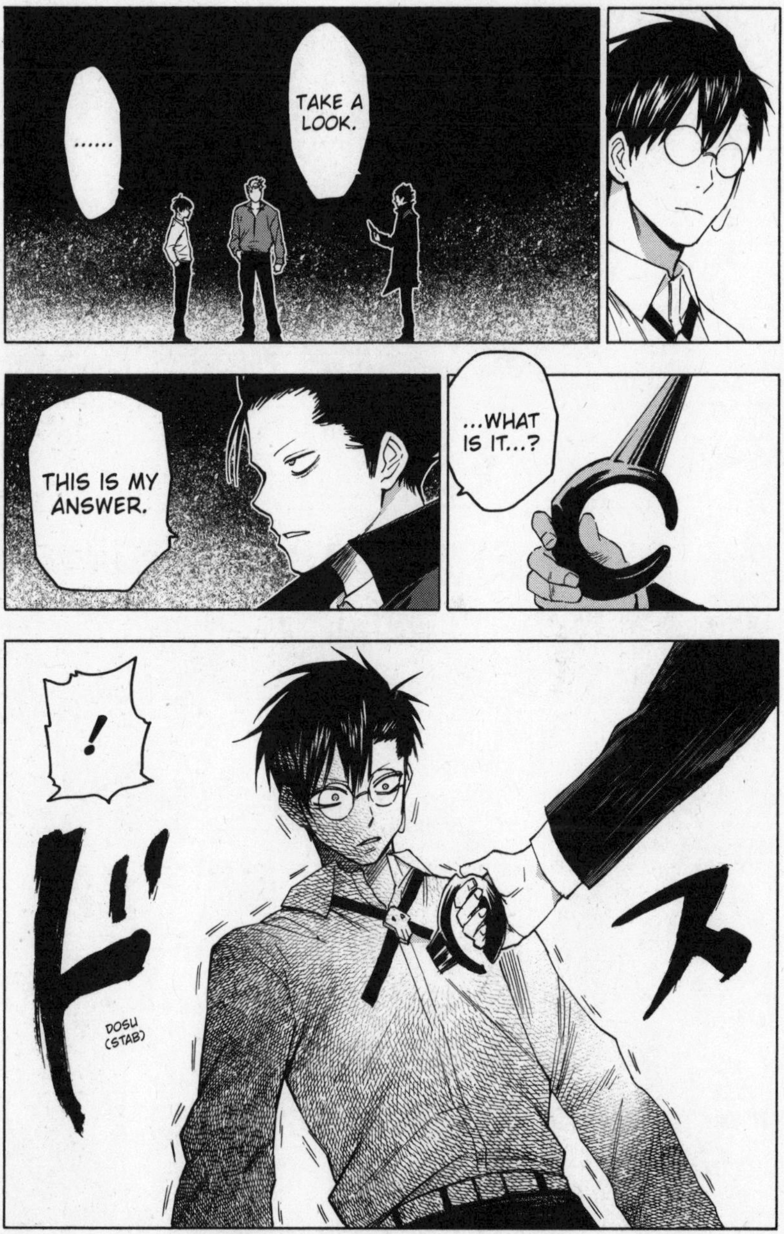
TAKE A LOOK.
......
...WHAT IS IT...?
THIS IS MY ANSWER.
!
ドス
DOSU (STAB)

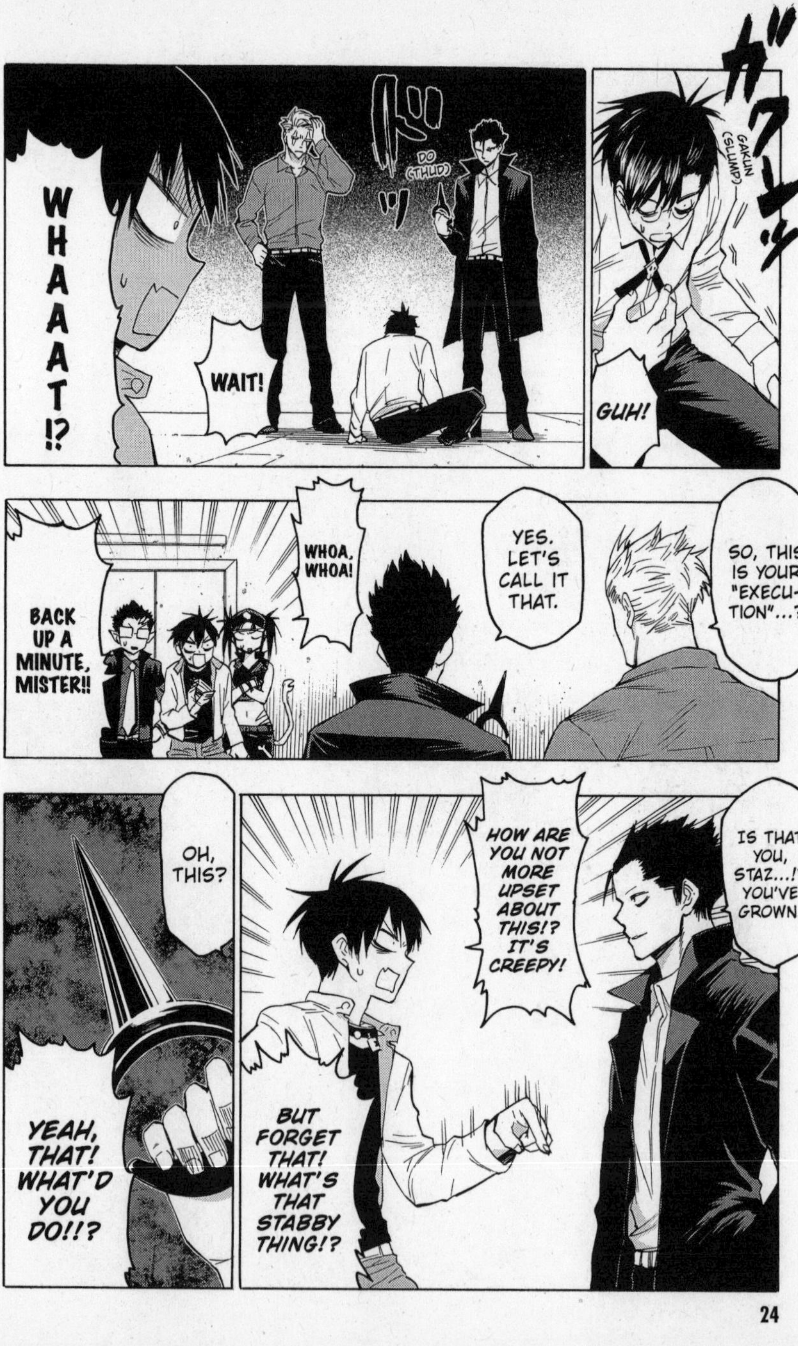
GAKUN (SLUMP)
GUH!
DO (THUD)
WAIT!
WHAAAAT!?
SO, THIS IS YOUR "EXECUTION"...?
YES. LET'S CALL IT THAT.
WHOA, WHOA!
BACK UP A MINUTE, MISTER!!
IS THAT YOU, STAZ...!? YOU'VE GROWN.
HOW ARE YOU NOT MORE UPSET ABOUT THIS!? IT'S CREEPY!
BUT FORGET THAT! WHAT'S THAT STABBY THING!?
OH, THIS?
YEAH, THAT! WHAT'D YOU DO!!?

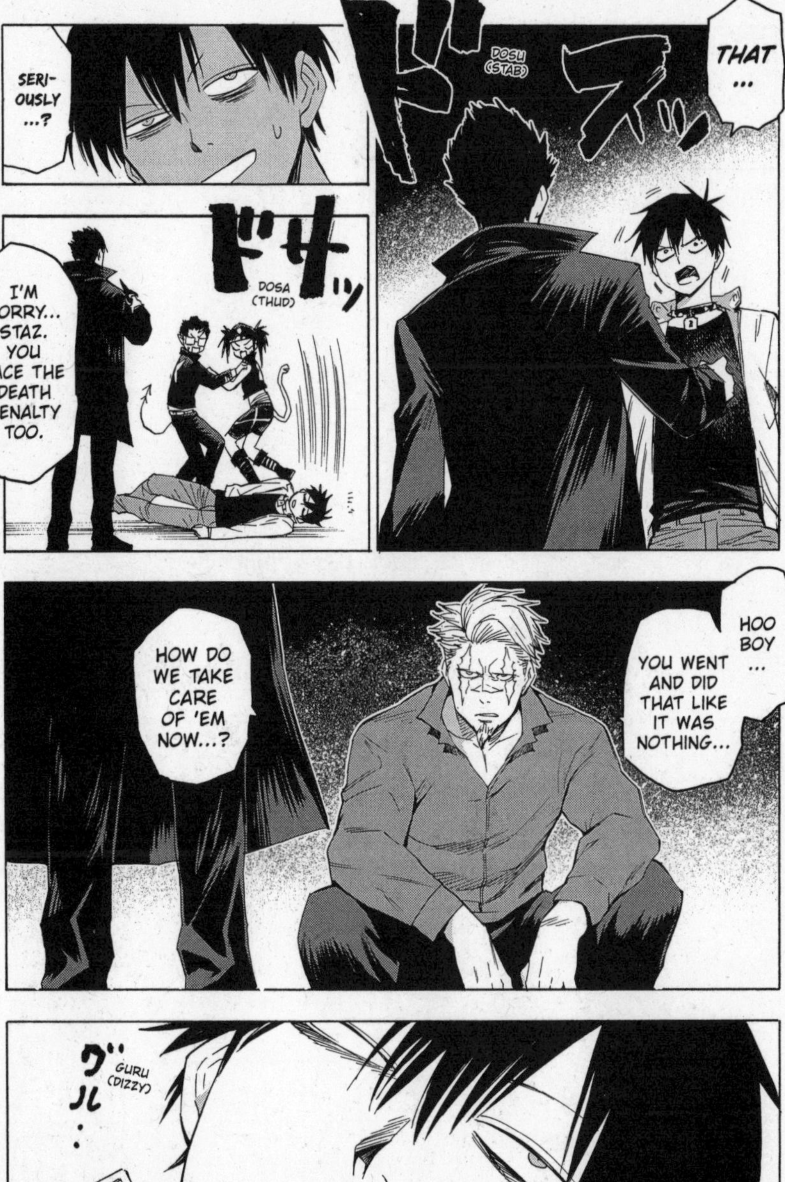
THAT ...
DOSU (STAB)
SERI-OUSLY ...?
I'M SORRY... STAZ. YOU FACE THE DEATH PENALTY TOO.
DOSA (THUD)
HOO BOY ... YOU WENT AND DID THAT LIKE IT WAS NOTHING...
HOW DO WE TAKE CARE OF 'EM NOW...?
GURU (DIZZY)

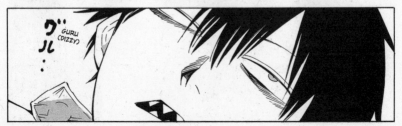

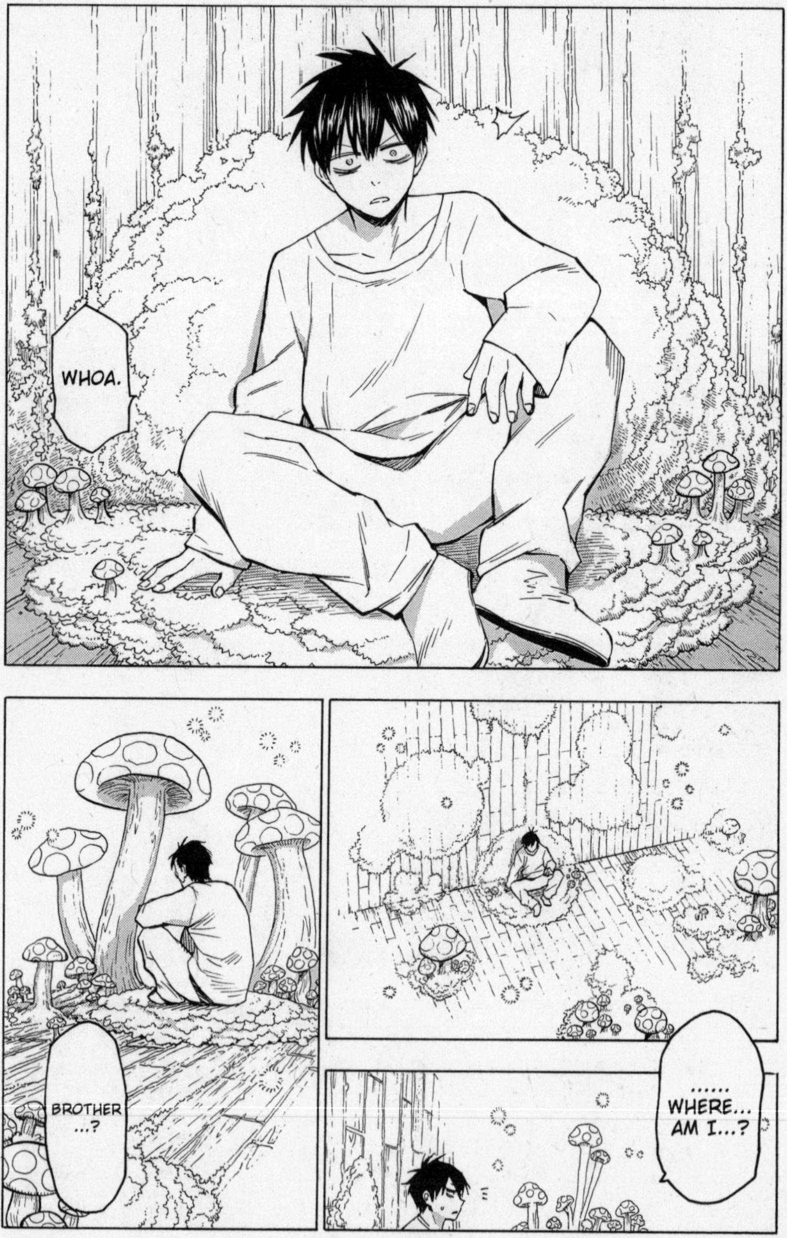
WHOA.
...... WHERE... AM I...?
BROTHER ...?

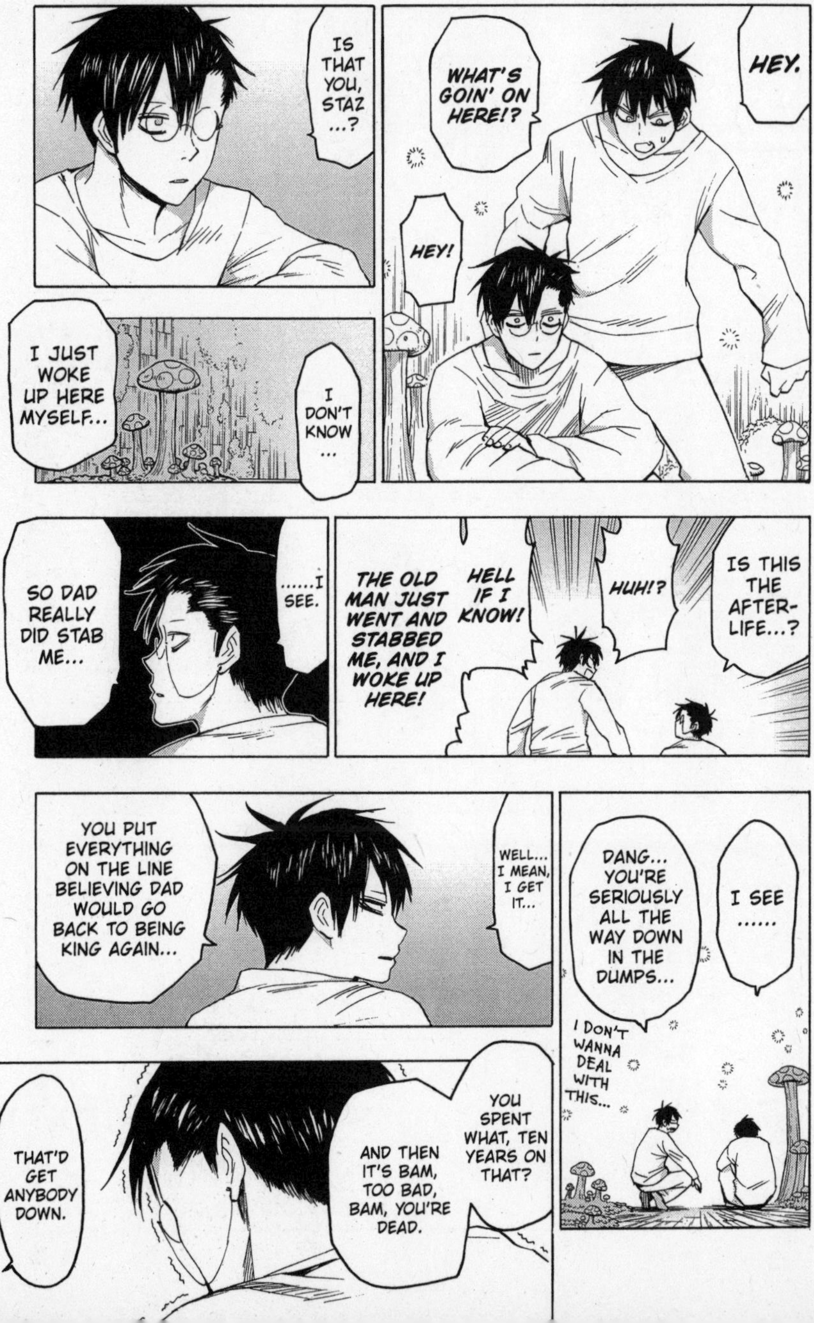
HEY.
WHAT'S GOIN' ON HERE!?
HEY!
IS THAT YOU, STAZ ...?
I DON'T KNOW ...
I JUST WOKE UP HERE MYSELF...
IS THIS THE AFTER-LIFE...?
HUH!?
HELL IF I KNOW!
THE OLD MAN JUST WENT AND STABBED ME, AND I WOKE UP HERE!
......I SEE.
SO DAD REALLY DID STAB ME...
I SEE ......
DANG... YOU'RE SERIOUSLY ALL THE WAY DOWN IN THE DUMPS...
I DON'T WANNA DEAL WITH THIS...
WELL... I MEAN, I GET IT...
YOU PUT EVERYTHING ON THE LINE BELIEVING DAD WOULD GO BACK TO BEING KING AGAIN...
YOU SPENT WHAT, TEN YEARS ON THAT?
AND THEN IT'S BAM, TOO BAD, BAM, YOU'RE DEAD.
THAT'D GET ANYBODY DOWN.

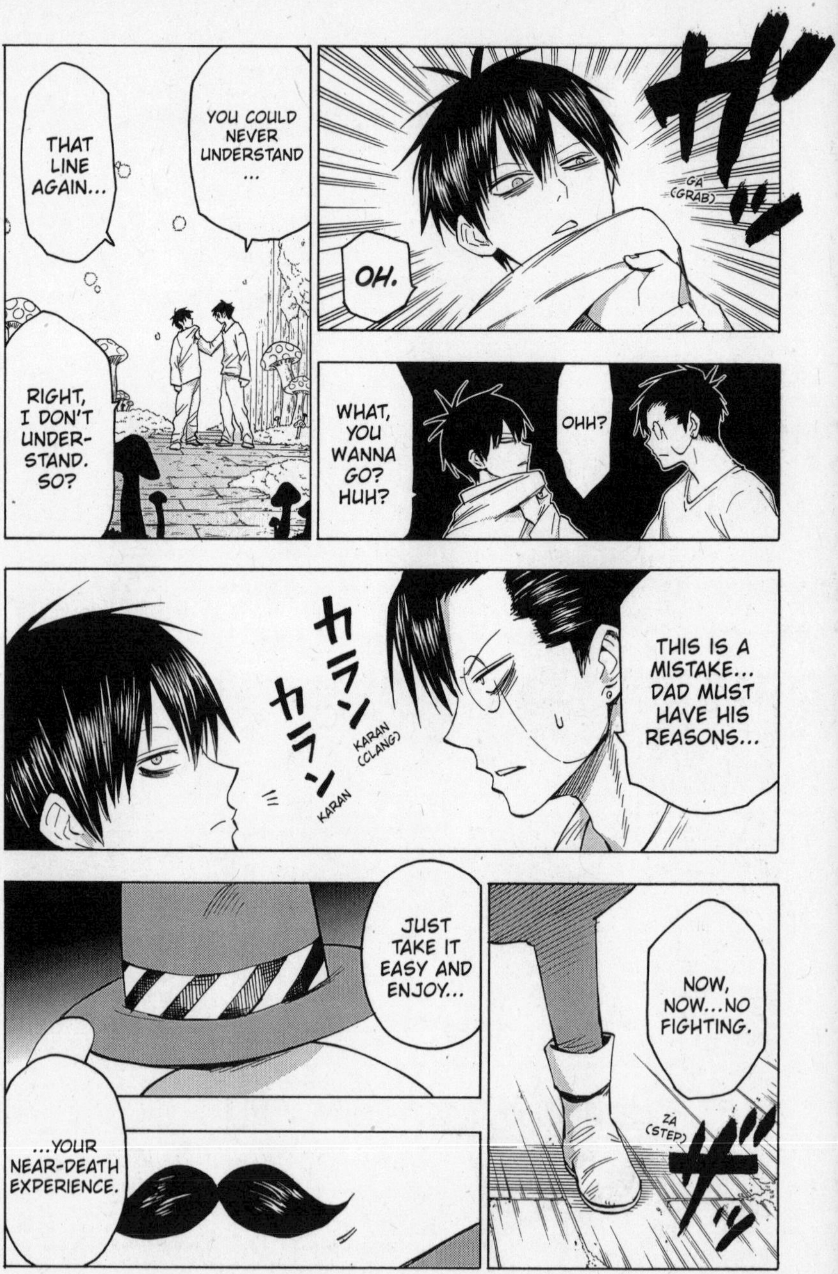
GA (GRAB)
OH.
OHH?
WHAT, YOU WANNA GO? HUH?
YOU COULD NEVER UNDERSTAND...
THAT LINE AGAIN...
RIGHT, I DON'T UNDER-STAND. SO?
THIS IS A MISTAKE... DAD MUST HAVE HIS REASONS...
カラン
KARAN (CLANG)
カラン
KARAN
NOW, NOW...NO FIGHTING.
ZA (STEP)
JUST TAKE IT EASY AND ENJOY...
...YOUR NEAR-DEATH EXPERIENCE.

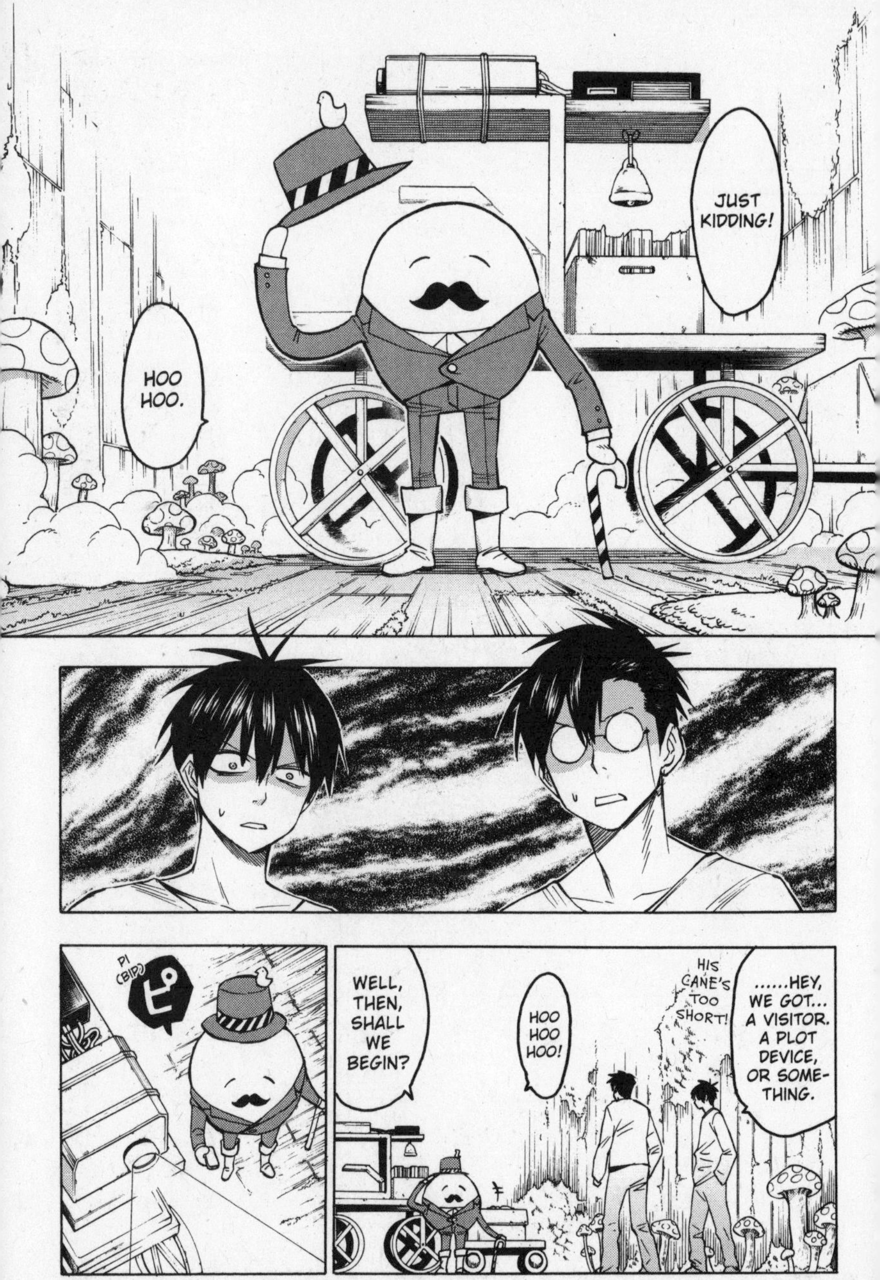
JUST KIDDING!
HOO HOO.
......HEY, WE GOT... A VISITOR. A PLOT DEVICE, OR SOMETHING.
HIS CANE'S TOO SHORT!
HOO HOO HOO!
WELL, THEN, SHALL WE BEGIN?
PI (BIP)
ピ

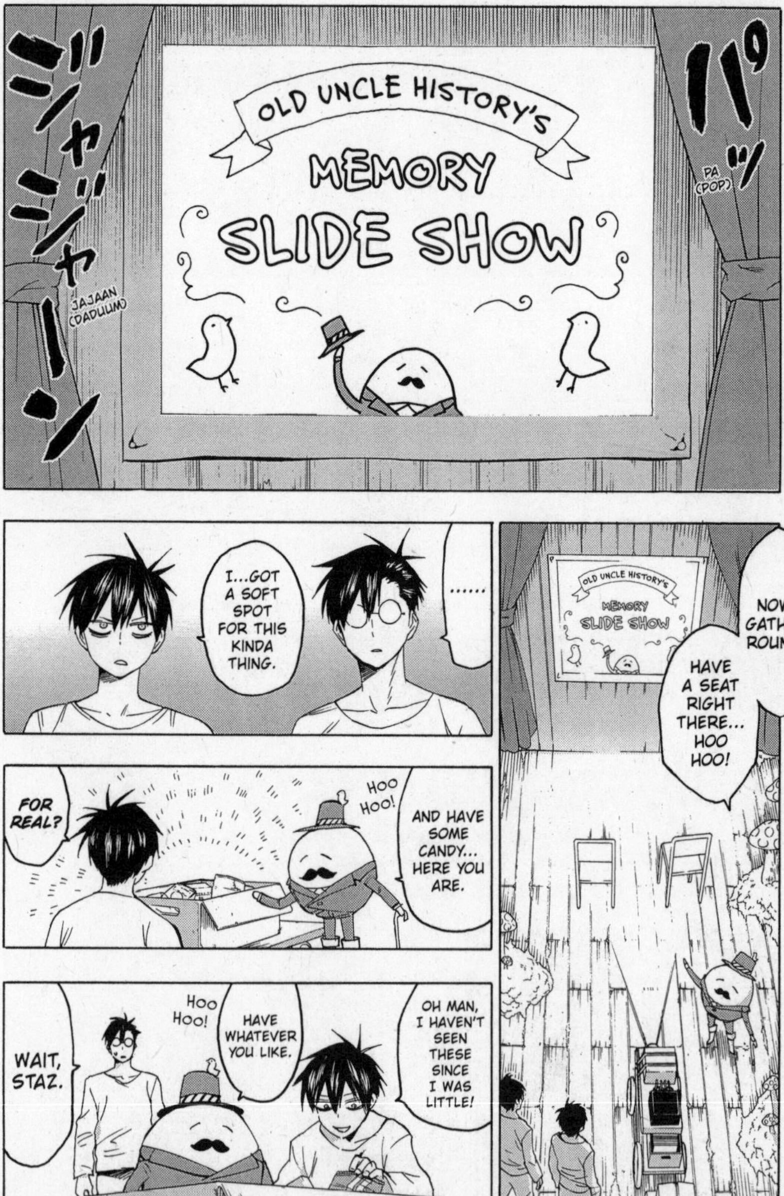
パッ
PA (POP)
OLD UNCLE HISTORY'S
MEMORY
SLIDE SHOW
ジャジャーン
JAJAAN (DADUUM)
OLD UNCLE HISTORY'S MEMORY SLIDE SHOW
NOW, GATHER ROUND!
HAVE A SEAT RIGHT THERE... HOO HOO!
......
I...GOT A SOFT SPOT FOR THIS KINDA THING.
AND HAVE SOME CANDY... HERE YOU ARE.
HOO HOO!
FOR REAL?
OH MAN, I HAVEN'T SEEN THESE SINCE I WAS LITTLE!
HAVE WHATEVER YOU LIKE.
HOO HOO!
WAIT, STAZ.

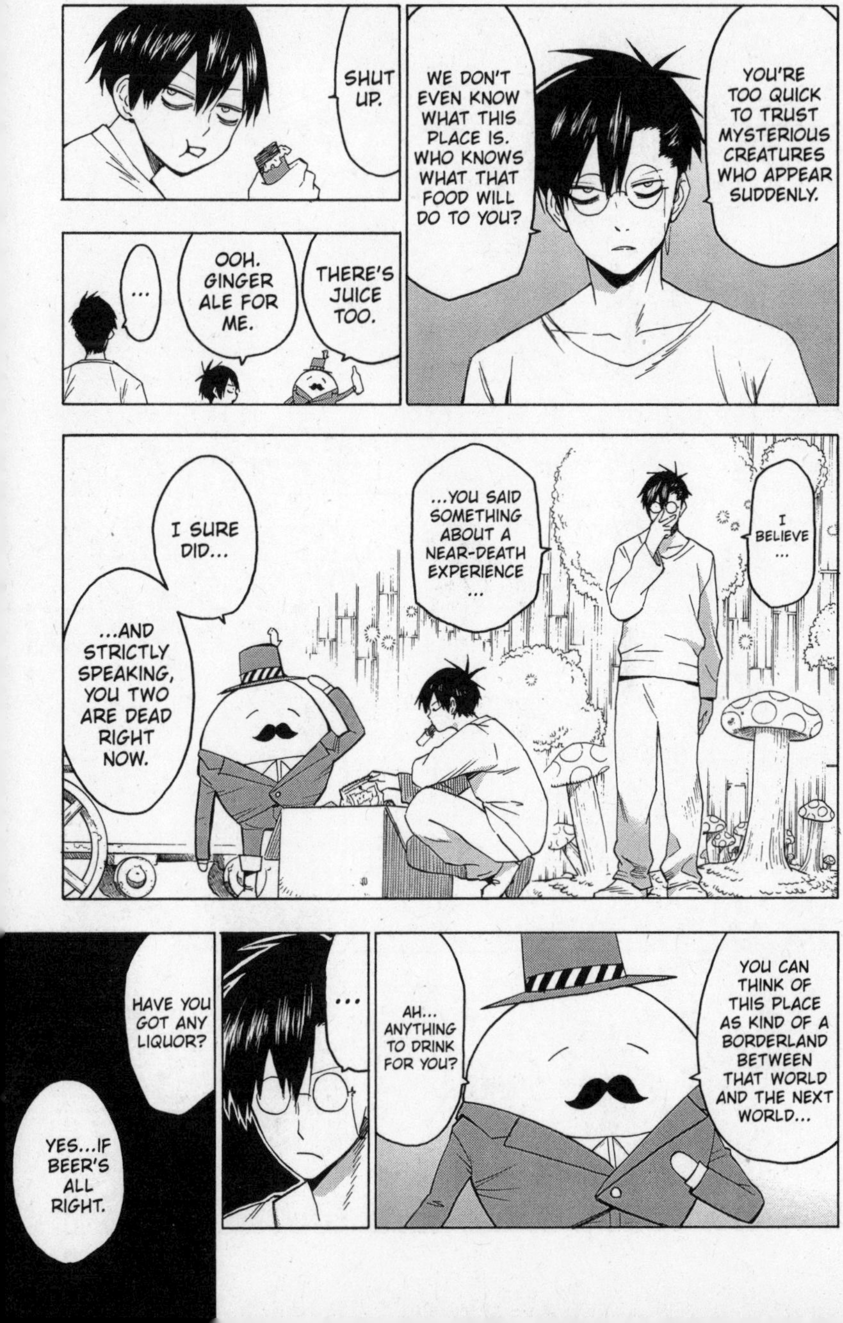
YOU'RE TOO QUICK TO TRUST MYSTERIOUS CREATURES WHO APPEAR SUDDENLY.
WE DON'T EVEN KNOW WHAT THIS PLACE IS. WHO KNOWS WHAT THAT FOOD WILL DO TO YOU?
SHUT UP.
THERE'S JUICE TOO.
OOH. GINGER ALE FOR ME.
...
I BELIEVE ...
...YOU SAID SOMETHING ABOUT A NEAR-DEATH EXPERIENCE ...
I SURE DID...
...AND STRICTLY SPEAKING, YOU TWO ARE DEAD RIGHT NOW.
YOU CAN THINK OF THIS PLACE AS KIND OF A BORDERLAND BETWEEN THAT WORLD AND THE NEXT WORLD...
AH... ANYTHING TO DRINK FOR YOU?
...
HAVE YOU GOT ANY LIQUOR?
YES...IF BEER'S ALL RIGHT.

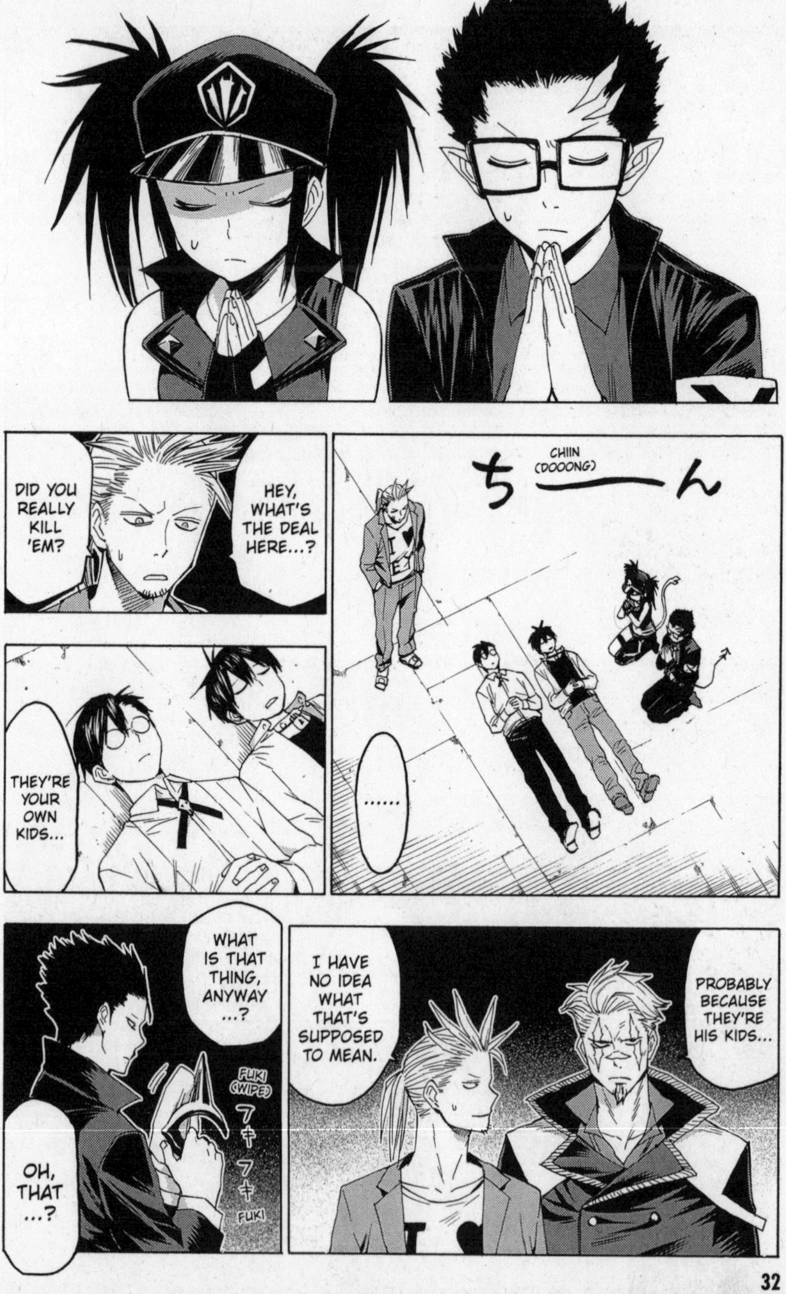
CHIIN (DOOONG)
ち——ん
......
HEY, WHAT'S THE DEAL HERE...?
DID YOU REALLY KILL 'EM?
THEY'RE YOUR OWN KIDS...
PROBABLY BECAUSE THEY'RE HIS KIDS...
I HAVE NO IDEA WHAT THAT'S SUPPOSED TO MEAN.
WHAT IS THAT THING, ANYWAY ...?
FUKI (WIPE)
フキフキ
FUKI
OH, THAT ...?

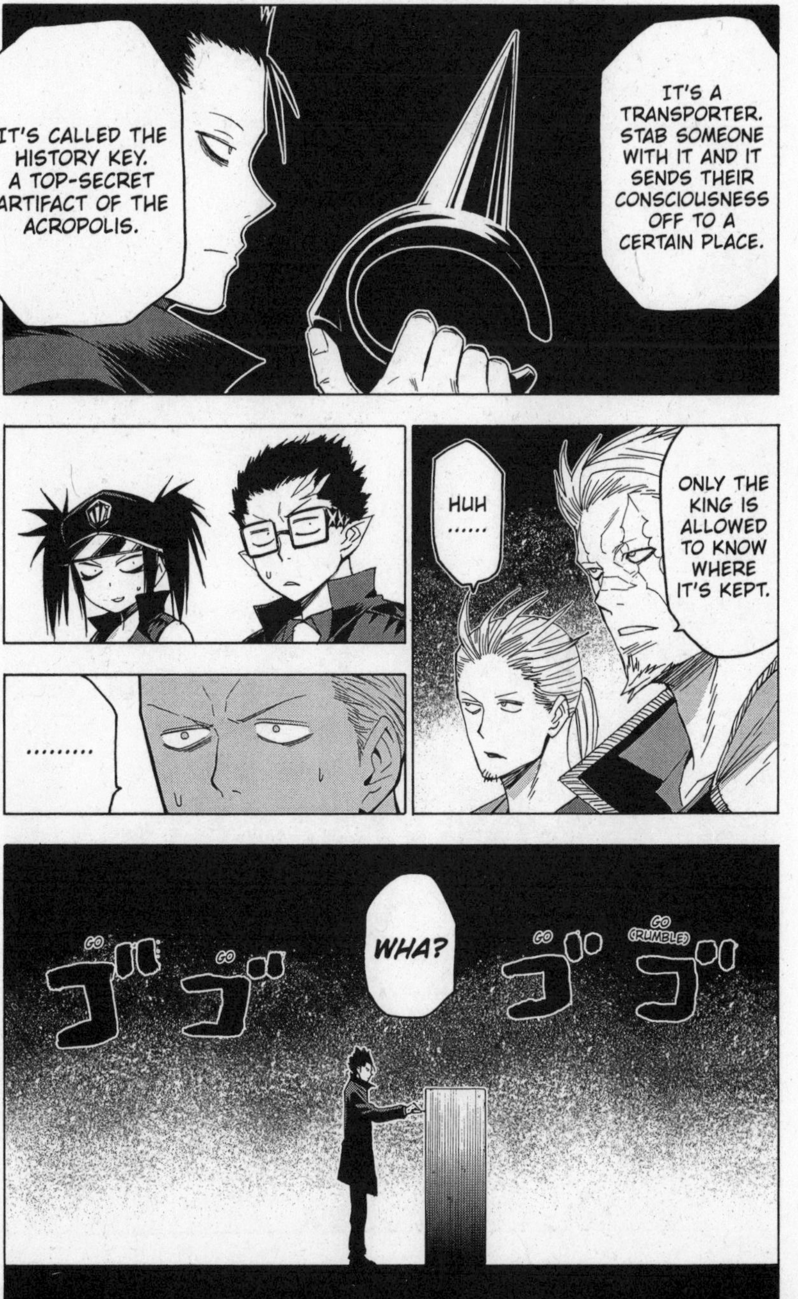
IT'S A TRANSPORTER. STAB SOMEONE WITH IT AND IT SENDS THEIR CONSCIOUSNESS OFF TO A CERTAIN PLACE.
IT'S CALLED THE HISTORY KEY. A TOP-SECRET ARTIFACT OF THE ACROPOLIS.
ONLY THE KING IS ALLOWED TO KNOW WHERE IT'S KEPT.
HUH ......
....
GO (RUMBLE)
GO
WHA?
GO
GO

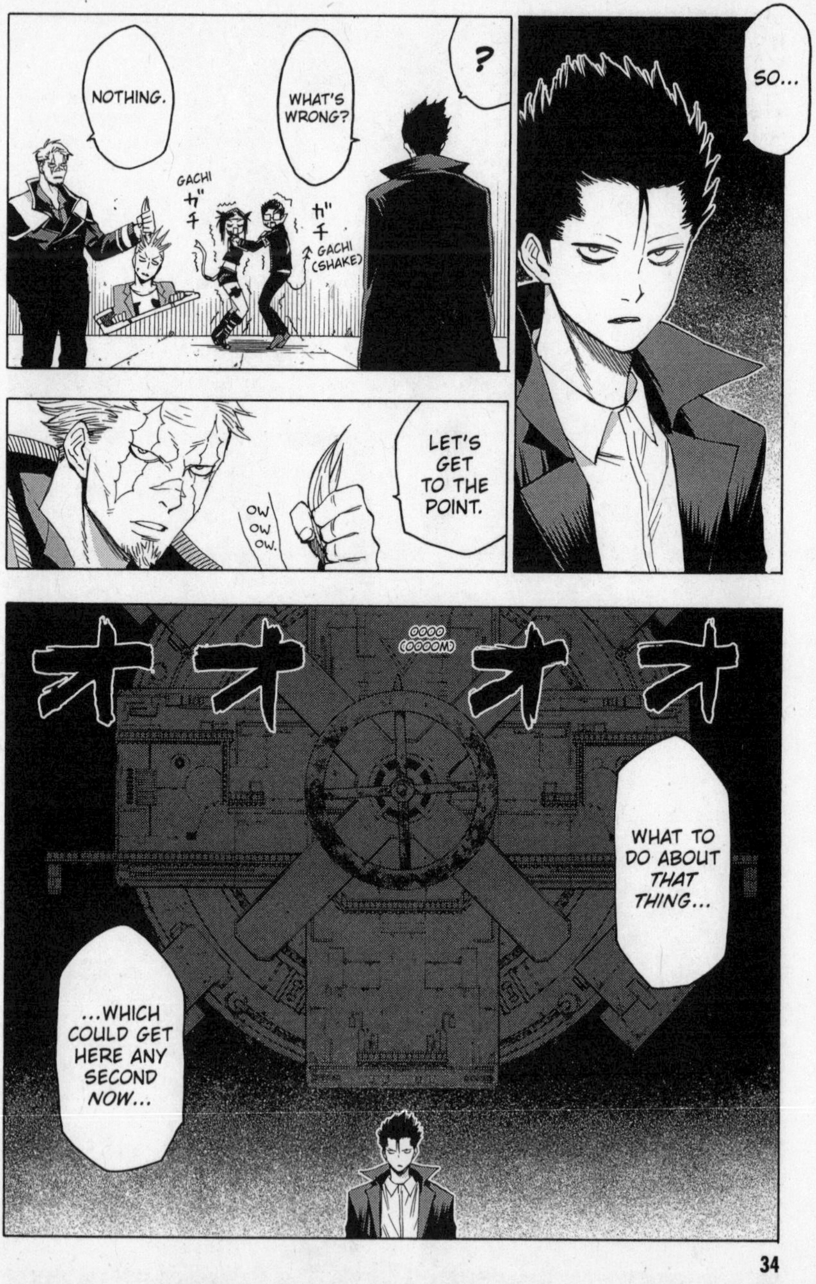

SO...
?
WHAT'S WRONG?
NOTHING.
GACHI ガチ
ガチ GACHI (SHAKE)
LET'S GET TO THE POINT.
OW OW OW.
オオオオ
OOOO (OOOOM)
WHAT TO DO ABOUT *THAT THING*...
...WHICH COULD GET HERE ANY SECOND *NOW*...

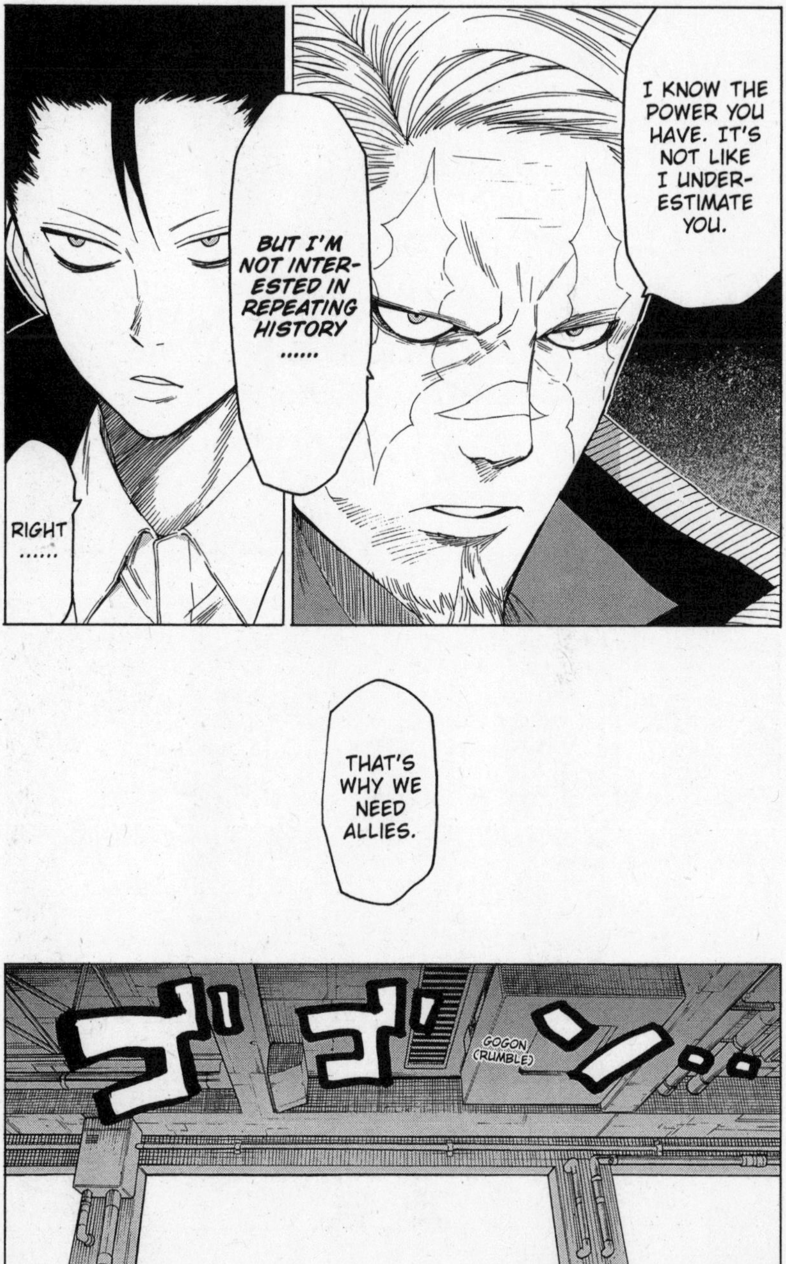
I KNOW THE POWER YOU HAVE. IT'S NOT LIKE I UNDER-ESTIMATE YOU.
BUT I'M NOT INTER-ESTED IN REPEATING HISTORY ......
RIGHT ......
THAT'S WHY WE NEED ALLIES.
ゴゴン
GOGON (RUMBLE)

GOPO
(BLUP)

PO

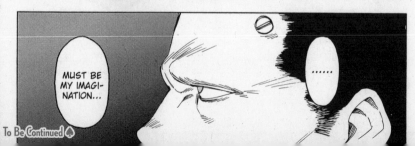

MUST BE
MY IMAGI-
NATION...

......

BLOOD LAD

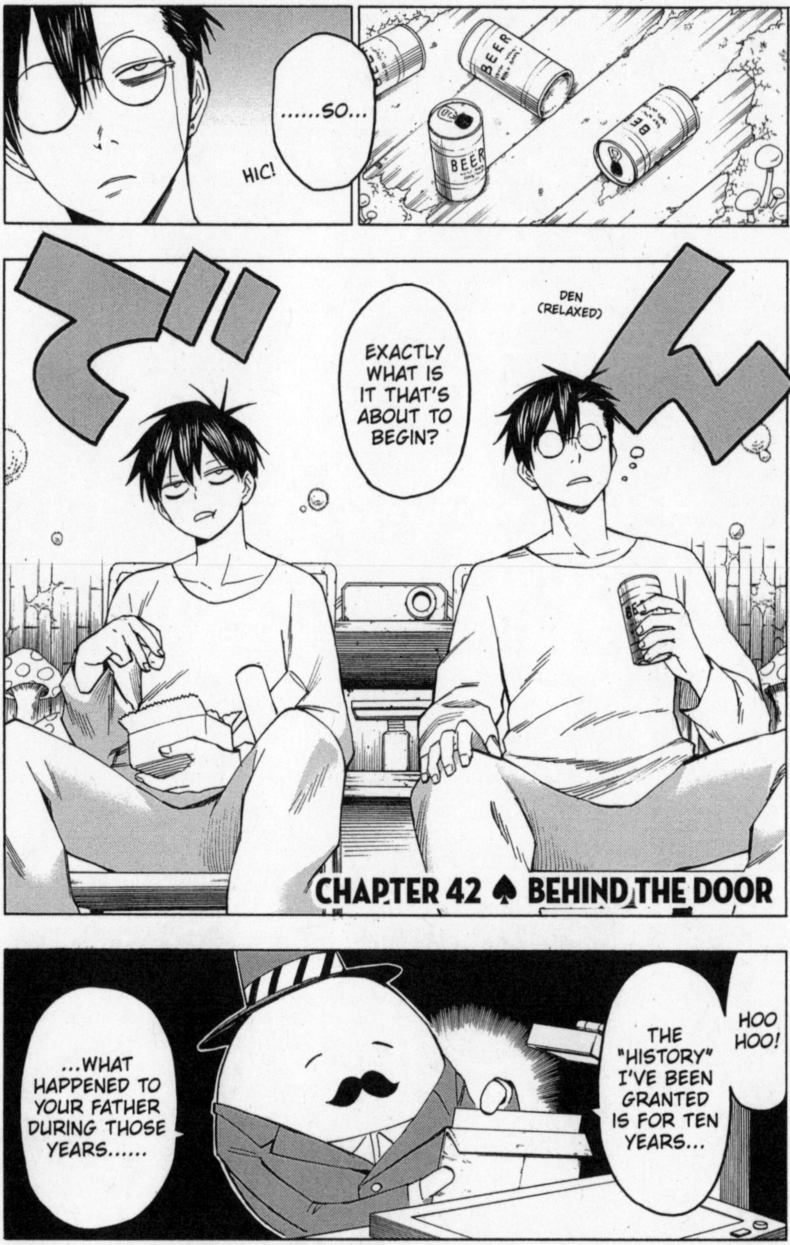

BEER
......SO...
HIC!
DEN (RELAXED)
EXACTLY WHAT IS IT THAT'S ABOUT TO BEGIN?
CHAPTER 42 ♠ BEHIND THE DOOR
HOO HOO!
THE "HISTORY" I'VE BEEN GRANTED IS FOR TEN YEARS...
...WHAT HAPPENED TO YOUR FATHER DURING THOSE YEARS......

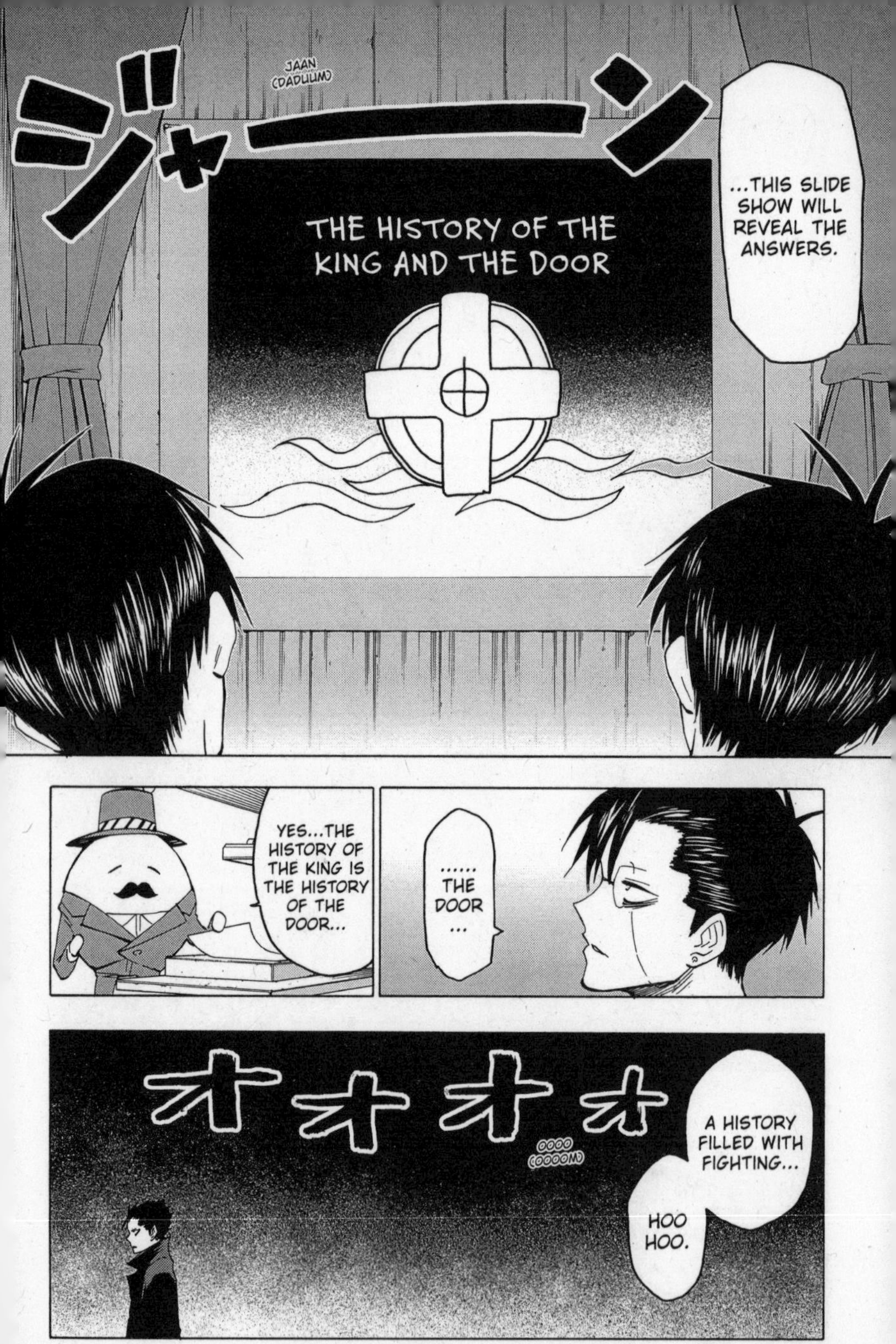
...THIS SLIDE SHOW WILL REVEAL THE ANSWERS.
JAAN (DADUUM)
THE HISTORY OF THE KING AND THE DOOR
...... THE DOOR ...
YES...THE HISTORY OF THE KING IS THE HISTORY OF THE DOOR...
A HISTORY FILLED WITH FIGHTING...
HOO HOO.
OOOO (OOOOM)

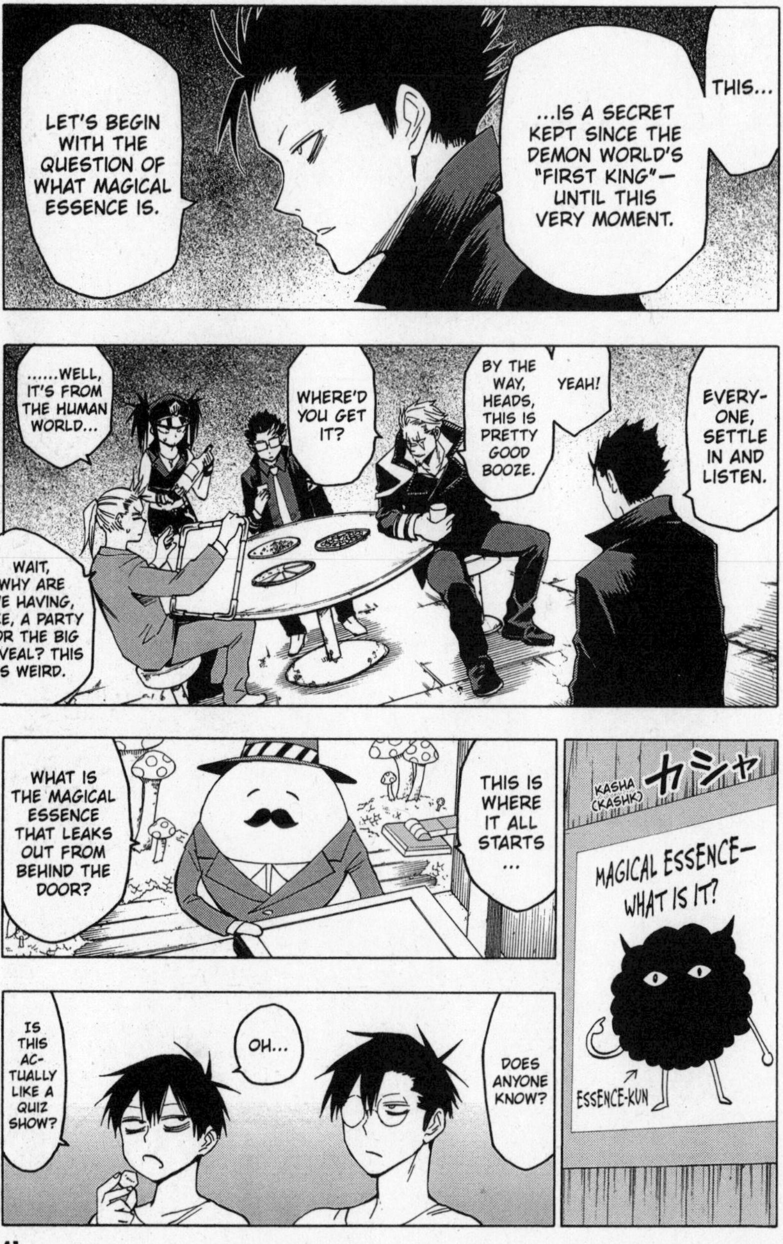
THIS...
...IS A SECRET KEPT SINCE THE DEMON WORLD'S "FIRST KING"—UNTIL THIS VERY MOMENT.
LET'S BEGIN WITH THE QUESTION OF WHAT MAGICAL ESSENCE IS.
EVERY-ONE, SETTLE IN AND LISTEN.
YEAH!
BY THE WAY, HEADS, THIS IS PRETTY GOOD BOOZE.
WHERE'D YOU GET IT?
......WELL, IT'S FROM THE HUMAN WORLD...
WAIT, WHY ARE WE HAVING, LIKE, A PARTY FOR THE BIG REVEAL? THIS IS WEIRD.
カシャ
KASHA (KASHK)
MAGICAL ESSENCE—WHAT IS IT?
ESSENCE-KUN
THIS IS WHERE IT ALL STARTS ...
WHAT IS THE MAGICAL ESSENCE THAT LEAKS OUT FROM BEHIND THE DOOR?
DOES ANYONE KNOW?
OH...
IS THIS ACTUALLY LIKE A QUIZ SHOW?

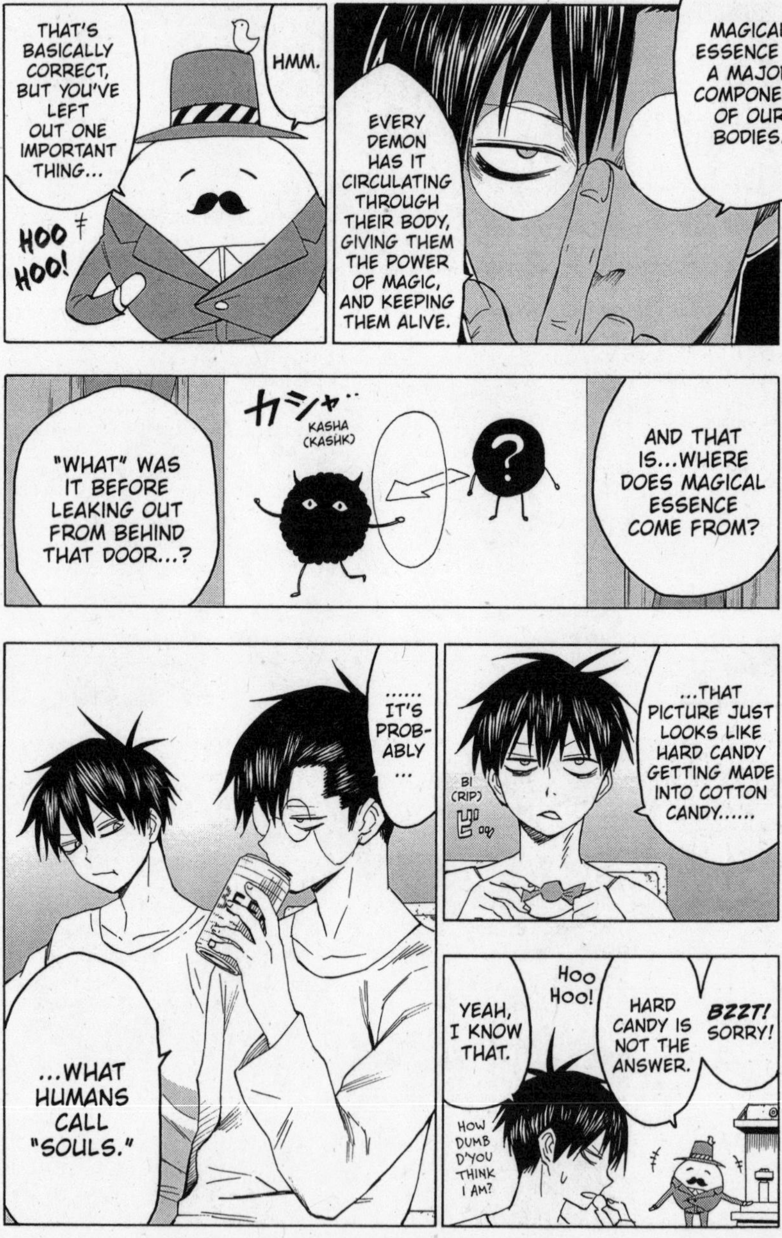
MAGICAL ESSENCE IS A MAJOR COMPONENT OF OUR BODIES.
EVERY DEMON HAS IT CIRCULATING THROUGH THEIR BODY, GIVING THEM THE POWER OF MAGIC, AND KEEPING THEM ALIVE.
HMM.
THAT'S BASICALLY CORRECT, BUT YOU'VE LEFT OUT ONE IMPORTANT THING...
HOO HOO!
AND THAT IS...WHERE DOES MAGICAL ESSENCE COME FROM?
カシャ‥
KASHA (KASHK)
"WHAT" WAS IT BEFORE LEAKING OUT FROM BEHIND THAT DOOR...?
...THAT PICTURE JUST LOOKS LIKE HARD CANDY GETTING MADE INTO COTTON CANDY......
ビッ
BI (RIP)
BZZT! SORRY!
HARD CANDY IS NOT THE ANSWER.
HOO HOO!
YEAH, I KNOW THAT.
HOW DUMB D'YOU THINK I AM?
...... IT'S PROB-ABLY ...
...WHAT HUMANS CALL "SOULS."

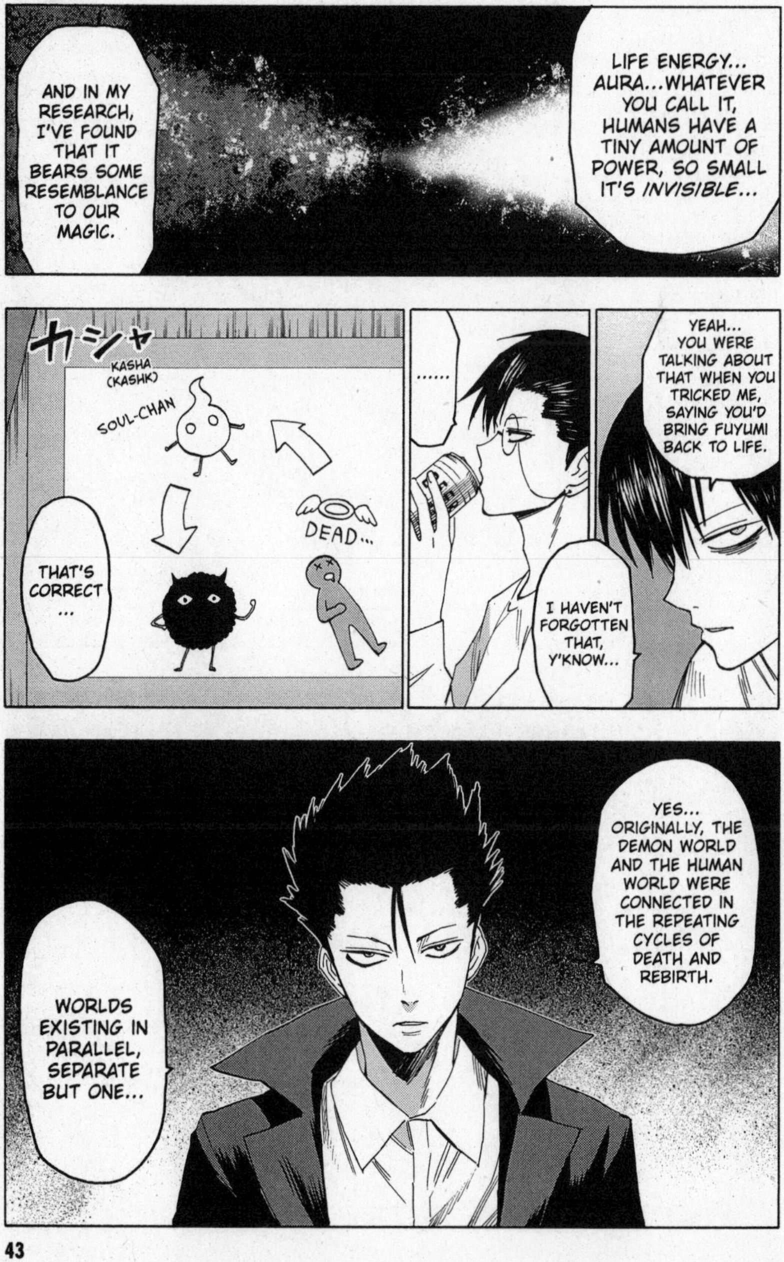
LIFE ENERGY... AURA...WHATEVER YOU CALL IT, HUMANS HAVE A TINY AMOUNT OF POWER, SO SMALL IT'S *INVISIBLE*...
AND IN MY RESEARCH, I'VE FOUND THAT IT BEARS SOME RESEMBLANCE TO OUR MAGIC.
YEAH... YOU WERE TALKING ABOUT THAT WHEN YOU TRICKED ME, SAYING YOU'D BRING FUYUMI BACK TO LIFE.
I HAVEN'T FORGOTTEN THAT, Y'KNOW...
......
カシャ
KASHA (KASHK)
SOUL-CHAN
DEAD...
THAT'S CORRECT ...
YES... ORIGINALLY, THE DEMON WORLD AND THE HUMAN WORLD WERE CONNECTED IN THE REPEATING CYCLES OF DEATH AND REBIRTH.
WORLDS EXISTING IN PARALLEL, SEPARATE BUT ONE...

カシャ
KASHA (KASHK)
ALIVE!
HUMAN WORLD
DEAD
THE SOULS OF HUMANS WHO DIED BECAME MAGICAL ESSENCE AND FLOWED INTO THE DEMON WORLD...
DEAD
DEMON WORLD
ALIVE!
...AND THE MAGICAL POWER OF DEMONS WHO DIED WOULD FLOW BACK INTO THE HUMAN WORLD...
THAT WAS THE CYCLE.
BUT...... WE DEMONS ...
ズ ZU (ZMMM)
ズ ZU
ズ ZU
...BUILT A "DAM" FOR THE MAGICAL ESSENCE—THE DOOR.
WHY ...?
BECAUSE WE WERE AFRAID...OF THE EVER-INCREASING NUMBERS OF HUMANS... AND THEIR DEATHS.
...AFRAID THAT WE WOULD BE DROWNED BY THE TORRENT OF MAGICAL ESSENCE.

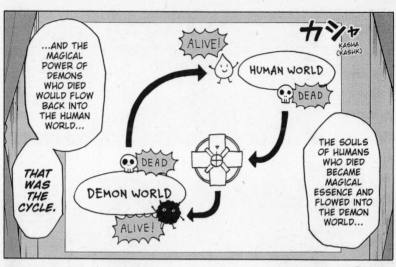

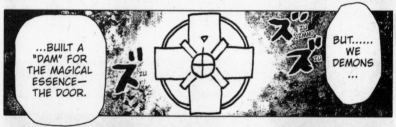

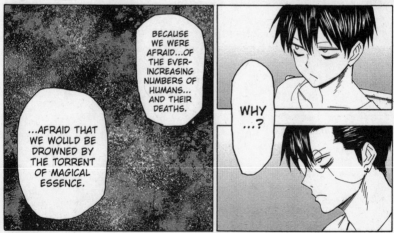

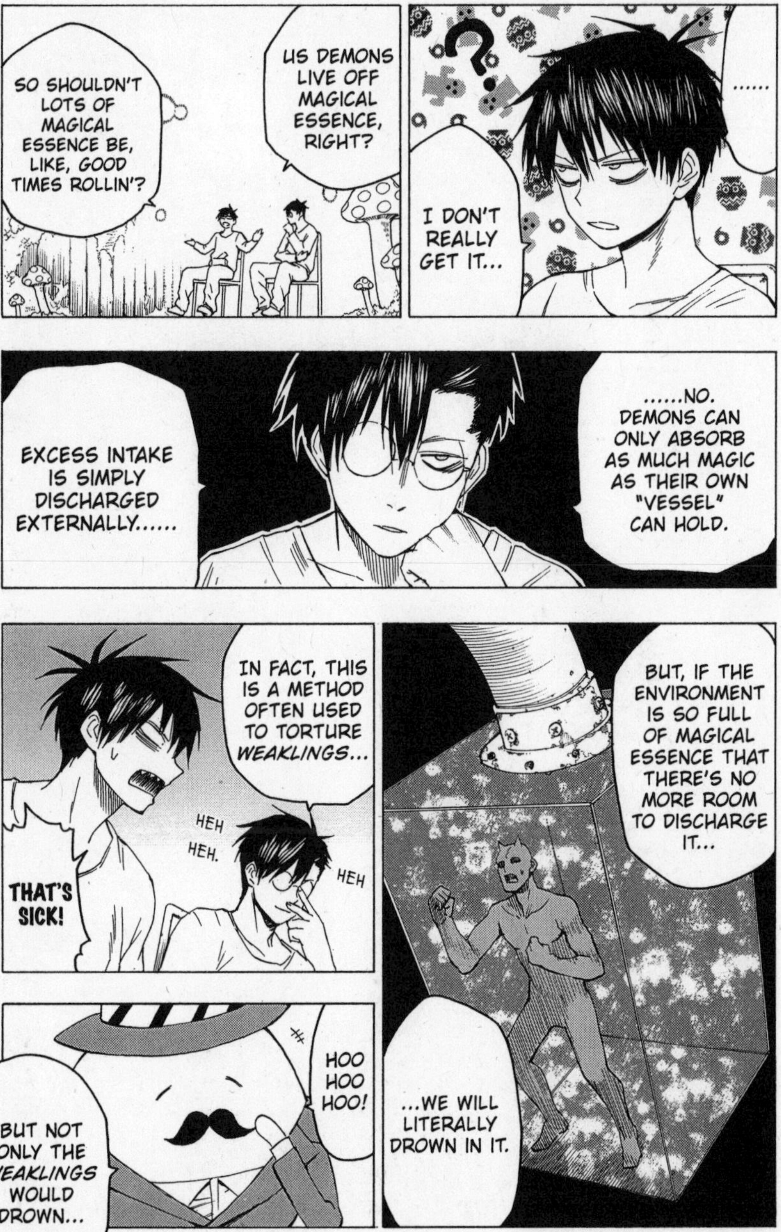
......
I DON'T REALLY GET IT...
US DEMONS LIVE OFF MAGICAL ESSENCE, RIGHT?
SO SHOULDN'T LOTS OF MAGICAL ESSENCE BE, LIKE, GOOD TIMES ROLLIN'?
......NO. DEMONS CAN ONLY ABSORB AS MUCH MAGIC AS THEIR OWN "VESSEL" CAN HOLD.
EXCESS INTAKE IS SIMPLY DISCHARGED EXTERNALLY......
BUT, IF THE ENVIRONMENT IS SO FULL OF MAGICAL ESSENCE THAT THERE'S NO MORE ROOM TO DISCHARGE IT...
...WE WILL LITERALLY DROWN IN IT.
IN FACT, THIS IS A METHOD OFTEN USED TO TORTURE *WEAKLINGS*...
HEH
HEH.
HEH
THAT'S SICK!
HOO HOO HOO!
BUT NOT ONLY THE *WEAKLINGS* WOULD DROWN...

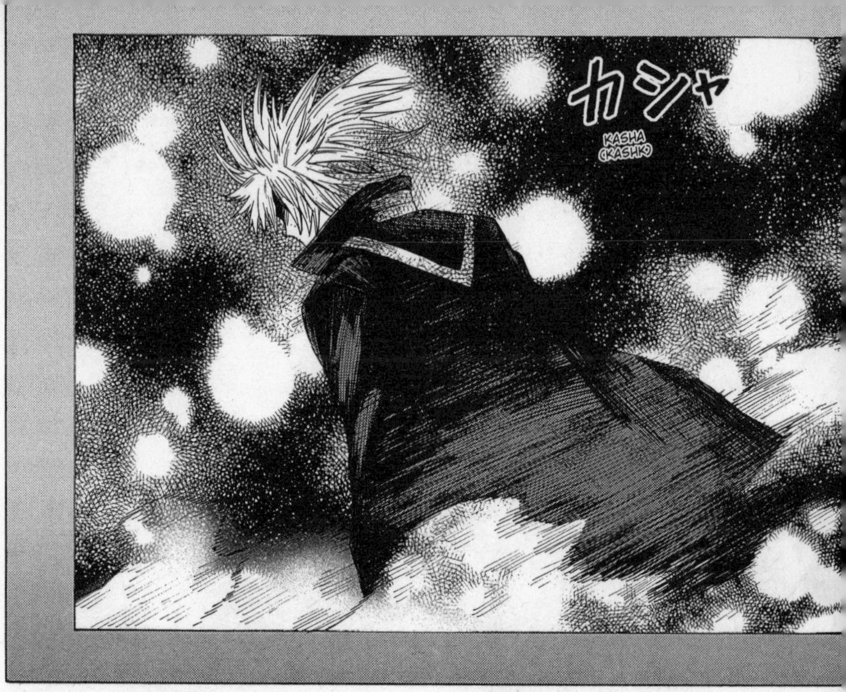
カシャ
KASHA (KASHK)
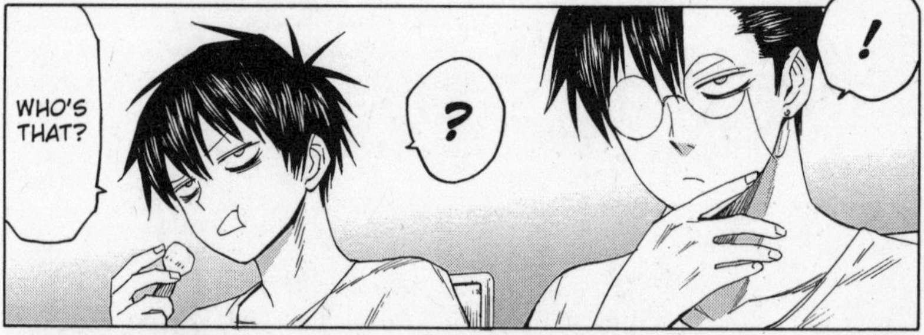
!
?
WHO'S THAT?
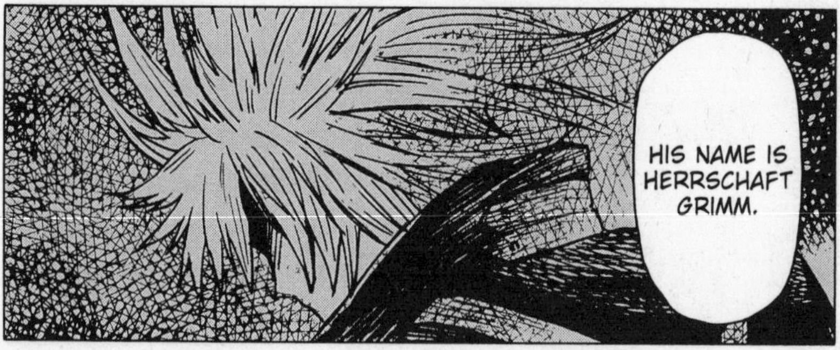
HIS NAME IS HERRSCHAFT GRIMM.

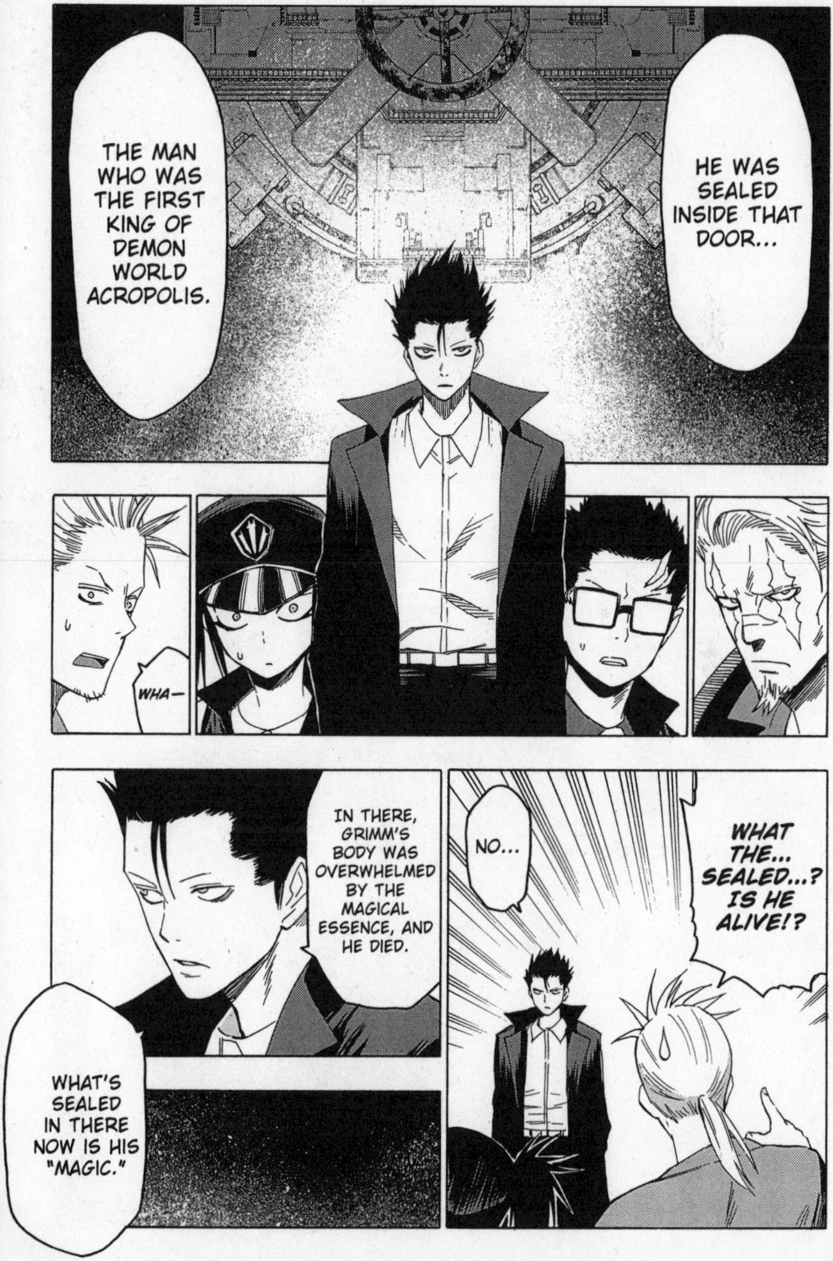
HE WAS SEALED INSIDE THAT DOOR...
THE MAN WHO WAS THE FIRST KING OF DEMON WORLD ACROPOLIS.
WHA—
WHAT THE... SEALED...? IS HE ALIVE!?
NO...
IN THERE, GRIMM'S BODY WAS OVERWHELMED BY THE MAGICAL ESSENCE, AND HE DIED.
WHAT'S SEALED IN THERE NOW IS HIS "MAGIC."

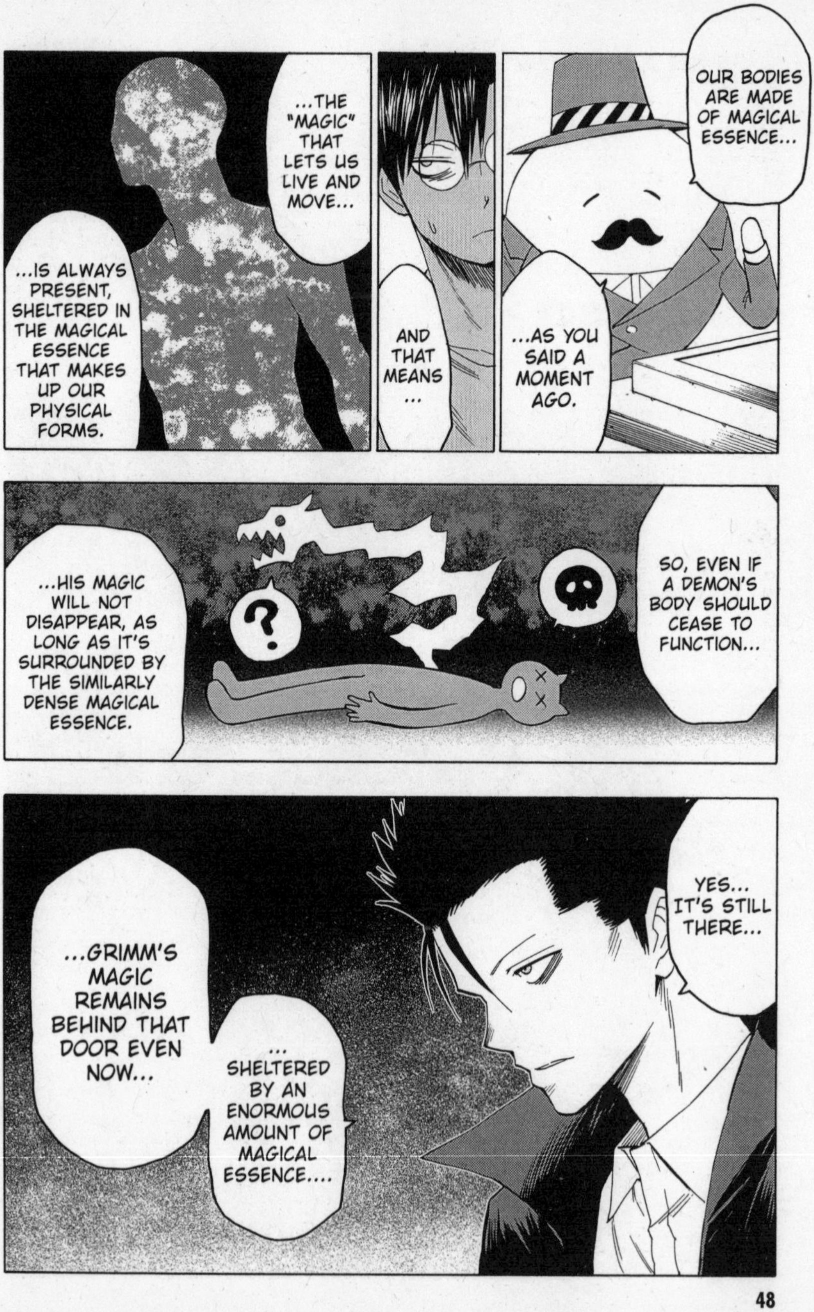
OUR BODIES ARE MADE OF MAGICAL ESSENCE...
...AS YOU SAID A MOMENT AGO.
AND THAT MEANS ...
...THE "MAGIC" THAT LETS US LIVE AND MOVE...
...IS ALWAYS PRESENT, SHELTERED IN THE MAGICAL ESSENCE THAT MAKES UP OUR PHYSICAL FORMS.
SO, EVEN IF A DEMON'S BODY SHOULD CEASE TO FUNCTION...
...HIS MAGIC WILL NOT DISAPPEAR, AS LONG AS IT'S SURROUNDED BY THE SIMILARLY DENSE MAGICAL ESSENCE.
YES... IT'S STILL THERE...
...GRIMM'S MAGIC REMAINS BEHIND THAT DOOR EVEN NOW...
... SHELTERED BY AN ENORMOUS AMOUNT OF MAGICAL ESSENCE....

BOTTLE: YAMAZAKI

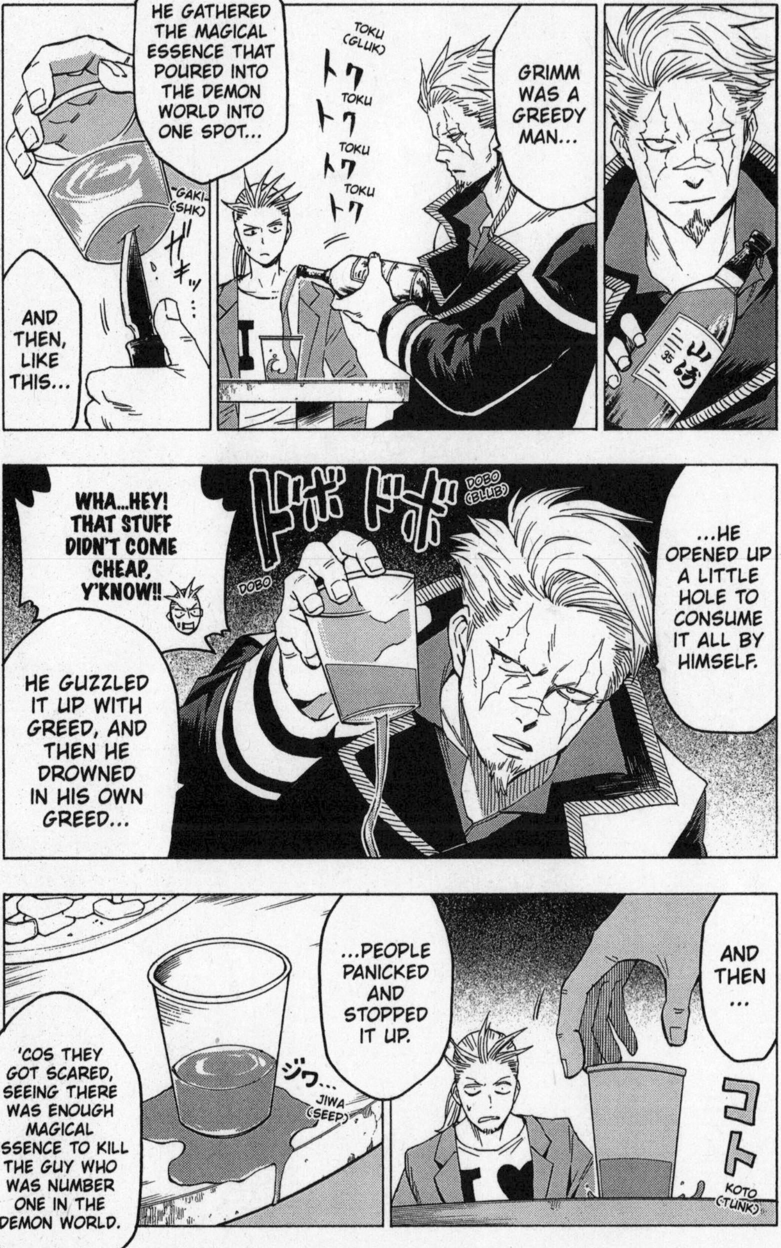

GRIMM WAS A GREEDY MAN...
TOKU (GLUK) TOKU TOKU TOKU
HE GATHERED THE MAGICAL ESSENCE THAT POURED INTO THE DEMON WORLD INTO ONE SPOT...
GAKI (SHK)
AND THEN, LIKE THIS...
...HE OPENED UP A LITTLE HOLE TO CONSUME IT ALL BY HIMSELF.
DOBO (BLUB) DOBO
WHA...HEY! THAT STUFF DIDN'T COME CHEAP, Y'KNOW!!
HE GUZZLED IT UP WITH GREED, AND THEN HE DROWNED IN HIS OWN GREED...
AND THEN...
...PEOPLE PANICKED AND STOPPED IT UP.
KOTO (TUNK)
JIWA (SEEP)
'COS THEY GOT SCARED, SEEING THERE WAS ENOUGH MAGICAL ESSENCE TO KILL THE GUY WHO WAS NUMBER ONE IN THE DEMON WORLD.

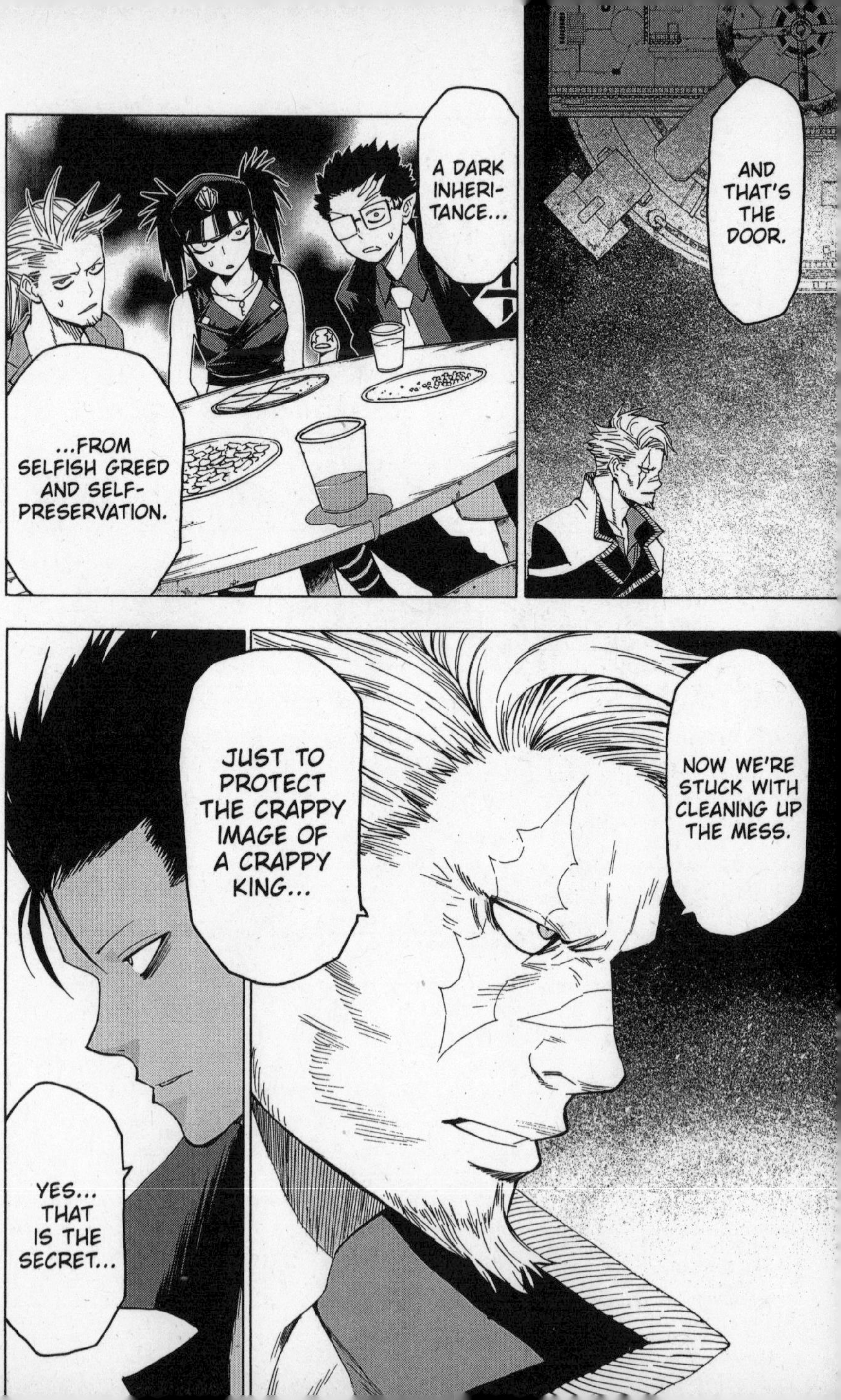
AND THAT'S THE DOOR.
A DARK INHERI- TANCE...
...FROM SELFISH GREED AND SELF- PRESERVATION.
NOW WE'RE STUCK WITH CLEANING UP THE MESS.
JUST TO PROTECT THE CRAPPY IMAGE OF A CRAPPY KING...
YES... THAT IS THE SECRET...

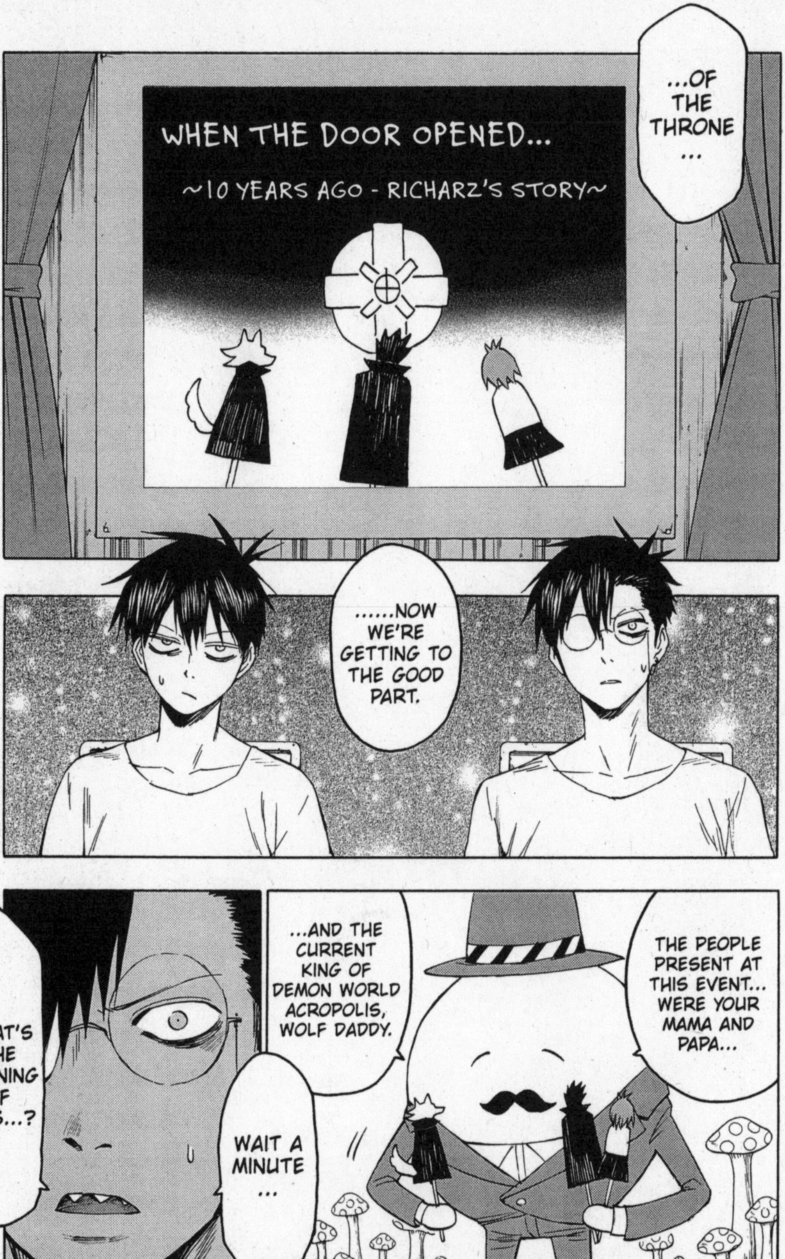
...OF THE THRONE...
WHEN THE DOOR OPENED...
~10 YEARS AGO - RICHARZ'S STORY~
......NOW WE'RE GETTING TO THE GOOD PART.
THE PEOPLE PRESENT AT THIS EVENT... WERE YOUR MAMA AND PAPA...
...AND THE CURRENT KING OF DEMON WORLD ACROPOLIS, WOLF DADDY.
WAIT A MINUTE...
WHAT'S THE MEANING OF THIS...?

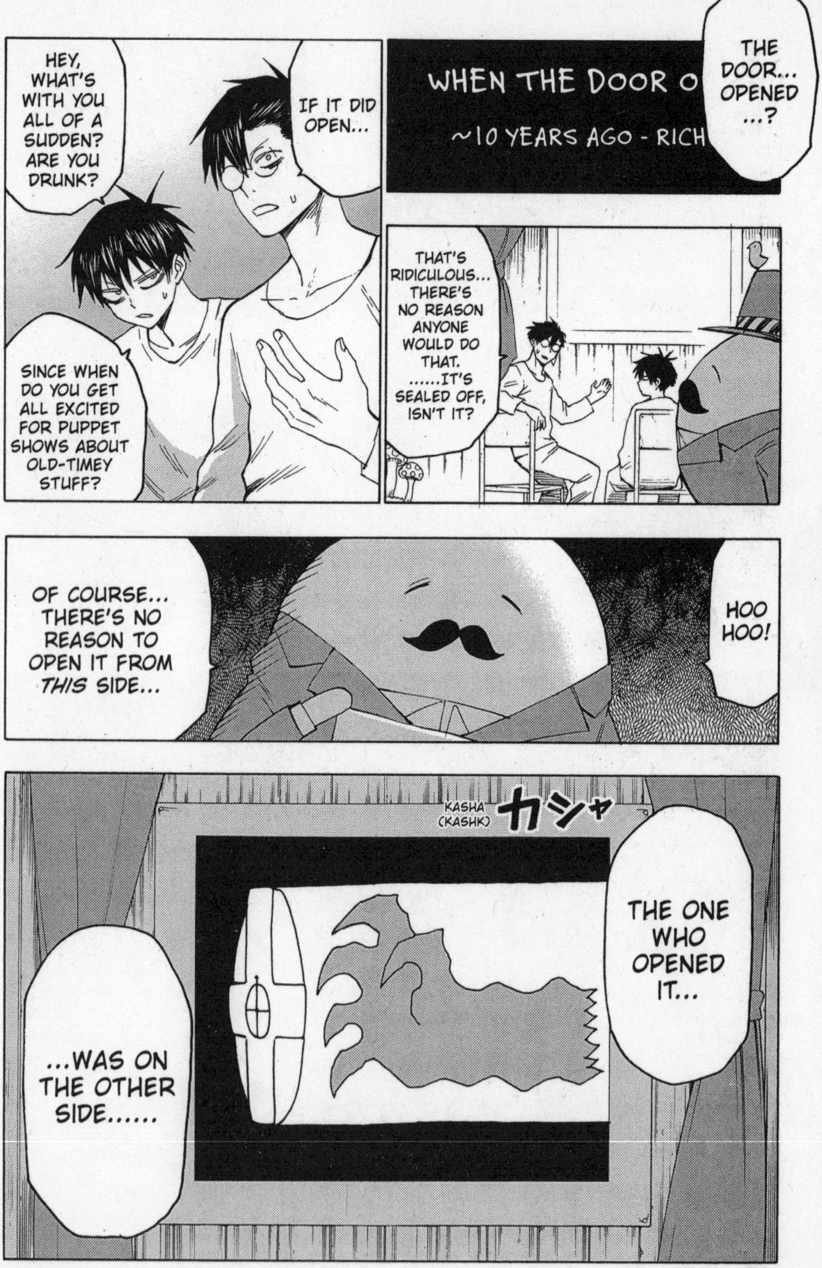
WHEN THE DOOR O
~10 YEARS AGO - RICH
THE DOOR... OPENED ...?
THAT'S RIDICULOUS... THERE'S NO REASON ANYONE WOULD DO THAT. ......IT'S SEALED OFF, ISN'T IT?
IF IT DID OPEN...
HEY, WHAT'S WITH YOU ALL OF A SUDDEN? ARE YOU DRUNK?
SINCE WHEN DO YOU GET ALL EXCITED FOR PUPPET SHOWS ABOUT OLD-TIMEY STUFF?
HOO HOO!
OF COURSE... THERE'S NO REASON TO OPEN IT FROM *THIS* SIDE...
KASHA (KASHK)
カシャ
THE ONE WHO OPENED IT...
...WAS ON THE OTHER SIDE......

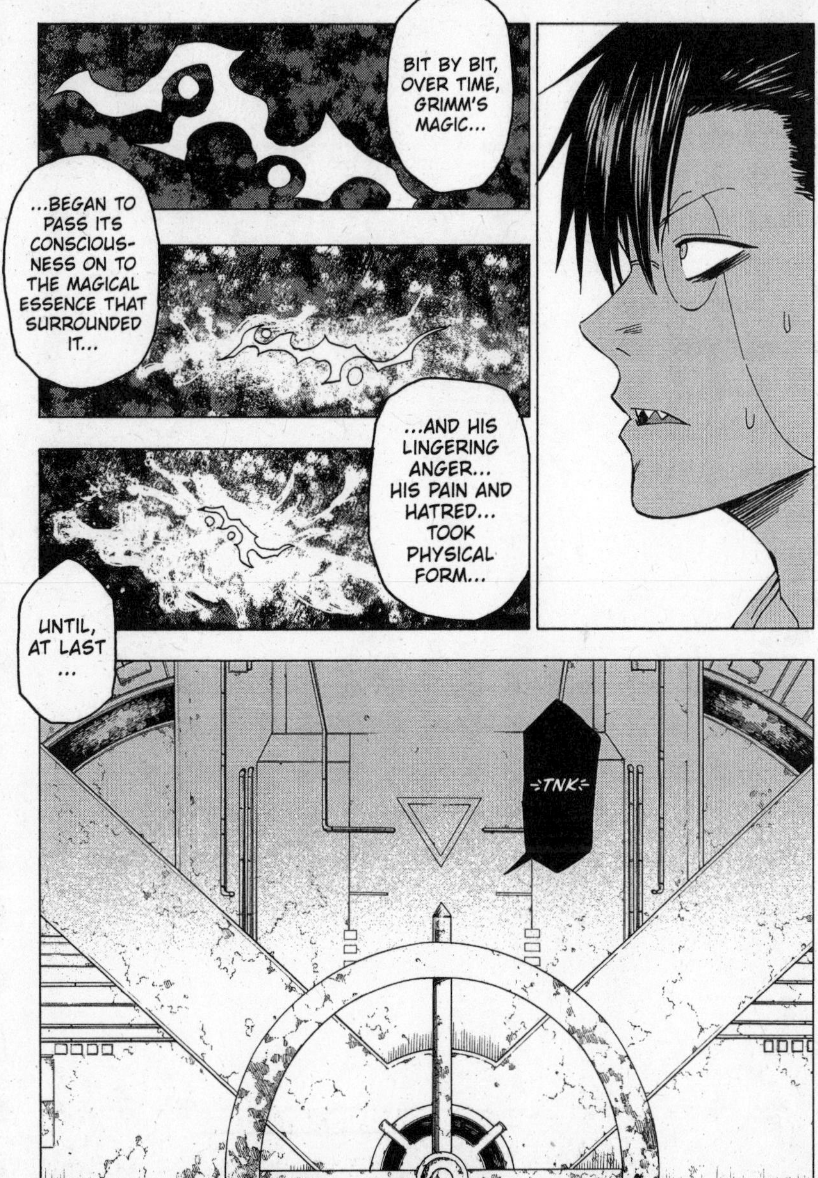
BIT BY BIT, OVER TIME, GRIMM'S MAGIC...
...BEGAN TO PASS ITS CONSCIOUSNESS ON TO THE MAGICAL ESSENCE THAT SURROUNDED IT...
...AND HIS LINGERING ANGER... HIS PAIN AND HATRED... TOOK PHYSICAL FORM...
UNTIL, AT LAST...
TNK

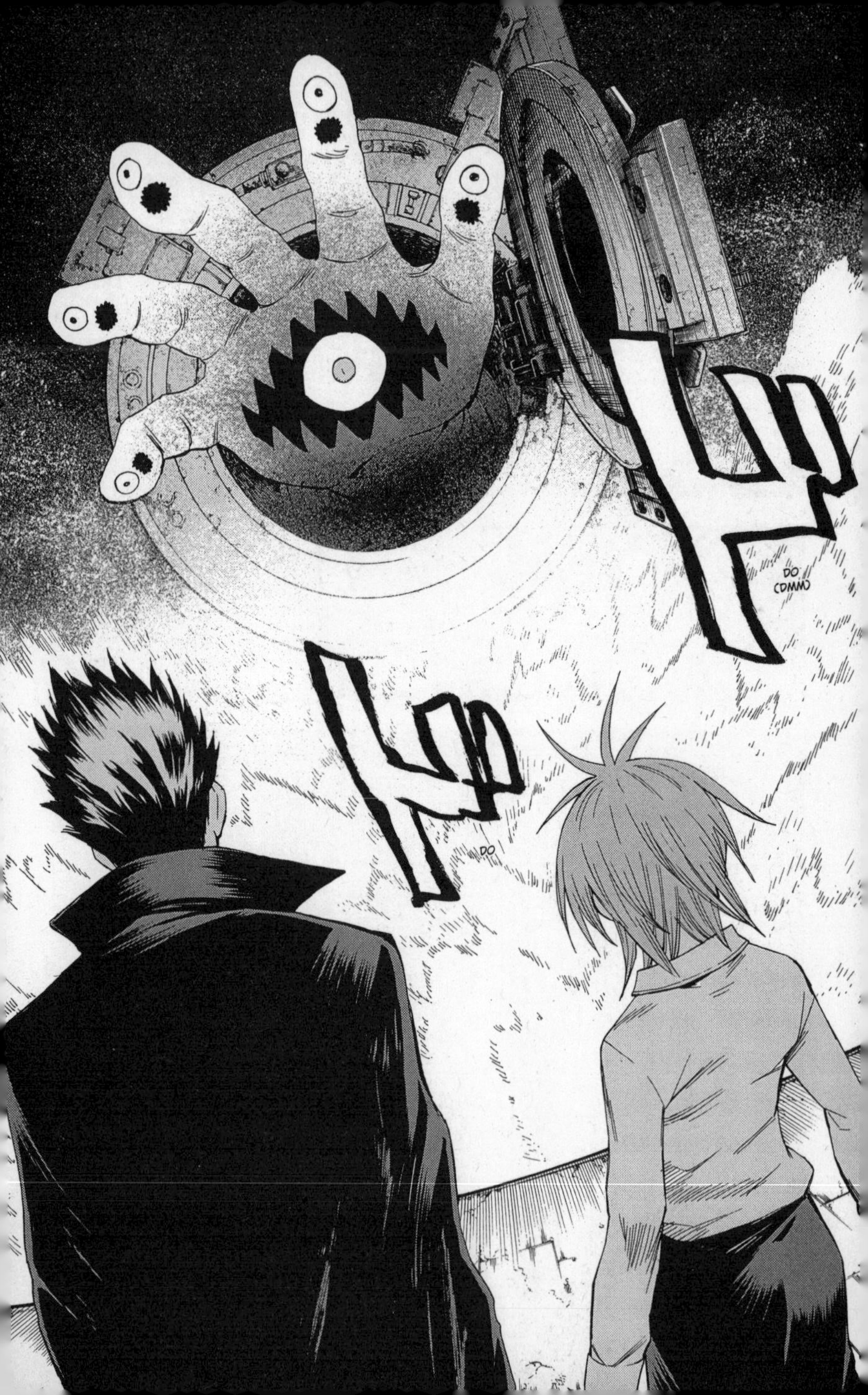
DO
(DMM)
DO

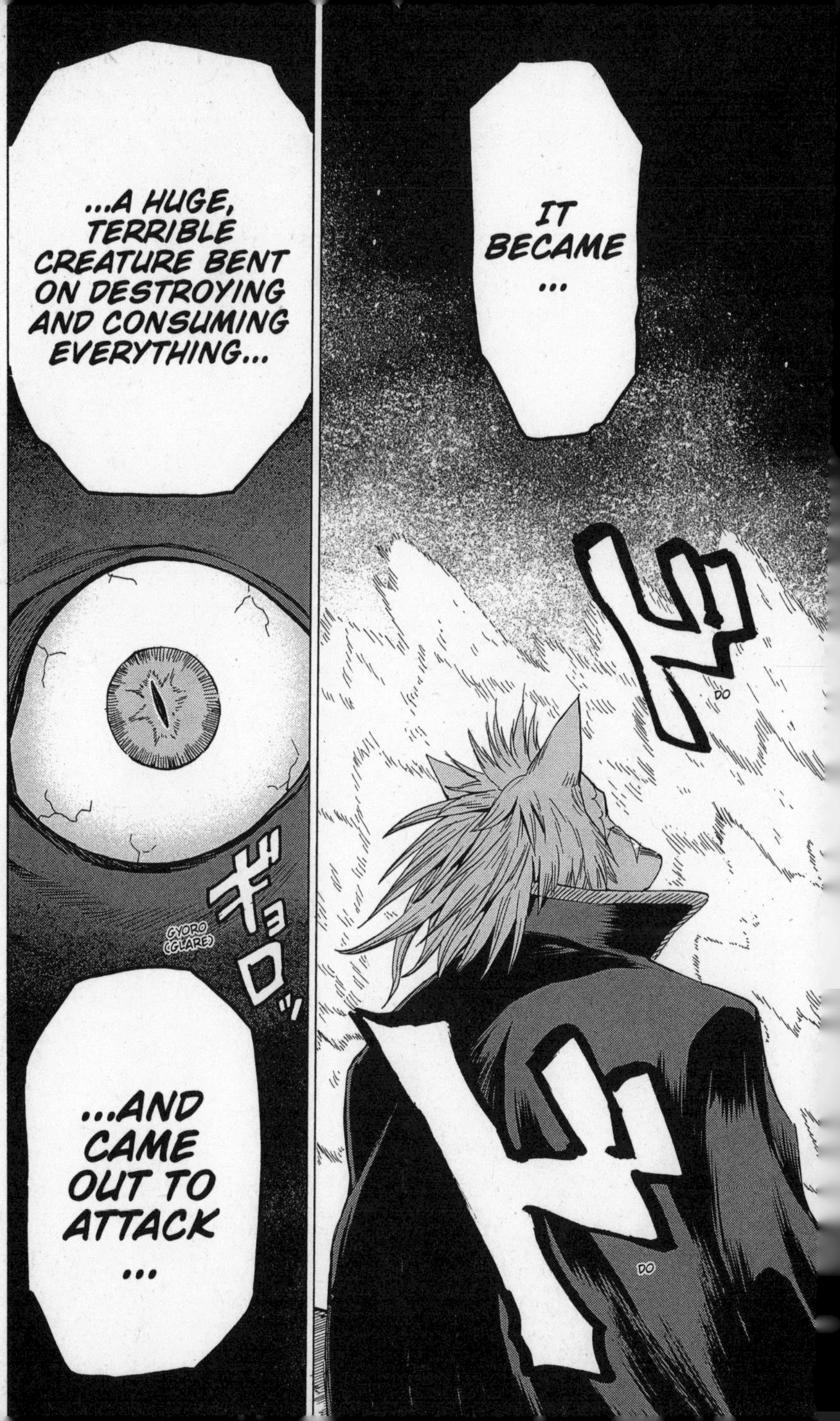
IT BECAME ...
DO
DO
...A HUGE, TERRIBLE CREATURE BENT ON DESTROYING AND CONSUMING EVERYTHING...
ギョロッ
GYORO (GLARE)
...AND CAME OUT TO ATTACK ...

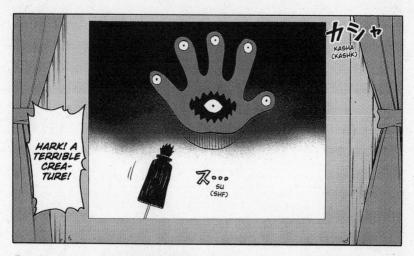

カシャ
KASHA (KASHK)
HARK! A TERRIBLE CREATURE!
ス…
SU (SHF)
IT IS THE KING'S DUTY TO RID THE WORLD OF IT COMPLETELY!
IS EVERYONE READY!?
KAWA
KAWA (WIGGLE)
OKAY! I'LL DRAW ITS ATTENTION!
WOOF! I'LL SHUT THE DOOR SO IT CAN'T ESCAPE BACK INSIDE!
SU
LET'S DO THIS!
AAAH!
BAM BAM BAM BAM!
NOW, RICHARZ!
DON'T LET IT GET AWAY, WOLF DADDY!
HEY ...
THERE! GET IT!
HEY, OLD-TIMER, HELLO...
HUFF! HUFF!
HUFF! HUFF!

SFX: PATA (FLAP) PATA

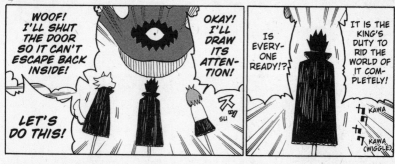

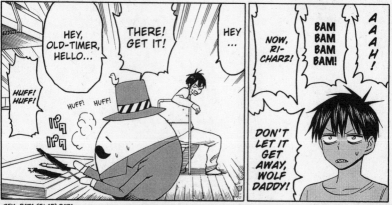

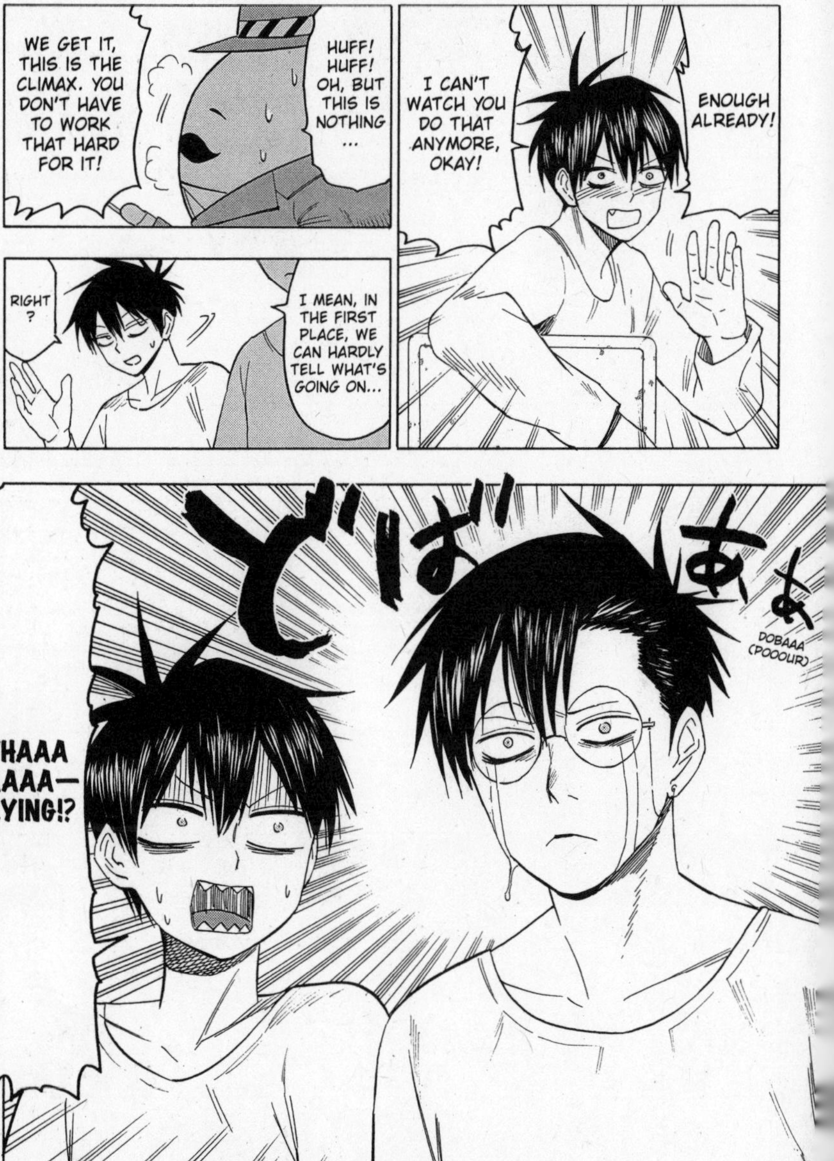
ENOUGH ALREADY!
I CAN'T WATCH YOU DO THAT ANYMORE, OKAY!
HUFF! HUFF! OH, BUT THIS IS NOTHING ...
WE GET IT, THIS IS THE CLIMAX. YOU DON'T HAVE TO WORK THAT HARD FOR IT!
I MEAN, IN THE FIRST PLACE, WE CAN HARDLY TELL WHAT'S GOING ON...
RIGHT ?
どばぁ
DOBAAA (POOOUR)
WHAAA AAAAA— CRYING!?

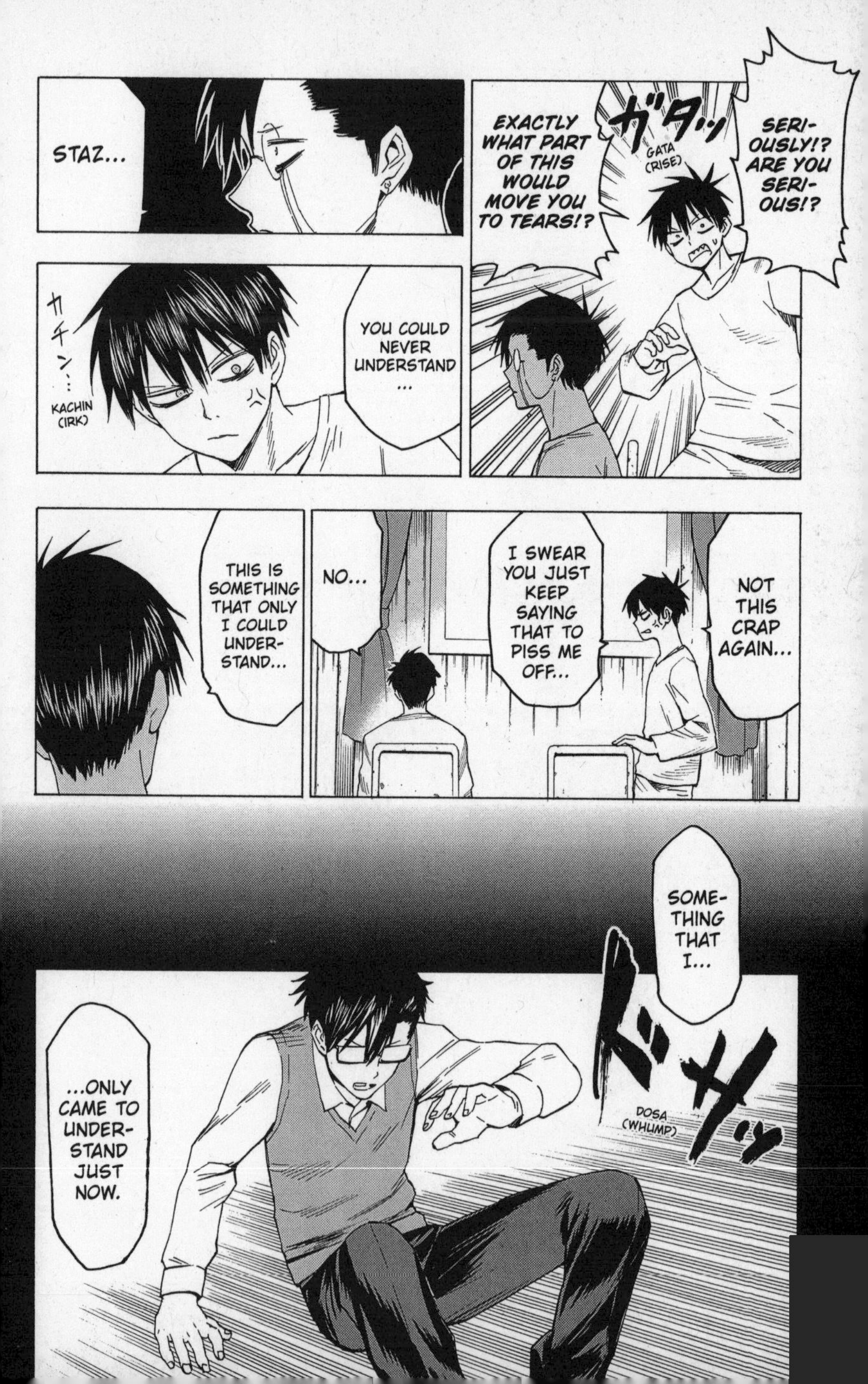
SERI-OUSLY!? ARE YOU SERI-OUS!?
ガタッ
GATA (RISE)
EXACTLY WHAT PART OF THIS WOULD MOVE YOU TO TEARS!?
STAZ...
YOU COULD NEVER UNDERSTAND ...
カチン…
KACHIN (IRK)
NOT THIS CRAP AGAIN...
I SWEAR YOU JUST KEEP SAYING THAT TO PISS ME OFF...
NO...
THIS IS SOMETHING THAT ONLY I COULD UNDER-STAND...
SOME-THING THAT I...
ドサッ
DOSA (WHUMP)
...ONLY CAME TO UNDER-STAND JUST NOW.

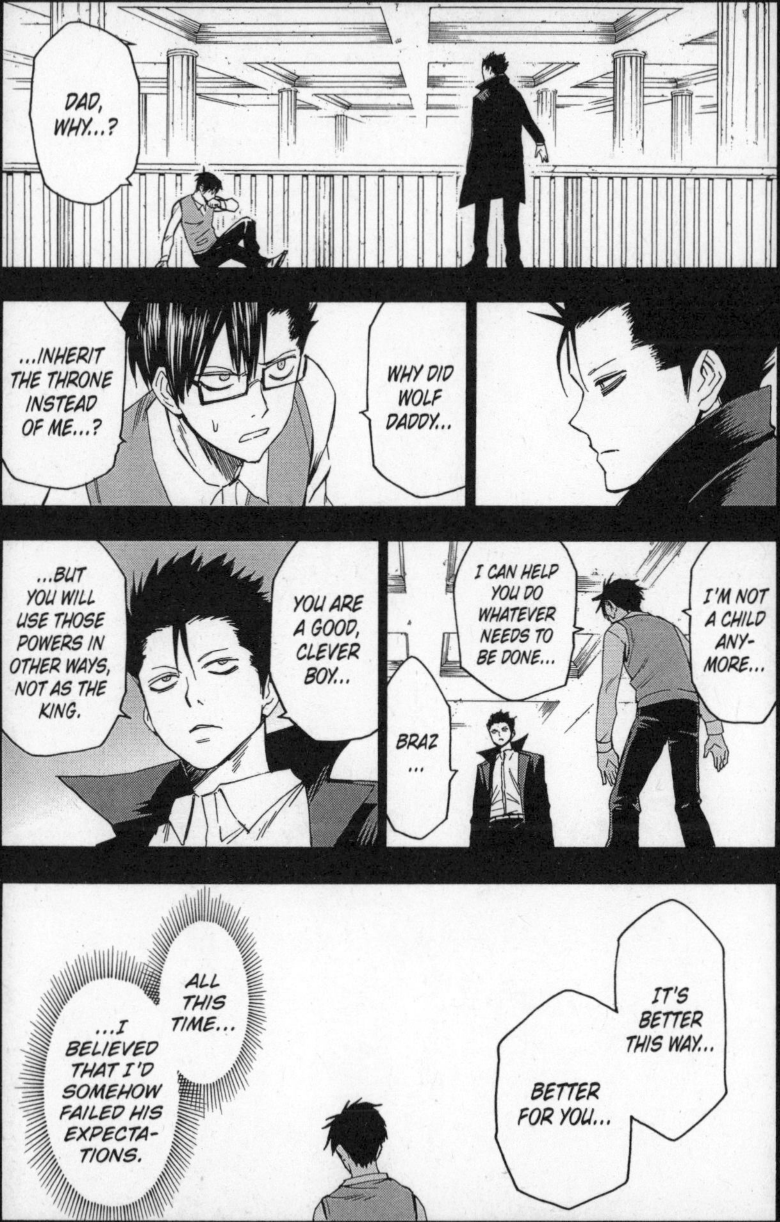
DAD, WHY...?
WHY DID WOLF DADDY...
...INHERIT THE THRONE INSTEAD OF ME...?
I'M NOT A CHILD ANY-MORE...
I CAN HELP YOU DO WHATEVER NEEDS TO BE DONE...
BRAZ ...
YOU ARE A GOOD, CLEVER BOY...
...BUT YOU WILL USE THOSE POWERS IN OTHER WAYS, NOT AS THE KING.
IT'S BETTER THIS WAY...
BETTER FOR YOU...
ALL THIS TIME...
...I BELIEVED THAT I'D SOMEHOW FAILED HIS EXPECTA-TIONS.

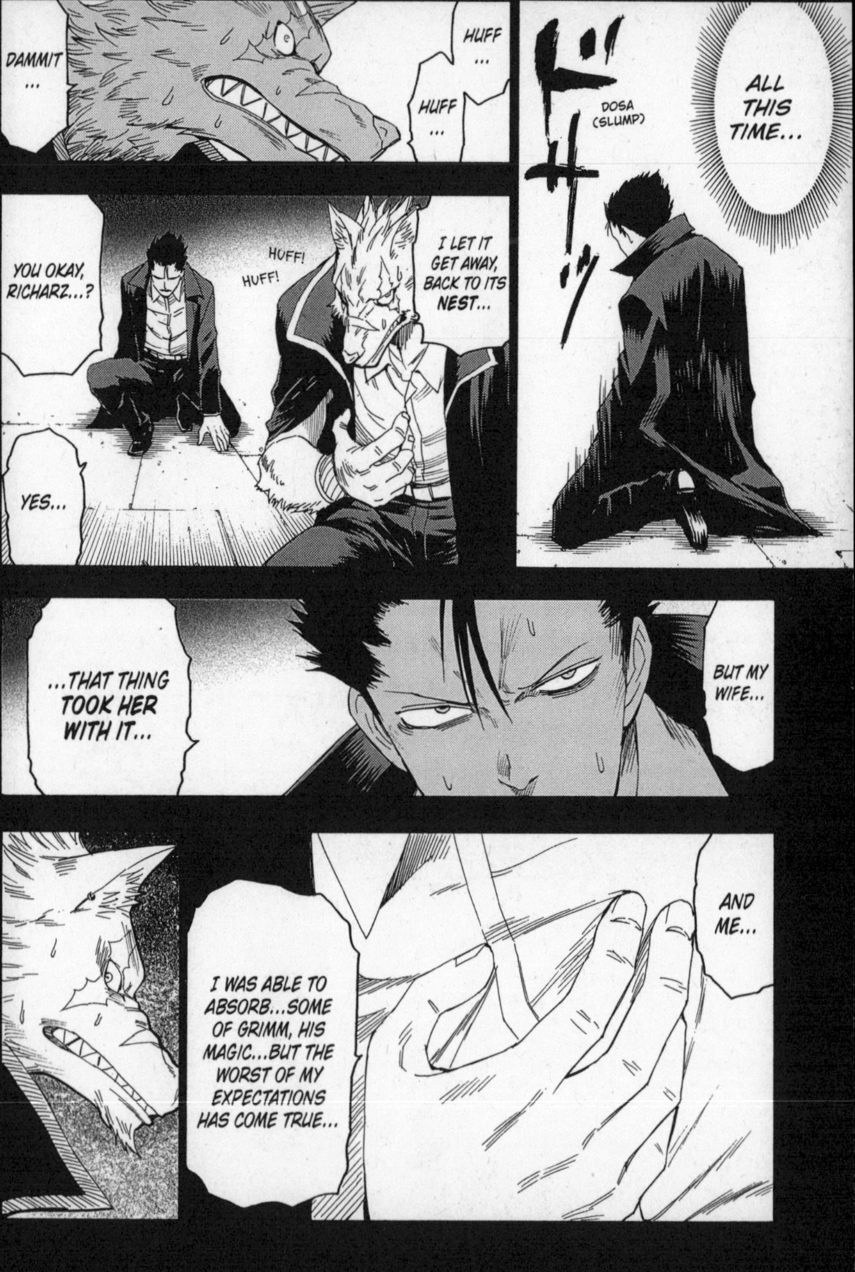
ALL THIS TIME...
DOSA (SLUMP)
HUFF ...
HUFF ...
DAMMIT ...
I LET IT GET AWAY, BACK TO ITS NEST...
HUFF!
HUFF!
YOU OKAY, RICHARZ...?
YES...
BUT MY WIFE...
...THAT THING TOOK HER WITH IT...
AND ME...
I WAS ABLE TO ABSORB...SOME OF GRIMM, HIS MAGIC...BUT THE WORST OF MY EXPECTATIONS HAS COME TRUE...

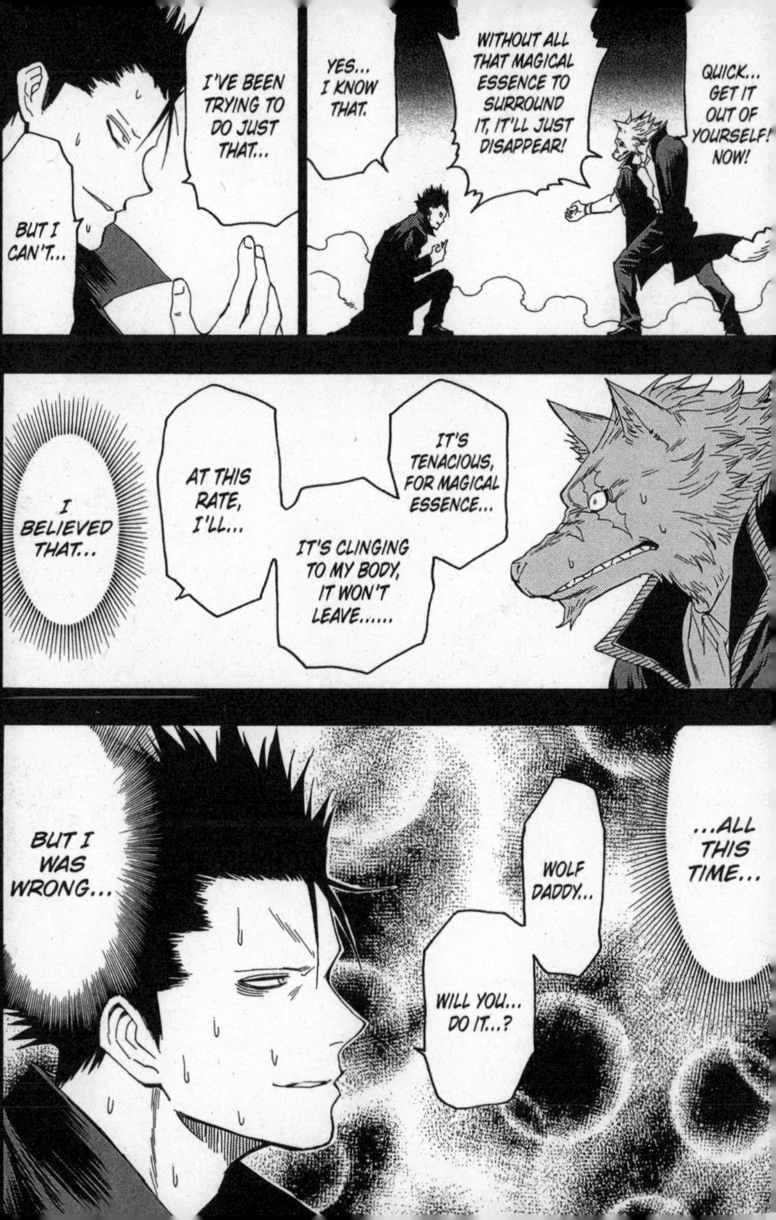
QUICK... GET IT OUT OF YOURSELF! NOW!
WITHOUT ALL THAT MAGICAL ESSENCE TO SURROUND IT, IT'LL JUST DISAPPEAR!
YES... I KNOW THAT.
I'VE BEEN TRYING TO DO JUST THAT...
BUT I CAN'T...
IT'S TENACIOUS, FOR MAGICAL ESSENCE...
IT'S CLINGING TO MY BODY, IT WON'T LEAVE......
AT THIS RATE, I'LL...
I BELIEVED THAT...
...ALL THIS TIME...
WOLF DADDY...
WILL YOU... DO IT...?
BUT I WAS WRONG...

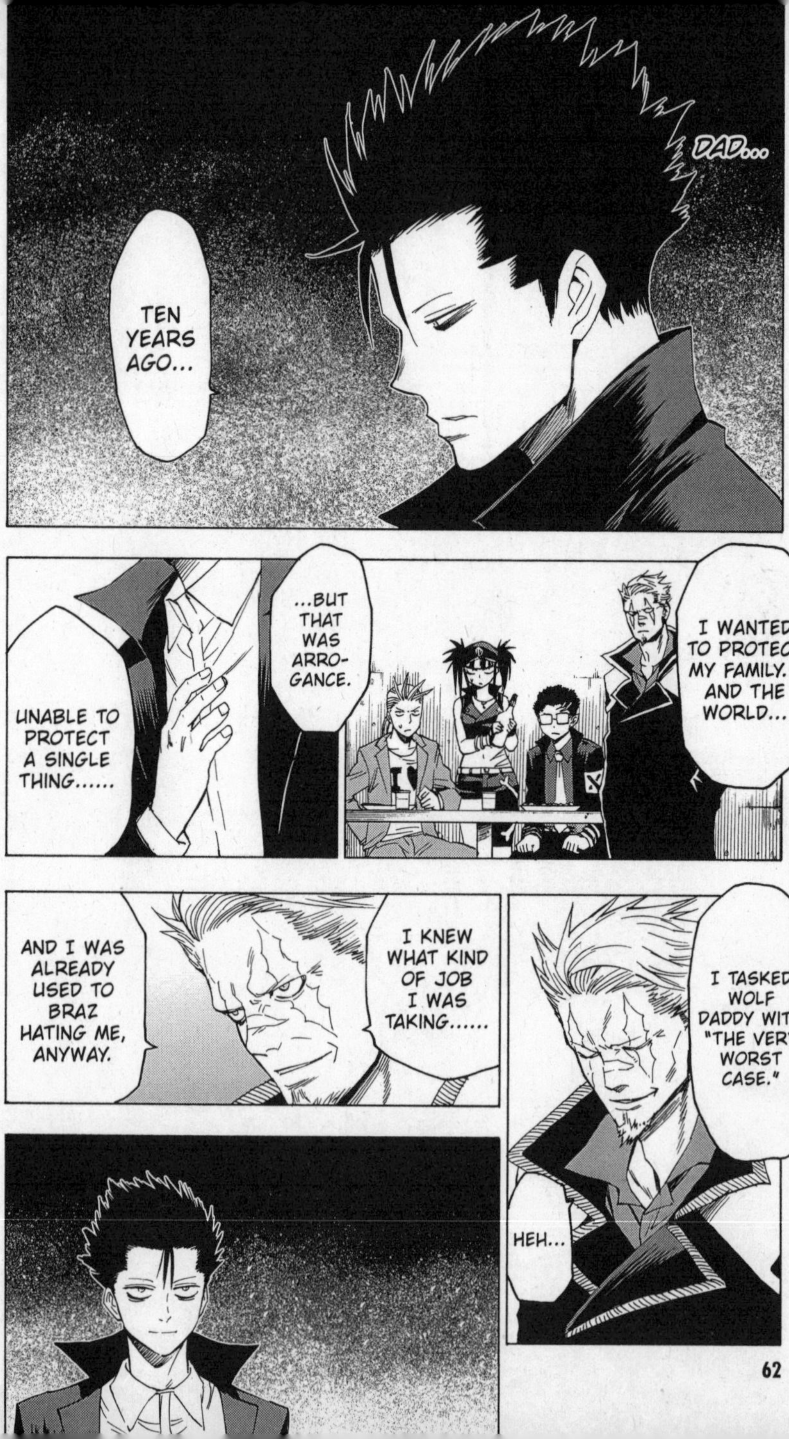
DAD...
TEN YEARS AGO...
I WANTED TO PROTECT MY FAMILY... AND THE WORLD...
...BUT THAT WAS ARROGANCE.
UNABLE TO PROTECT A SINGLE THING......
I TASKED WOLF DADDY WITH "THE VERY WORST CASE."
HEH...
I KNEW WHAT KIND OF JOB I WAS TAKING......
AND I WAS ALREADY USED TO BRAZ HATING ME, ANYWAY.

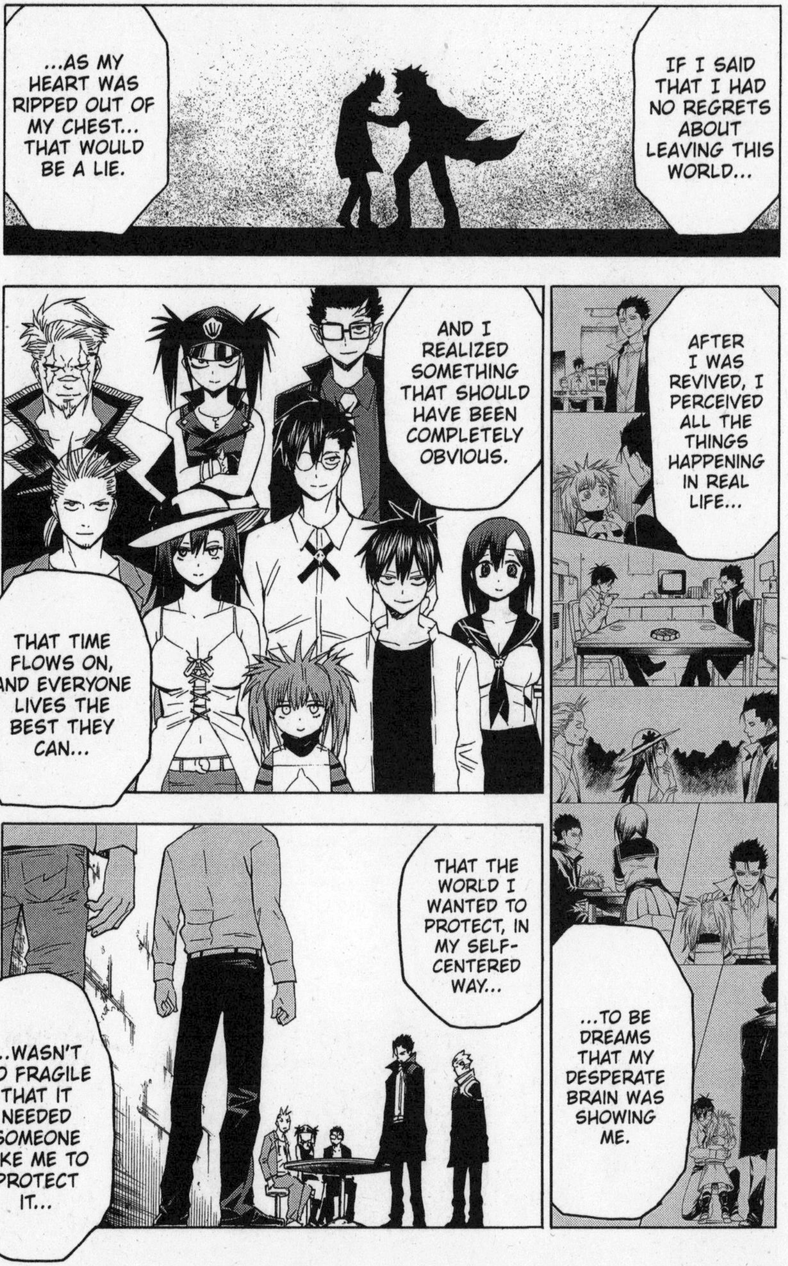
IF I SAID THAT I HAD NO REGRETS ABOUT LEAVING THIS WORLD...
...AS MY HEART WAS RIPPED OUT OF MY CHEST... THAT WOULD BE A LIE.
AFTER I WAS REVIVED, I PERCEIVED ALL THE THINGS HAPPENING IN REAL LIFE...
...TO BE DREAMS THAT MY DESPERATE BRAIN WAS SHOWING ME.
AND I REALIZED SOMETHING THAT SHOULD HAVE BEEN COMPLETELY OBVIOUS.
THAT TIME FLOWS ON, AND EVERYONE LIVES THE BEST THEY CAN...
THAT THE WORLD I WANTED TO PROTECT, IN MY SELF-CENTERED WAY...
...WASN'T SO FRAGILE THAT IT NEEDED SOMEONE LIKE ME TO PROTECT IT...

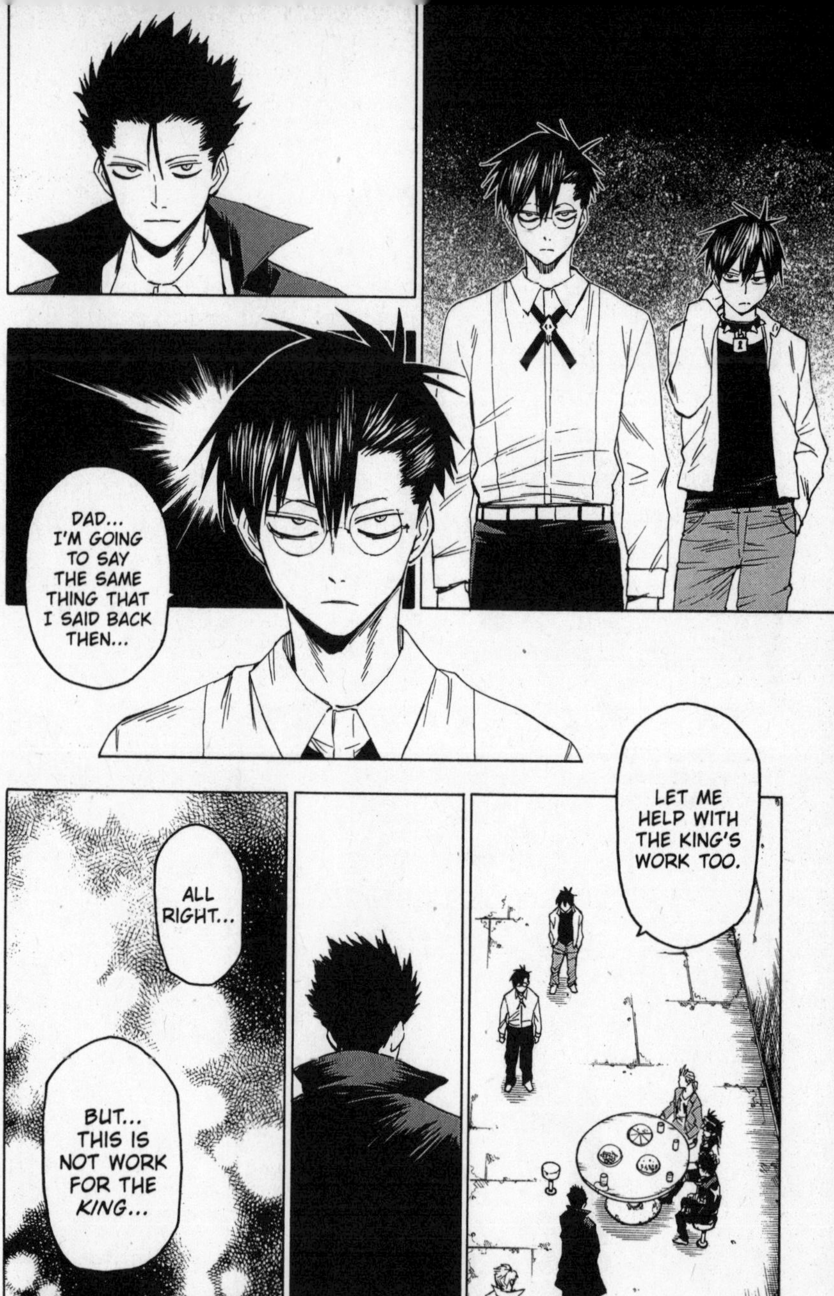
DAD... I'M GOING TO SAY THE SAME THING THAT I SAID BACK THEN...
LET ME HELP WITH THE KING'S WORK TOO.
ALL RIGHT...
BUT... THIS IS NOT WORK FOR THE *KING*...

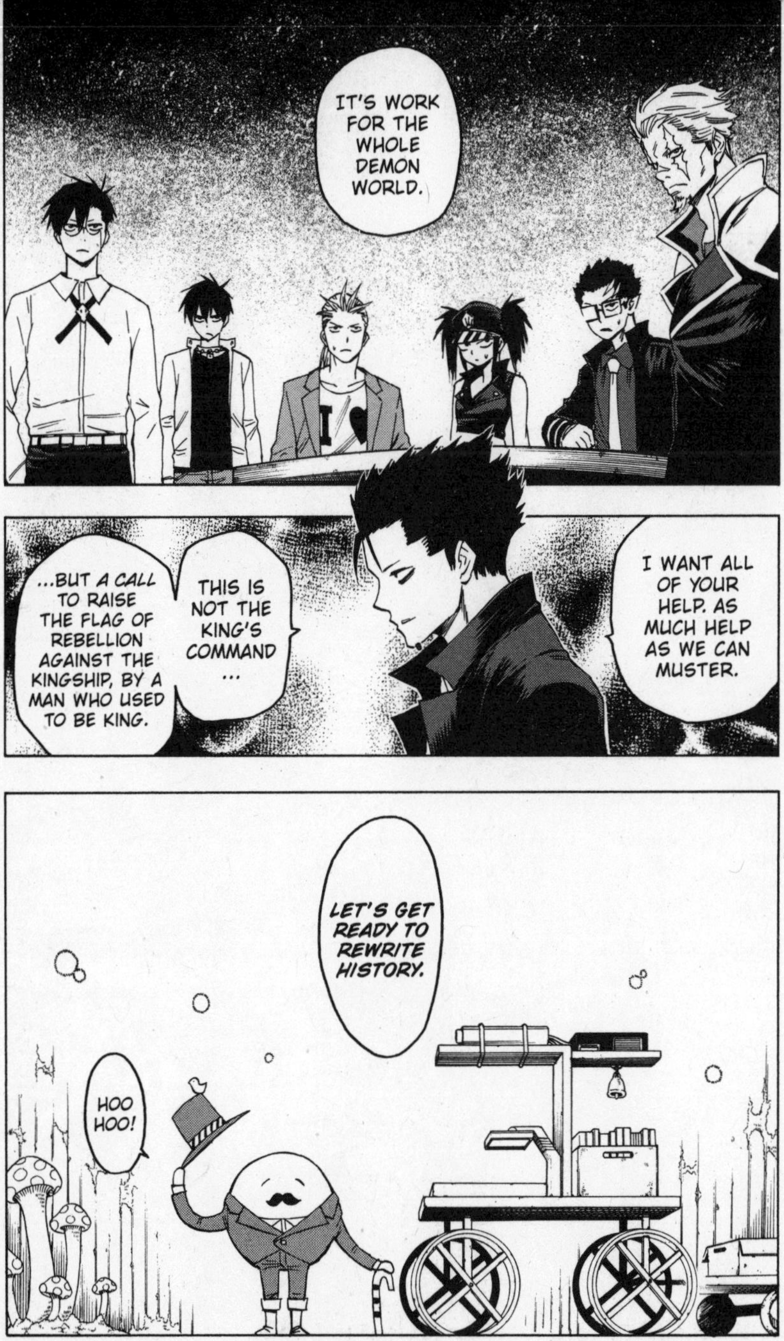
IT'S WORK FOR THE WHOLE DEMON WORLD.
I WANT ALL OF YOUR HELP. AS MUCH HELP AS WE CAN MUSTER.
THIS IS NOT THE KING'S COMMAND ...
...BUT A CALL TO RAISE THE FLAG OF REBELLION AGAINST THE KINGSHIP, BY A MAN WHO USED TO BE KING.
LET'S GET READY TO REWRITE HISTORY.
HOO HOO!

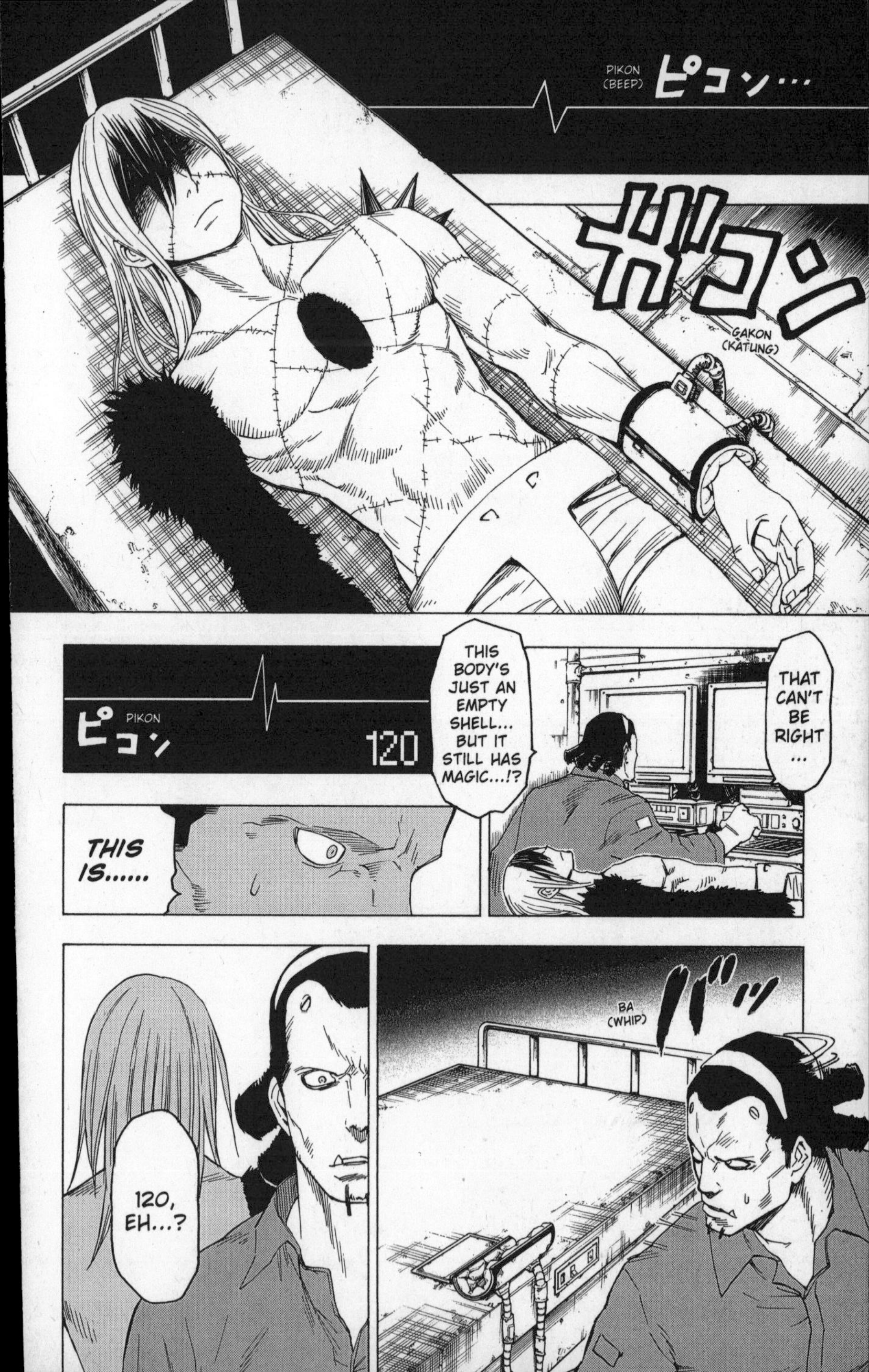
PIKON (BEEP)
ピコン…
ガコン
GAKON (KATUNG)
THAT CAN'T BE RIGHT...
THIS BODY'S JUST AN EMPTY SHELL... BUT IT STILL HAS MAGIC...!?
ピコン
PIKON
120
THIS IS......
バッ
BA (WHIP)
120, EH...?

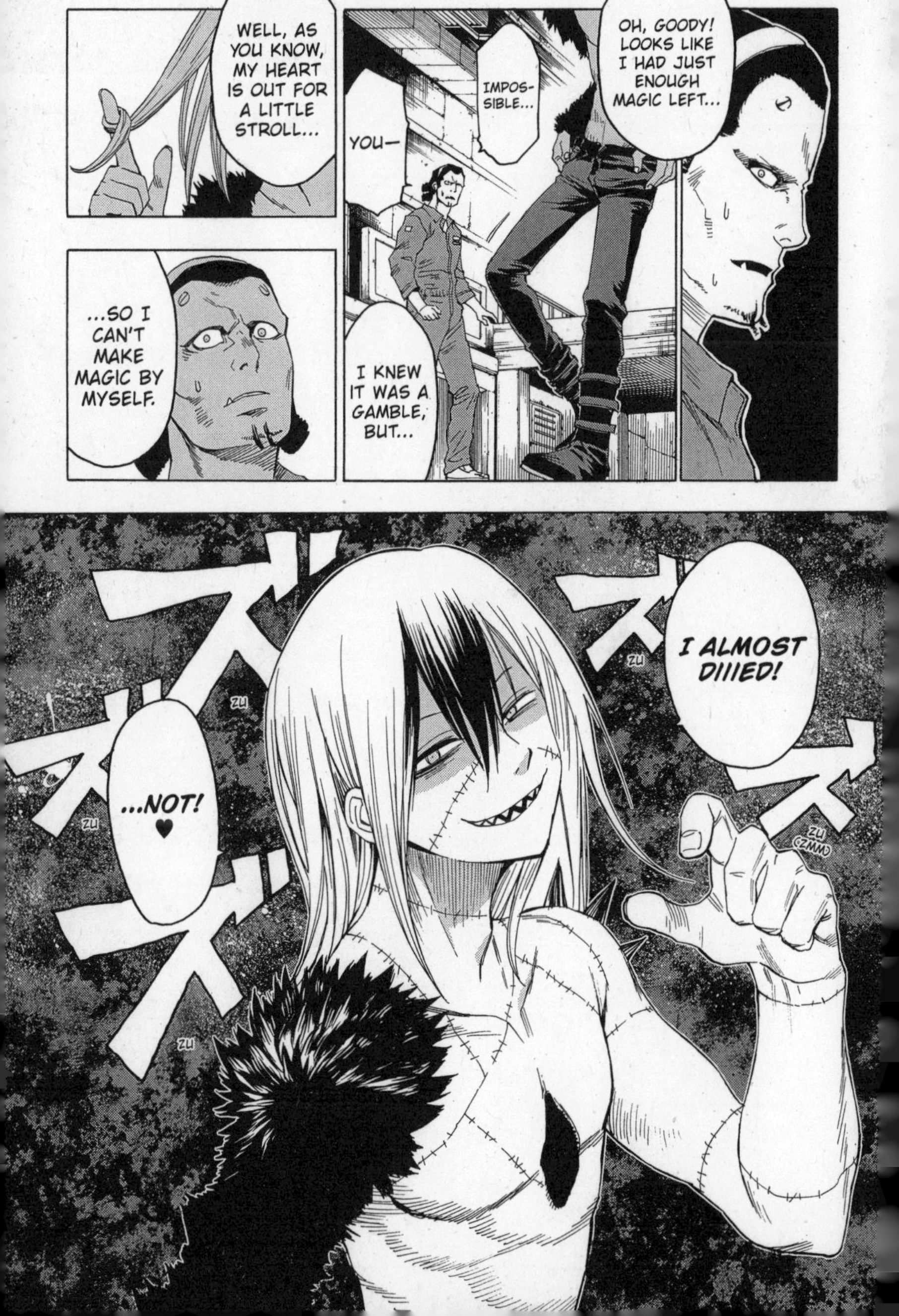
OH, GOODY! LOOKS LIKE I HAD JUST ENOUGH MAGIC LEFT...
IMPOS-SIBLE...
YOU—
I KNEW IT WAS A GAMBLE, BUT...
WELL, AS YOU KNOW, MY HEART IS OUT FOR A LITTLE STROLL...
...SO I CAN'T MAKE MAGIC BY MYSELF.
ZU
ZU (ZMMM)
I ALMOST DIIIED!
ZU
ZU
ZU
...NOT! ♥

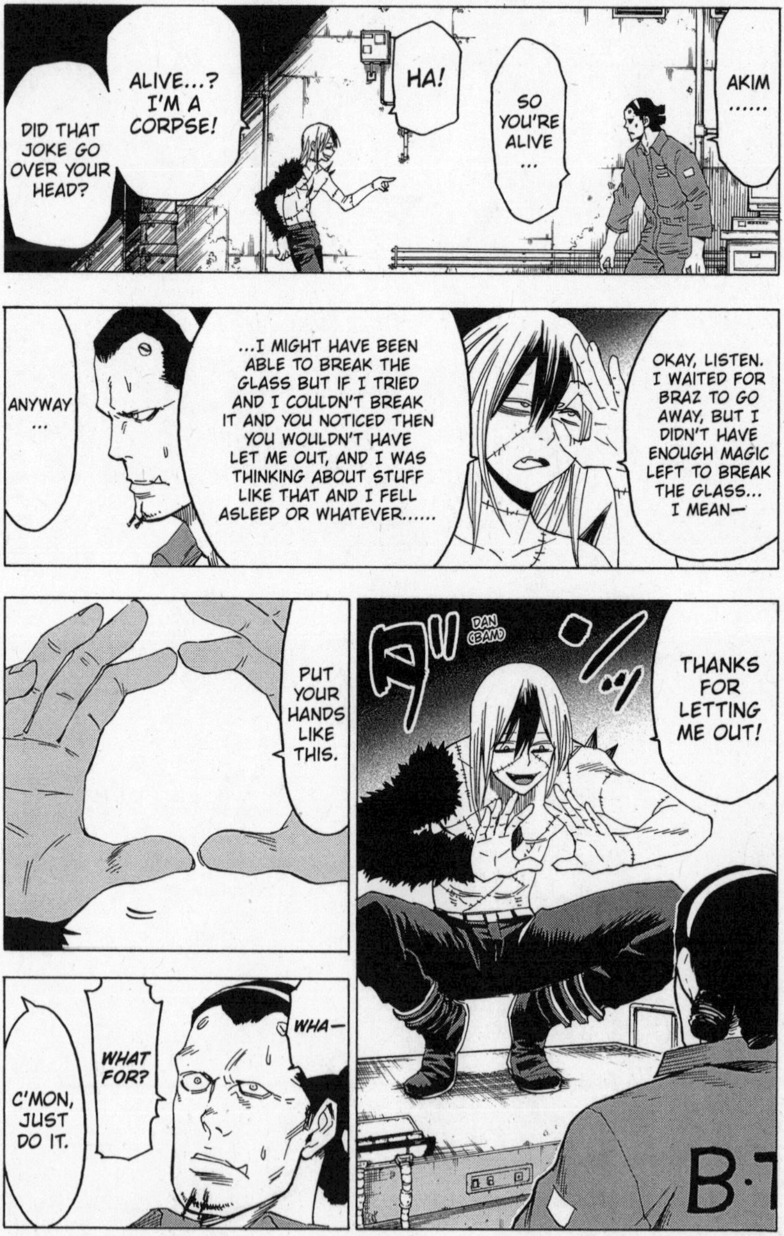
AKIM ......
SO YOU'RE ALIVE ...
HA!
ALIVE...? I'M A CORPSE!
DID THAT JOKE GO OVER YOUR HEAD?
OKAY, LISTEN. I WAITED FOR BRAZ TO GO AWAY, BUT I DIDN'T HAVE ENOUGH MAGIC LEFT TO BREAK THE GLASS... I MEAN—
...I MIGHT HAVE BEEN ABLE TO BREAK THE GLASS BUT IF I TRIED AND I COULDN'T BREAK IT AND YOU NOTICED THEN YOU WOULDN'T HAVE LET ME OUT, AND I WAS THINKING ABOUT STUFF LIKE THAT AND I FELL ASLEEP OR WHATEVER......
ANYWAY ...
DAN (BAM)
THANKS FOR LETTING ME OUT!
PUT YOUR HANDS LIKE THIS.
WHA—
WHAT FOR?
C'MON, JUST DO IT.

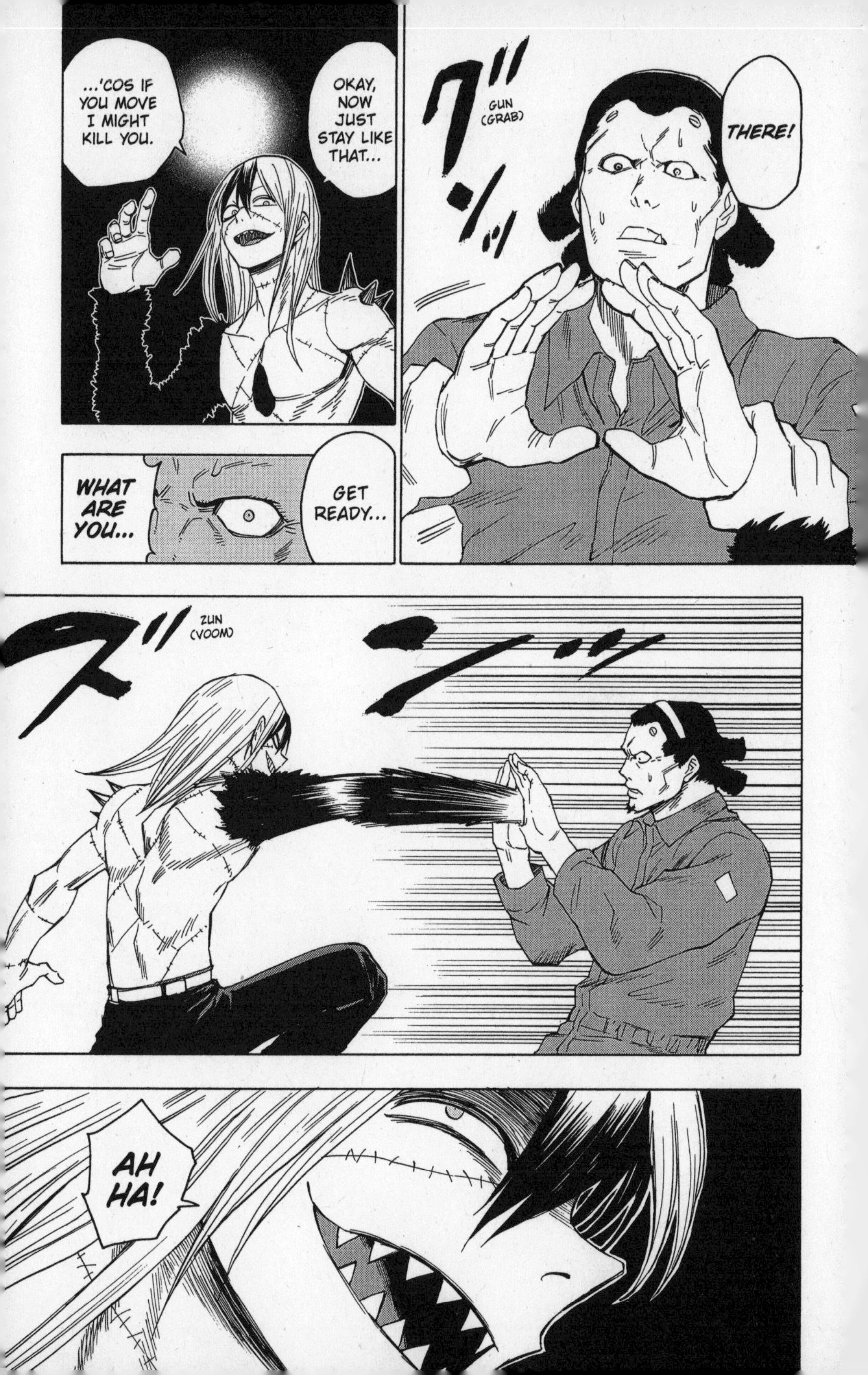
GUN (GRAB)
THERE!
OKAY, NOW JUST STAY LIKE THAT...
...'COS IF YOU MOVE I MIGHT KILL YOU.
GET READY...
WHAT ARE YOU...
ZUN (VOOM)
AH HA!

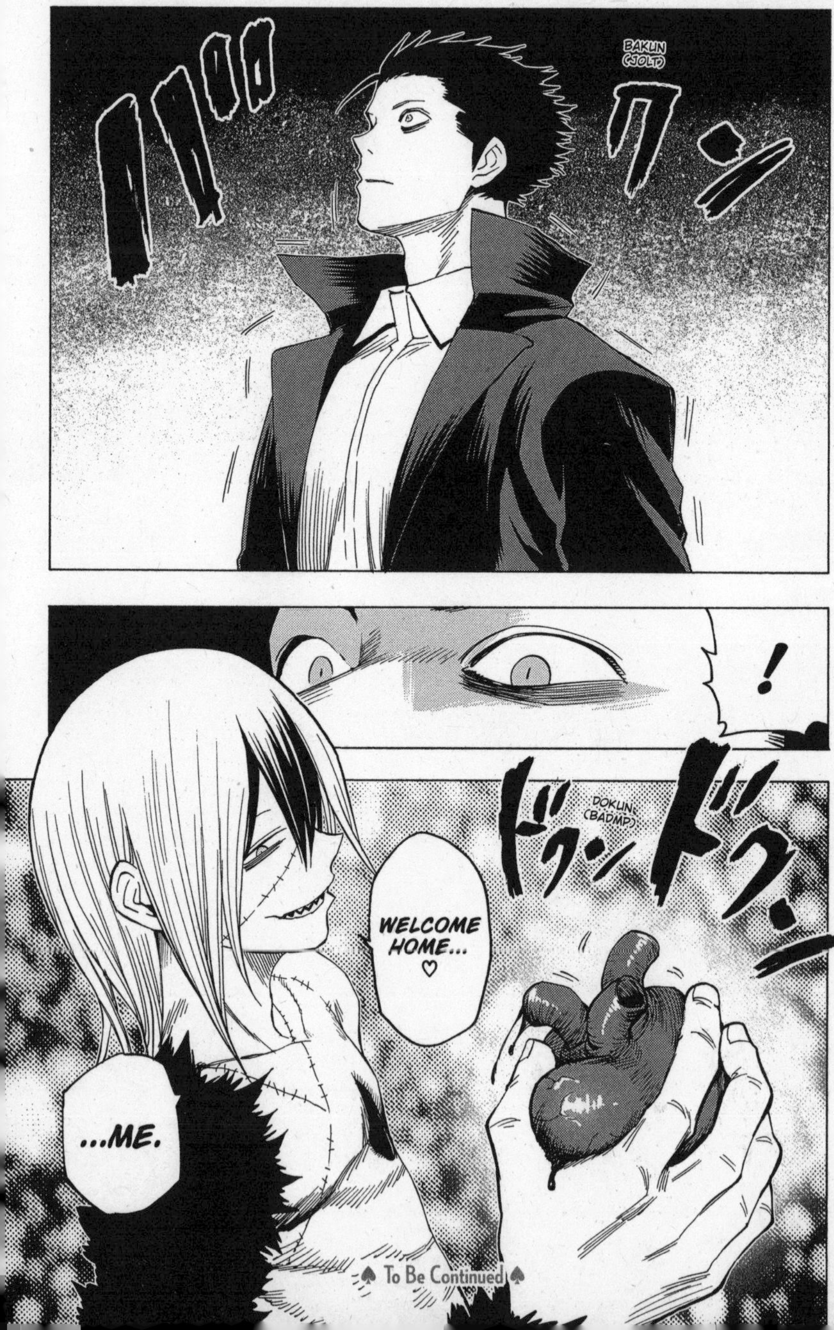
BAKUN (JOLT)
!
DOKUN (BADMP)
WELCOME HOME... ♡
...ME.
To Be Continued

BLOOD LAD

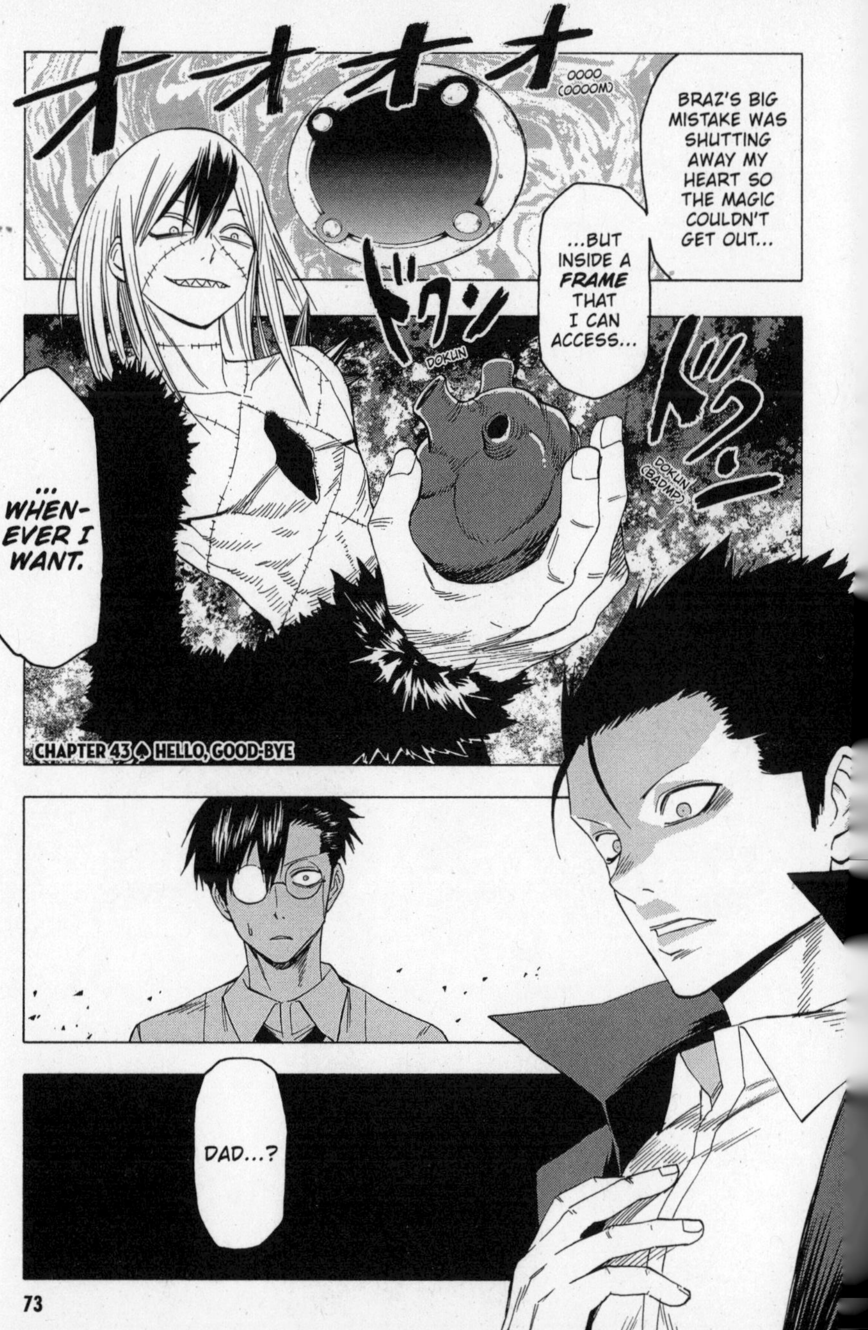
オオオオ
OOOO (OOOOM)
BRAZ'S BIG MISTAKE WAS SHUTTING AWAY MY HEART SO THE MAGIC COULDN'T GET OUT...
...BUT INSIDE A FRAME THAT I CAN ACCESS...
ドクン
DOKUN (BADMP)
ドクン
DOKUN
...WHEN-EVER I WANT.
CHAPTER 43 ♠ HELLO, GOOD-BYE
DAD...?

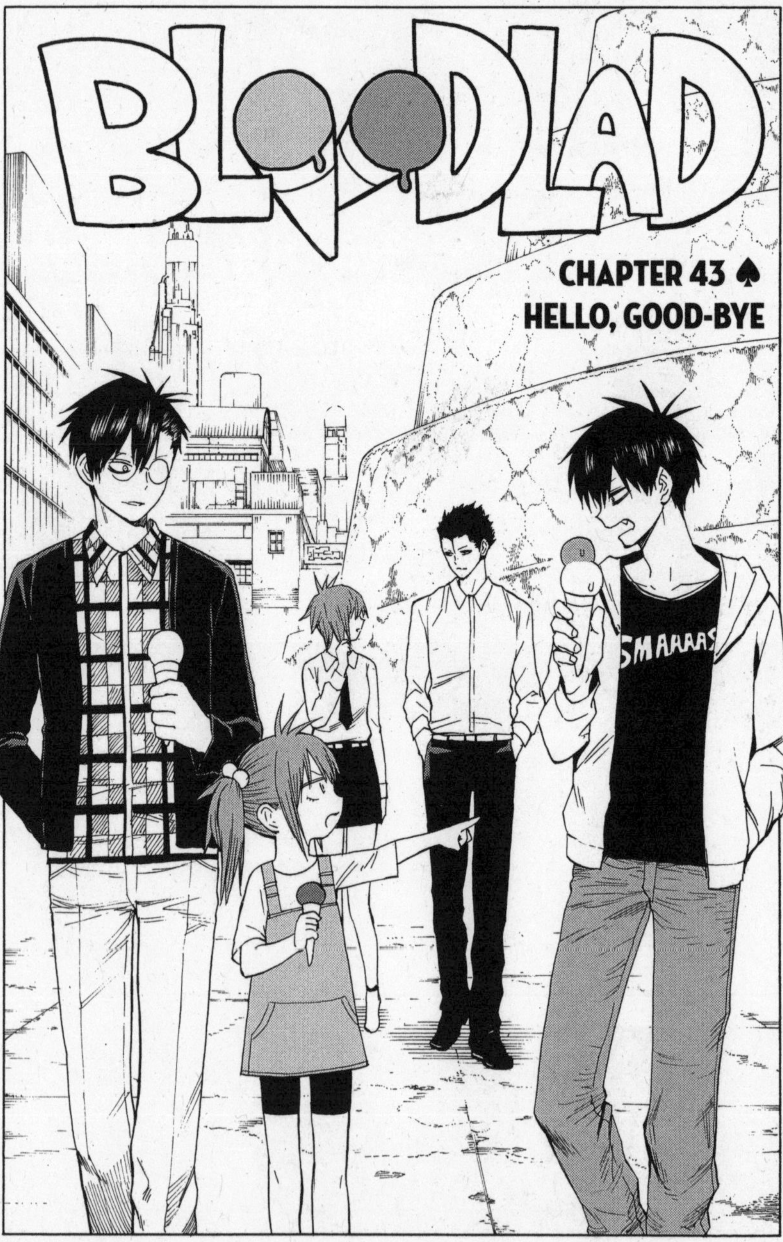
BLOOD LAD
CHAPTER 43 ♠
HELLO, GOOD-BYE

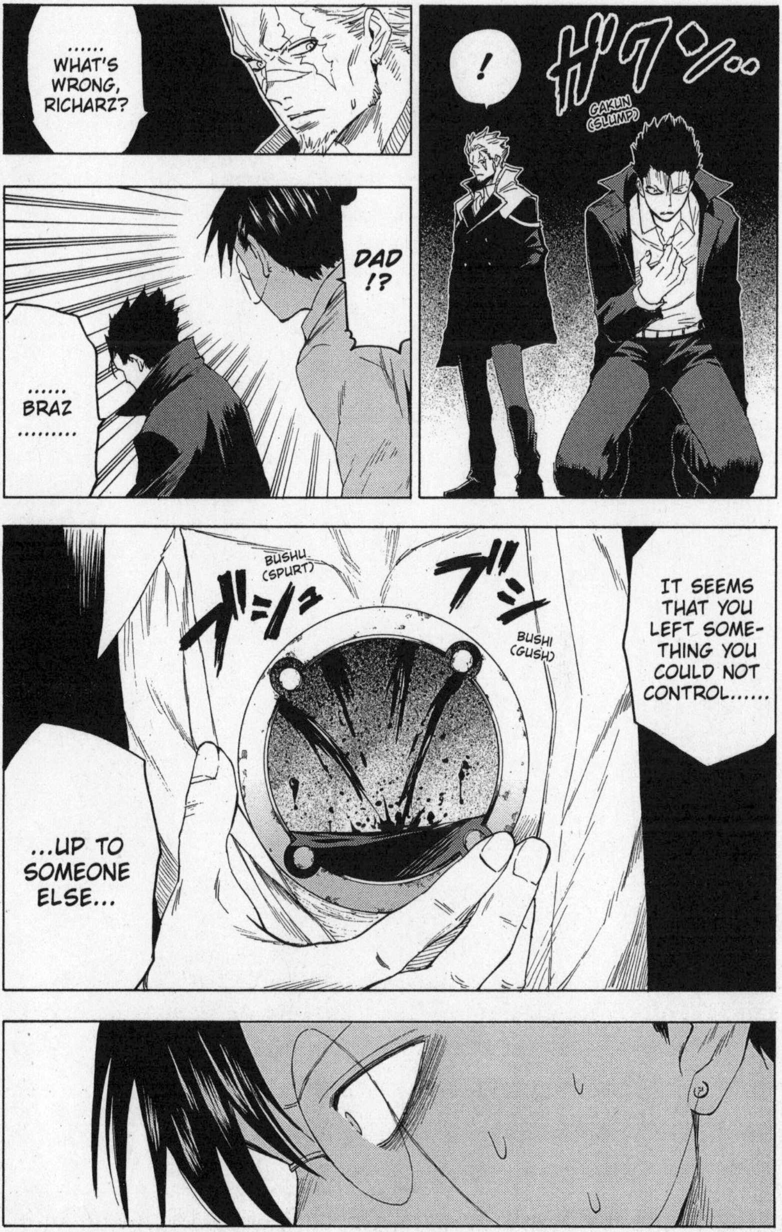
!
ガクン
GAKUN (SLUMP)
...... WHAT'S WRONG, RICHARZ?
DAD !?
...... BRAZ ....
IT SEEMS THAT YOU LEFT SOME-THING YOU COULD NOT CONTROL......
ブシ
BUSHI (GUSH)
ブシュ
BUSHU (SPURT)
...UP TO SOMEONE ELSE...

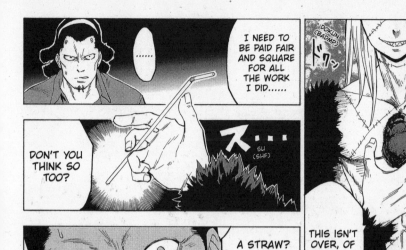

DOKUN (BADMP)
ドクン
THIS ISN'T OVER, OF COURSE...
I NEED TO BE PAID FAIR AND SQUARE FOR ALL THE WORK I DID......
......
ス...
SU (SHF)
DON'T YOU THINK SO TOO?
A STRAW? ...WHAT ARE YOU UP TO...
I'M THE ONE WHO MADE THAT MAGIC CIRCULATE...
ZU (SLURP)
ズッ
トプン
TOPUN (PLISH)
...SO IT'S MINE.

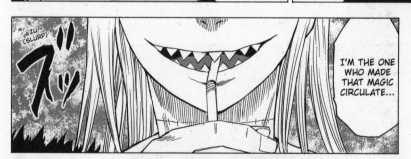

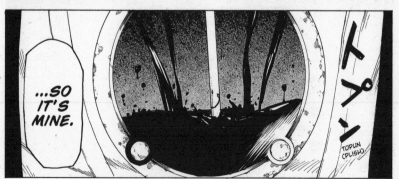

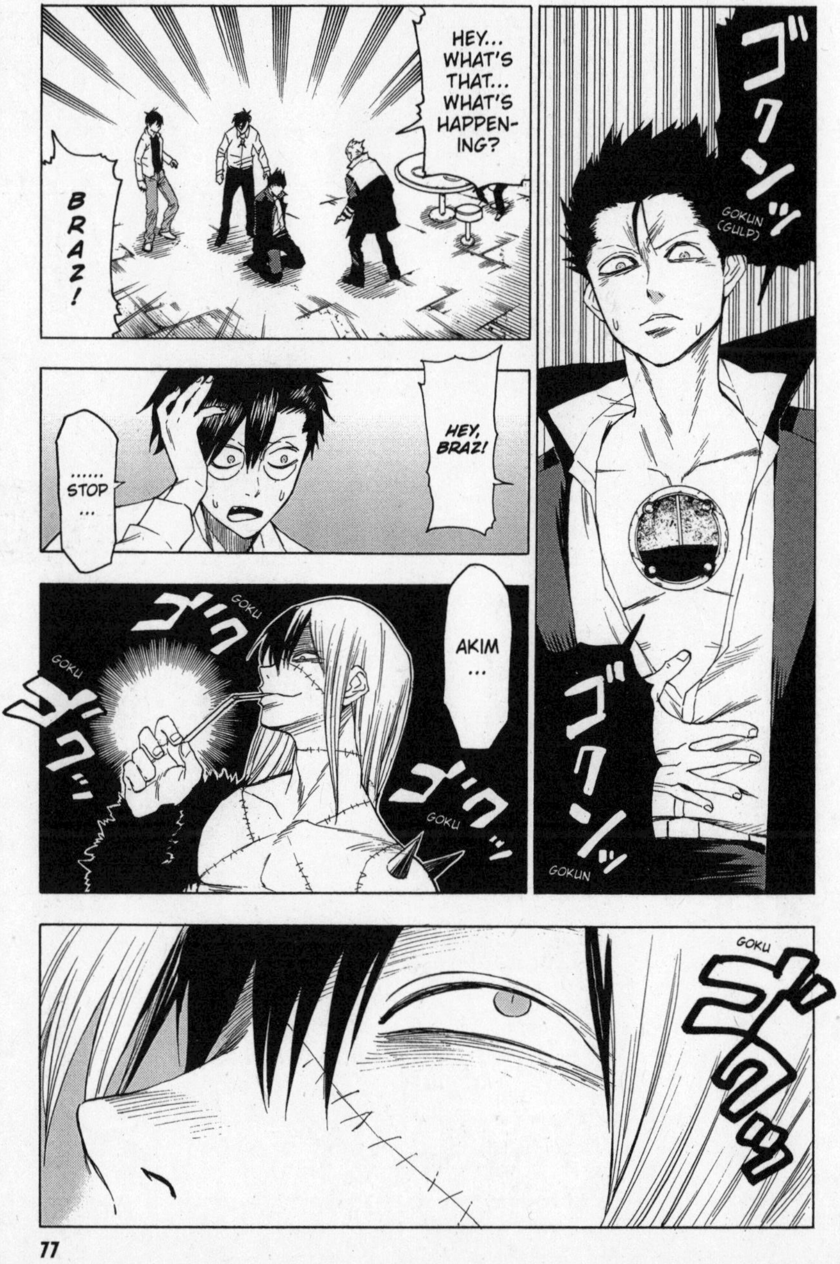

ゴクンッ
GOKUN (GULP)
ゴクンッ
GOKUN
HEY... WHAT'S THAT... WHAT'S HAPPEN-ING?
BRAZ!
HEY, BRAZ!
...... STOP ...
AKIM ...
GOKU
GOKU
GOKU
GOKU

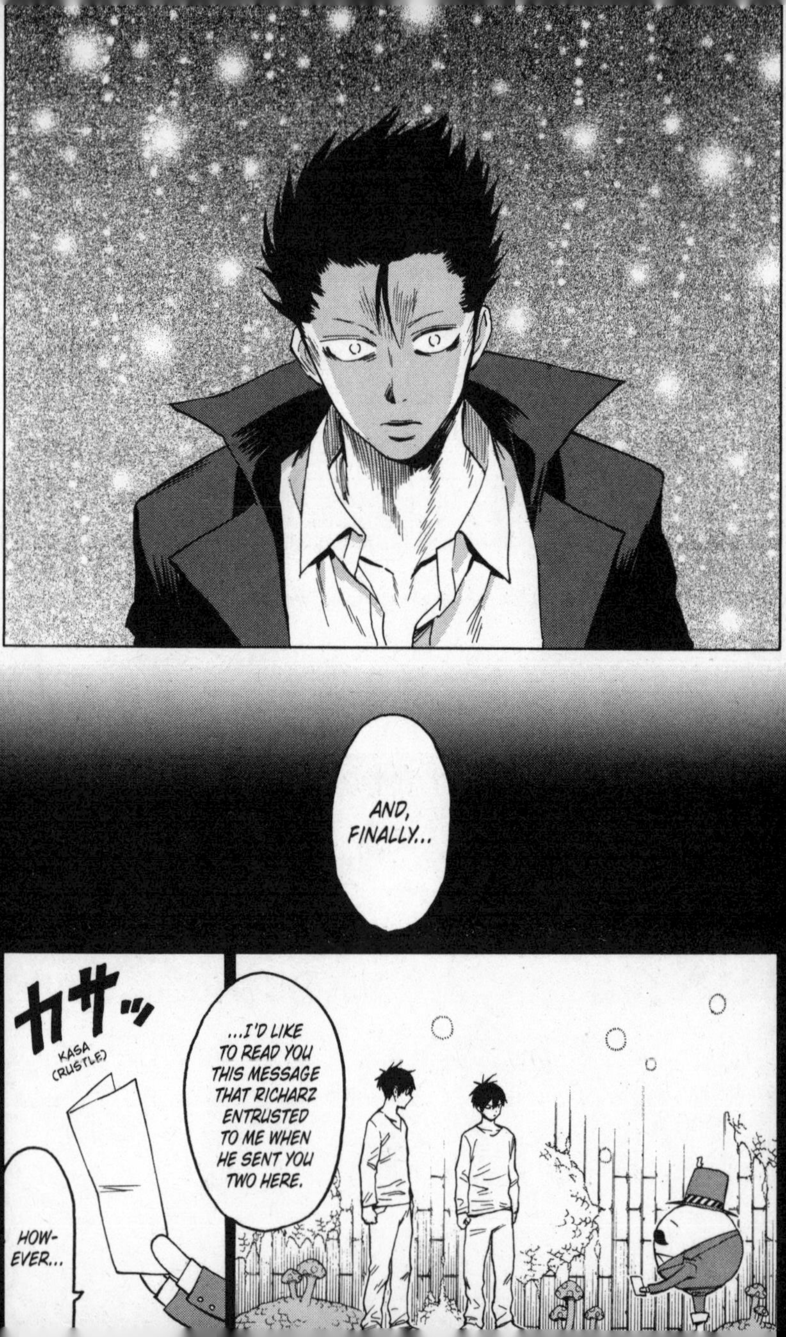
AND, FINALLY...
...I'D LIKE TO READ YOU THIS MESSAGE THAT RICHARZ ENTRUSTED TO ME WHEN HE SENT YOU TWO HERE.
カサッ
KASA (RUSTLE)
HOW-EVER...

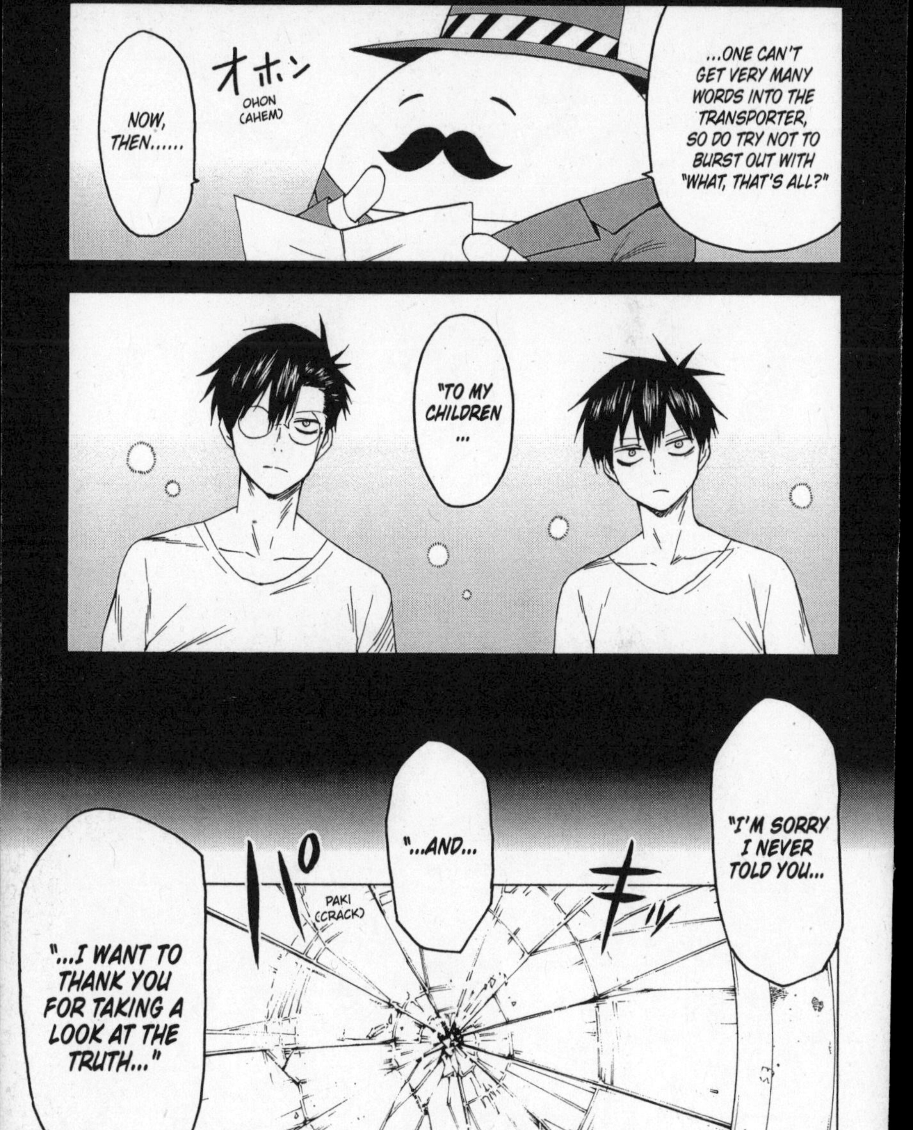
...ONE CAN'T GET VERY MANY WORDS INTO THE TRANSPORTER, SO DO TRY NOT TO BURST OUT WITH "WHAT, THAT'S ALL?"
オホン
OHON (AHEM)
NOW, THEN......
"TO MY CHILDREN ...
"I'M SORRY I NEVER TOLD YOU...
パキッ
PAKI (CRACK)
"...AND...
"...I WANT TO THANK YOU FOR TAKING A LOOK AT THE TRUTH..."

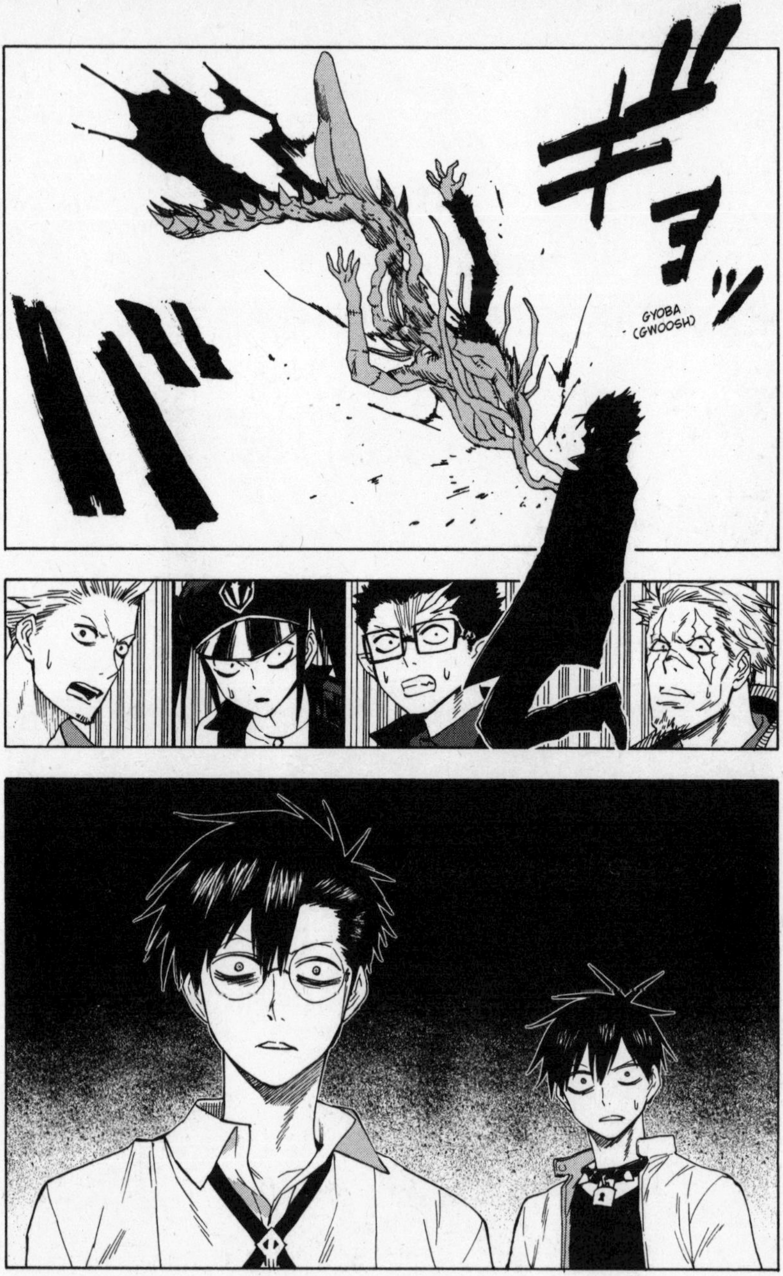
ギョッ
GYOBA (GWOOSH)
バ

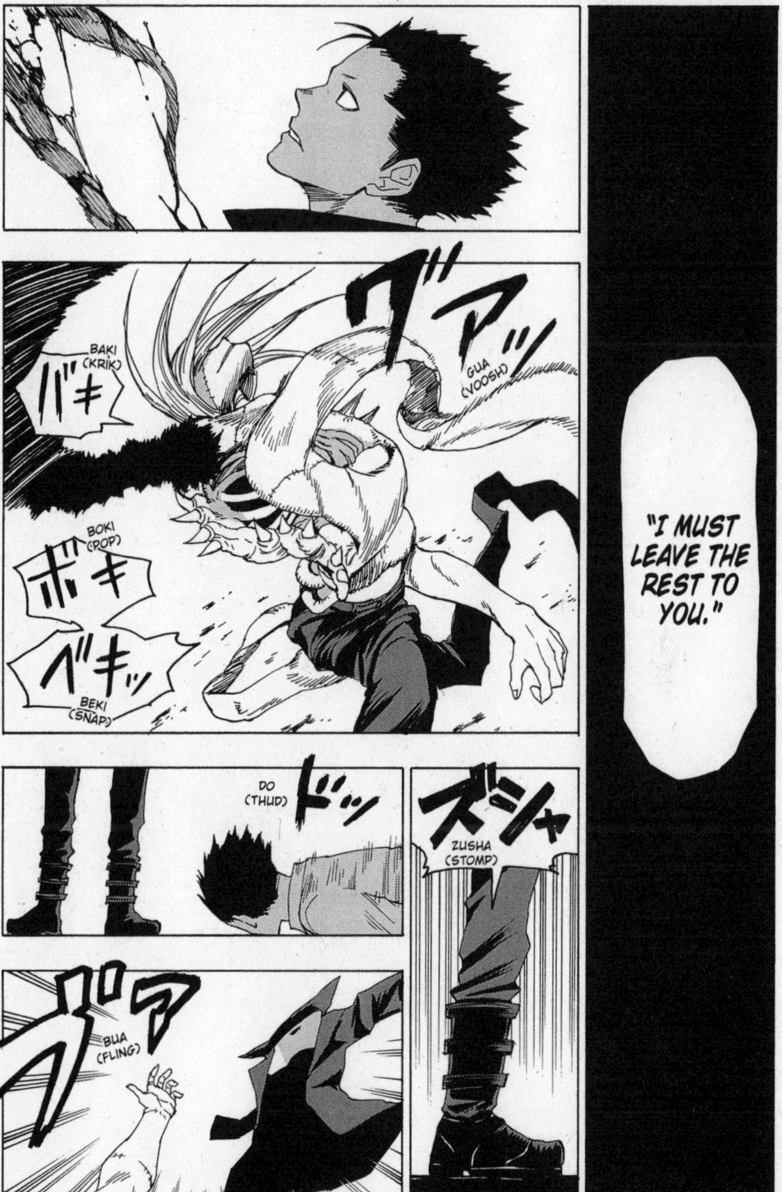
"I MUST LEAVE THE REST TO YOU."
ヴアッ
GUA (VOOSH)
バキ
BAKI (KRIK)
ボキ
BOKI (POP)
ベキッ
BEKI (SNAP)
ズシャ
ZUSHA (STOMP)
ドッ
DO (THUD)
ブア
BUA (FLING)

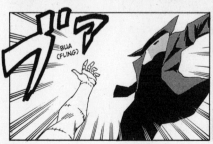

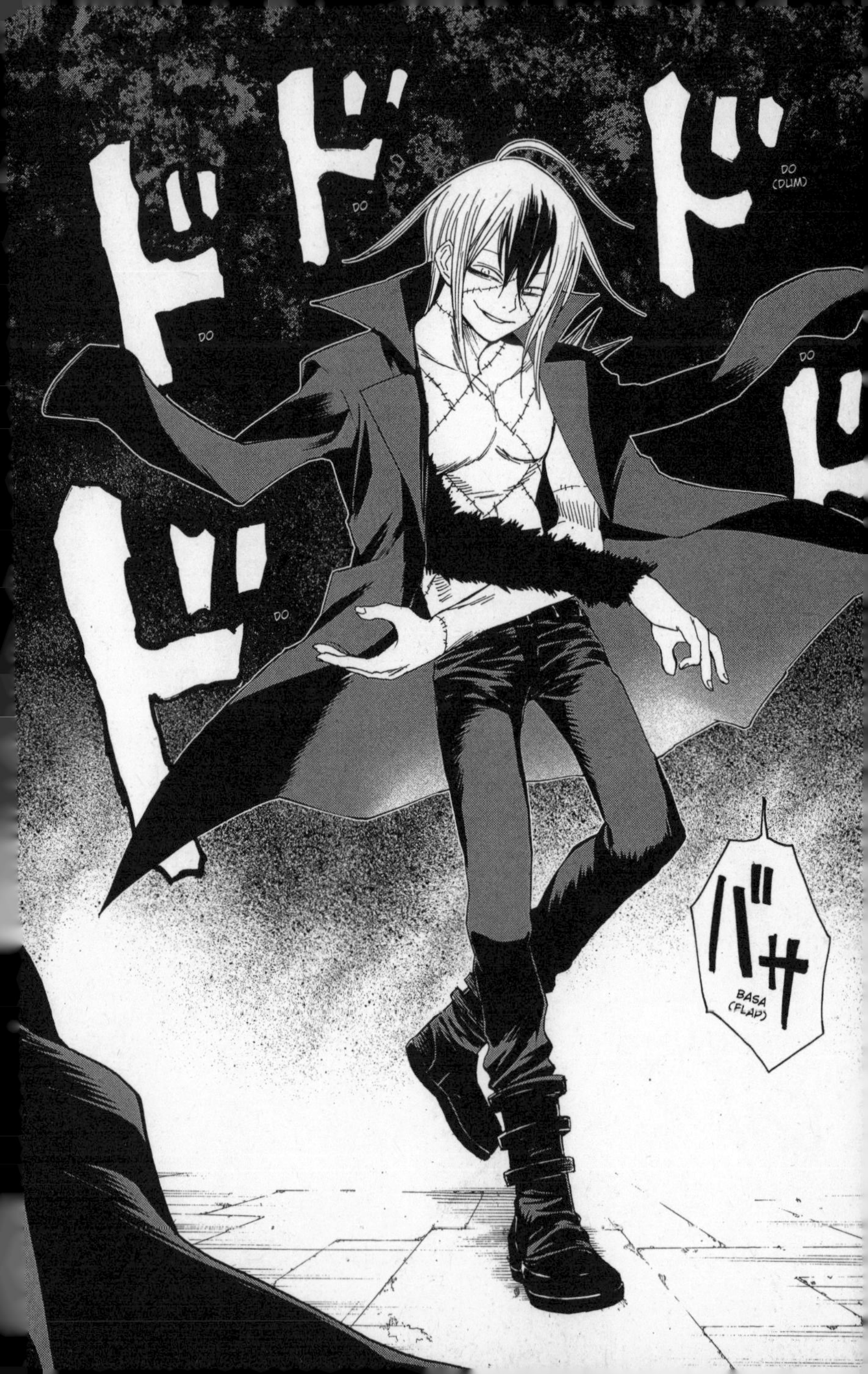

ド
DO (DUM)
ド
DO
ド
DO
ド
DO
ド
DO
バサ
BASA (FLAP)

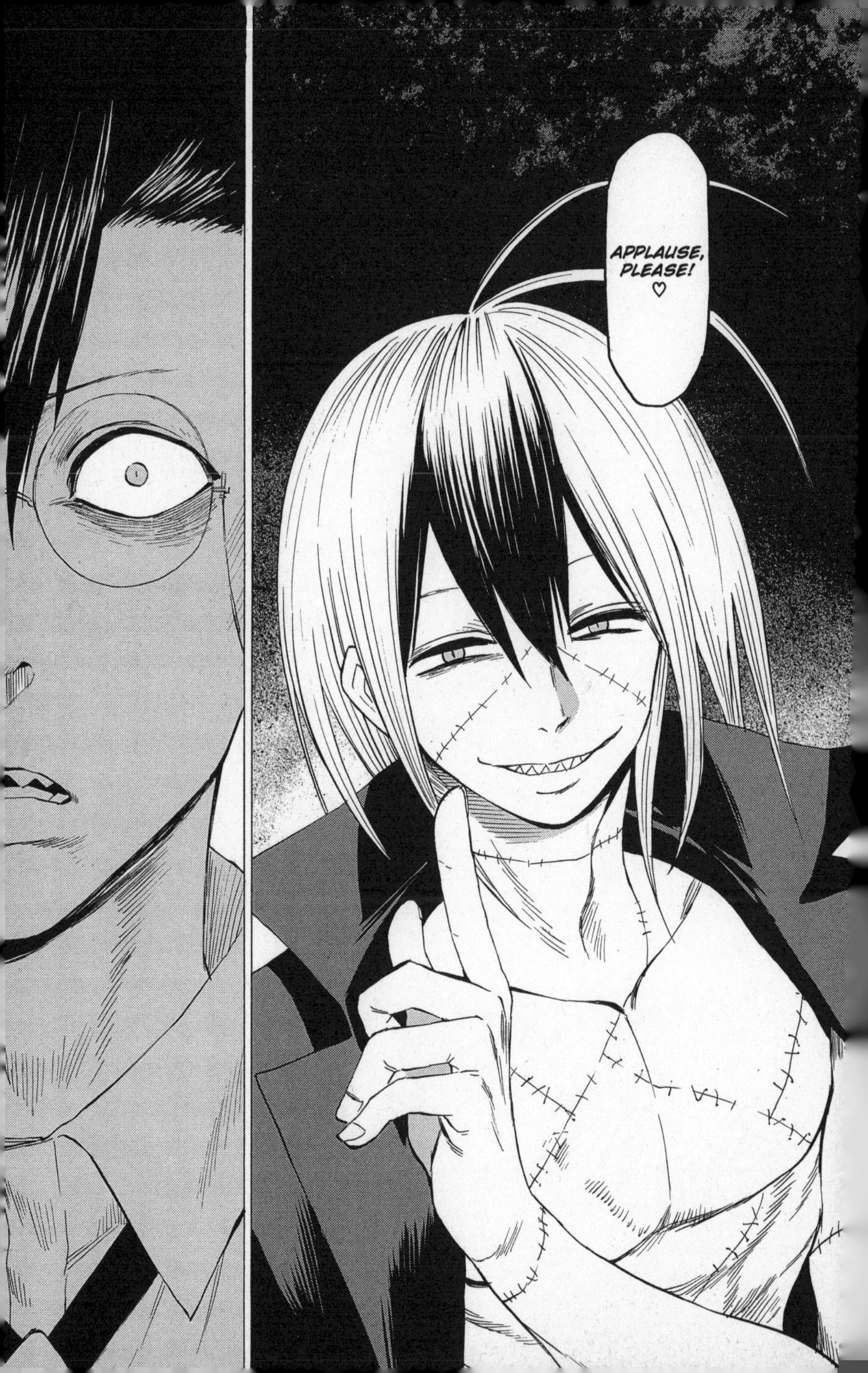
APPLAUSE, PLEASE! ♡

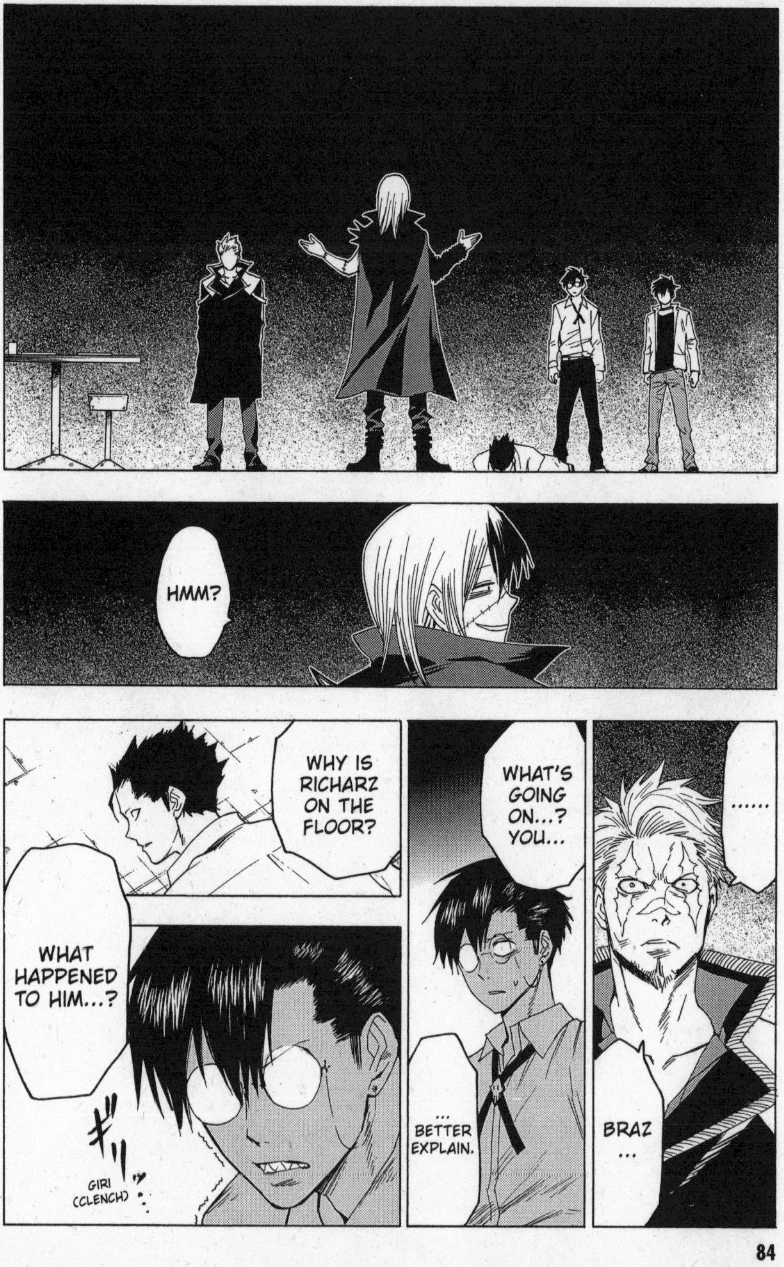
HMM?
......
BRAZ ...
WHAT'S GOING ON...? YOU...
... BETTER EXPLAIN.
WHY IS RICHARZ ON THE FLOOR?
WHAT HAPPENED TO HIM...?
GIRI (CLENCH)

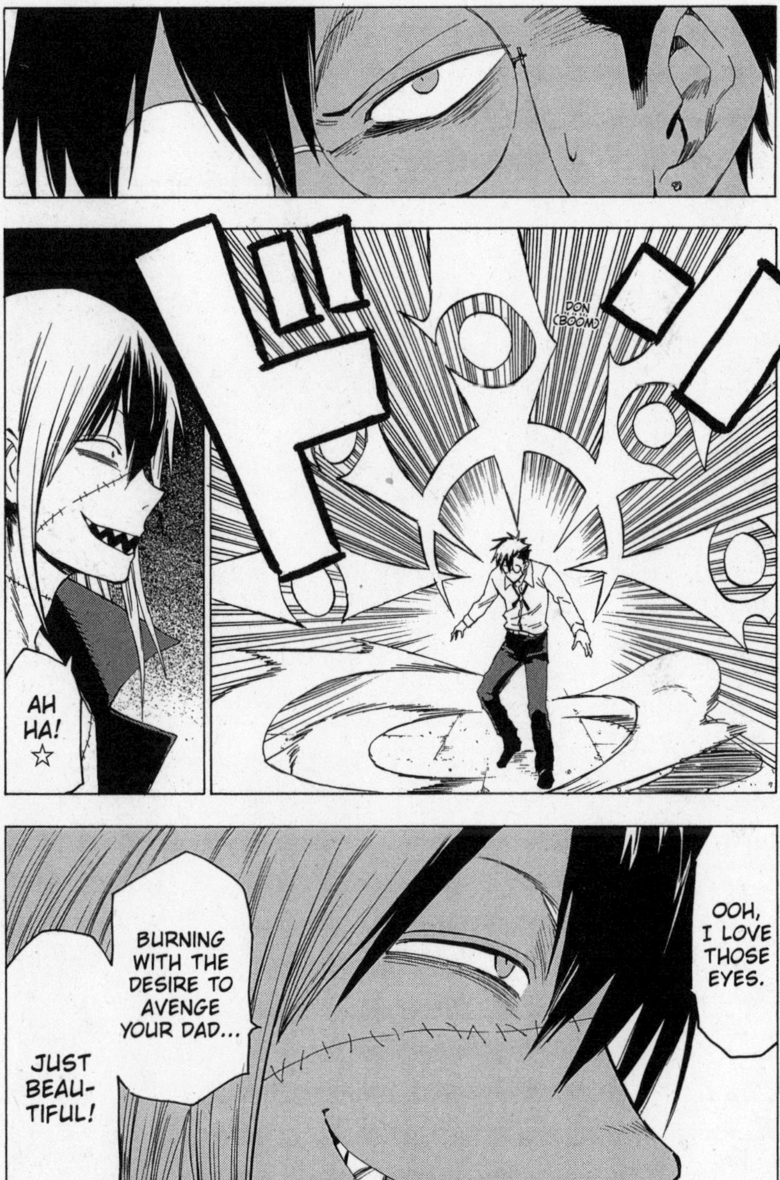
DON (BOOM)
AH HA! ☆
OOH, I LOVE THOSE EYES.
BURNING WITH THE DESIRE TO AVENGE YOUR DAD...
JUST BEAU-TIFUL!

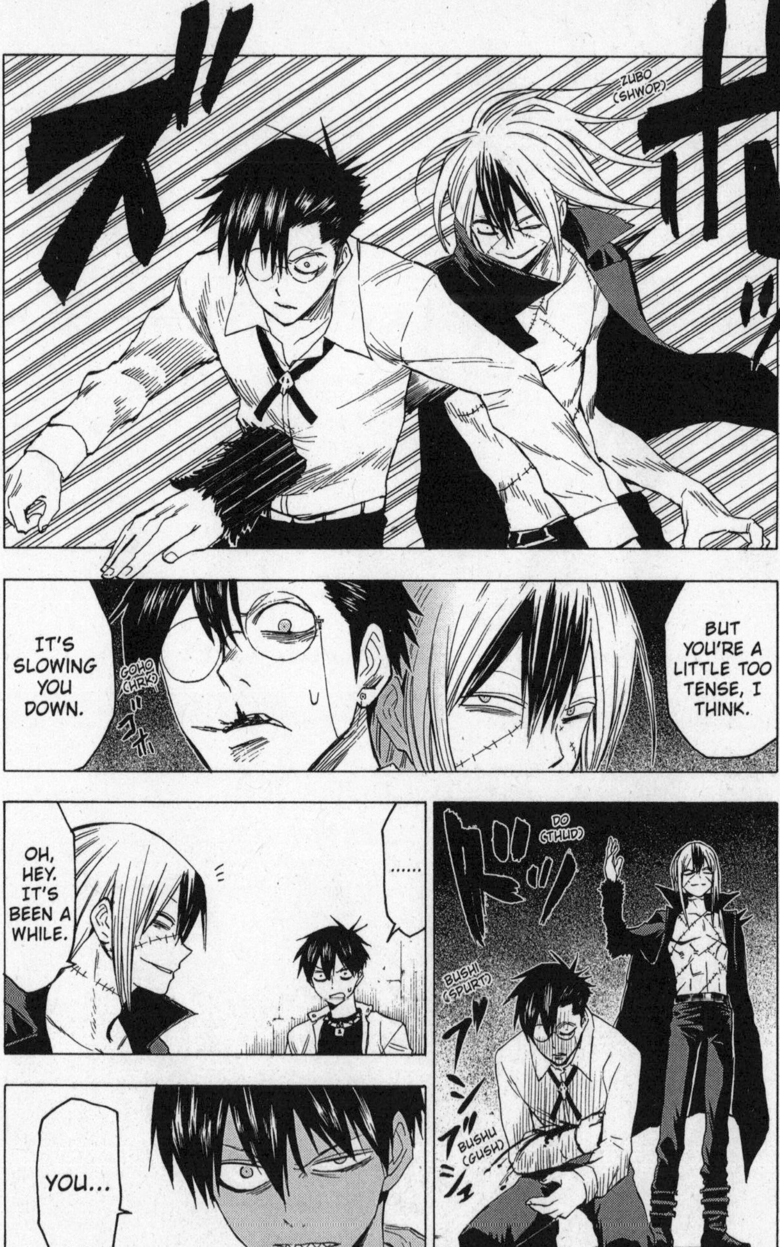
ZUBO (SHWOP)
BUT YOU'RE A LITTLE TOO TENSE, I THINK.
GOHO (HRK)
IT'S SLOWING YOU DOWN.
DO (THUD)
BUSHI (SPURT)
BUSHU (GUSH)
......
OH, HEY. IT'S BEEN A WHILE.
YOU...

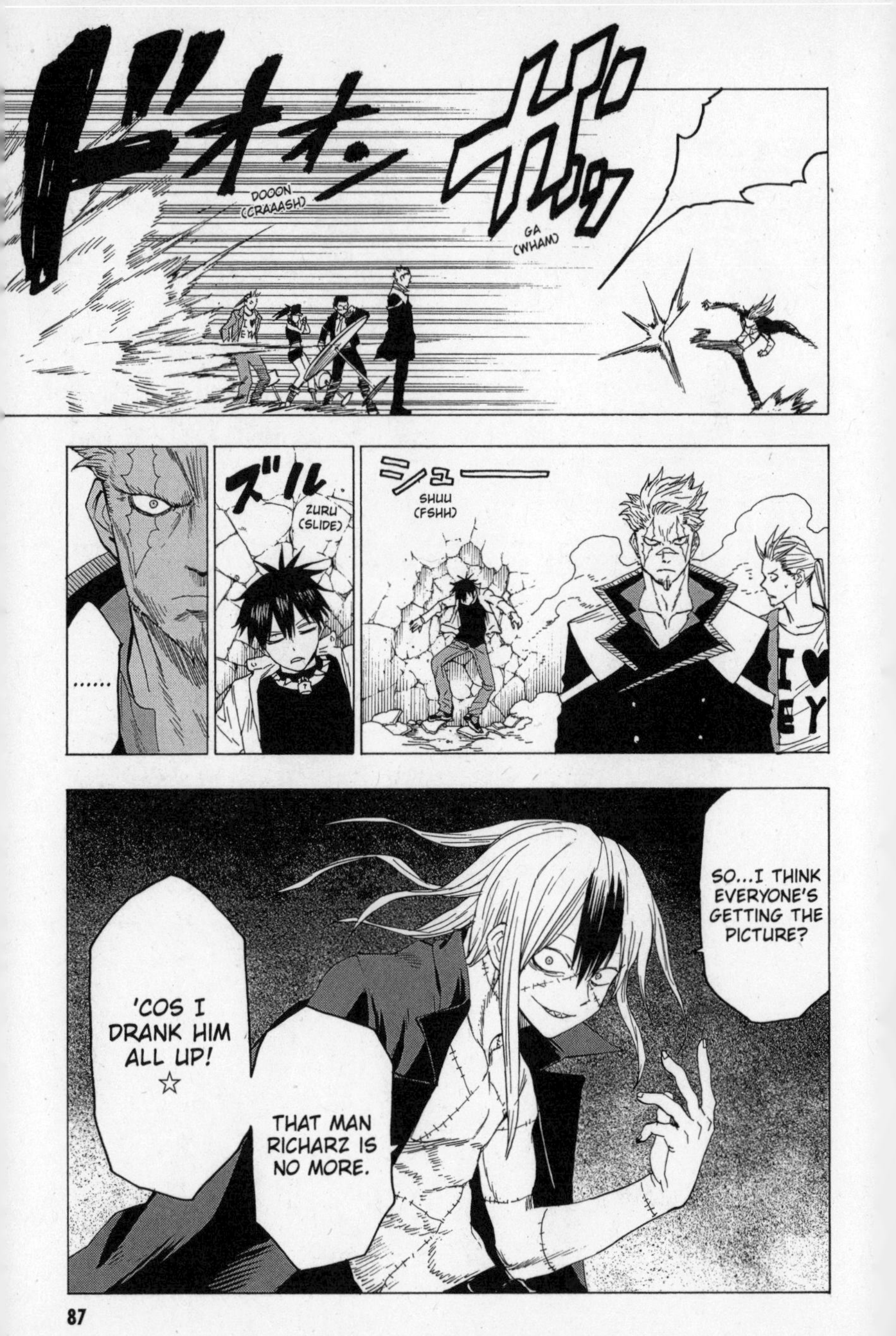
ガンッ
GA (WHAM)
ドオオン
DOOON (CRAAASH)
シュー
SHUU (FSHH)
ズル
ZURU (SLIDE)
......
SO...I THINK EVERYONE'S GETTING THE PICTURE?
THAT MAN RICHARZ IS NO MORE.
'COS I DRANK HIM ALL UP! ☆

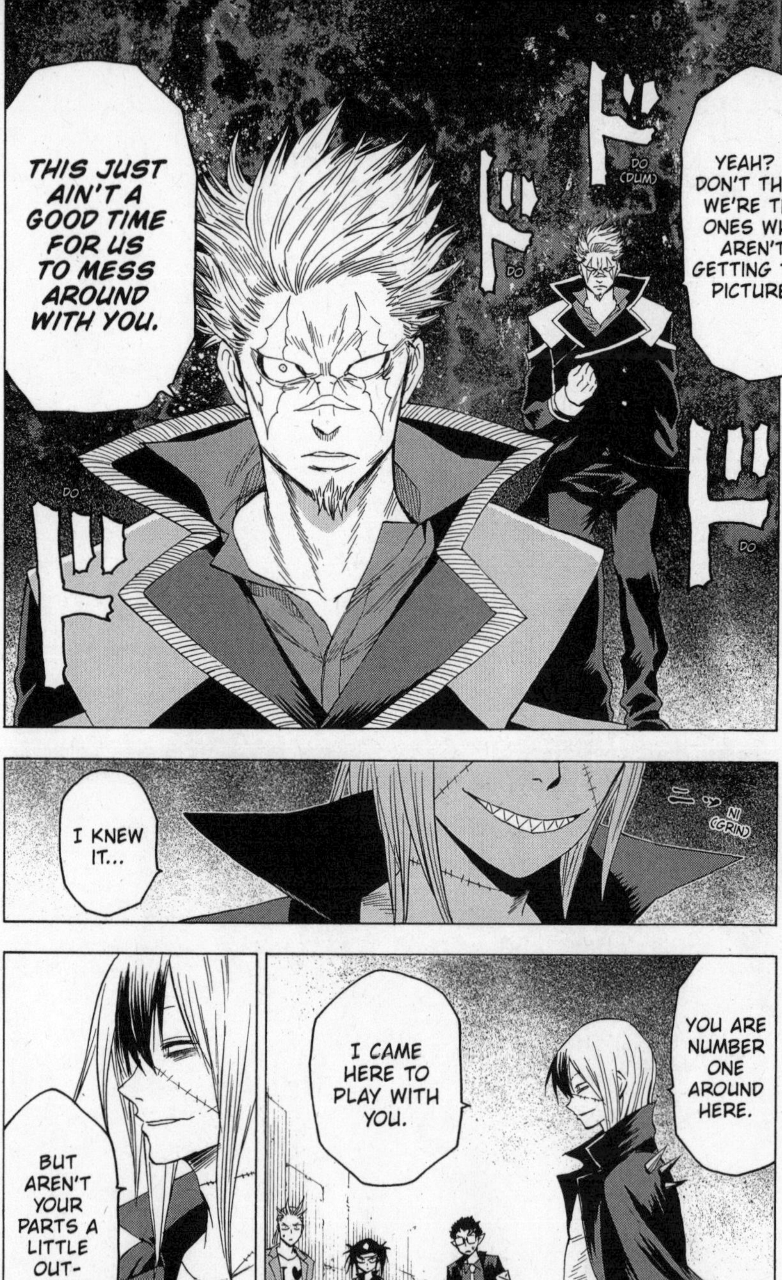
YEAH? I DON'T THINK WE'RE THE ONES WHO AREN'T GETTING THE PICTURE.
DO (DUM)
DO
THIS JUST AIN'T A GOOD TIME FOR US TO MESS AROUND WITH YOU.
DO
DO
NI (GRIN)
I KNEW IT...
YOU ARE NUMBER ONE AROUND HERE.
I CAME HERE TO PLAY WITH YOU.
BUT AREN'T YOUR PARTS A LITTLE OUT-DATED?

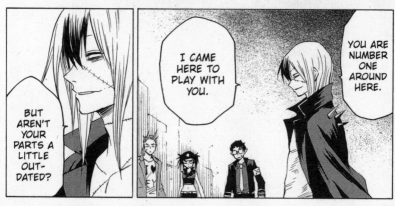

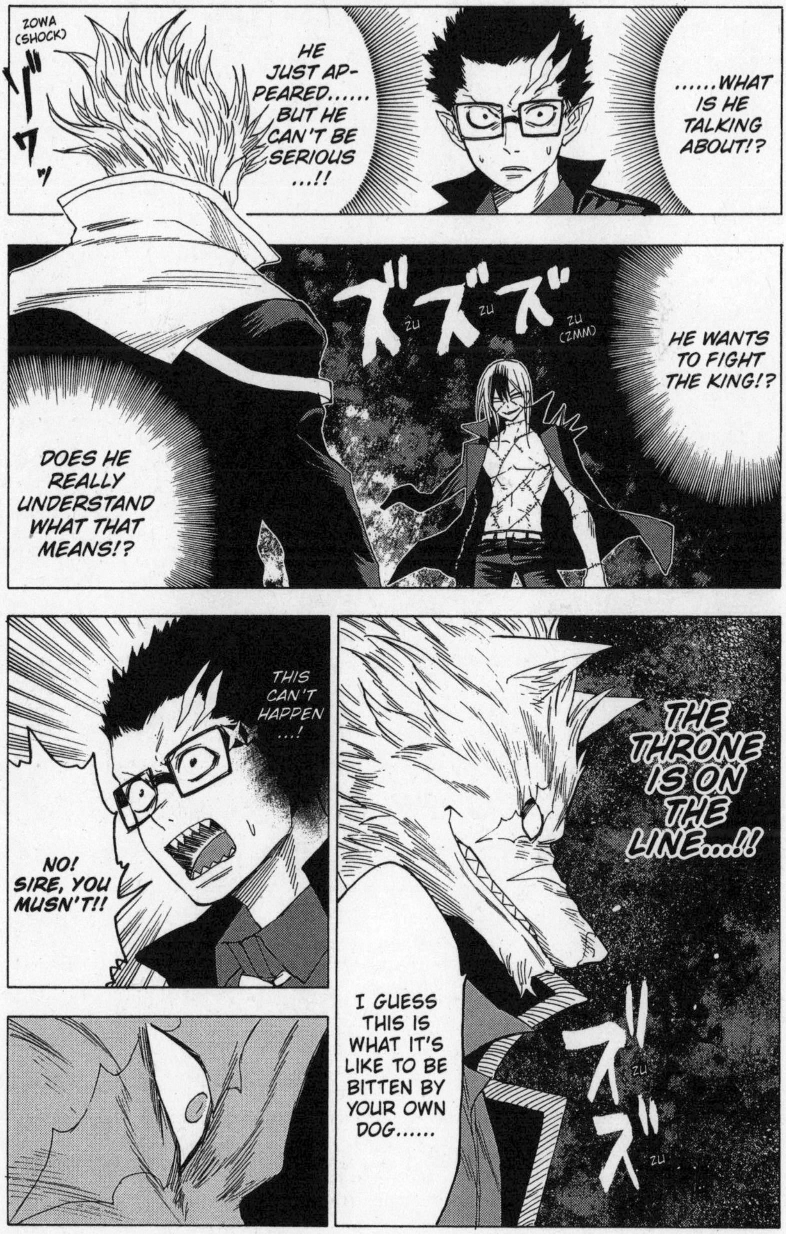
......WHAT IS HE TALKING ABOUT!?
HE JUST AP-PEARED...... BUT HE CAN'T BE SERIOUS...!!
ZOWA (SHOCK)
HE WANTS TO FIGHT THE KING!?
ZU ZU ZU (ZMM)
DOES HE REALLY UNDERSTAND WHAT THAT MEANS!?
THE THRONE IS ON THE LINE...!!
I GUESS THIS IS WHAT IT'S LIKE TO BE BITTEN BY YOUR OWN DOG......
ZU ZU
THIS CAN'T HAPPEN...!
NO! SIRE, YOU MUSN'T!!

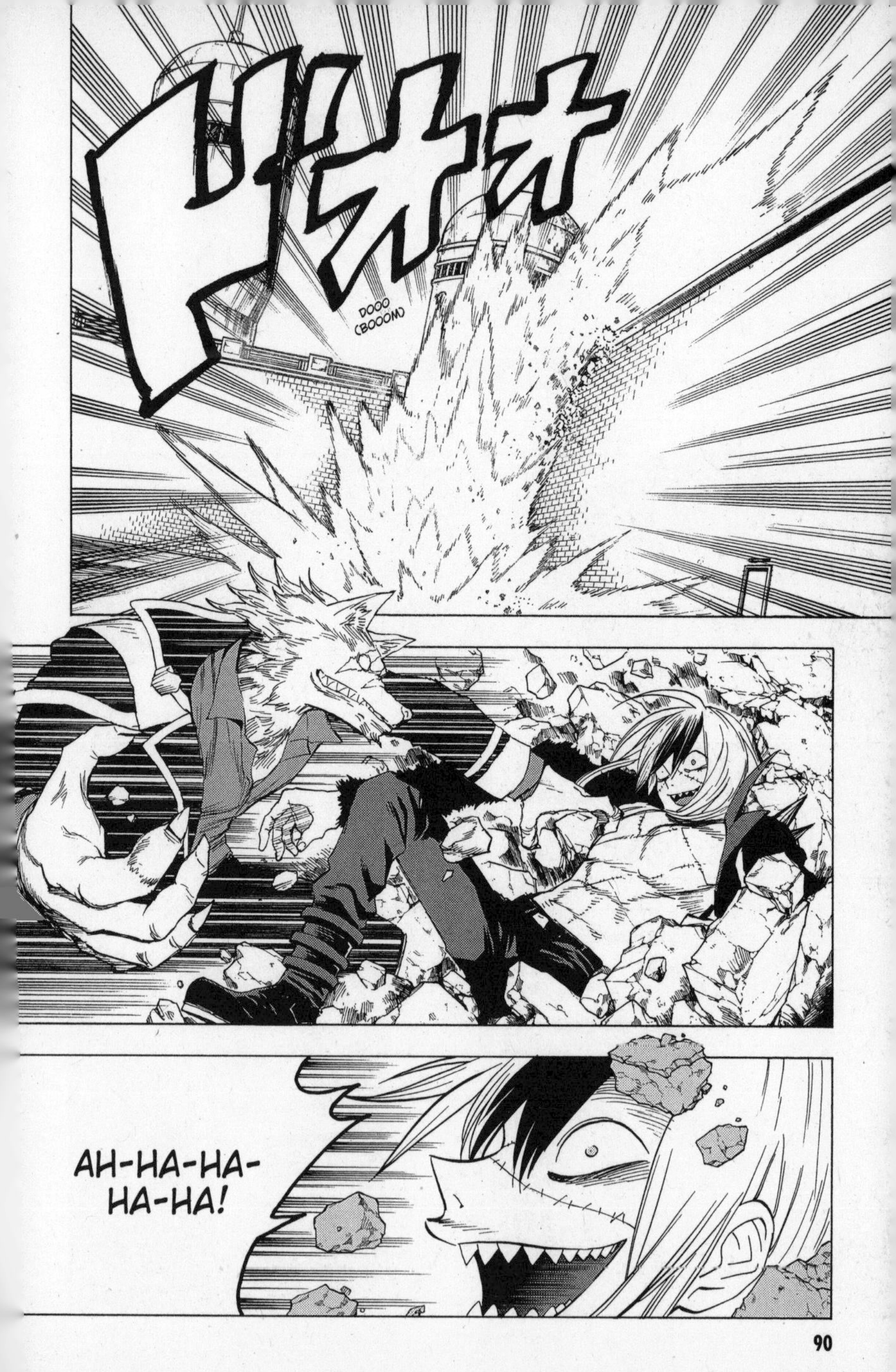
DOOO
(BOOOM)
AH-HA-HA-
HA-HA!

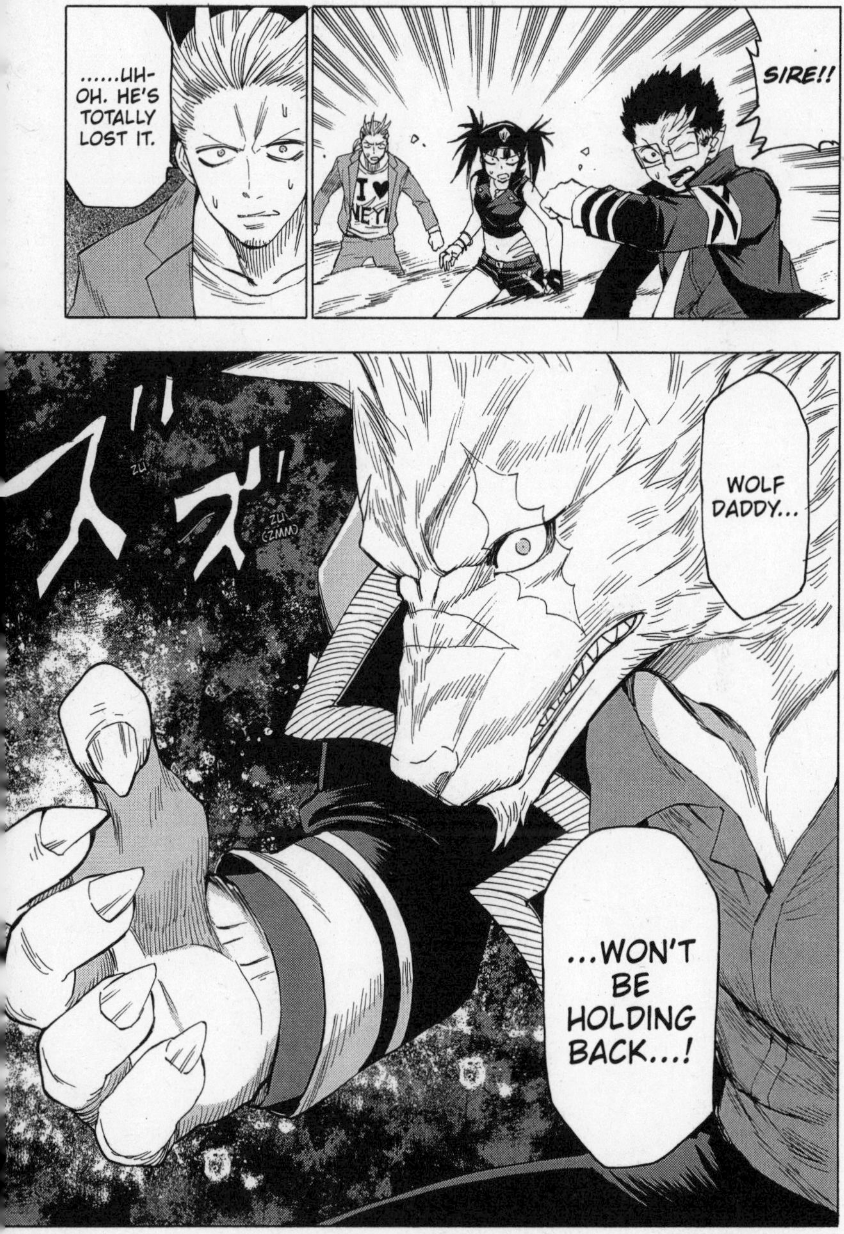
SIRE!!
......UH-OH. HE'S TOTALLY LOST IT.
WOLF DADDY...
...WON'T BE HOLDING BACK...!
ズズ
ZU
ZU (ZMMM)

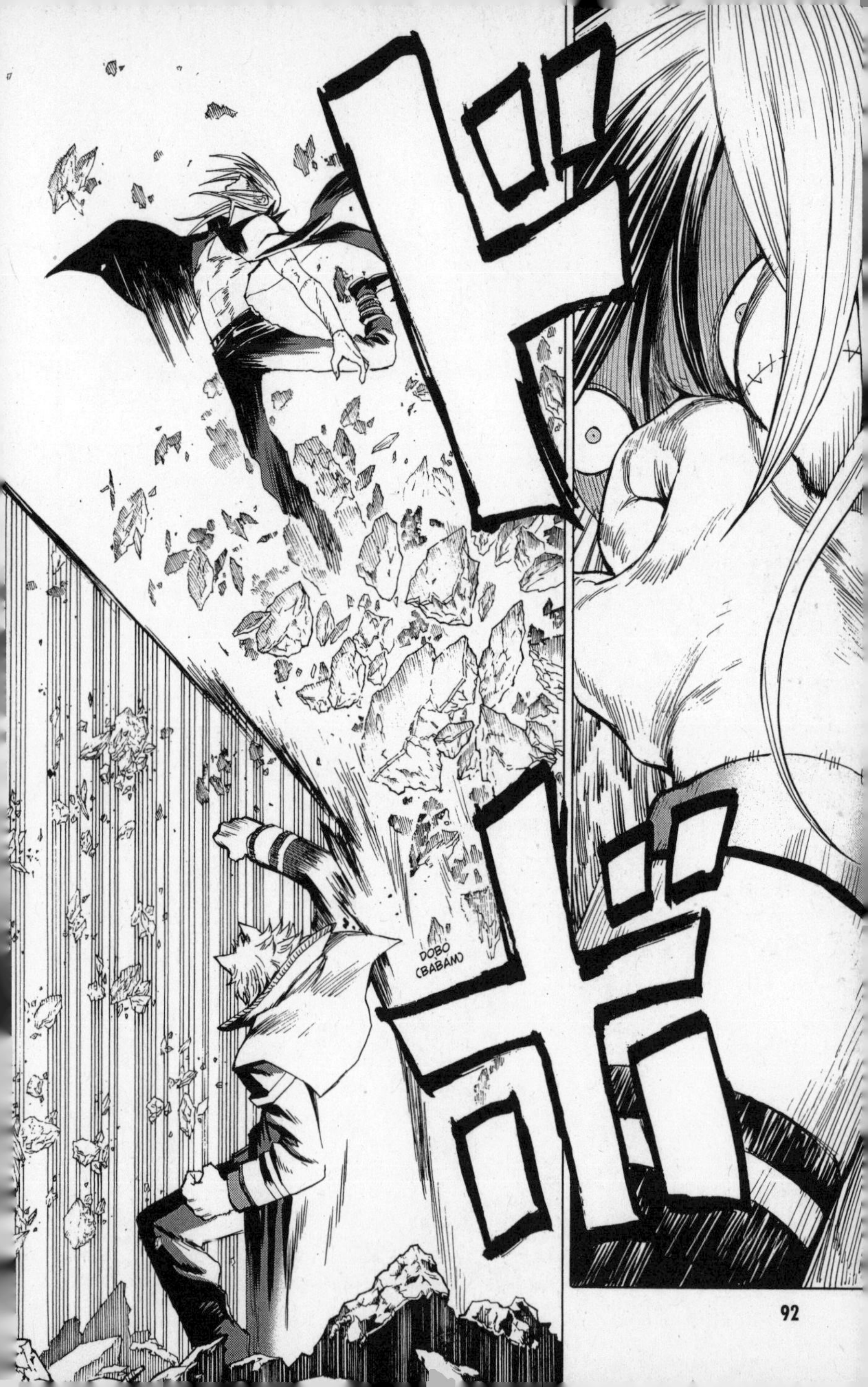
DOBO
(BABAM)

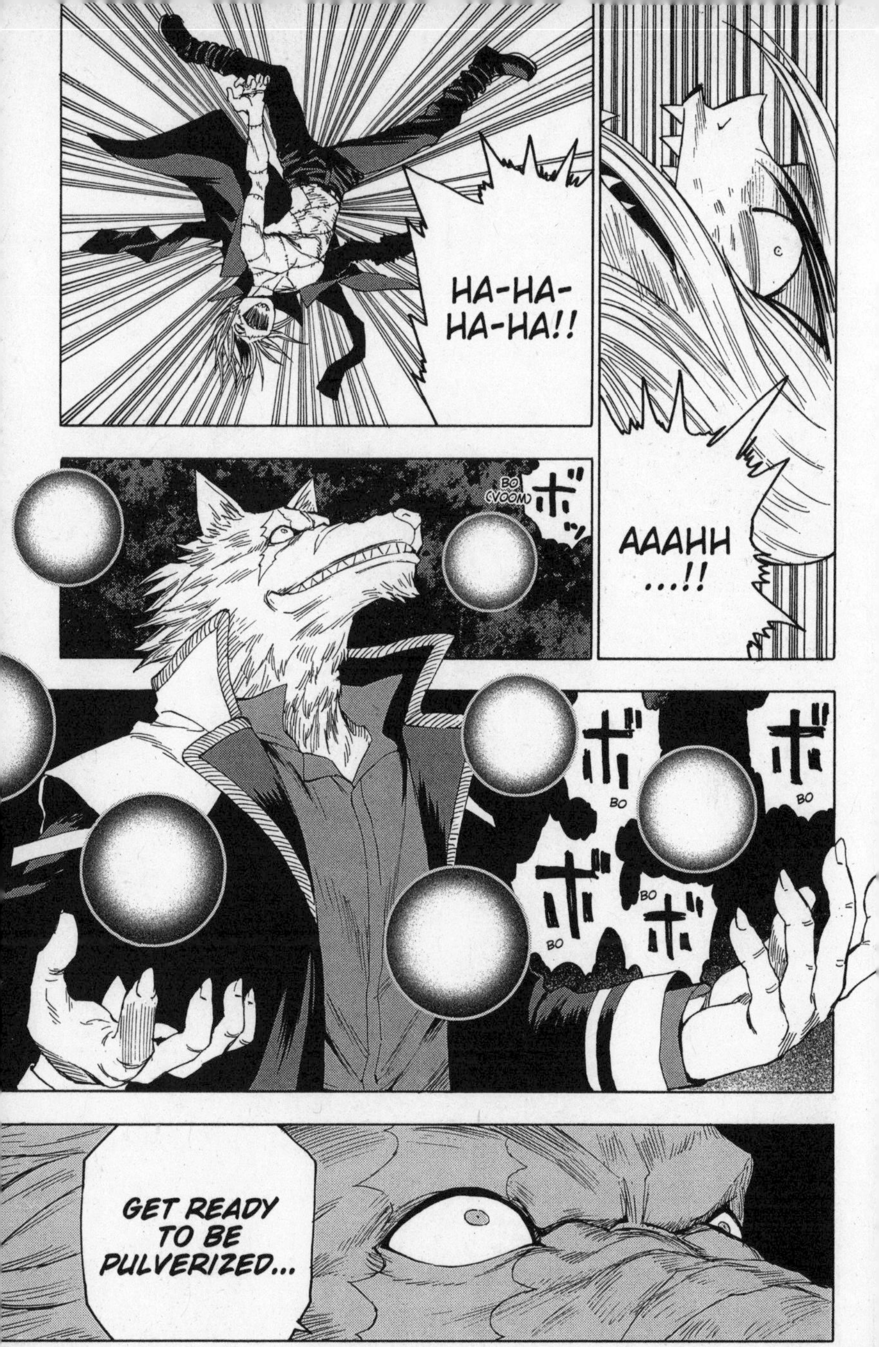
AAAHH ...!!
HA-HA-HA-HA!!
ボッ BO (VOOM)
ボ BO
ボ BO
ボ BO
ボ BO
GET READY TO BE PULVERIZED...

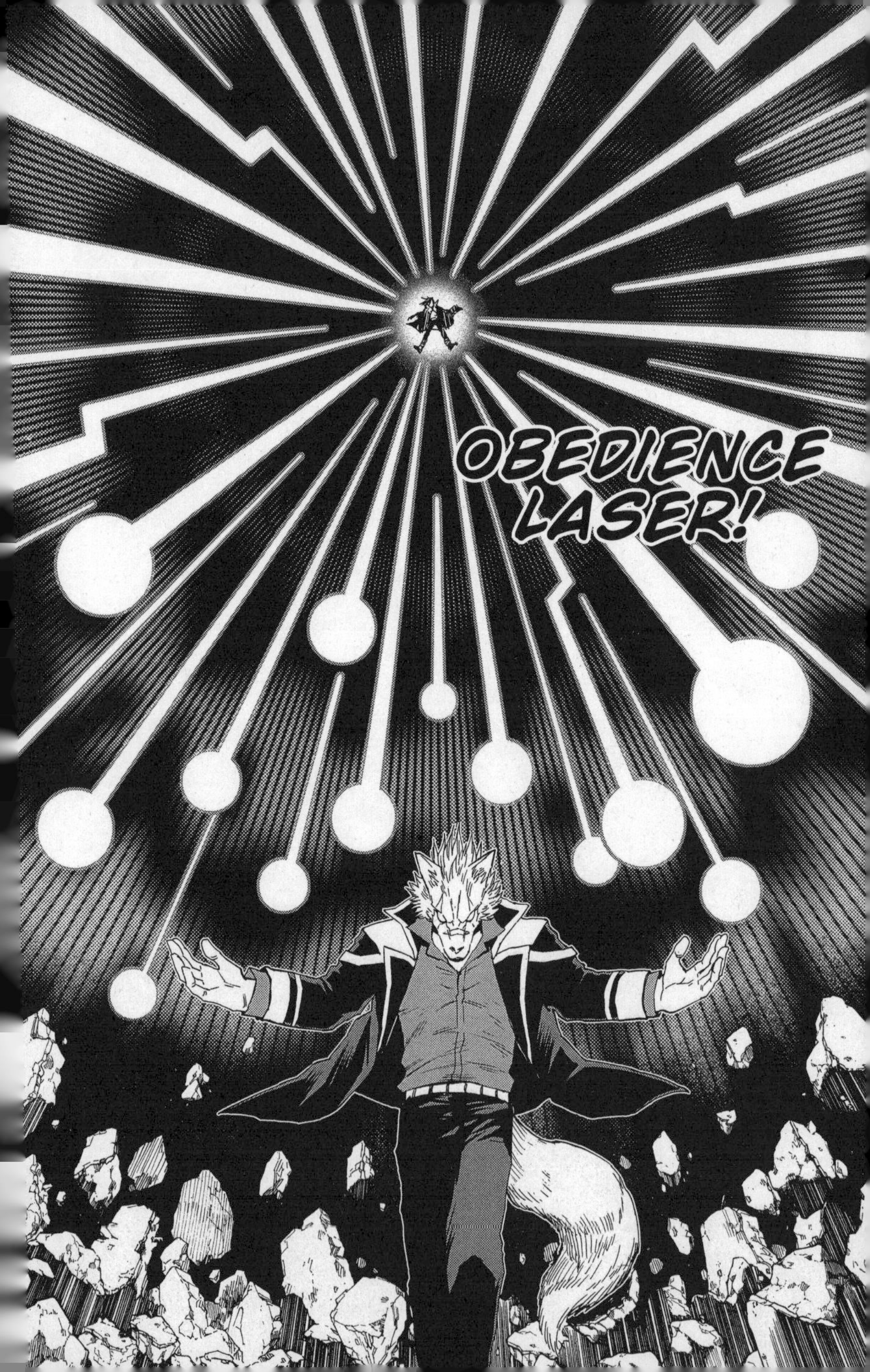
OBEDIENCE LASER!

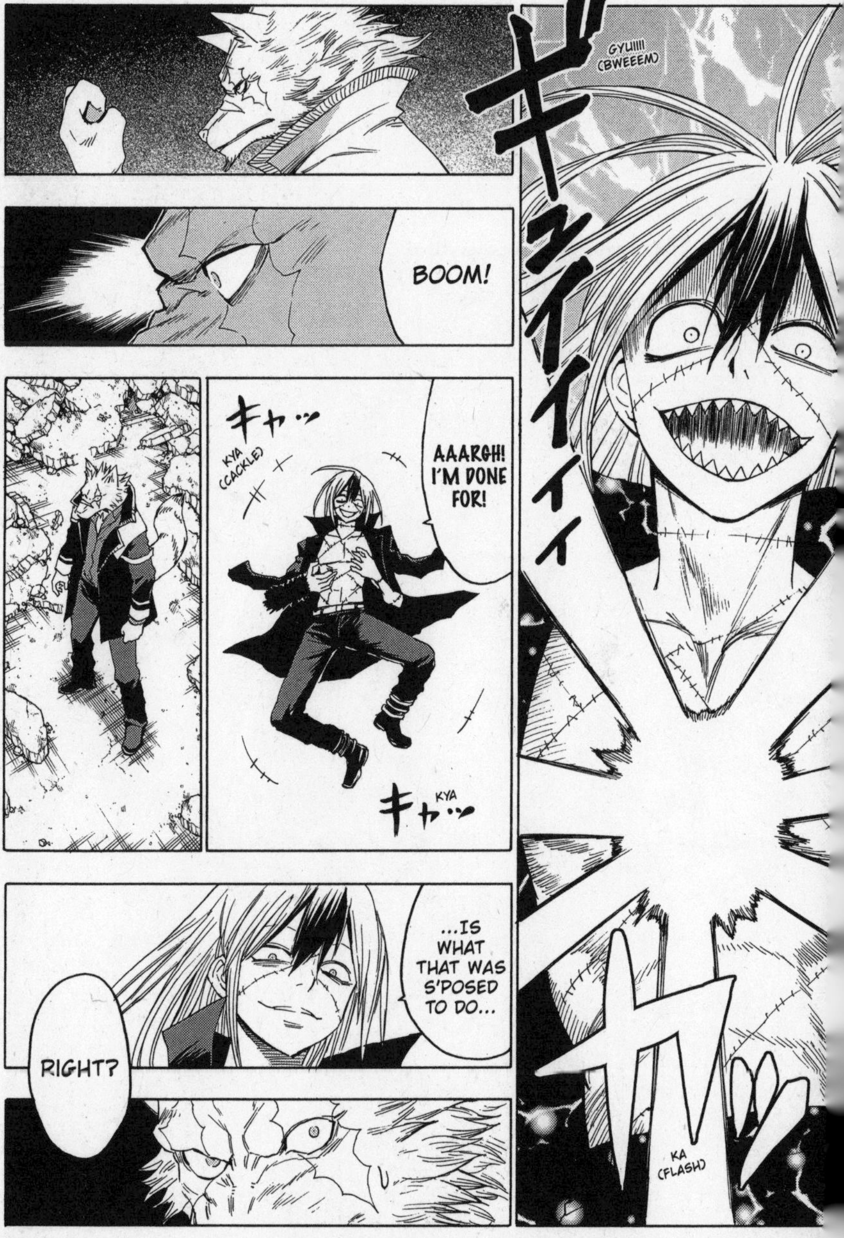
ギュイイイ
GYUIIII (BWEEEM)
カッ
KA (FLASH)
BOOM!
キャッ
KYA (CACKLE)
AAARGH! I'M DONE FOR!
キャッ
KYA
...IS WHAT THAT WAS S'POSED TO DO...
RIGHT?

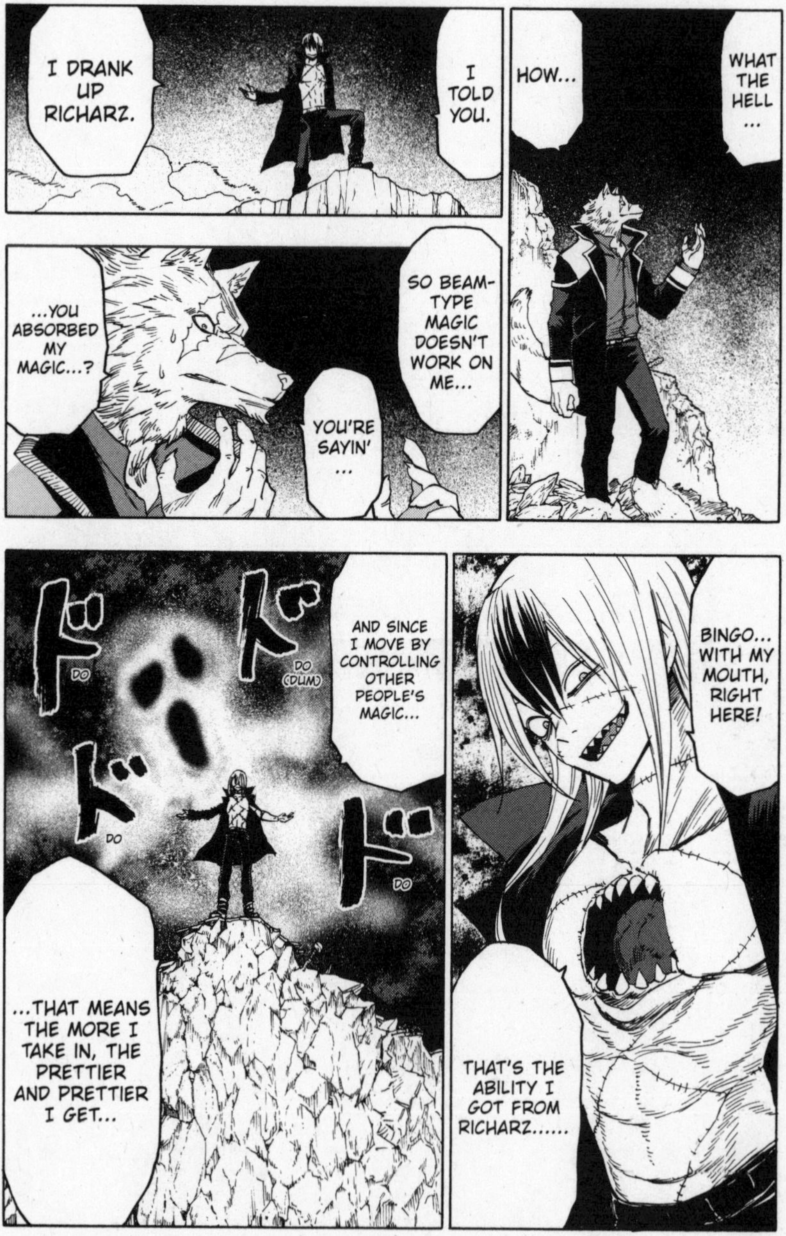
WHAT THE HELL ...
HOW...
I TOLD YOU.
I DRANK UP RICHARZ.
SO BEAM-TYPE MAGIC DOESN'T WORK ON ME...
YOU'RE SAYIN' ...
...YOU ABSORBED MY MAGIC...?
BINGO... WITH MY MOUTH, RIGHT HERE!
THAT'S THE ABILITY I GOT FROM RICHARZ......
AND SINCE I MOVE BY CONTROLLING OTHER PEOPLE'S MAGIC...
ド DO (DUM)
ド DO
ド DO
ド DO
...THAT MEANS THE MORE I TAKE IN, THE PRETTIER AND PRETTIER I GET...

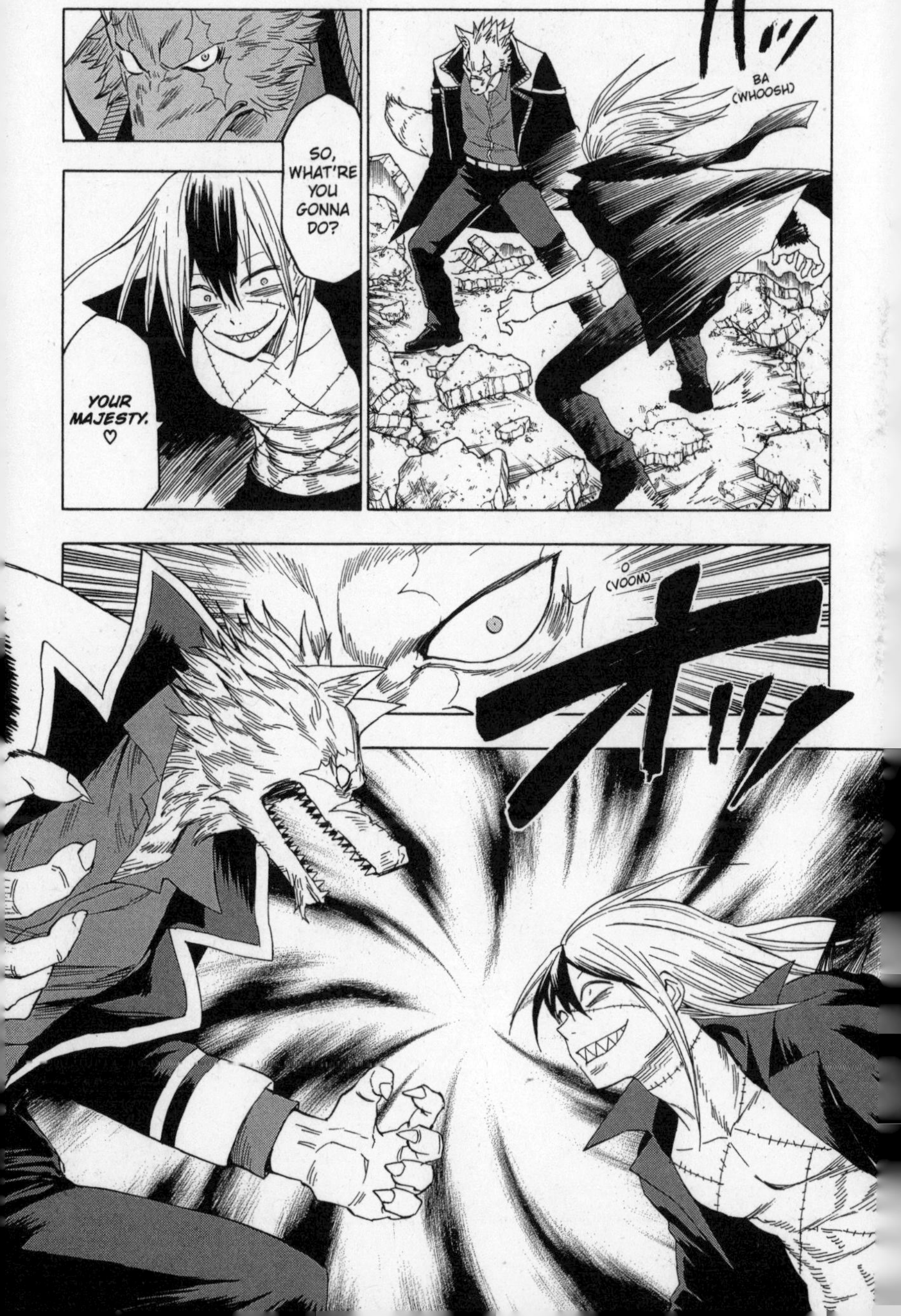
バッ
BA (WHOOSH)
SO, WHAT'RE YOU GONNA DO?
YOUR MAJESTY. ♡
オッ
O (VOOM)

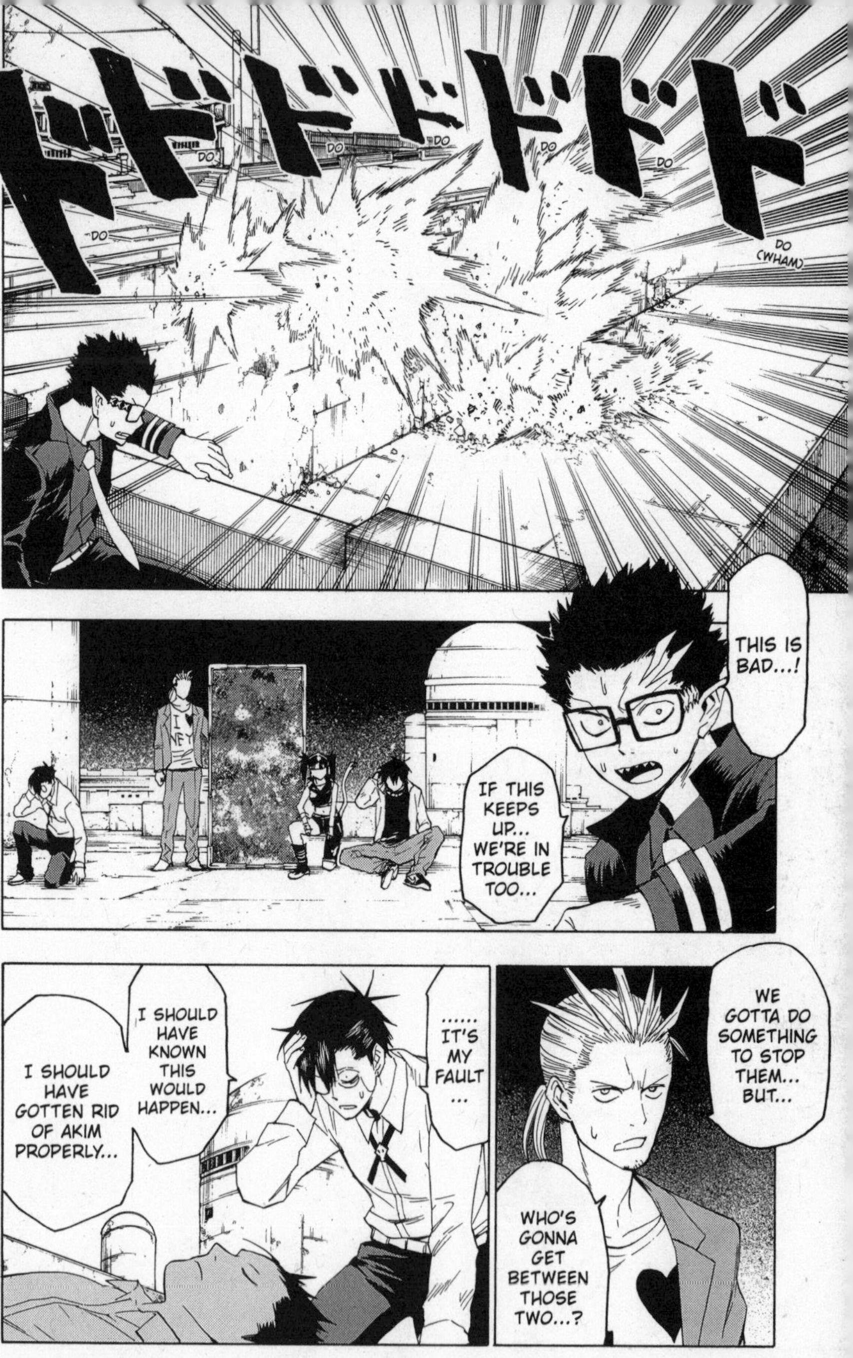
ドドドドドドド
DO DO DO DO DO DO
DO (WHAM)
THIS IS BAD...!
IF THIS KEEPS UP... WE'RE IN TROUBLE TOO...
WE GOTTA DO SOMETHING TO STOP THEM... BUT...
WHO'S GONNA GET BETWEEN THOSE TWO...?
......IT'S MY FAULT...
I SHOULD HAVE KNOWN THIS WOULD HAPPEN...
I SHOULD HAVE GOTTEN RID OF AKIM PROPERLY...

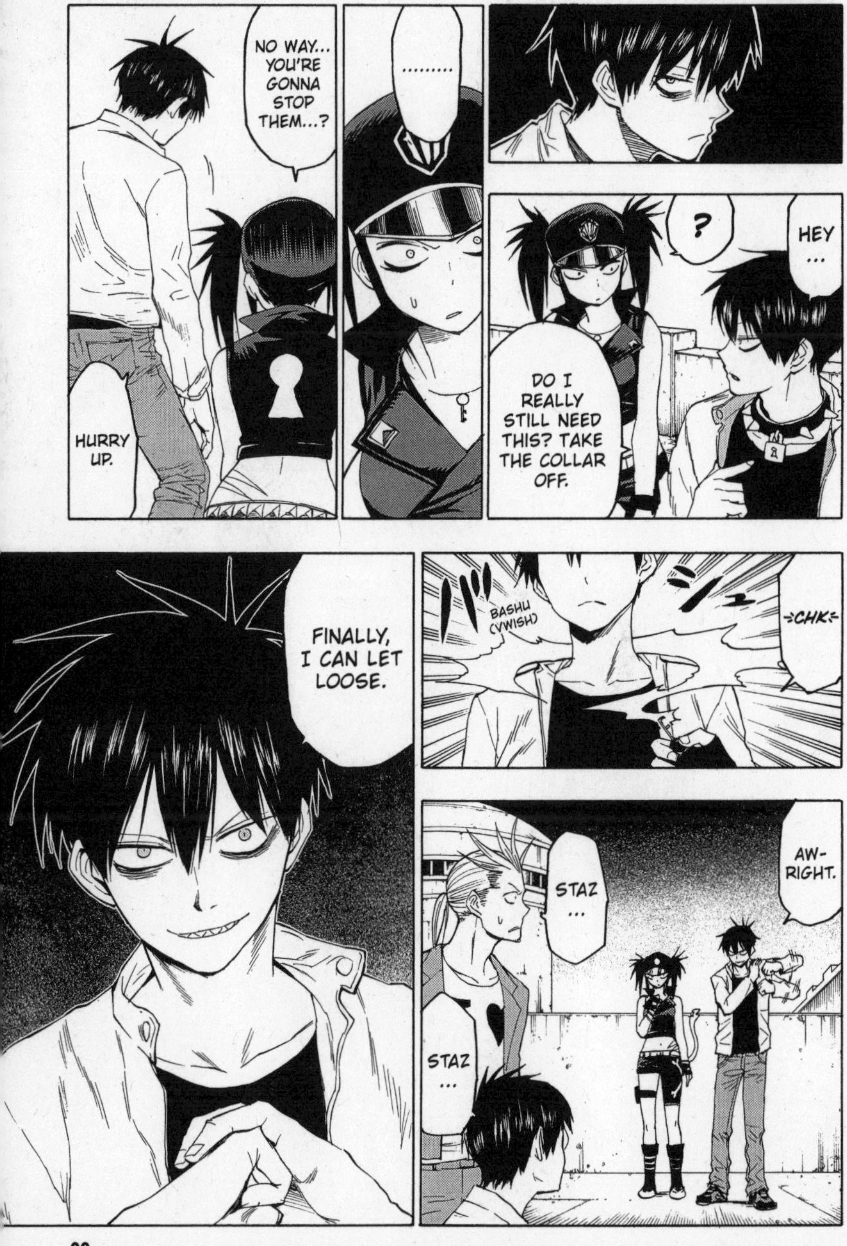
HEY ...
?
DO I REALLY STILL NEED THIS? TAKE THE COLLAR OFF.
....
NO WAY... YOU'RE GONNA STOP THEM...?
HURRY UP.
=CHK=
BASHU (VWISH)
AW-RIGHT.
STAZ ...
STAZ ...
FINALLY, I CAN LET LOOSE.

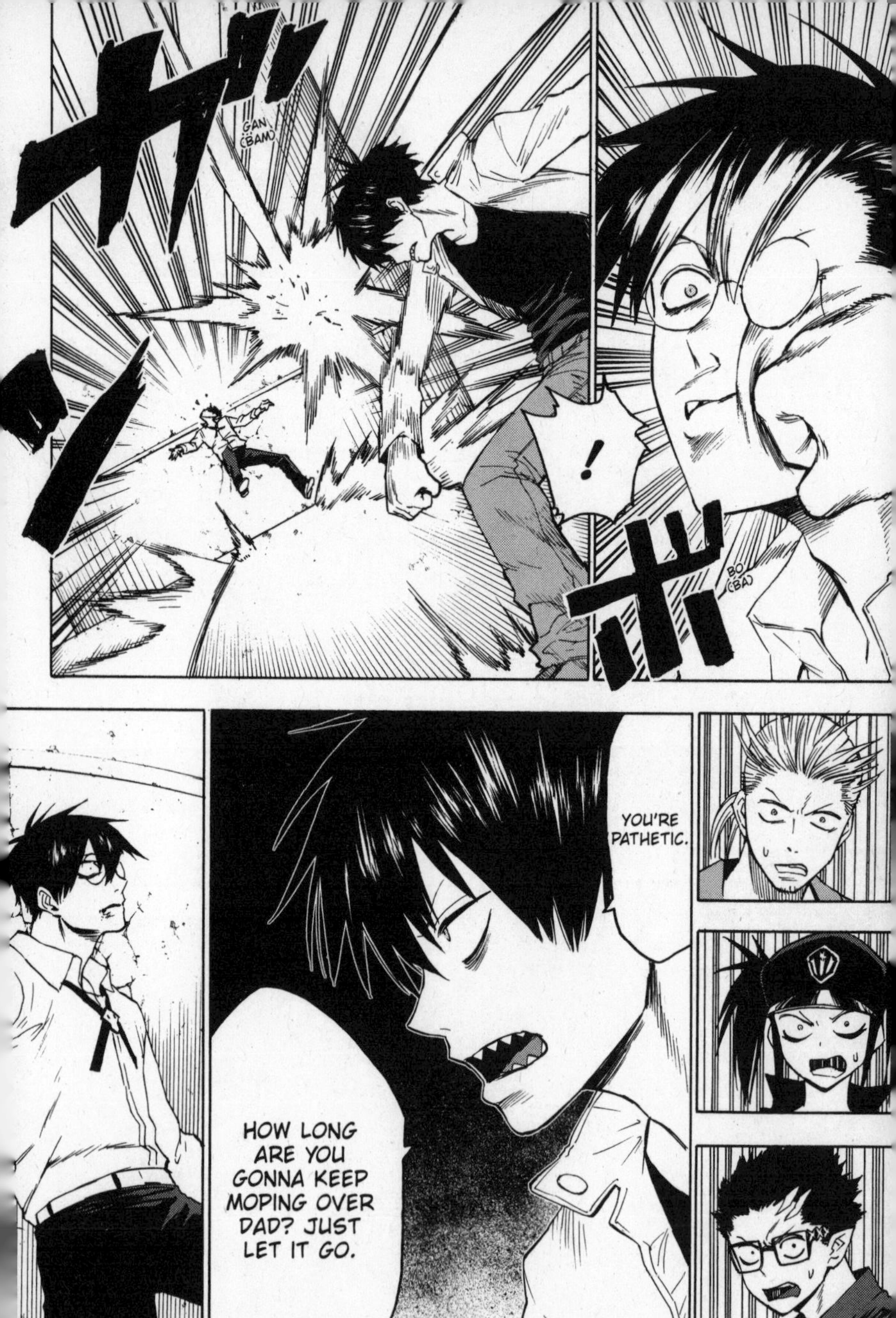
!
BO (BA)
GAN (BAM)
YOU'RE PATHETIC.
HOW LONG ARE YOU GONNA KEEP MOPING OVER DAD? JUST LET IT GO.

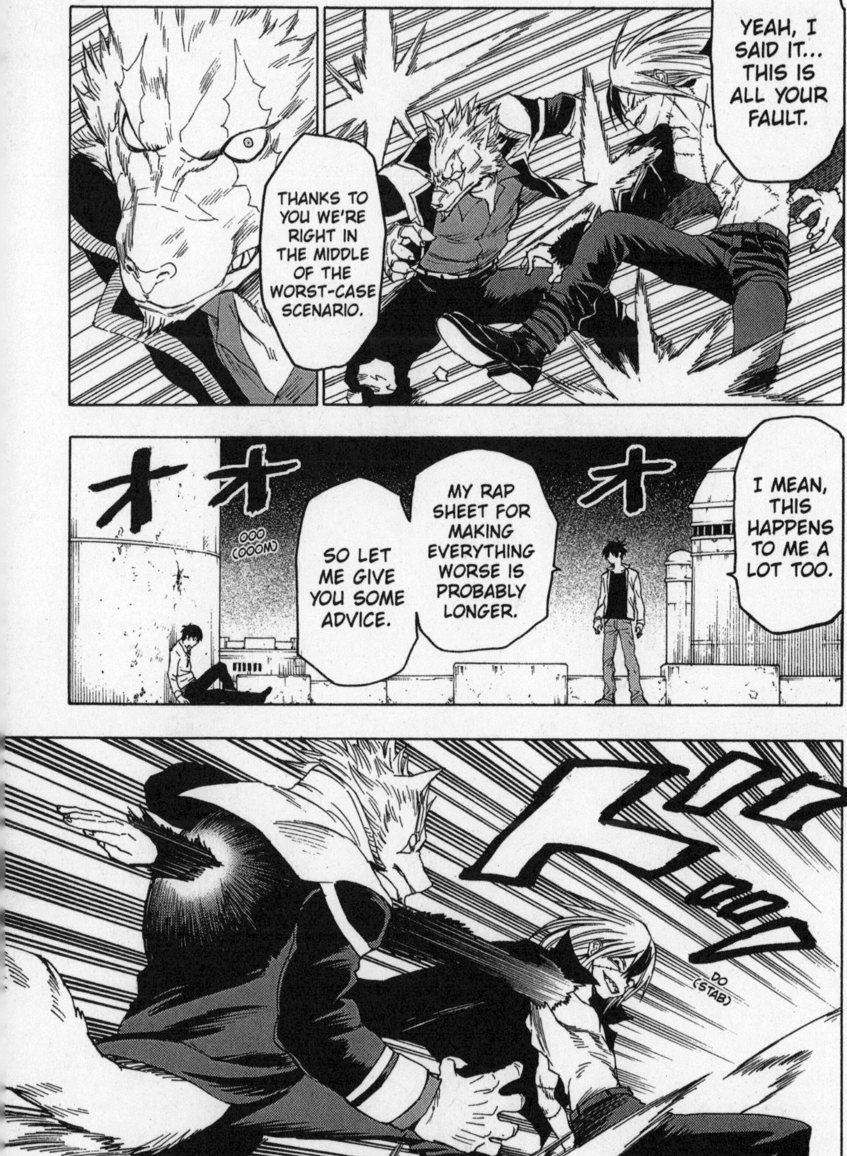
YEAH, I SAID IT... THIS IS ALL YOUR FAULT.
THANKS TO YOU WE'RE RIGHT IN THE MIDDLE OF THE WORST-CASE SCENARIO.
I MEAN, THIS HAPPENS TO ME A LOT TOO.
MY RAP SHEET FOR MAKING EVERYTHING WORSE IS PROBABLY LONGER.
SO LET ME GIVE YOU SOME ADVICE.
OOO (OOOM)
DO (STAB)

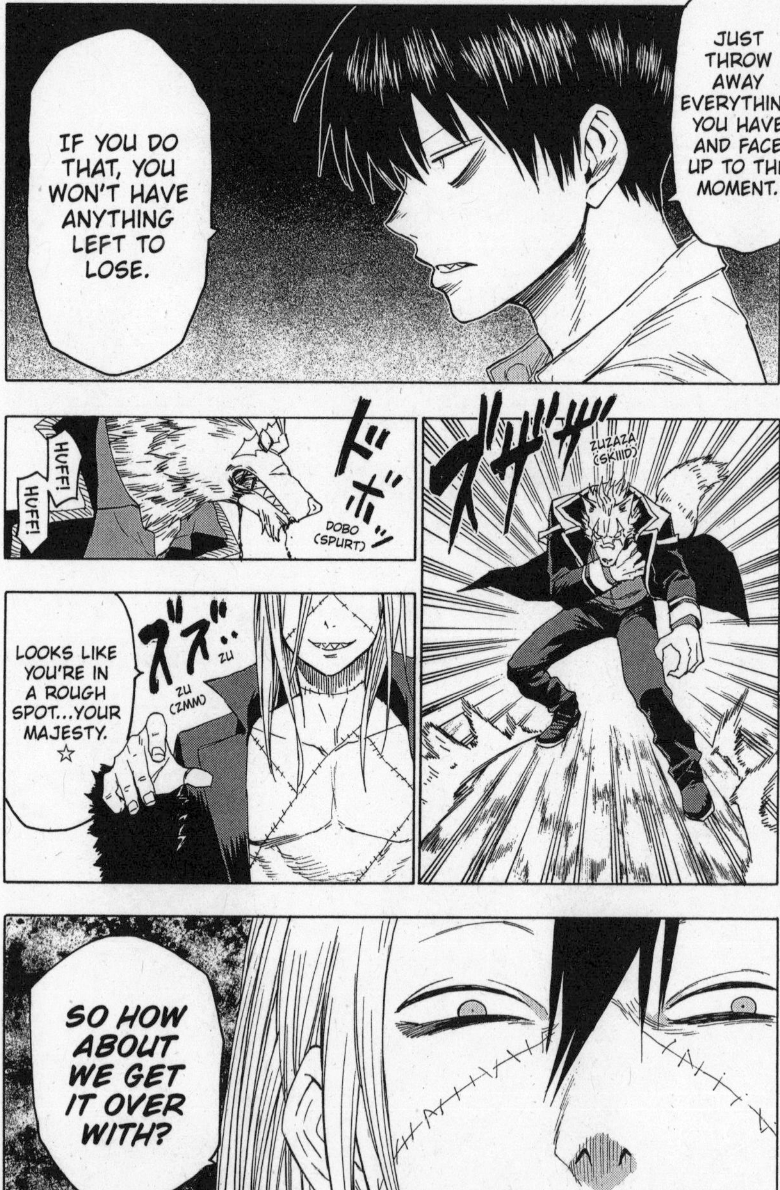
JUST THROW AWAY EVERYTHING YOU HAVE AND FACE UP TO THE MOMENT.
IF YOU DO THAT, YOU WON'T HAVE ANYTHING LEFT TO LOSE.
ズザザ
ZUZAZA (SKIIID)
ドボッ
DOBO (SPURT)
HUFF!
HUFF!
ズズ
ZU
ZU (ZMM)
LOOKS LIKE YOU'RE IN A ROUGH SPOT...YOUR MAJESTY. ☆
SO HOW ABOUT WE GET IT OVER WITH?

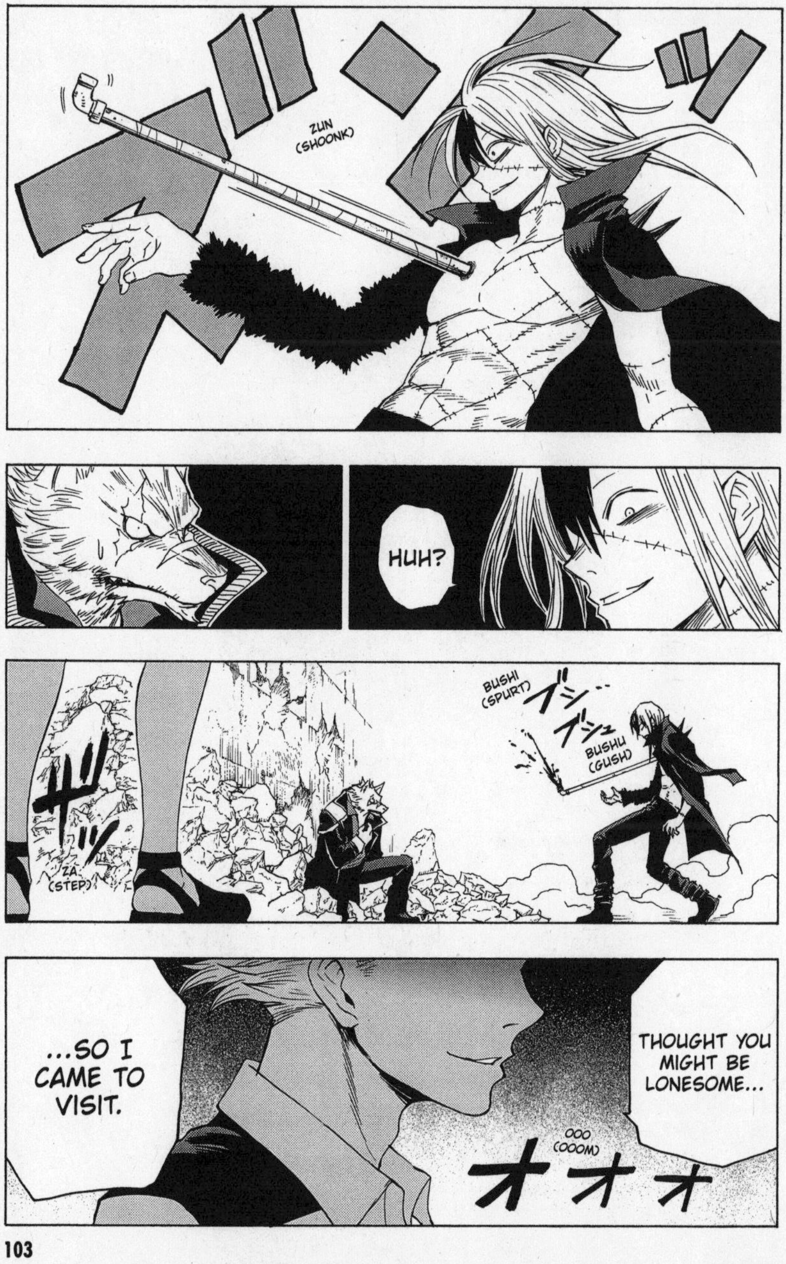
ZUN (SHOONK)
HUH?
BUSHI (SPURT)
BUSHU (GUSH)
ZA (STEP)
THOUGHT YOU MIGHT BE LONESOME...
OOO (OOOM)
...SO I CAME TO VISIT.

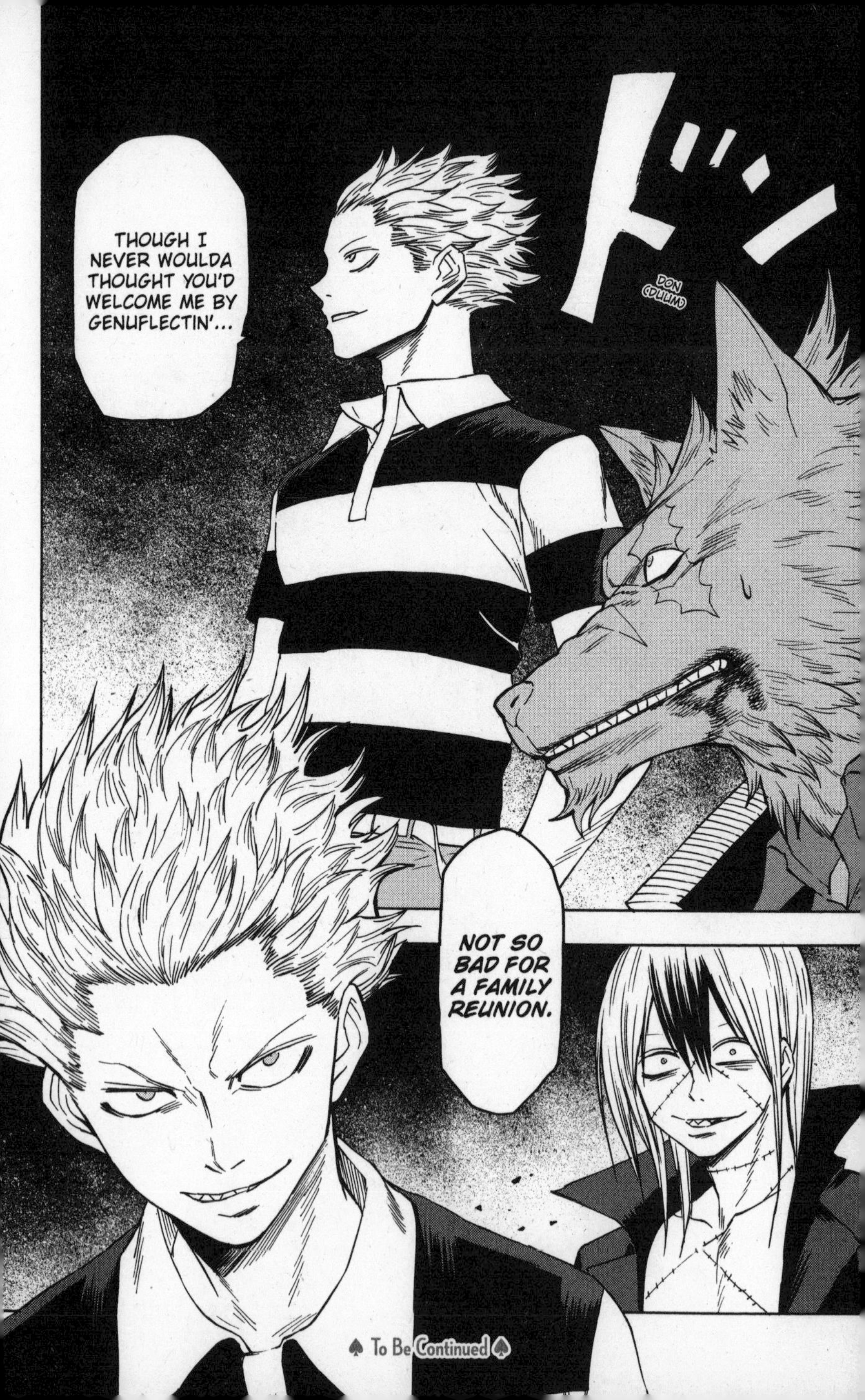
DON (DUUN)
THOUGH I NEVER WOULDA THOUGHT YOU'D WELCOME ME BY GENUFLECTIN'...
NOT SO BAD FOR A FAMILY REUNION.
To Be Continued

BLOOD LAD

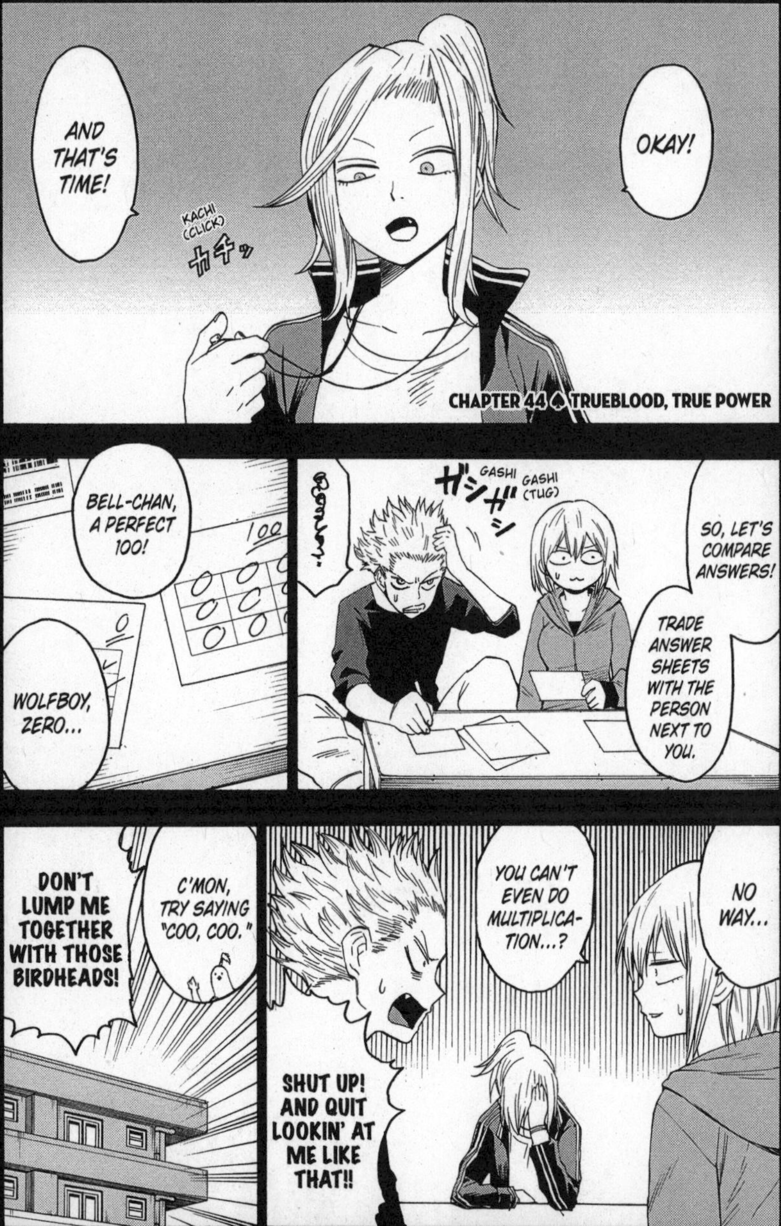
OKAY!
AND THAT'S TIME!
KACHI (CLICK)
CHAPTER 44 ♠ TRUEBLOOD, TRUE POWER
SO, LET'S COMPARE ANSWERS!
TRADE ANSWER SHEETS WITH THE PERSON NEXT TO YOU.
GASHI GASHI (TUG)
BELL-CHAN, A PERFECT 100!
100
WOLFBOY, ZERO...
0
NO WAY...
YOU CAN'T EVEN DO MULTIPLICATION...?
SHUT UP! AND QUIT LOOKIN' AT ME LIKE THAT!!
C'MON, TRY SAYING "COO, COO."
DON'T LUMP ME TOGETHER WITH THOSE BIRDHEADS!

BLOOD LAD

CHAPTER 44 ♠ TRUEBLOOD, TRUE POWER

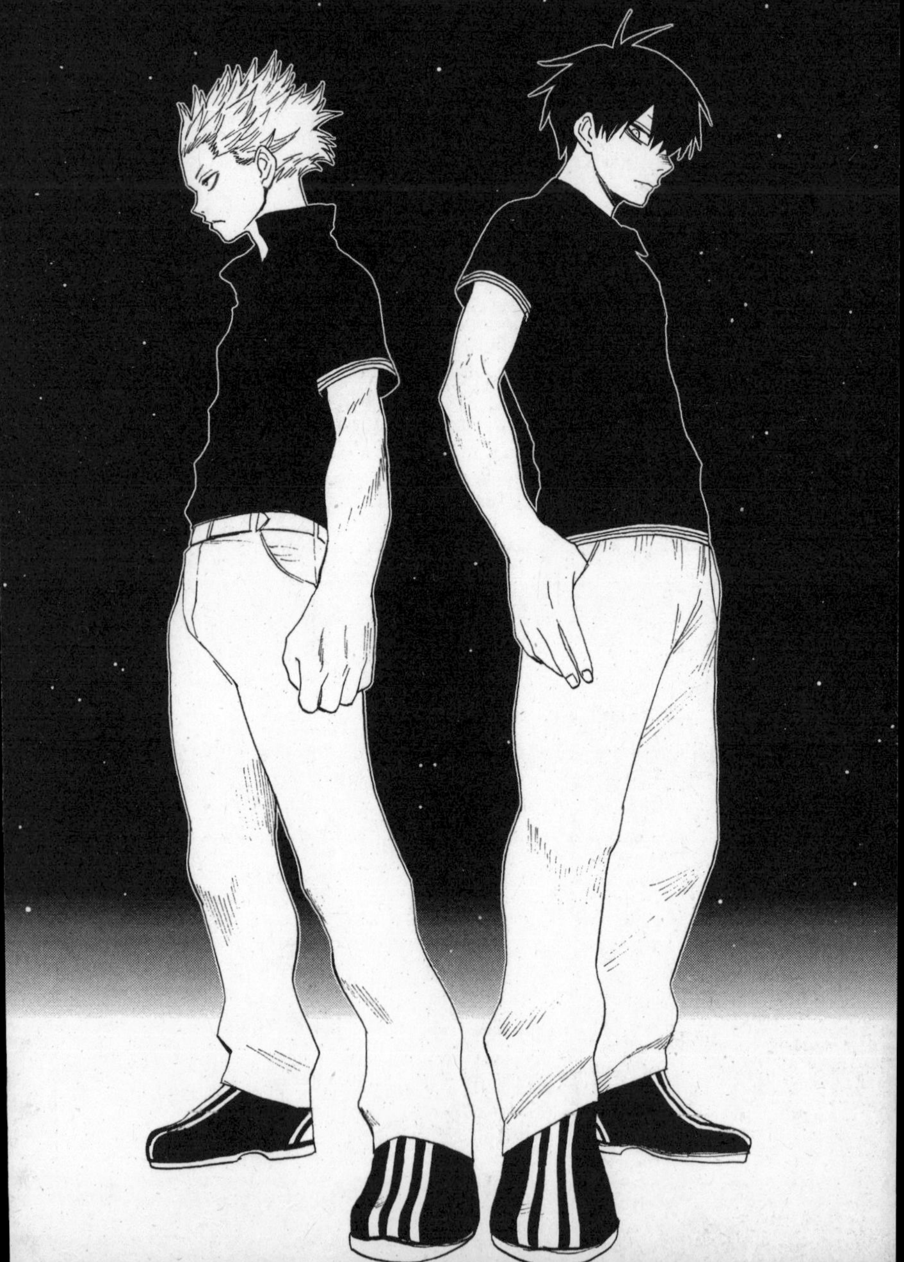

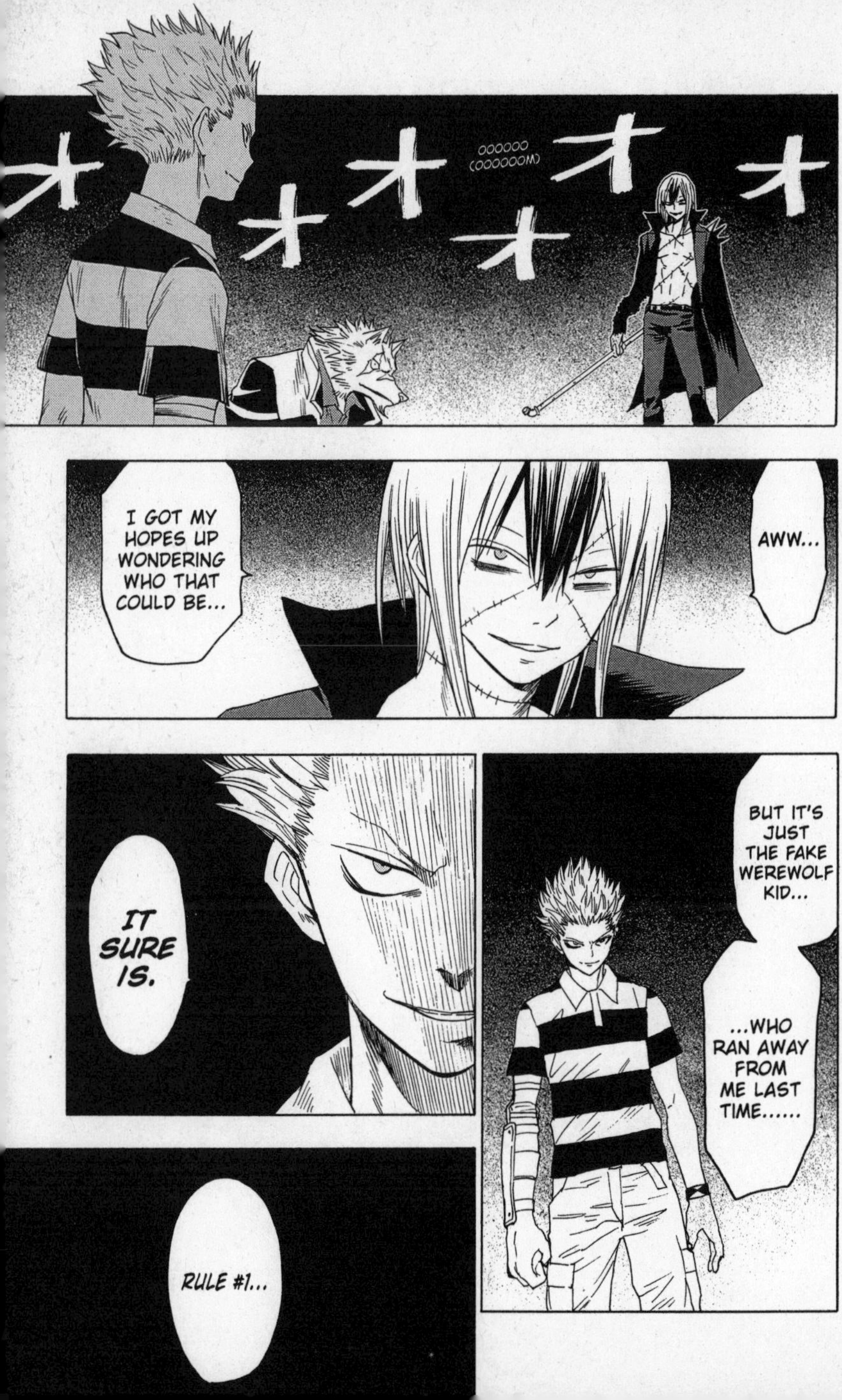
OOOOOO (OOOOOOM)
AWW...
I GOT MY HOPES UP WONDERING WHO THAT COULD BE...
BUT IT'S JUST THE FAKE WEREWOLF KID...
...WHO RAN AWAY FROM ME LAST TIME......
IT SURE IS.
RULE #1...

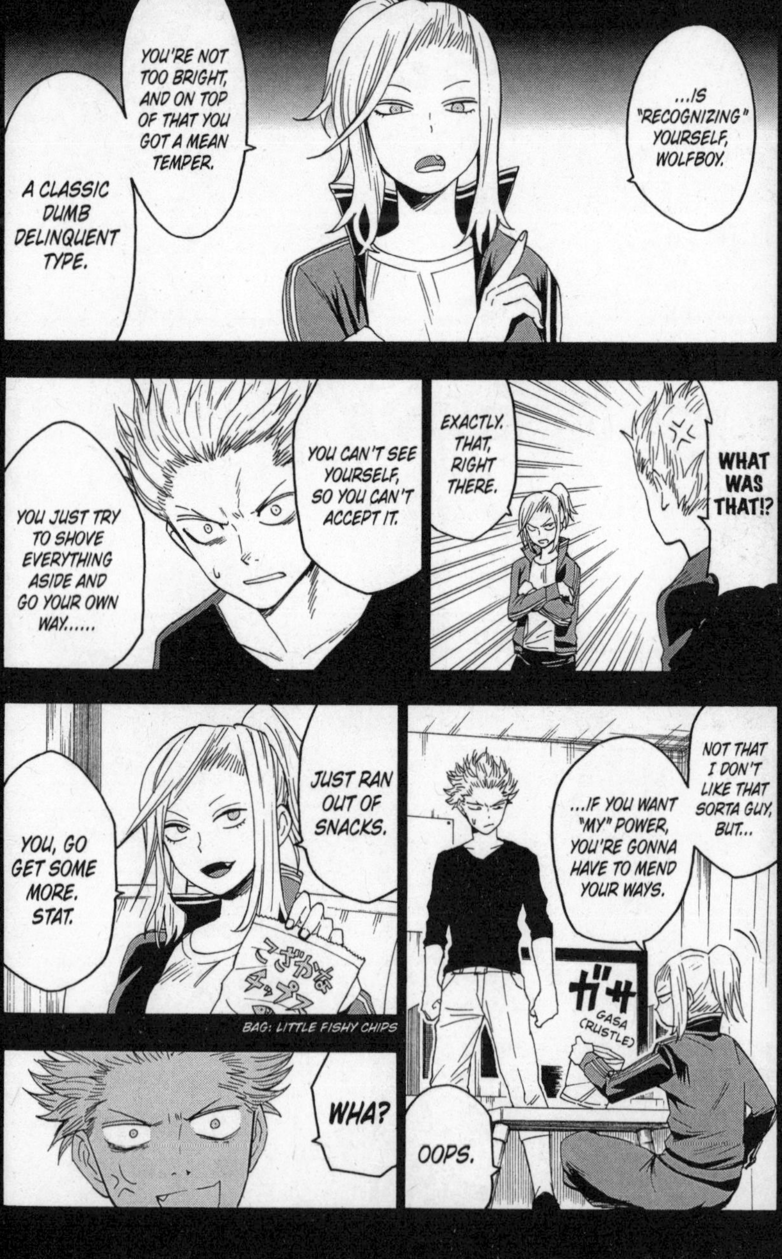
...IS "RECOGNIZING" YOURSELF, WOLFBOY.
YOU'RE NOT TOO BRIGHT, AND ON TOP OF THAT YOU GOT A MEAN TEMPER.
A CLASSIC DUMB DELINQUENT TYPE.
WHAT WAS THAT!?
EXACTLY. THAT, RIGHT THERE.
YOU CAN'T SEE YOURSELF, SO YOU CAN'T ACCEPT IT.
YOU JUST TRY TO SHOVE EVERYTHING ASIDE AND GO YOUR OWN WAY......
NOT THAT I DON'T LIKE THAT SORTA GUY, BUT...
...IF YOU WANT "MY" POWER, YOU'RE GONNA HAVE TO MEND YOUR WAYS.
ガサ
GASA (RUSTLE)
OOPS.
JUST RAN OUT OF SNACKS.
YOU, GO GET SOME MORE. STAT.
こざかな チップス
BAG: LITTLE FISHY CHIPS
WHA?

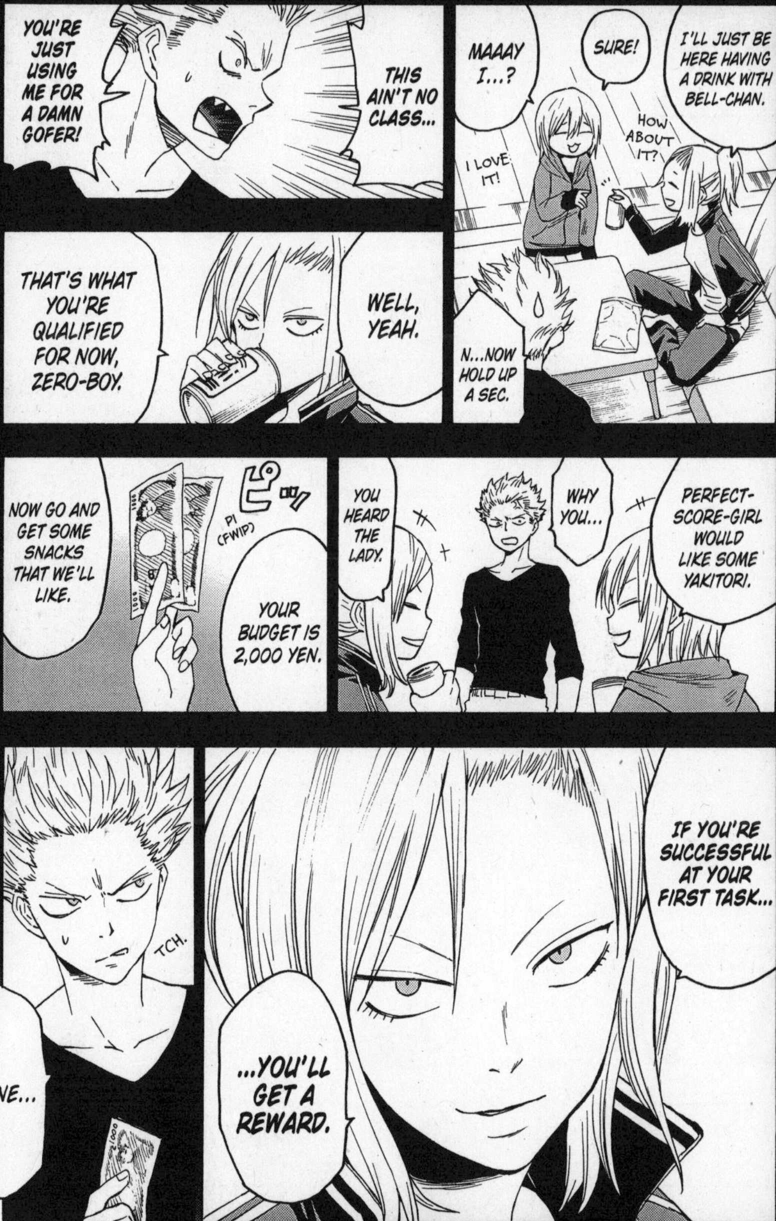
I'LL JUST BE HERE HAVING A DRINK WITH BELL-CHAN.
SURE!
MAAAY I...?
HOW ABOUT IT?
I LOVE IT!
N...NOW HOLD UP A SEC.
THIS AIN'T NO CLASS...
YOU'RE JUST USING ME FOR A DAMN GOFER!
WELL, YEAH.
THAT'S WHAT YOU'RE QUALIFIED FOR NOW, ZERO-BOY.
PERFECT-SCORE-GIRL WOULD LIKE SOME YAKITORI.
WHY YOU...
YOU HEARD THE LADY.
ピッ
PI (FWIP)
NOW GO AND GET SOME SNACKS THAT WE'LL LIKE.
YOUR BUDGET IS 2,000 YEN.
IF YOU'RE SUCCESSFUL AT YOUR FIRST TASK...
...YOU'LL GET A REWARD.
TCH.
FINE...

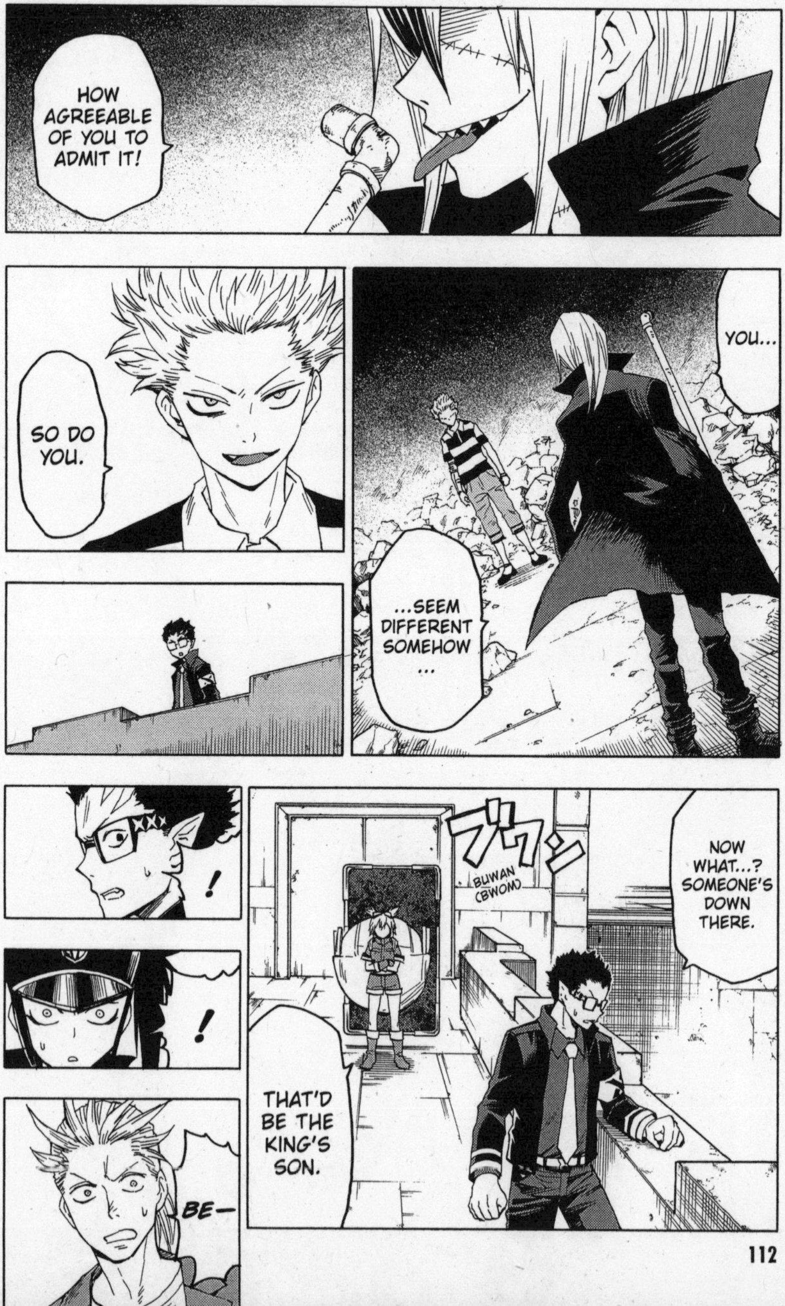
HOW AGREEABLE OF YOU TO ADMIT IT!
YOU...
...SEEM DIFFERENT SOMEHOW ...
SO DO YOU.
BUWAN (BWOM)
NOW WHAT...? SOMEONE'S DOWN THERE.
THAT'D BE THE KING'S SON.
!
!
BE—

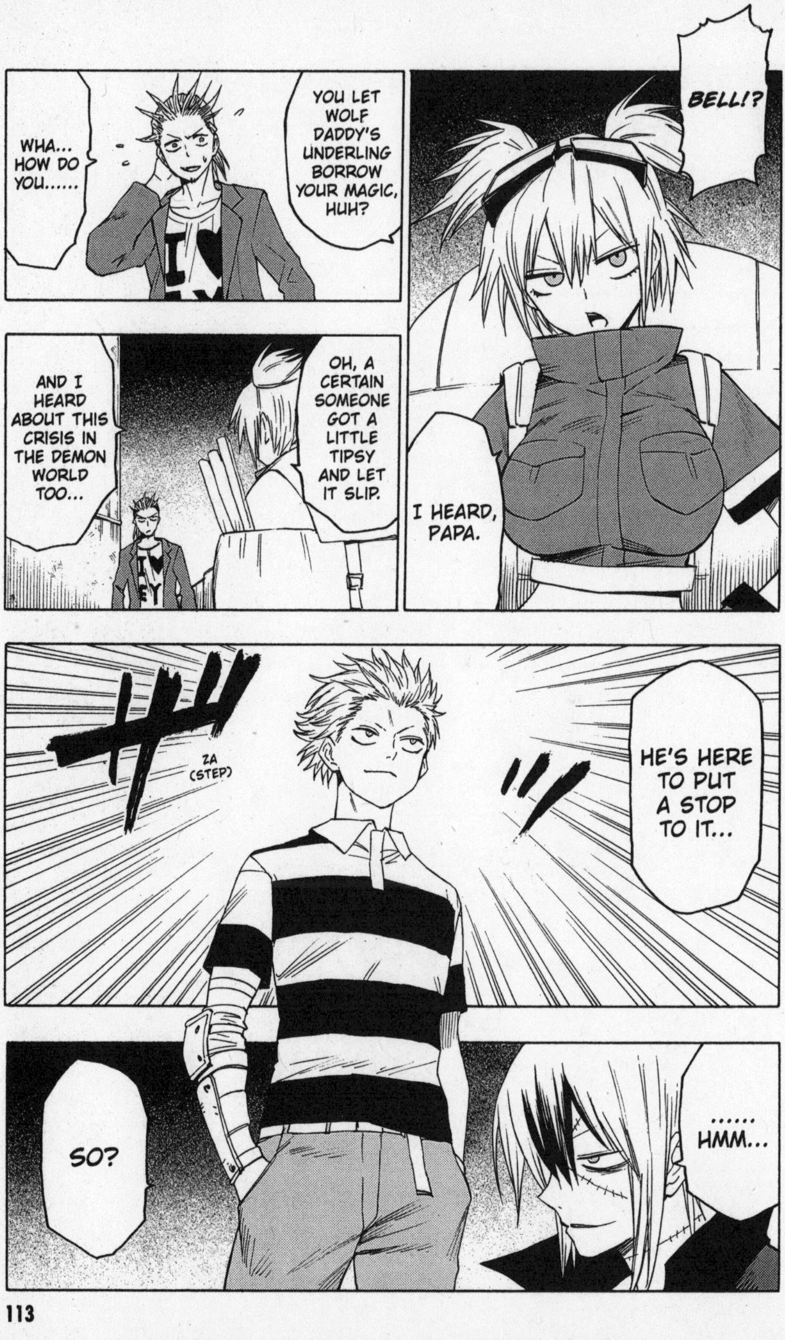
BELL!?
I HEARD, PAPA.
YOU LET WOLF DADDY'S UNDERLING BORROW YOUR MAGIC, HUH?
WHA... HOW DO YOU......
OH, A CERTAIN SOMEONE GOT A LITTLE TIPSY AND LET IT SLIP.
AND I HEARD ABOUT THIS CRISIS IN THE DEMON WORLD TOO...
HE'S HERE TO PUT A STOP TO IT...
ZA (STEP)
...... HMM...
SO?

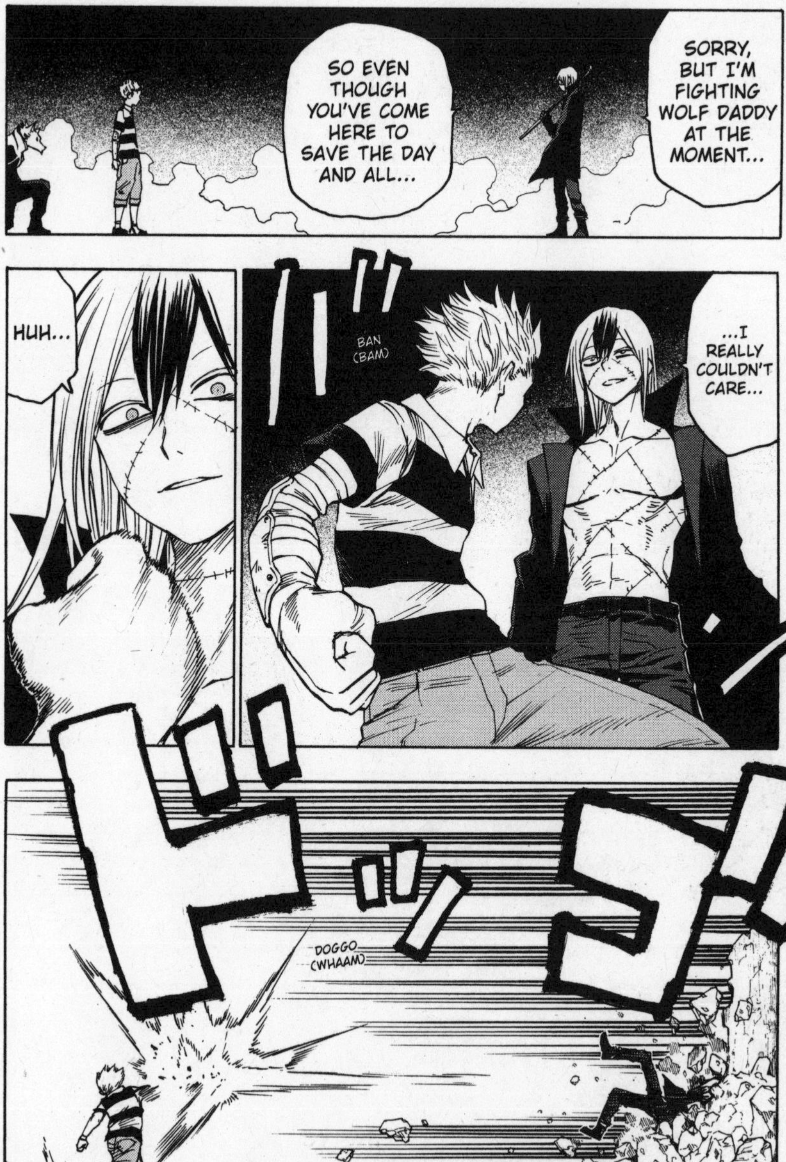
SORRY, BUT I'M FIGHTING WOLF DADDY AT THE MOMENT...
SO EVEN THOUGH YOU'VE COME HERE TO SAVE THE DAY AND ALL...
...I REALLY COULDN'T CARE...
BAN (BAM)
HUH...
DOGGO (WHAAM)

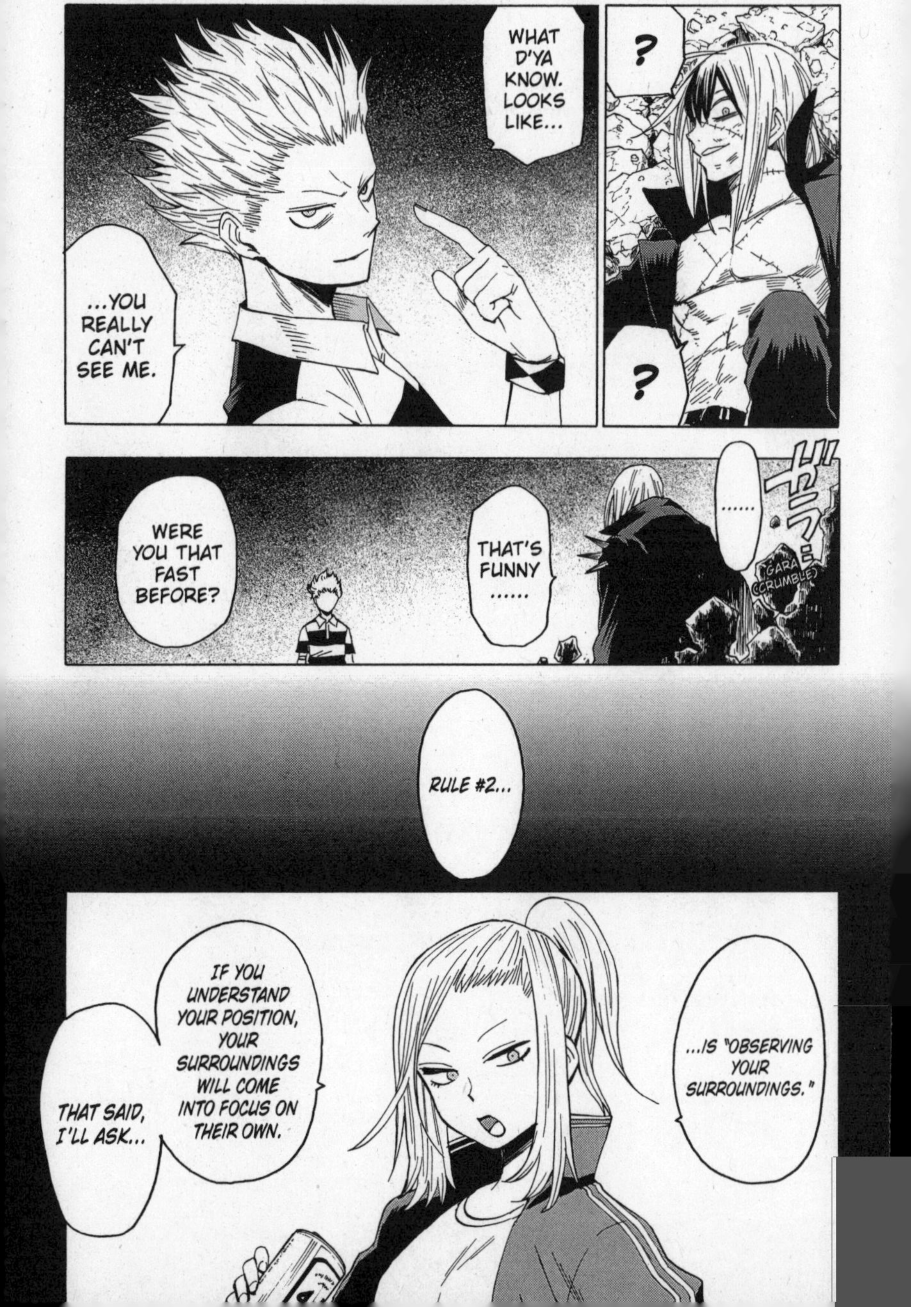
?
?
WHAT D'YA KNOW. LOOKS LIKE...
...YOU REALLY CAN'T SEE ME.
......
GARA (CRUMBLE)
THAT'S FUNNY ......
WERE YOU THAT FAST BEFORE?
RULE #2...
...IS "OBSERVING YOUR SURROUNDINGS."
IF YOU UNDERSTAND YOUR POSITION, YOUR SURROUNDINGS WILL COME INTO FOCUS ON THEIR OWN.
THAT SAID, I'LL ASK...

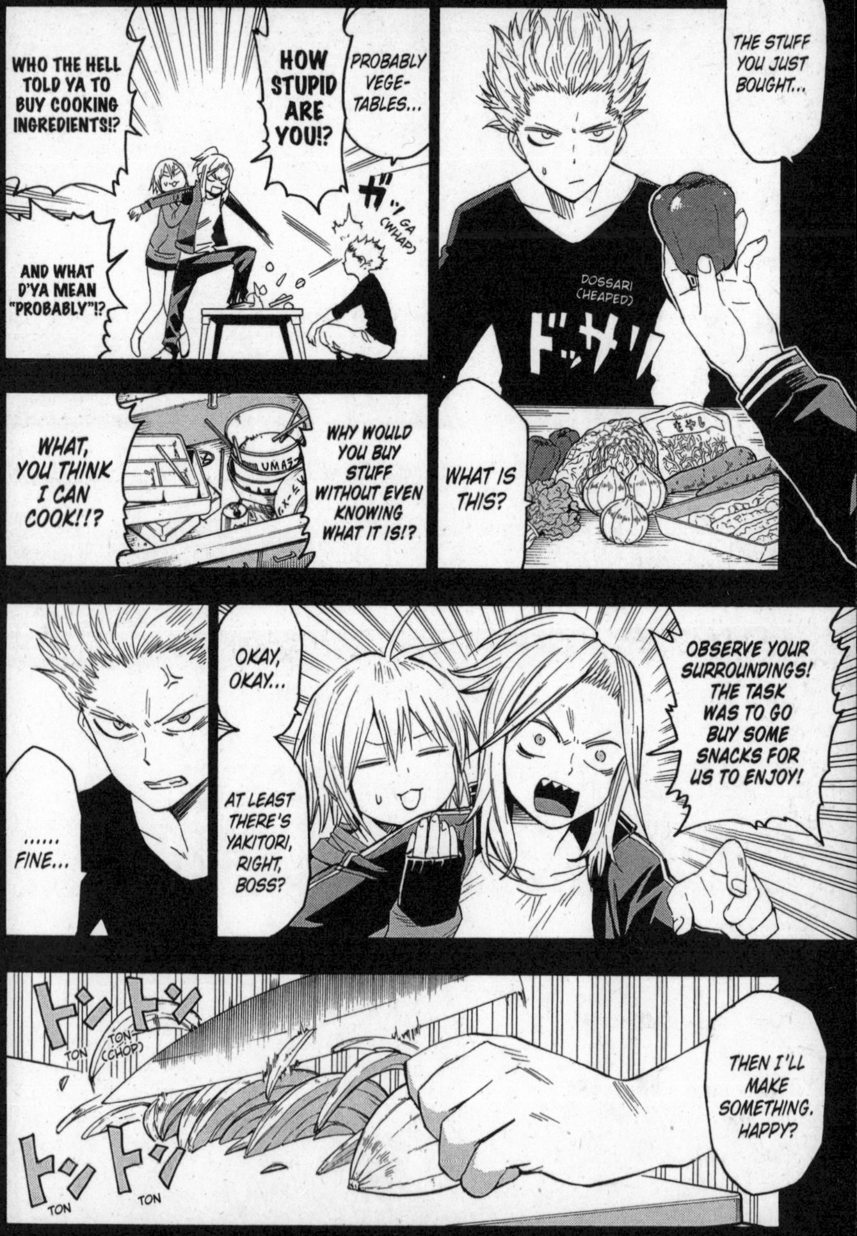
THE STUFF YOU JUST BOUGHT...
DOSSARI (HEAPED)
ドッサリ
WHAT IS THIS?
PROBABLY VEGETABLES...
HOW STUPID ARE YOU!?
ガッ
GA (WHAP)
WHO THE HELL TOLD YA TO BUY COOKING INGREDIENTS!?
AND WHAT D'YA MEAN "PROBABLY"!?
WHY WOULD YOU BUY STUFF WITHOUT EVEN KNOWING WHAT IT IS!?
WHAT, YOU THINK I CAN COOK!!?
OBSERVE YOUR SURROUNDINGS! THE TASK WAS TO GO BUY SOME SNACKS FOR US TO ENJOY!
OKAY, OKAY...
AT LEAST THERE'S YAKITORI, RIGHT, BOSS?
......FINE...
THEN I'LL MAKE SOMETHING. HAPPY?
トントン
TON TON (CHOP)
トントン
TON TON

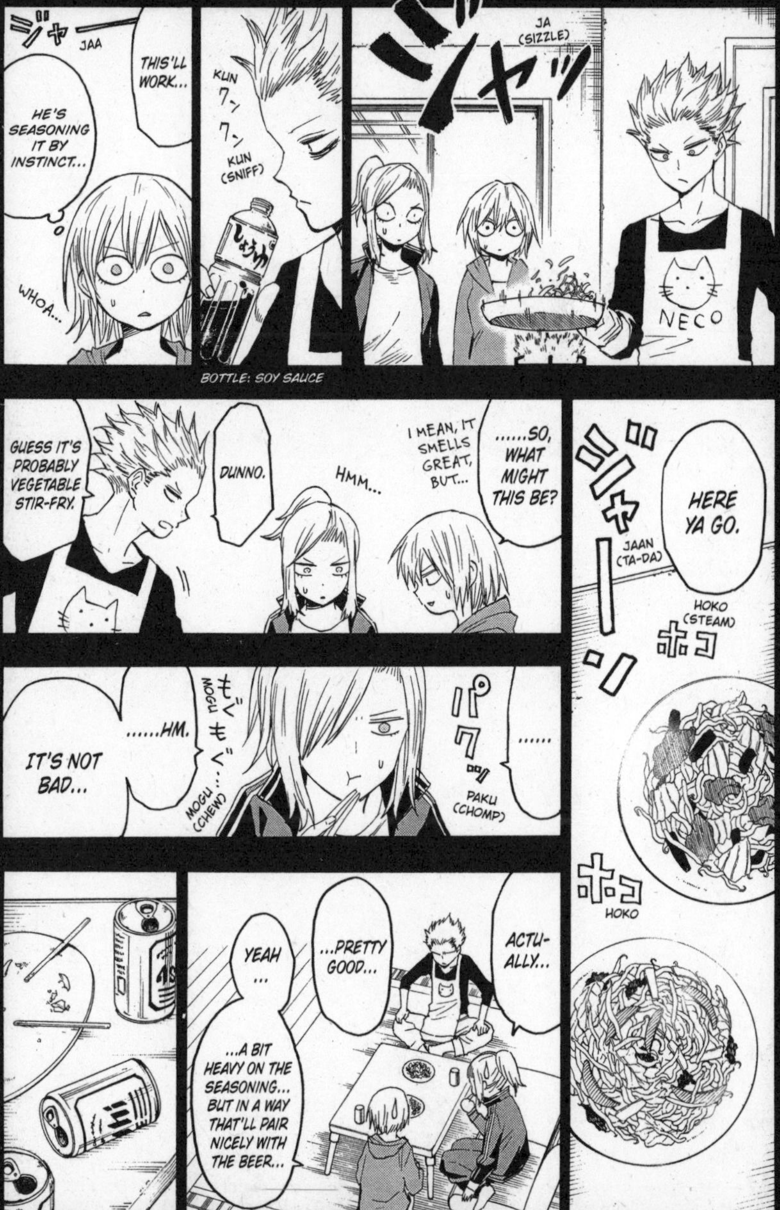
ジャッ
JA (SIZZLE)
クン クン
KUN
KUN (SNIFF)
ジャー
JAA
THIS'LL WORK...
HE'S SEASONING IT BY INSTINCT...
WHOA...
BOTTLE: SOY SAUCE
ジャーン
JAAN (TA-DA)
HERE YA GO.
ホコ
HOKO (STEAM)
ホコ
HOKO
......SO, WHAT MIGHT THIS BE?
I MEAN, IT SMELLS GREAT, BUT...
HMM...
DUNNO.
GUESS IT'S PROBABLY VEGETABLE STIR-FRY.
......
パクッ
PAKU (CHOMP)
もぐ もぐ...
MOGU
MOGU (CHEW)
......HM.
IT'S NOT BAD...
ACTU-ALLY...
...PRETTY GOOD...
YEAH ...
...A BIT HEAVY ON THE SEASONING... BUT IN A WAY THAT'LL PAIR NICELY WITH THE BEER...

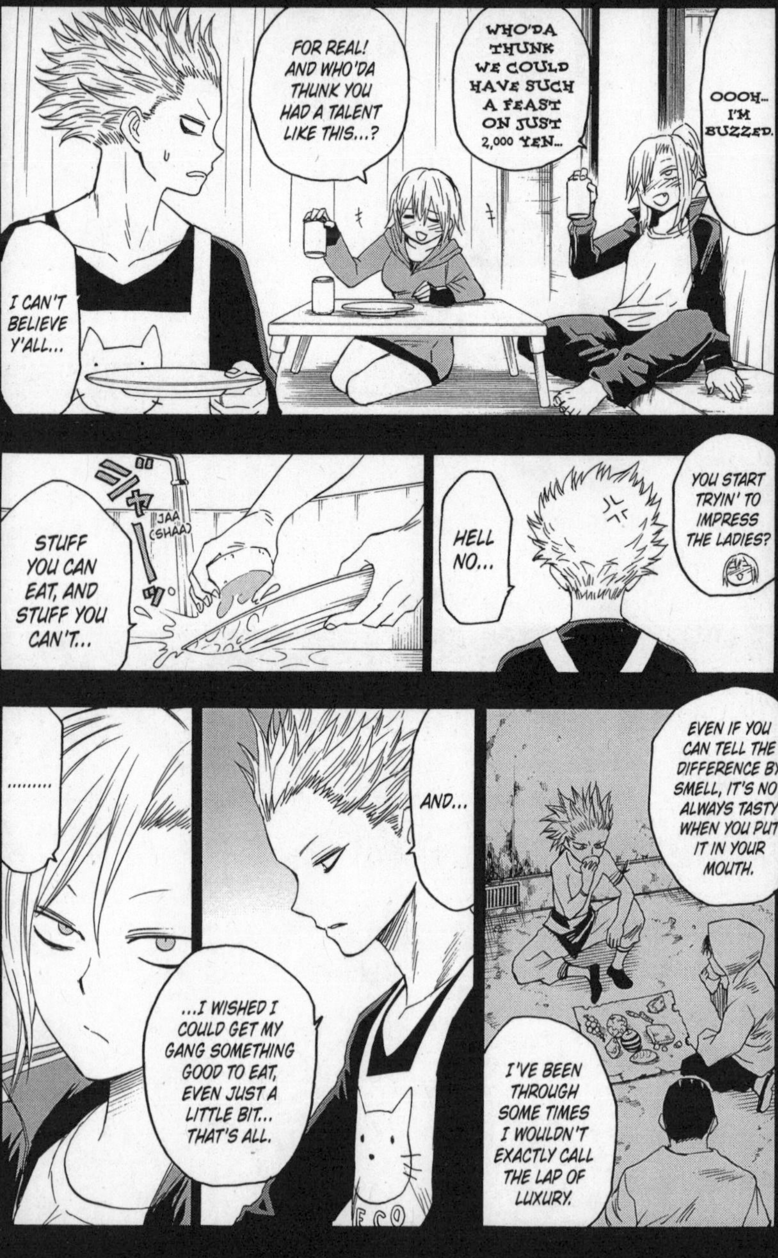
OOOH... I'M BUZZED.
WHO'DA THUNK WE COULD HAVE SUCH A FEAST ON JUST 2,000 YEN...
FOR REAL! AND WHO'DA THUNK YOU HAD A TALENT LIKE THIS...?
I CAN'T BELIEVE Y'ALL...
YOU START TRYIN' TO IMPRESS THE LADIES?
HELL NO...
JAA (SHAA)
STUFF YOU CAN EAT, AND STUFF YOU CAN'T...
EVEN IF YOU CAN TELL THE DIFFERENCE BY SMELL, IT'S NOT ALWAYS TASTY WHEN YOU PUT IT IN YOUR MOUTH.
I'VE BEEN THROUGH SOME TIMES I WOULDN'T EXACTLY CALL THE LAP OF LUXURY.
AND...
...I WISHED I COULD GET MY GANG SOMETHING GOOD TO EAT, EVEN JUST A LITTLE BIT... THAT'S ALL.
....

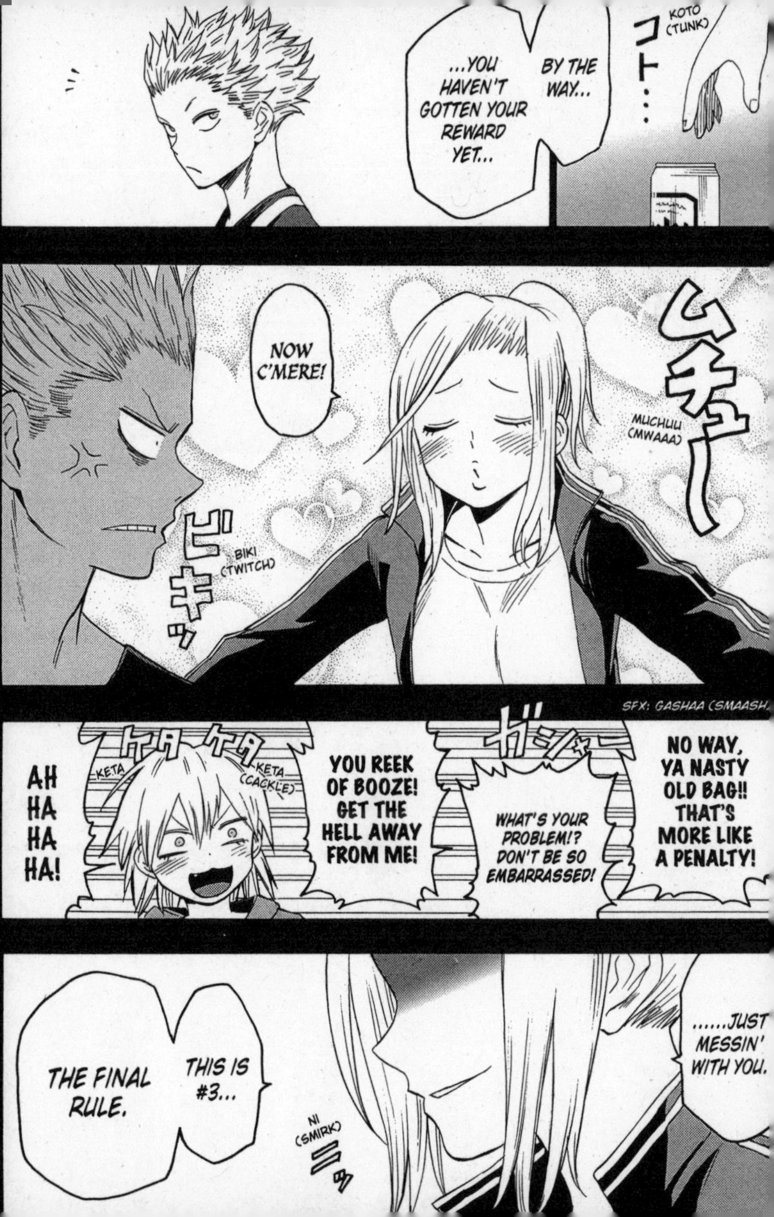
KOTO (TUNK)
コト…
BY THE WAY...
...YOU HAVEN'T GOTTEN YOUR REWARD YET...
MUCHUU (MWAAA)
NOW C'MERE!
BIKI (TWITCH)
SFX: GASHAA (SMAASH)
NO WAY, YA NASTY OLD BAG!! THAT'S MORE LIKE A PENALTY!
WHAT'S YOUR PROBLEM!? DON'T BE SO EMBARRASSED!
YOU REEK OF BOOZE! GET THE HELL AWAY FROM ME!
KETA KETA (CACKLE)
AH HA HA HA!
......JUST MESSIN' WITH YOU.
NI (SMIRK)
THIS IS #3...
THE FINAL RULE.

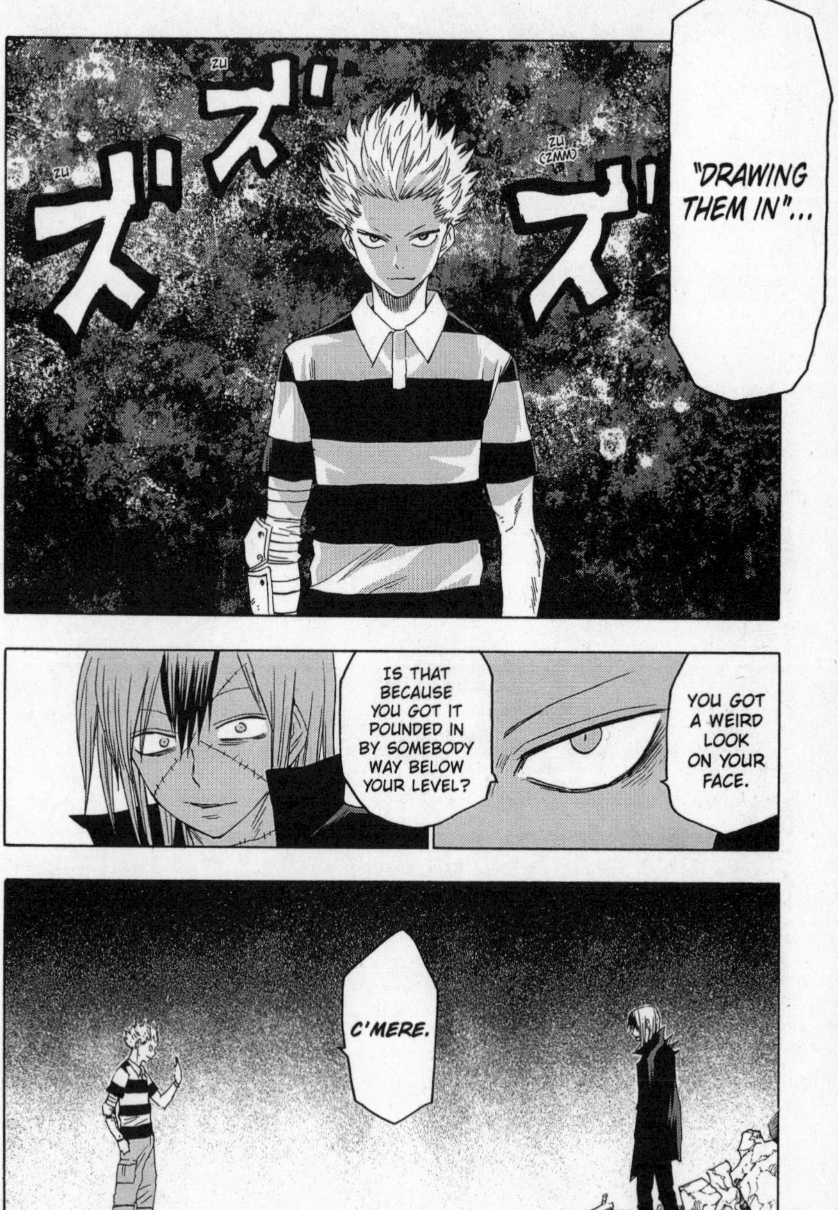
"DRAWING THEM IN"...
ZU (ZMM)
ZU
ZU
YOU GOT A WEIRD LOOK ON YOUR FACE.
IS THAT BECAUSE YOU GOT IT POUNDED IN BY SOMEBODY WAY BELOW YOUR LEVEL?
C'MERE.

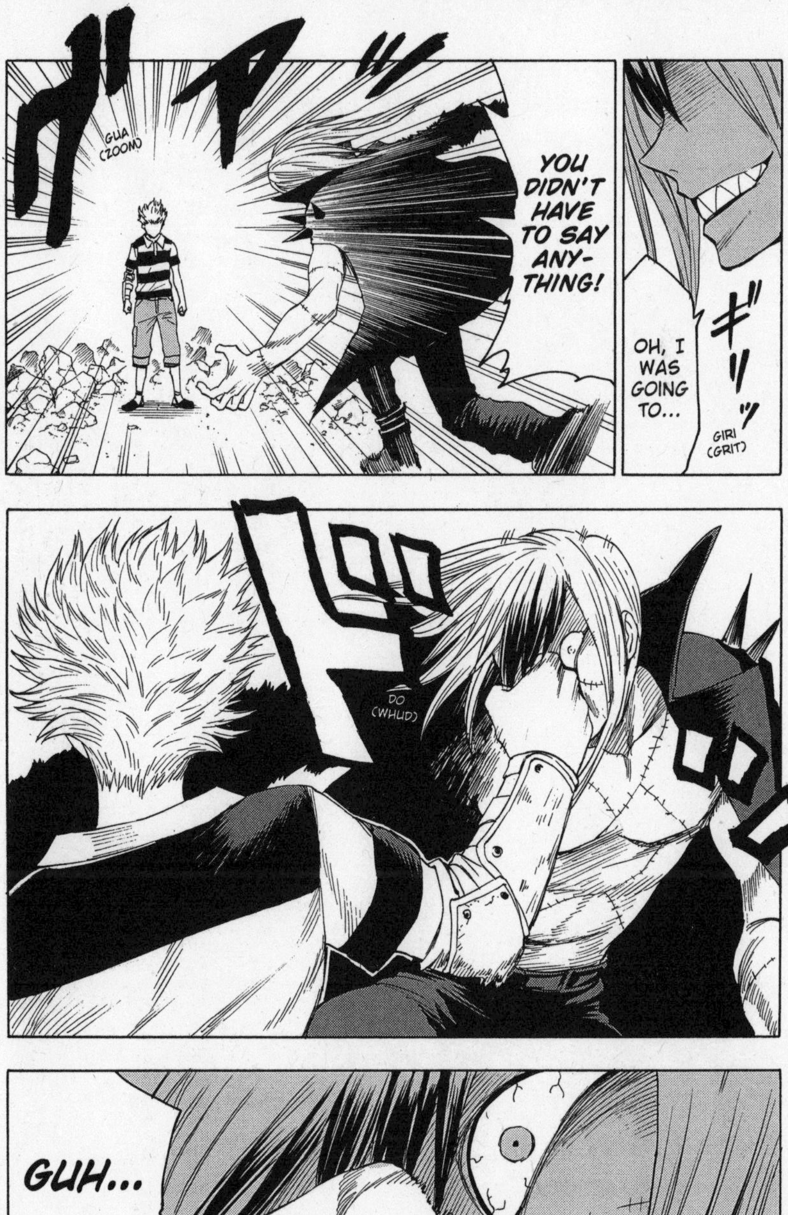
OH, I WAS GOING TO...
GIRI (GRIT)
YOU DIDN'T HAVE TO SAY ANYTHING!
GUA (ZOOM)
DO (WHUD)
GUH...

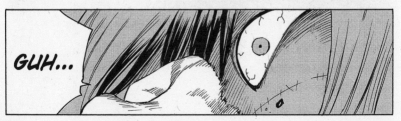

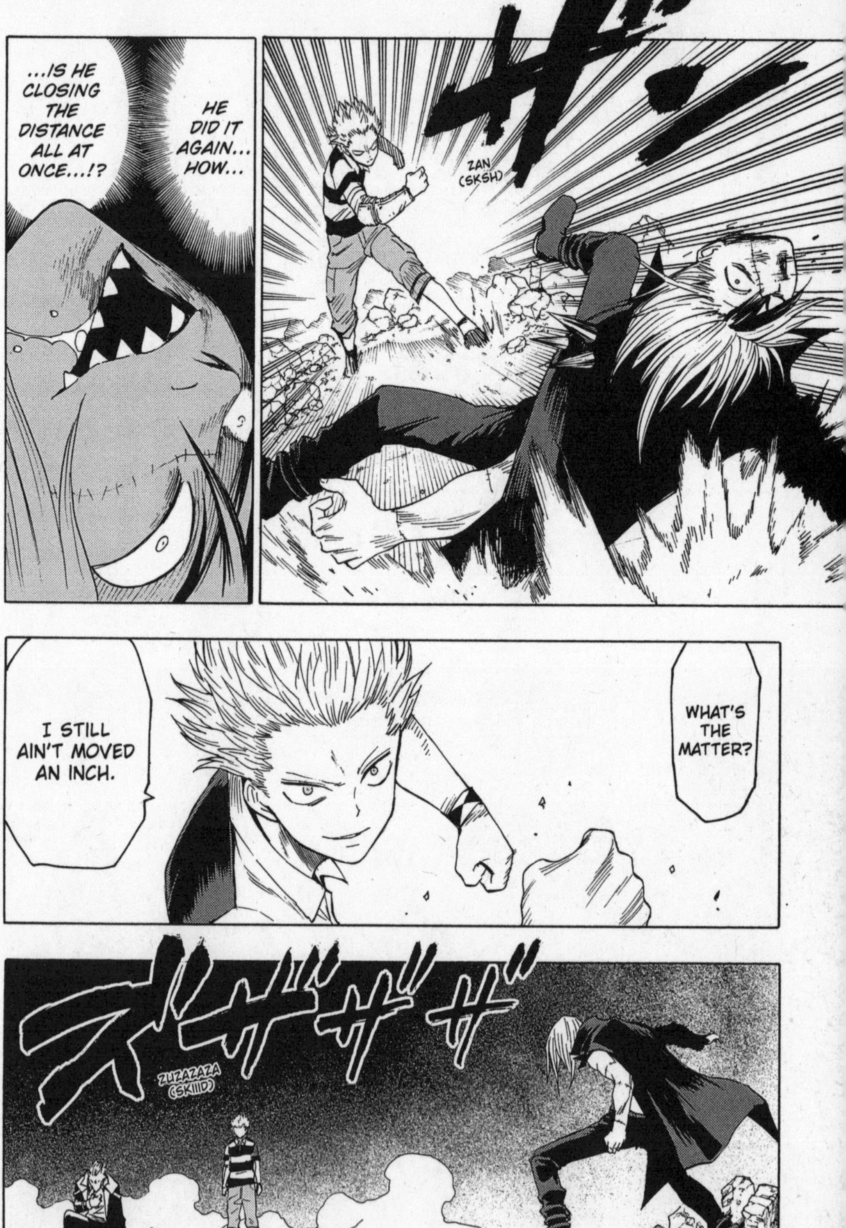
ZAN (SKSH)
HE DID IT AGAIN... HOW...
...IS HE CLOSING THE DISTANCE ALL AT ONCE...!?
WHAT'S THE MATTER?
I STILL AIN'T MOVED AN INCH.
ZUZAZAZA (SKIIID)

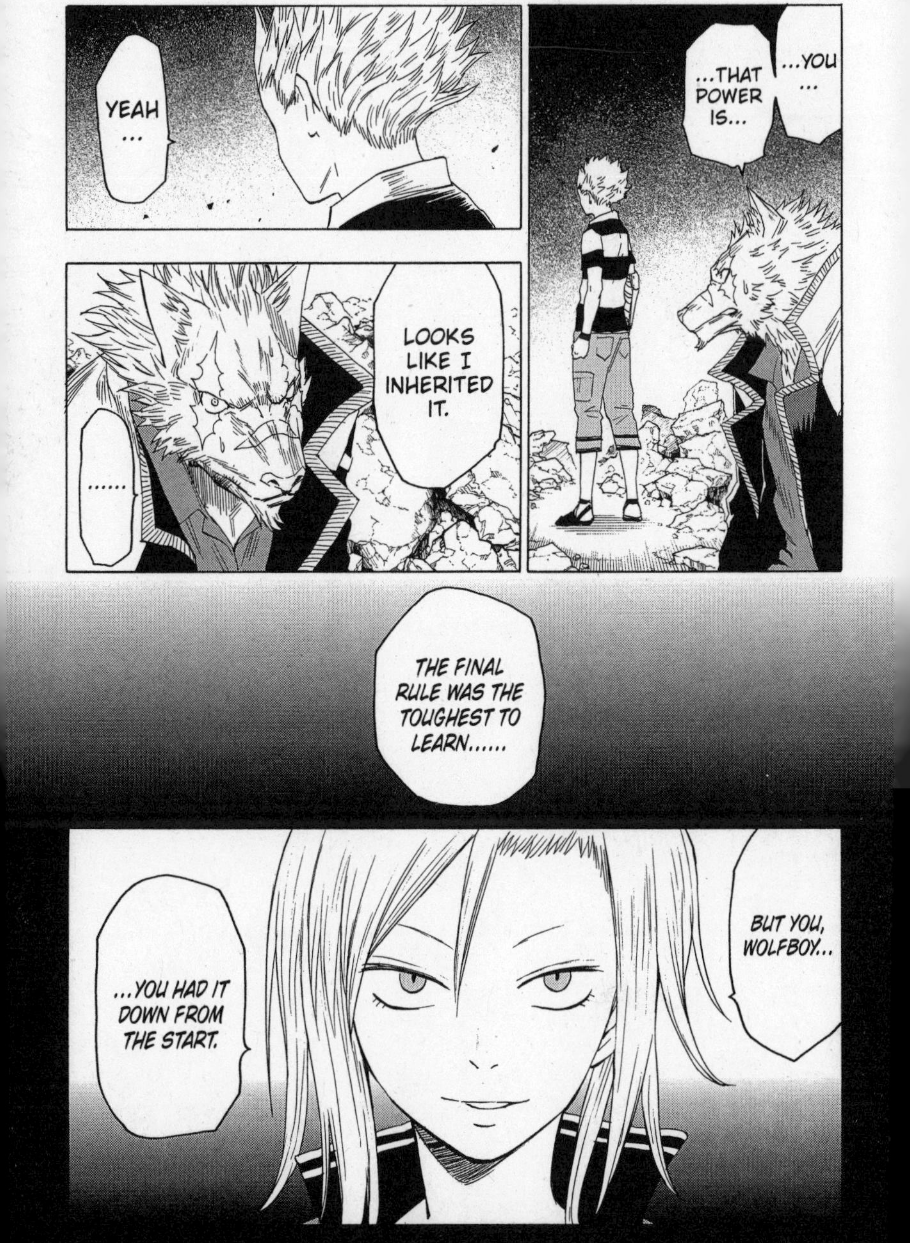
...YOU ...
...THAT POWER IS...
YEAH ...
LOOKS LIKE I INHERITED IT.
......
THE FINAL RULE WAS THE TOUGHEST TO LEARN......
BUT YOU, WOLFBOY...
...YOU HAD IT DOWN FROM THE START.

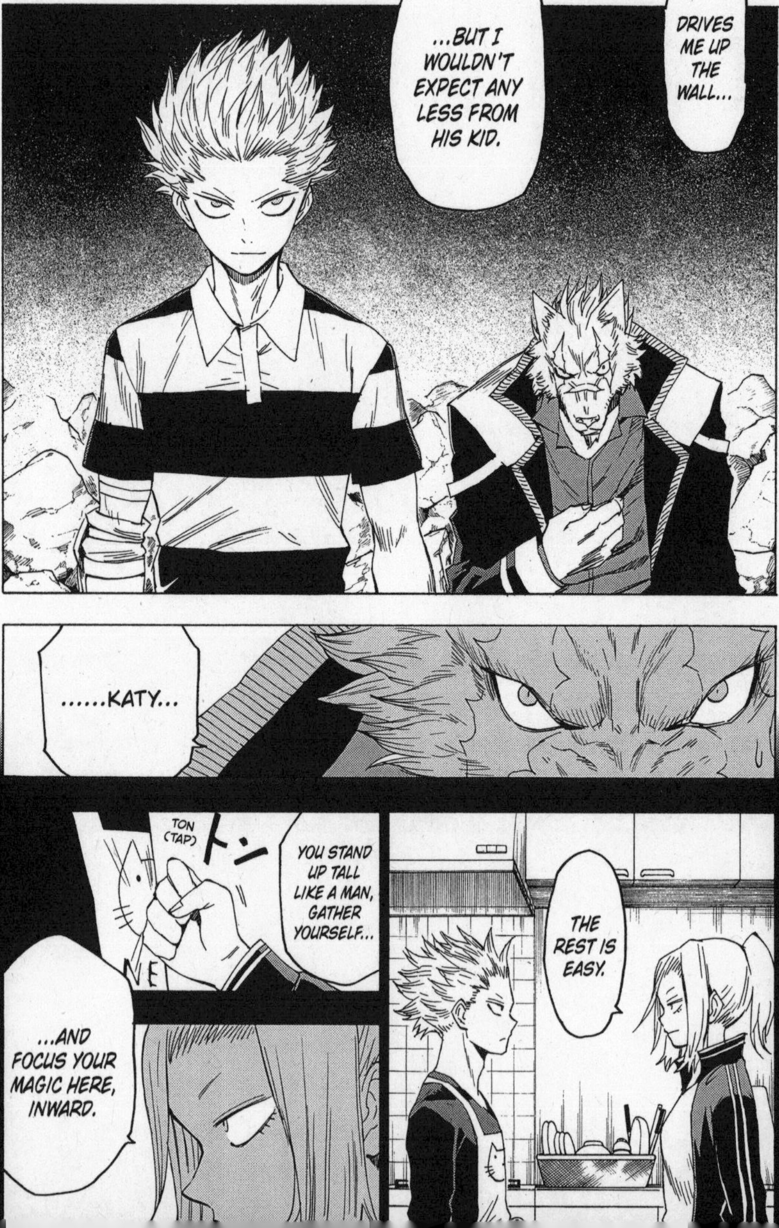
DRIVES ME UP THE WALL...
...BUT I WOULDN'T EXPECT ANY LESS FROM HIS KID.
......KATY...
THE REST IS EASY.
TON (TAP)
YOU STAND UP TALL LIKE A MAN, GATHER YOURSELF...
...AND FOCUS YOUR MAGIC HERE, INWARD.

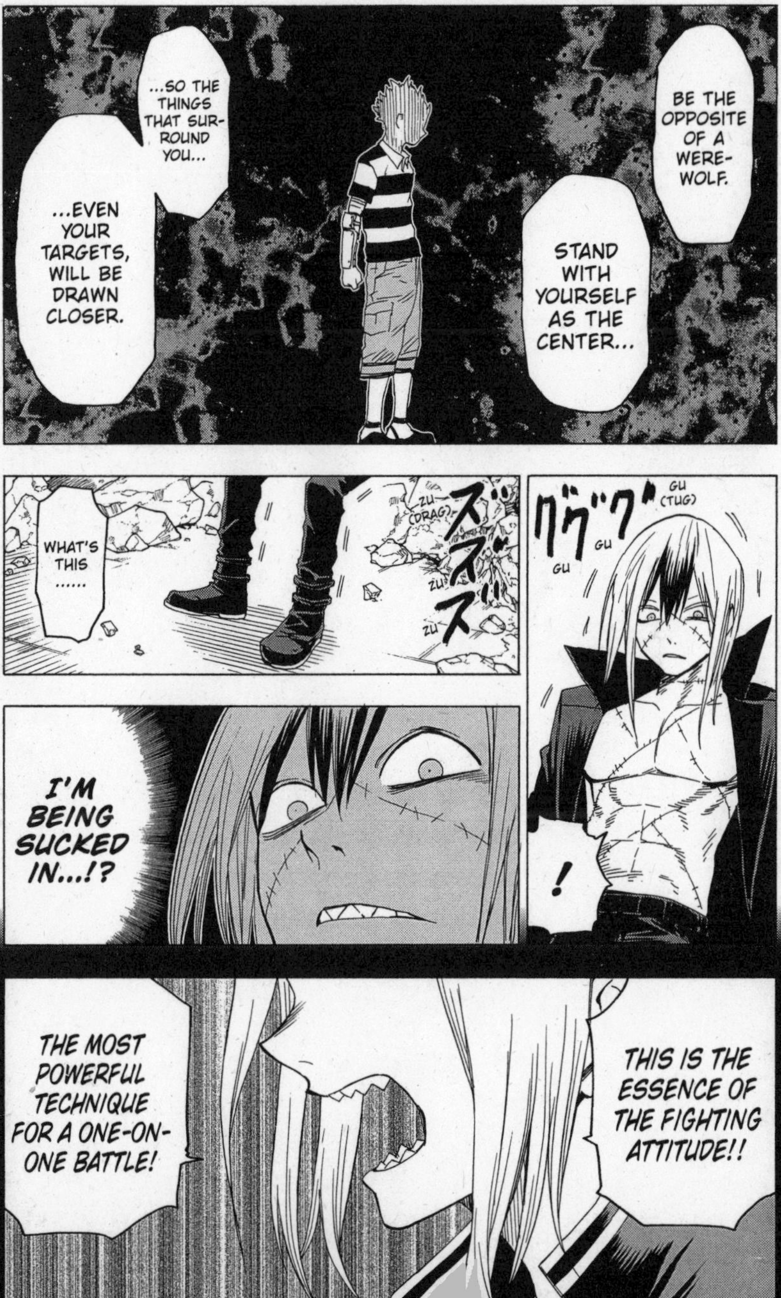
BE THE OPPOSITE OF A WERE-WOLF.
STAND WITH YOURSELF AS THE CENTER...
...SO THE THINGS THAT SUR-ROUND YOU...
...EVEN YOUR TARGETS, WILL BE DRAWN CLOSER.
グググ
GU (TUG) GU GU
!
ズズズ
ZU (DRAG) ZU ZU
WHAT'S THIS ......
I'M BEING SUCKED IN...!?
THIS IS THE ESSENCE OF THE FIGHTING ATTITUDE!!
THE MOST POWERFUL TECHNIQUE FOR A ONE-ON-ONE BATTLE!

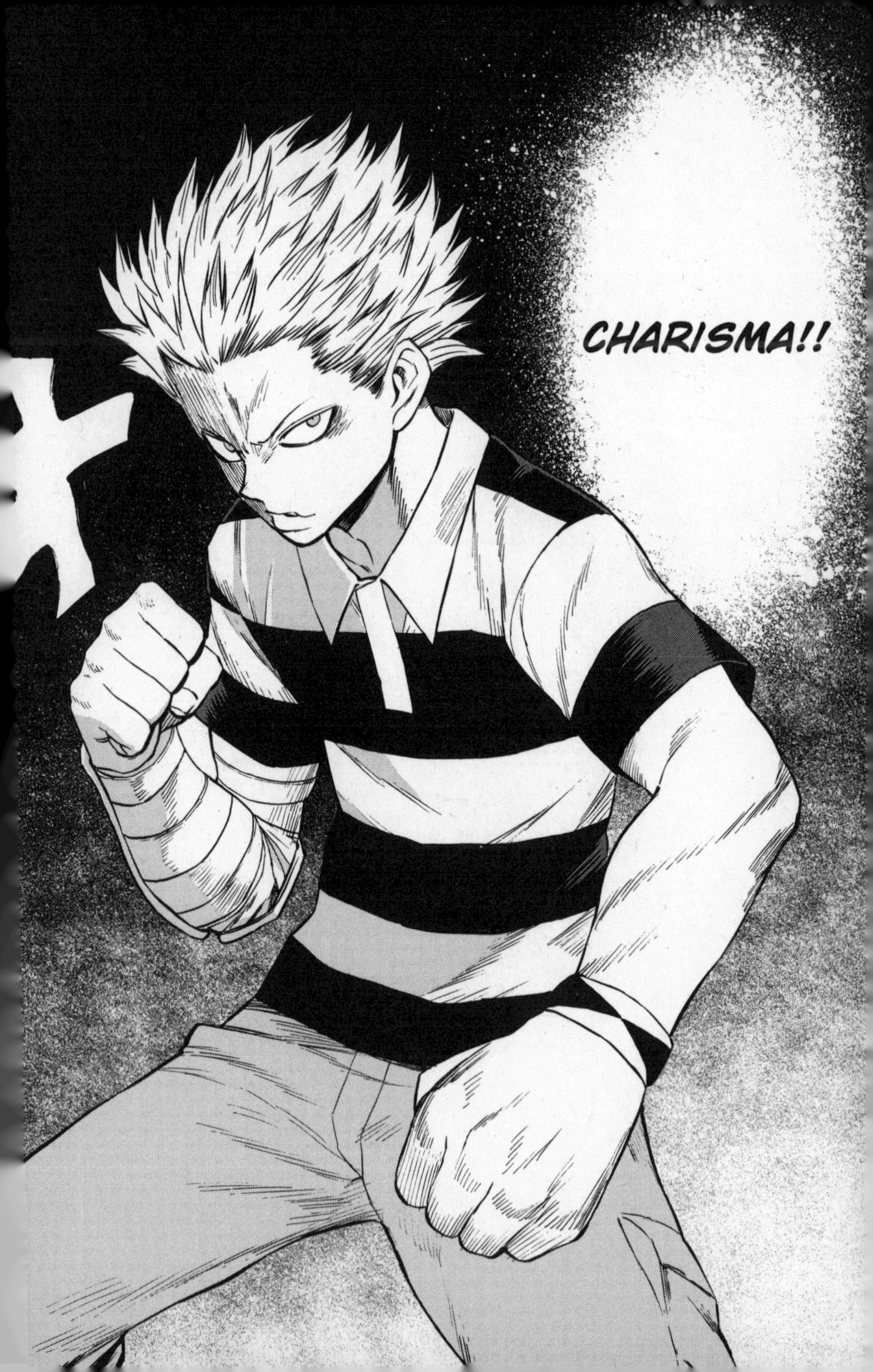
CHARISMA!!

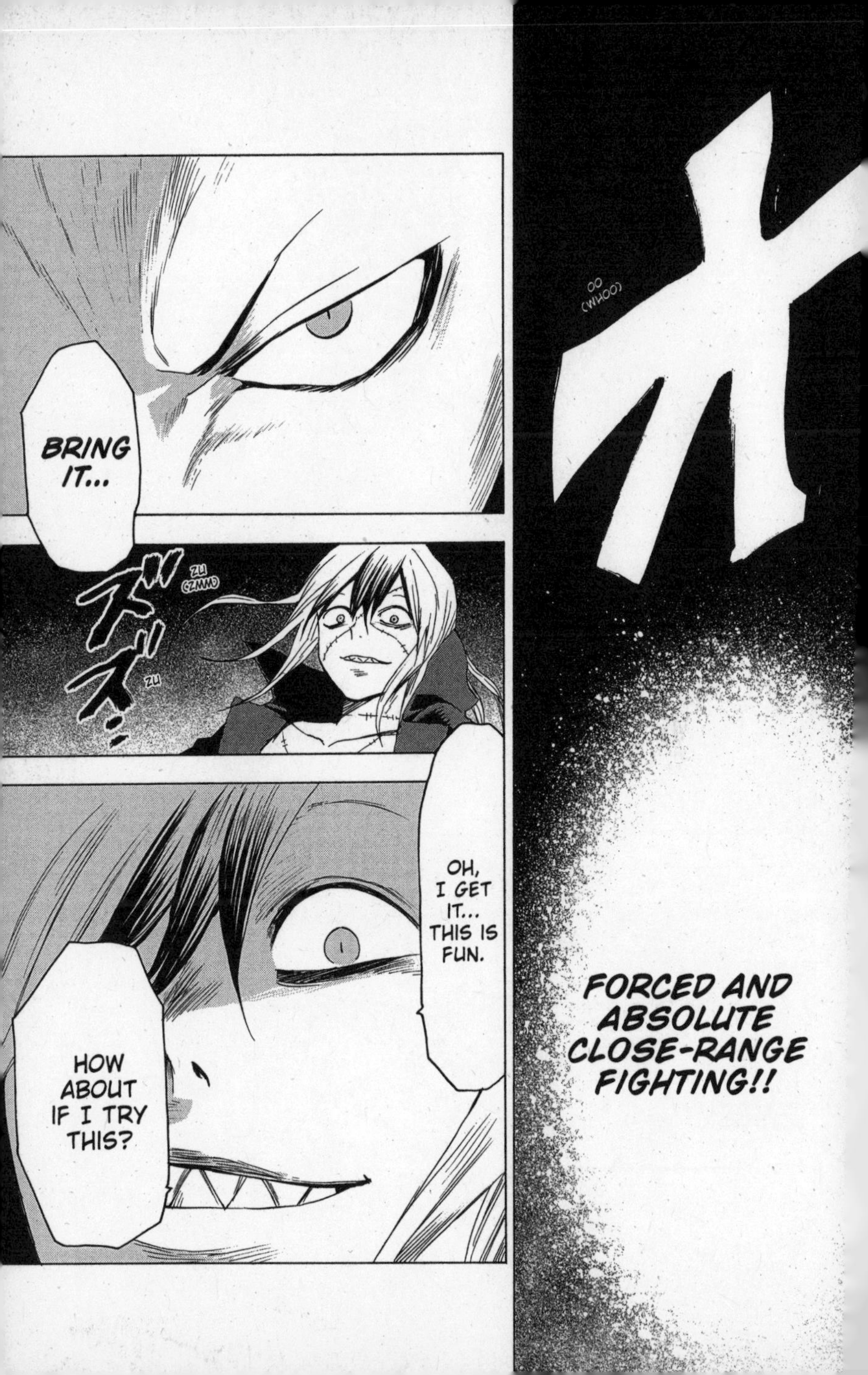
OO (WHOO)
FORCED AND ABSOLUTE CLOSE-RANGE FIGHTING!!
BRING IT...
ZU (ZMMM)
ZU
OH, I GET IT... THIS IS FUN.
HOW ABOUT IF I TRY THIS?

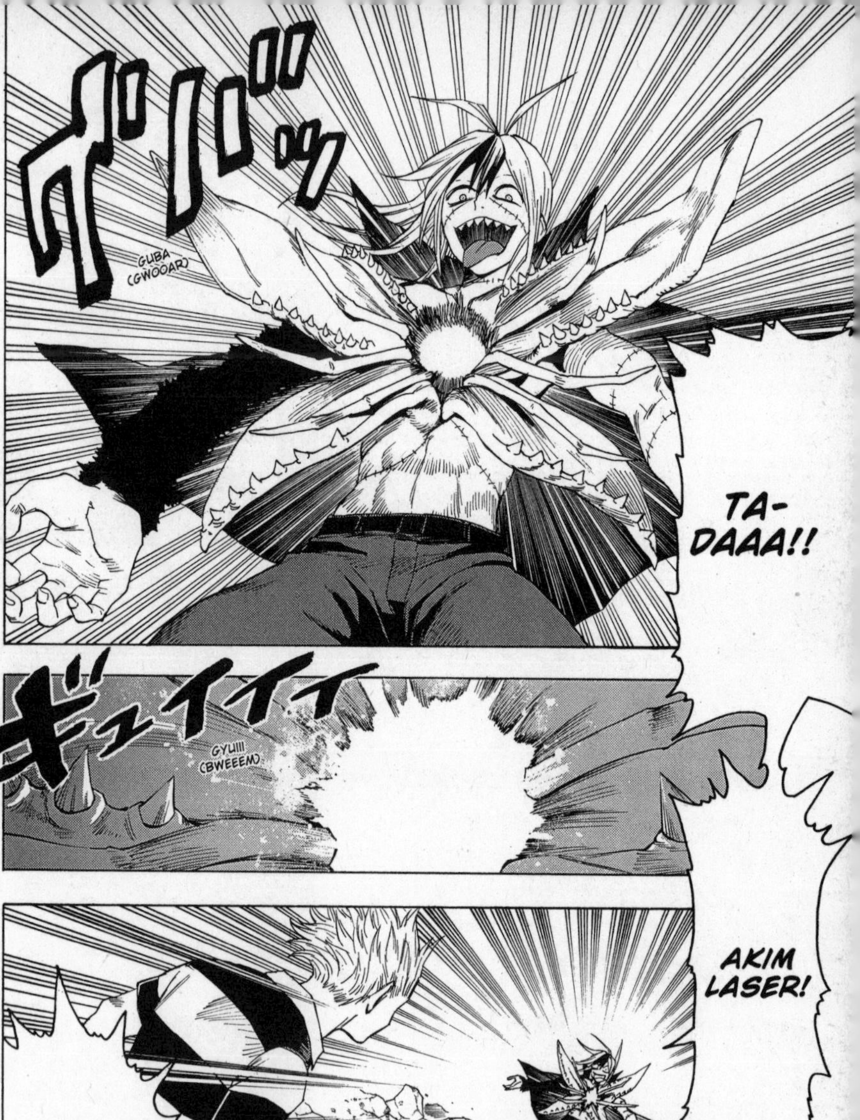

グバッ
GUBA (GWOOAR)
TA-DAAA!!
ギュイイイ
GYUIII (BWEEEM)
AKIM LASER!
FIRE!!

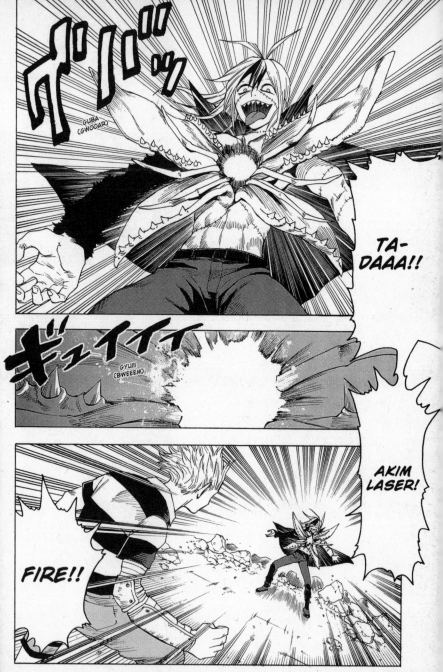

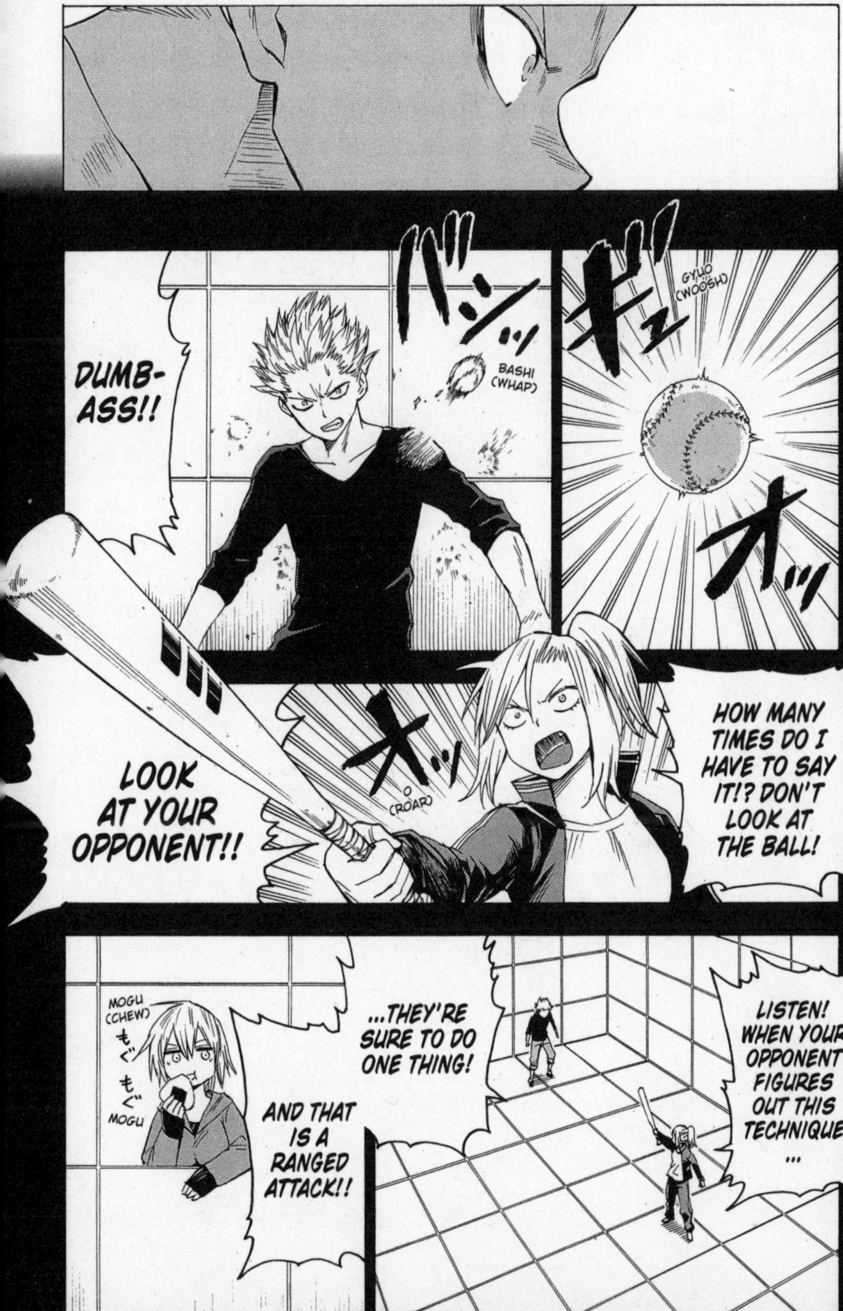

ギュオッ
GYUO (WOOSH)
バシッ
BASHI (WHAP)
DUMB-ASS!!
HOW MANY TIMES DO I HAVE TO SAY IT!? DON'T LOOK AT THE BALL!
オッ
O (ROAR)
LOOK AT YOUR OPPONENT!!
LISTEN! WHEN YOUR OPPONENT FIGURES OUT THIS TECHNIQUE ...
...THEY'RE SURE TO DO ONE THING!
AND THAT IS A RANGED ATTACK!!
MOGU (CHEW)
もぐ もぐ
MOGU

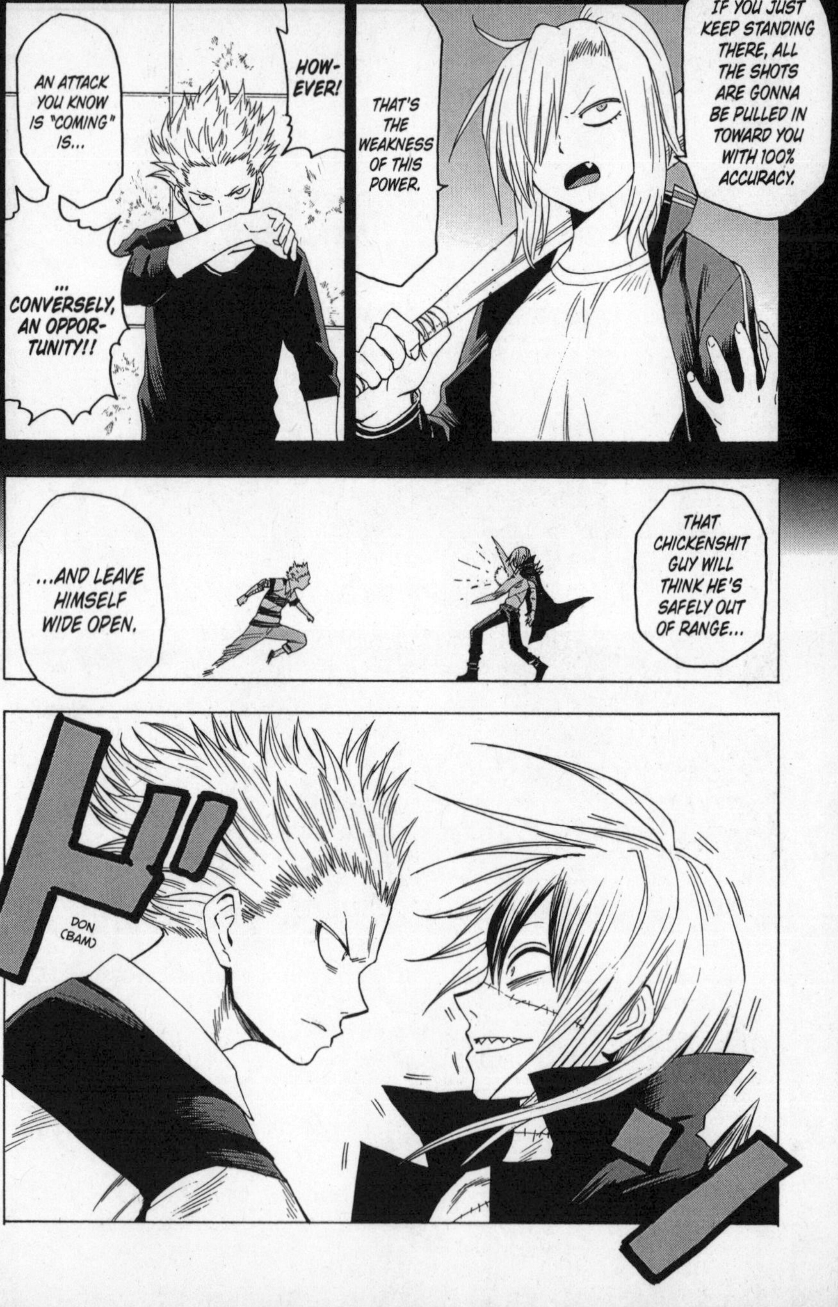
IF YOU JUST KEEP STANDING THERE, ALL THE SHOTS ARE GONNA BE PULLED IN TOWARD YOU WITH 100% ACCURACY.
THAT'S THE WEAKNESS OF THIS POWER.
HOW-EVER!
AN ATTACK YOU KNOW IS "COMING" IS...
...CONVERSELY, AN OPPORTUNITY!!
THAT CHICKENSHIT GUY WILL THINK HE'S SAFELY OUT OF RANGE...
...AND LEAVE HIMSELF WIDE OPEN.
DON (BAM)

SO BEFORE HE GETS TO SHOW OFF...

...YOU TAKE HIM OUT WITH ONE HIT.

DOBA (SPLTCH)

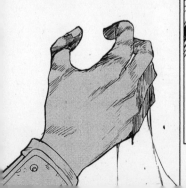

WHA...

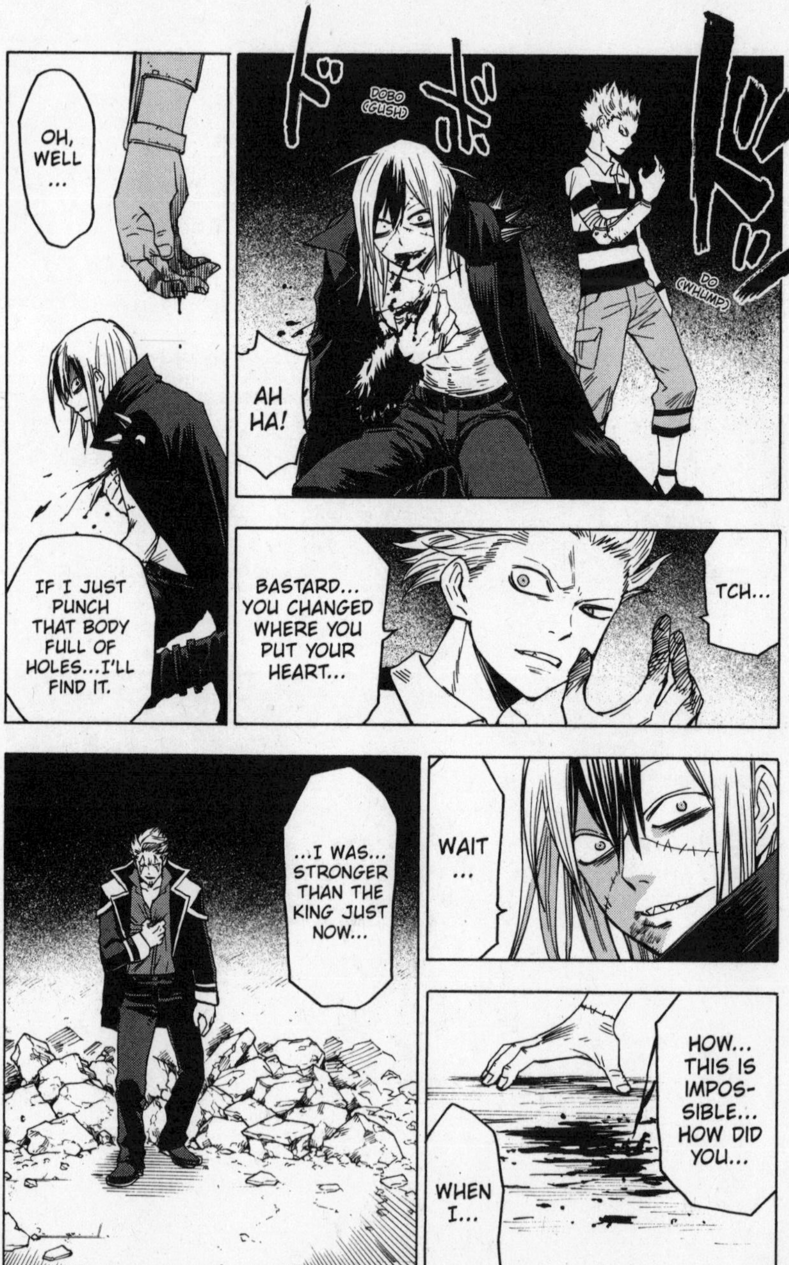
DOBO (GUSH)
DO (WHLIMP)
AH HA!
TCH...
BASTARD... YOU CHANGED WHERE YOU PUT YOUR HEART...
OH, WELL ...
IF I JUST PUNCH THAT BODY FULL OF HOLES...I'LL FIND IT.
WAIT ...
HOW... THIS IS IMPOSSIBLE... HOW DID YOU...
WHEN I...
...I WAS... STRONGER THAN THE KING JUST NOW...

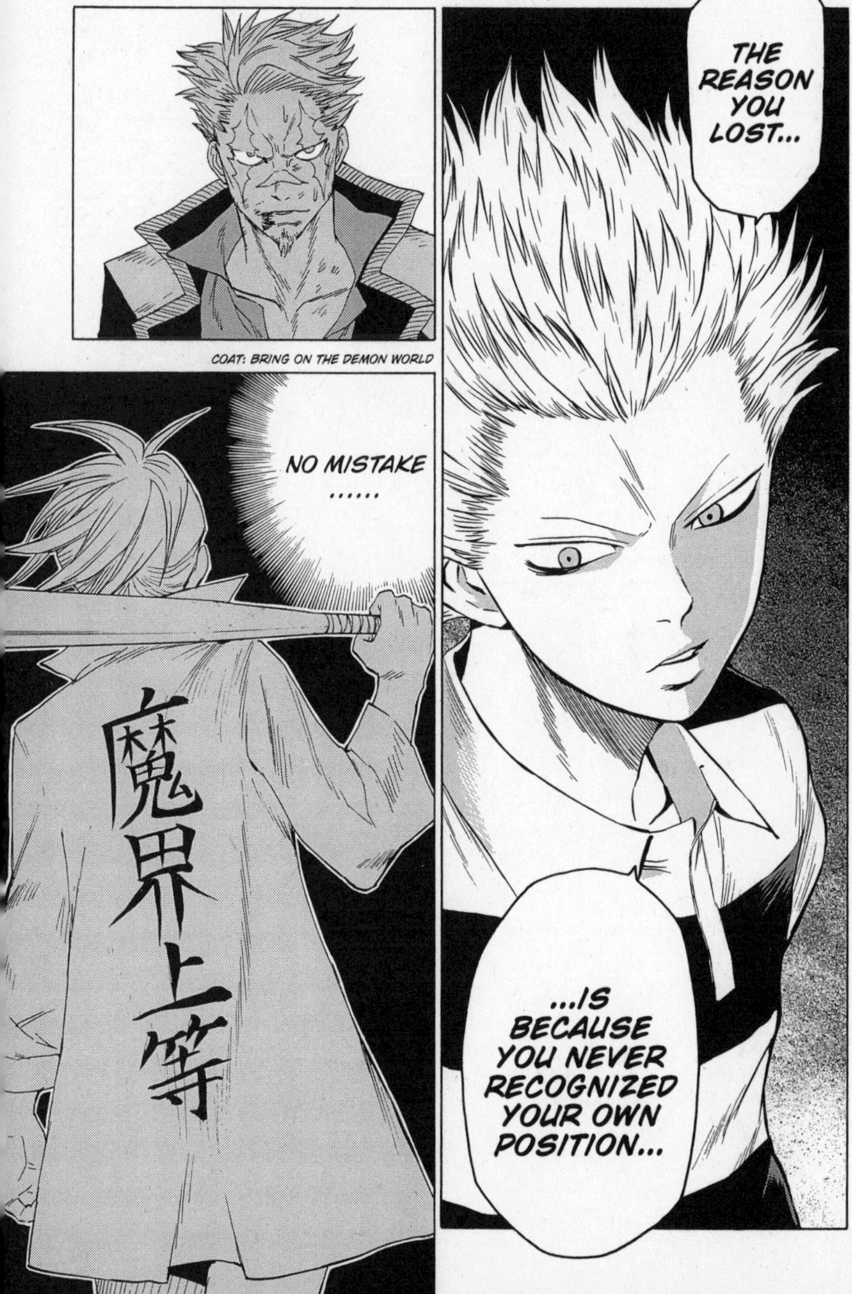
THE REASON YOU LOST...
...IS BECAUSE YOU NEVER RECOGNIZED YOUR OWN POSITION...
COAT: BRING ON THE DEMON WORLD
NO MISTAKE ......
魔界上等

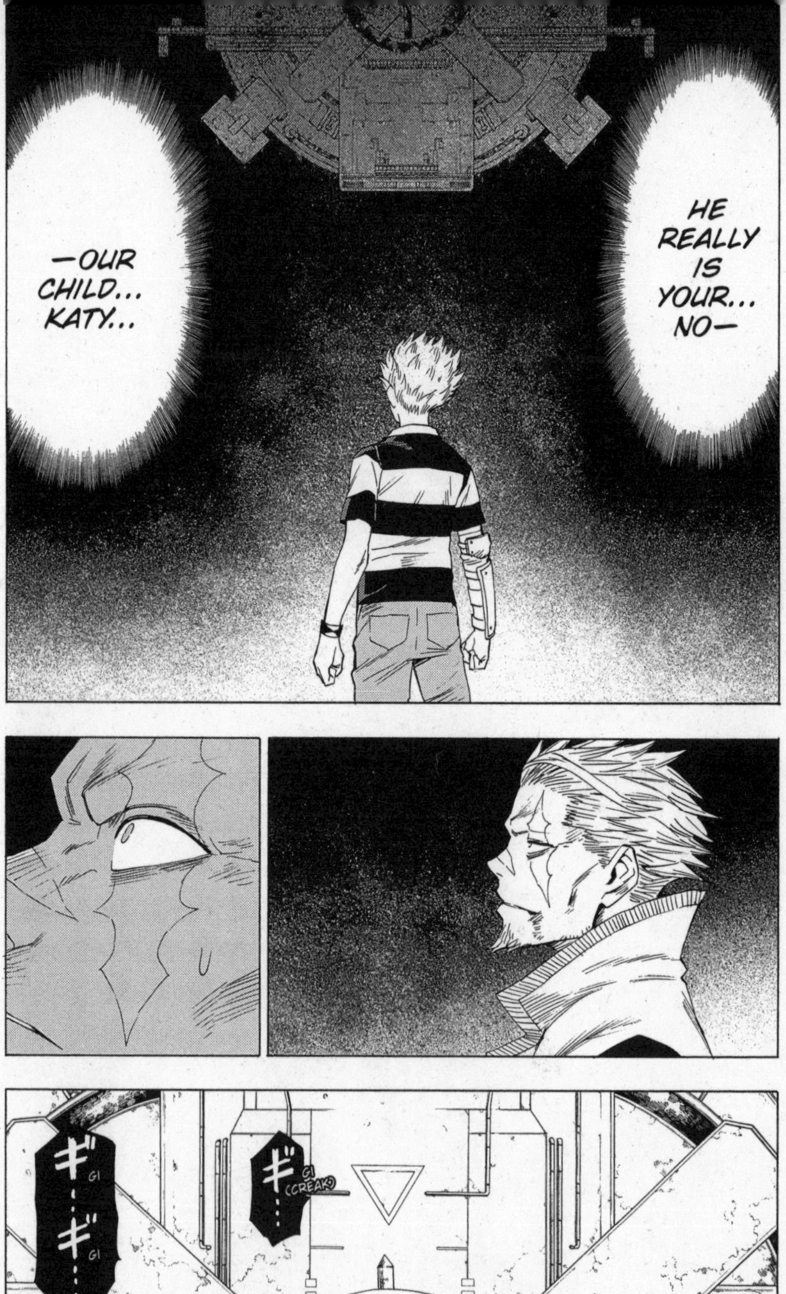
HE REALLY IS YOUR... NO—
—OUR CHILD... KATY...
ギ GI (CREAK)
ギ GI
ギ GI

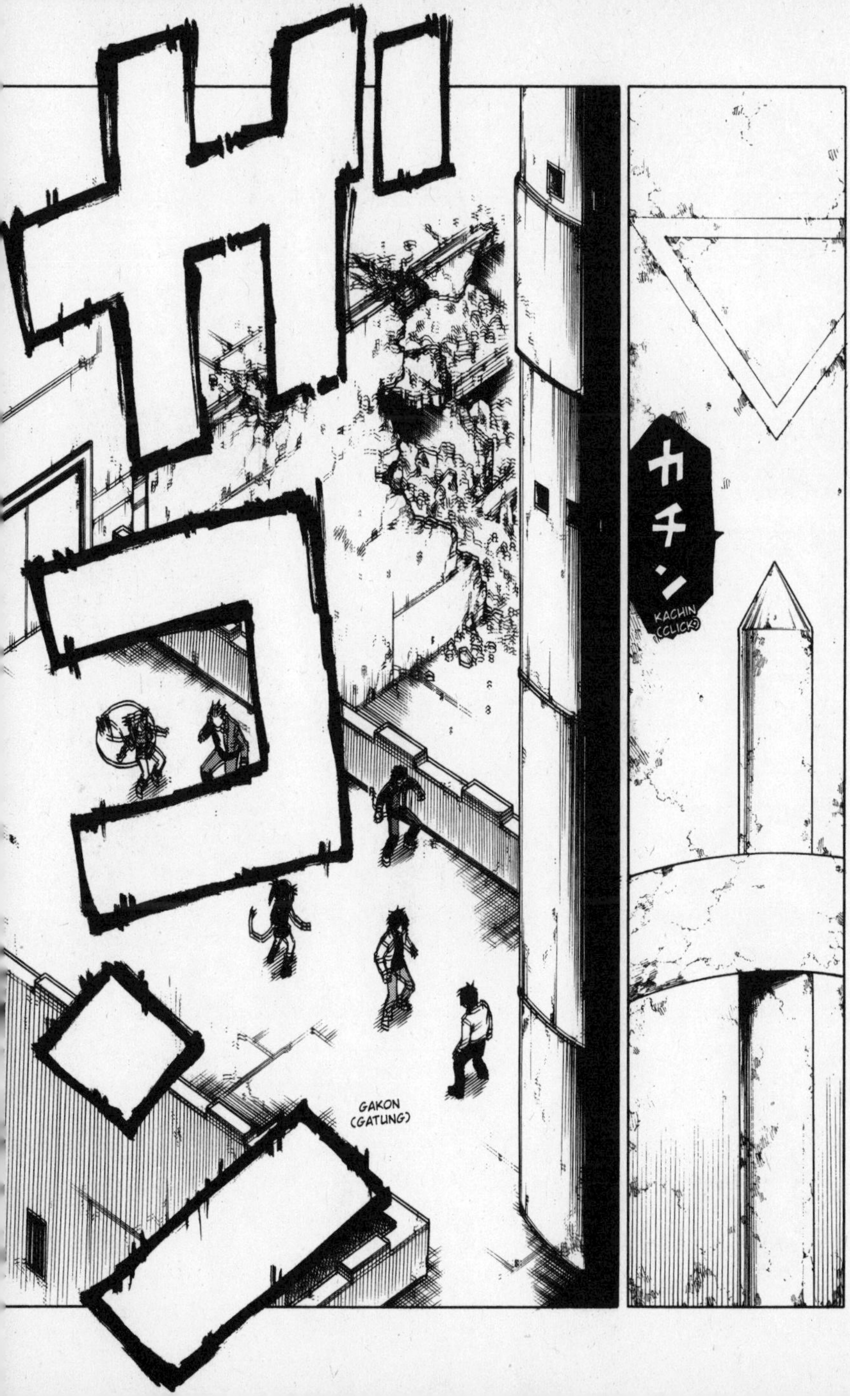
カチン
KACHIN (CLICK)
ガコン
GAKON (GATUNG)

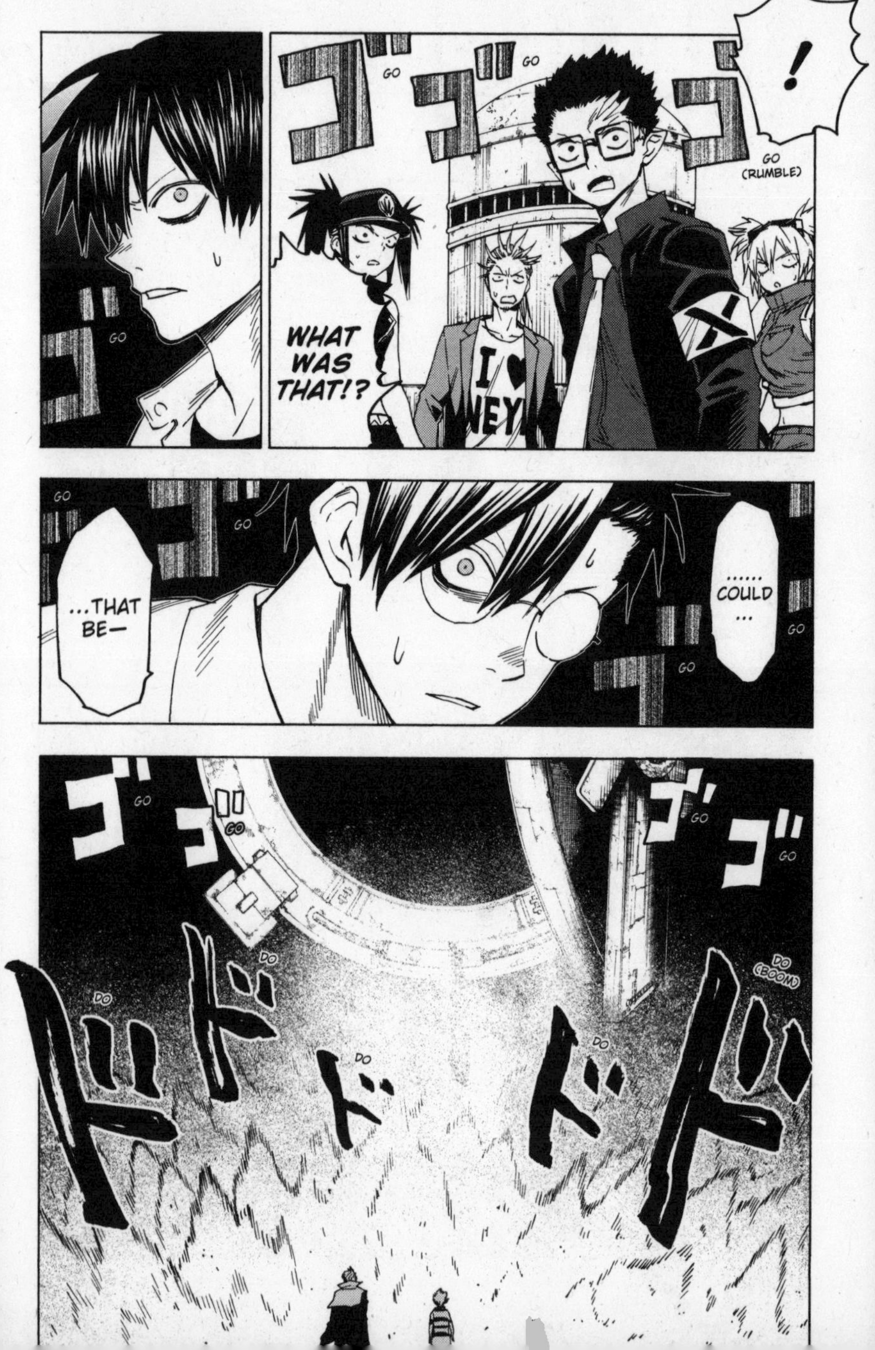
!
GO
GO
GO (RUMBLE)
WHAT WAS THAT!?
GO
......COULD ...
...THAT BE—
GO
GO
GO
GO
GO
GO
GO
GO
DO (BOOM)
DO
DO
DO
DO

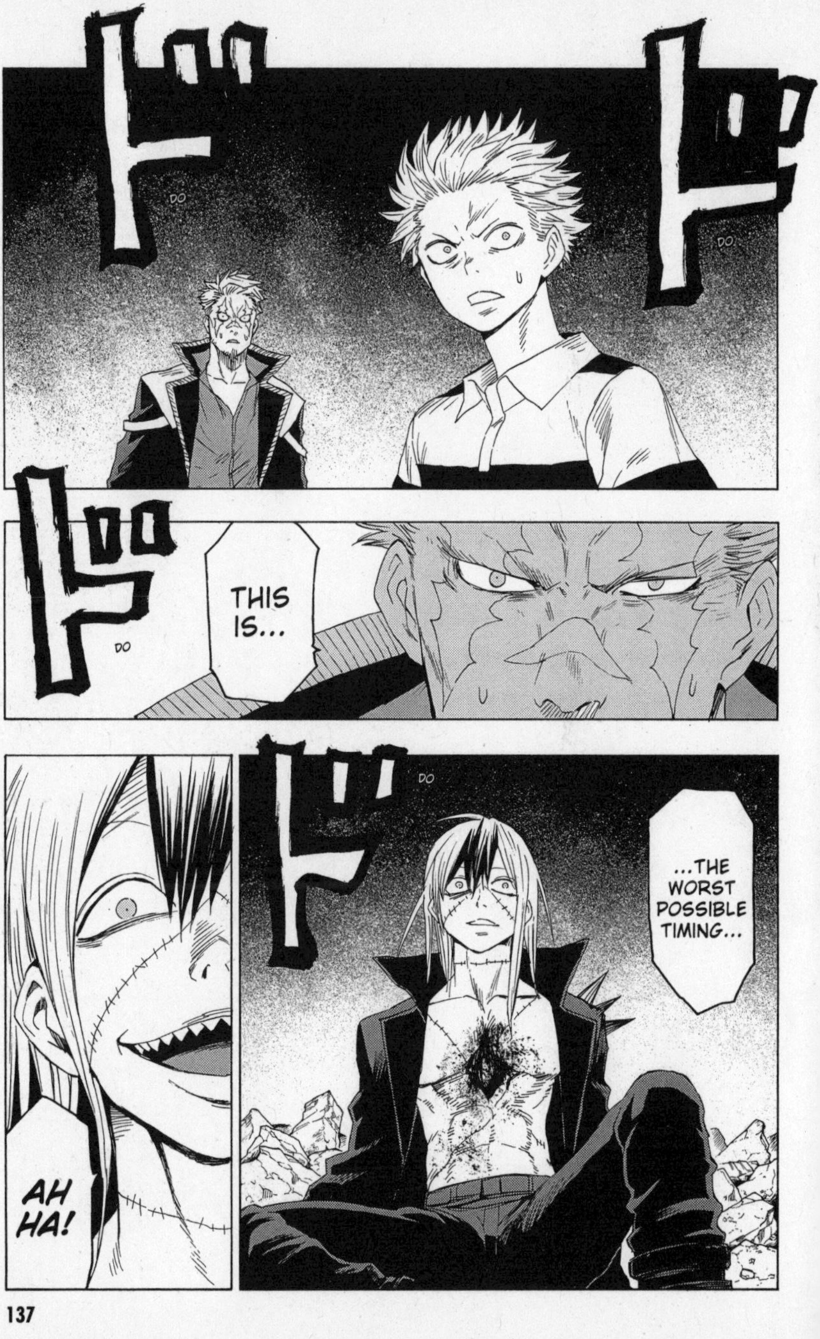
DO
DO
DO
THIS IS...
DO
...THE WORST POSSIBLE TIMING...
AH HA!

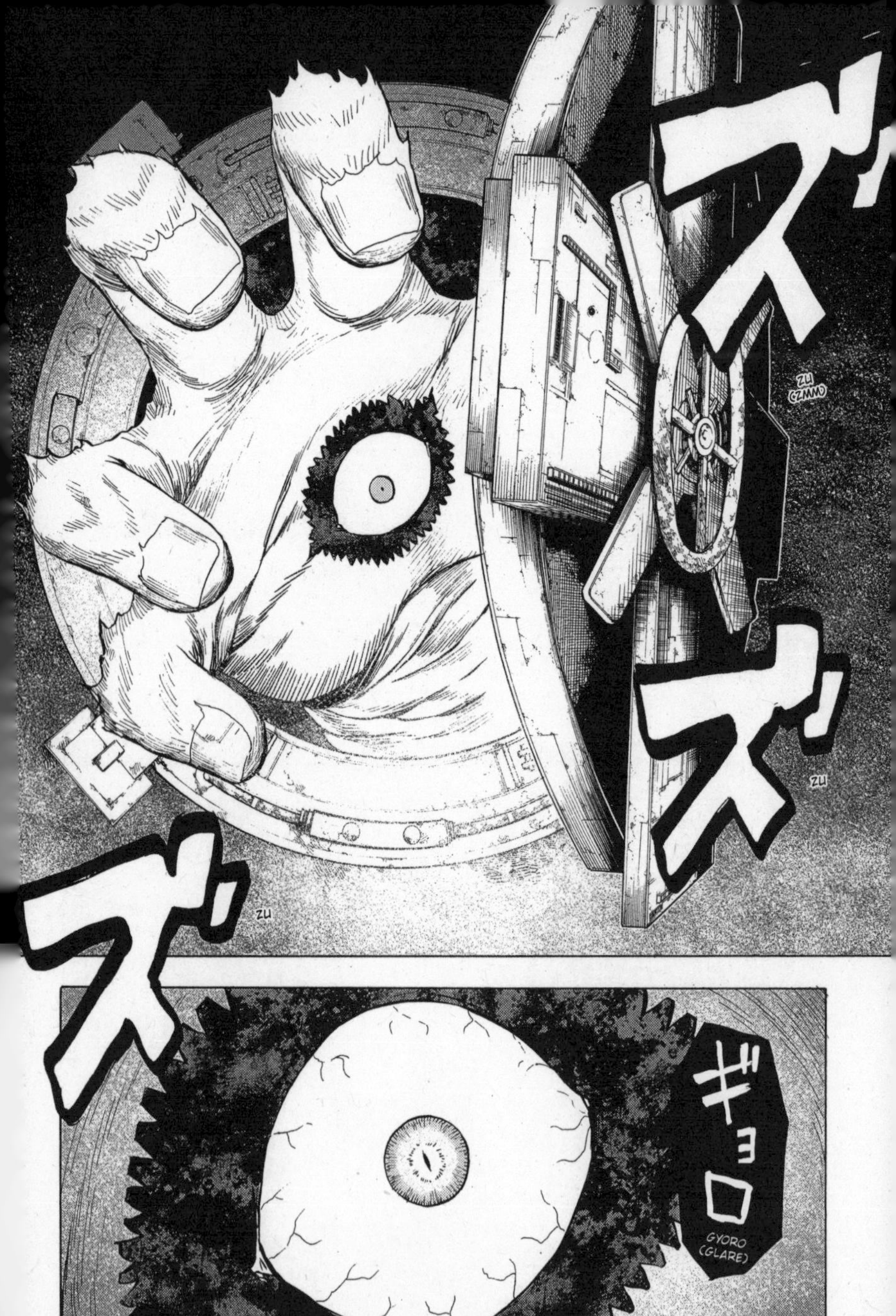
ズ
ZU (ZWM)
ズ
ZU
ズ
ZU
ギョロ
GYORO (GLARE)

♠ To Be Continued ♠

BLOOD LAD

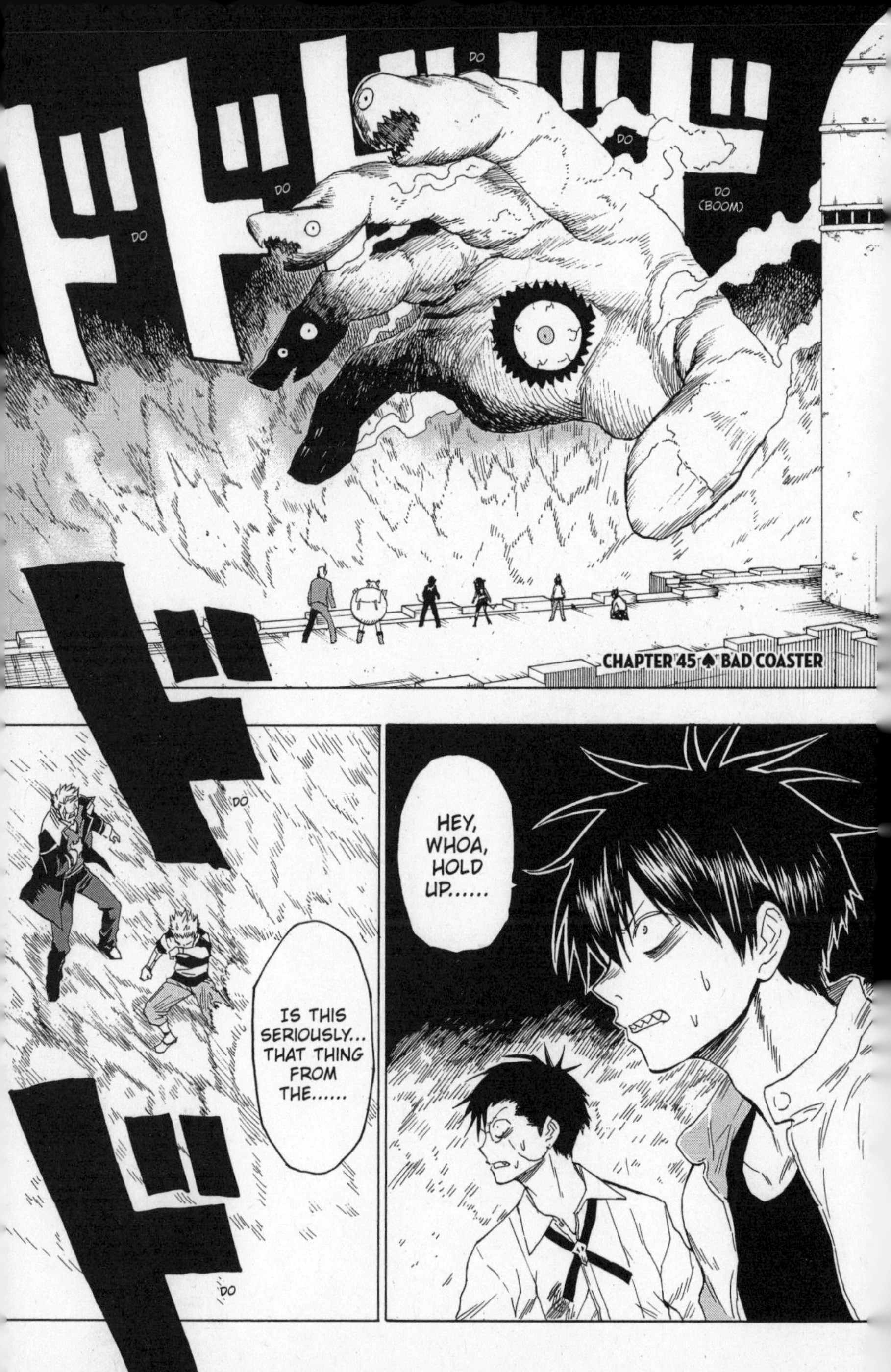
DO (BOOM)
DO
DO
DO
DO
CHAPTER 45 BAD COASTER
HEY, WHOA, HOLD UP......
DO
IS THIS SERIOUSLY... THAT THING FROM THE......
DO

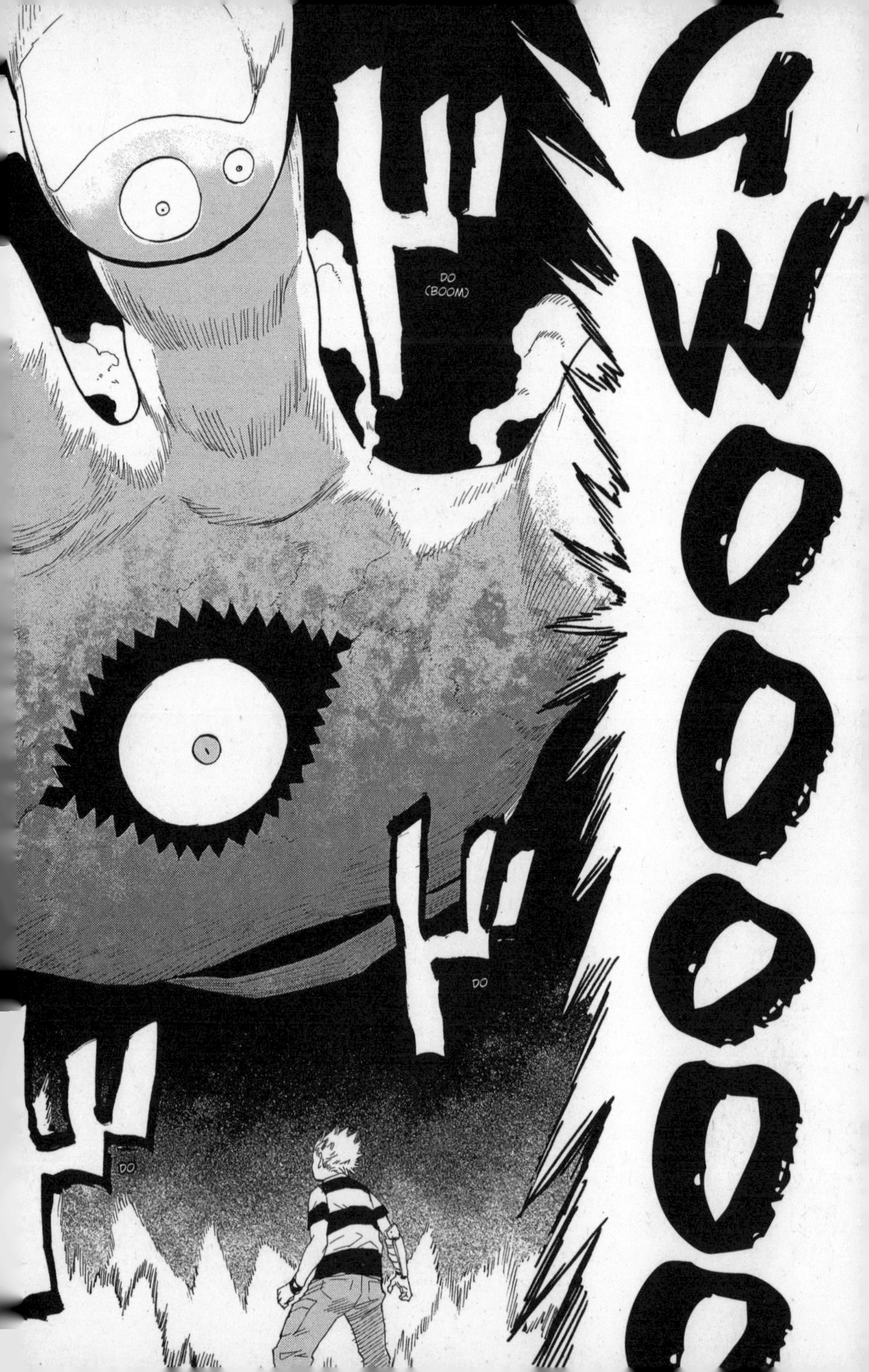
aWOOOOOO
DO
(BOOM)
DO
DO

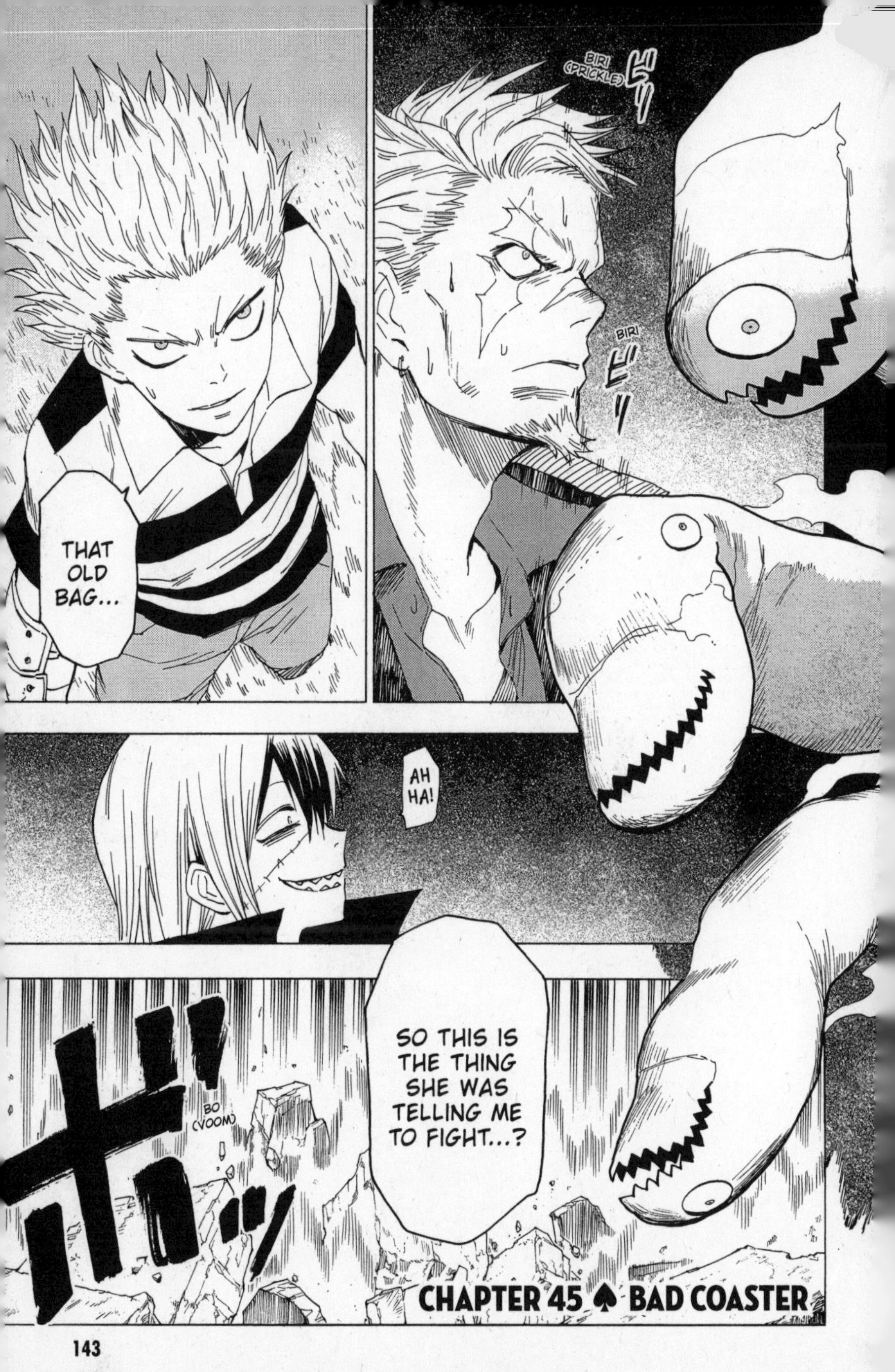
BIRI (PRICKLE)
BIRI
THAT OLD BAG...
AH HA!
SO THIS IS THE THING SHE WAS TELLING ME TO FIGHT...?
BO (VOOM)
CHAPTER 45 ♠ BAD COASTER

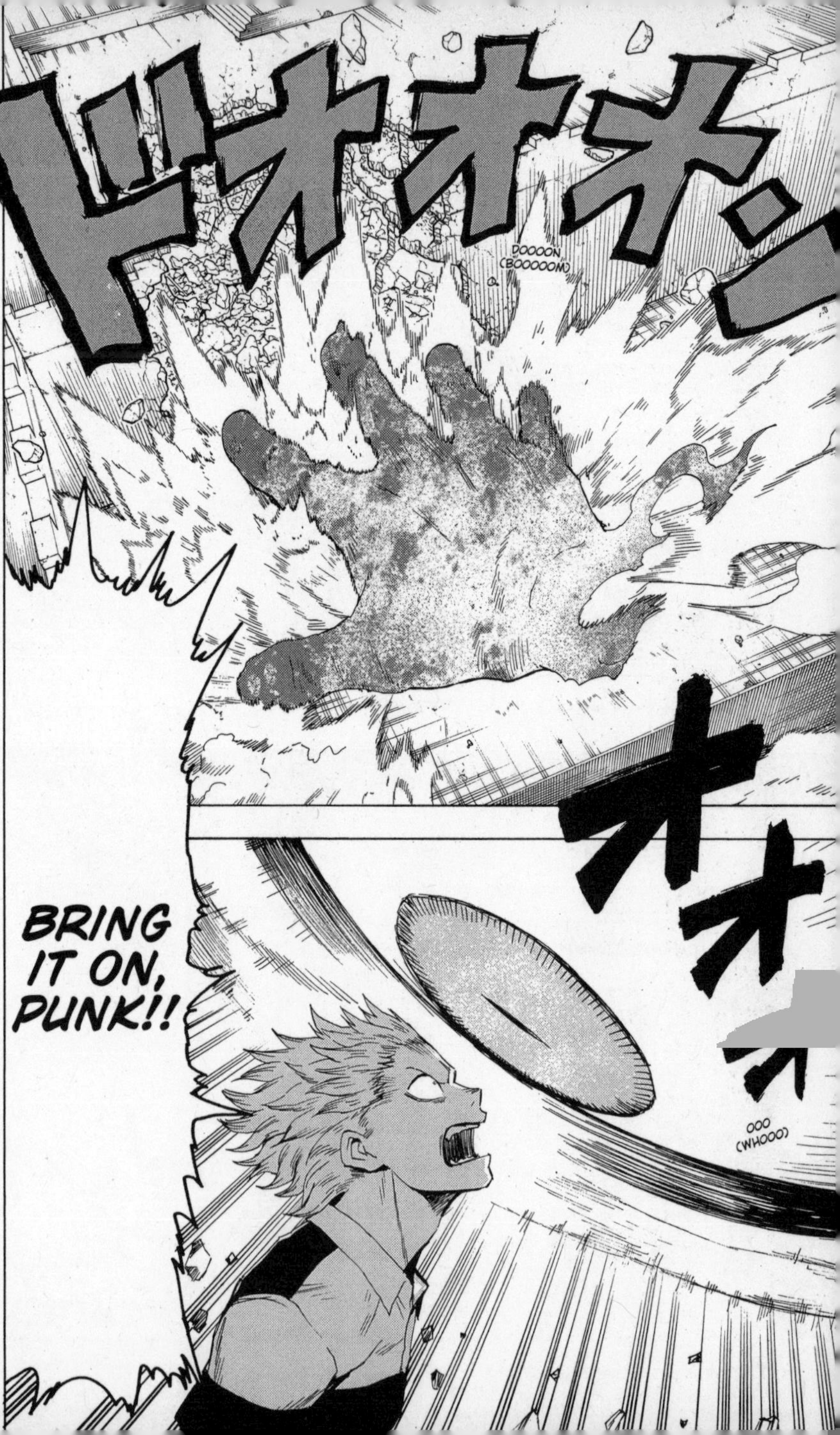
DOOOON (BOOOOOM)
OOO (WHOOO)
BRING IT ON, PUNK!!

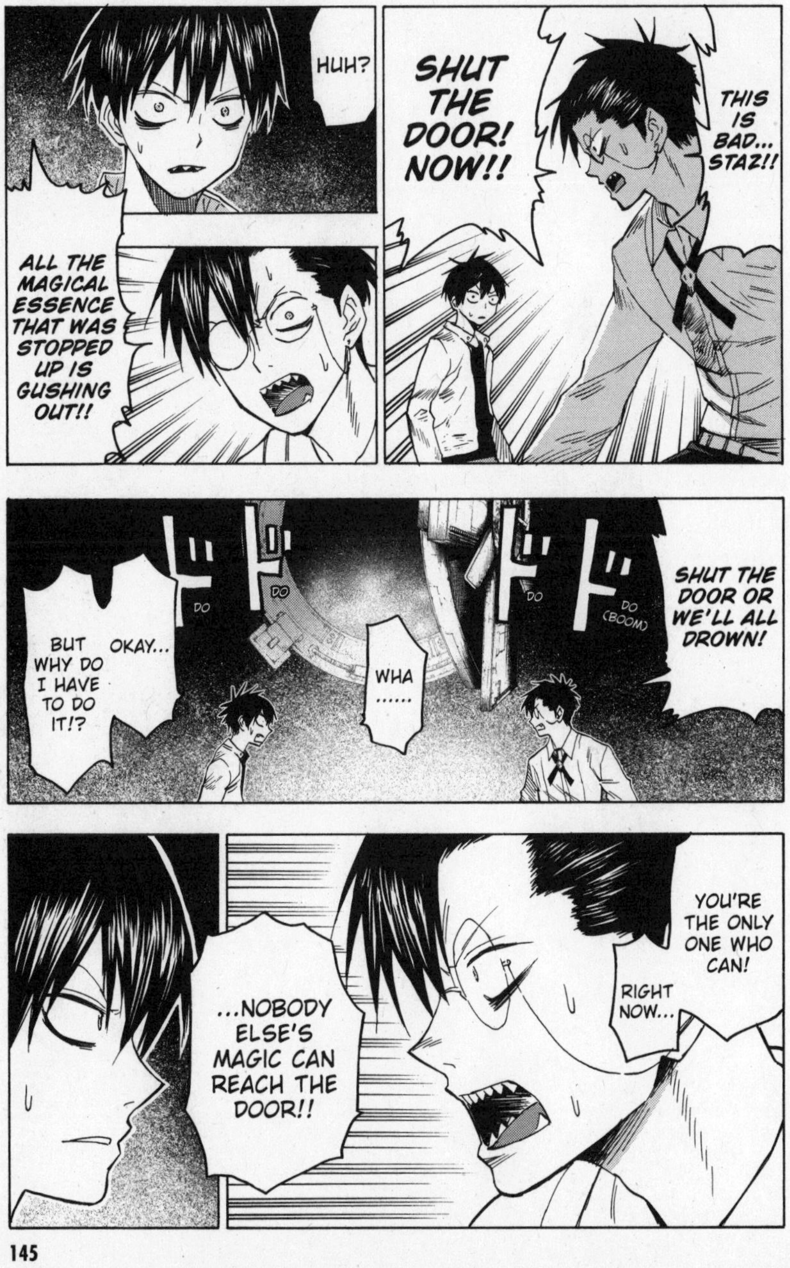
THIS IS BAD... STAZ!!
SHUT THE DOOR! NOW!!
HUH?
ALL THE MAGICAL ESSENCE THAT WAS STOPPED UP IS GUSHING OUT!!
SHUT THE DOOR OR WE'LL ALL DROWN!
DO (BOOM)
DO
WHA ......
DO
DO
OKAY...
BUT WHY DO I HAVE TO DO IT!?
YOU'RE THE ONLY ONE WHO CAN!
RIGHT NOW...
...NOBODY ELSE'S MAGIC CAN REACH THE DOOR!!

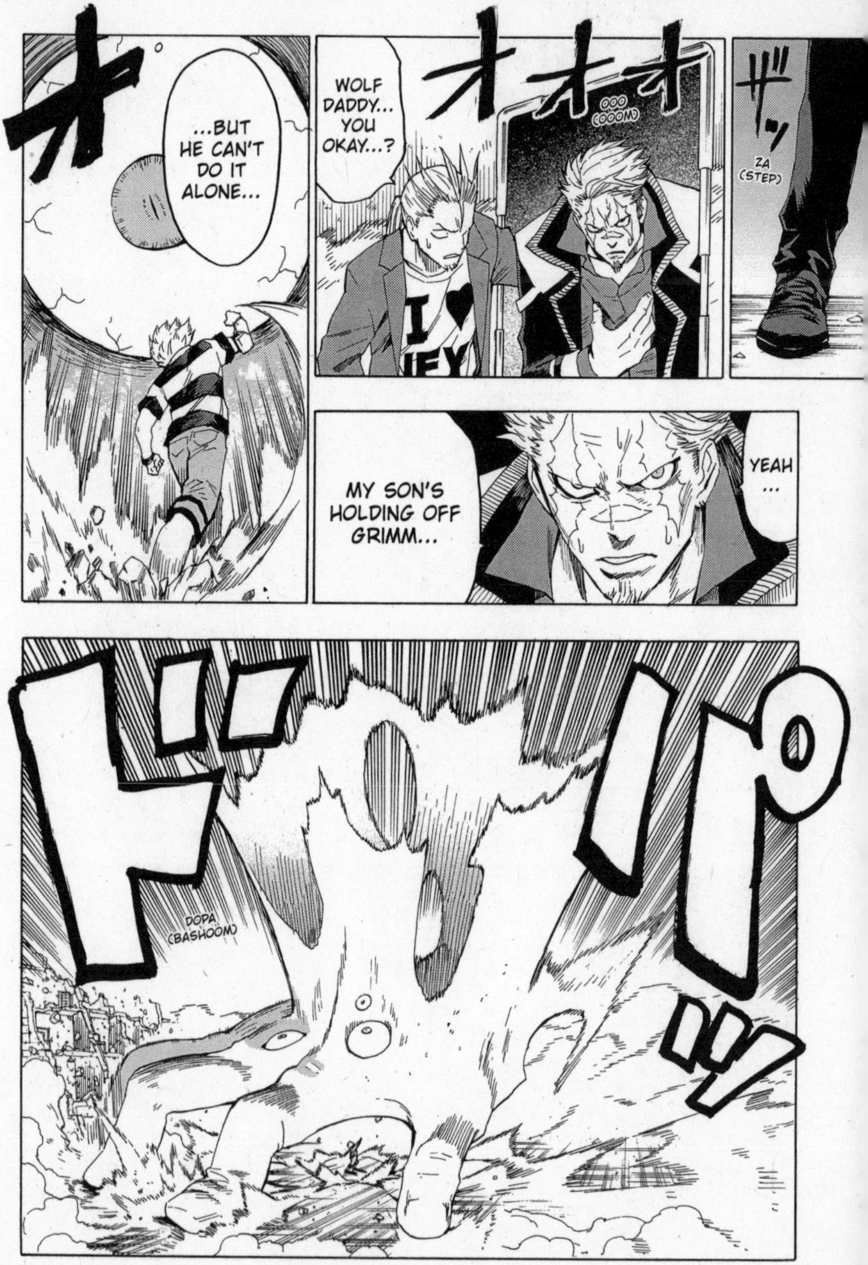

ZA (STEP)
OOO (OOOM)
WOLF DADDY... YOU OKAY...?
YEAH ...
MY SON'S HOLDING OFF GRIMM...
...BUT HE CAN'T DO IT ALONE...
DOPA (BASHOOM)

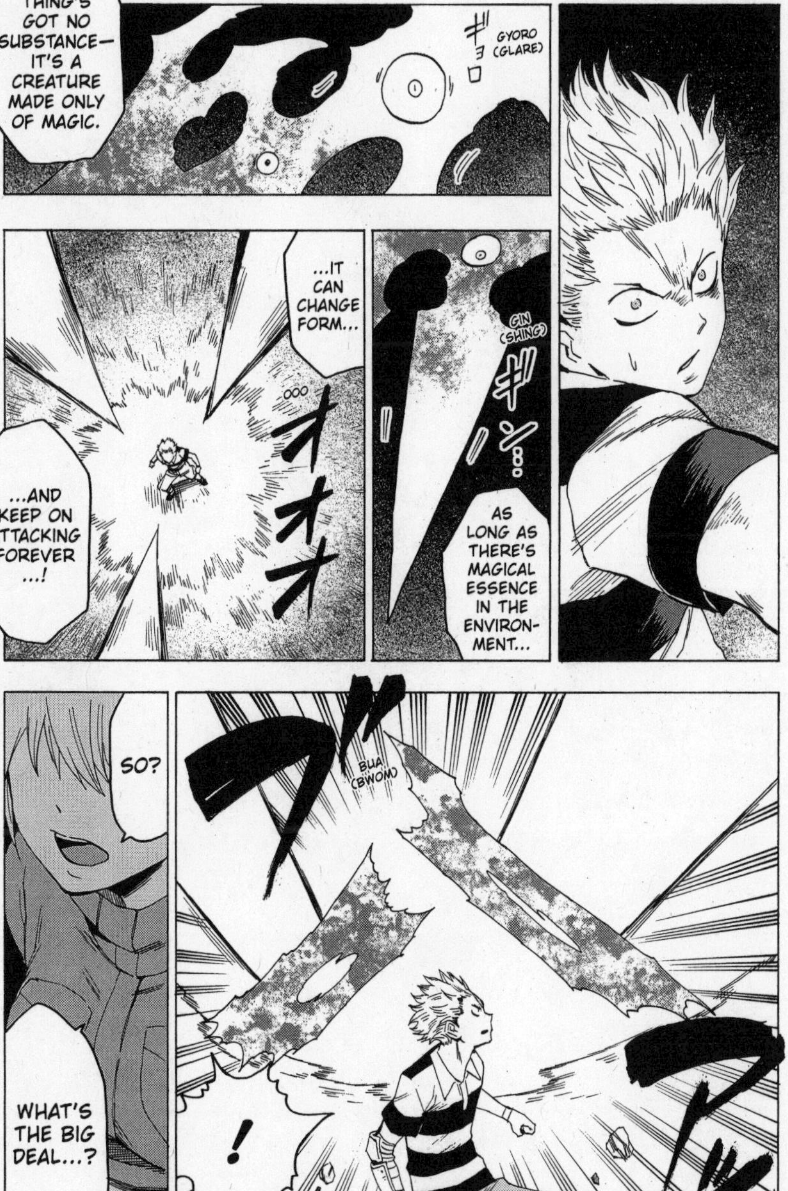
THAT THING'S GOT NO SUBSTANCE—IT'S A CREATURE MADE ONLY OF MAGIC.
GYORO (GLARE)
GIN (SHING)
AS LONG AS THERE'S MAGICAL ESSENCE IN THE ENVIRONMENT...
...IT CAN CHANGE FORM...
OOO
...AND KEEP ON ATTACKING FOREVER...!
BUA (BWOM)
!
SO?
WHAT'S THE BIG DEAL...?

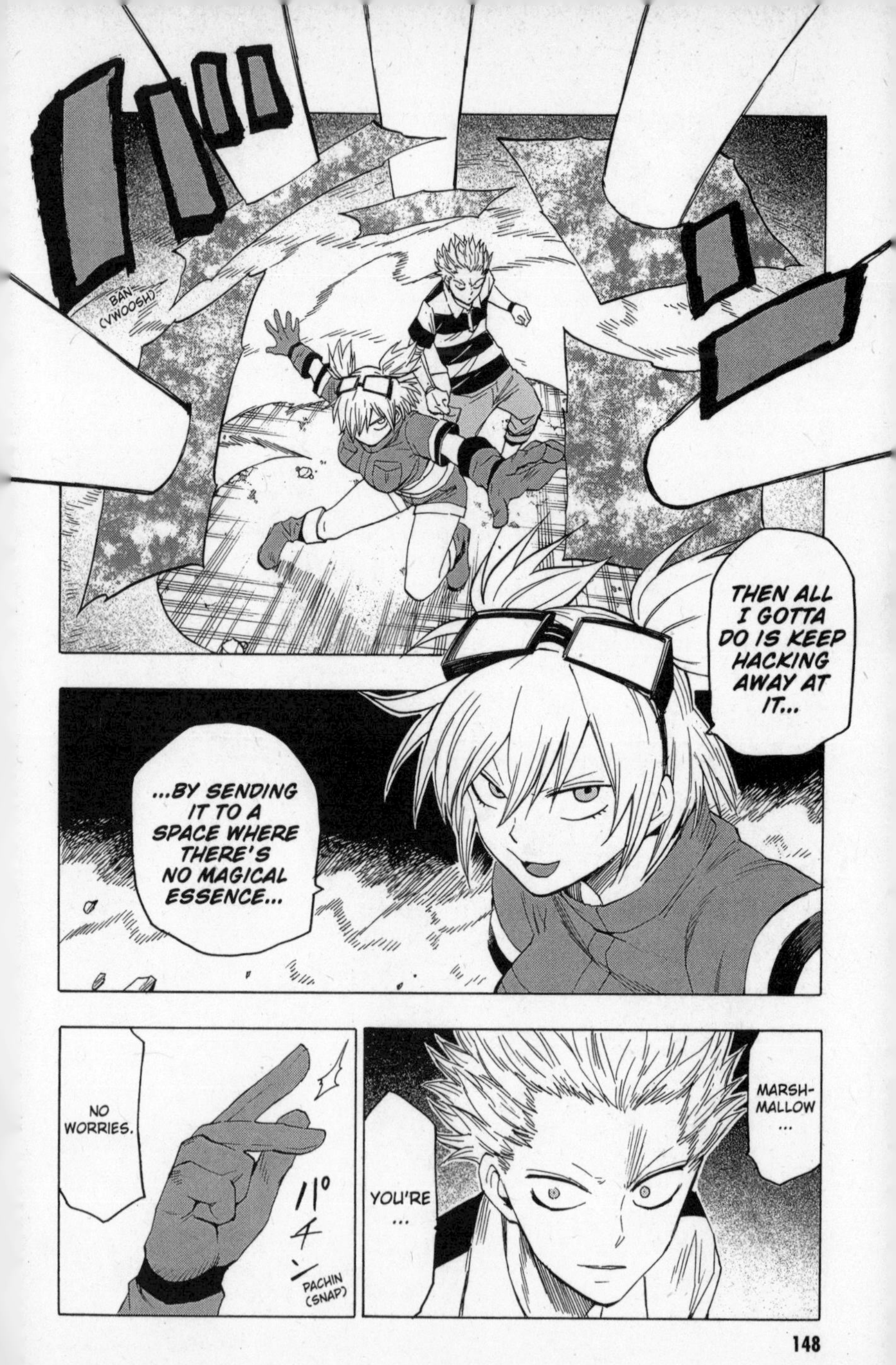
BAN (VWOOSH)
THEN ALL I GOTTA DO IS KEEP HACKING AWAY AT IT...
...BY SENDING IT TO A SPACE WHERE THERE'S NO MAGICAL ESSENCE...
MARSH-MALLOW...
YOU'RE...
NO WORRIES.
PACHIN (SNAP)

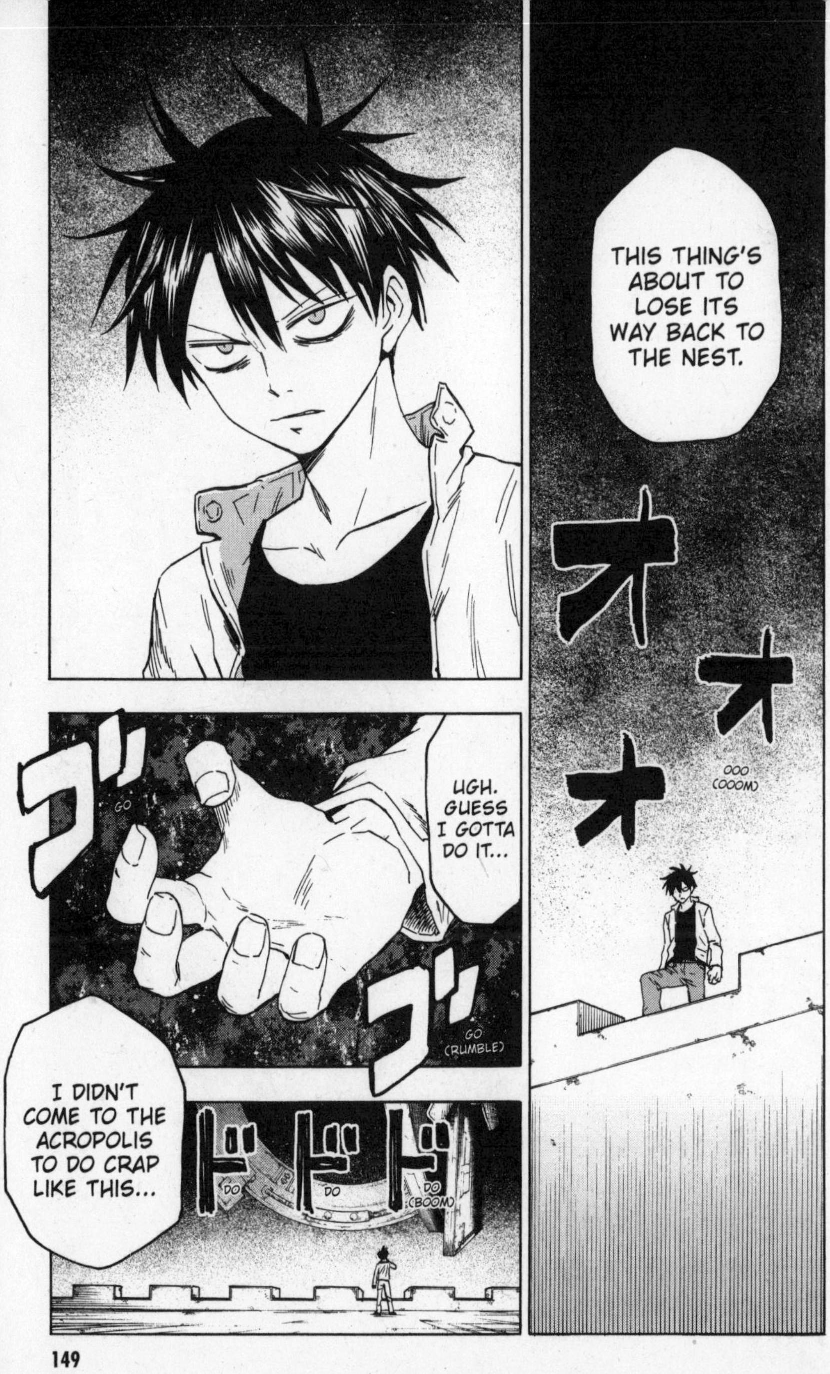
THIS THING'S ABOUT TO LOSE ITS WAY BACK TO THE NEST.
オオオ
OOO (OOOM)
ゴ
GO
UGH. GUESS I GOTTA DO IT...
ゴ
GO (RUMBLE)
I DIDN'T COME TO THE ACROPOLIS TO DO CRAP LIKE THIS...
ドドド
DO DO DO (BOOM)

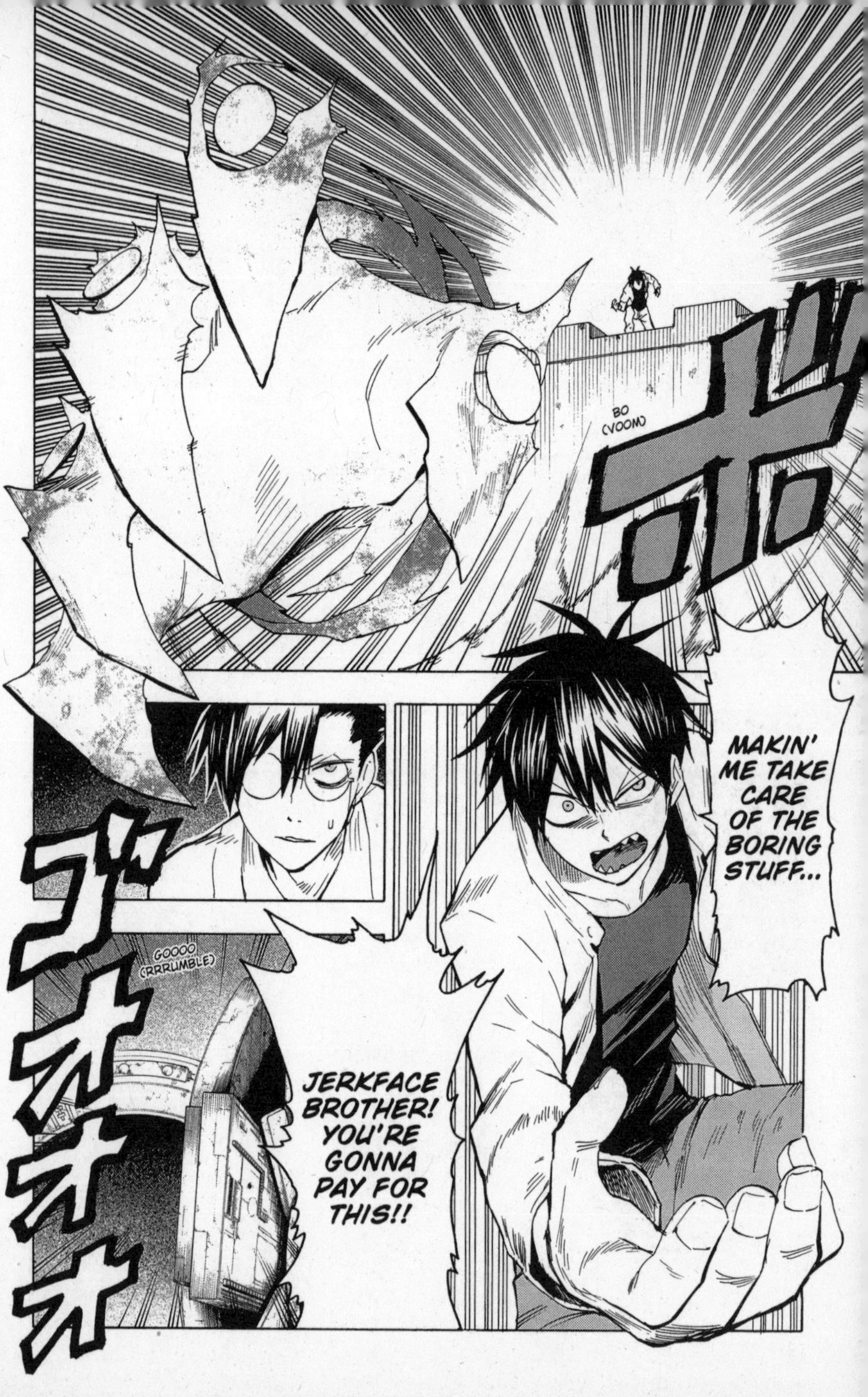

BO
(VOOM)
MAKIN' ME TAKE CARE OF THE BORING STUFF...
JERKFACE BROTHER! YOU'RE GONNA PAY FOR THIS!!
GOOOO
(RRRUMBLE)

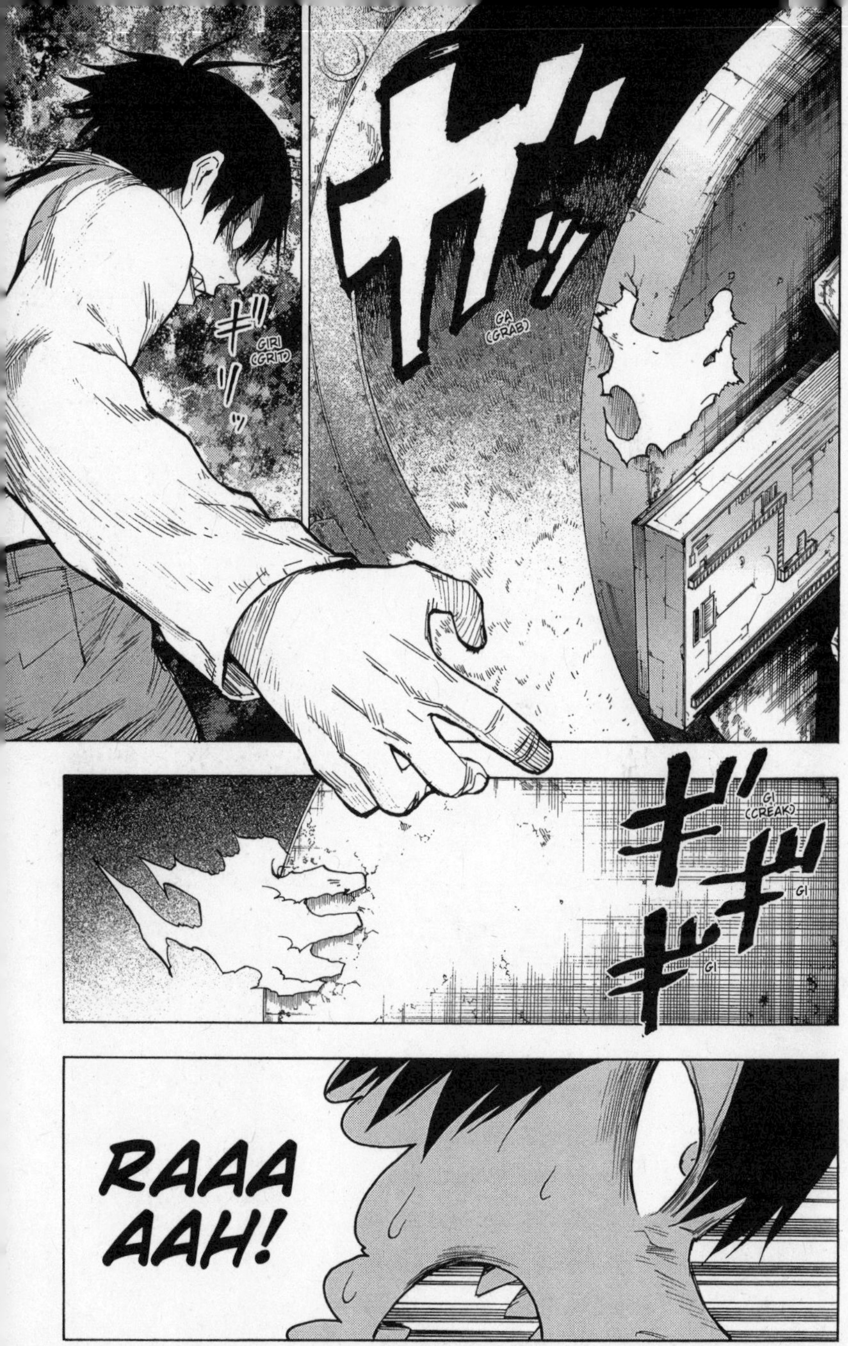
GA
(GRAB)
GIRI
(GRIT)
GI
(CREAK)
GI
GI
RAAA
AAH!

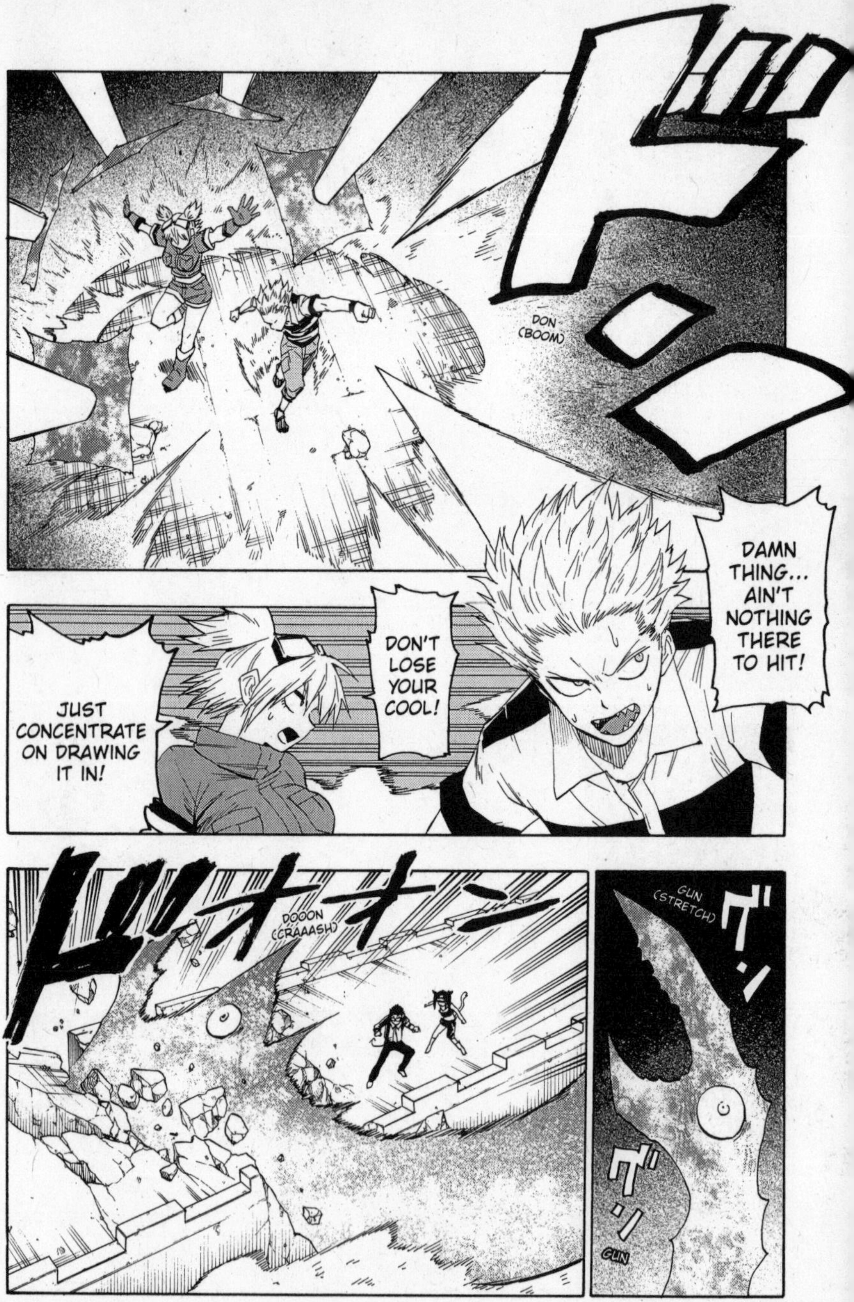
DON (BOOM)
DAMN THING... AIN'T NOTHING THERE TO HIT!
DON'T LOSE YOUR COOL!
JUST CONCENTRATE ON DRAWING IT IN!
GUN (STRETCH)
GUN
DOOON (CRAAASH)

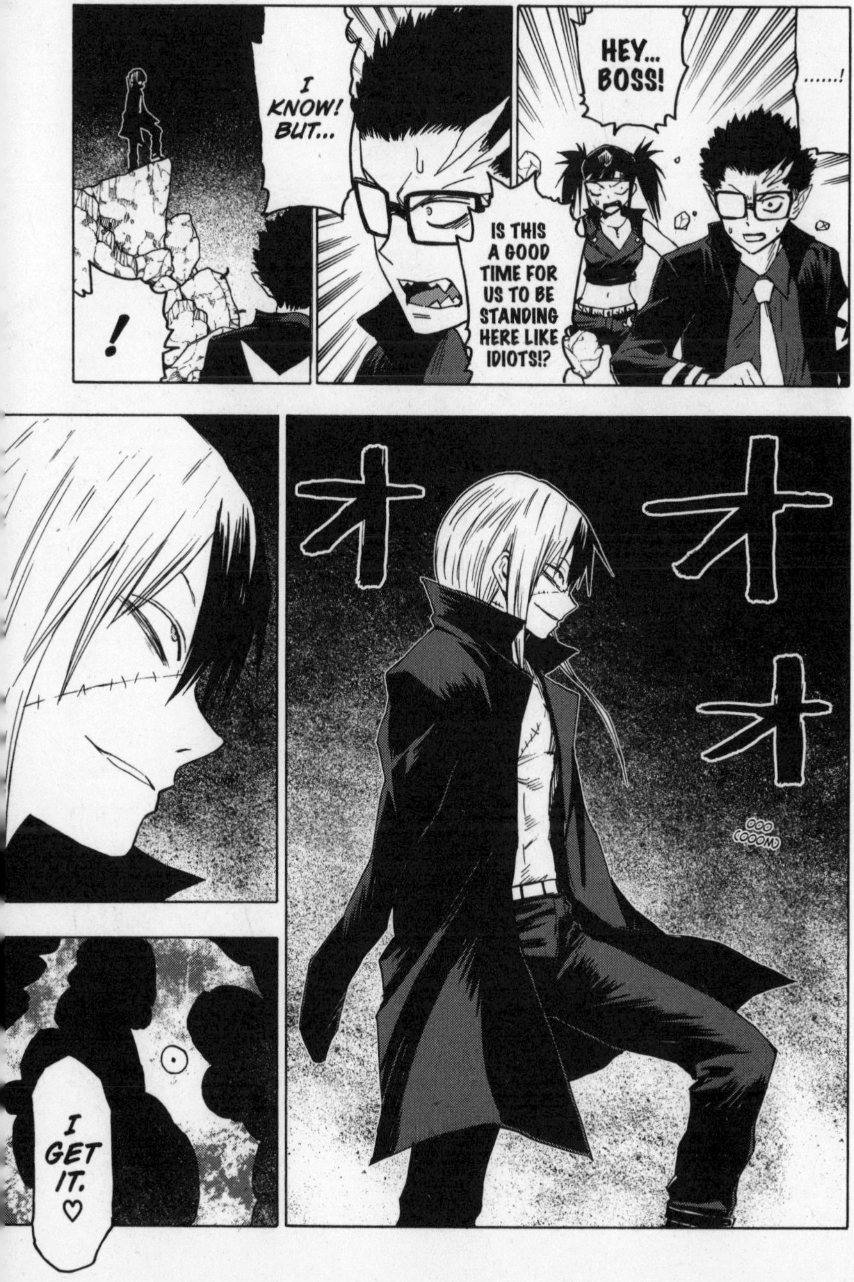
HEY... BOSS!
......!
IS THIS A GOOD TIME FOR US TO BE STANDING HERE LIKE IDIOTS!?
I KNOW! BUT...
!
オオオ
OOO (OOOM)
I GET IT. ♡

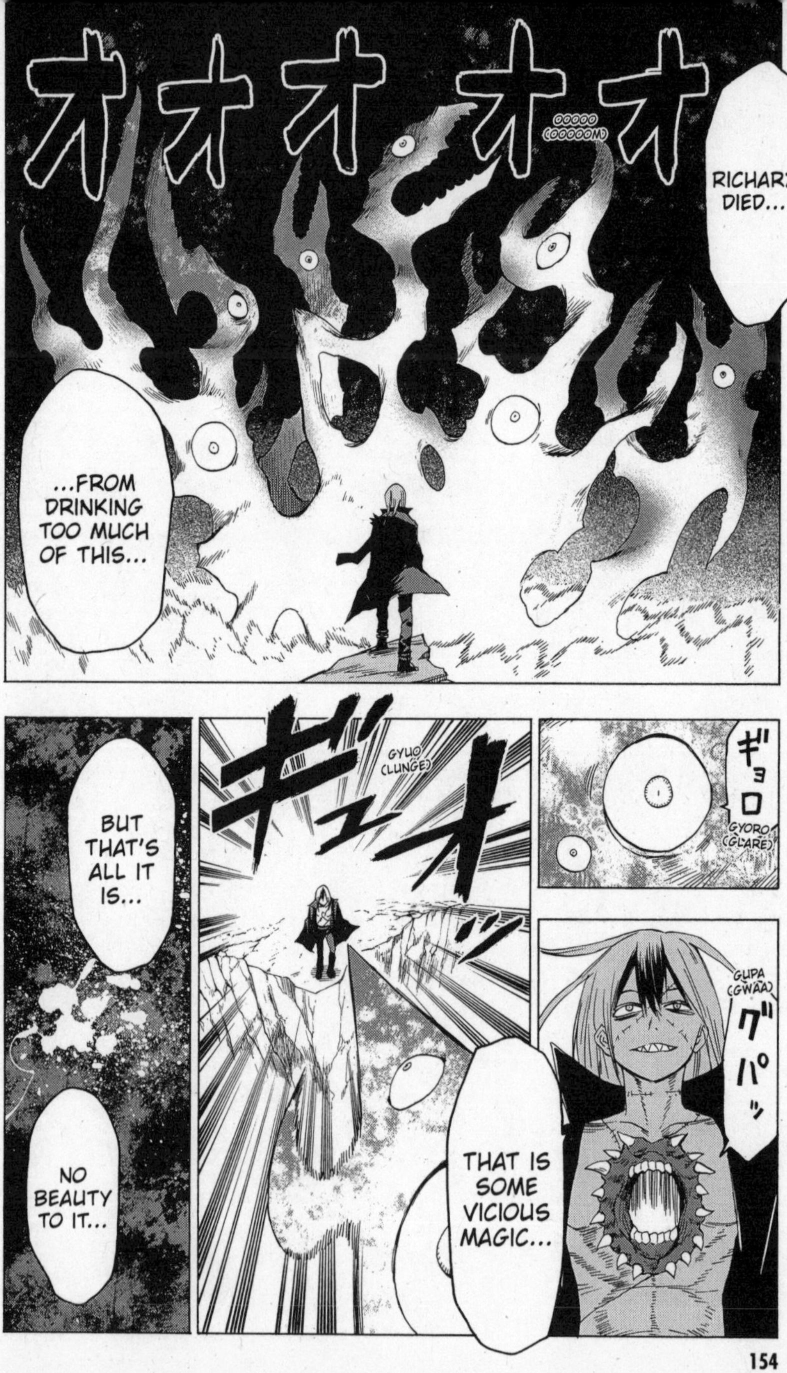
オオオオオ
OOOOO (OOOOON)
RICHARZ DIED...
...FROM DRINKING TOO MUCH OF THIS...
ギョロ
GYORO (GLARE)
グパッ
GUPA (GWAA)
THAT IS SOME VICIOUS MAGIC...
ギュオッ
GYUO (LUNGE)
BUT THAT'S ALL IT IS...
NO BEAUTY TO IT...

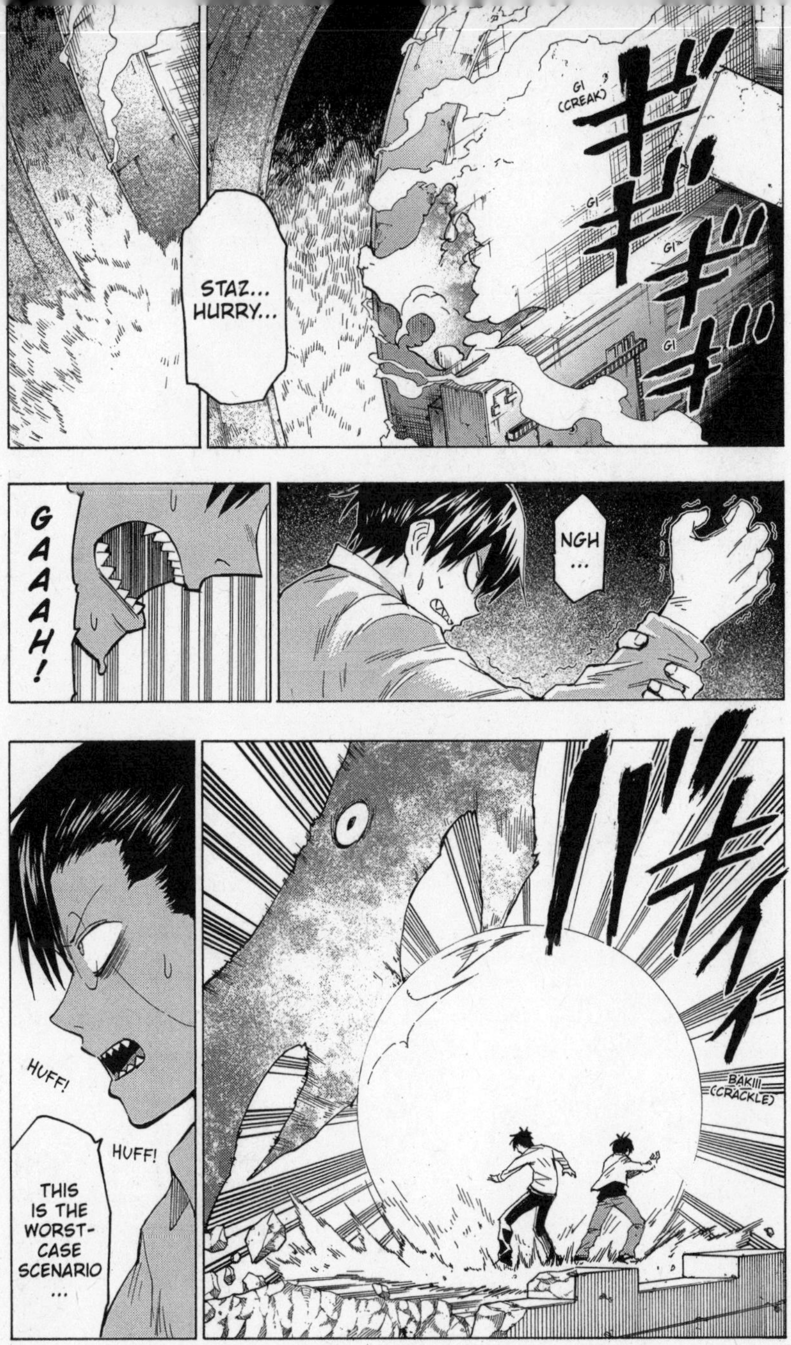
GI (CREAK)
GI
GI
GI
STAZ... HURRY...
NGH ...
GAAAAH!
BAKIII (CRACKLE)
HUFF!
HUFF!
THIS IS THE WORST-CASE SCENARIO ...

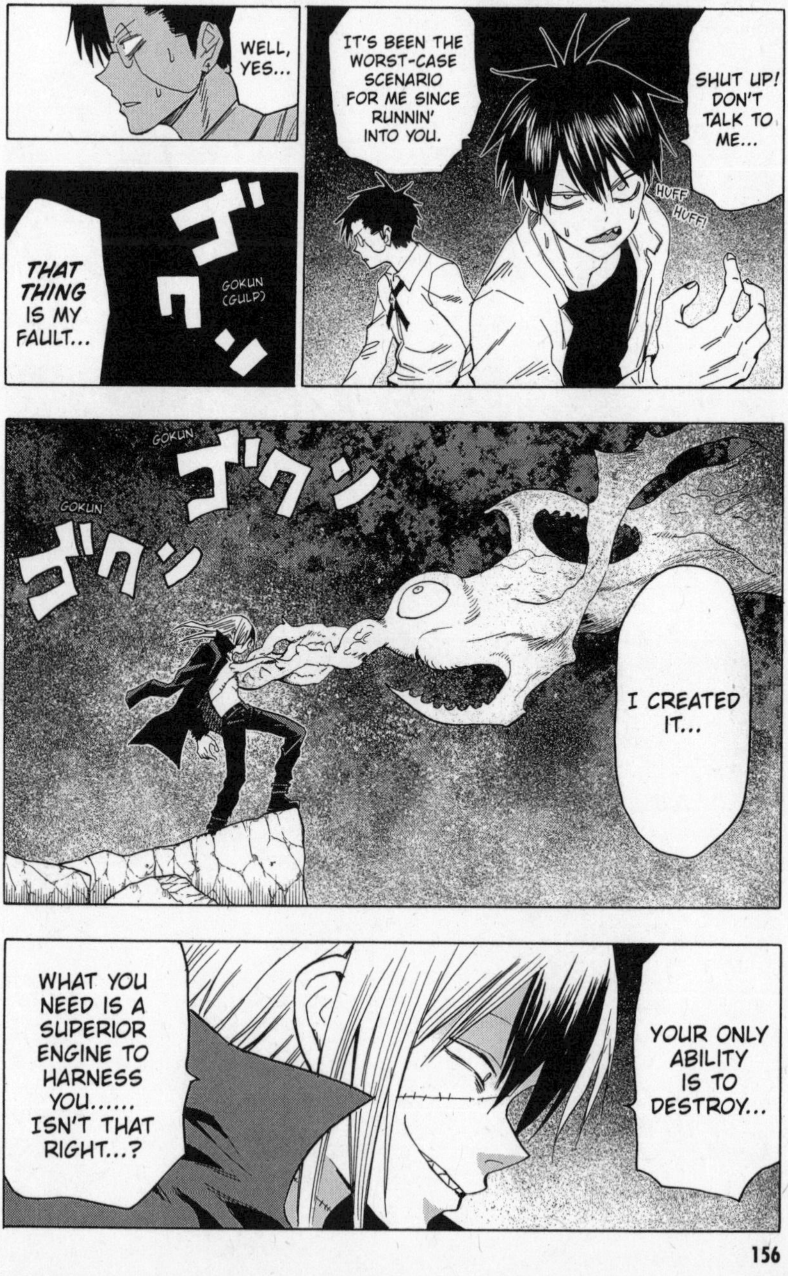
SHUT UP! DON'T TALK TO ME...
HUFF HUFF!
IT'S BEEN THE WORST-CASE SCENARIO FOR ME SINCE RUNNIN' INTO YOU.
WELL, YES...
ゴクッ
GOKUN (GULP)
THAT THING IS MY FAULT...
ゴクン
GOKUN
ゴクン
GOKUN
I CREATED IT...
YOUR ONLY ABILITY IS TO DESTROY...
WHAT YOU NEED IS A SUPERIOR ENGINE TO HARNESS YOU...... ISN'T THAT RIGHT...?

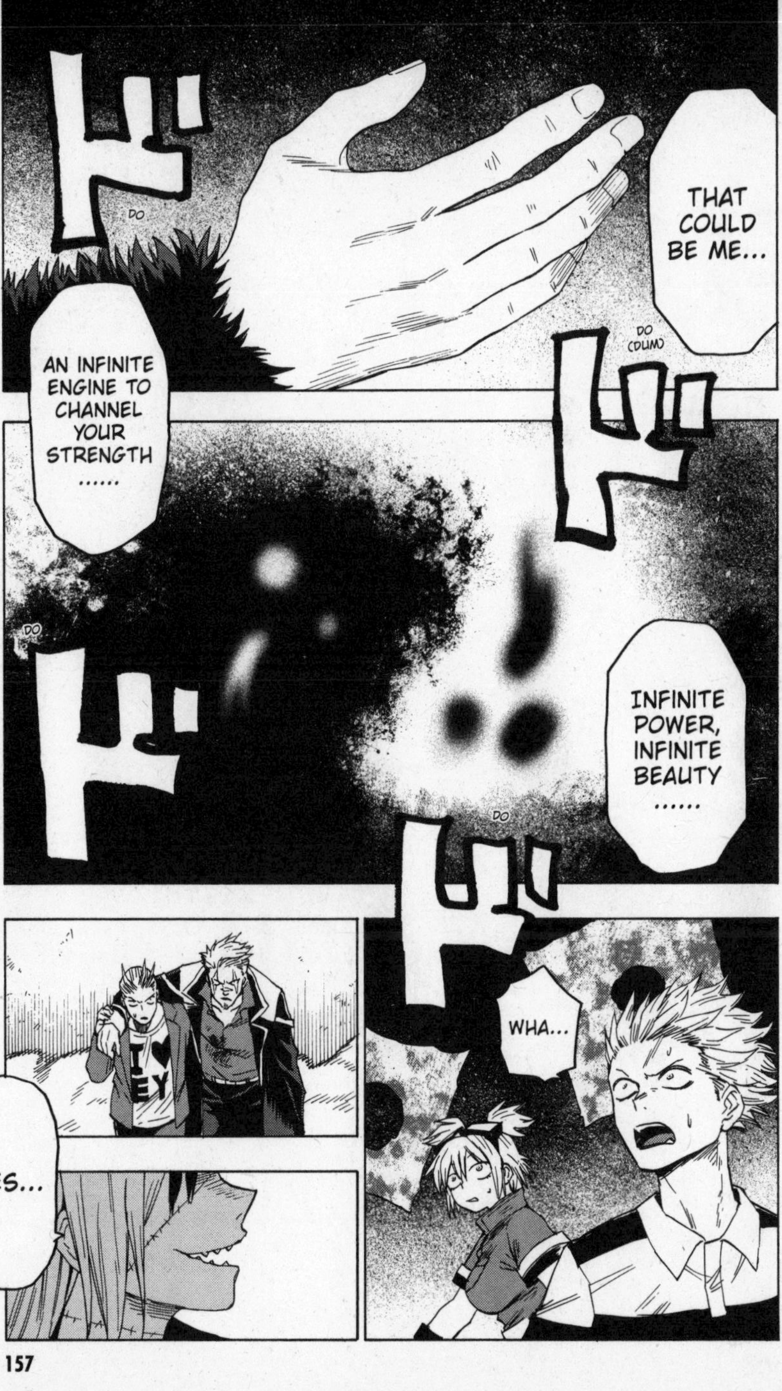
THAT COULD BE ME...
DO
DO (DUM)
AN INFINITE ENGINE TO CHANNEL YOUR STRENGTH ......
INFINITE POWER, INFINITE BEAUTY ......
DO
DO
WHA...
YES...

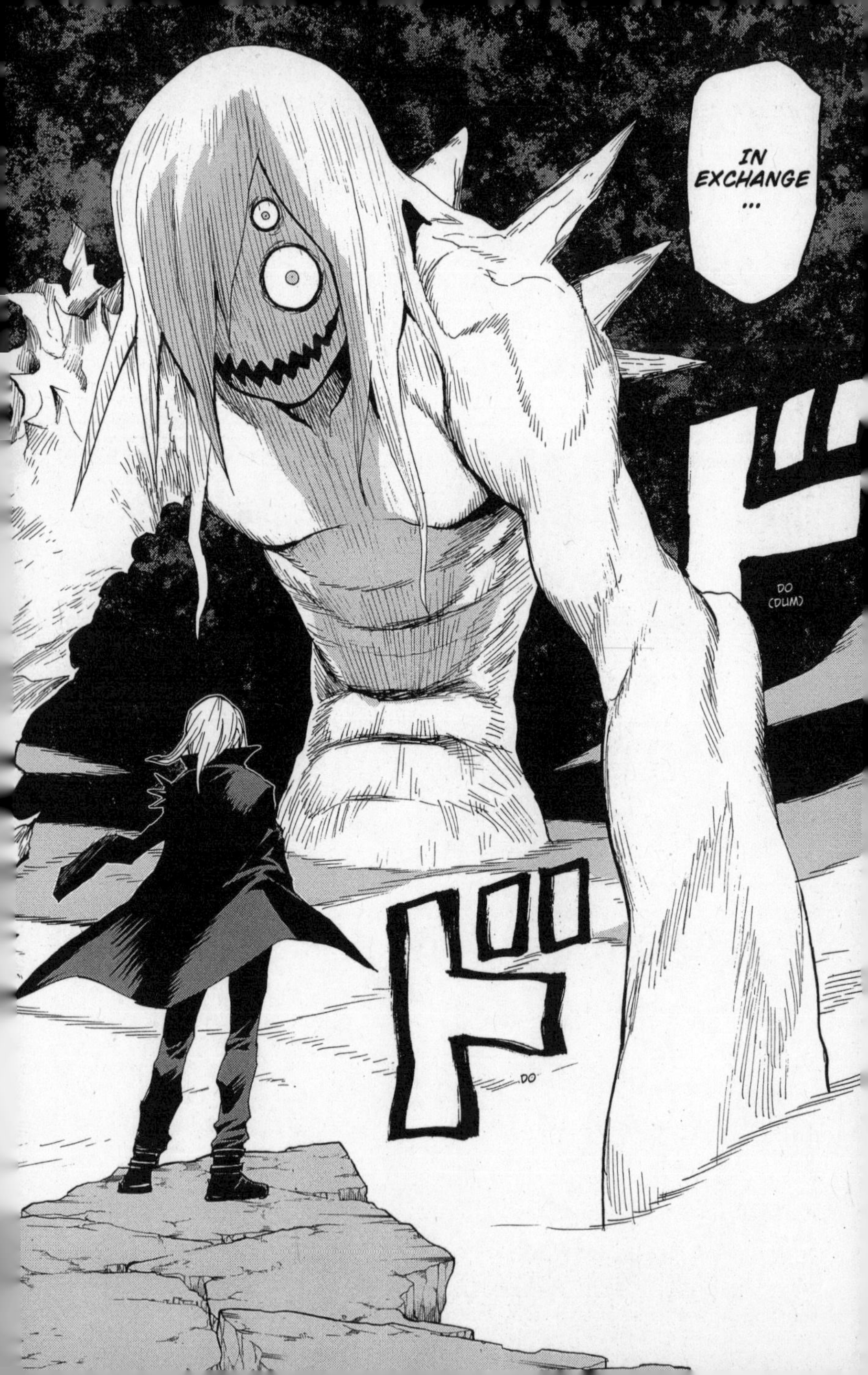
IN EXCHANGE ...
DO (DUM)
DO

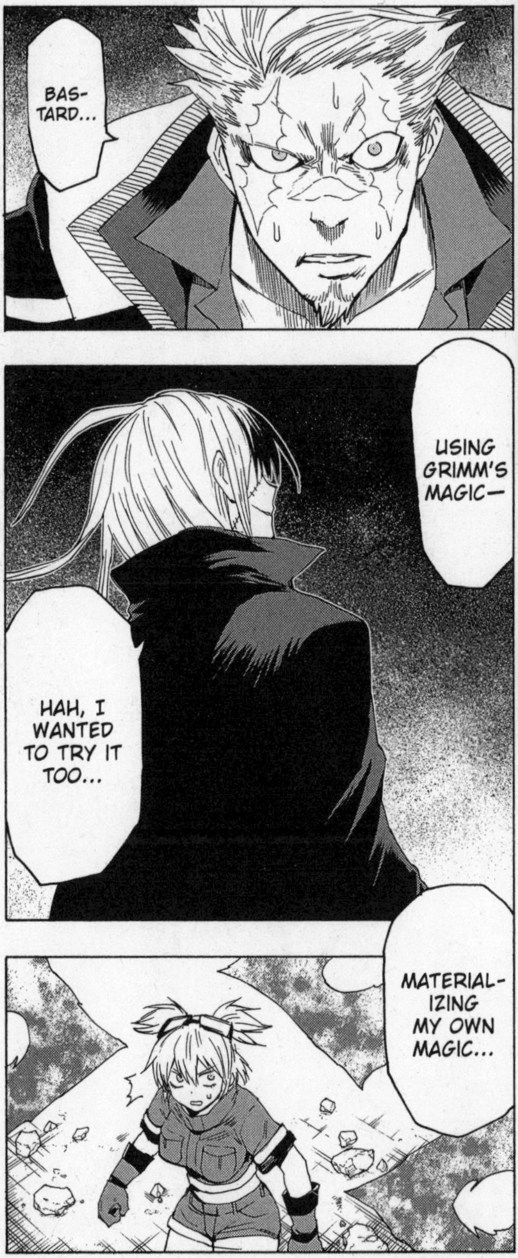
BAS-TARD...
USING GRIMM'S MAGIC—
HAH, I WANTED TO TRY IT TOO...
MATERIAL-IZING MY OWN MAGIC...

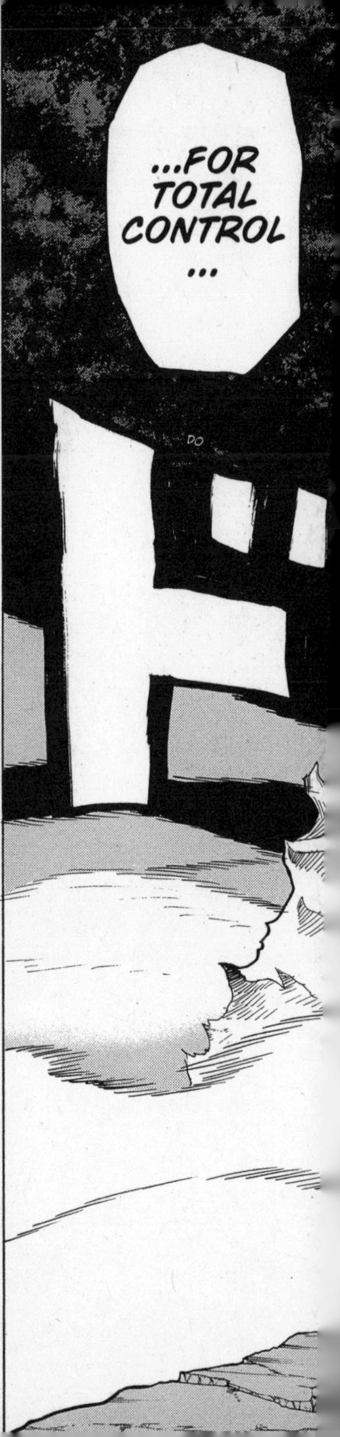
...FOR TOTAL CONTROL ...
DO

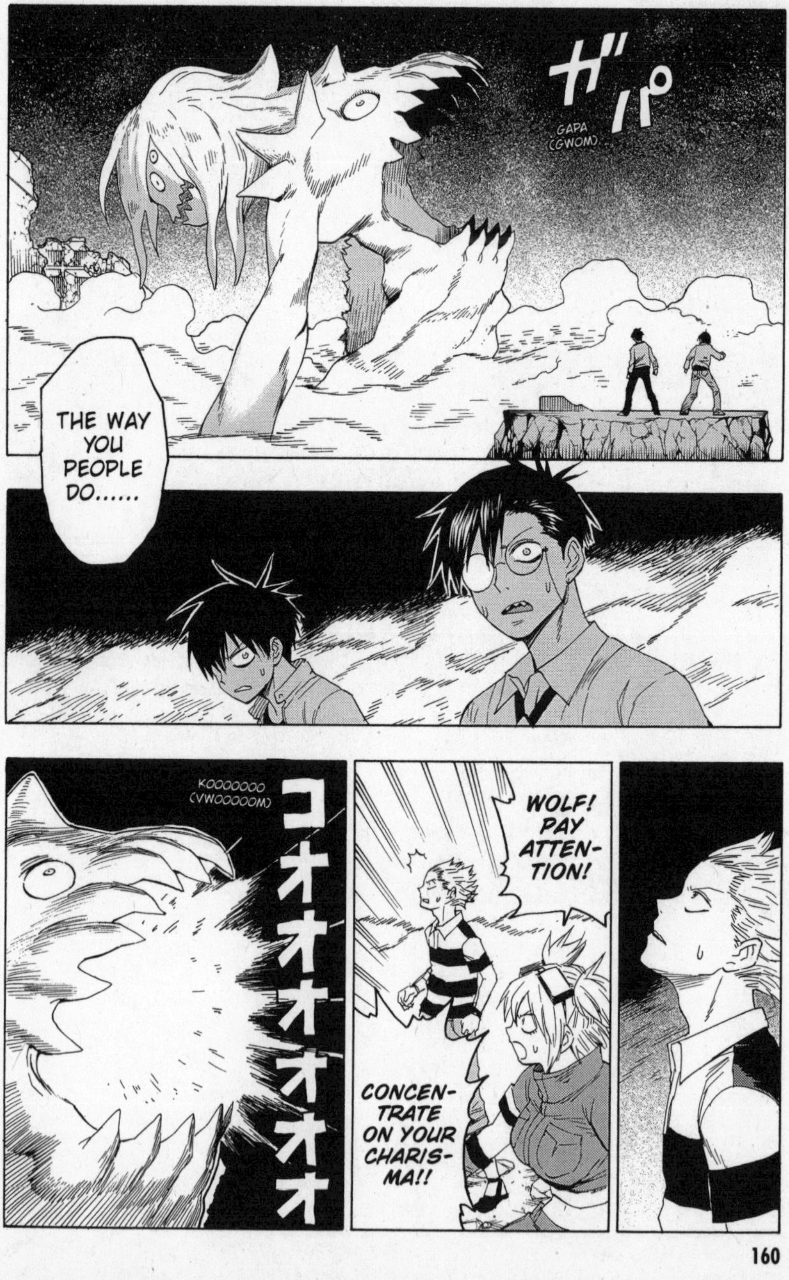
ガパ
GAPA (GWOM)
THE WAY YOU PEOPLE DO......
WOLF! PAY ATTENTION!
CONCENTRATE ON YOUR CHARISMA!!
コオオオオオオ
KOOOOOOO (VWOOOOOM)

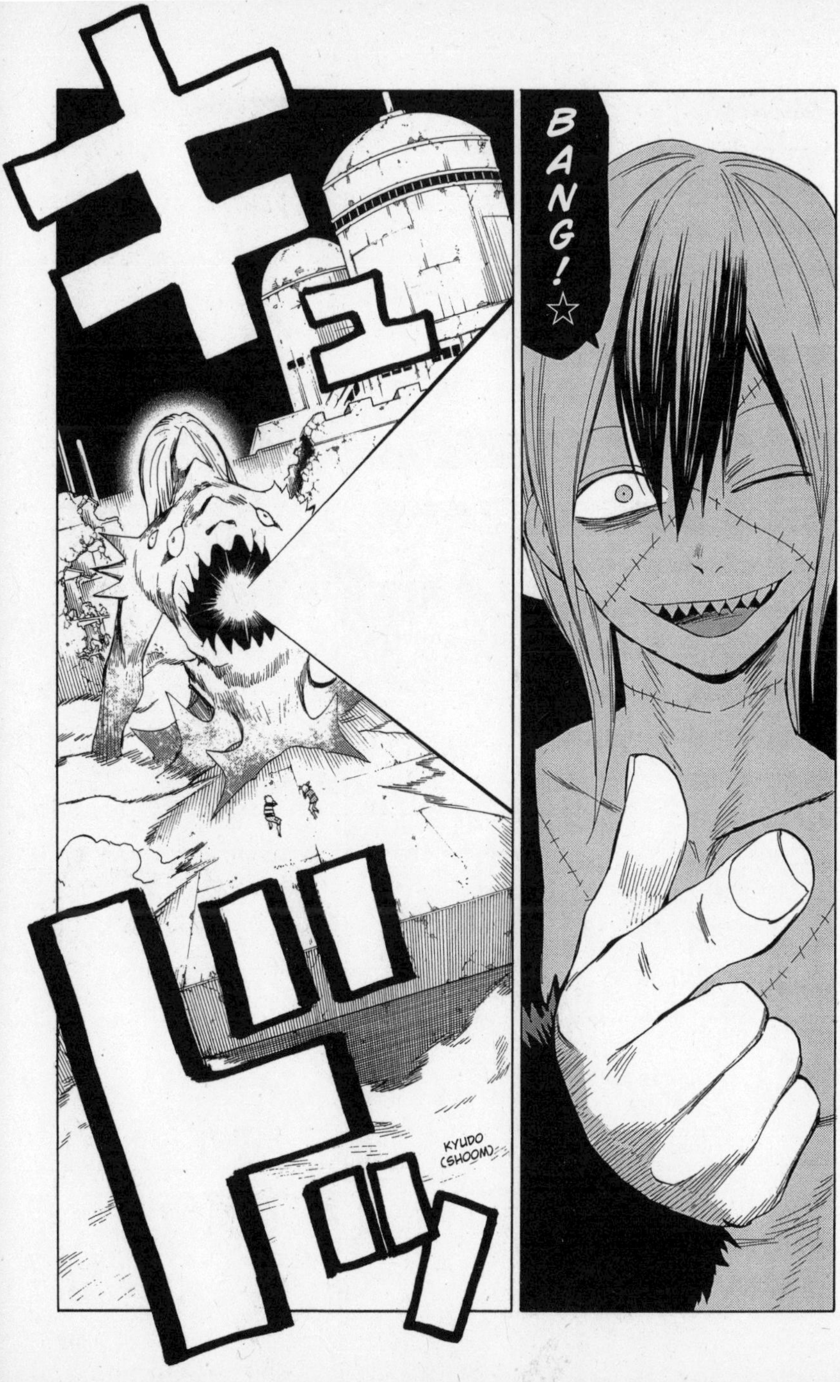
BANG!☆
キュ
ドッ
KYUDO
(SHOOM)

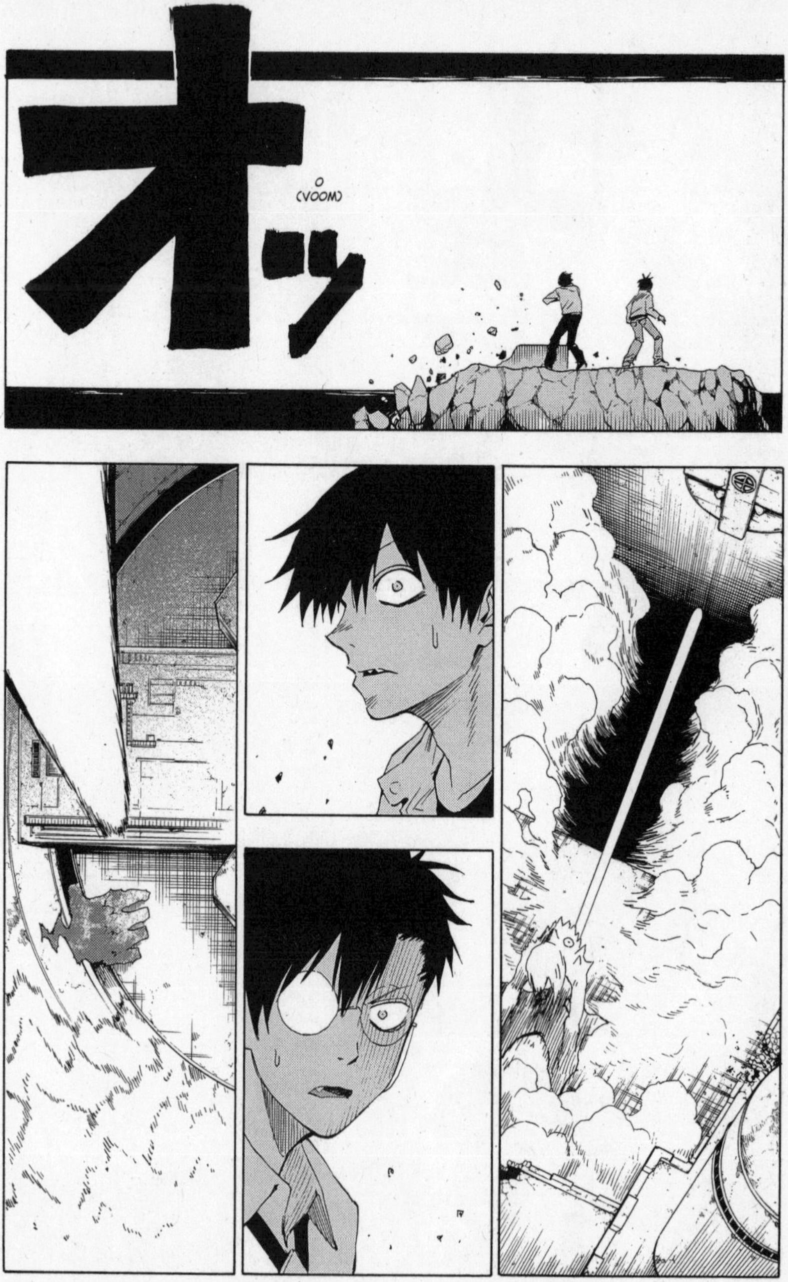
オッ
O
(VOOM)

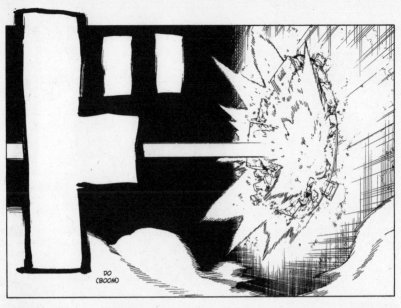

DO
(BOOM)

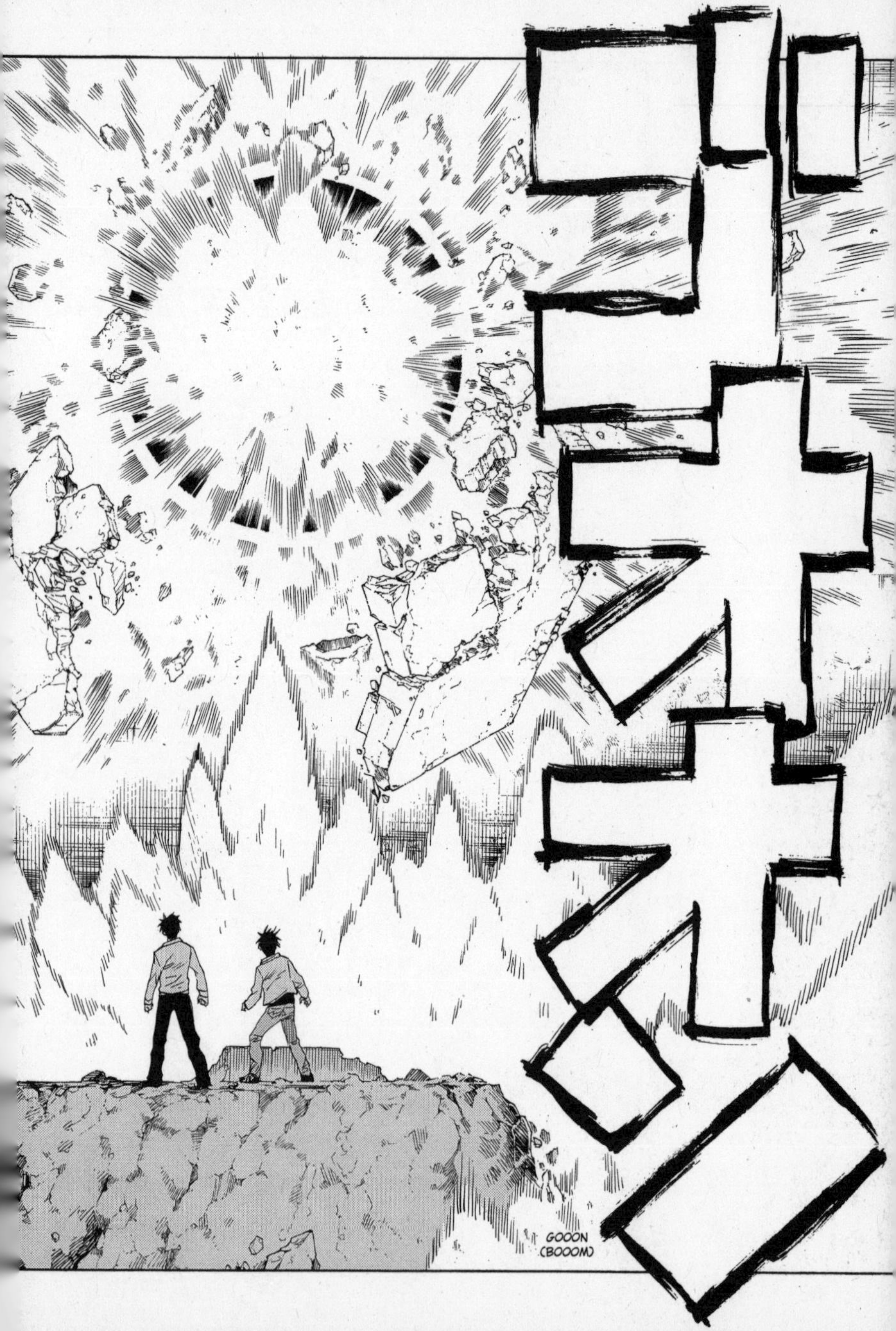
ゴオオン
GOOON
(BOOOM)

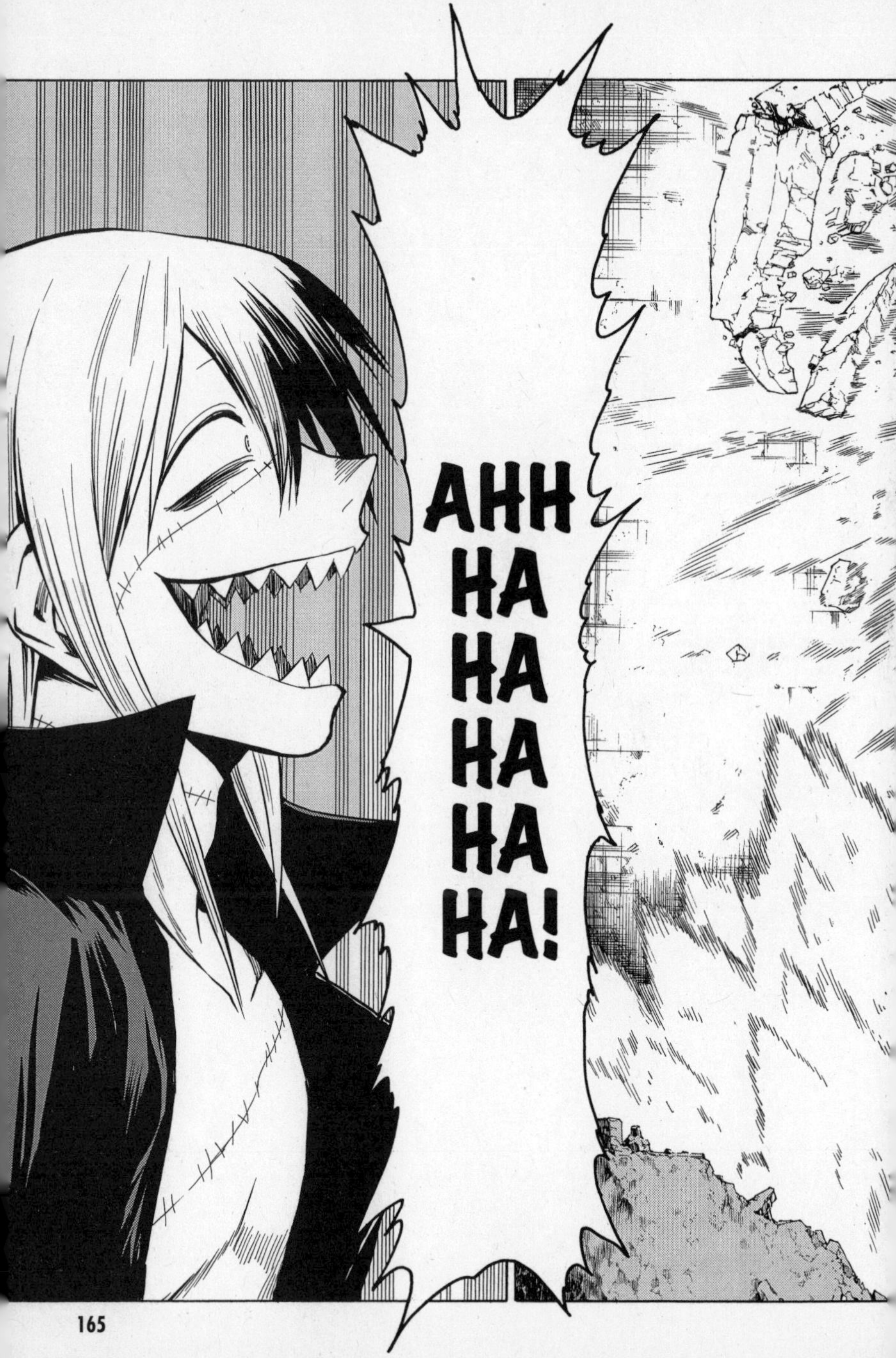
AHH HA HA HA HA HA!

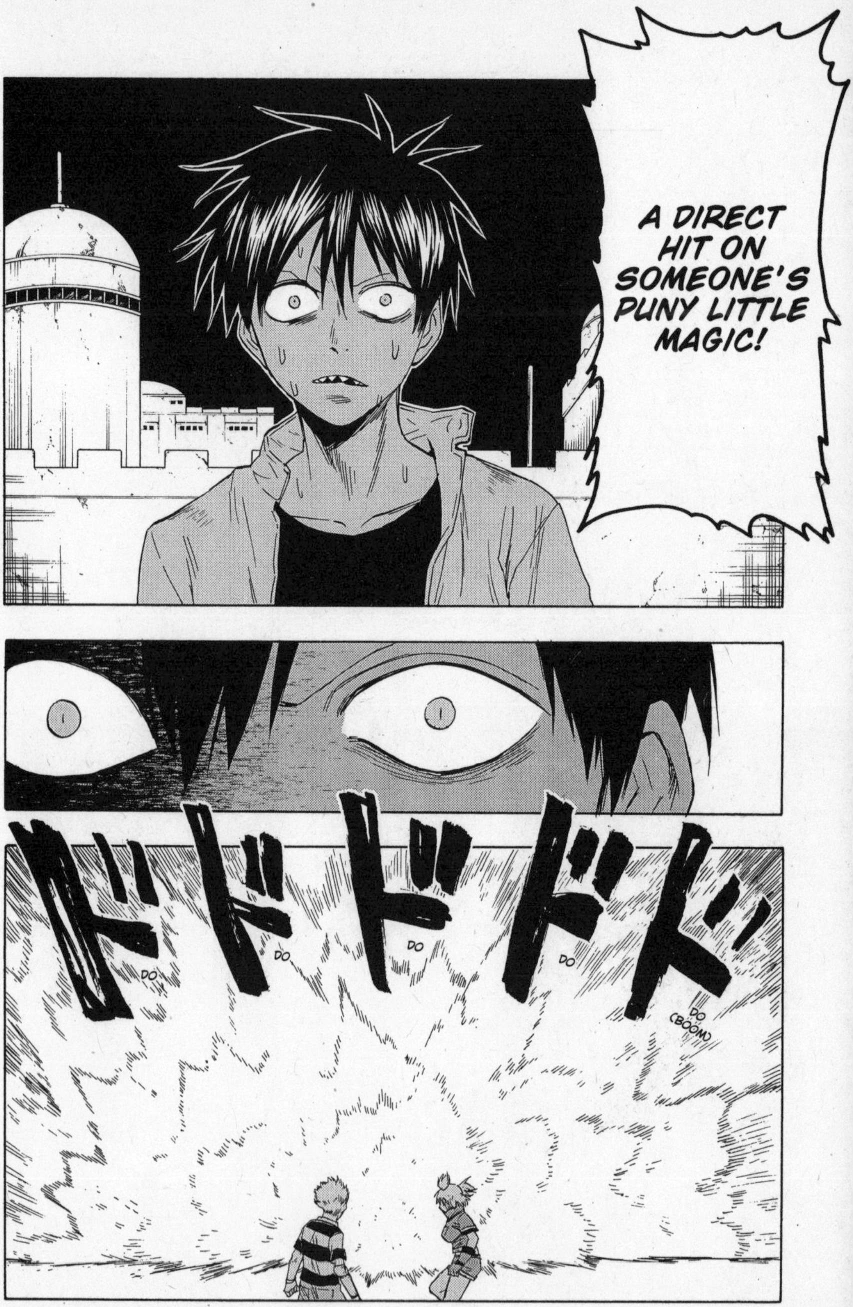
A DIRECT HIT ON SOMEONE'S PUNY LITTLE MAGIC!
DO DO DO DO DO (BOOM)

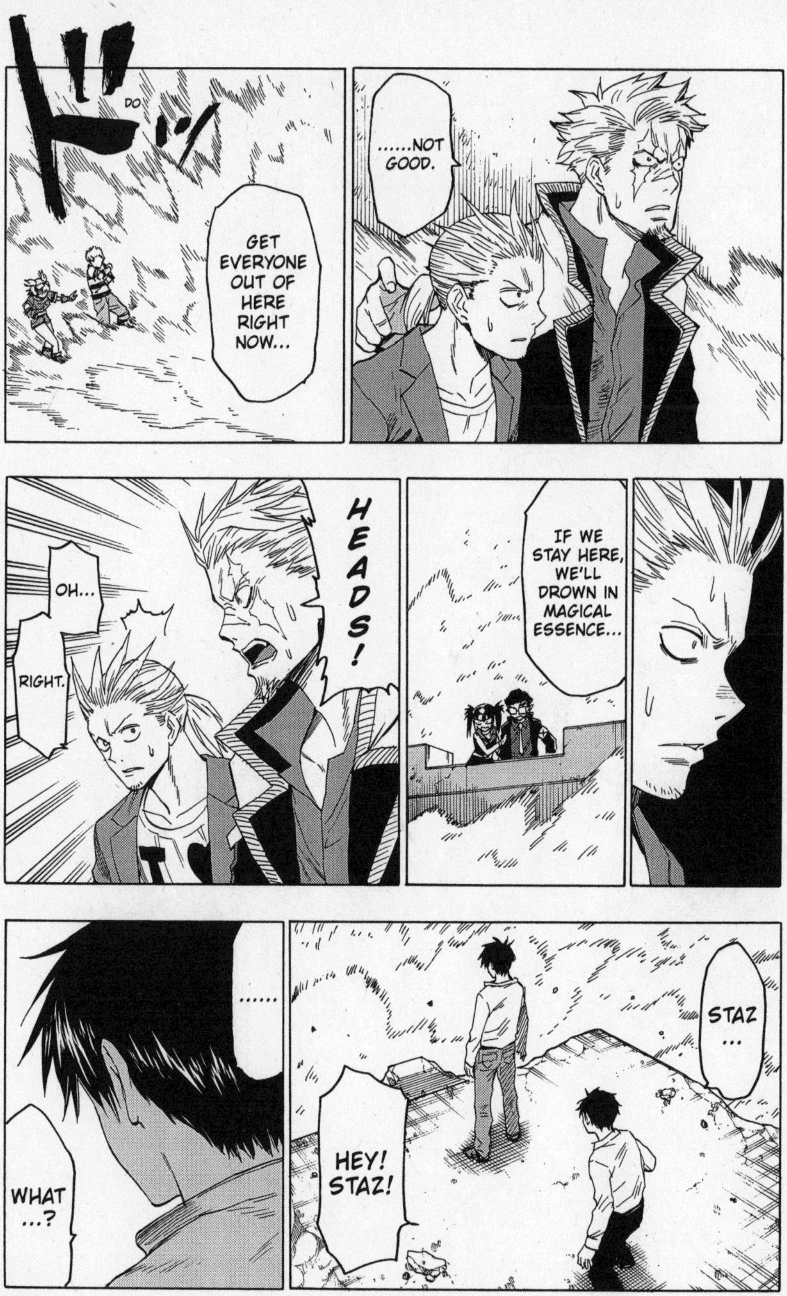
......NOT GOOD.
GET EVERYONE OUT OF HERE RIGHT NOW...
ドッ
DO
IF WE STAY HERE, WE'LL DROWN IN MAGICAL ESSENCE...
HEADS!
OH...
RIGHT.
STAZ...
HEY! STAZ!
......
WHAT...?

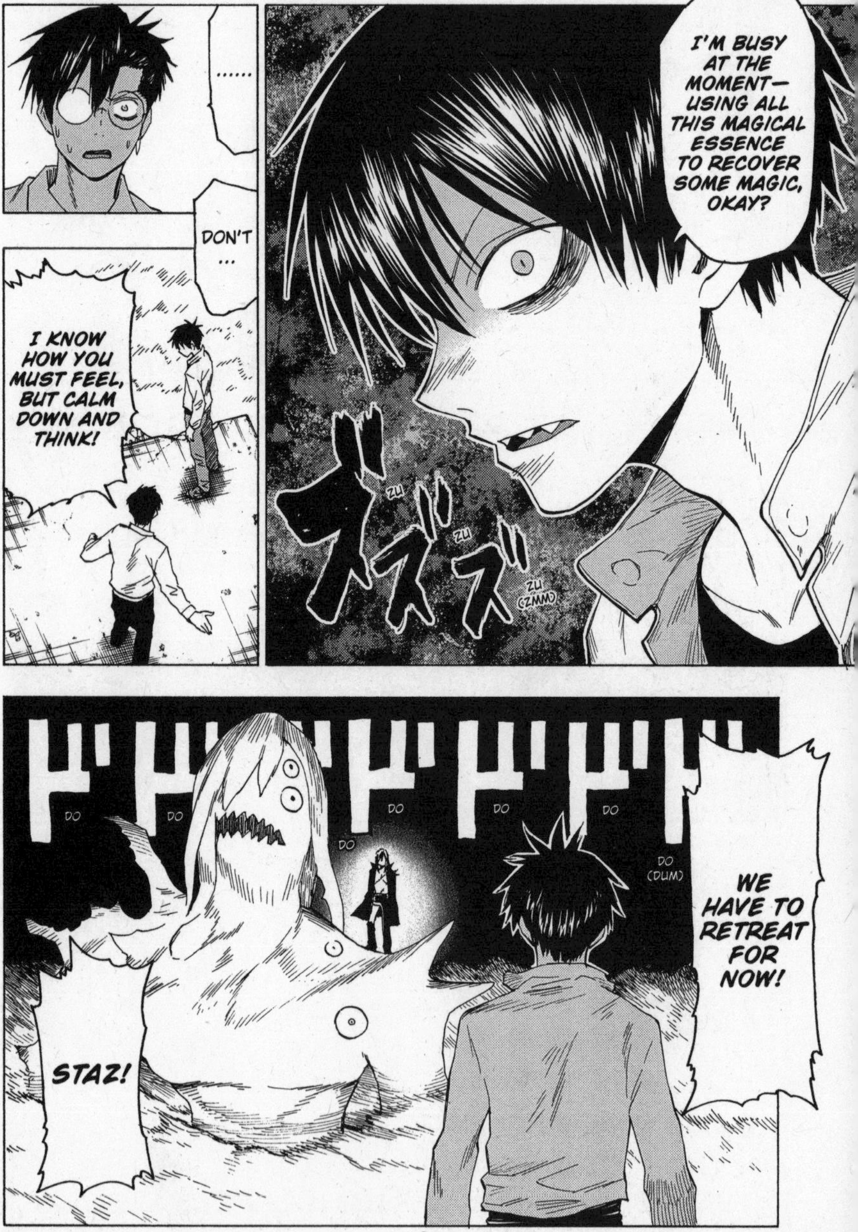
I'M BUSY AT THE MOMENT—USING ALL THIS MAGICAL ESSENCE TO RECOVER SOME MAGIC, OKAY?
ZU ZU ZU (ZMM)
......
DON'T ...
I KNOW HOW YOU MUST FEEL, BUT CALM DOWN AND THINK!
DO DO DO DO DO DO DO (DUM)
WE HAVE TO RETREAT FOR NOW!
STAZ!

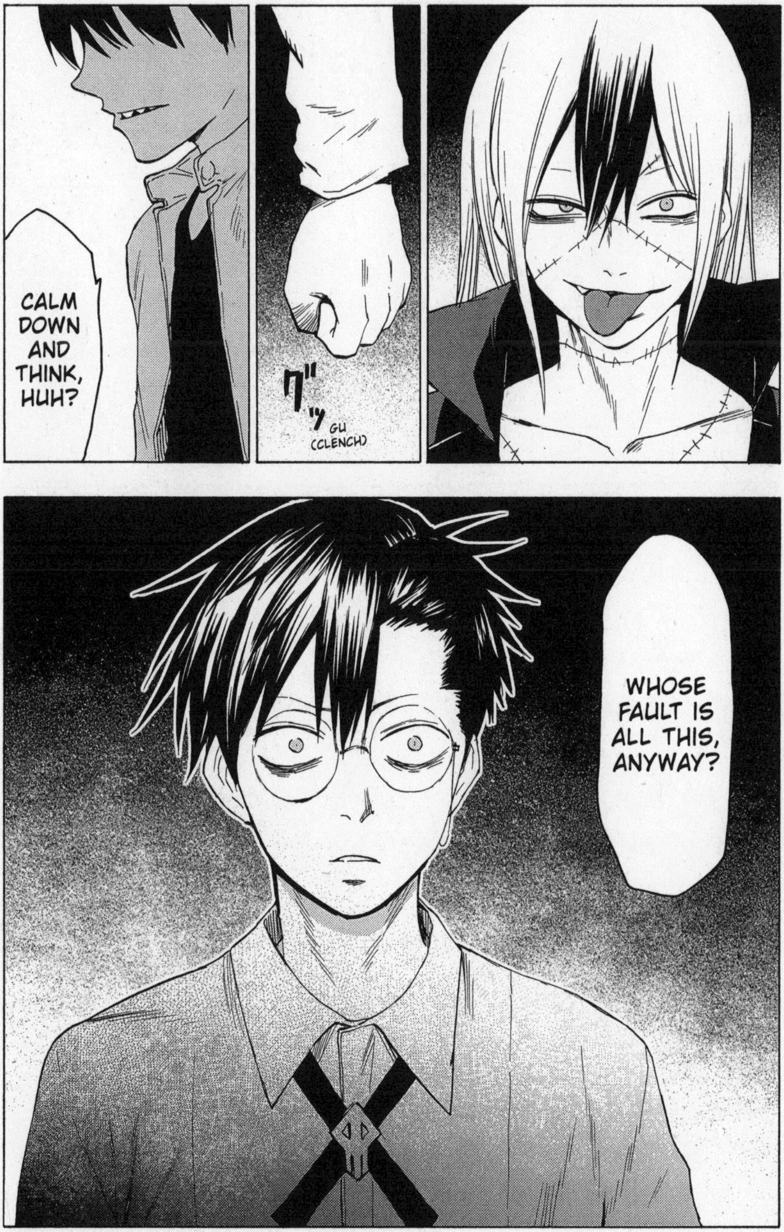
グッ
GU (CLENCH)
CALM DOWN AND THINK, HUH?
WHOSE FAULT IS ALL THIS, ANYWAY?

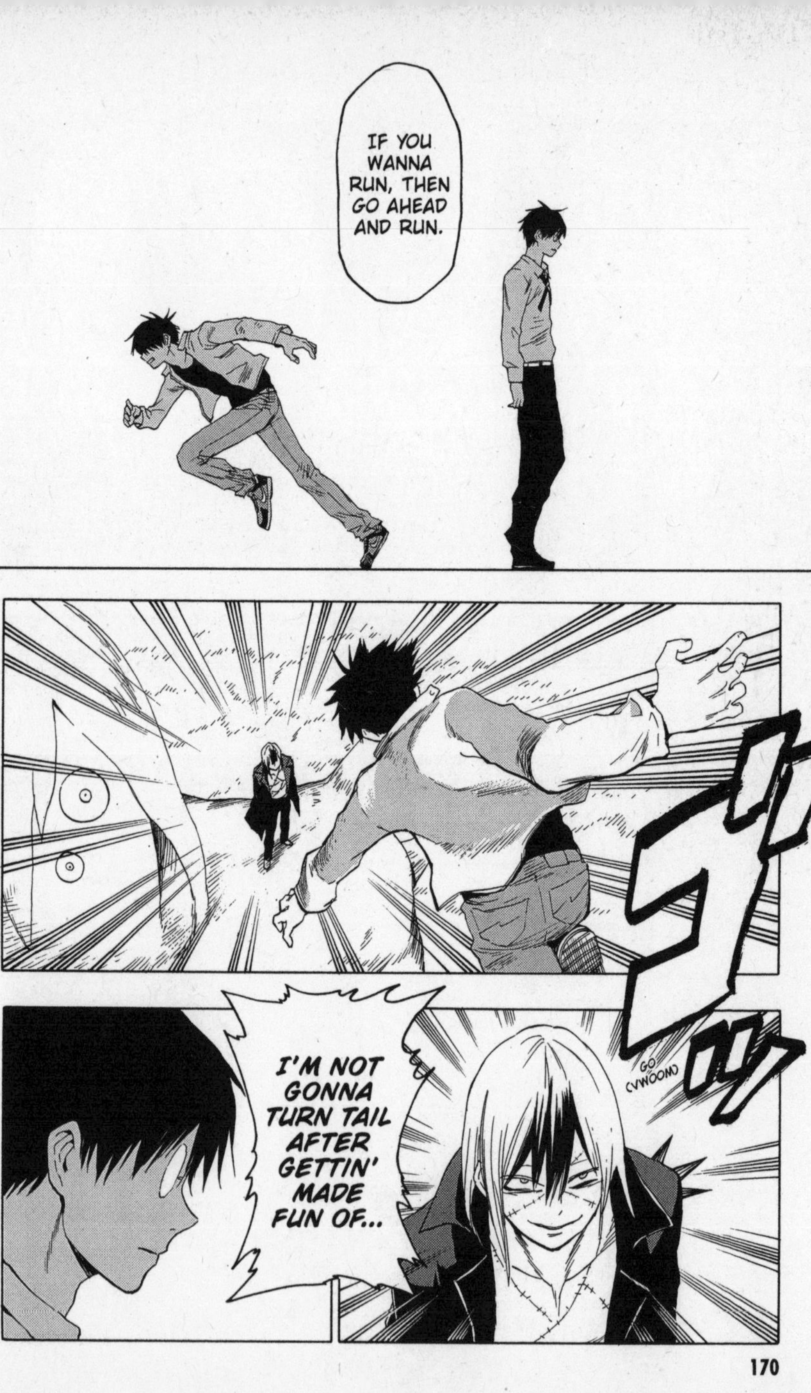
IF YOU WANNA RUN, THEN GO AHEAD AND RUN.
GO (VWOOM)
I'M NOT GONNA TURN TAIL AFTER GETTIN' MADE FUN OF...

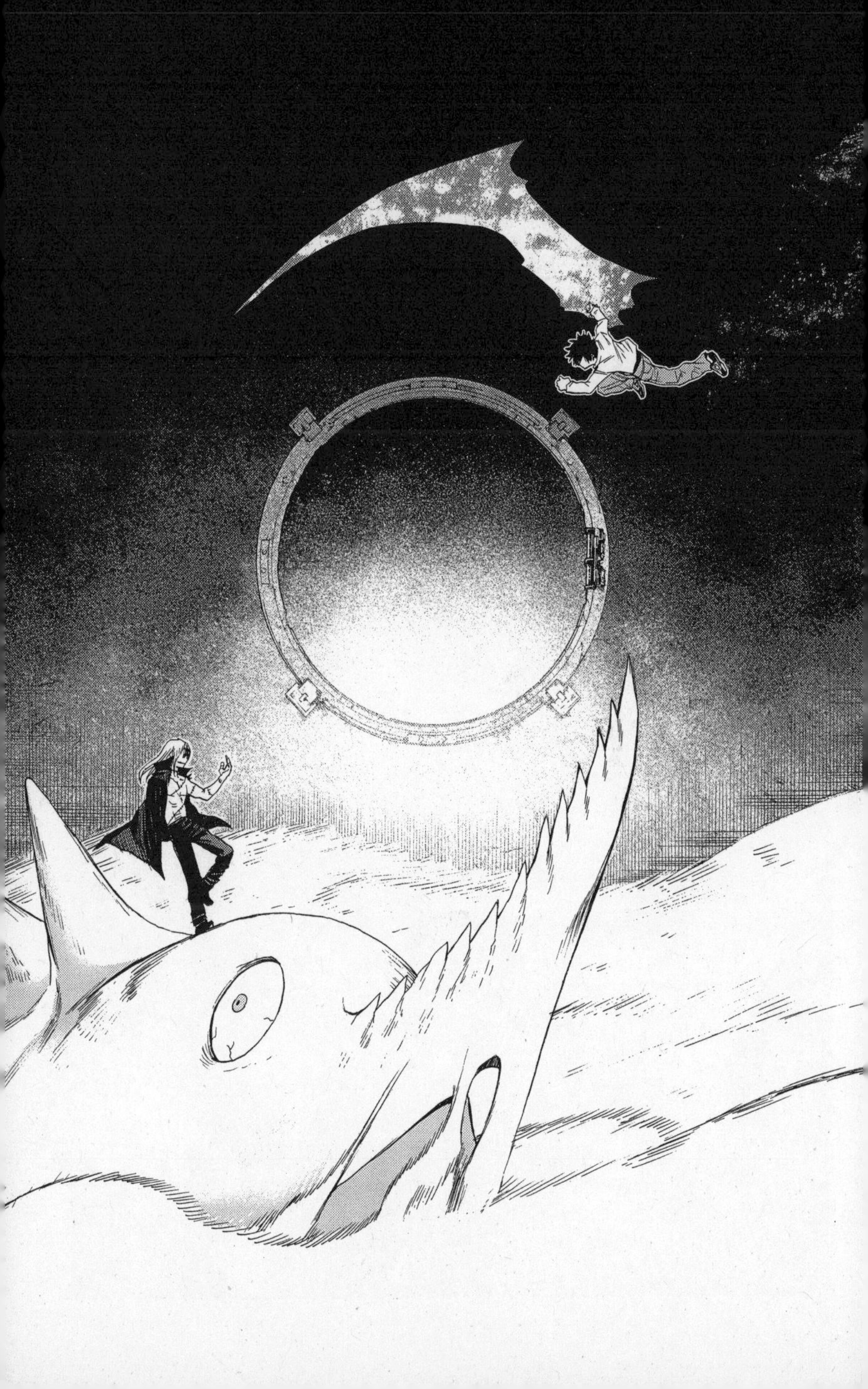

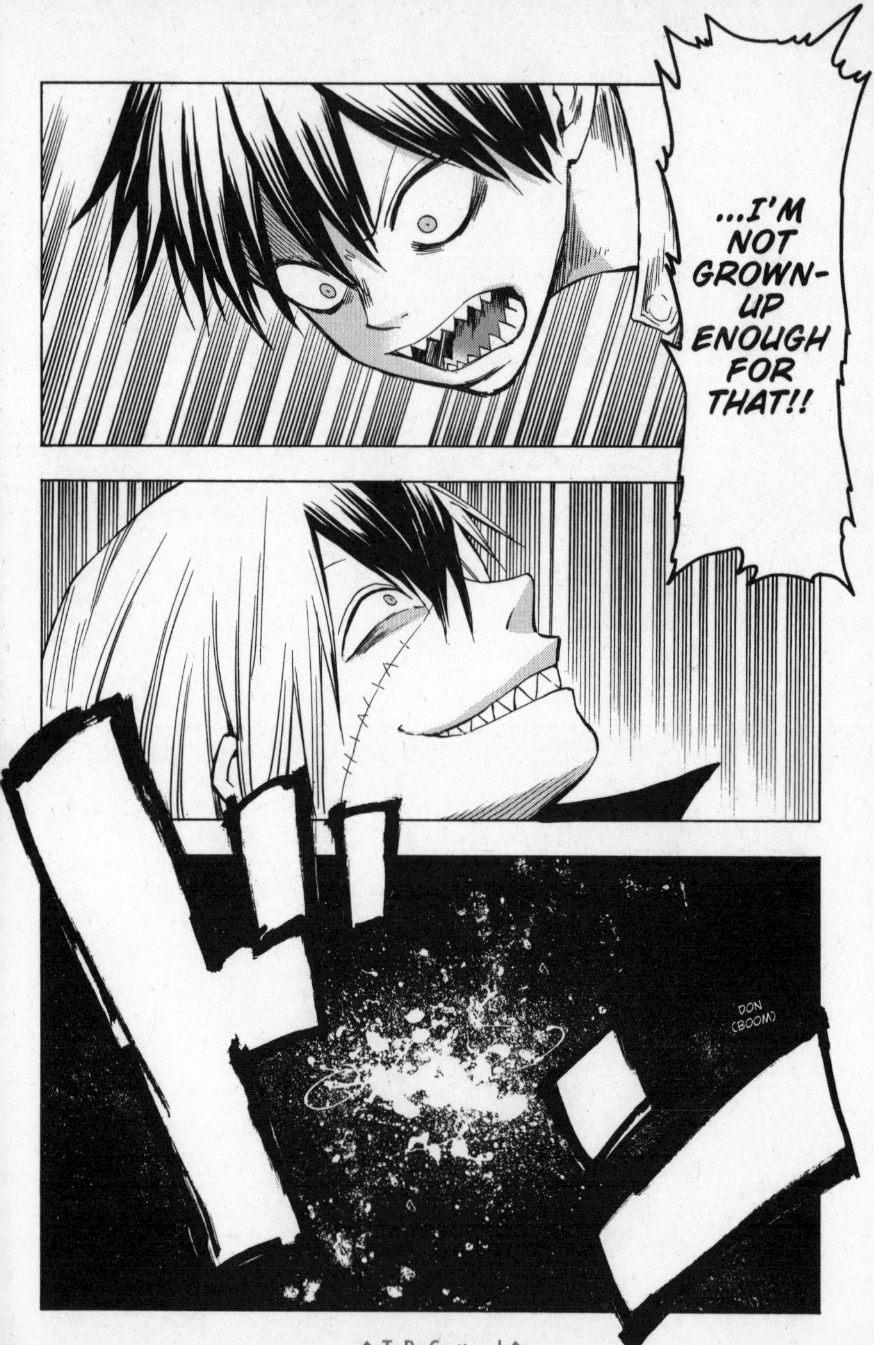
...I'M NOT GROWN-UP ENOUGH FOR THAT!!
DON (BOOM)

To Be Continued

HOO
HOO!

to be
continued

BLOOD LAD

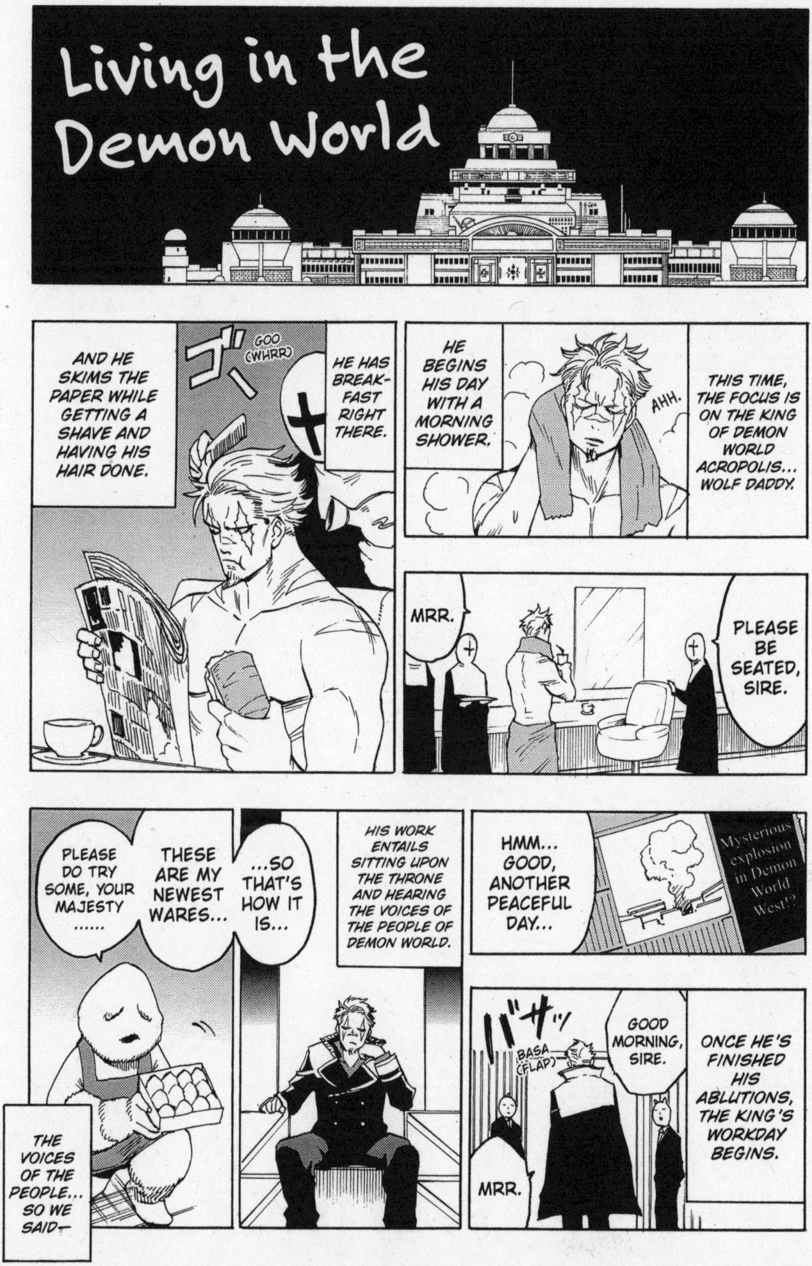
Living in the Demon World
THIS TIME, THE FOCUS IS ON THE KING OF DEMON WORLD ACROPOLIS... WOLF DADDY.
AHH.
HE BEGINS HIS DAY WITH A MORNING SHOWER.
PLEASE BE SEATED, SIRE.
MRR.
HE HAS BREAK-FAST RIGHT THERE.
GOO (WHRR)
AND HE SKIMS THE PAPER WHILE GETTING A SHAVE AND HAVING HIS HAIR DONE.
Mysterious explosion in Demon World West!?
HMM... GOOD, ANOTHER PEACEFUL DAY...
ONCE HE'S FINISHED HIS ABLUTIONS, THE KING'S WORKDAY BEGINS.
GOOD MORNING, SIRE.
BASA (FLAP)
MRR.
HIS WORK ENTAILS SITTING UPON THE THRONE AND HEARING THE VOICES OF THE PEOPLE OF DEMON WORLD.
...SO THAT'S HOW IT IS...
THESE ARE MY NEWEST WARES...
PLEASE DO TRY SOME, YOUR MAJESTY ......
THE VOICES OF THE PEOPLE... SO WE SAID—

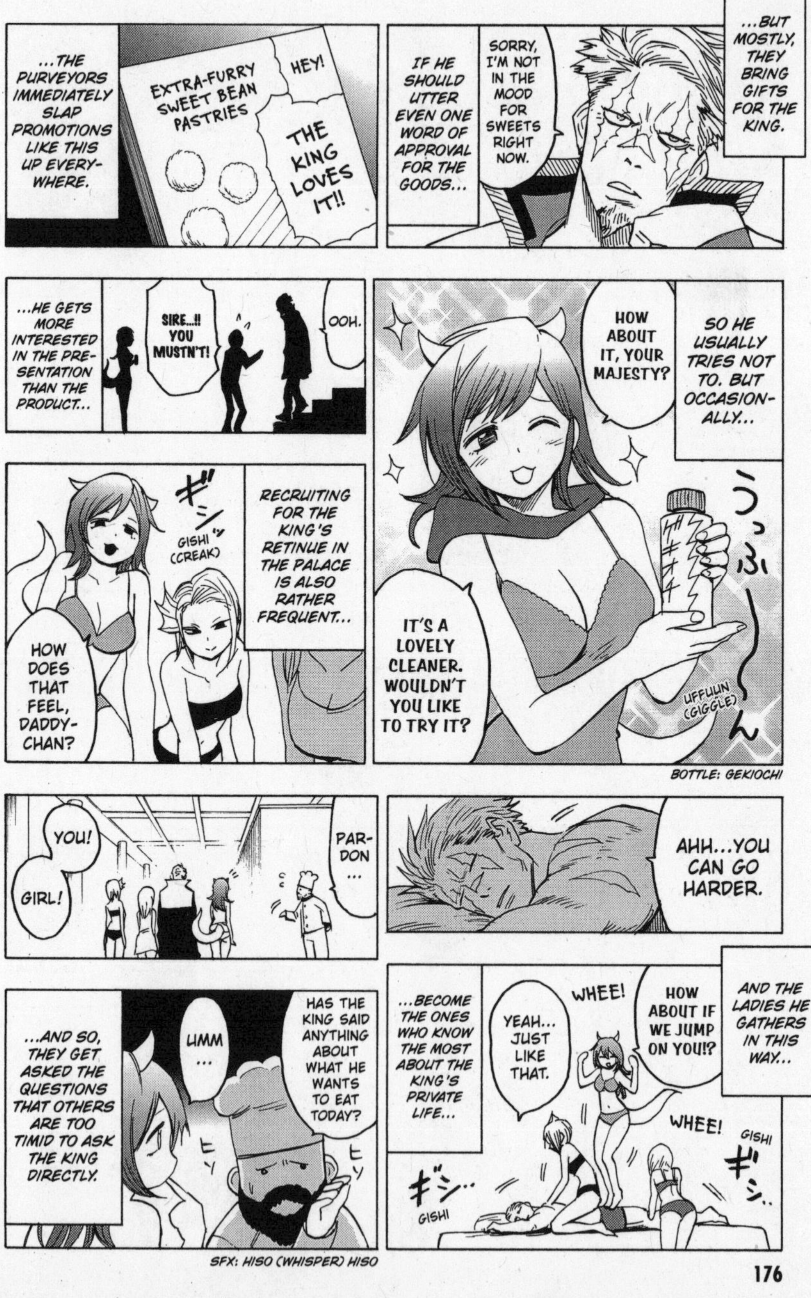
...BUT MOSTLY, THEY BRING GIFTS FOR THE KING.
SORRY, I'M NOT IN THE MOOD FOR SWEETS RIGHT NOW.
IF HE SHOULD UTTER EVEN ONE WORD OF APPROVAL FOR THE GOODS...
HEY!
EXTRA-FURRY SWEET BEAN PASTRIES
THE KING LOVES IT!!
...THE PURVEYORS IMMEDIATELY SLAP PROMOTIONS LIKE THIS UP EVERY-WHERE.
SO HE USUALLY TRIES NOT TO. BUT OCCASION-ALLY...
HOW ABOUT IT, YOUR MAJESTY?
うっふ～ん
UFFUUN (GIGGLE)
IT'S A LOVELY CLEANER. WOULDN'T YOU LIKE TO TRY IT?
OOH.
SIRE...!! YOU MUSTN'T!
...HE GETS MORE INTERESTED IN THE PRE-SENTATION THAN THE PRODUCT...
RECRUITING FOR THE KING'S RETINUE IN THE PALACE IS ALSO RATHER FREQUENT...
ギシッ
GISHI (CREAK)
HOW DOES THAT FEEL, DADDY-CHAN?
AHH...YOU CAN GO HARDER.
PAR-DON...
YOU!
GIRL!
AND THE LADIES HE GATHERS IN THIS WAY...
HOW ABOUT IF WE JUMP ON YOU!?
WHEE!
YEAH... JUST LIKE THAT.
WHEE!
GISHI
ギシ..
ギシ..
GISHI
...BECOME THE ONES WHO KNOW THE MOST ABOUT THE KING'S PRIVATE LIFE...
HAS THE KING SAID ANYTHING ABOUT WHAT HE WANTS TO EAT TODAY?
UMM...
ヒソ
ヒソ
...AND SO, THEY GET ASKED THE QUESTIONS THAT OTHERS ARE TOO TIMID TO ASK THE KING DIRECTLY.

BOTTLE: GEKIOCHI

SFX: HISO (WHISPER) HISO

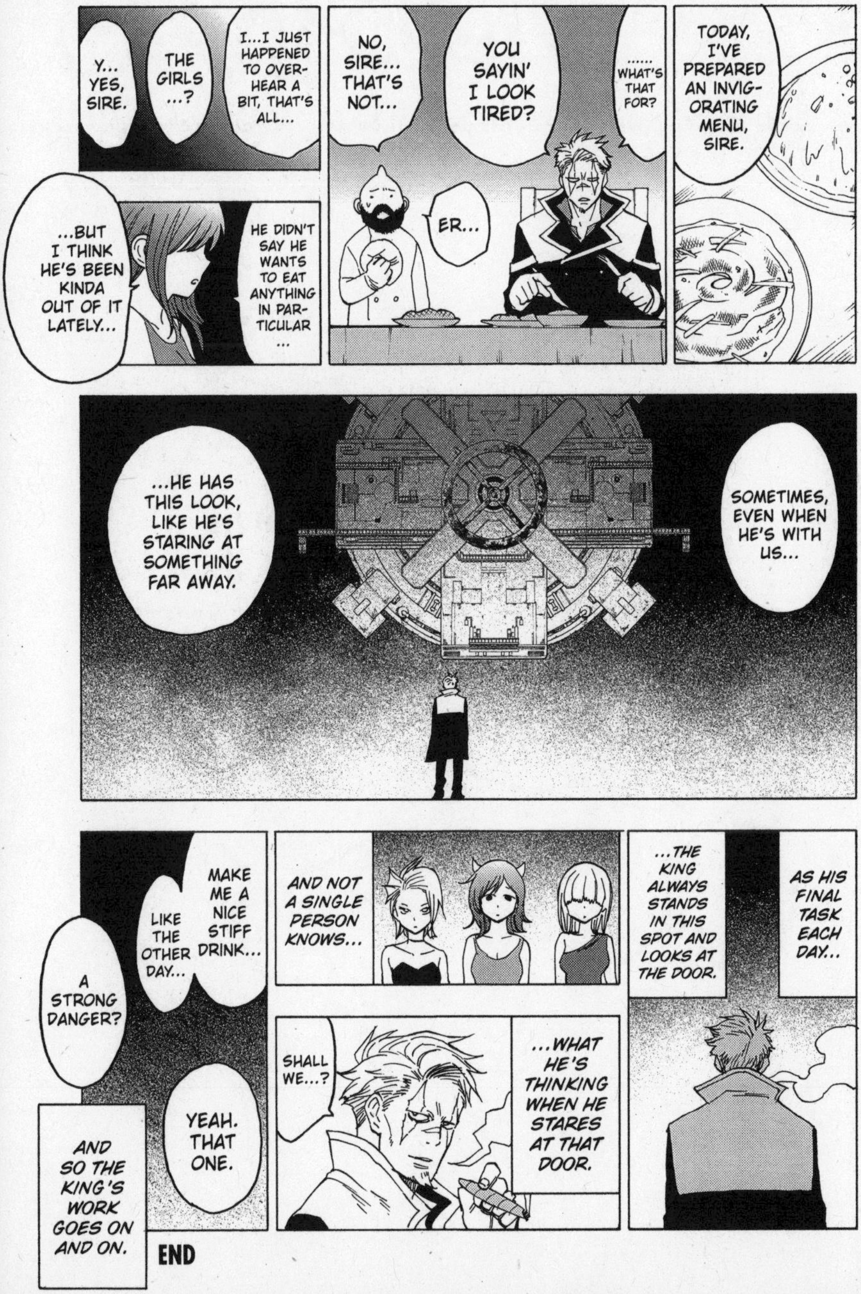
TODAY, I'VE PREPARED AN INVIGORATING MENU, SIRE.
......WHAT'S THAT FOR?
YOU SAYIN' I LOOK TIRED?
NO, SIRE... THAT'S NOT...
ER...
I...I JUST HAPPENED TO OVERHEAR A BIT, THAT'S ALL...
THE GIRLS ...?
Y... YES, SIRE.
HE DIDN'T SAY HE WANTS TO EAT ANYTHING IN PARTICULAR ...
...BUT I THINK HE'S BEEN KINDA OUT OF IT LATELY...
SOMETIMES, EVEN WHEN HE'S WITH US...
...HE HAS THIS LOOK, LIKE HE'S STARING AT SOMETHING FAR AWAY.
AS HIS FINAL TASK EACH DAY...
...THE KING ALWAYS STANDS IN THIS SPOT AND LOOKS AT THE DOOR.
AND NOT A SINGLE PERSON KNOWS...
...WHAT HE'S THINKING WHEN HE STARES AT THAT DOOR.
SHALL WE...?
MAKE ME A NICE STIFF DRINK...
LIKE THE OTHER DAY...
A STRONG DANGER?
YEAH. THAT ONE.
AND SO THE KING'S WORK GOES ON AND ON.
END

BLOOD LAD 9

These images appeared under the jacket of the original edition of *Blood Lad*!

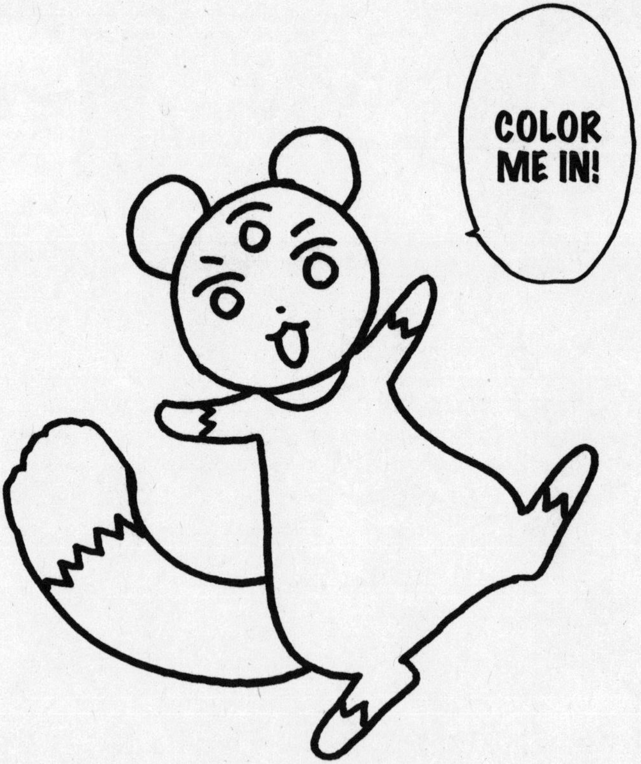
COLOR ME IN!

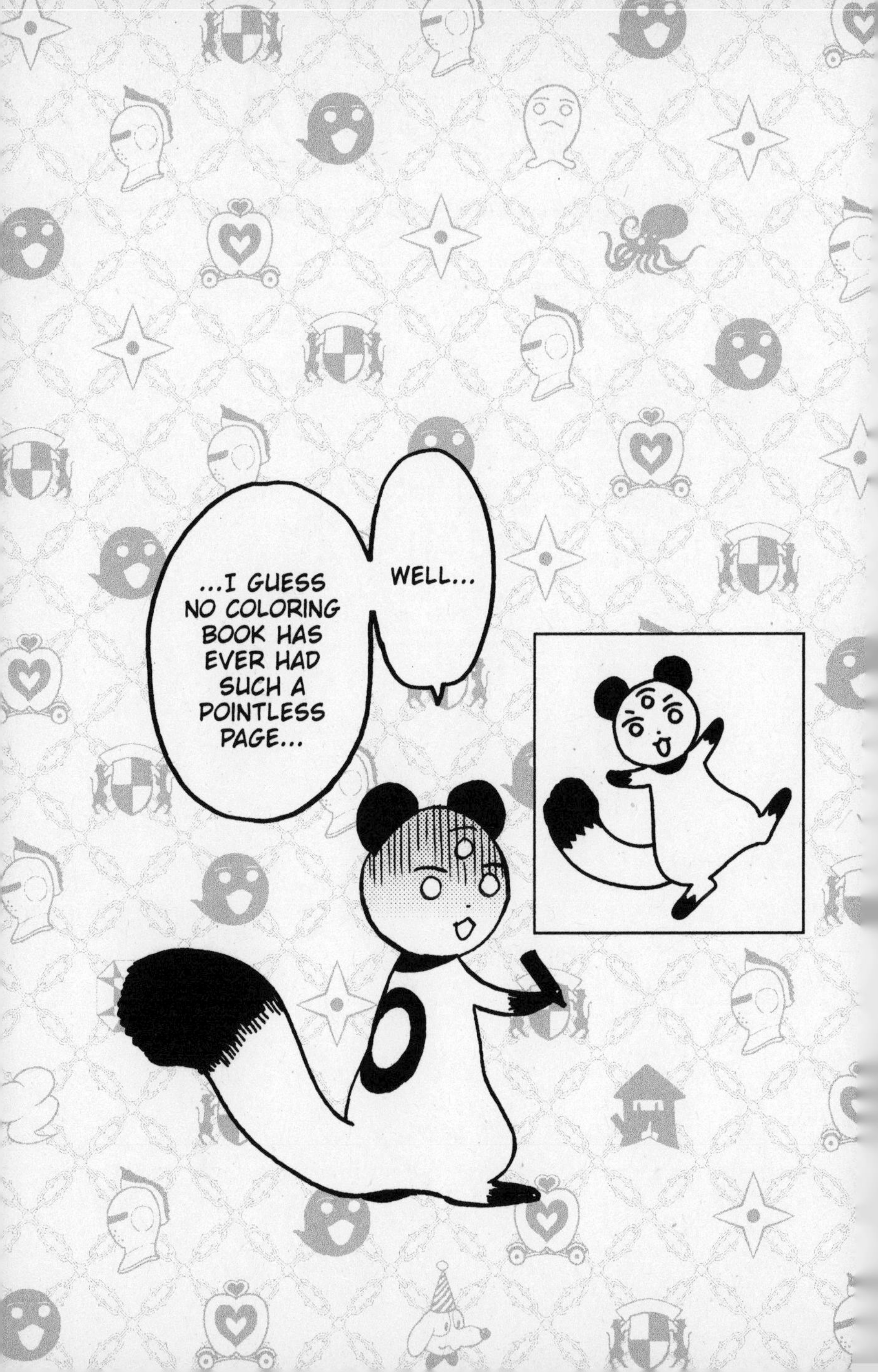
WELL...
...I GUESS NO COLORING BOOK HAS EVER HAD SUCH A POINTLESS PAGE...

BLOOD LAD

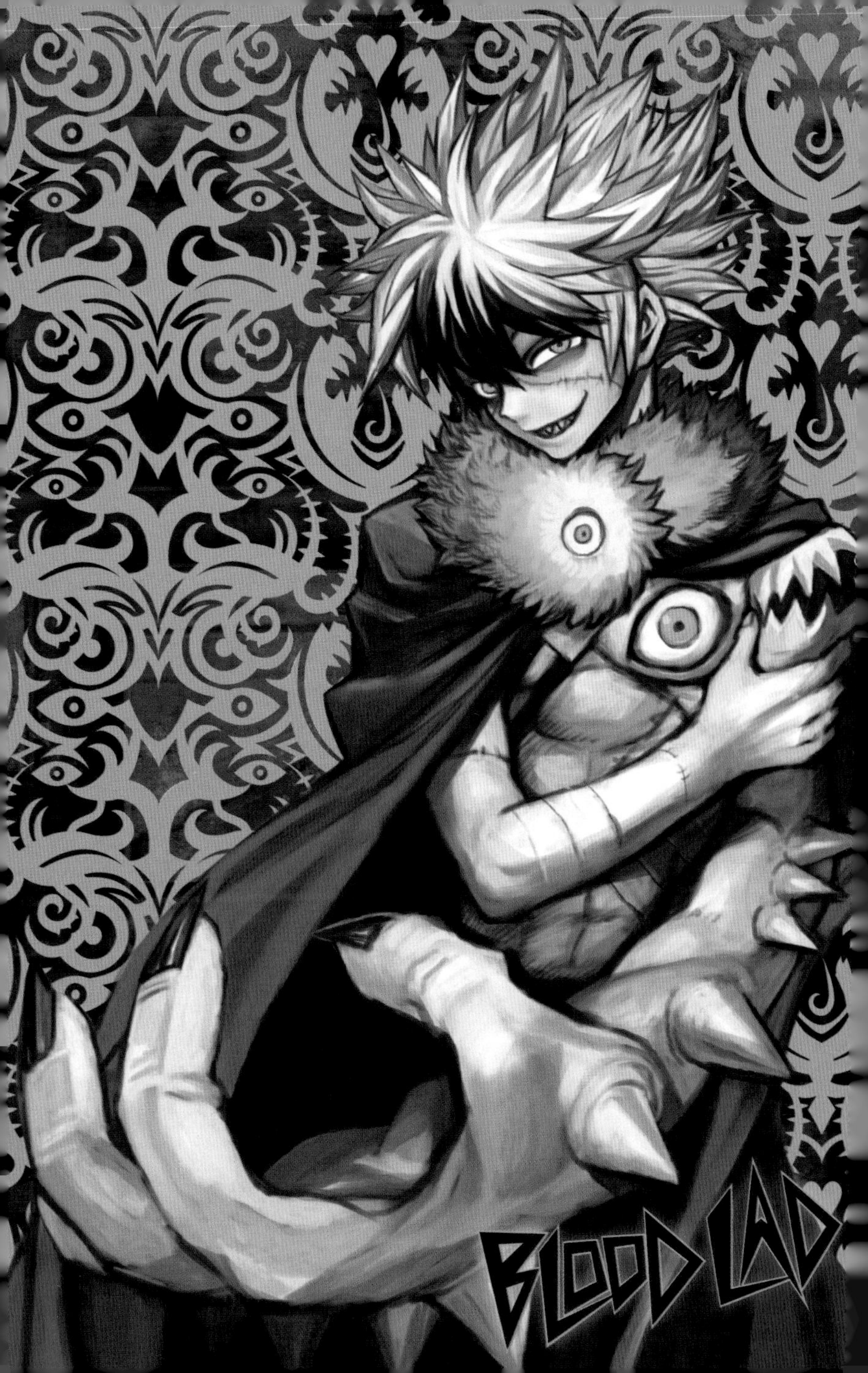
BLOOD LAD

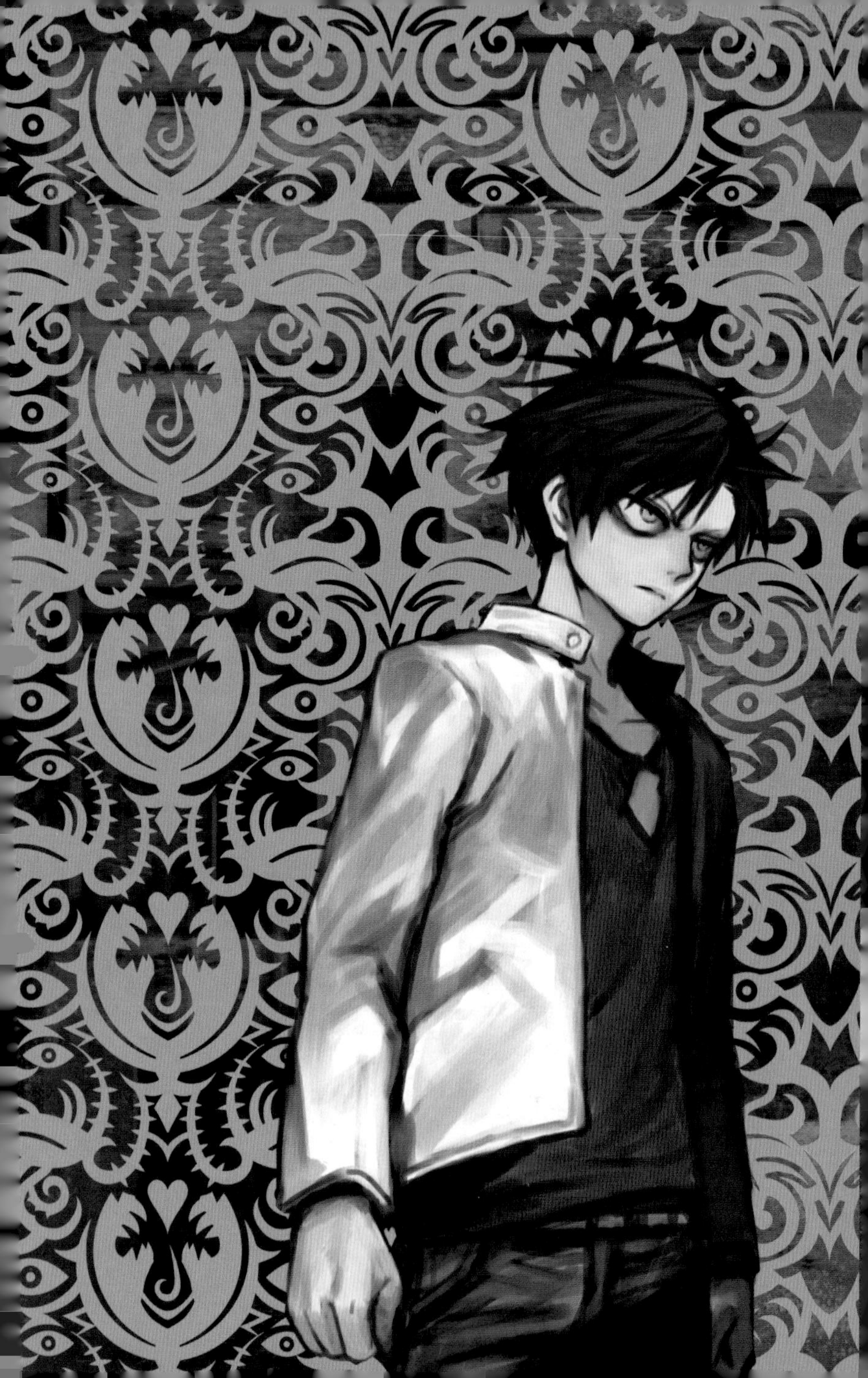

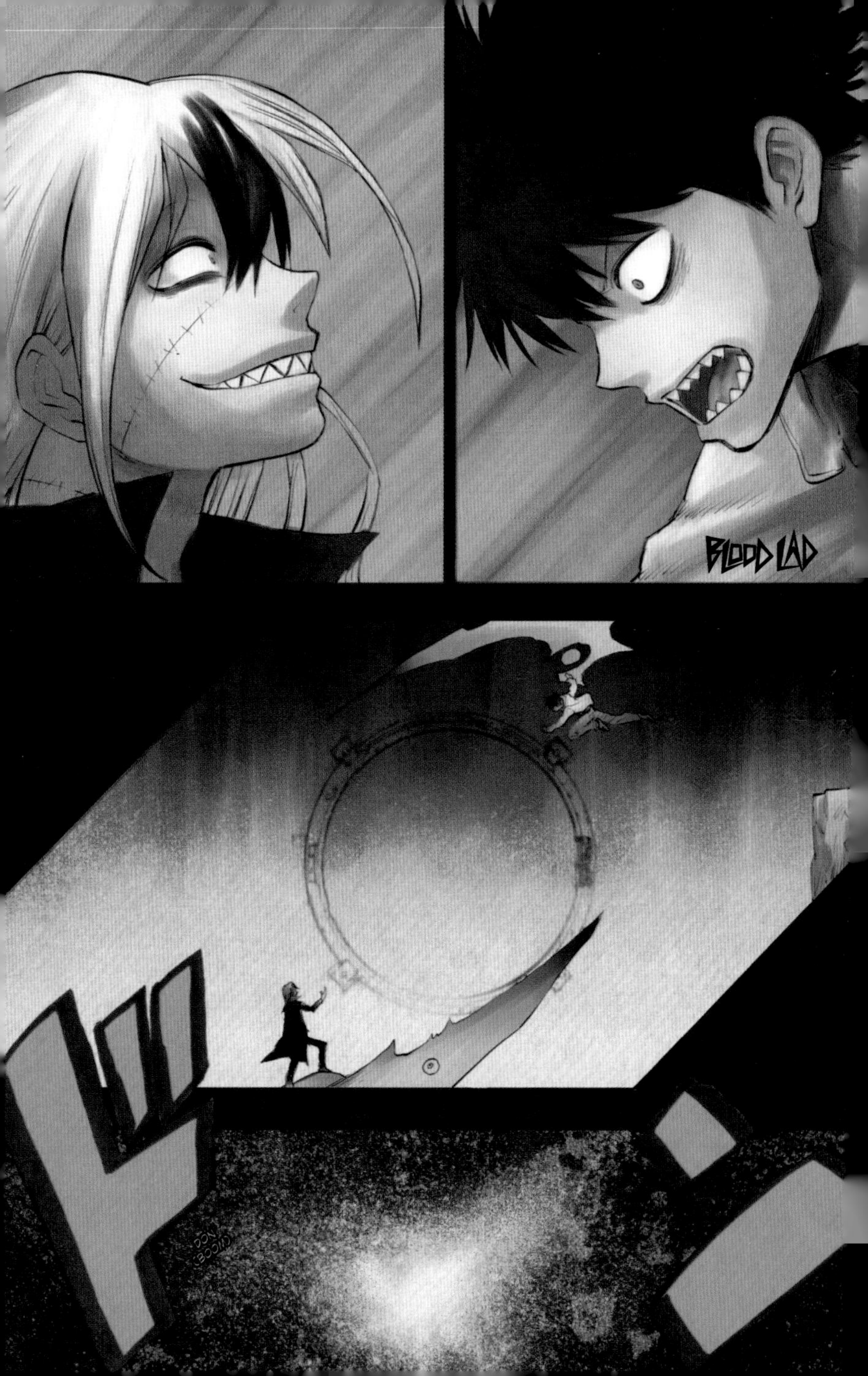
BLOOD LAD
DON
(BOOM)

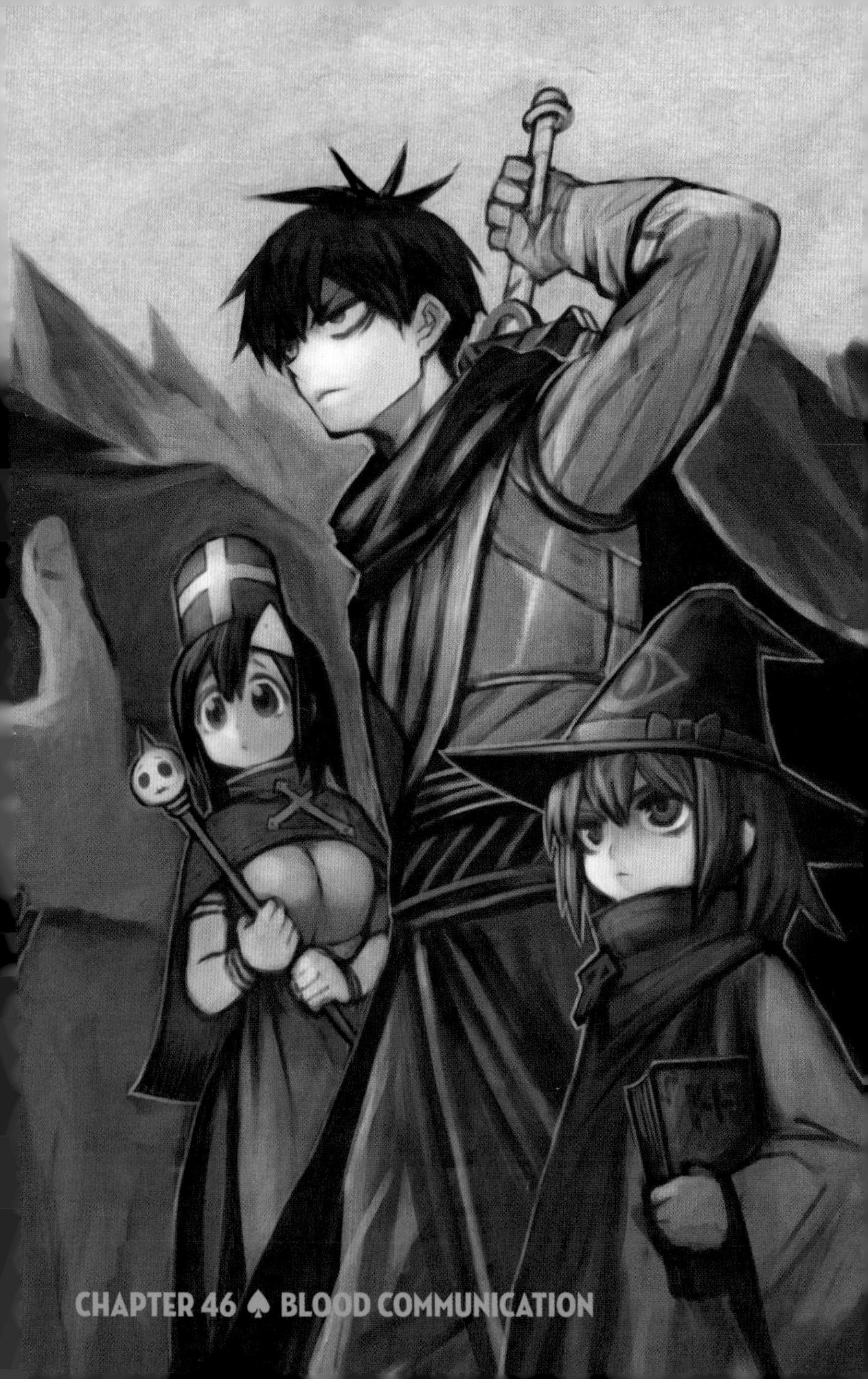

CHAPTER 46 ♠ BLOOD COMMUNICATION

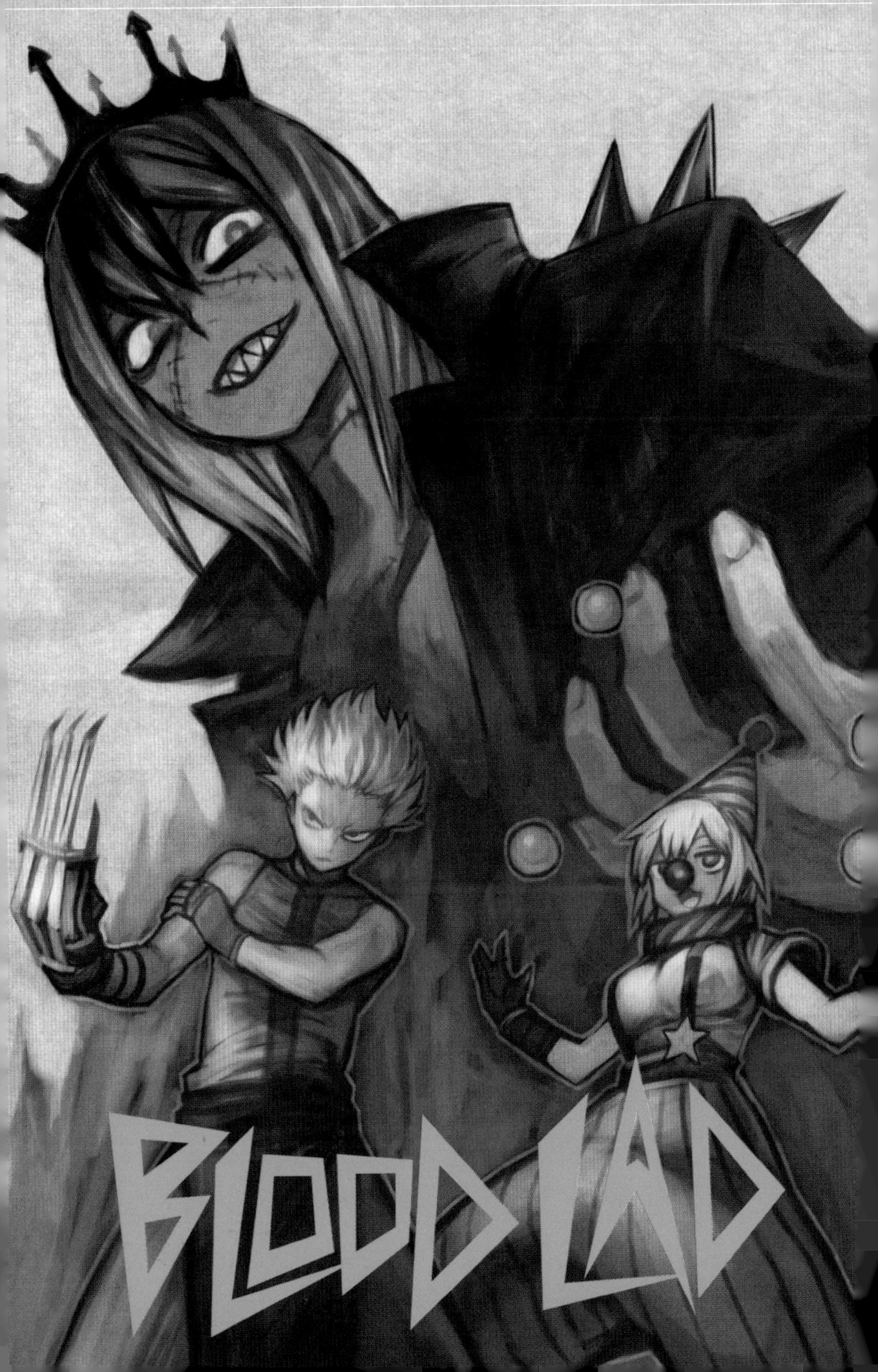
BLOOD LAD

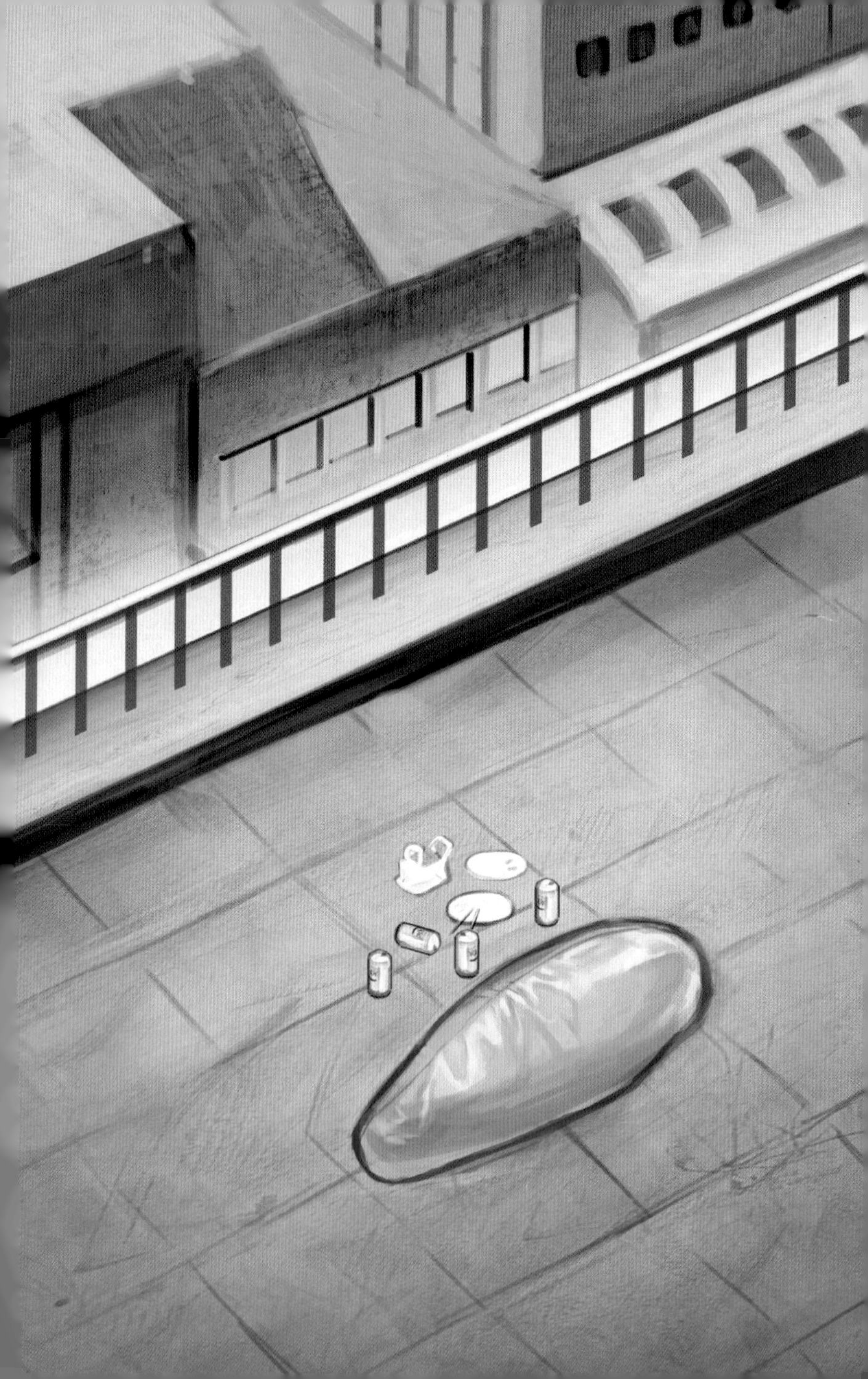

SIGN: CAFÉ THIRD EYE

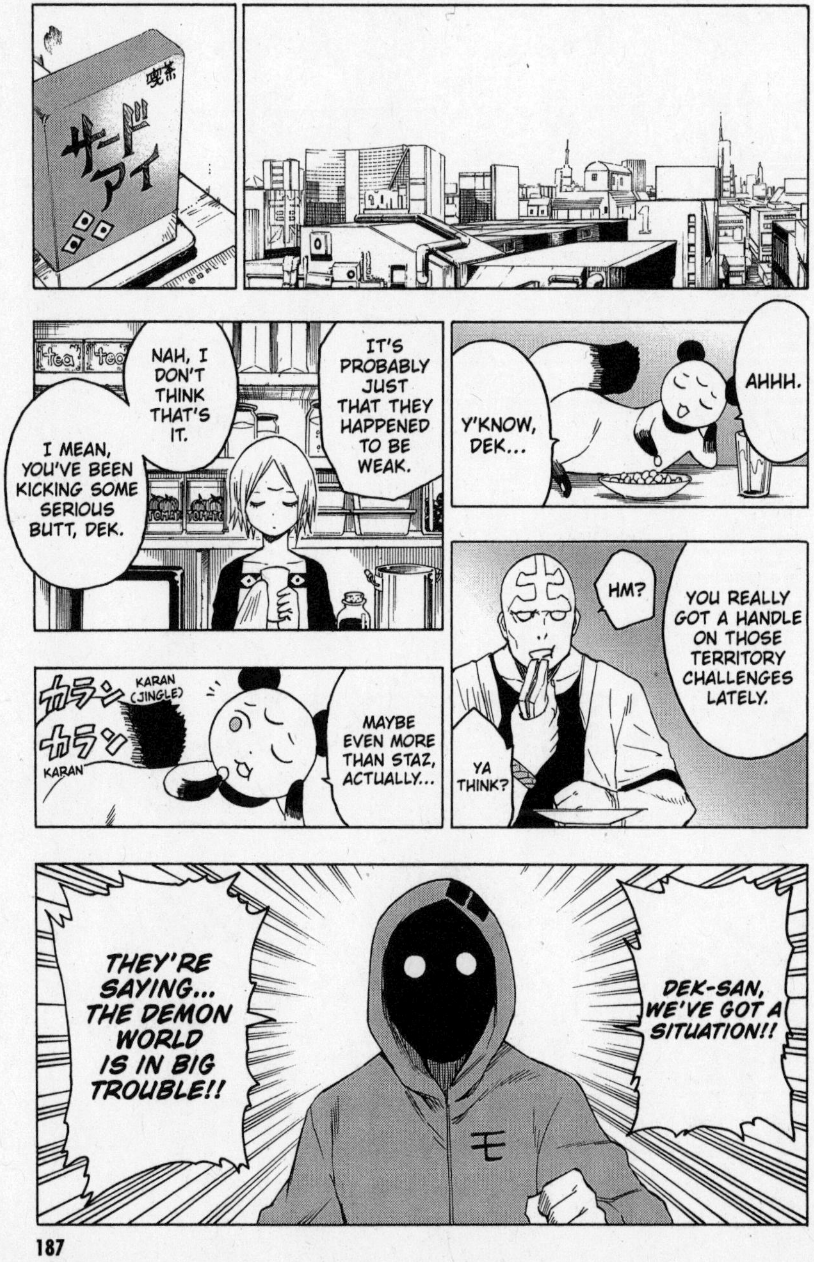
喫茶
サードアイ
AHHH.
Y'KNOW, DEK...
YOU REALLY GOT A HANDLE ON THOSE TERRITORY CHALLENGES LATELY.
HM?
YA THINK?
IT'S PROBABLY JUST THAT THEY HAPPENED TO BE WEAK.
NAH, I DON'T THINK THAT'S IT.
I MEAN, YOU'VE BEEN KICKING SOME SERIOUS BUTT, DEK.
MAYBE EVEN MORE THAN STAZ, ACTUALLY...
カラン KARAN (JINGLE)
カラン KARAN
DEK-SAN, WE'VE GOT A SITUATION!!
THEY'RE SAYING... THE DEMON WORLD IS IN BIG TROUBLE!!

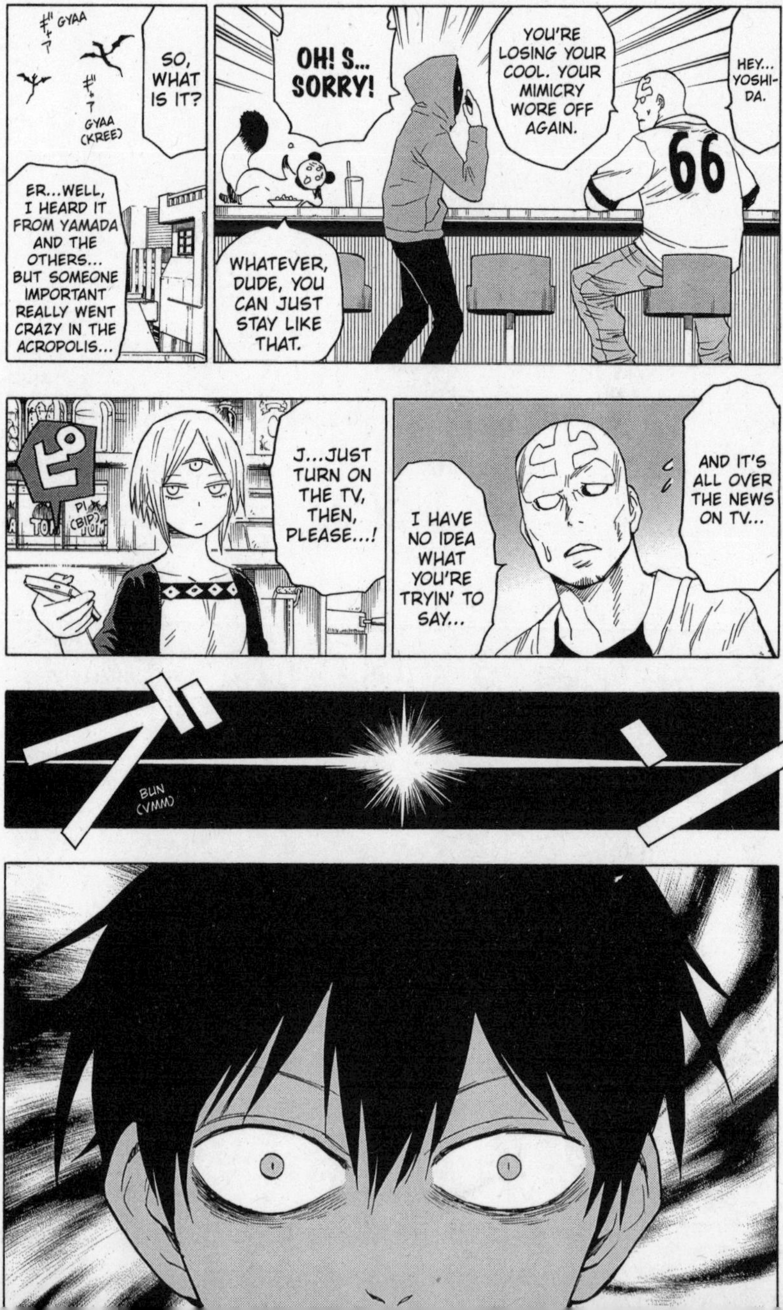
HEY... YOSHIDA.
YOU'RE LOSING YOUR COOL. YOUR MIMICRY WORE OFF AGAIN.
OH! S... SORRY!
WHATEVER, DUDE, YOU CAN JUST STAY LIKE THAT.
SO, WHAT IS IT?
GYAA
GYAA (KREE)
ER...WELL, I HEARD IT FROM YAMADA AND THE OTHERS... BUT SOMEONE IMPORTANT REALLY WENT CRAZY IN THE ACROPOLIS...
AND IT'S ALL OVER THE NEWS ON TV...
I HAVE NO IDEA WHAT YOU'RE TRYIN' TO SAY...
J...JUST TURN ON THE TV, THEN, PLEASE...!
PI (BIP)
BUN (VMM)

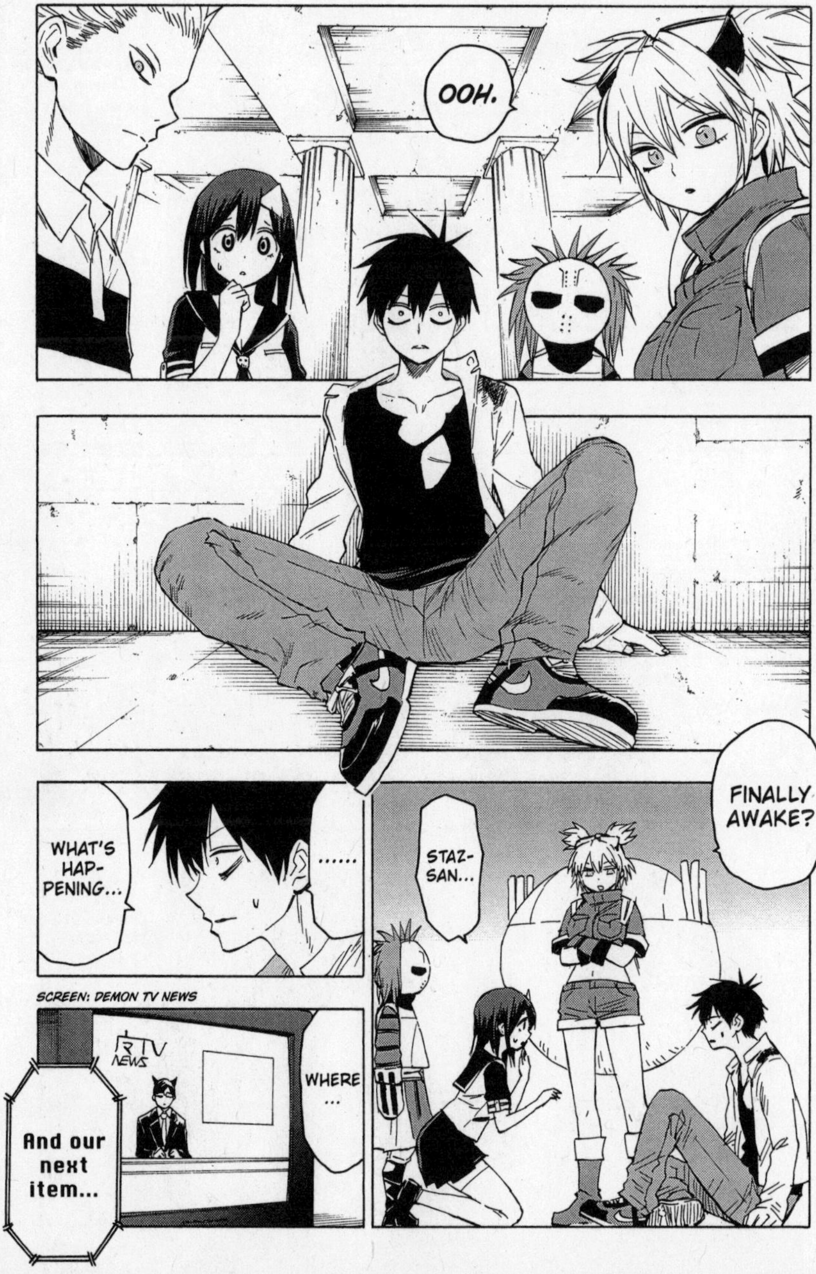
OOH.
FINALLY AWAKE?
STAZ-SAN...
WHERE ...
......
WHAT'S HAP-PENING...
SCREEN: DEMON TV NEWS
NEWS
And our next item...

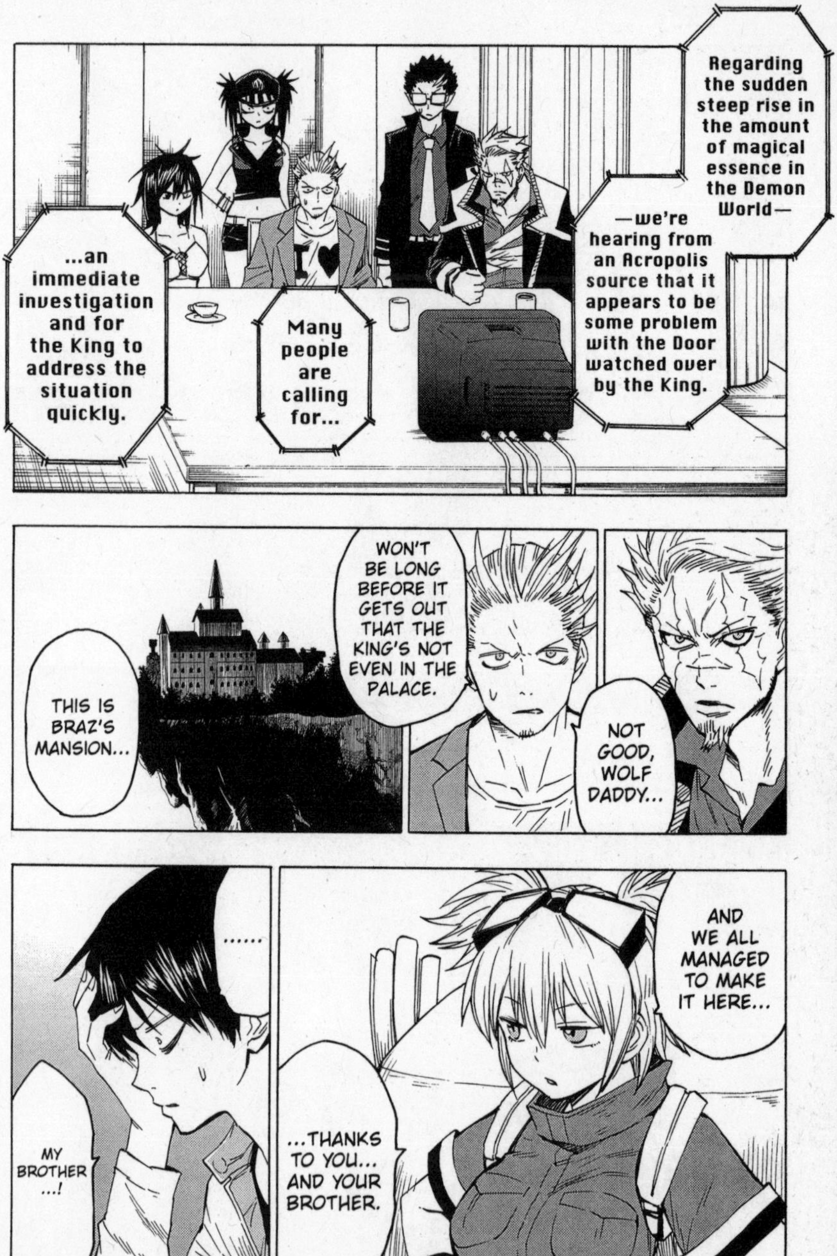
Regarding the sudden steep rise in the amount of magical essence in the Demon World—
—we're hearing from an Acropolis source that it appears to be some problem with the Door watched over by the King.
Many people are calling for...
...an immediate investigation and for the King to address the situation quickly.
WON'T BE LONG BEFORE IT GETS OUT THAT THE KING'S NOT EVEN IN THE PALACE.
NOT GOOD, WOLF DADDY...
THIS IS BRAZ'S MANSION...
AND WE ALL MANAGED TO MAKE IT HERE...
...THANKS TO YOU... AND YOUR BROTHER.
......
MY BROTHER ...!

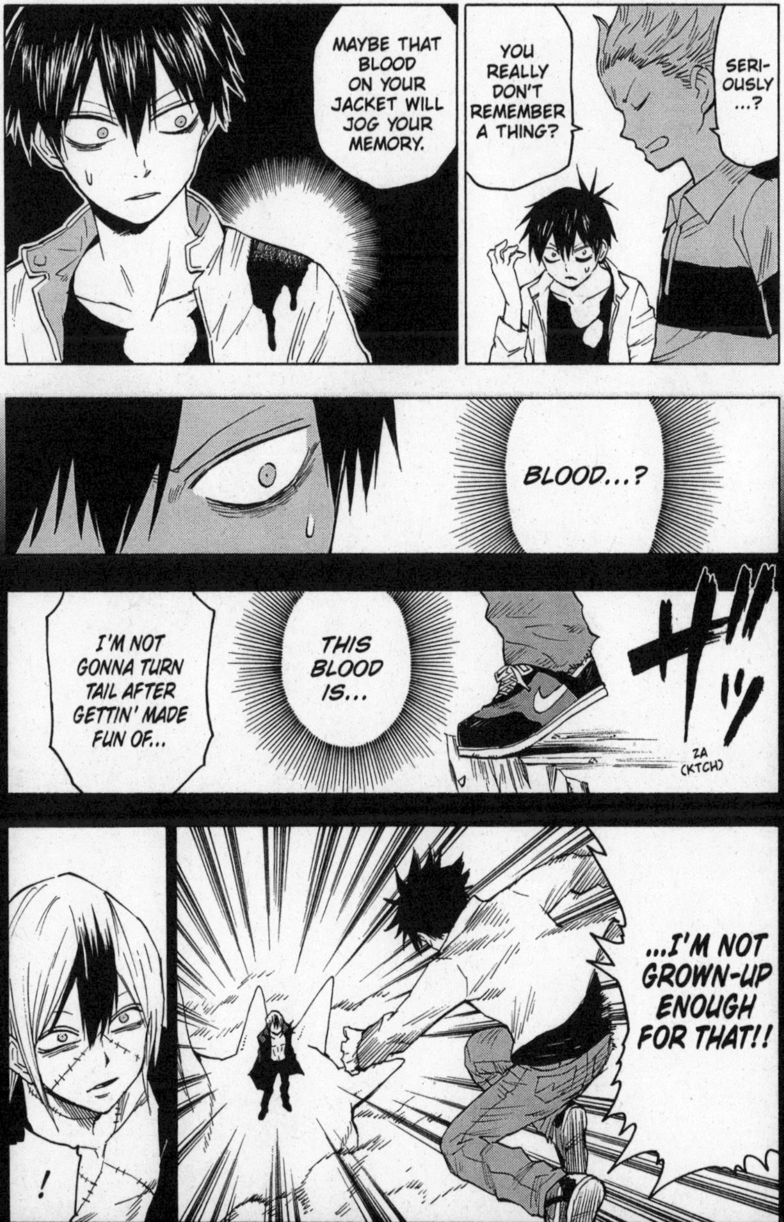
SERI-OUSLY...?
YOU REALLY DON'T REMEMBER A THING?
MAYBE THAT BLOOD ON YOUR JACKET WILL JOG YOUR MEMORY.
BLOOD...?
ザッ
ZA (KTCH)
THIS BLOOD IS...
I'M NOT GONNA TURN TAIL AFTER GETTIN' MADE FUN OF...
...I'M NOT GROWN-UP ENOUGH FOR THAT!!
!

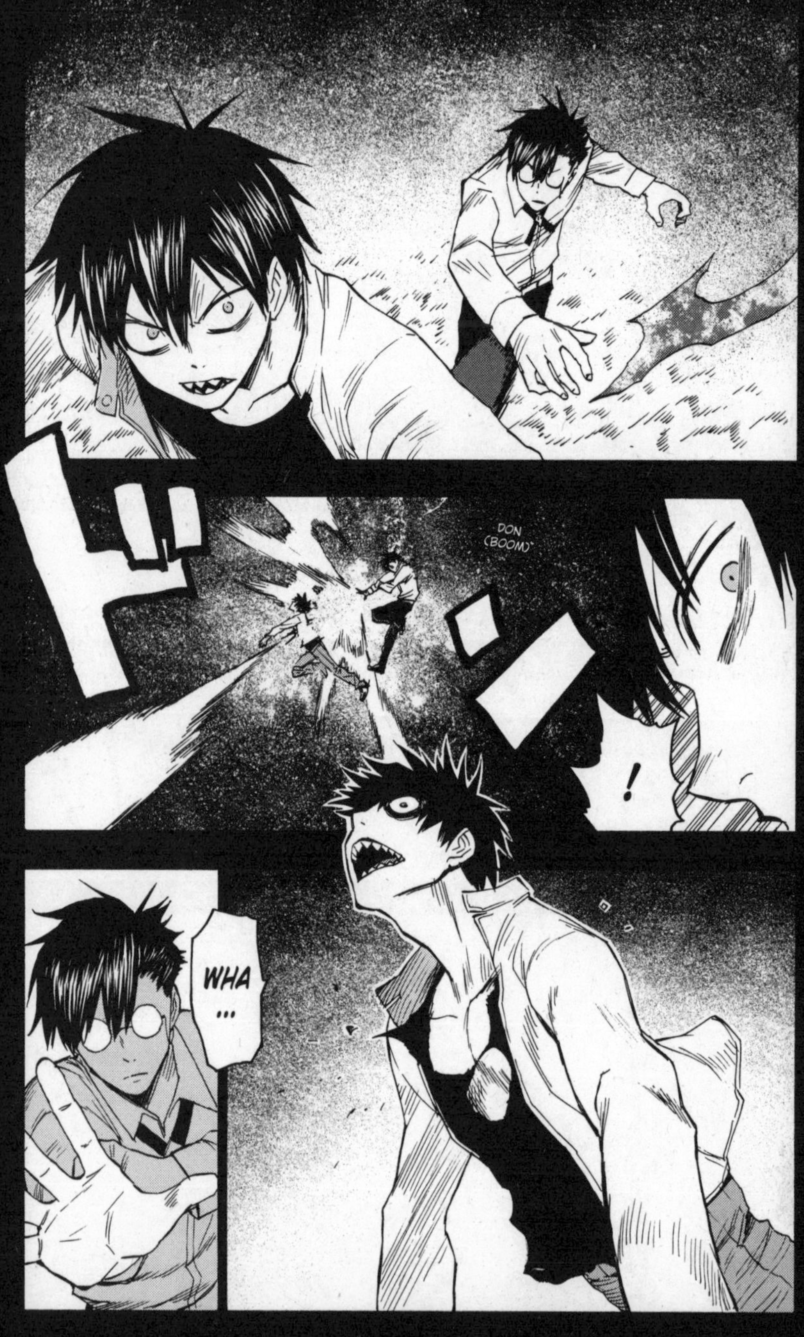
DON (BOOM)
!
WHA ...

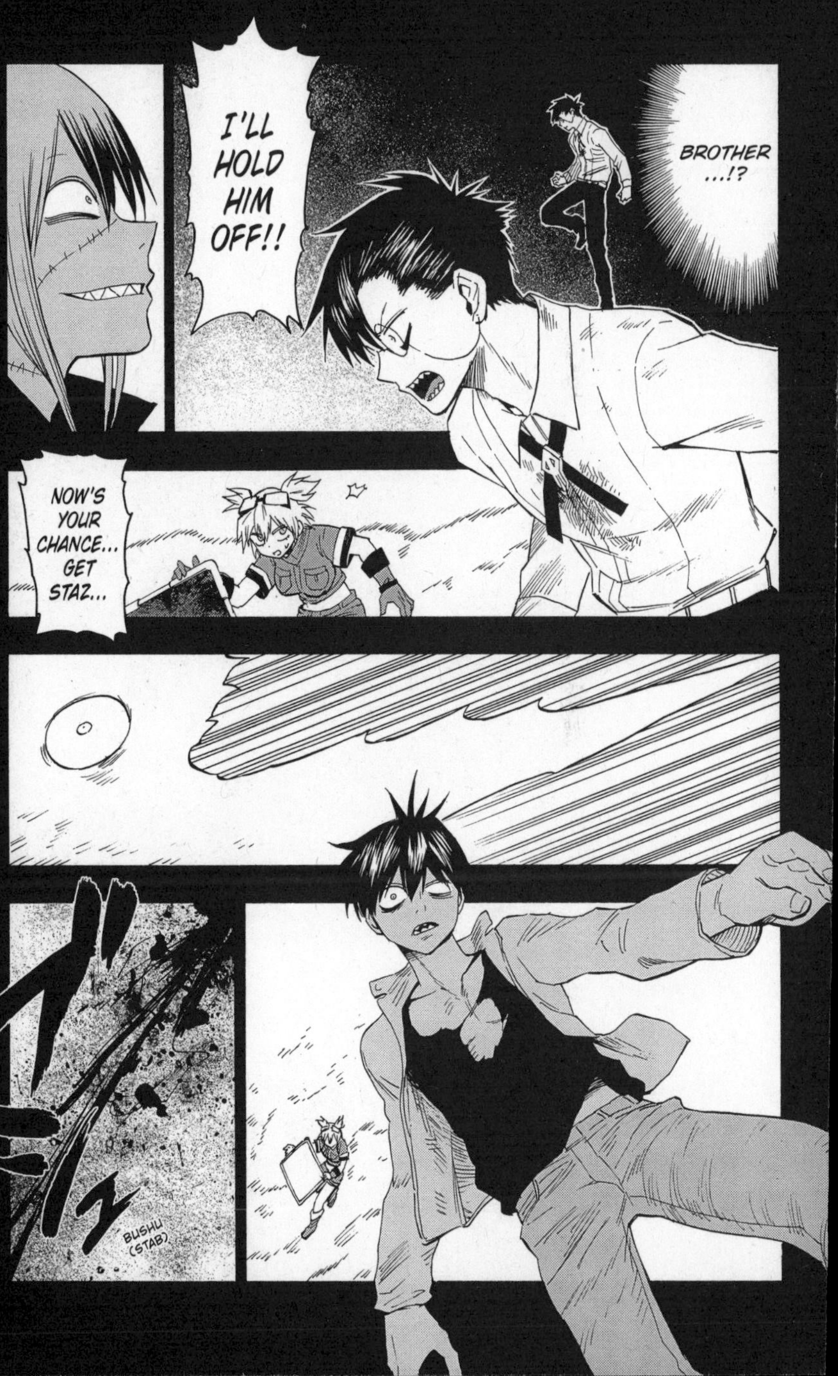
BROTHER ...!?
I'LL HOLD HIM OFF!!
NOW'S YOUR CHANCE... GET STAZ...
BUSHU (STAB)

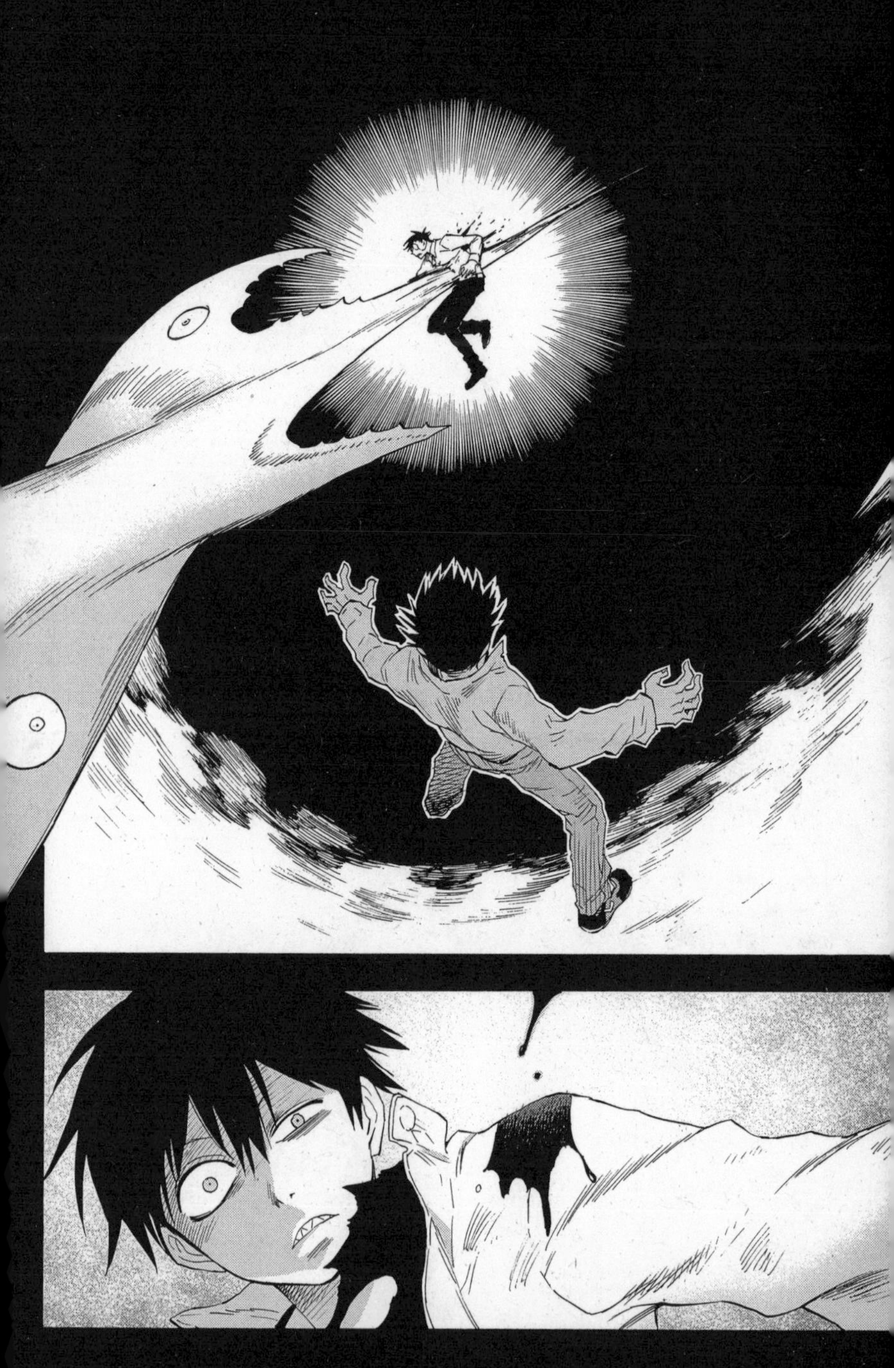

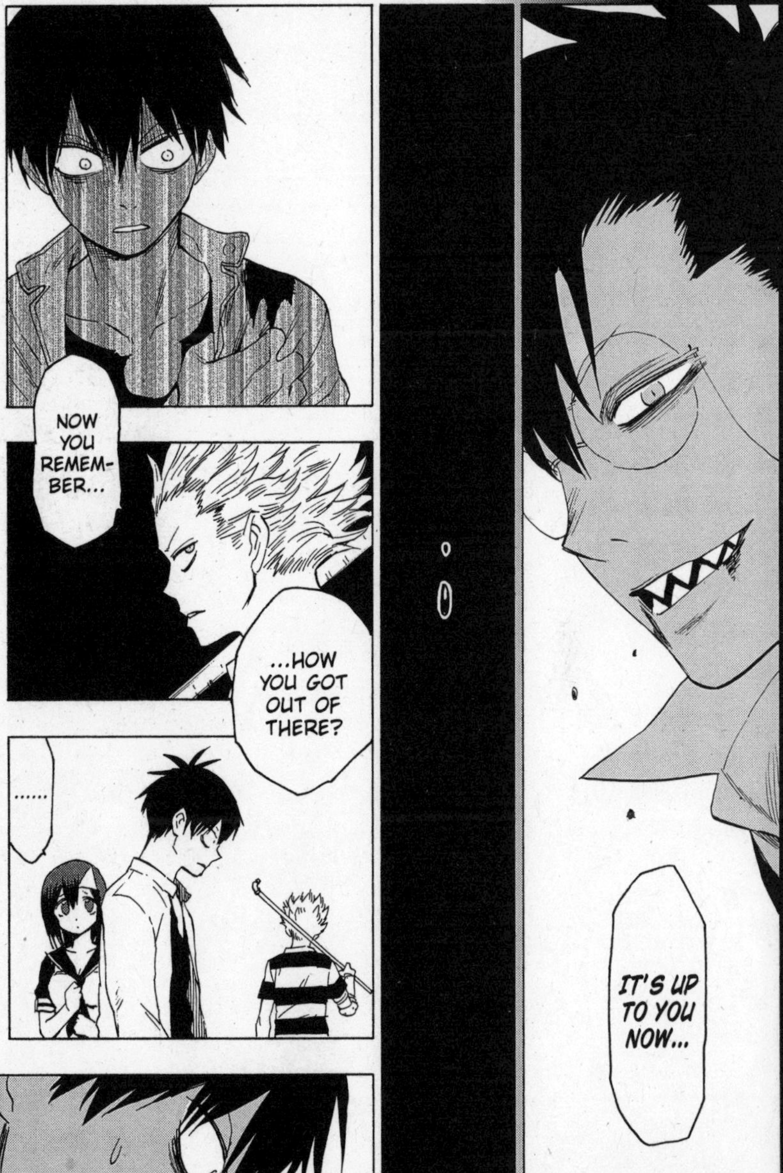
IT'S UP TO YOU NOW...
NOW YOU REMEMBER...
...HOW YOU GOT OUT OF THERE?
......

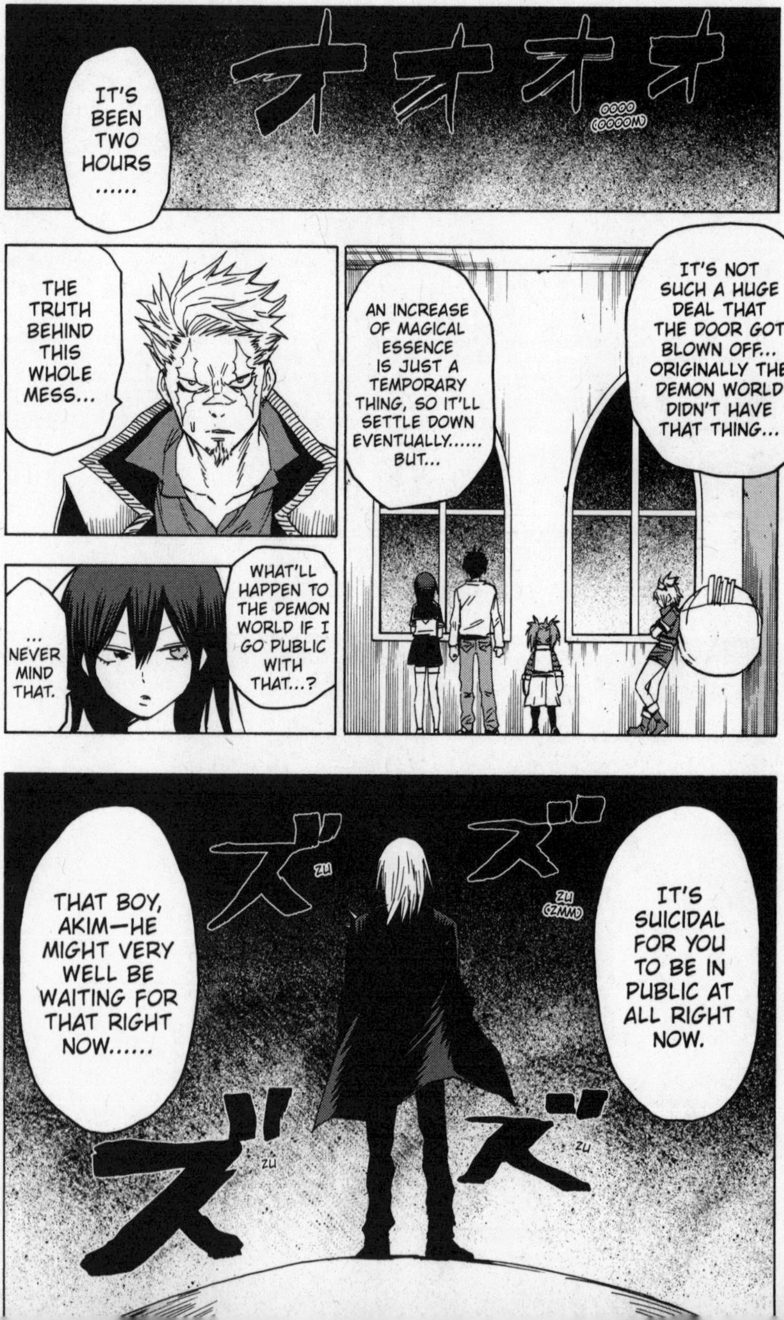
OOOO (OOOOM)
IT'S BEEN TWO HOURS ......
IT'S NOT SUCH A HUGE DEAL THAT THE DOOR GOT BLOWN OFF... ORIGINALLY THE DEMON WORLD DIDN'T HAVE THAT THING...
AN INCREASE OF MAGICAL ESSENCE IS JUST A TEMPORARY THING, SO IT'LL SETTLE DOWN EVENTUALLY...... BUT...
THE TRUTH BEHIND THIS WHOLE MESS...
WHAT'LL HAPPEN TO THE DEMON WORLD IF I GO PUBLIC WITH THAT...?
... NEVER MIND THAT.
IT'S SUICIDAL FOR YOU TO BE IN PUBLIC AT ALL RIGHT NOW.
ZU (ZMM)
ZU
THAT BOY, AKIM—HE MIGHT VERY WELL BE WAITING FOR THAT RIGHT NOW......
ZU
ZU

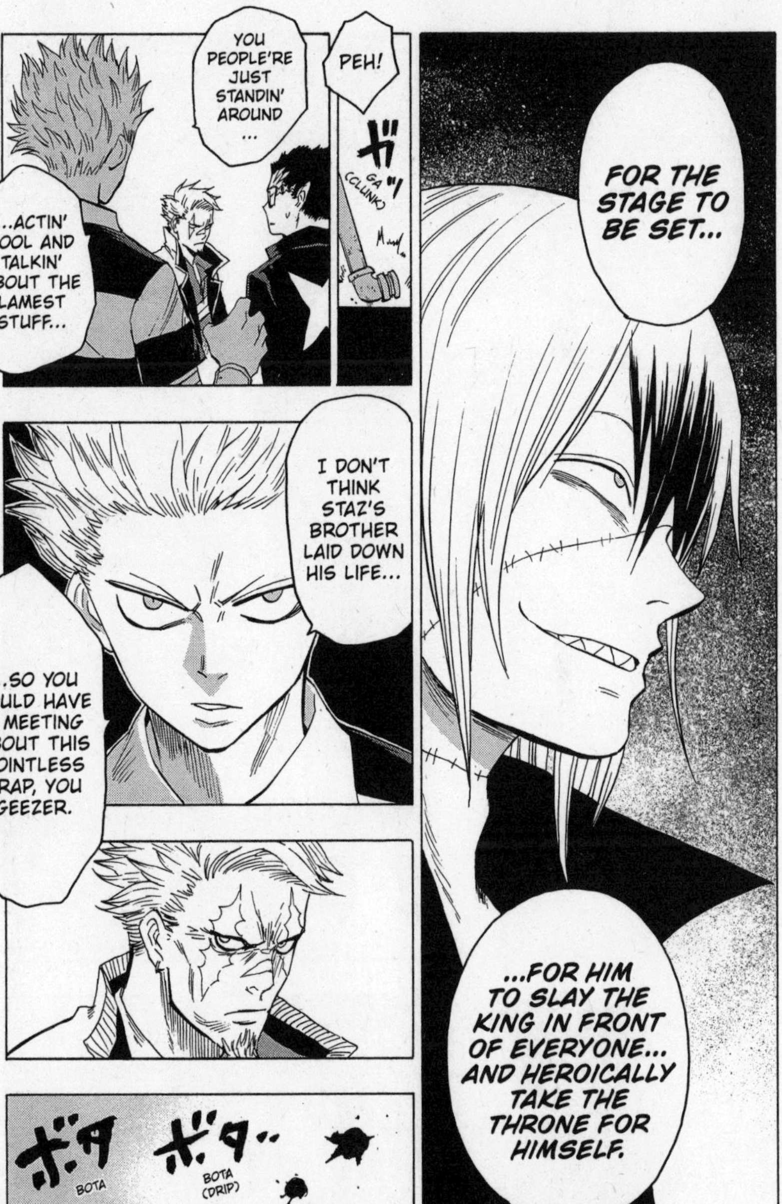
FOR THE STAGE TO BE SET...
...FOR HIM TO SLAY THE KING IN FRONT OF EVERYONE... AND HEROICALLY TAKE THE THRONE FOR HIMSELF.
PEH!
ガッ
GA (CLUNK)
YOU PEOPLE'RE JUST STANDIN' AROUND ...
...ACTIN' COOL AND TALKIN' ABOUT THE LAMEST STUFF...
I DON'T THINK STAZ'S BROTHER LAID DOWN HIS LIFE...
...SO YOU COULD HAVE A MEETING ABOUT THIS POINTLESS CRAP, YOU GEEZER.
ボタ
BOTA
ボタ
BOTA (DRIP)

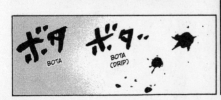

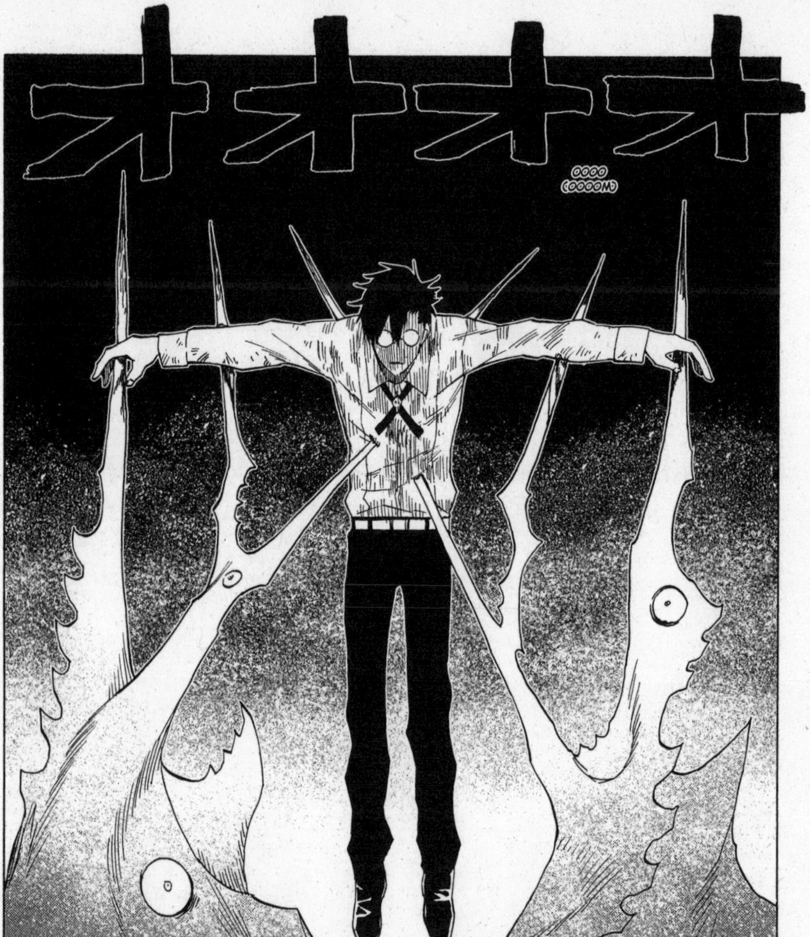
オオオオ
OOOO
(OOOON)

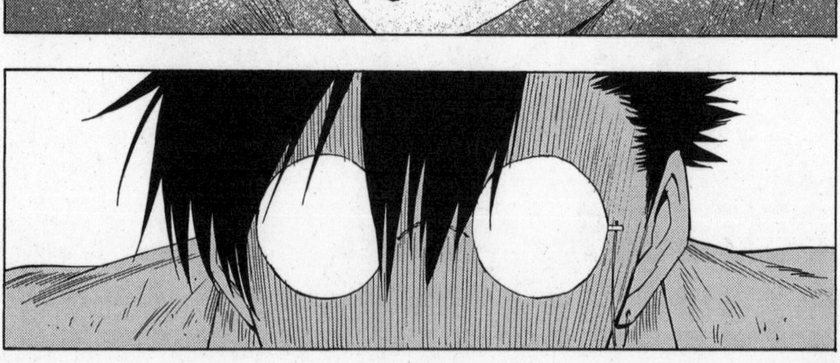

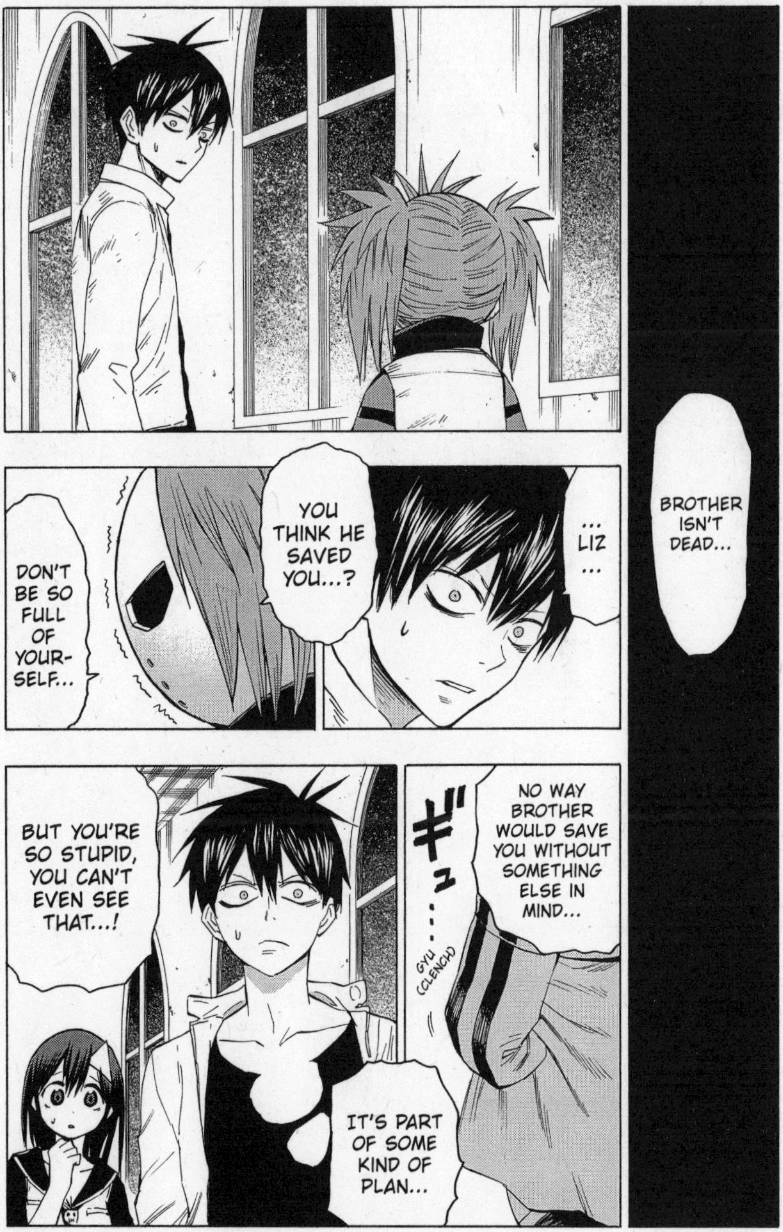
BROTHER ISN'T DEAD...
... LIZ ...
YOU THINK HE SAVED YOU...?
DON'T BE SO FULL OF YOURSELF...
NO WAY BROTHER WOULD SAVE YOU WITHOUT SOMETHING ELSE IN MIND...
ギュ...
GYU (CLENCH)
IT'S PART OF SOME KIND OF PLAN...
BUT YOU'RE SO STUPID, YOU CAN'T EVEN SEE THAT...!

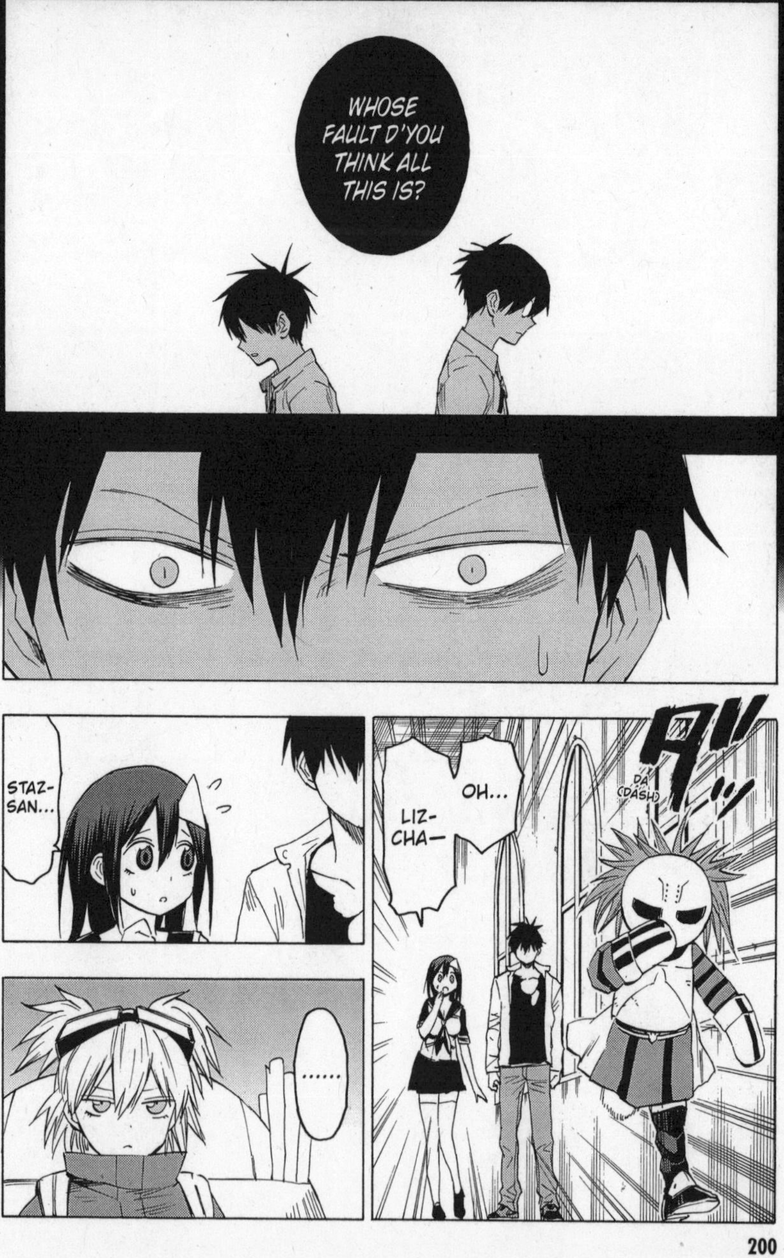
WHOSE FAULT D'YOU THINK ALL THIS IS?
DA (DASH)
OH... LIZ-CHA—
STAZ-SAN...
......

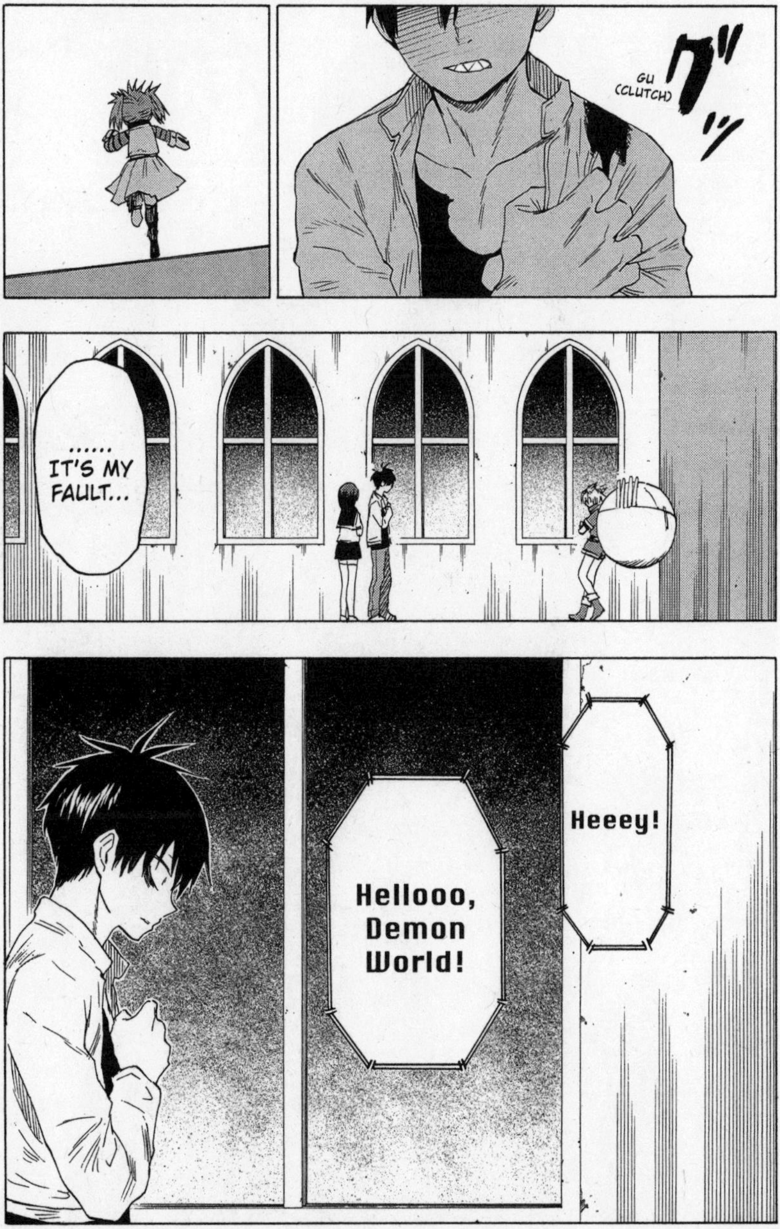
グッ
GU (CLUTCH)
...... IT'S MY FAULT...
Heeey!
Hellooo, Demon World!

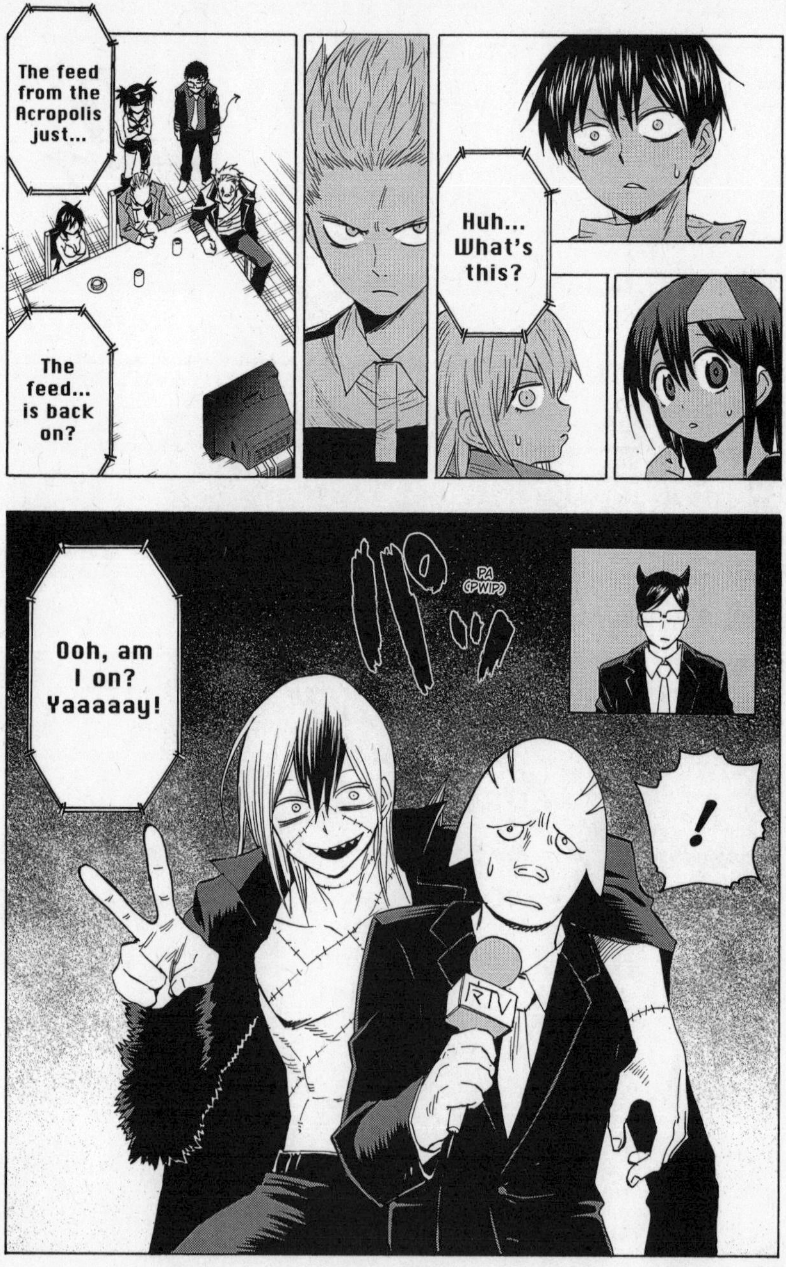
Huh... What's this?
The feed from the Acropolis just...
The feed... is back on?
PA (PWIP)
Ooh, am I on? Yaaaaay!
!
RTV

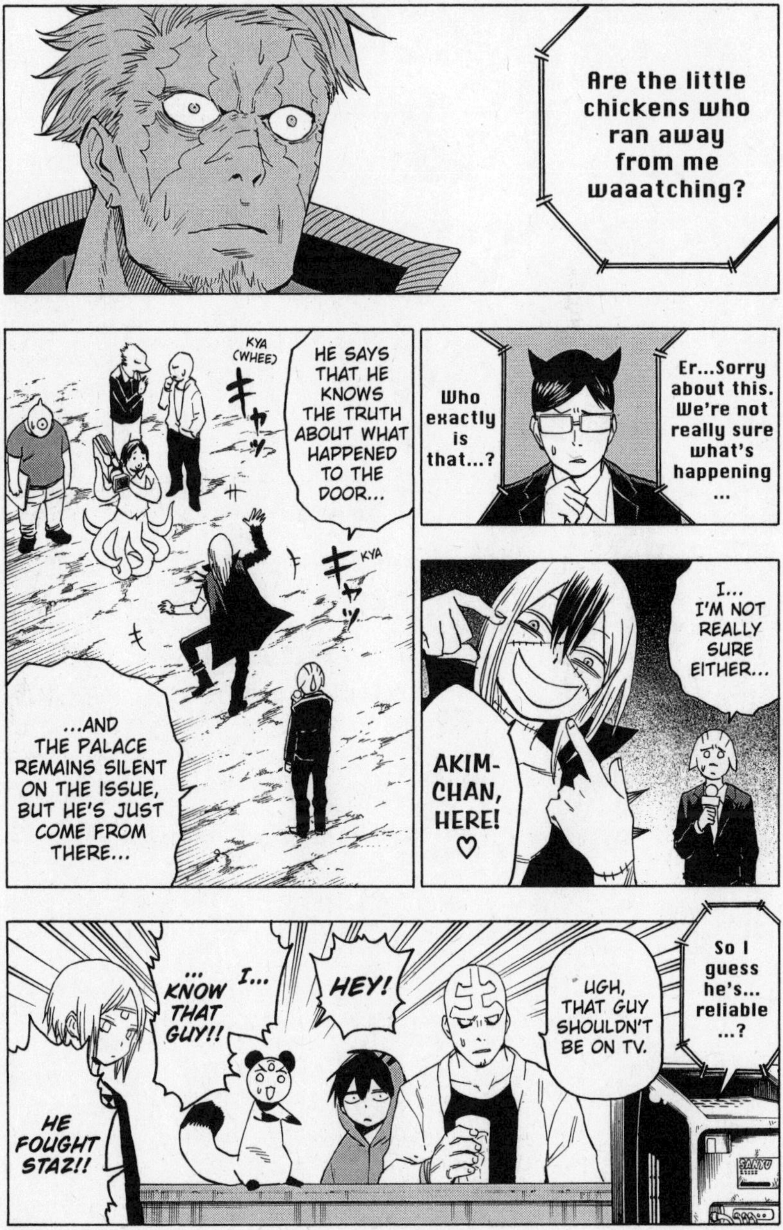

Are the little chickens who ran away from me waaatching?
Er...Sorry about this. We're not really sure what's happening...
Who exactly is that...?
I... I'M NOT REALLY SURE EITHER...
AKIM-CHAN, HERE! ♡
HE SAYS THAT HE KNOWS THE TRUTH ABOUT WHAT HAPPENED TO THE DOOR...
KYA (WHEE)
KYA
...AND THE PALACE REMAINS SILENT ON THE ISSUE, BUT HE'S JUST COME FROM THERE...
So I guess he's... reliable...?
UGH, THAT GUY SHOULDN'T BE ON TV.
HEY!
I...
...KNOW THAT GUY!!
HE FOUGHT STAZ!!

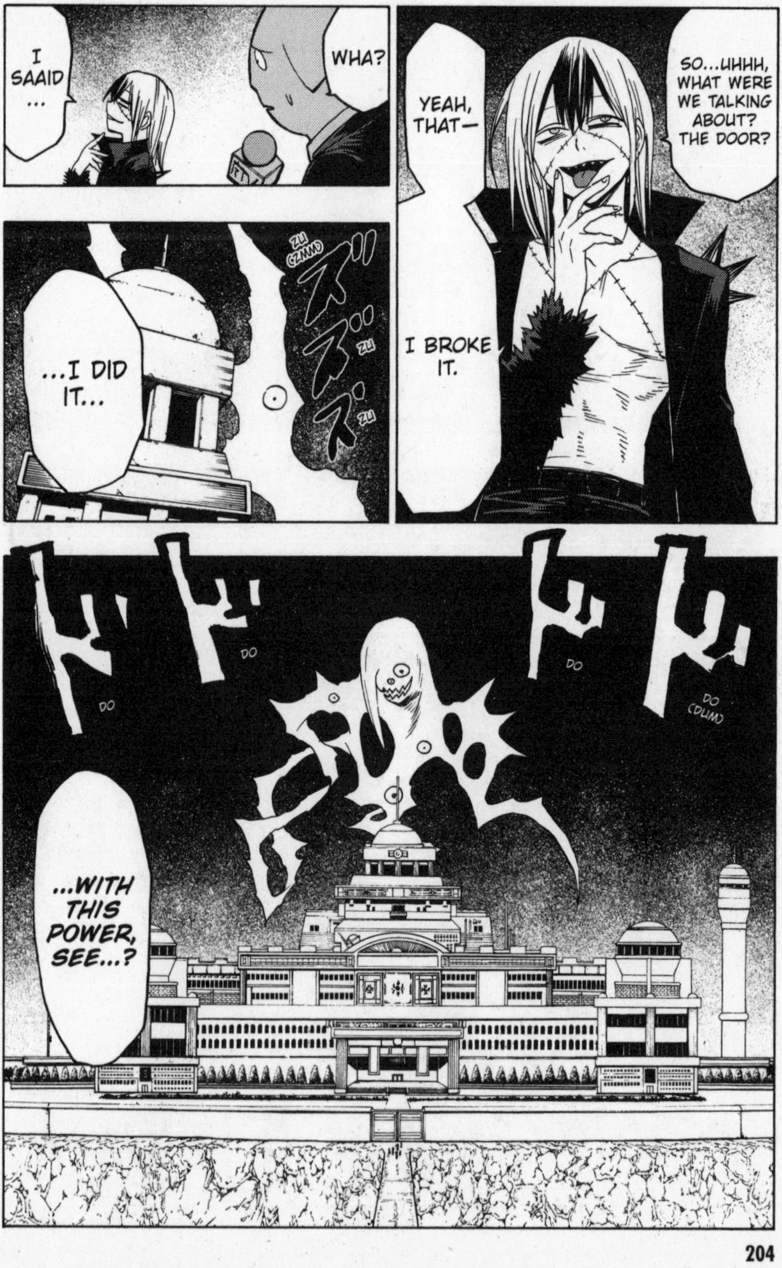
SO...UHHH, WHAT WERE WE TALKING ABOUT? THE DOOR?
YEAH, THAT—
I BROKE IT.
WHA?
I SAAID ...
ZU (ZWMM)
ZU
ZU
...I DID IT...
DO
DO
DO
DO (DUM)
...WITH THIS POWER, SEE...?

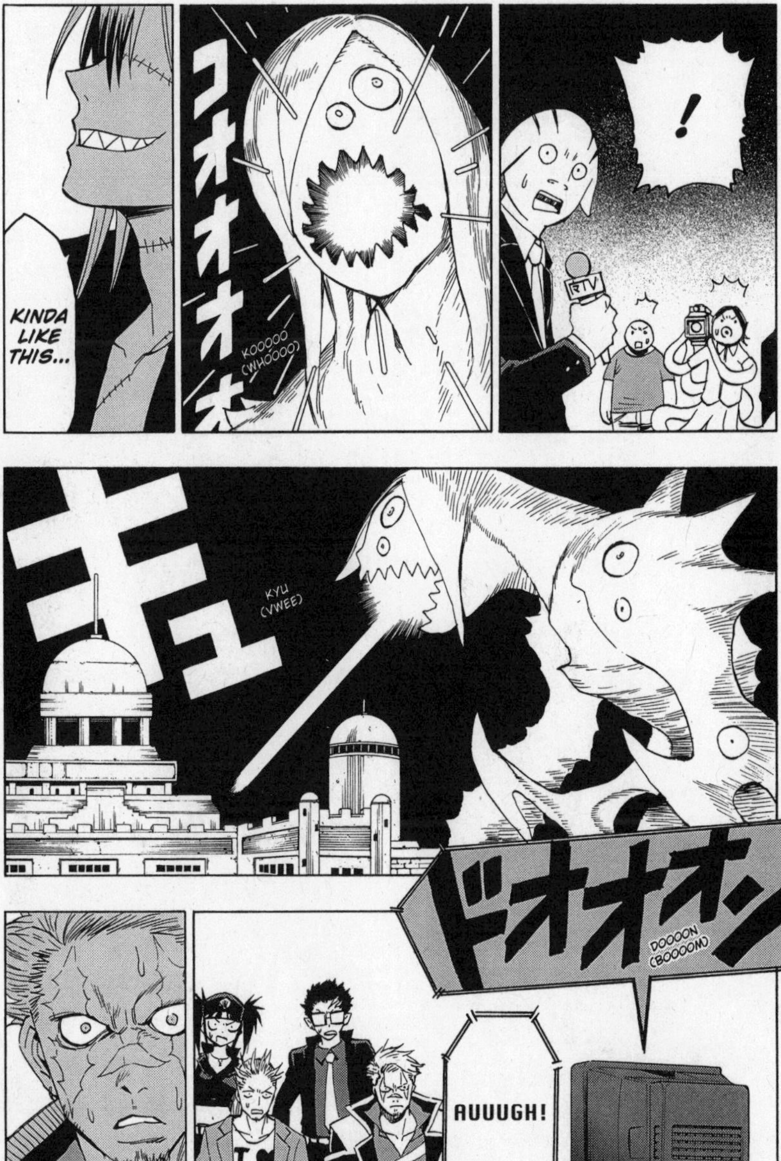
!
コオオオオ
KOOOOO (WHOOOO)
KINDA LIKE THIS...
キュ
KYU (VWEE)
ドオオオン
DOOOON (BOOOOM)
AUUUGH!

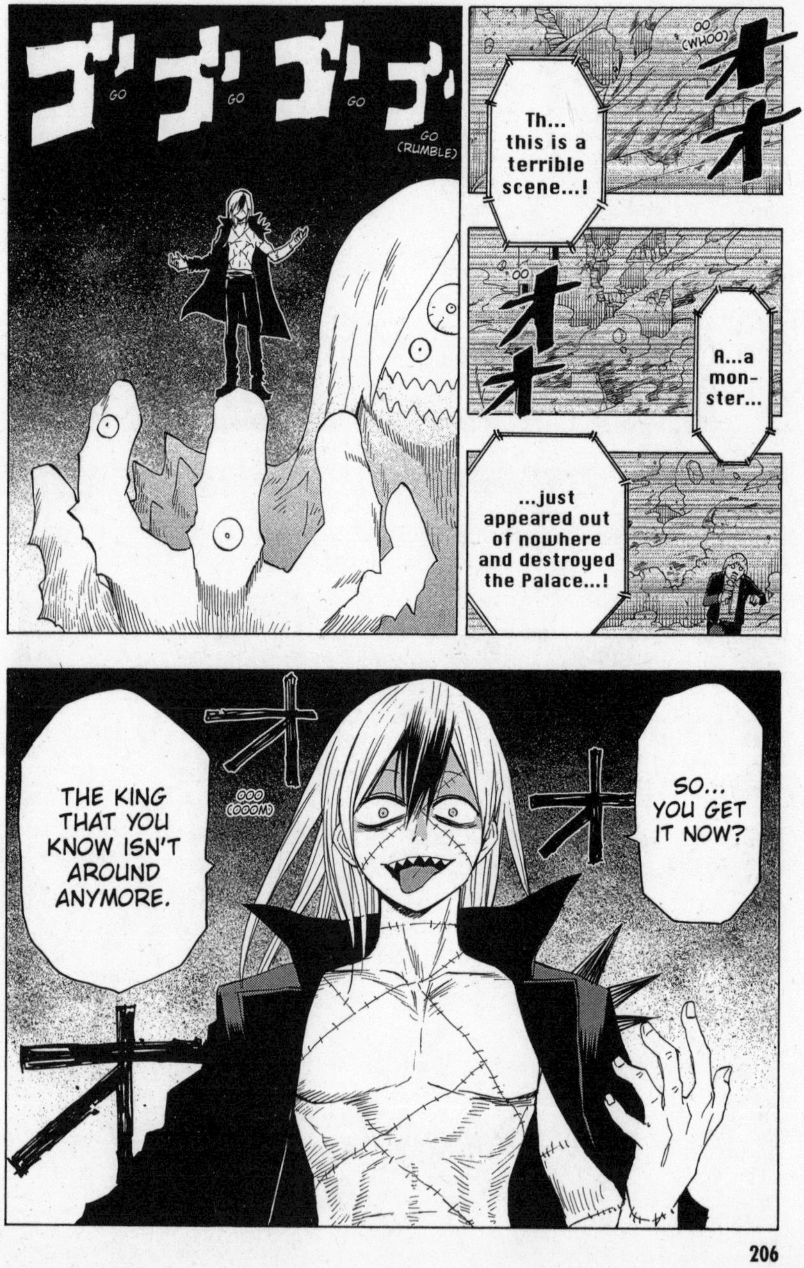
オオ
OO (WHOO)
Th... this is a terrible scene...!
オオ
OO
A...a monster...
...just appeared out of nowhere and destroyed the Palace...!
ゴゴゴゴ
GO GO GO GO (RUMBLE)
SO... YOU GET IT NOW?
オオオ
OOO (OOOM)
THE KING THAT YOU KNOW ISN'T AROUND ANYMORE.

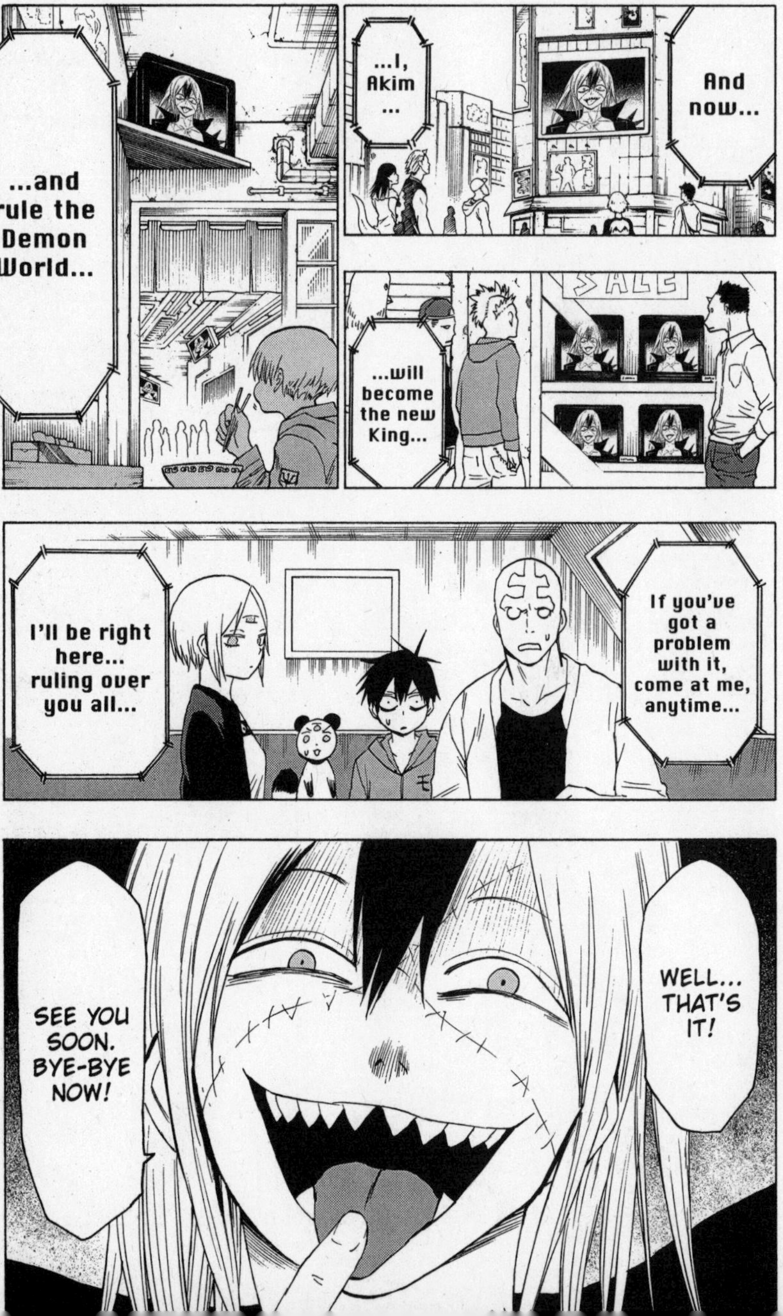
And now...
...I, Akim ...
...will become the new King...
...and rule the Demon World...
If you've got a problem with it, come at me, anytime...
I'll be right here... ruling over you all...
WELL... THAT'S IT!
SEE YOU SOON. BYE-BYE NOW!

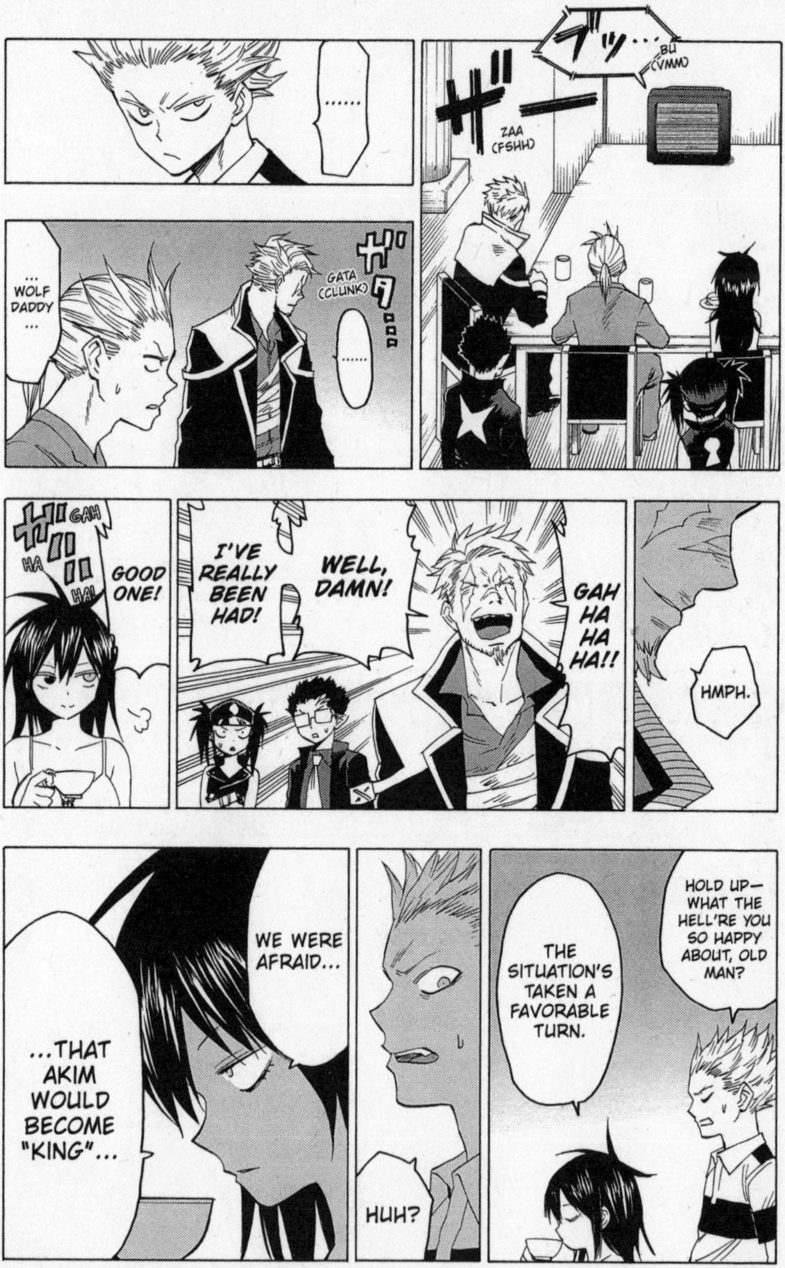
ブッ…
BU (VMM)
ザー
ZAA (FSHH)
......
ガタ
GATA (CLUNK)
......
... WOLF DADDY ...
HMPH.
GAH HA HA HA!!
WELL, DAMN!
I'VE REALLY BEEN HAD!
GAH HA HA!
GOOD ONE!
HOLD UP—WHAT THE HELL'RE YOU SO HAPPY ABOUT, OLD MAN?
THE SITUATION'S TAKEN A FAVORABLE TURN.
HUH?
WE WERE AFRAID...
...THAT AKIM WOULD BECOME "KING"...

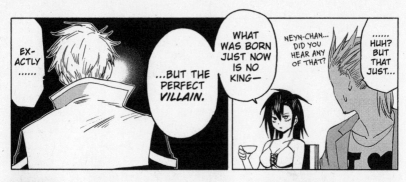

......HUH? BUT THAT JUST...
NEYN-CHAN... DID YOU HEAR ANY OF THAT?
WHAT WAS BORN JUST NOW IS NO KING—
...BUT THE PERFECT *VILLAIN.*
EX-ACTLY......
THE KING IS THE SYMBOL OF ABSOLUTE JUSTICE, THE FOUNDATION OF LAW AND ORDER IN THE DEMON WORLD.
THAT'S WHY EVERYONE LIVES THEIR LIVES IN ACCORDANCE WITH THE LAWS.
BUT...IF THE KING'S RIGHTEOUS-NESS SHOULD WAVER...?
THE KING WHO WAS SUPPOSED TO BE PROTECTING THE DEMON WORLD WAS ACTUALLY KEEPING A MONSTER THAT WOULD DESTROY IT BEHIND THE DOOR......
WHETHER WE LET THAT OUT OR KEEP IT A SECRET... THE PEOPLE OF THE DEMON WORLD CAN'T TRUST THEIR KING ANYMORE.

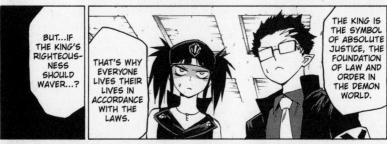

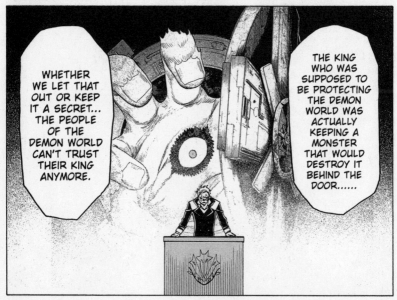

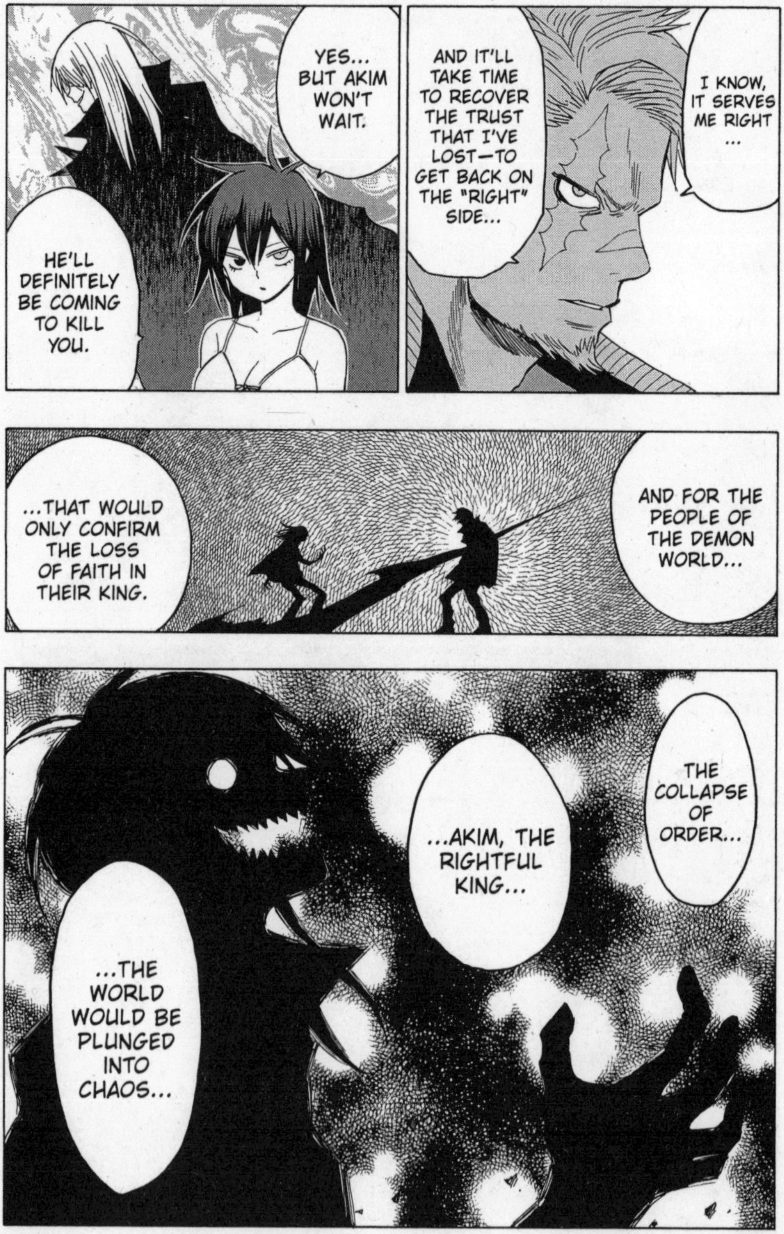
I KNOW, IT SERVES ME RIGHT ...
AND IT'LL TAKE TIME TO RECOVER THE TRUST THAT I'VE LOST—TO GET BACK ON THE "RIGHT" SIDE...
YES... BUT AKIM WON'T WAIT.
HE'LL DEFINITELY BE COMING TO KILL YOU.
AND FOR THE PEOPLE OF THE DEMON WORLD...
...THAT WOULD ONLY CONFIRM THE LOSS OF FAITH IN THEIR KING.
THE COLLAPSE OF ORDER...
...AKIM, THE RIGHTFUL KING...
...THE WORLD WOULD BE PLUNGED INTO CHAOS...

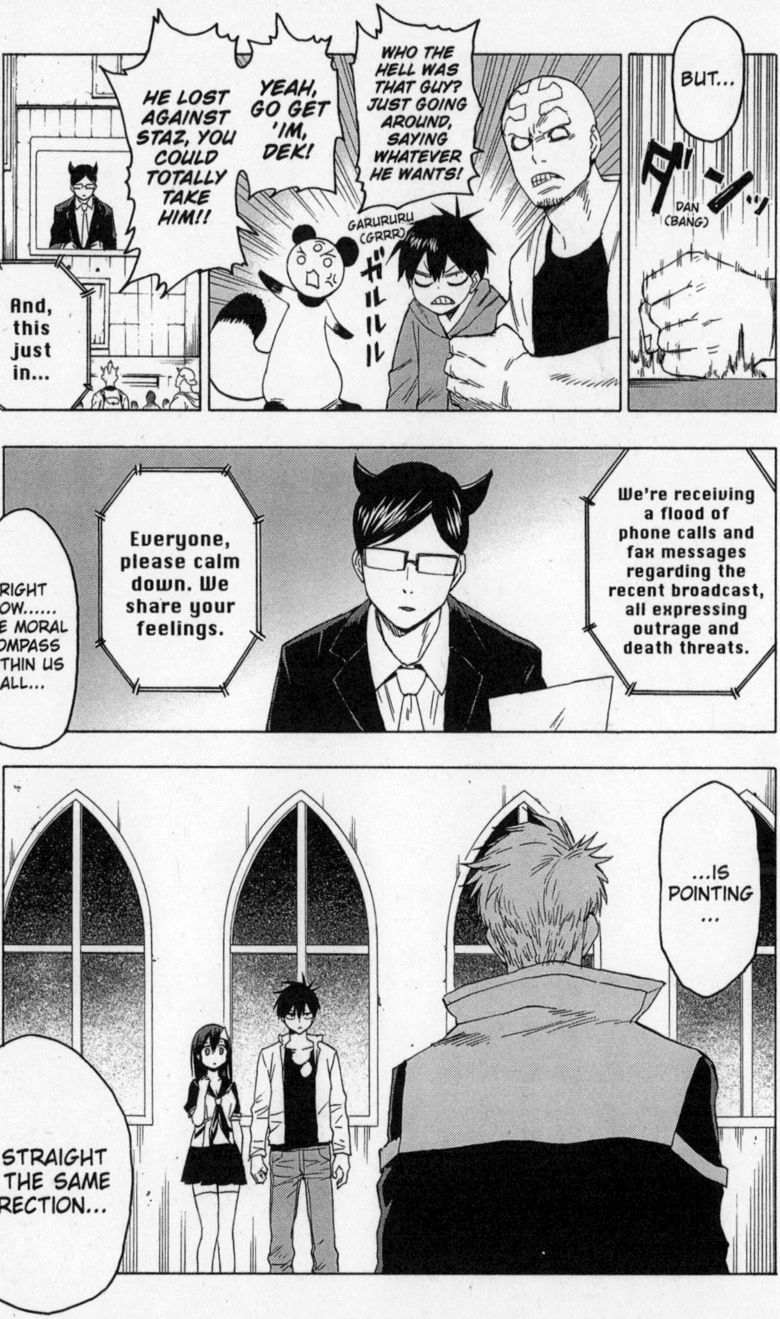
BUT...
ダンッ
DAN (BANG)
WHO THE HELL WAS THAT GUY? JUST GOING AROUND, SAYING WHATEVER HE WANTS!
YEAH, GO GET 'IM, DEK!
HE LOST AGAINST STAZ, YOU COULD TOTALLY TAKE HIM!!
ガルルル
GARURURU (GRRR)
And, this just in...
We're receiving a flood of phone calls and fax messages regarding the recent broadcast, all expressing outrage and death threats.
Everyone, please calm down. We share your feelings.
RIGHT NOW...... THE MORAL COMPASS WITHIN US ALL...
...IS POINTING ...
...STRAIGHT IN THE SAME DIRECTION...

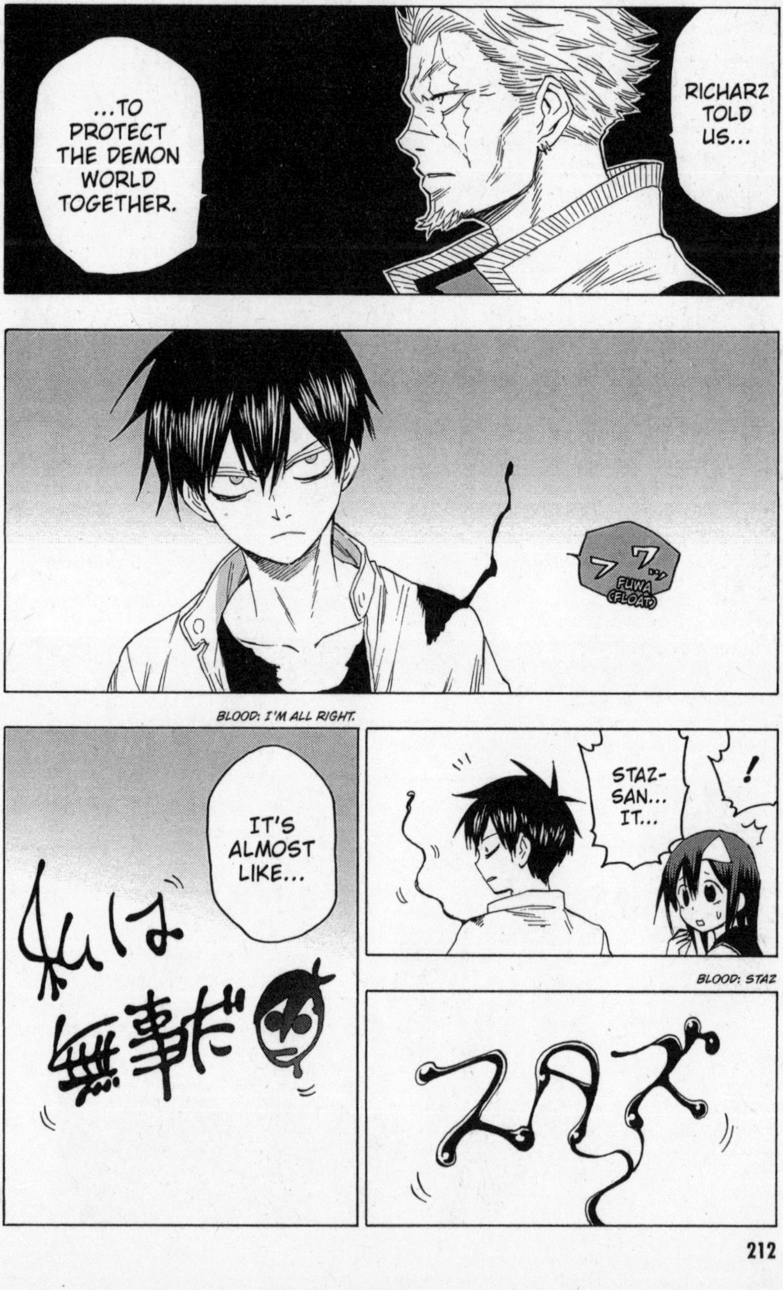
RICHARZ TOLD US...
...TO PROTECT THE DEMON WORLD TOGETHER.
フワッ
FUWA (FLOAT)
BLOOD: I'M ALL RIGHT.
STAZ-SAN... IT...
!
BLOOD: STAZ
スタズ
IT'S ALMOST LIKE...
私は無事だ

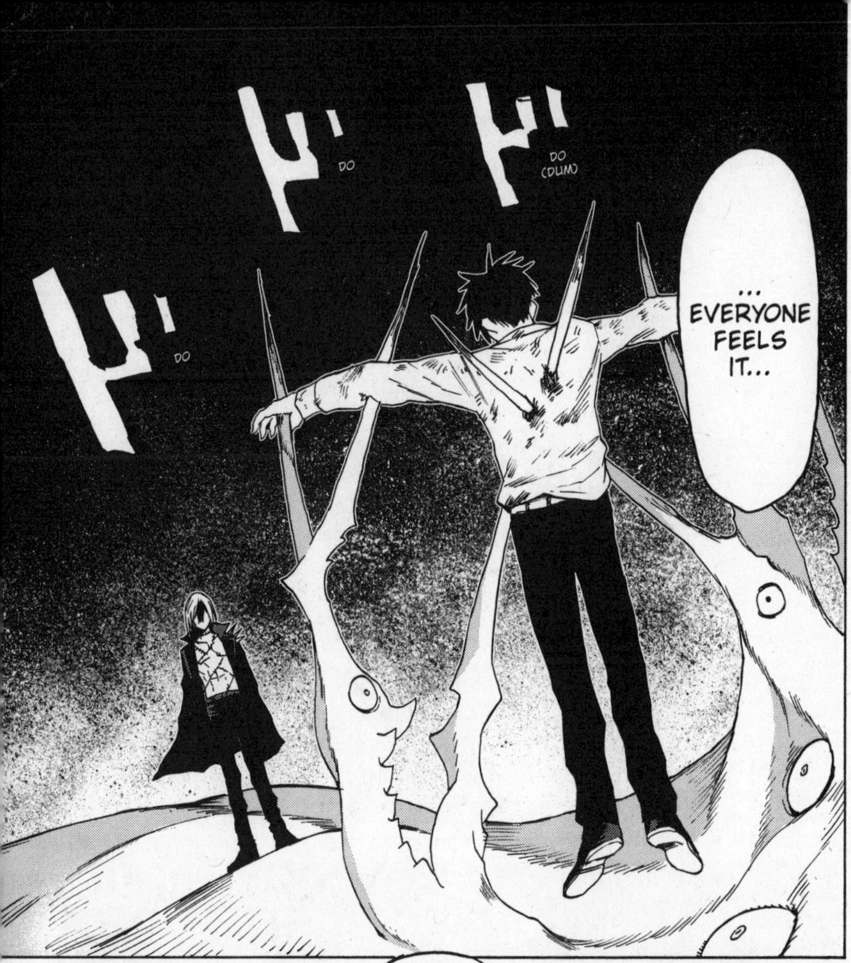
...EVERYONE FEELS IT...
DO (DUM)
DO
DO

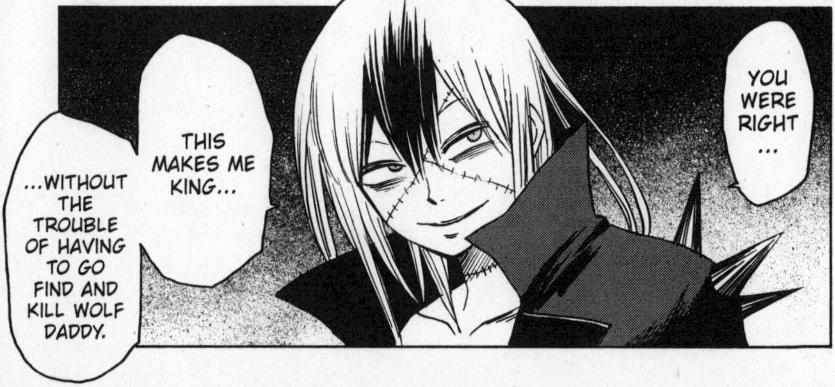
YOU WERE RIGHT ...
THIS MAKES ME KING...
...WITHOUT THE TROUBLE OF HAVING TO GO FIND AND KILL WOLF DADDY.

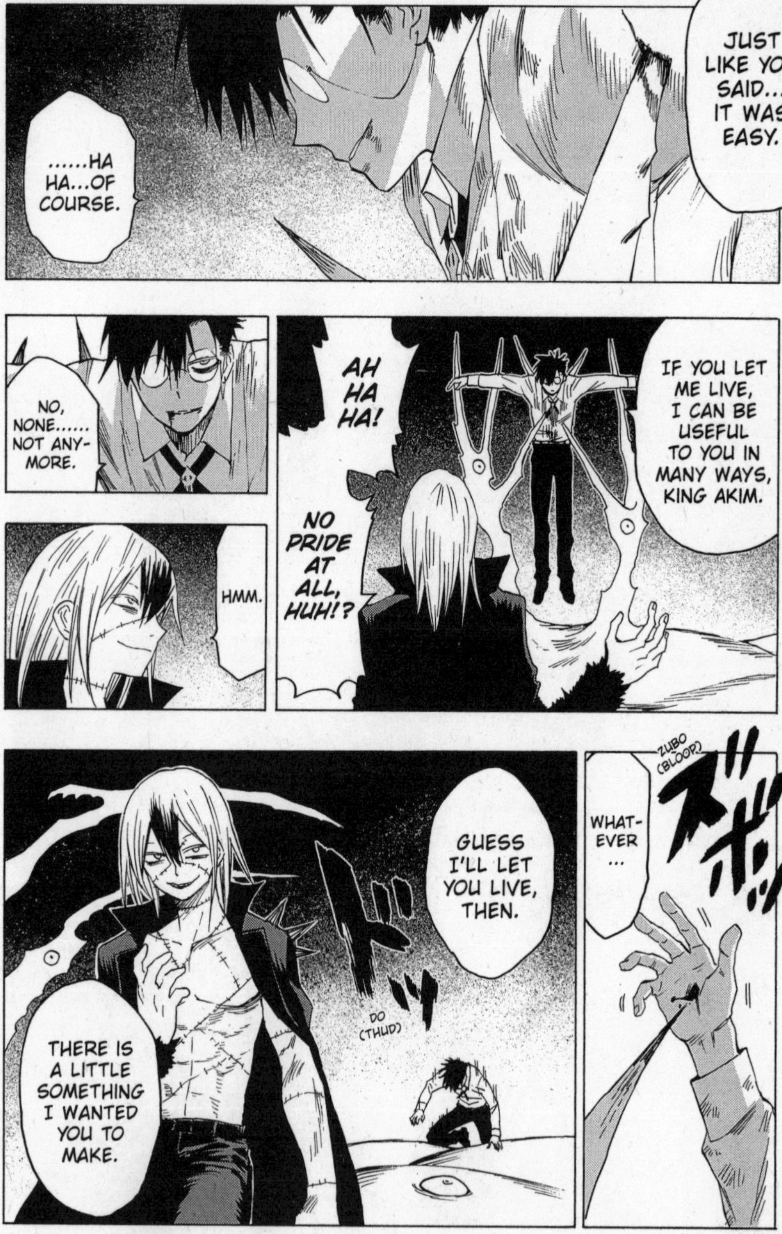
JUST LIKE YOU SAID... IT WAS EASY.
......HA HA...OF COURSE.
IF YOU LET ME LIVE, I CAN BE USEFUL TO YOU IN MANY WAYS, KING AKIM.
AH HA HA!
NO PRIDE AT ALL, HUH!?
NO, NONE...... NOT ANYMORE.
HMM.
ZUBO (BLOOP)
WHAT-EVER ...
GUESS I'LL LET YOU LIVE, THEN.
DO (THUD)
THERE IS A LITTLE SOMETHING I WANTED YOU TO MAKE.

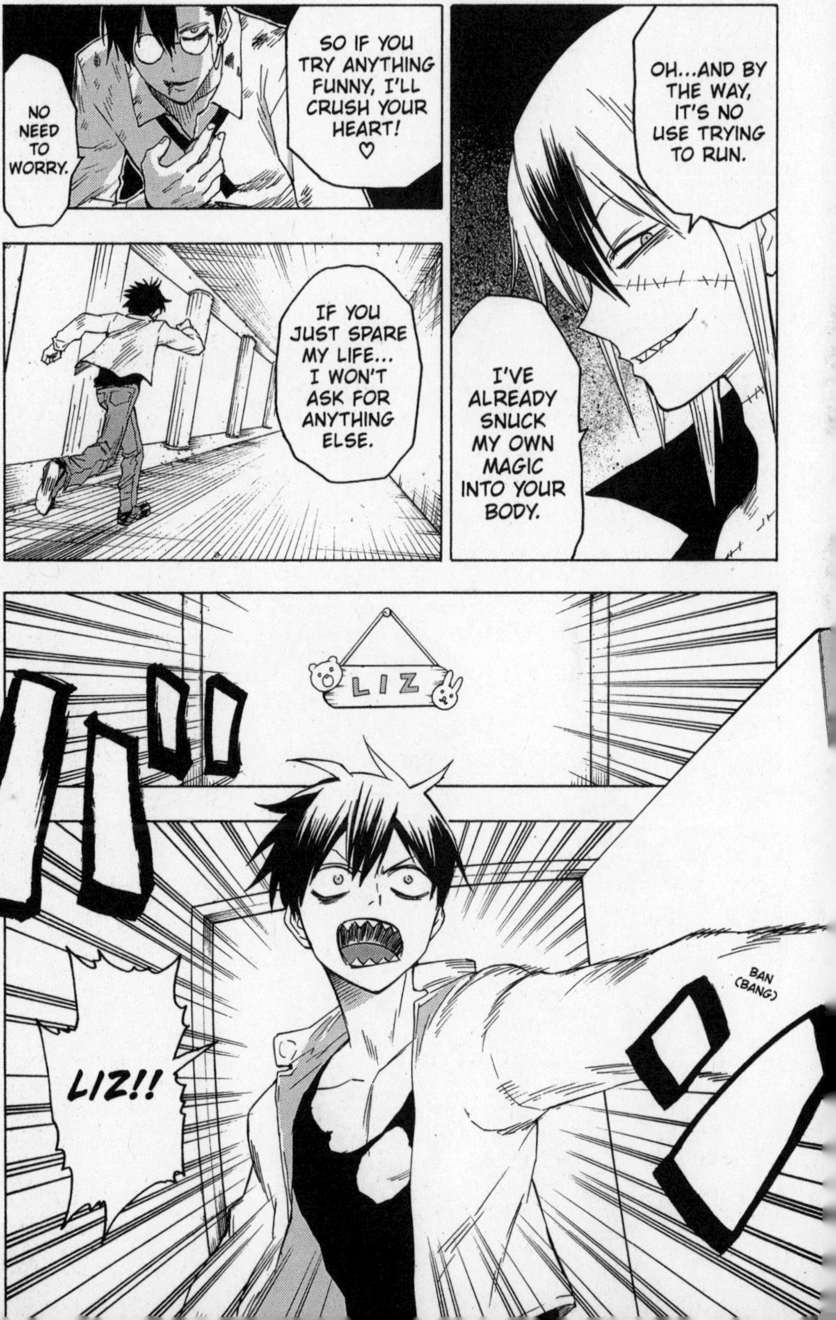
OH...AND BY THE WAY, IT'S NO USE TRYING TO RUN.
I'VE ALREADY SNUCK MY OWN MAGIC INTO YOUR BODY.
SO IF YOU TRY ANYTHING FUNNY, I'LL CRUSH YOUR HEART! ♡
NO NEED TO WORRY.
IF YOU JUST SPARE MY LIFE... I WON'T ASK FOR ANYTHING ELSE.
LIZ
BAN (BANG)
LIZ!!

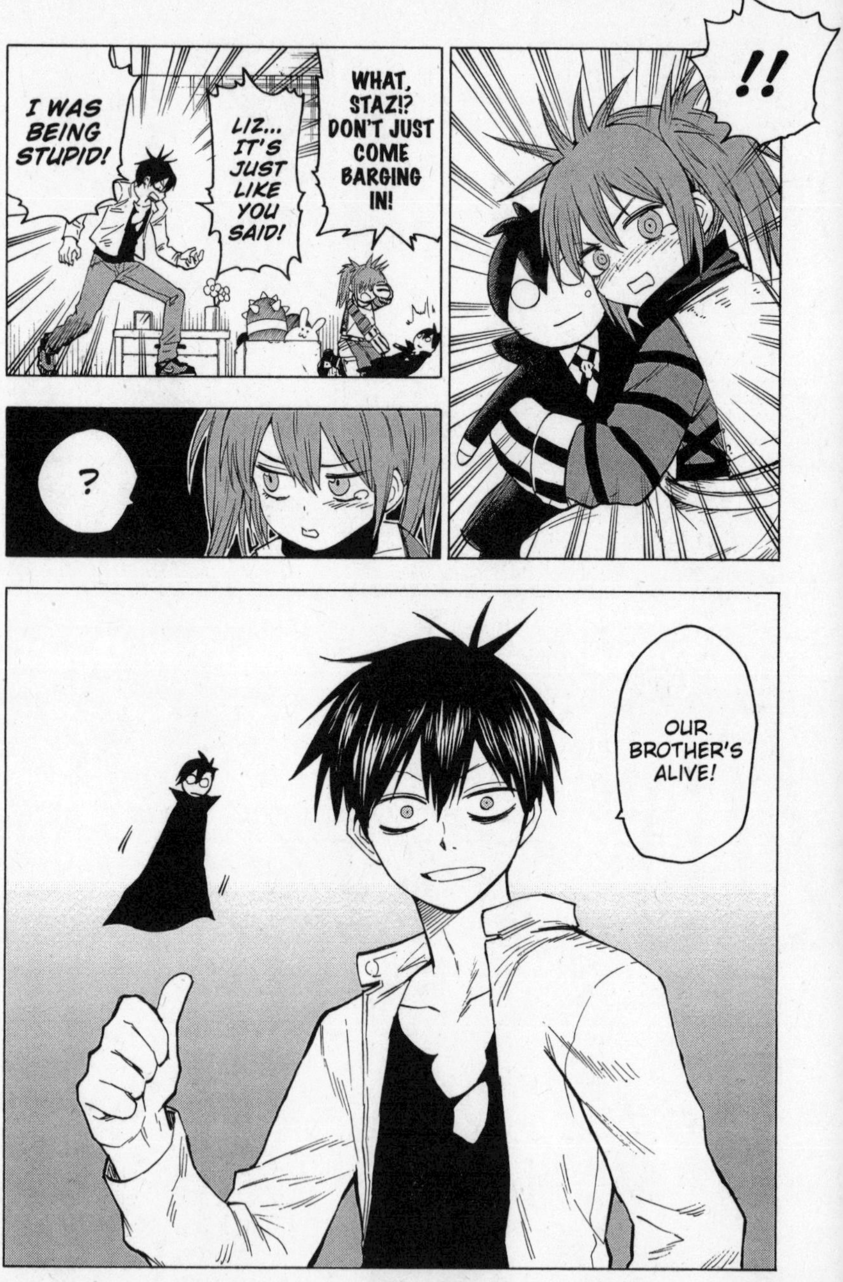
!!
WHAT, STAZ!? DON'T JUST COME BARGING IN!
LIZ... IT'S JUST LIKE YOU SAID!
I WAS BEING STUPID!
?
OUR BROTHER'S ALIVE!

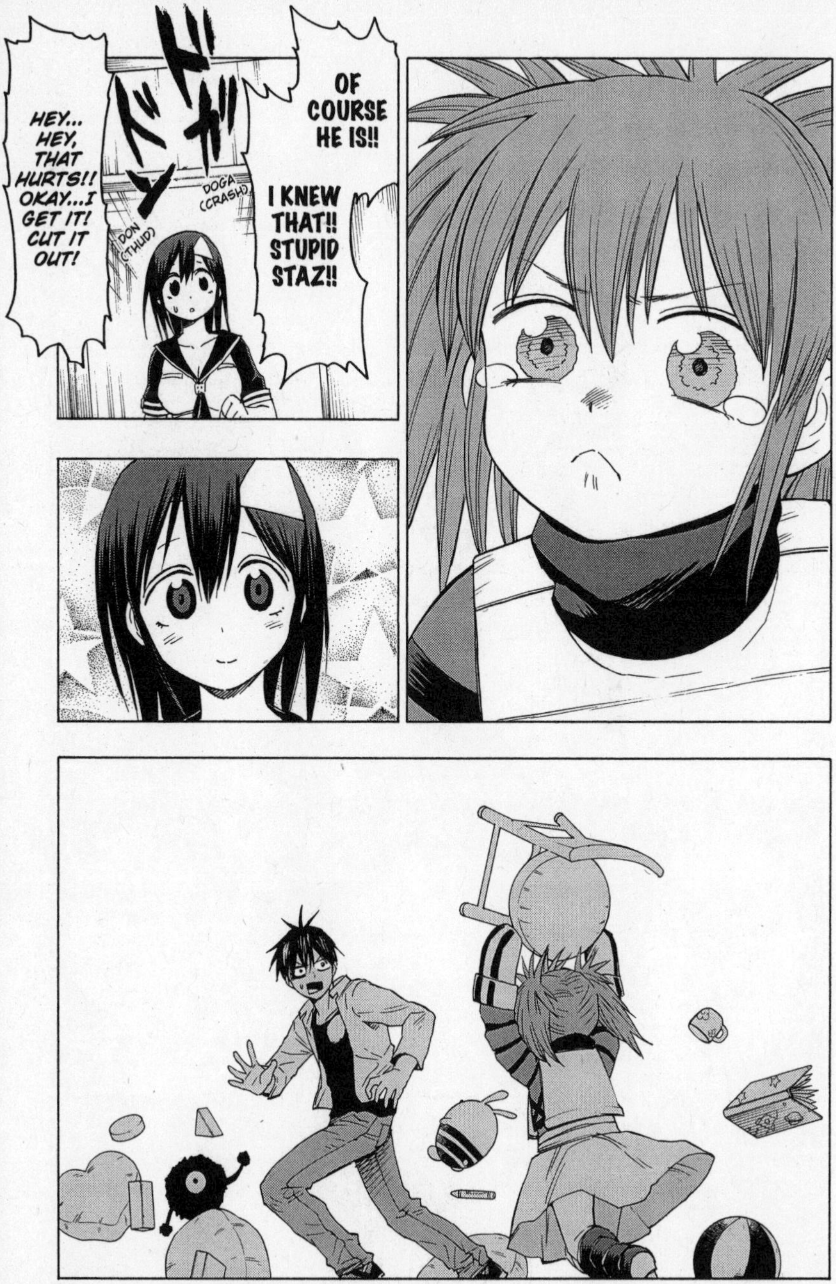
OF COURSE HE IS!!
I KNEW THAT!! STUPID STAZ!!
DOGA (CRASH)
DON (THUD)
HEY... HEY, THAT HURTS!! OKAY...I GET IT! CUT IT OUT!

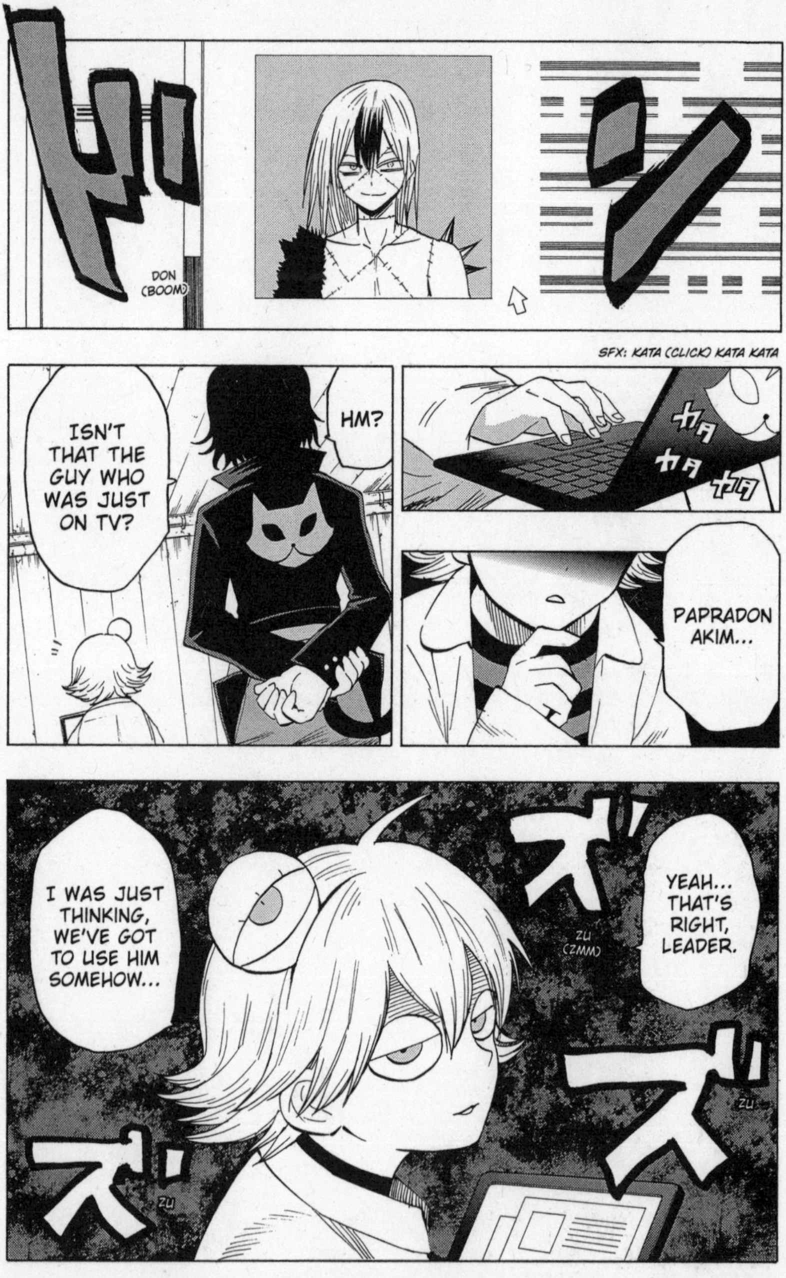
DON (BOOM)
SFX: KATA (CLICK) KATA KATA
PAPRADON AKIM...
HM?
ISN'T THAT THE GUY WHO WAS JUST ON TV?
YEAH... THAT'S RIGHT, LEADER.
ZU (ZMM)
I WAS JUST THINKING, WE'VE GOT TO USE HIM SOMEHOW...
ZU
ZU

♠ To Be Continued ♠

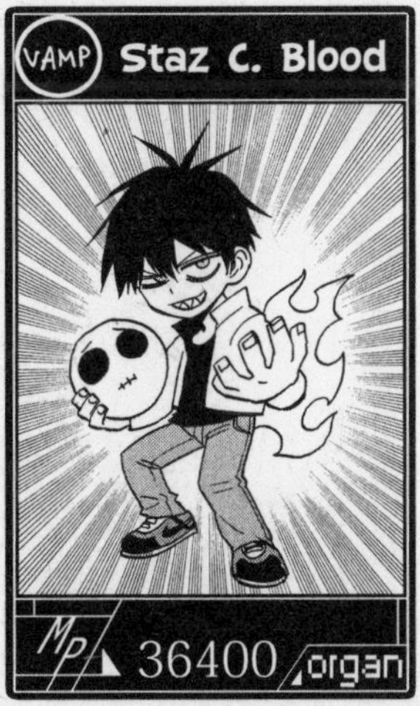
VAMP
Staz C. Blood
MP
36400
organ

BLOOD LAD

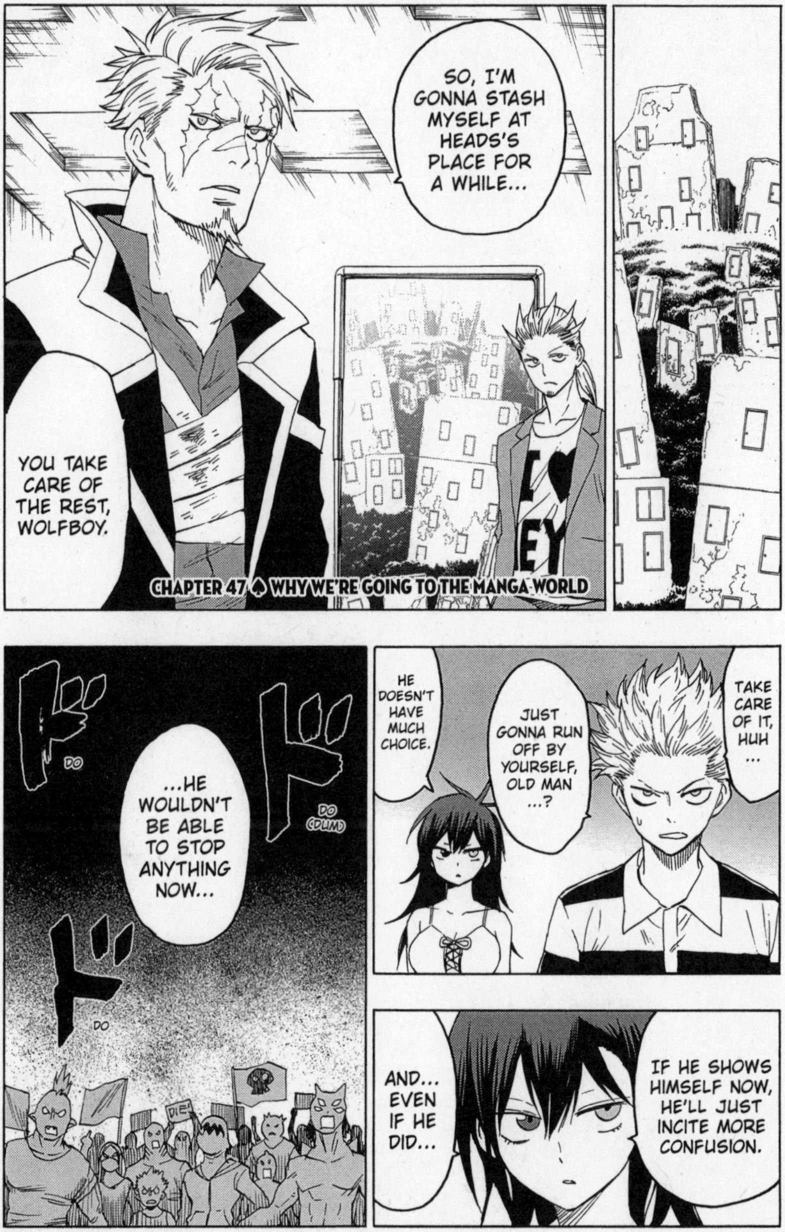
SO, I'M GONNA STASH MYSELF AT HEADS'S PLACE FOR A WHILE...
YOU TAKE CARE OF THE REST, WOLFBOY.
CHAPTER 47 ♠ WHY WE'RE GOING TO THE MANGA WORLD
TAKE CARE OF IT, HUH...
JUST GONNA RUN OFF BY YOURSELF, OLD MAN...?
HE DOESN'T HAVE MUCH CHOICE.
IF HE SHOWS HIMSELF NOW, HE'LL JUST INCITE MORE CONFUSION.
AND... EVEN IF HE DID...
DO (DUM)
DO
...HE WOULDN'T BE ABLE TO STOP ANYTHING NOW...
DO
DIE!

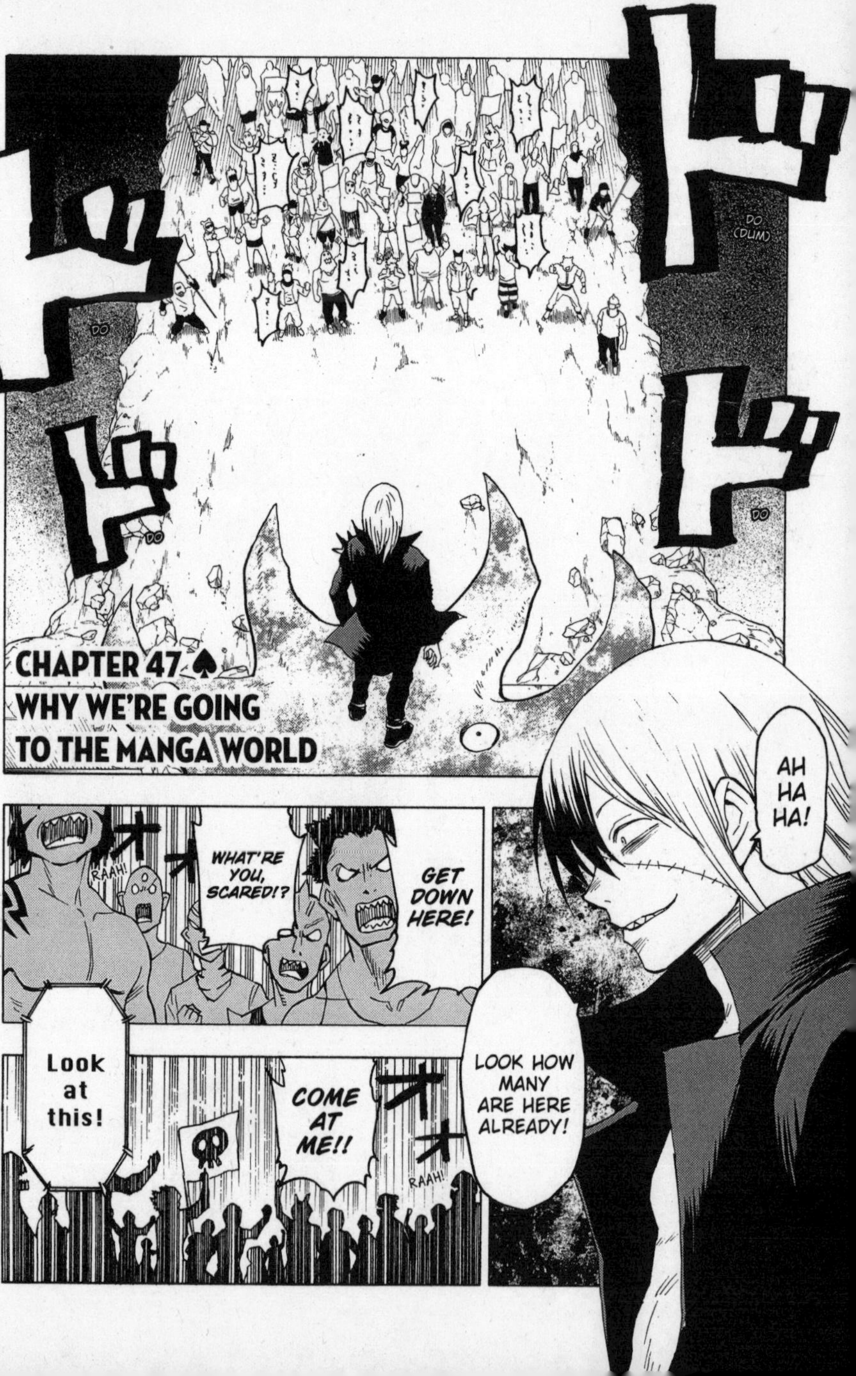
DO (DUM)
DO
DO
DO
CHAPTER 47 ♠ WHY WE'RE GOING TO THE MANGA WORLD
AH HA HA!
LOOK HOW MANY ARE HERE ALREADY!
GET DOWN HERE!
WHAT'RE YOU, SCARED!?
RAAH!
RAAH!
COME AT ME!!
Look at this!

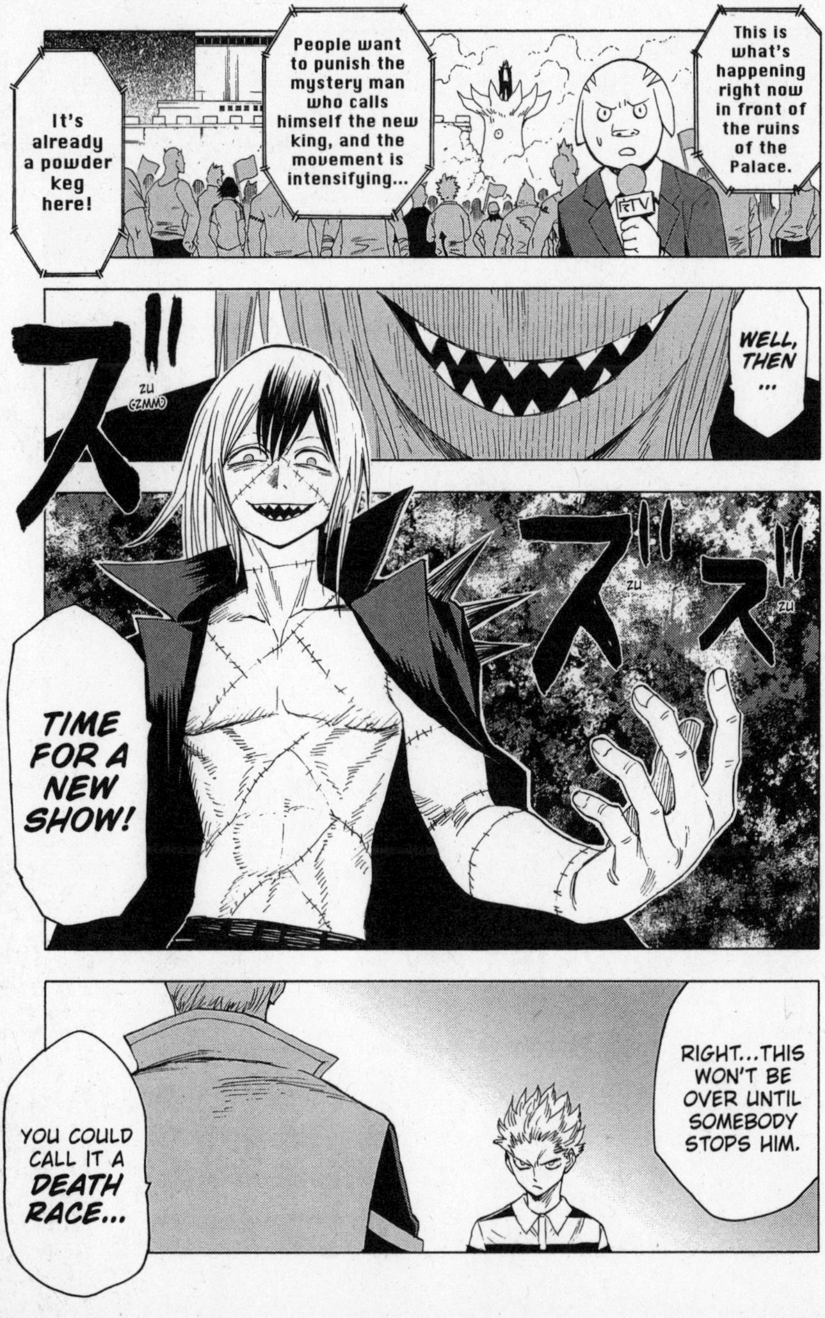
This is what's happening right now in front of the ruins of the Palace.
People want to punish the mystery man who calls himself the new king, and the movement is intensifying...
It's already a powder keg here!
RTV
WELL, THEN...
ZU (ZMM)
ZU
ZU
TIME FOR A NEW SHOW!
RIGHT...THIS WON'T BE OVER UNTIL SOMEBODY STOPS HIM.
YOU COULD CALL IT A DEATH RACE...

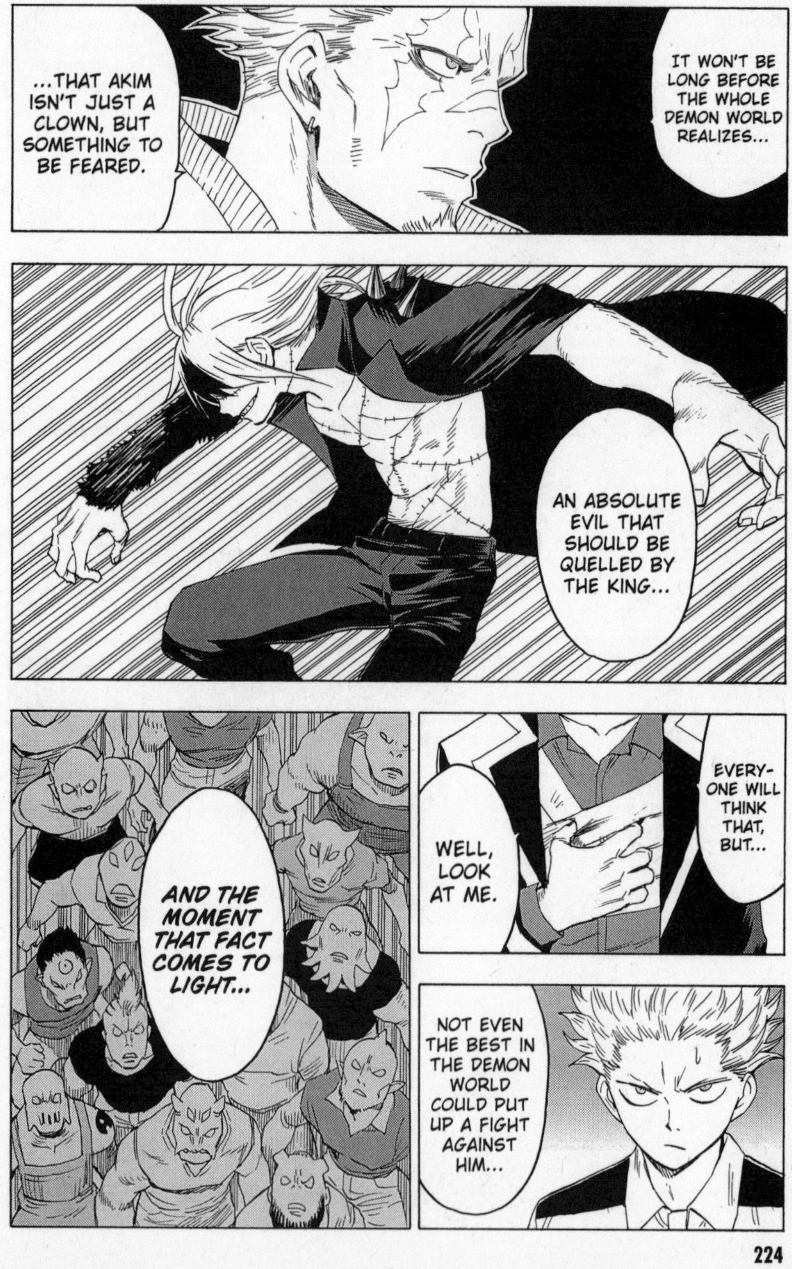
IT WON'T BE LONG BEFORE THE WHOLE DEMON WORLD REALIZES...
...THAT AKIM ISN'T JUST A CLOWN, BUT SOMETHING TO BE FEARED.
AN ABSOLUTE EVIL THAT SHOULD BE QUELLED BY THE KING...
EVERY-ONE WILL THINK THAT, BUT...
WELL, LOOK AT ME.
NOT EVEN THE BEST IN THE DEMON WORLD COULD PUT UP A FIGHT AGAINST HIM...
AND THE MOMENT THAT FACT COMES TO LIGHT...

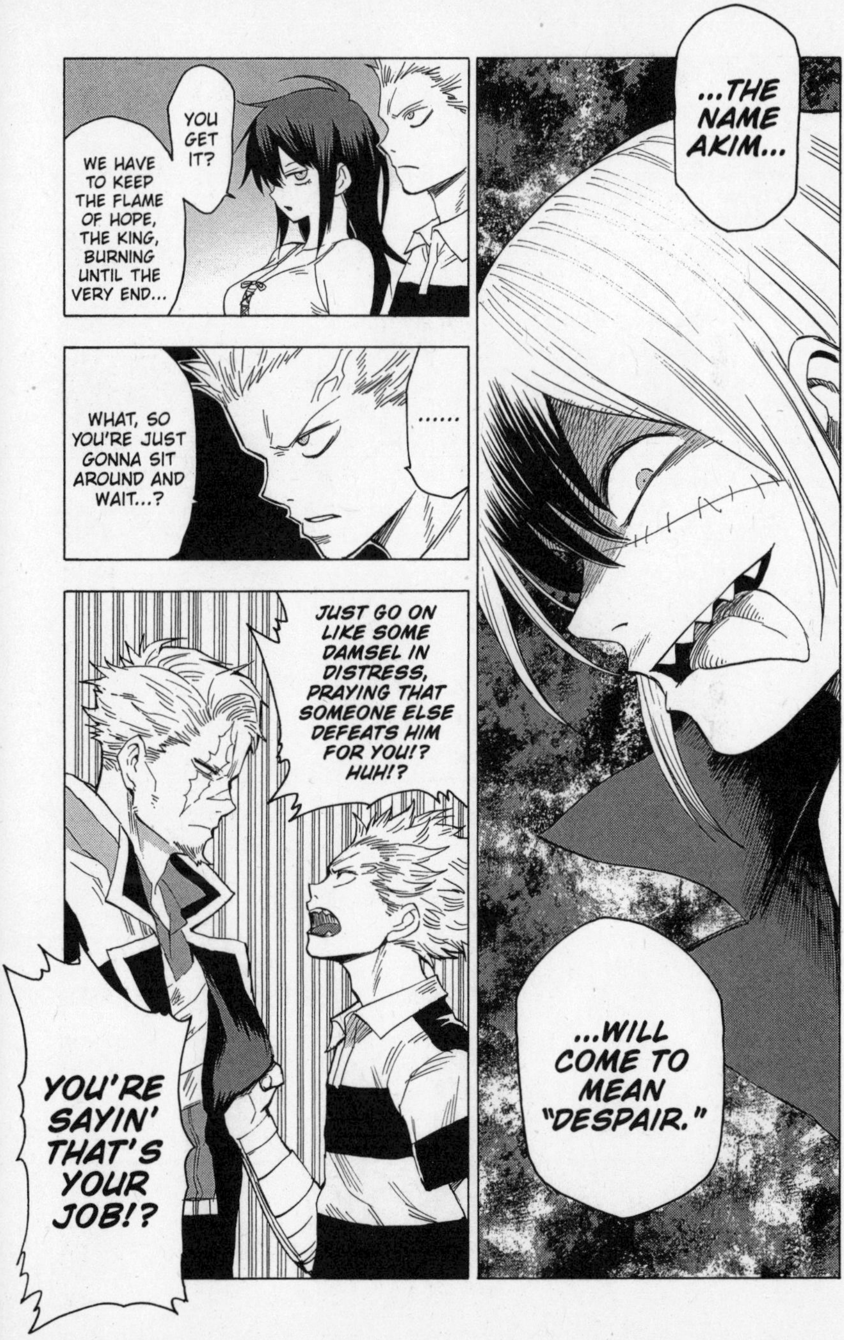
...THE NAME AKIM...
...WILL COME TO MEAN "DESPAIR."
YOU GET IT?
WE HAVE TO KEEP THE FLAME OF HOPE, THE KING, BURNING UNTIL THE VERY END...
......
WHAT, SO YOU'RE JUST GONNA SIT AROUND AND WAIT...?
JUST GO ON LIKE SOME DAMSEL IN DISTRESS, PRAYING THAT SOMEONE ELSE DEFEATS HIM FOR YOU!? HUH!?
YOU'RE SAYIN' THAT'S YOUR JOB!?

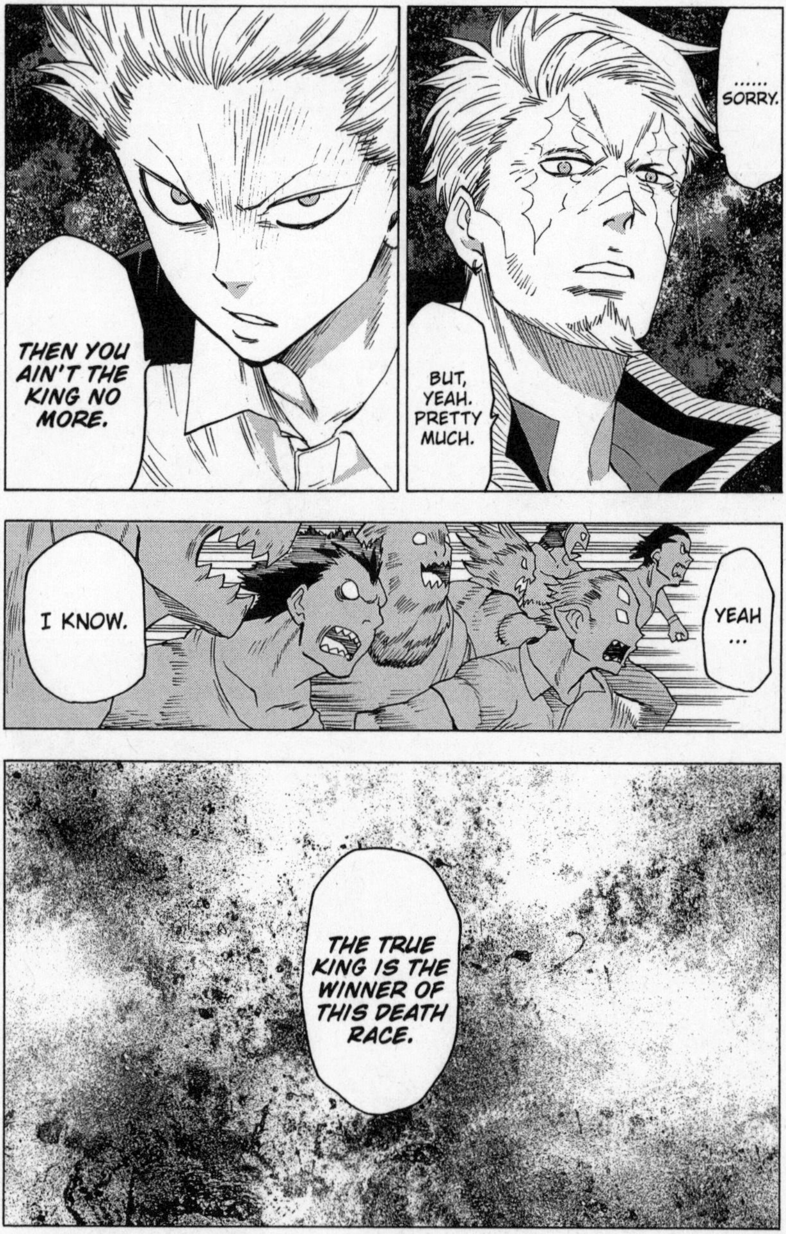
......SORRY.
BUT, YEAH. PRETTY MUCH.
THEN YOU AIN'T THE KING NO MORE.
YEAH ...
I KNOW.
THE TRUE KING IS THE WINNER OF THIS DEATH RACE.

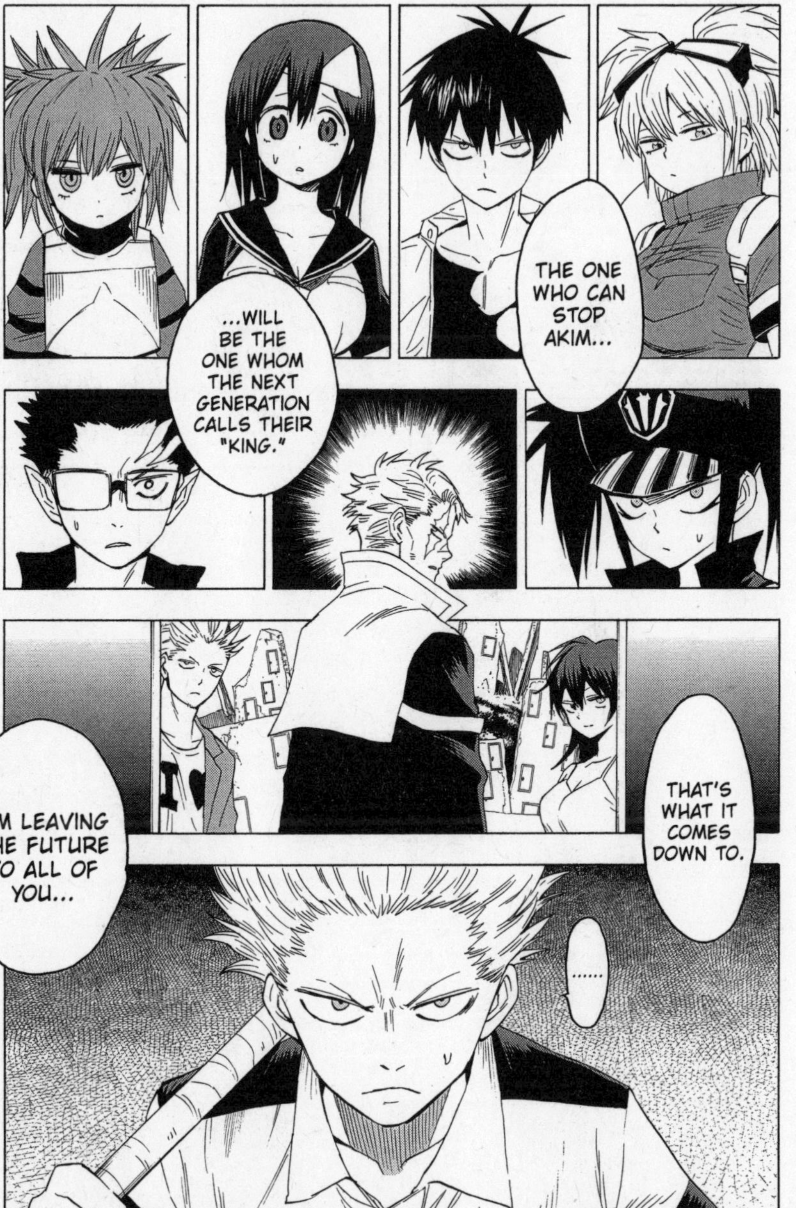
THE ONE WHO CAN STOP AKIM...
...WILL BE THE ONE WHOM THE NEXT GENERATION CALLS THEIR "KING."
THAT'S WHAT IT COMES DOWN TO.
I'M LEAVING THE FUTURE TO ALL OF YOU...
......

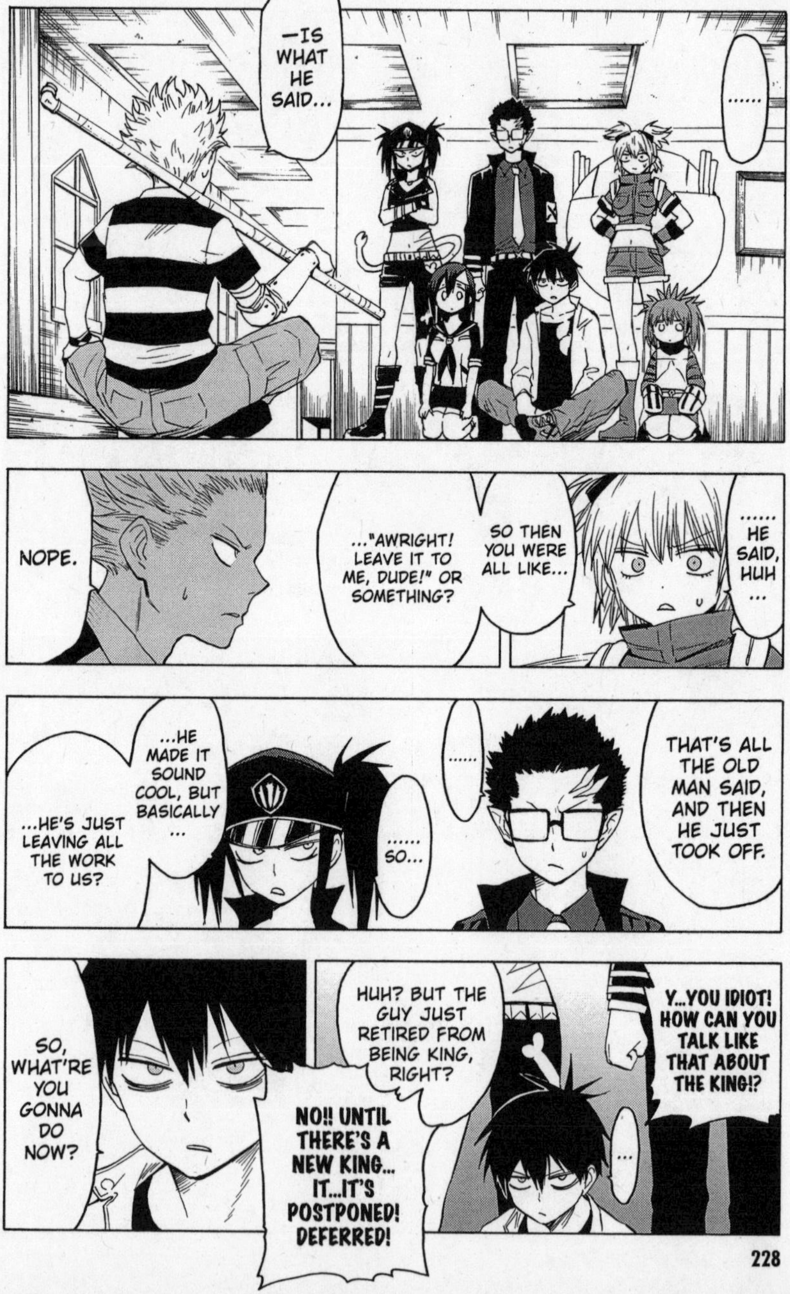
......
—IS WHAT HE SAID...
...... HE SAID, HUH ...
SO THEN YOU WERE ALL LIKE...
..."AWRIGHT! LEAVE IT TO ME, DUDE!" OR SOMETHING?
NOPE.
THAT'S ALL THE OLD MAN SAID, AND THEN HE JUST TOOK OFF.
......
...... SO...
...HE MADE IT SOUND COOL, BUT BASICALLY ...
...HE'S JUST LEAVING ALL THE WORK TO US?
Y...YOU IDIOT! HOW CAN YOU TALK LIKE THAT ABOUT THE KING!?
HUH? BUT THE GUY JUST RETIRED FROM BEING KING, RIGHT?
...
NO!! UNTIL THERE'S A NEW KING... IT...IT'S POSTPONED! DEFERRED!
SO, WHAT'RE YOU GONNA DO NOW?

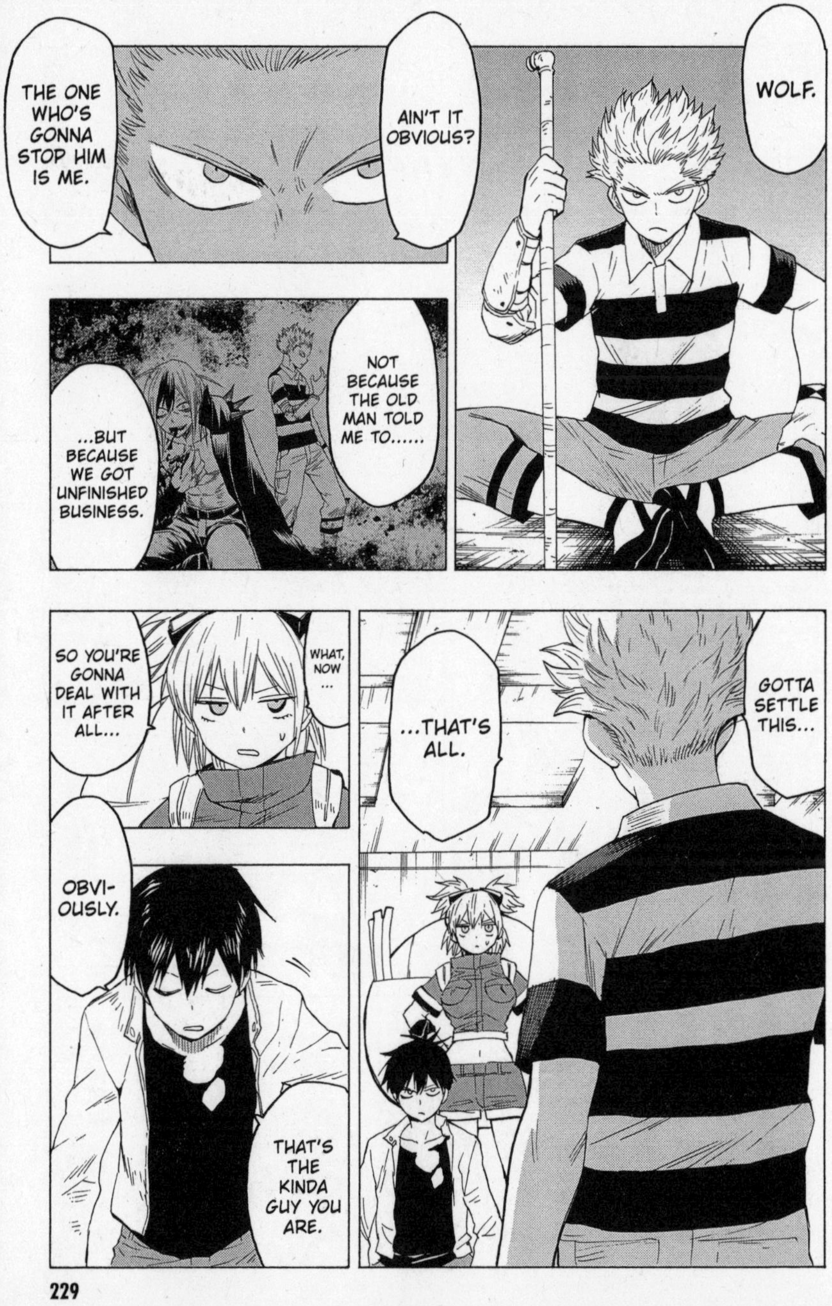
WOLF.
AIN'T IT OBVIOUS?
THE ONE WHO'S GONNA STOP HIM IS ME.
NOT BECAUSE THE OLD MAN TOLD ME TO......
...BUT BECAUSE WE GOT UNFINISHED BUSINESS.
GOTTA SETTLE THIS...
...THAT'S ALL.
WHAT, NOW ...
SO YOU'RE GONNA DEAL WITH IT AFTER ALL...
OBVIOUSLY.
THAT'S THE KINDA GUY YOU ARE.

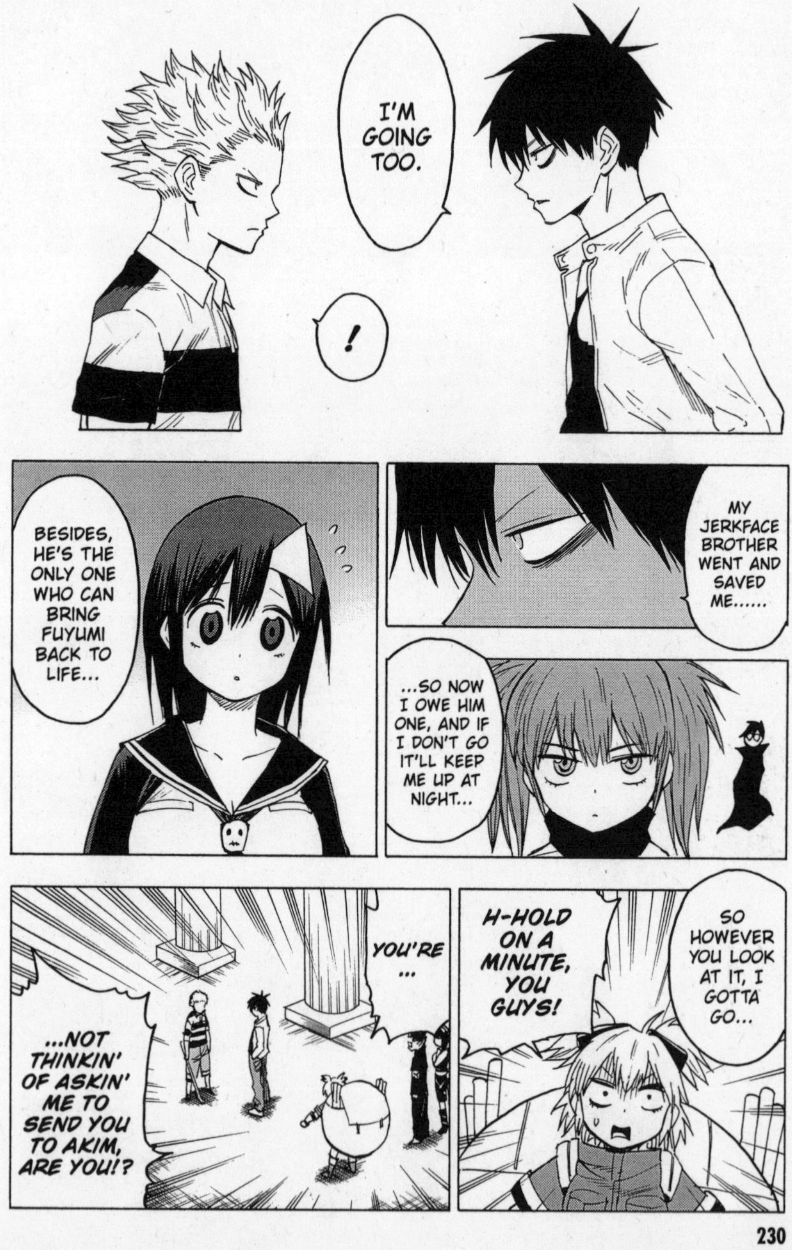
I'M GOING TOO.
!
MY JERKFACE BROTHER WENT AND SAVED ME......
...SO NOW I OWE HIM ONE, AND IF I DON'T GO IT'LL KEEP ME UP AT NIGHT...
BESIDES, HE'S THE ONLY ONE WHO CAN BRING FUYUMI BACK TO LIFE...
SO HOWEVER YOU LOOK AT IT, I GOTTA GO...
H-HOLD ON A MINUTE, YOU GUYS!
YOU'RE ...
...NOT THINKIN' OF ASKIN' ME TO SEND YOU TO AKIM, ARE YOU!?

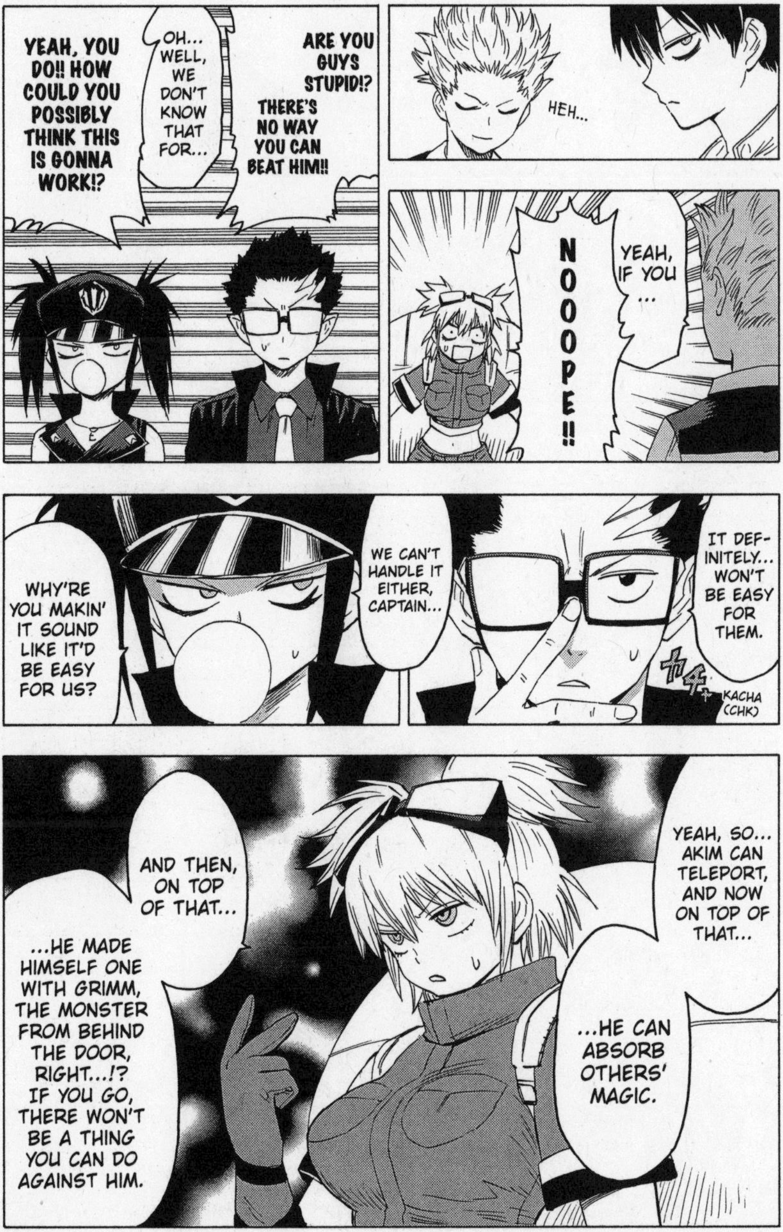
HEH...
YEAH, IF YOU...
NOOOOPE!!
ARE YOU GUYS STUPID!?
THERE'S NO WAY YOU CAN BEAT HIM!!
OH... WELL, WE DON'T KNOW THAT FOR...
YEAH, YOU DO!! HOW COULD YOU POSSIBLY THINK THIS IS GONNA WORK!?
IT DEFINITELY... WON'T BE EASY FOR THEM.
KACHA (CHK)
WE CAN'T HANDLE IT EITHER, CAPTAIN...
WHY'RE YOU MAKIN' IT SOUND LIKE IT'D BE EASY FOR US?
YEAH, SO... AKIM CAN TELEPORT, AND NOW ON TOP OF THAT...
...HE CAN ABSORB OTHERS' MAGIC.
AND THEN, ON TOP OF THAT...
...HE MADE HIMSELF ONE WITH GRIMM, THE MONSTER FROM BEHIND THE DOOR, RIGHT...!? IF YOU GO, THERE WON'T BE A THING YOU CAN DO AGAINST HIM.

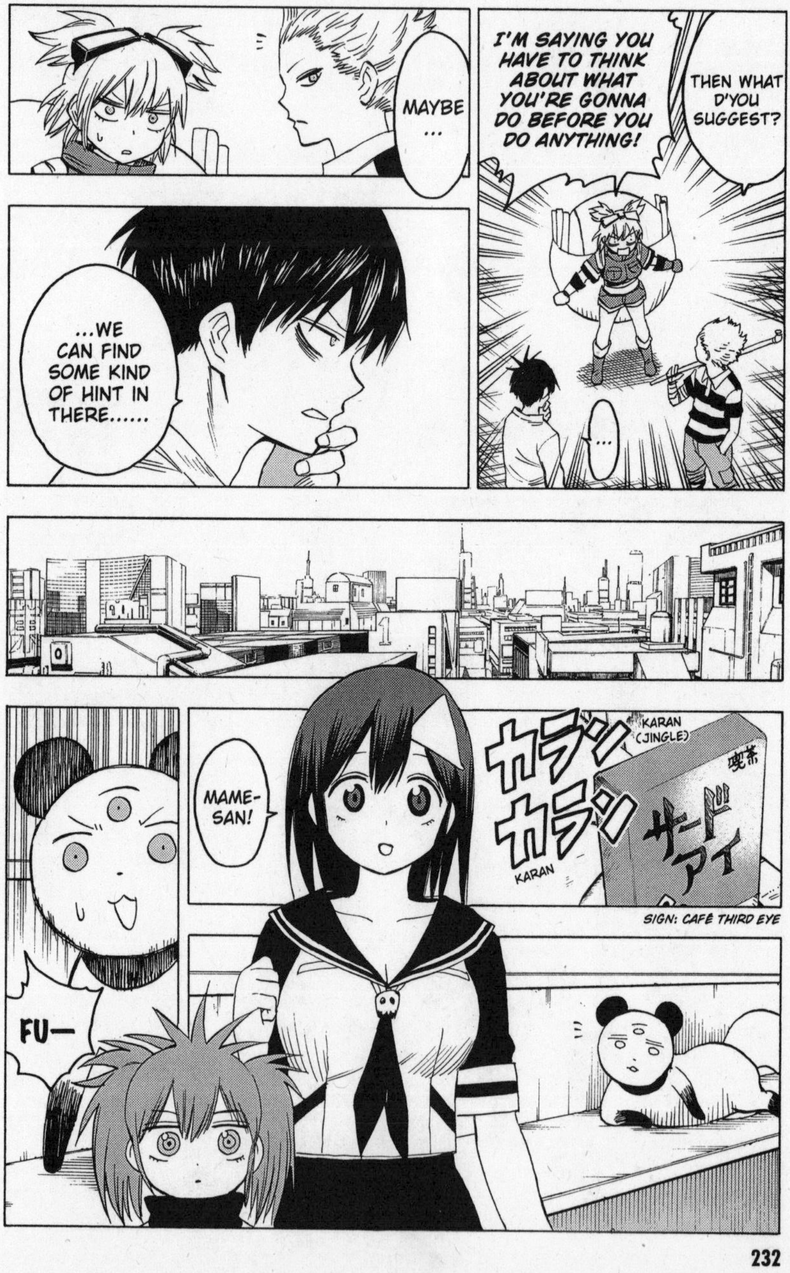
THEN WHAT D'YOU SUGGEST?
I'M SAYING YOU HAVE TO THINK ABOUT WHAT YOU'RE GONNA DO BEFORE YOU DO ANYTHING!
...
MAYBE ...
...WE CAN FIND SOME KIND OF HINT IN THERE......
カランカラン
KARAN (JINGLE) KARAN
喫茶 サードアイ
SIGN: CAFÉ THIRD EYE
MAME-SAN!
FU—

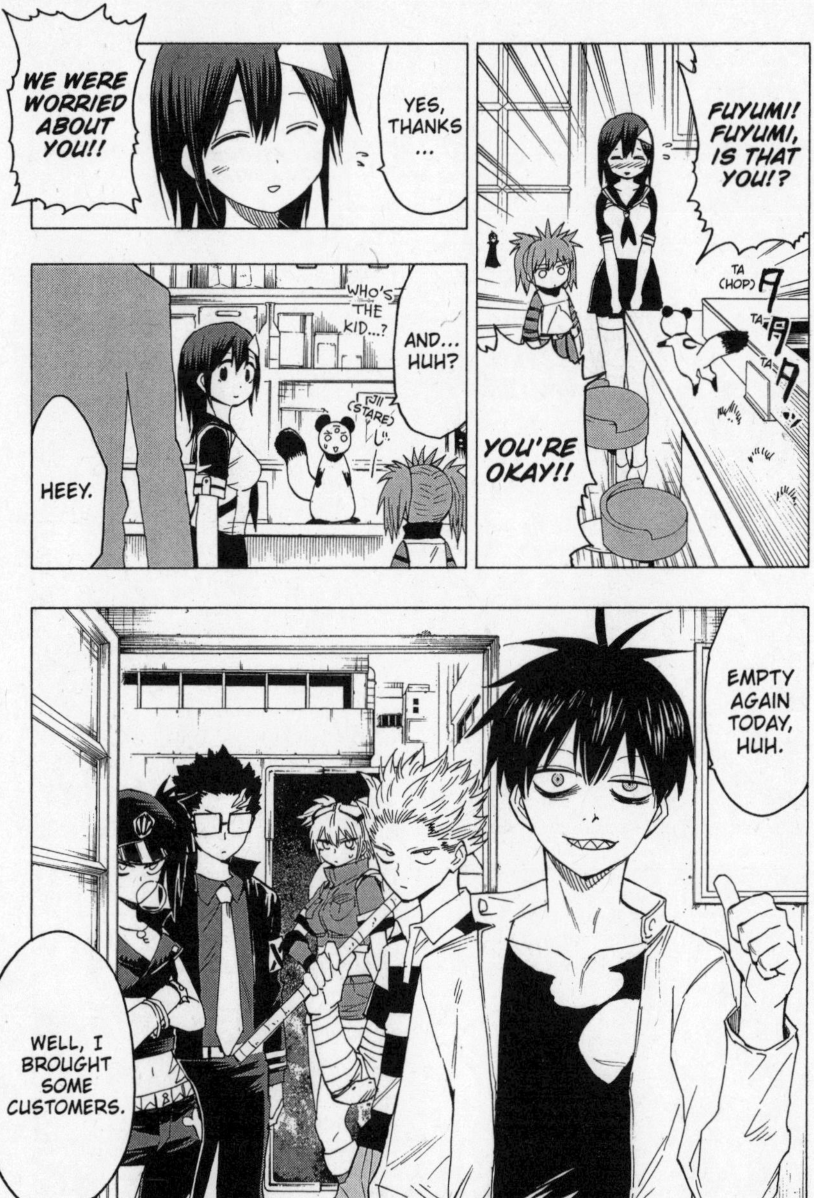

FUYUMI! FUYUMI, IS THAT YOU!?
TA (HOP)
TA
TA
YOU'RE OKAY!!
YES, THANKS ...
WE WERE WORRIED ABOUT YOU!!
AND... HUH?
WHO'S THE KID...?
(STARE)
HEEY.
EMPTY AGAIN TODAY, HUH.
WELL, I BROUGHT SOME CUSTOMERS.

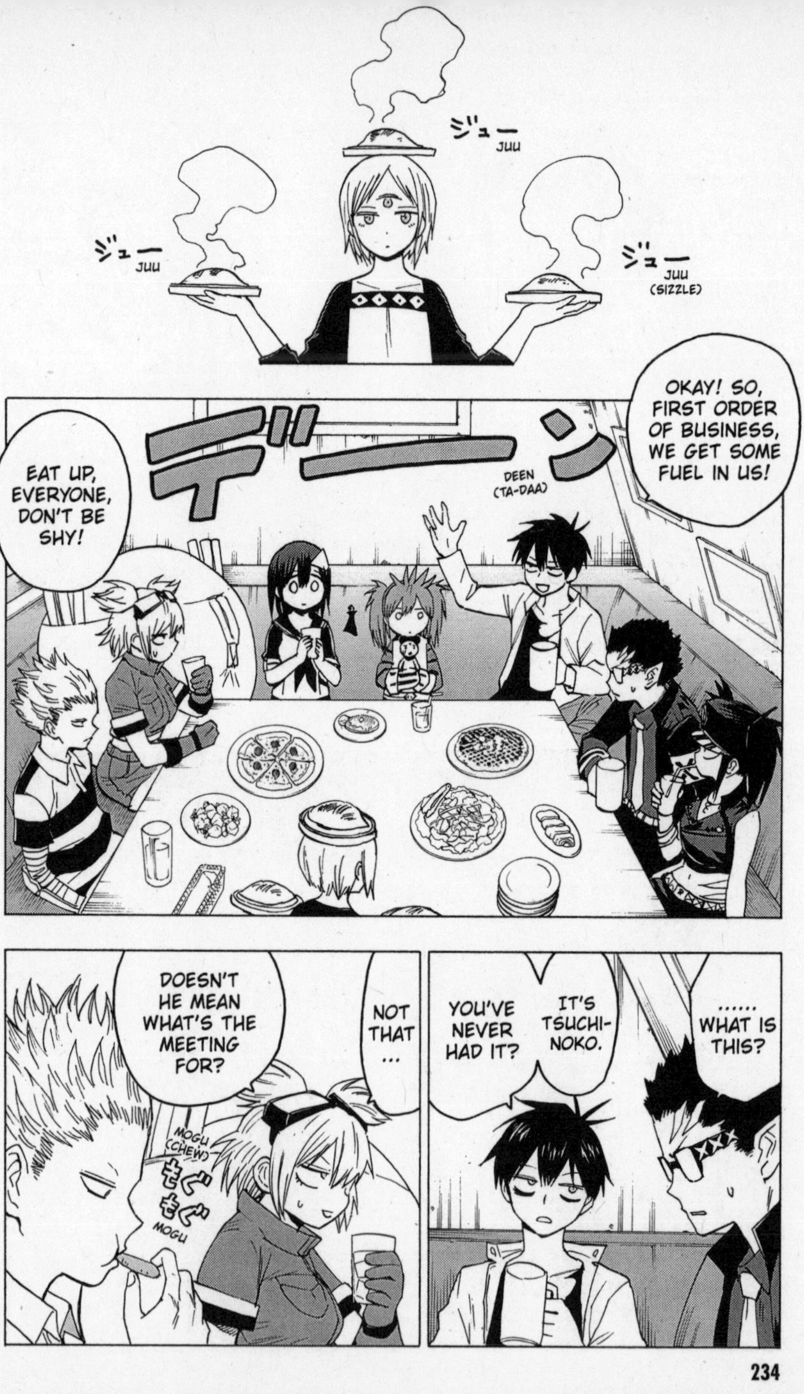
ジュー
JUU
ジュー
JUU
ジュー
JUU (SIZZLE)
OKAY! SO, FIRST ORDER OF BUSINESS, WE GET SOME FUEL IN US!
デーン
DEEN (TA-DAA)
EAT UP, EVERYONE, DON'T BE SHY!
...... WHAT IS THIS?
IT'S TSUCHINOKO.
YOU'VE NEVER HAD IT?
NOT THAT ...
DOESN'T HE MEAN WHAT'S THE MEETING FOR?
MOGU (CHEW)
もぐ もぐ
MOGU

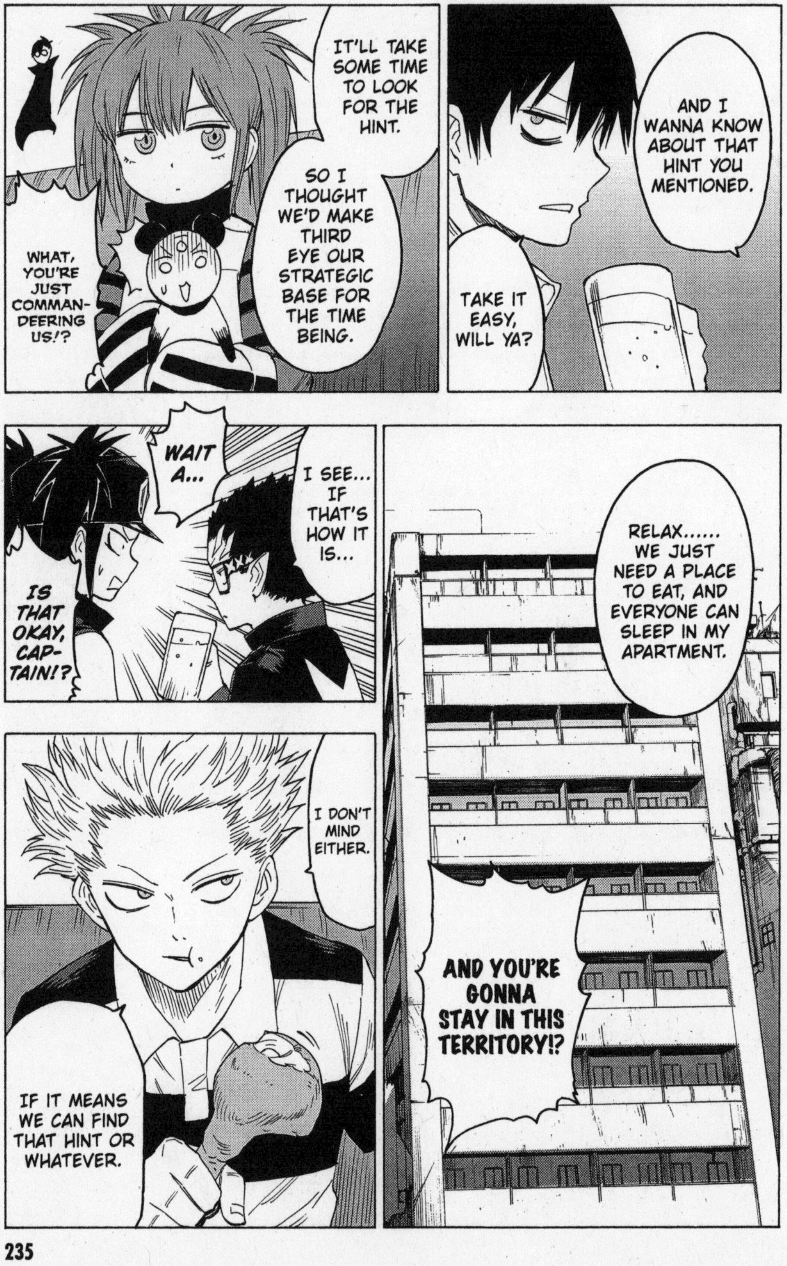
AND I WANNA KNOW ABOUT THAT HINT YOU MENTIONED.
TAKE IT EASY, WILL YA?
IT'LL TAKE SOME TIME TO LOOK FOR THE HINT.
SO I THOUGHT WE'D MAKE THIRD EYE OUR STRATEGIC BASE FOR THE TIME BEING.
WHAT, YOU'RE JUST COMMAN-DEERING US!?
RELAX...... WE JUST NEED A PLACE TO EAT, AND EVERYONE CAN SLEEP IN MY APARTMENT.
AND YOU'RE GONNA STAY IN THIS TERRITORY!?
I SEE... IF THAT'S HOW IT IS...
WAIT A...
IS THAT OKAY, CAP-TAIN!?
I DON'T MIND EITHER.
IF IT MEANS WE CAN FIND THAT HINT OR WHATEVER.

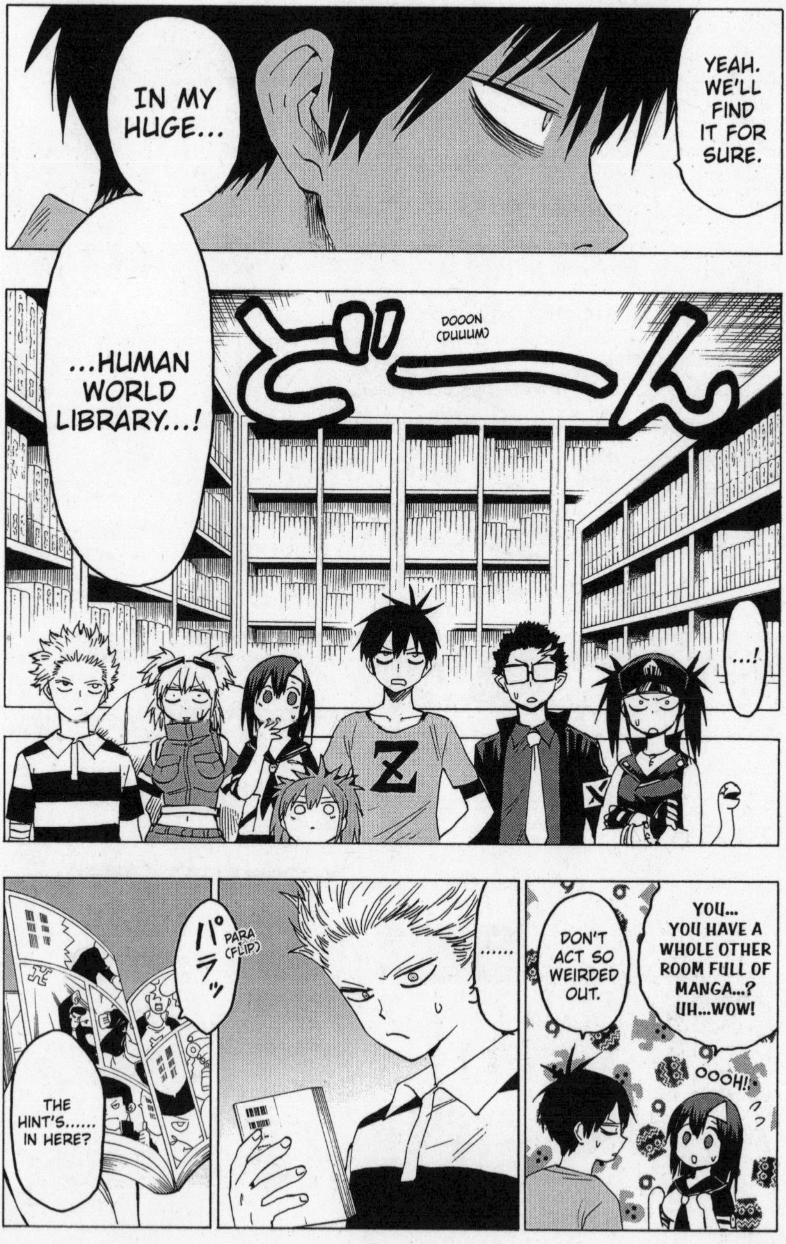
YEAH. WE'LL FIND IT FOR SURE.
IN MY HUGE...
...HUMAN WORLD LIBRARY...!
どーん
DOOON (DUUUM)
...!
YOU... YOU HAVE A WHOLE OTHER ROOM FULL OF MANGA...? UH...WOW!
OOOH!
DON'T ACT SO WEIRDED OUT.
......
パラッ
PARA (FLIP)
THE HINT'S...... IN HERE?

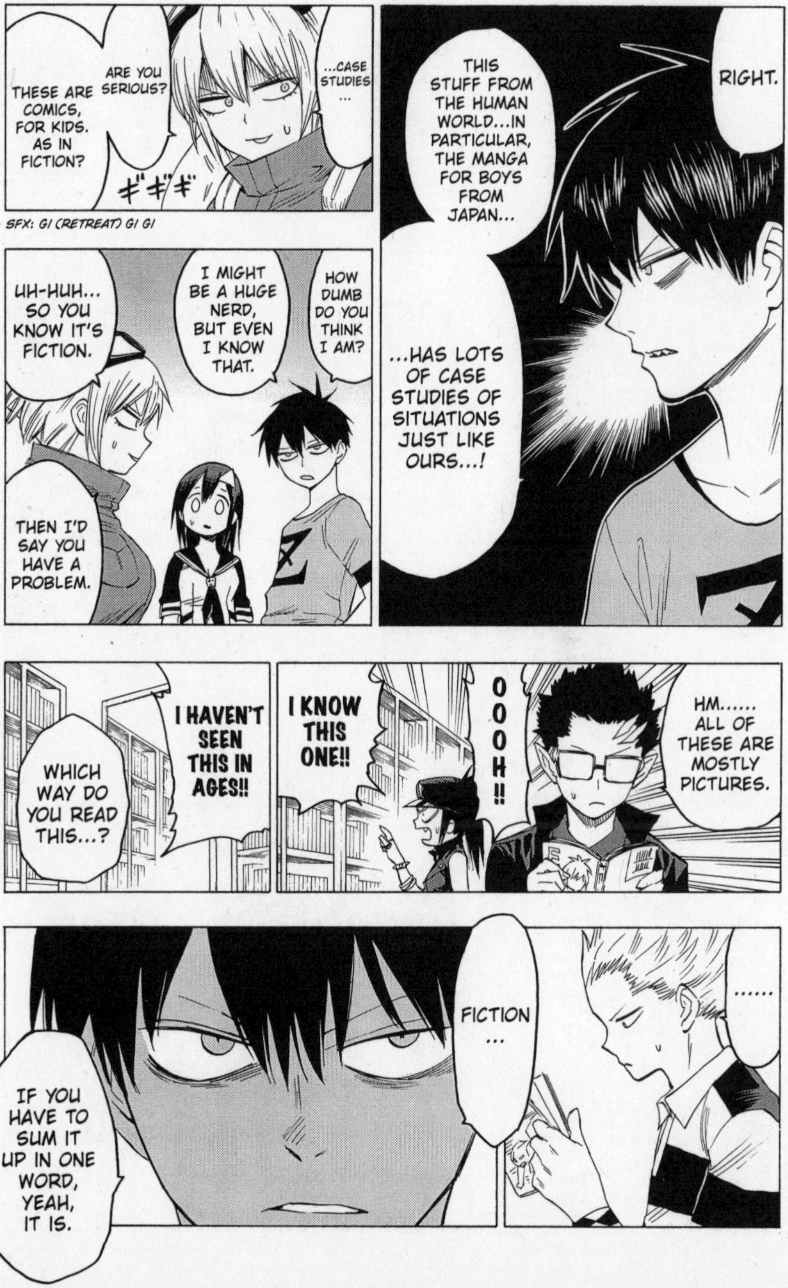
RIGHT.
THIS STUFF FROM THE HUMAN WORLD...IN PARTICULAR, THE MANGA FOR BOYS FROM JAPAN...
...HAS LOTS OF CASE STUDIES OF SITUATIONS JUST LIKE OURS...!
...CASE STUDIES...
ARE YOU SERIOUS?
THESE ARE COMICS, FOR KIDS. AS IN FICTION?
ギギギ
SFX: GI (RETREAT) GI GI
HOW DUMB DO YOU THINK I AM?
I MIGHT BE A HUGE NERD, BUT EVEN I KNOW THAT.
UH-HUH... SO YOU KNOW IT'S FICTION.
THEN I'D SAY YOU HAVE A PROBLEM.
HM...... ALL OF THESE ARE MOSTLY PICTURES.
OOOOH!!
I KNOW THIS ONE!!
I HAVEN'T SEEN THIS IN AGES!!
WHICH WAY DO YOU READ THIS...?
......
FICTION...
IF YOU HAVE TO SUM IT UP IN ONE WORD, YEAH, IT IS.

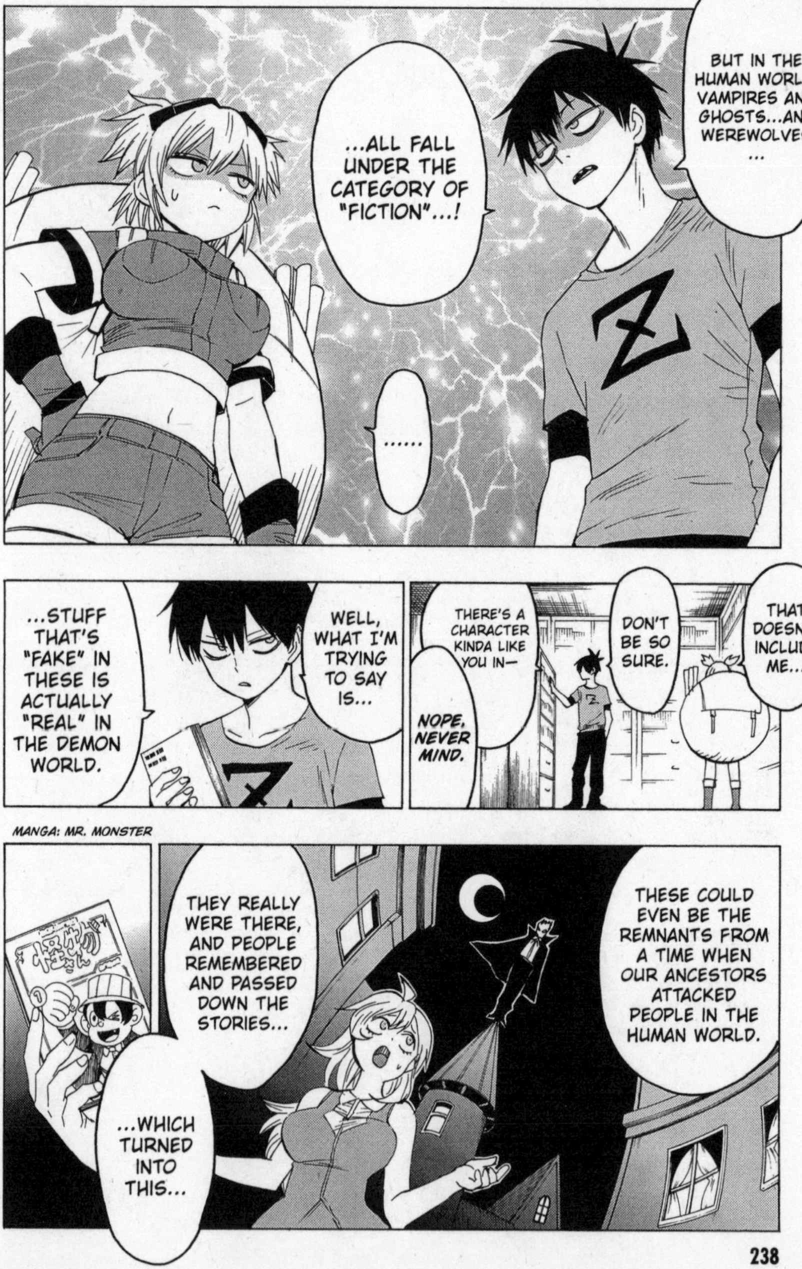
BUT IN THE HUMAN WORLD, VAMPIRES AND GHOSTS...AND WEREWOLVES ...
...ALL FALL UNDER THE CATEGORY OF "FICTION"...!
......
THAT DOESN'T INCLUDE ME...
DON'T BE SO SURE.
THERE'S A CHARACTER KINDA LIKE YOU IN—
NOPE, NEVER MIND.
WELL, WHAT I'M TRYING TO SAY IS...
...STUFF THAT'S "FAKE" IN THESE IS ACTUALLY "REAL" IN THE DEMON WORLD.
MANGA: MR. MONSTER
THESE COULD EVEN BE THE REMNANTS FROM A TIME WHEN OUR ANCESTORS ATTACKED PEOPLE IN THE HUMAN WORLD.
THEY REALLY WERE THERE, AND PEOPLE REMEMBERED AND PASSED DOWN THE STORIES...
...WHICH TURNED INTO THIS...

MANGA: BAD FRUIT

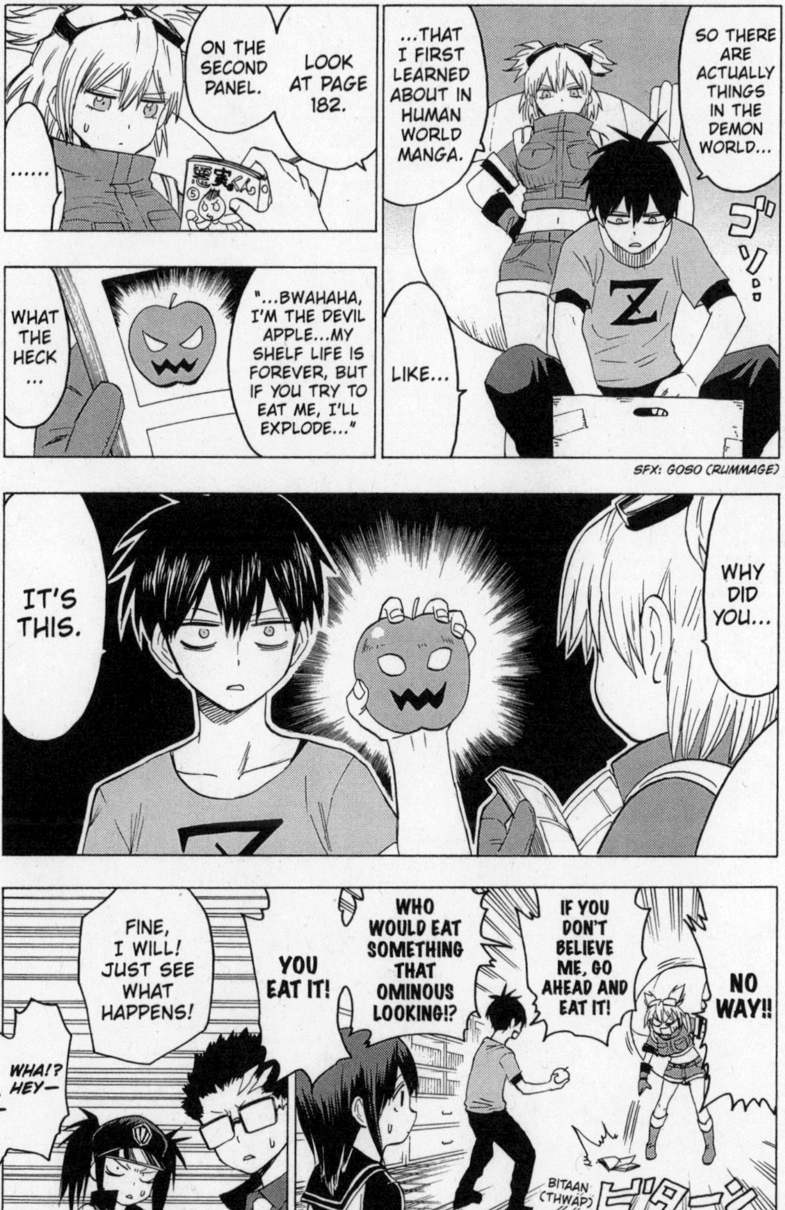
SO THERE ARE ACTUALLY THINGS IN THE DEMON WORLD...
...THAT I FIRST LEARNED ABOUT IN HUMAN WORLD MANGA.
LIKE...
ゴソ
LOOK AT PAGE 182.
ON THE SECOND PANEL.
......
"...BWAHAHA, I'M THE DEVIL APPLE...MY SHELF LIFE IS FOREVER, BUT IF YOU TRY TO EAT ME, I'LL EXPLODE..."
WHAT THE HECK ...
WHY DID YOU...
IT'S THIS.
NO WAY!!
IF YOU DON'T BELIEVE ME, GO AHEAD AND EAT IT!
WHO WOULD EAT SOMETHING THAT OMINOUS LOOKING!?
YOU EAT IT!
FINE, I WILL! JUST SEE WHAT HAPPENS!
WHA!? HEY—
NO... WAI—
BITAAN (THWAP)
ビターン

SFX: GOSO (RUMMAGE)

SFX: GUSSHO (DRENCHED)

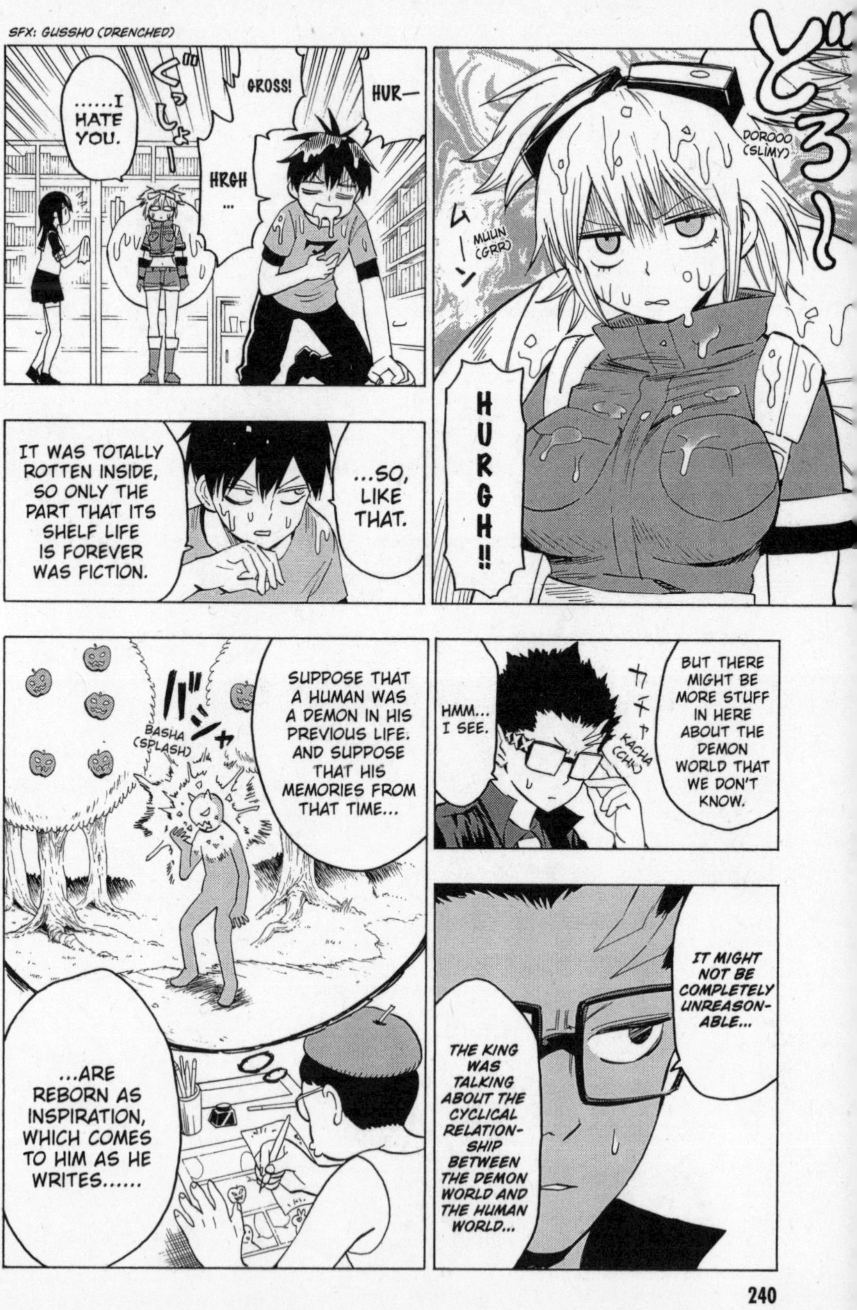
DOROOO (SLIMY)
MUUN (GRR)
HURGH!!
HUR—
GROSS!
......I HATE YOU.
HRGH ...
...SO, LIKE THAT.
IT WAS TOTALLY ROTTEN INSIDE, SO ONLY THE PART THAT ITS SHELF LIFE IS FOREVER WAS FICTION.
BUT THERE MIGHT BE MORE STUFF IN HERE ABOUT THE DEMON WORLD THAT WE DON'T KNOW.
KACHA (CHK)
HMM... I SEE.
IT MIGHT NOT BE COMPLETELY UNREASON-ABLE...
THE KING WAS TALKING ABOUT THE CYCLICAL RELATION-SHIP BETWEEN THE DEMON WORLD AND THE HUMAN WORLD...
SUPPOSE THAT A HUMAN WAS A DEMON IN HIS PREVIOUS LIFE. AND SUPPOSE THAT HIS MEMORIES FROM THAT TIME...
BASHA (SPLASH)
...ARE REBORN AS INSPIRATION, WHICH COMES TO HIM AS HE WRITES......

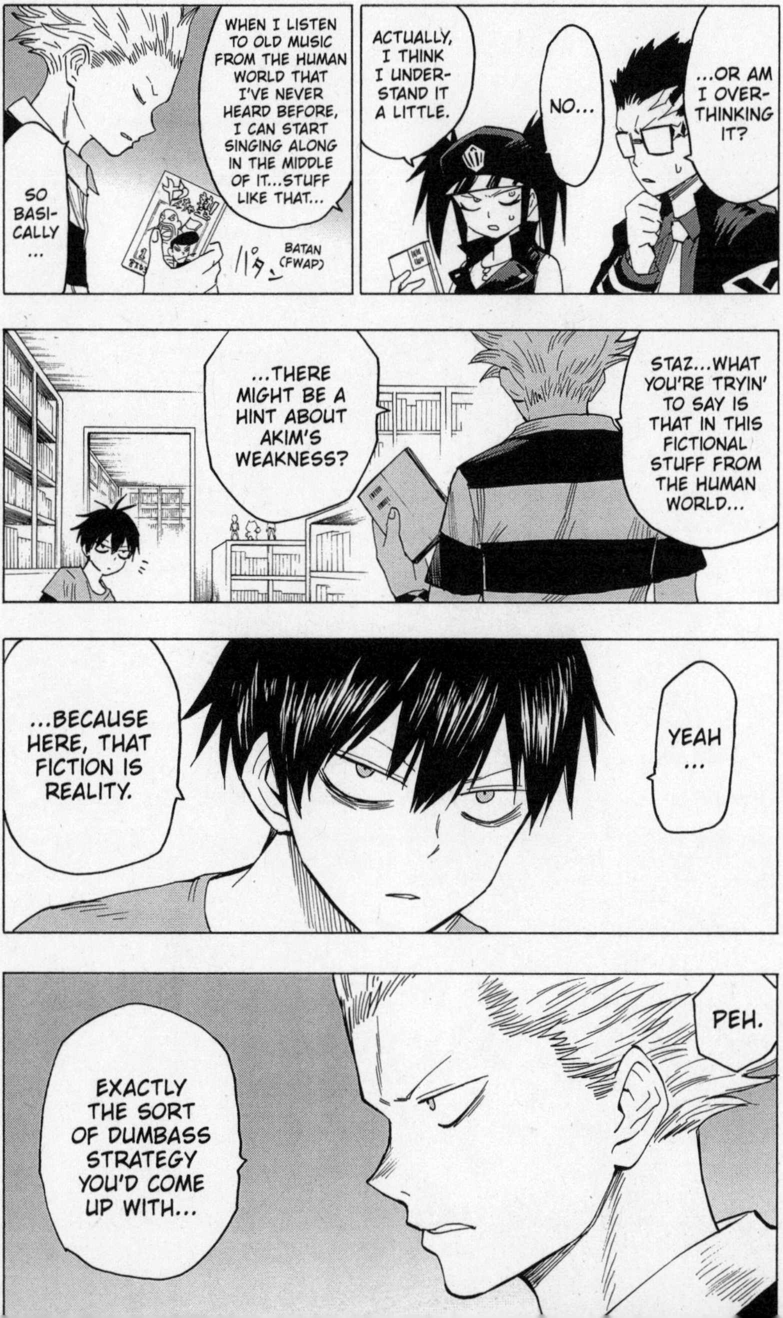

...OR AM I OVER-THINKING IT?
NO...
ACTUALLY, I THINK I UNDER-STAND IT A LITTLE.
WHEN I LISTEN TO OLD MUSIC FROM THE HUMAN WORLD THAT I'VE NEVER HEARD BEFORE, I CAN START SINGING ALONG IN THE MIDDLE OF IT...STUFF LIKE THAT...
BATAN (FWAP)
SO BASI-CALLY...
STAZ...WHAT YOU'RE TRYIN' TO SAY IS THAT IN THIS FICTIONAL STUFF FROM THE HUMAN WORLD...
...THERE MIGHT BE A HINT ABOUT AKIM'S WEAKNESS?
YEAH...
...BECAUSE HERE, THAT FICTION IS REALITY.
PEH.
EXACTLY THE SORT OF DUMBASS STRATEGY YOU'D COME UP WITH...

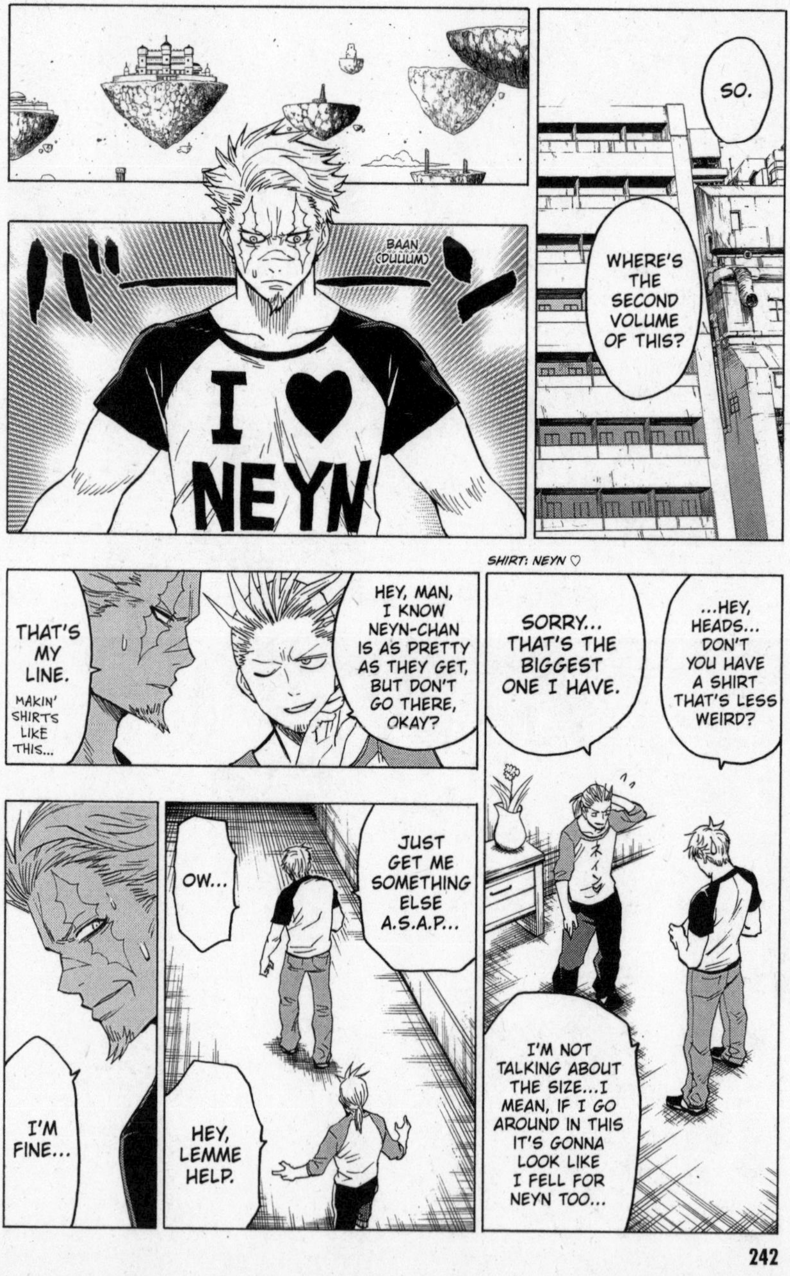
SO.
WHERE'S THE SECOND VOLUME OF THIS?
BAAN (DUUUM)
I ♥ NEYN
SHIRT: NEYN ♡
...HEY, HEADS... DON'T YOU HAVE A SHIRT THAT'S LESS WEIRD?
SORRY... THAT'S THE BIGGEST ONE I HAVE.
I'M NOT TALKING ABOUT THE SIZE...I MEAN, IF I GO AROUND IN THIS IT'S GONNA LOOK LIKE I FELL FOR NEYN TOO...
HEY, MAN, I KNOW NEYN-CHAN IS AS PRETTY AS THEY GET, BUT DON'T GO THERE, OKAY?
THAT'S MY LINE.
MAKIN' SHIRTS LIKE THIS...
JUST GET ME SOMETHING ELSE A.S.A.P...
OW...
HEY, LEMME HELP.
I'M FINE...

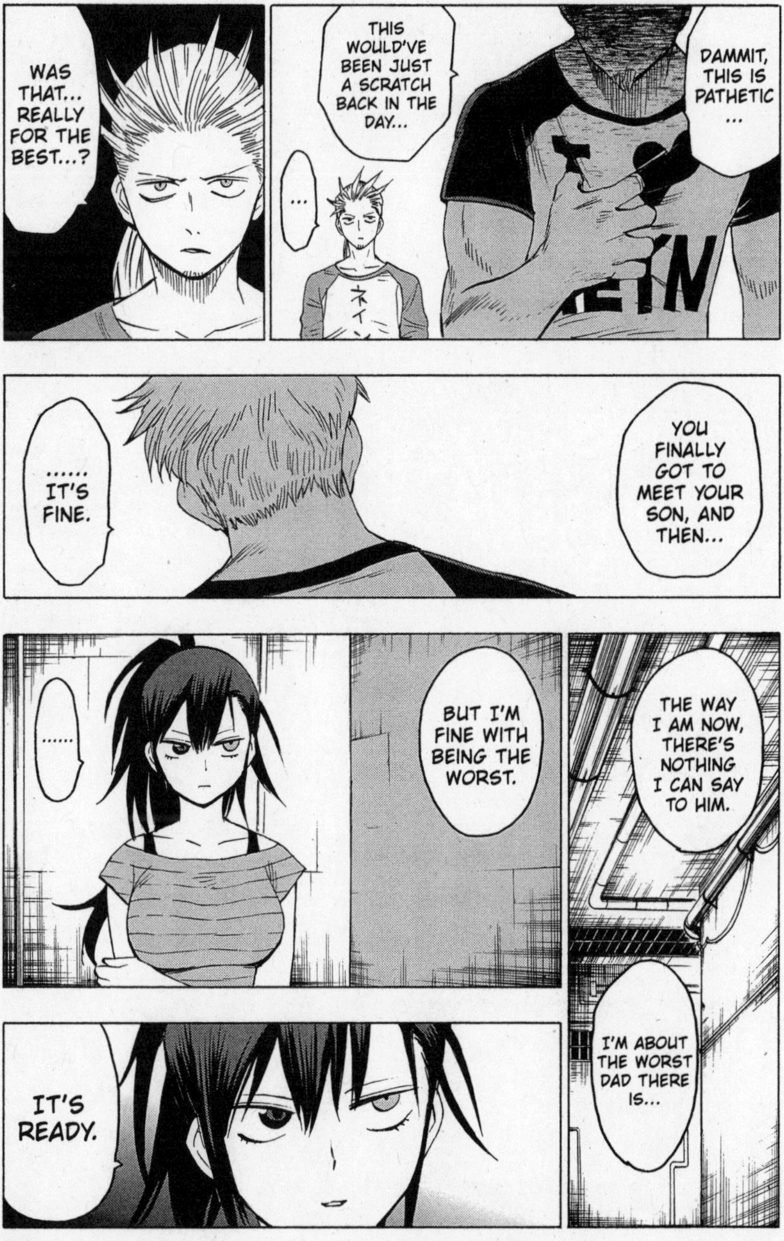
DAMMIT, THIS IS PATHETIC ...
THIS WOULD'VE BEEN JUST A SCRATCH BACK IN THE DAY...
...
WAS THAT... REALLY FOR THE BEST...?
YOU FINALLY GOT TO MEET YOUR SON, AND THEN...
...... IT'S FINE.
THE WAY I AM NOW, THERE'S NOTHING I CAN SAY TO HIM.
I'M ABOUT THE WORST DAD THERE IS...
BUT I'M FINE WITH BEING THE WORST.
......
IT'S READY.

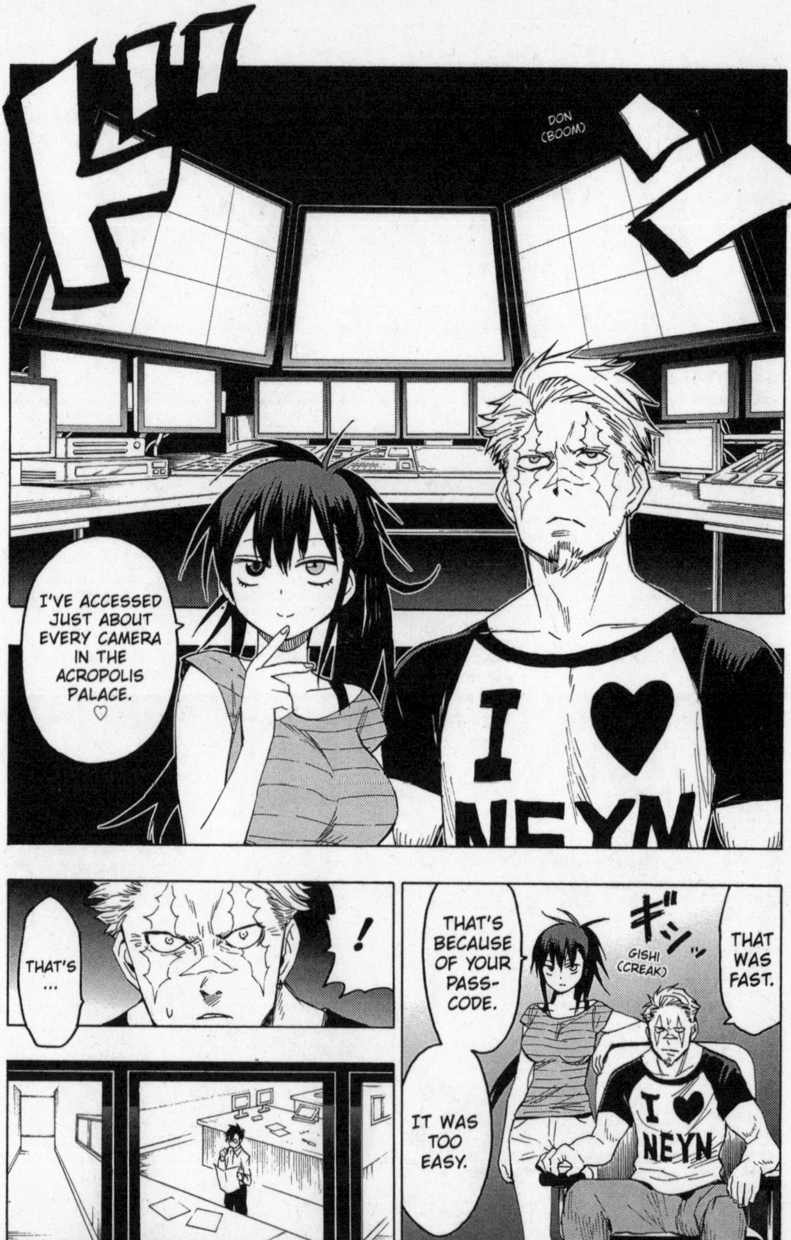

DON (BOOM)
I'VE ACCESSED JUST ABOUT EVERY CAMERA IN THE ACROPOLIS PALACE. ♡
THAT WAS FAST.
GISHI (CREAK)
THAT'S BECAUSE OF YOUR PASS-CODE.
IT WAS TOO EASY.
!
THAT'S ...

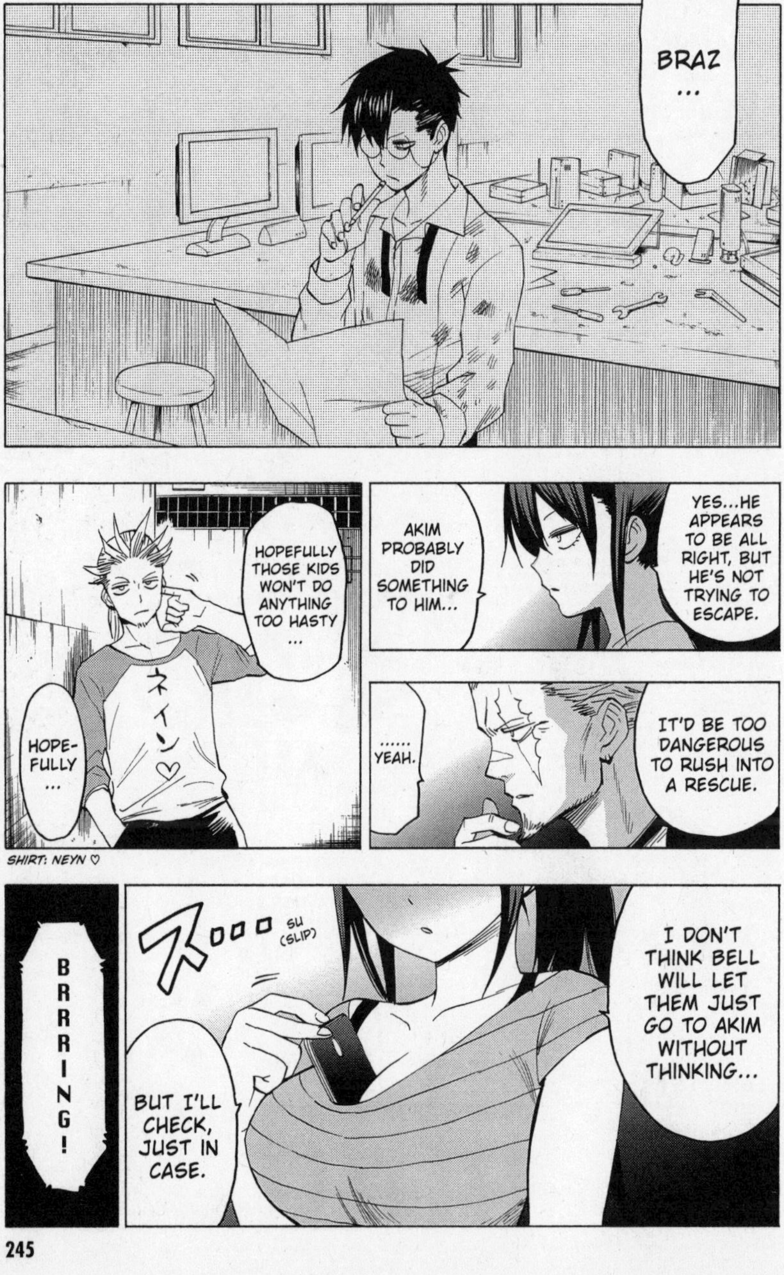
BRAZ...
YES...HE APPEARS TO BE ALL RIGHT, BUT HE'S NOT TRYING TO ESCAPE.
AKIM PROBABLY DID SOMETHING TO HIM...
IT'D BE TOO DANGEROUS TO RUSH INTO A RESCUE.
......YEAH.
HOPEFULLY THOSE KIDS WON'T DO ANYTHING TOO HASTY...
HOPE-FULLY...
I DON'T THINK BELL WILL LET THEM JUST GO TO AKIM WITHOUT THINKING...
SU (SLIP)
BUT I'LL CHECK, JUST IN CASE.
BRRRING!

SHIRT: NEYN ♡

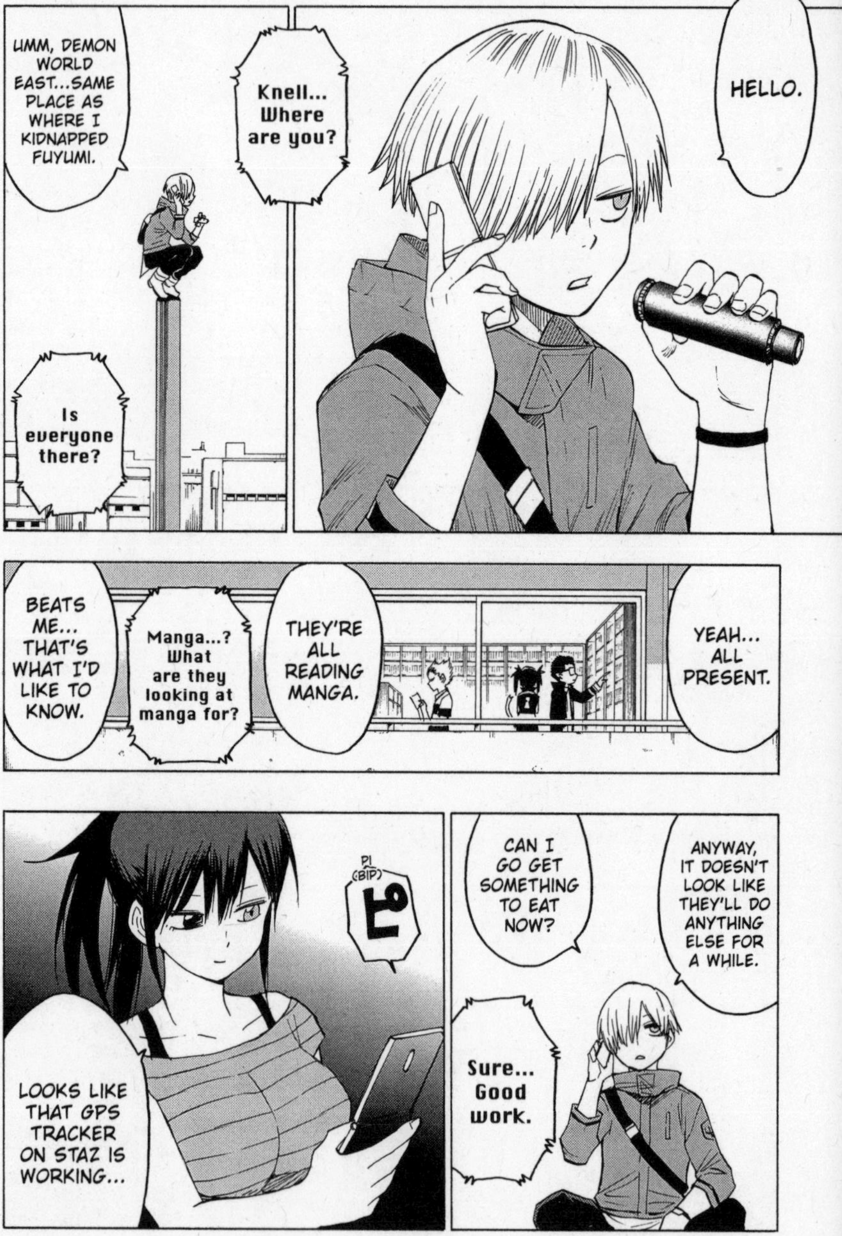
HELLO.
Knell... Where are you?
UMM, DEMON WORLD EAST...SAME PLACE AS WHERE I KIDNAPPED FUYUMI.
Is everyone there?
YEAH... ALL PRESENT.
THEY'RE ALL READING MANGA.
Manga...? What are they looking at manga for?
BEATS ME... THAT'S WHAT I'D LIKE TO KNOW.
ANYWAY, IT DOESN'T LOOK LIKE THEY'LL DO ANYTHING ELSE FOR A WHILE.
CAN I GO GET SOMETHING TO EAT NOW?
Sure... Good work.
PI (BIP)
LOOKS LIKE THAT GPS TRACKER ON STAZ IS WORKING...

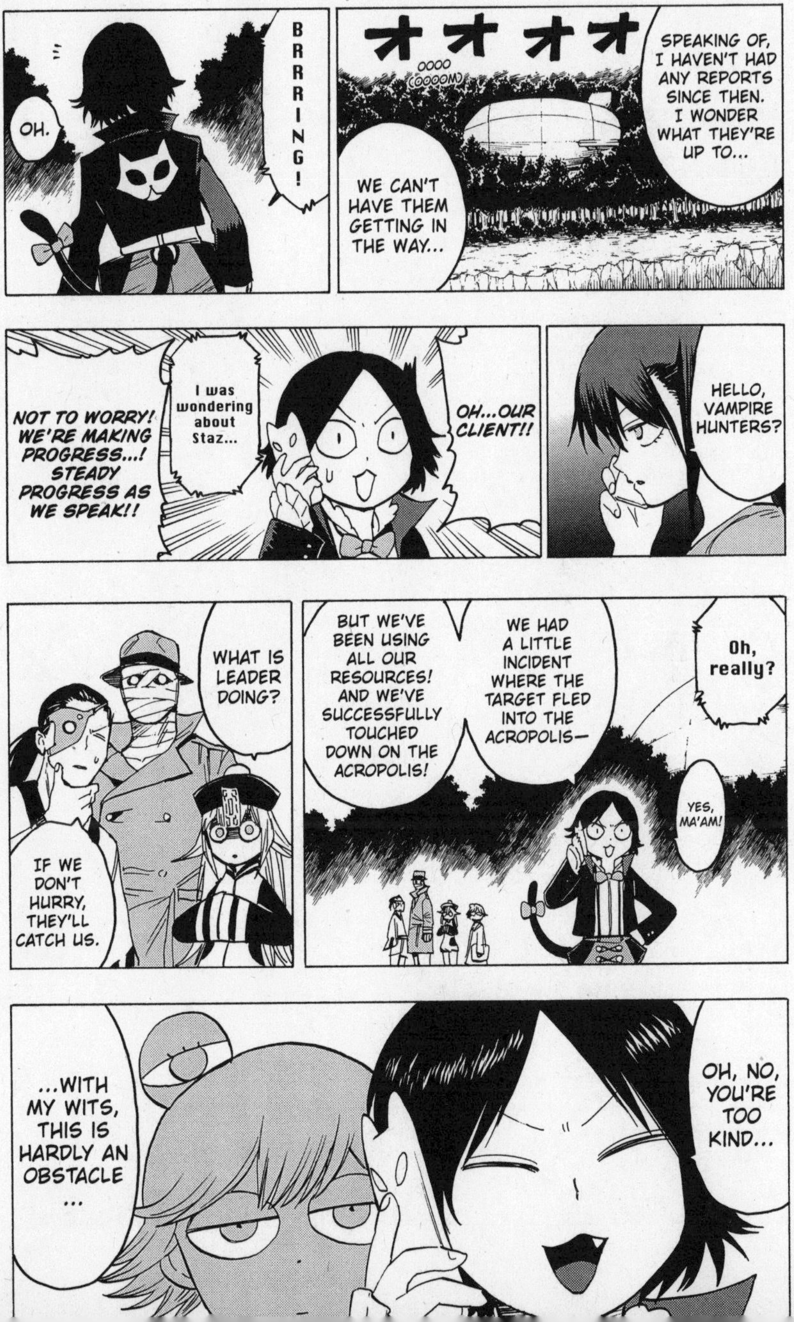
オオオオ
OOOO (OOOOM)
SPEAKING OF, I HAVEN'T HAD ANY REPORTS SINCE THEN. I WONDER WHAT THEY'RE UP TO...
WE CAN'T HAVE THEM GETTING IN THE WAY...
BRRRING!
OH.
HELLO, VAMPIRE HUNTERS?
OH...OUR CLIENT!!
I was wondering about Staz...
NOT TO WORRY! WE'RE MAKING PROGRESS...! STEADY PROGRESS AS WE SPEAK!!
Oh, really?
WE HAD A LITTLE INCIDENT WHERE THE TARGET FLED INTO THE ACROPOLIS—
YES, MA'AM!
BUT WE'VE BEEN USING ALL OUR RESOURCES! AND WE'VE SUCCESSFULLY TOUCHED DOWN ON THE ACROPOLIS!
WHAT IS LEADER DOING?
IF WE DON'T HURRY, THEY'LL CATCH US.
OH, NO, YOU'RE TOO KIND...
...WITH MY WITS, THIS IS HARDLY AN OBSTACLE ...

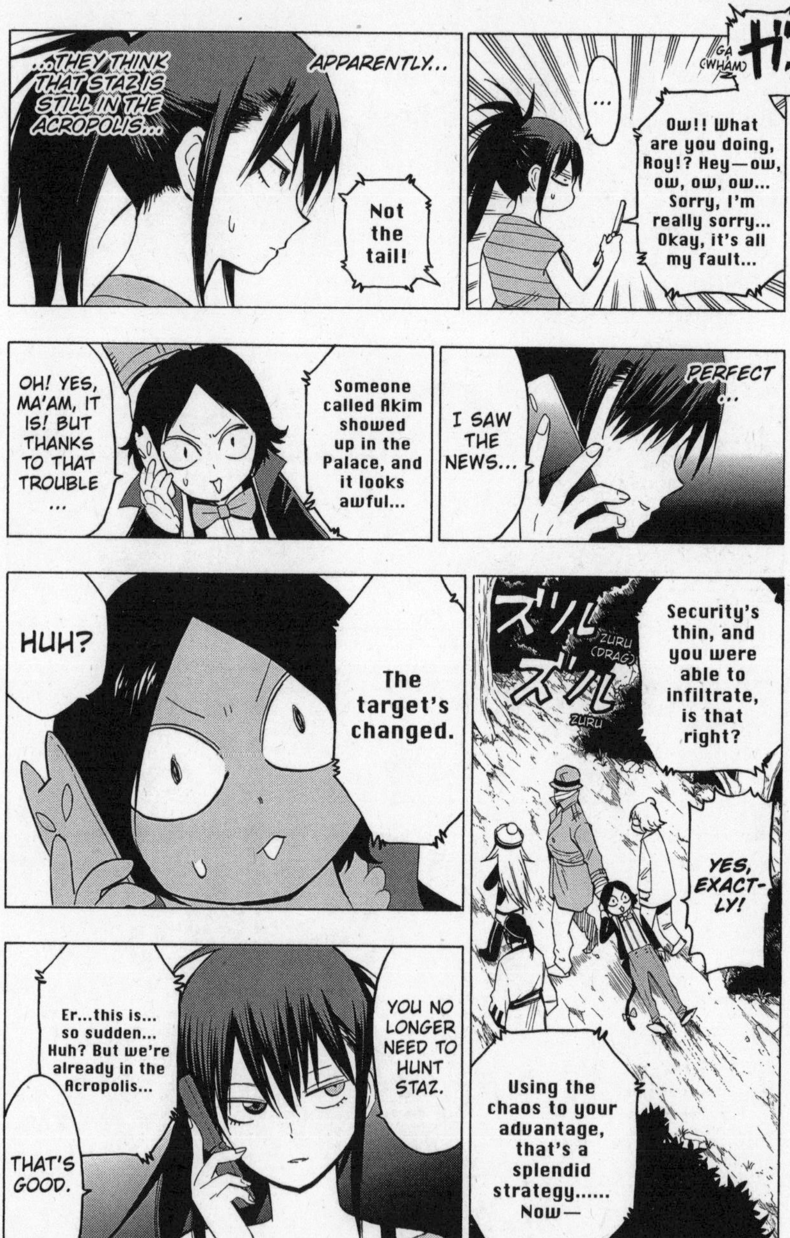

ガッ
GA (WHAM)
...
Ow!! What are you doing, Roy!? Hey—ow, ow, ow, ow... Sorry, I'm really sorry... Okay, it's all my fault...
APPARENTLY...
...THEY THINK THAT STAZ IS STILL IN THE ACROPOLIS...
Not the tail!
PERFECT...
I SAW THE NEWS...
Someone called Akim showed up in the Palace, and it looks awful...
OH! YES, MA'AM, IT IS! BUT THANKS TO THAT TROUBLE...
ズル
ZURU (DRAG)
ズル
ZURU
Security's thin, and you were able to infiltrate, is that right?
YES, EXACTLY!
Using the chaos to your advantage, that's a splendid strategy...... Now—
HUH?
The target's changed.
YOU NO LONGER NEED TO HUNT STAZ.
Er...this is... so sudden... Huh? But we're already in the Acropolis...
THAT'S GOOD.

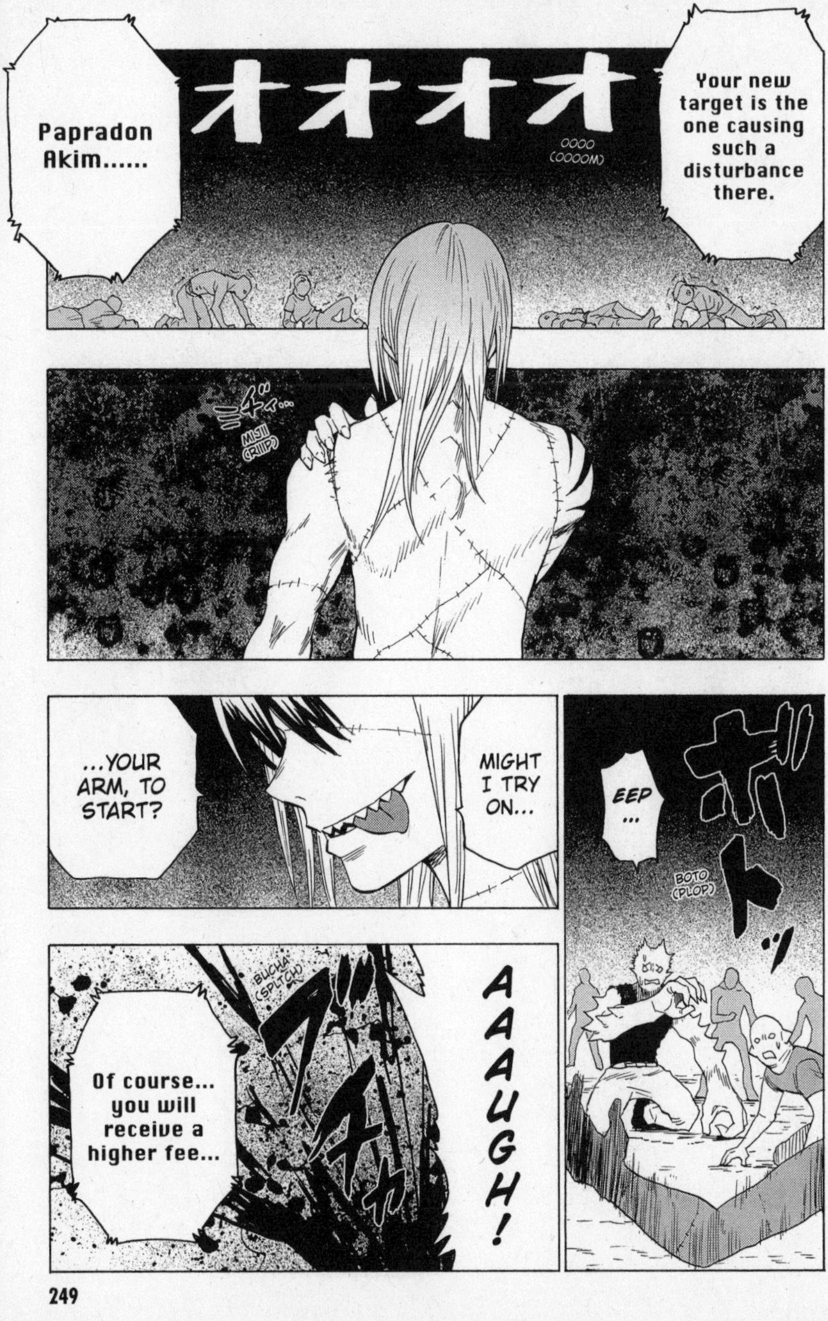
Your new target is the one causing such a disturbance there.
オオオオ
OOOO (OOOOM)
Papradon Akim......
MIJI (RIIIP)
EEP...
BOTO (PLOP)
MIGHT I TRY ON...
...YOUR ARM, TO START?
AAAAUGH!
BUCHA (SPLTCH)
Of course... you will receive a higher fee...

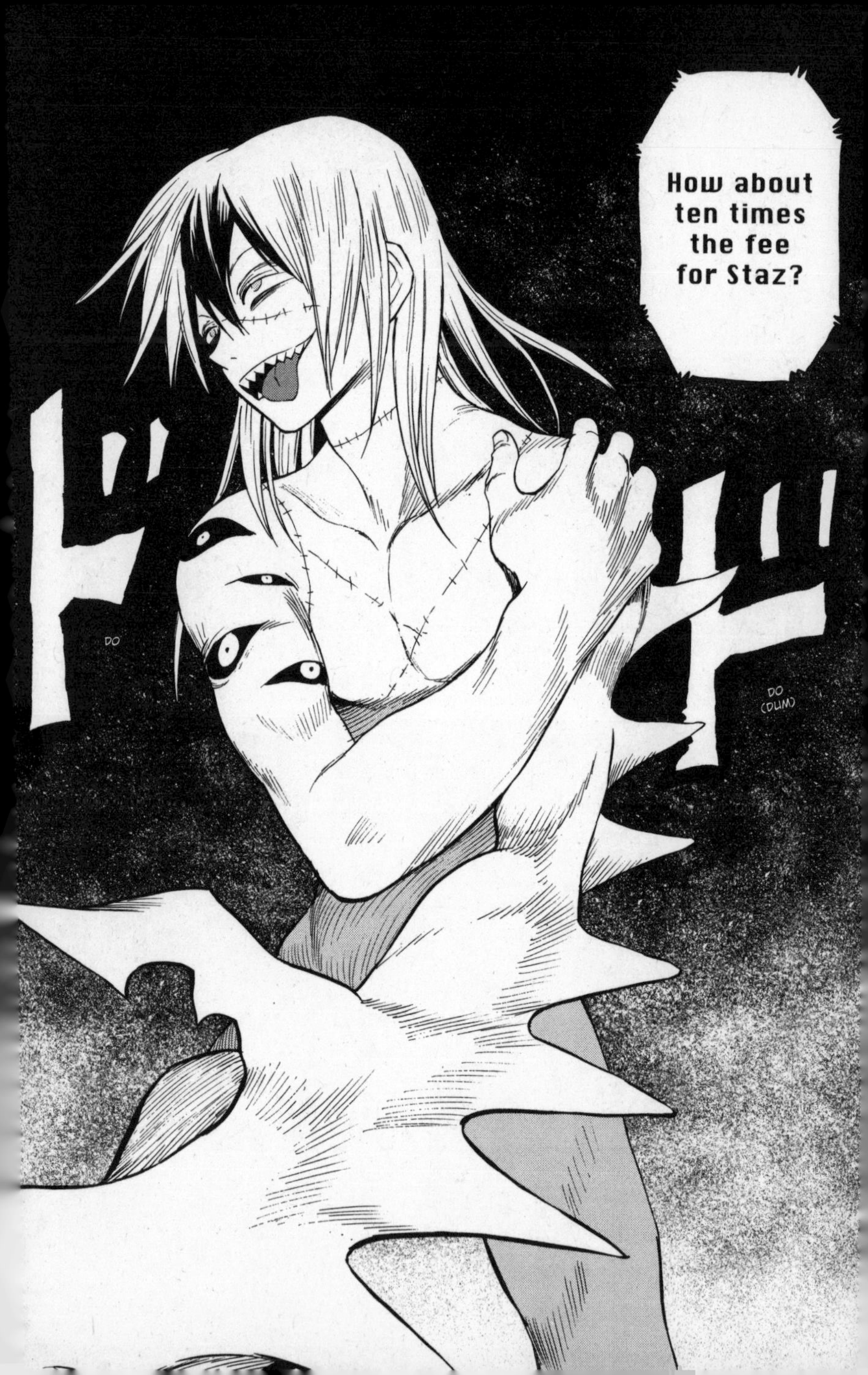
How about ten times the fee for Staz?
DO
DO (DUM)

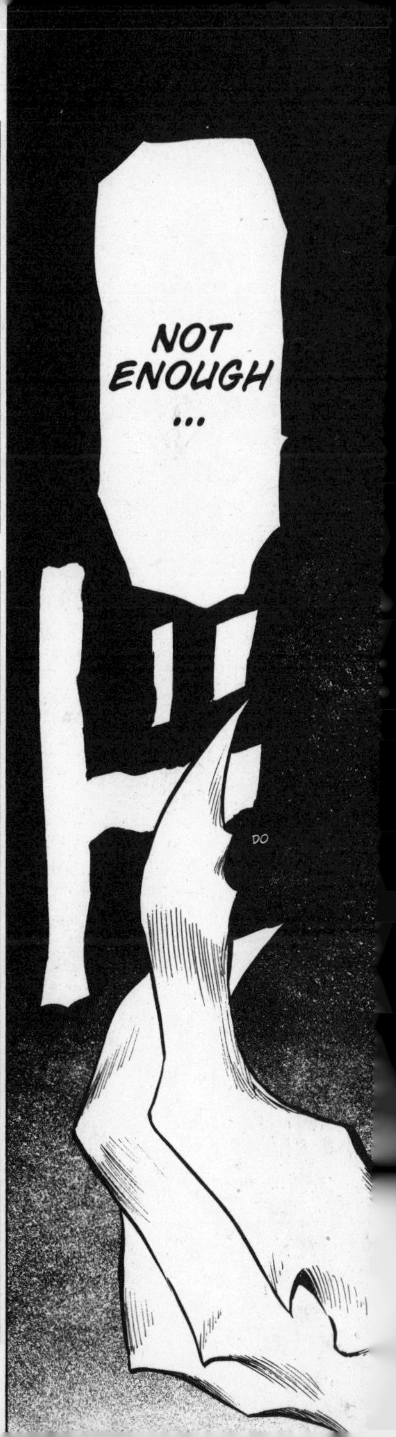
NOT ENOUGH ...
DO

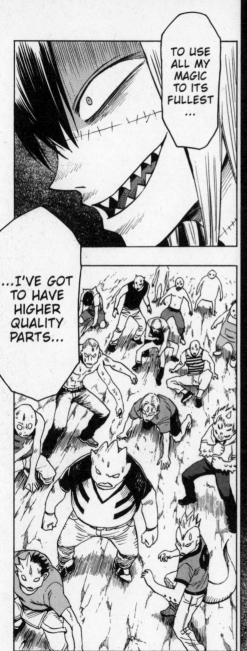

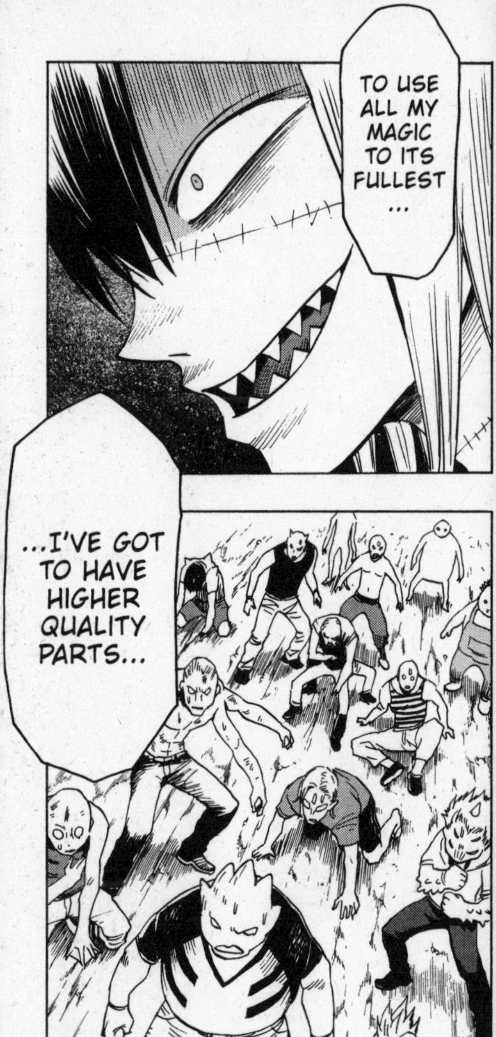
TO USE ALL MY MAGIC TO ITS FULLEST ...
...I'VE GOT TO HAVE HIGHER QUALITY PARTS...

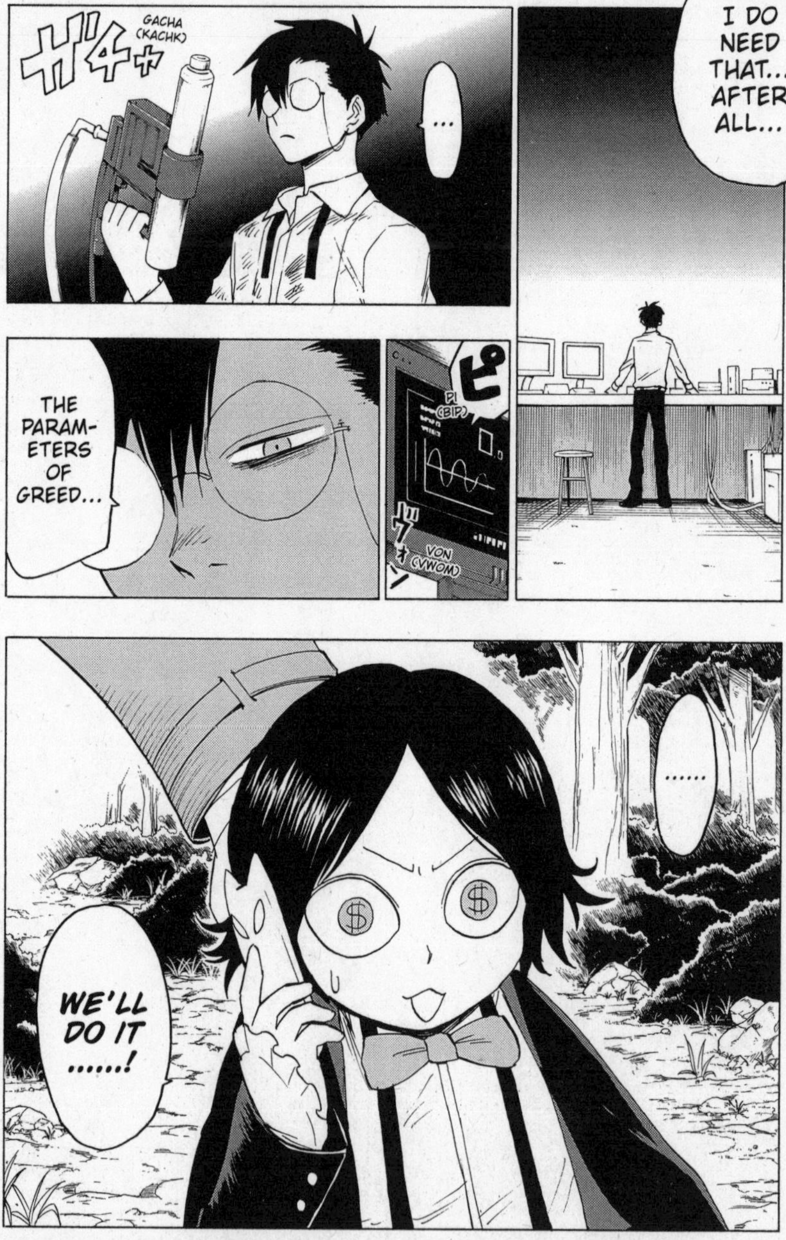
I DO NEED THAT... AFTER ALL...
GACHA (KACHK)
...
PI (BIP)
VON (VWOM)
THE PARAMETERS OF GREED...
......
WE'LL DO IT ......!

♠ To Be Continued ♠

WERE Wolfboy

MP ▲ 19800 /organ

BLOOD LAD

BLOODLAD

CHAPTER 48 ♠
WHY EVEN THE MANGA WORLD ISN'T THAT EASY

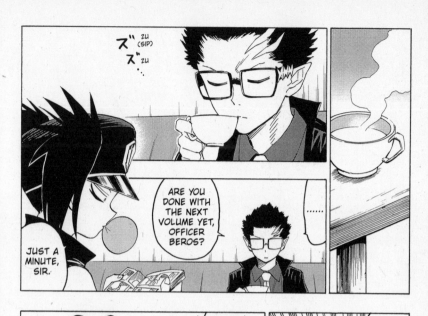

ズ ZU (SIP)
ズ ZU
......
ARE YOU DONE WITH THE NEXT VOLUME YET, OFFICER BEROS?
JUST A MINUTE, SIR.
THIS IS A GOOD PART...
...THEY FINALLY FIND OUT WHO THAT MYSTERIOUS FIGURE IS... AND IT'S...
NOOO! DON'T TELL ME!!
...FROM THAT THING THREE YEARS AGO...
I TOLD YOU NOT TO TELL ME!!
WELL, YOU REALLY WANTED TO KNOW, CAPTAIN, SO I THOUGHT I SHOULD JUST TELL YOU.
I WANT TO READ IT FOR MYSELF!
...
HEY, WOLF...

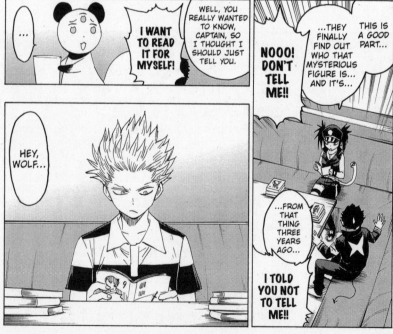

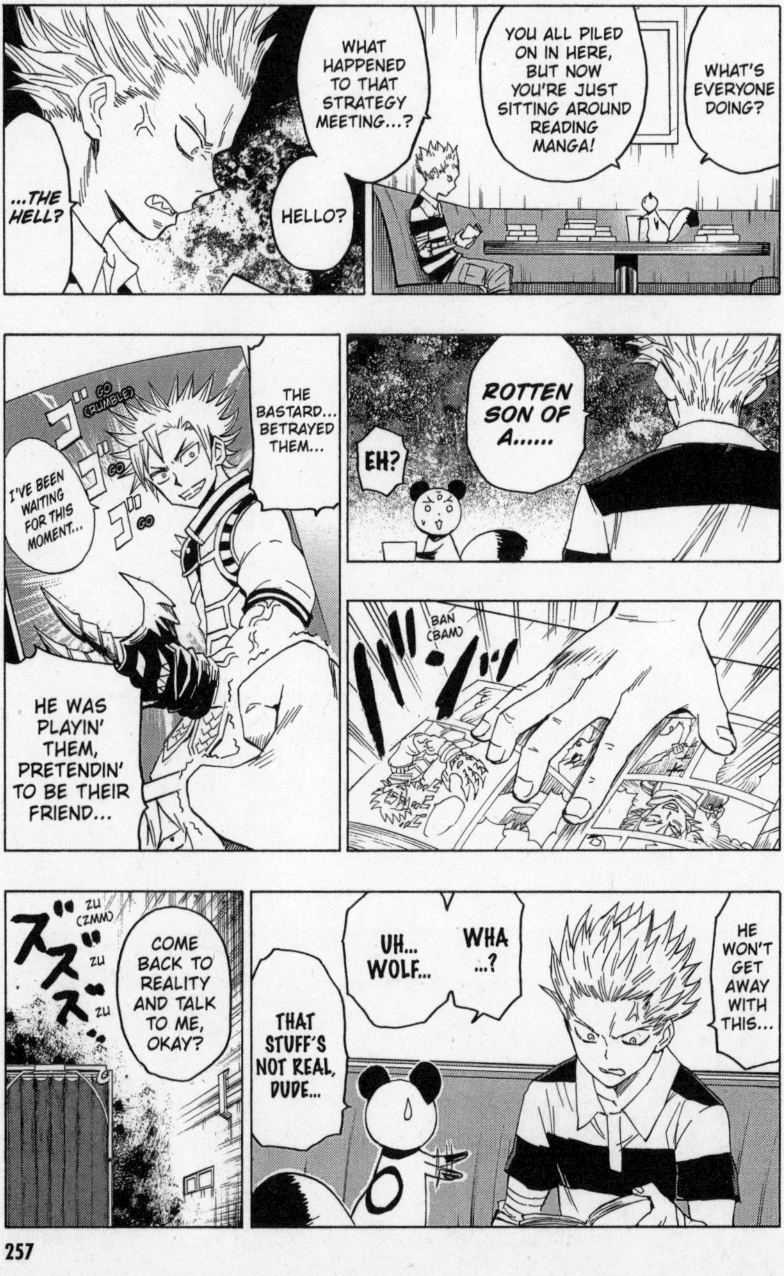
WHAT'S EVERYONE DOING?
YOU ALL PILED ON IN HERE, BUT NOW YOU'RE JUST SITTING AROUND READING MANGA!
WHAT HAPPENED TO THAT STRATEGY MEETING...?
HELLO?
...THE HELL?
ROTTEN SON OF A......
EH?
BAN (BAM)
THE BASTARD... BETRAYED THEM...
GO (RUMBLE) GO GO
I'VE BEEN WAITING FOR THIS MOMENT...
HE WAS PLAYIN' THEM, PRETENDIN' TO BE THEIR FRIEND...
HE WON'T GET AWAY WITH THIS...
WHA ...?
UH... WOLF...
THAT STUFF'S NOT REAL, DUDE...
ZU (ZMMM) ZU ZU
COME BACK TO REALITY AND TALK TO ME, OKAY?

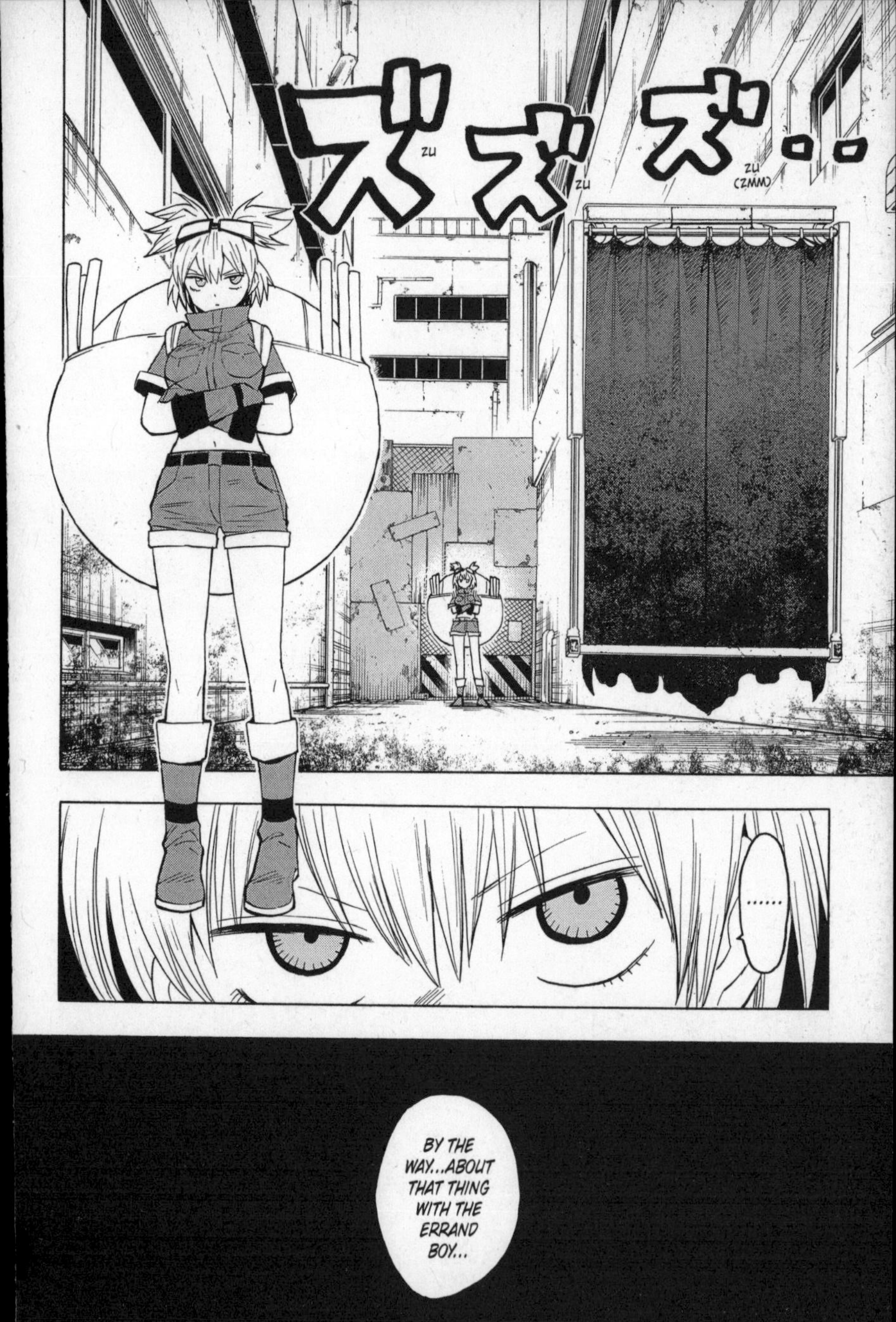
ズズズ...
ZU ZU ZU (ZMM)
......
BY THE WAY...ABOUT THAT THING WITH THE ERRAND BOY...

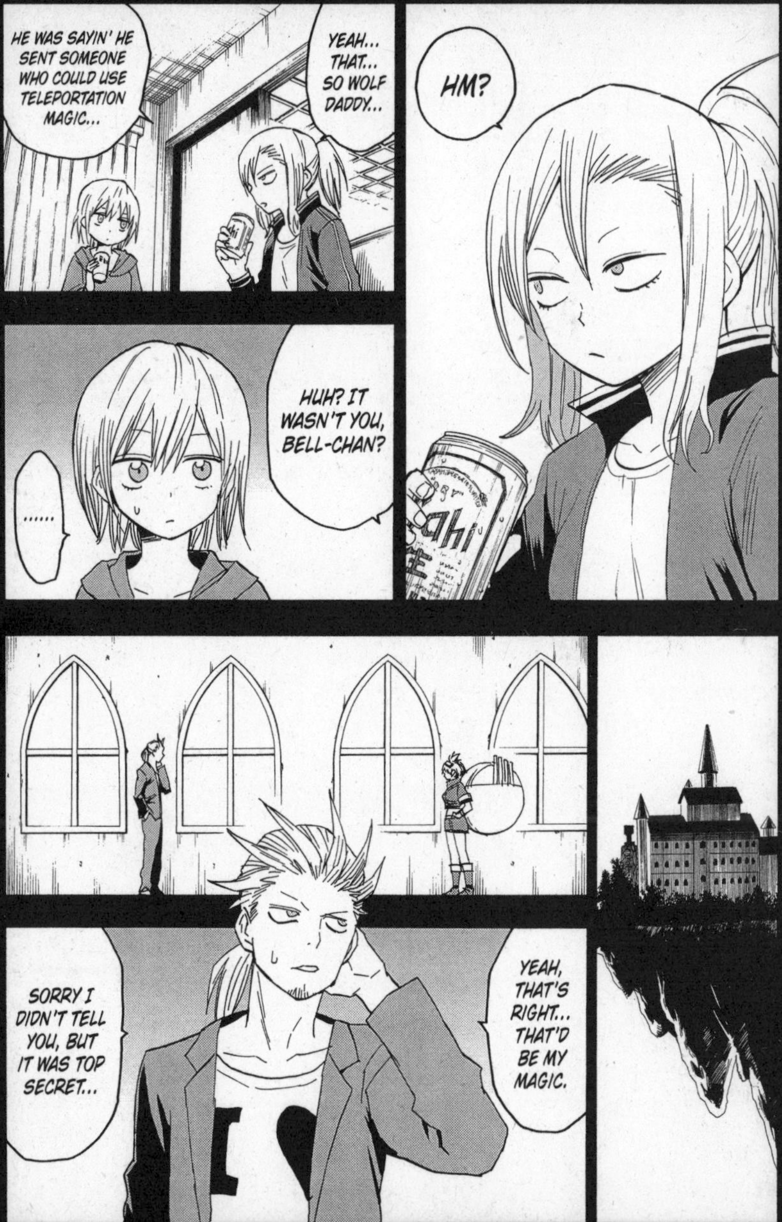
HM?
YEAH... THAT... SO WOLF DADDY...
HE WAS SAYIN' HE SENT SOMEONE WHO COULD USE TELEPORTATION MAGIC...
HUH? IT WASN'T YOU, BELL-CHAN?
......
YEAH, THAT'S RIGHT... THAT'D BE MY MAGIC.
SORRY I DIDN'T TELL YOU, BUT IT WAS TOP SECRET...

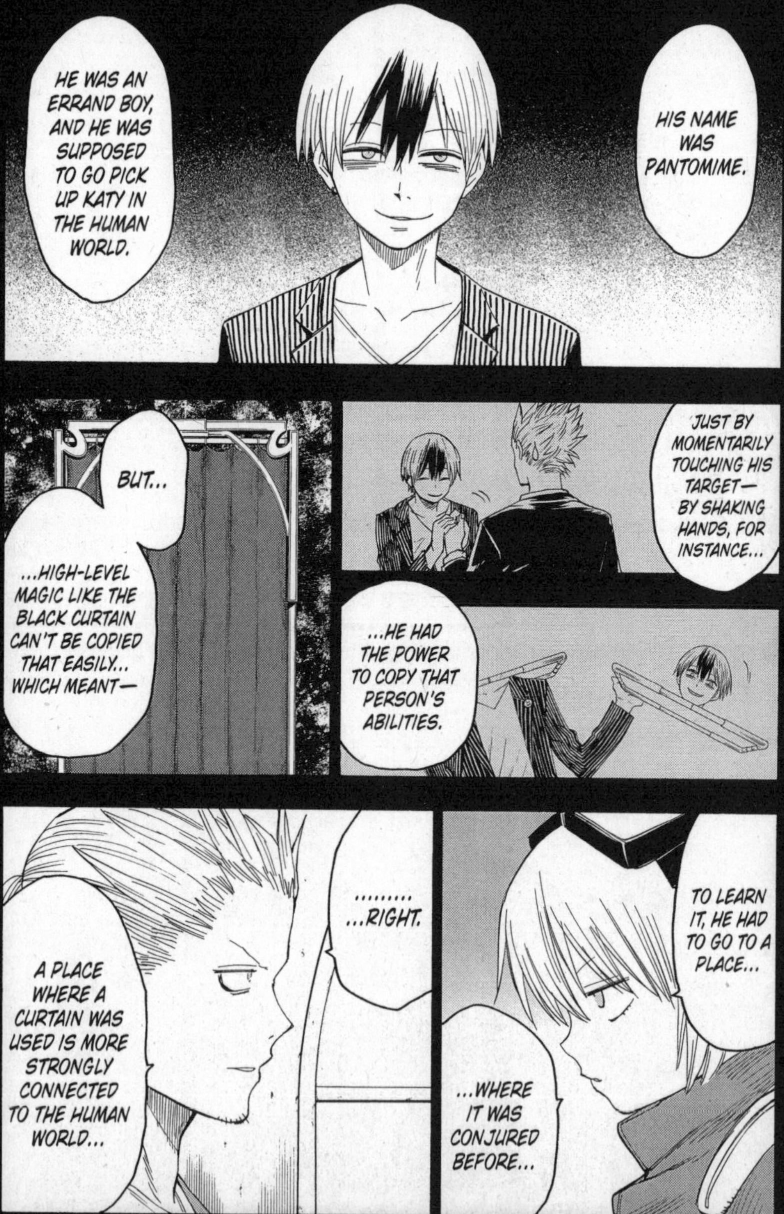
HIS NAME WAS PANTOMIME.
HE WAS AN ERRAND BOY, AND HE WAS SUPPOSED TO GO PICK UP KATY IN THE HUMAN WORLD.
JUST BY MOMENTARILY TOUCHING HIS TARGET—BY SHAKING HANDS, FOR INSTANCE...
...HE HAD THE POWER TO COPY THAT PERSON'S ABILITIES.
BUT...
...HIGH-LEVEL MAGIC LIKE THE BLACK CURTAIN CAN'T BE COPIED THAT EASILY... WHICH MEANT—
TO LEARN IT, HE HAD TO GO TO A PLACE...
...WHERE IT WAS CONJURED BEFORE...
....RIGHT.
A PLACE WHERE A CURTAIN WAS USED IS MORE STRONGLY CONNECTED TO THE HUMAN WORLD...

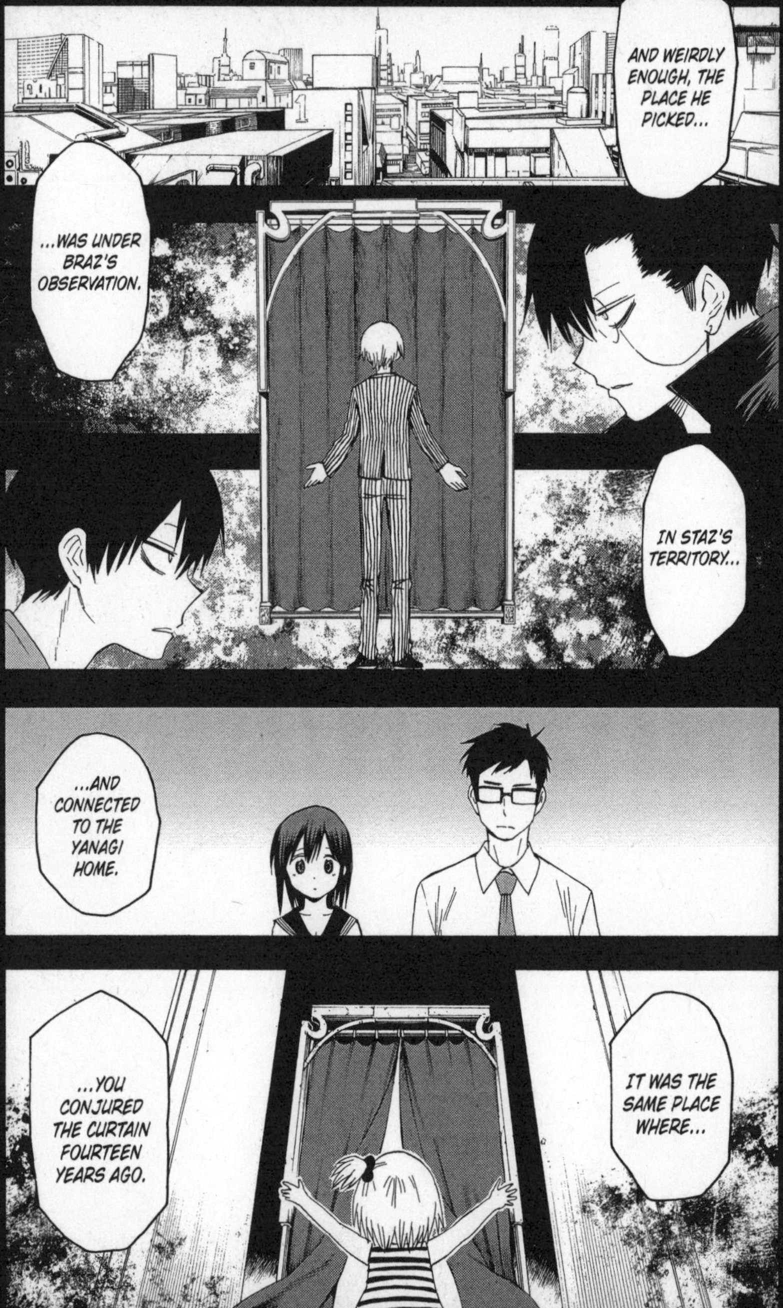
AND WEIRDLY ENOUGH, THE PLACE HE PICKED...
...WAS UNDER BRAZ'S OBSERVATION.
IN STAZ'S TERRITORY...
...AND CONNECTED TO THE YANAGI HOME.
IT WAS THE SAME PLACE WHERE...
...YOU CONJURED THE CURTAIN FOURTEEN YEARS AGO.

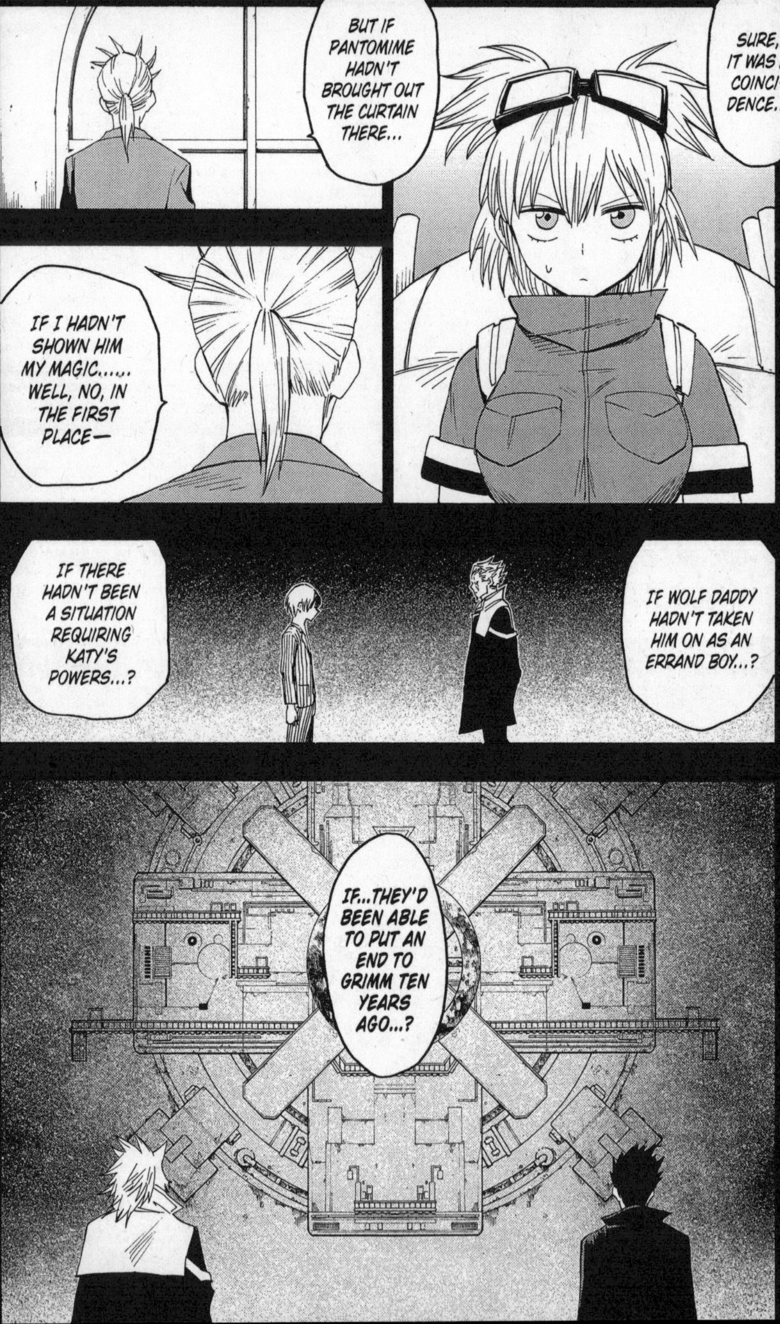
SURE, IT WAS A COINCIDENCE...
BUT IF PANTOMIME HADN'T BROUGHT OUT THE CURTAIN THERE...
IF I HADN'T SHOWN HIM MY MAGIC...... WELL, NO, IN THE FIRST PLACE—
IF WOLF DADDY HADN'T TAKEN HIM ON AS AN ERRAND BOY...?
IF THERE HADN'T BEEN A SITUATION REQUIRING KATY'S POWERS...?
IF...THEY'D BEEN ABLE TO PUT AN END TO GRIMM TEN YEARS AGO...?

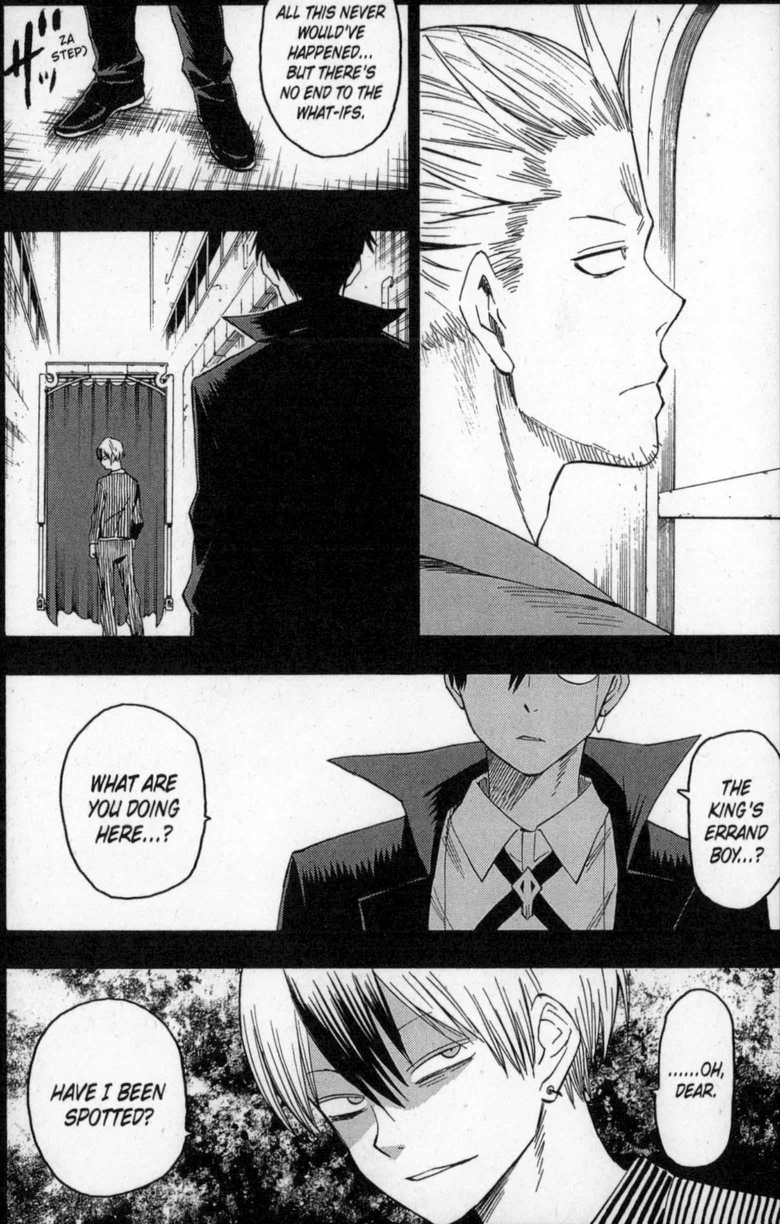
ALL THIS NEVER WOULD'VE HAPPENED... BUT THERE'S NO END TO THE WHAT-IFS.
ZA STEP)
THE KING'S ERRAND BOY...?
WHAT ARE YOU DOING HERE...?
......OH, DEAR.
HAVE I BEEN SPOTTED?

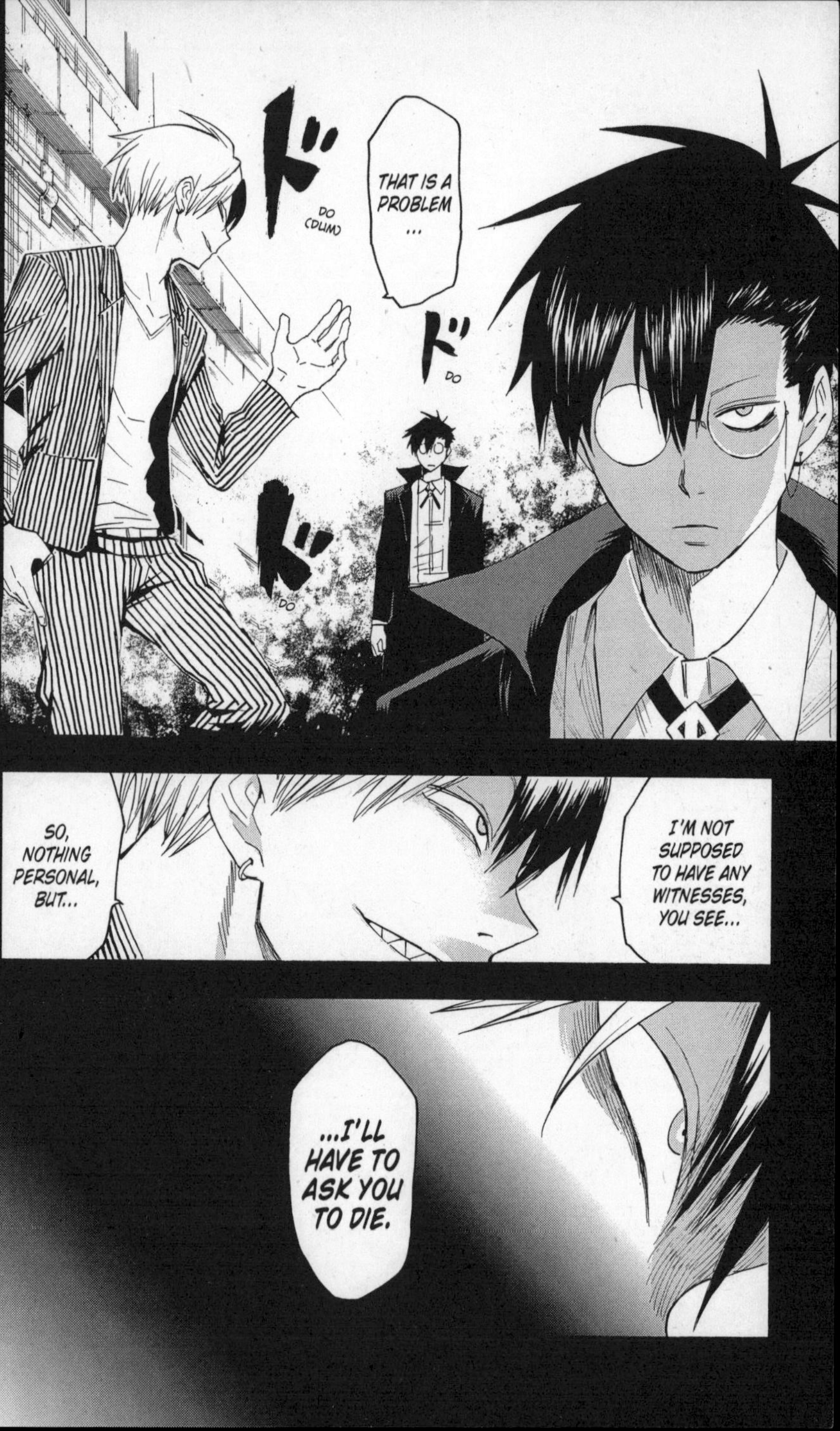
THAT IS A PROBLEM ...
ド
DO (DUM)
ド
DO
ド
DO
I'M NOT SUPPOSED TO HAVE ANY WITNESSES, YOU SEE...
SO, NOTHING PERSONAL, BUT...
...I'LL HAVE TO ASK YOU TO DIE.

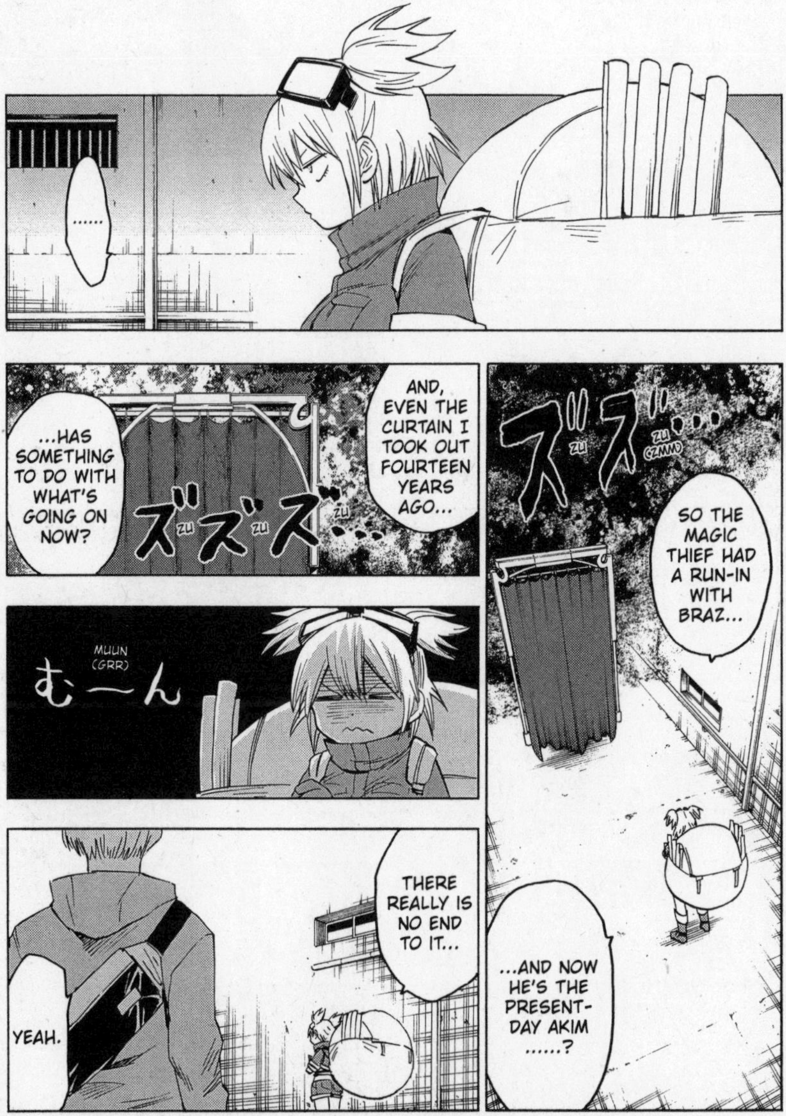
......
ズズ…
ZU ZU (ZMM)
SO THE MAGIC THIEF HAD A RUN-IN WITH BRAZ...
...AND NOW HE'S THE PRESENT-DAY AKIM ......?
AND, EVEN THE CURTAIN I TOOK OUT FOURTEEN YEARS AGO...
ズズズ…
ZU ZU ZU
...HAS SOMETHING TO DO WITH WHAT'S GOING ON NOW?
むーん
MUUN (GRR)
THERE REALLY IS NO END TO IT...
YEAH.

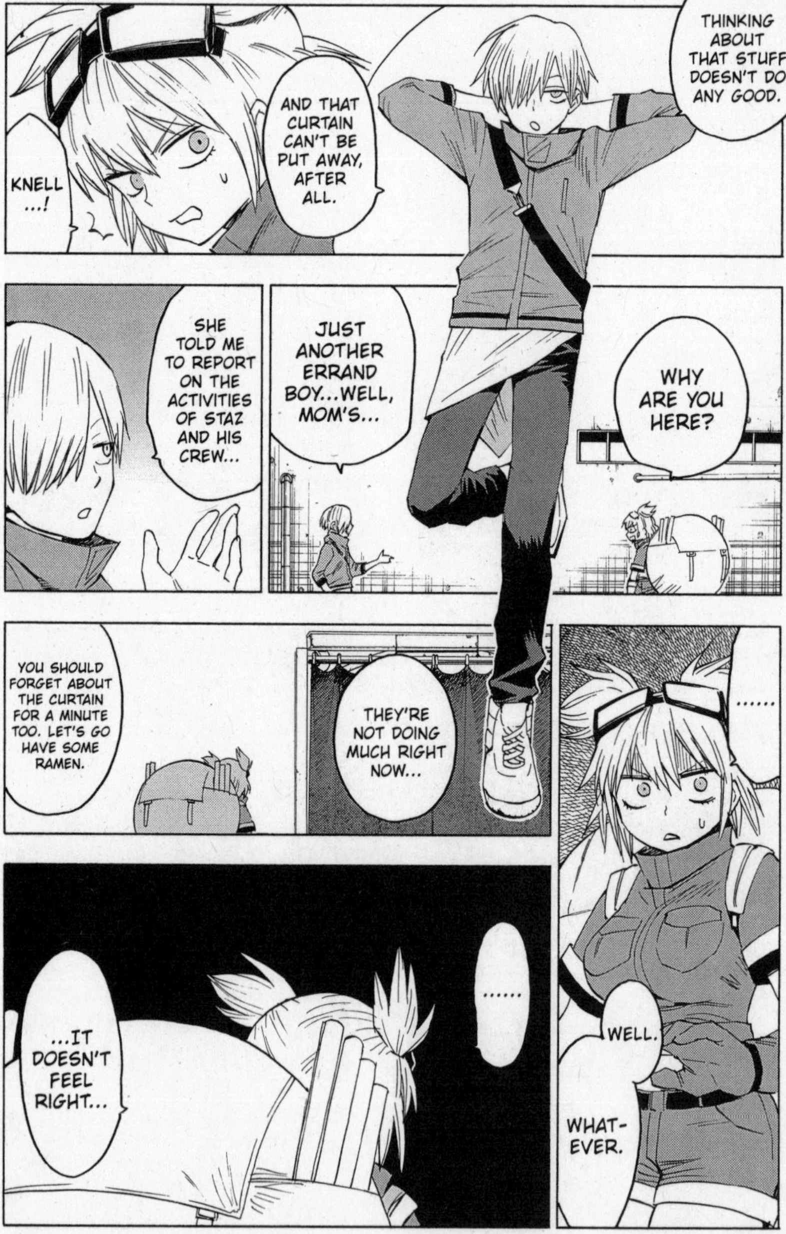
THINKING ABOUT THAT STUFF DOESN'T DO ANY GOOD.
AND THAT CURTAIN CAN'T BE PUT AWAY, AFTER ALL.
KNELL ...!
WHY ARE YOU HERE?
JUST ANOTHER ERRAND BOY...WELL, MOM'S...
SHE TOLD ME TO REPORT ON THE ACTIVITIES OF STAZ AND HIS CREW...
......
WELL.
WHAT-EVER.
THEY'RE NOT DOING MUCH RIGHT NOW...
YOU SHOULD FORGET ABOUT THE CURTAIN FOR A MINUTE TOO. LET'S GO HAVE SOME RAMEN.
......
...IT DOESN'T FEEL RIGHT...

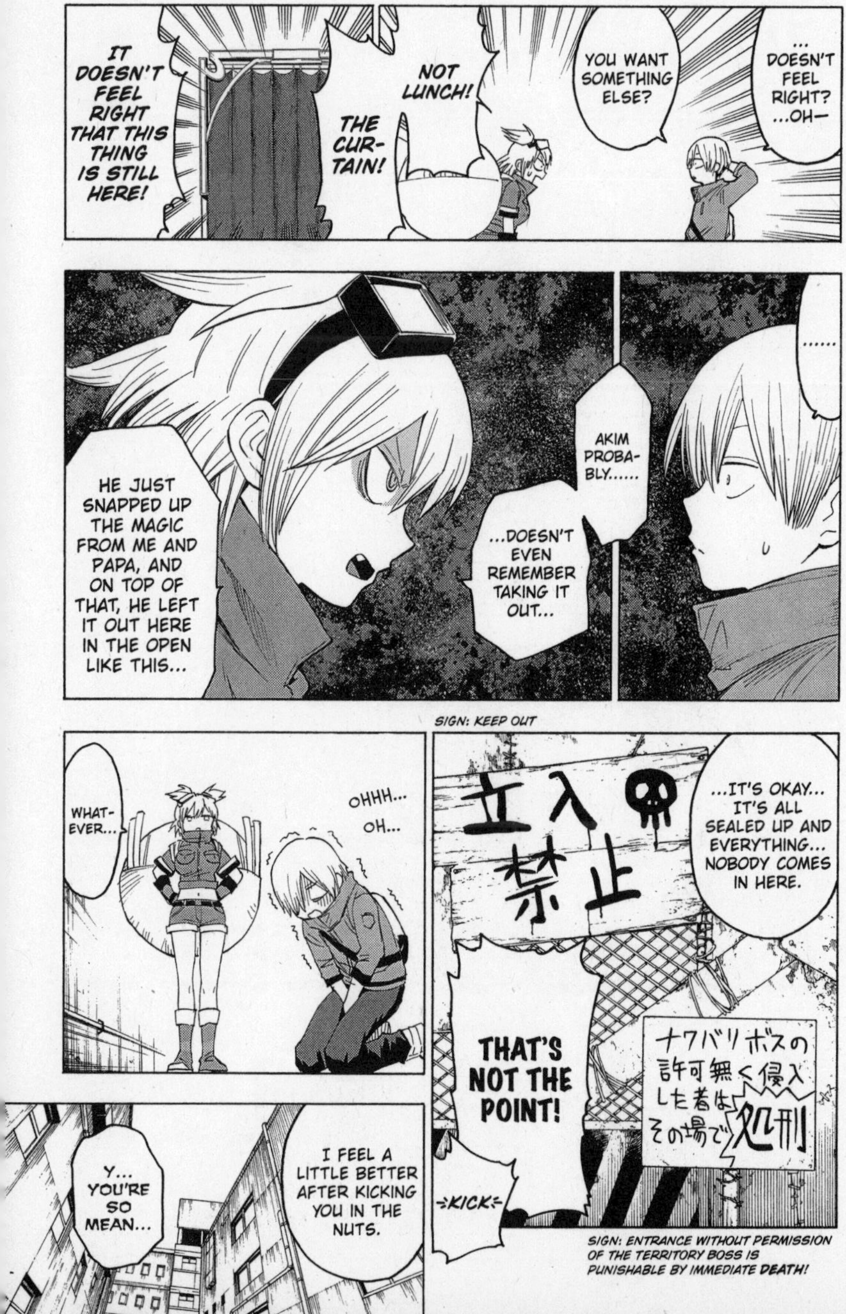
...DOESN'T FEEL RIGHT? ...OH—
YOU WANT SOMETHING ELSE?
NOT LUNCH!
THE CURTAIN!
IT DOESN'T FEEL RIGHT THAT THIS THING IS STILL HERE!
......
AKIM PROBABLY......
...DOESN'T EVEN REMEMBER TAKING IT OUT...
HE JUST SNAPPED UP THE MAGIC FROM ME AND PAPA, AND ON TOP OF THAT, HE LEFT IT OUT HERE IN THE OPEN LIKE THIS...
...IT'S OKAY... IT'S ALL SEALED UP AND EVERYTHING... NOBODY COMES IN HERE.
立入禁止
ナワバリボスの許可無く侵入した者はその場で処刑
THAT'S NOT THE POINT!
KICK
OHHH... OH...
WHATEVER...
I FEEL A LITTLE BETTER AFTER KICKING YOU IN THE NUTS.
Y... YOU'RE SO MEAN...

SIGN: KEEP OUT

SIGN: ENTRANCE WITHOUT PERMISSION OF THE TERRITORY BOSS IS PUNISHABLE BY IMMEDIATE DEATH!

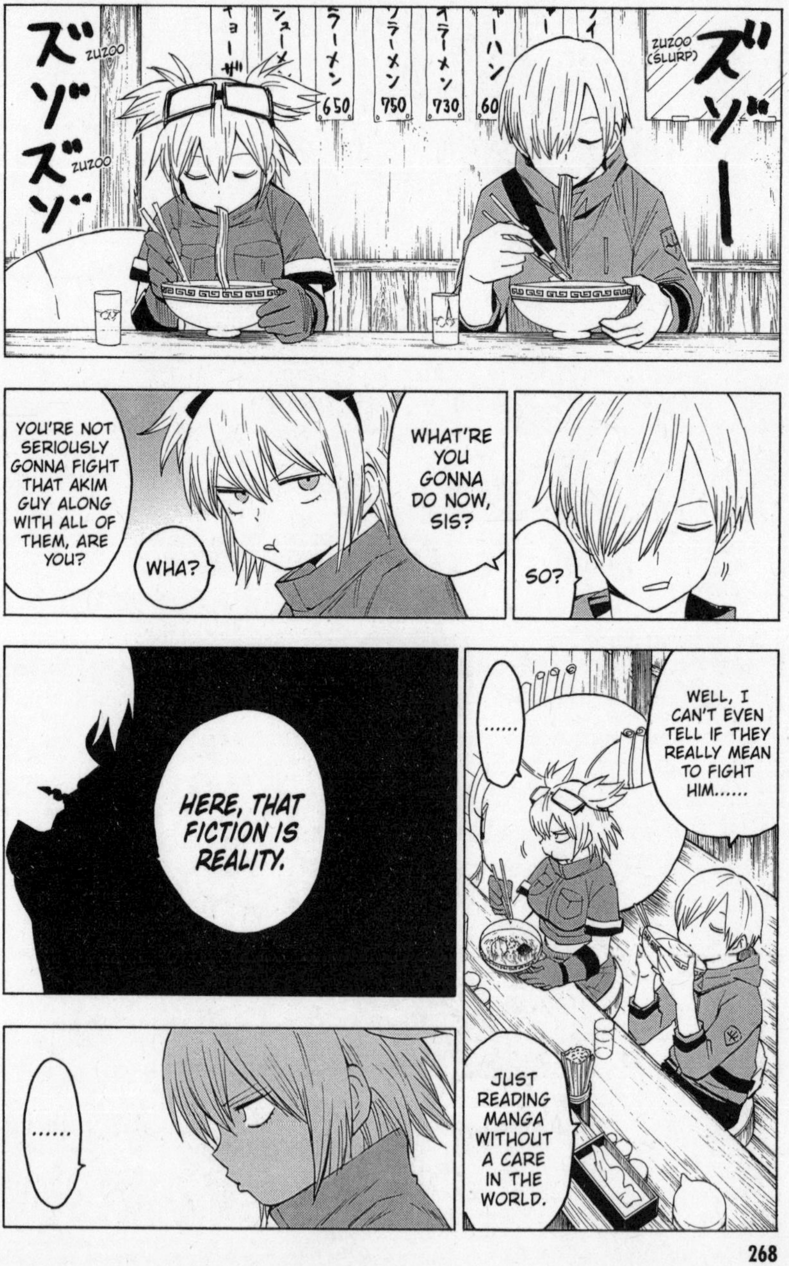
ZUZOO (SLURP)
ZUZOO
ZUZOO
SO?
WHAT'RE YOU GONNA DO NOW, SIS?
YOU'RE NOT SERIOUSLY GONNA FIGHT THAT AKIM GUY ALONG WITH ALL OF THEM, ARE YOU?
WHA?
WELL, I CAN'T EVEN TELL IF THEY REALLY MEAN TO FIGHT HIM......
......
JUST READING MANGA WITHOUT A CARE IN THE WORLD.
HERE, THAT FICTION IS REALITY.
......

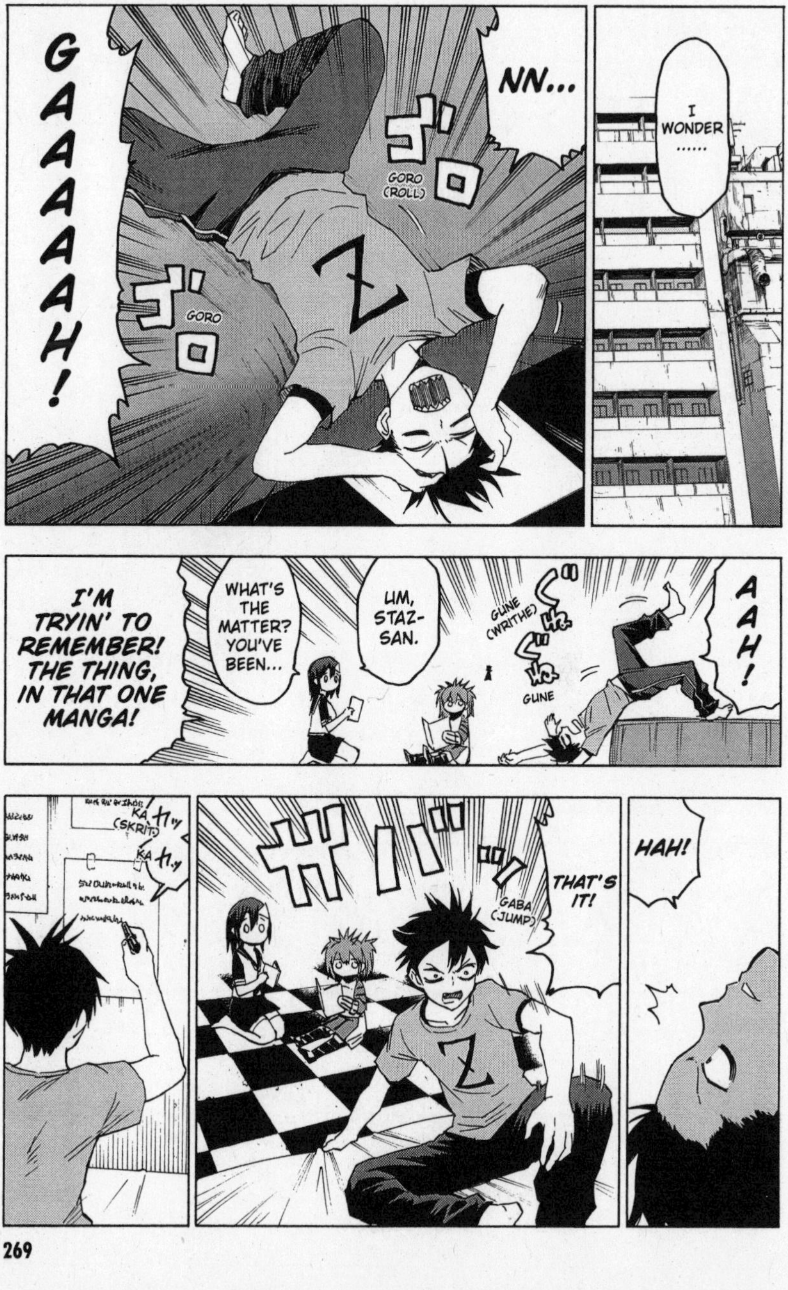
I WONDER ......
NN...
GORO (ROLL)
GORO
GAAAAAAAH!
AAH!
GUNE (WRITHE)
GUNE
UM, STAZ-SAN.
WHAT'S THE MATTER? YOU'VE BEEN...
I'M TRYIN' TO REMEMBER! THE THING, IN THAT ONE MANGA!
HAH!
THAT'S IT!
GABA (JUMP)
KA (SKRIT)
KA

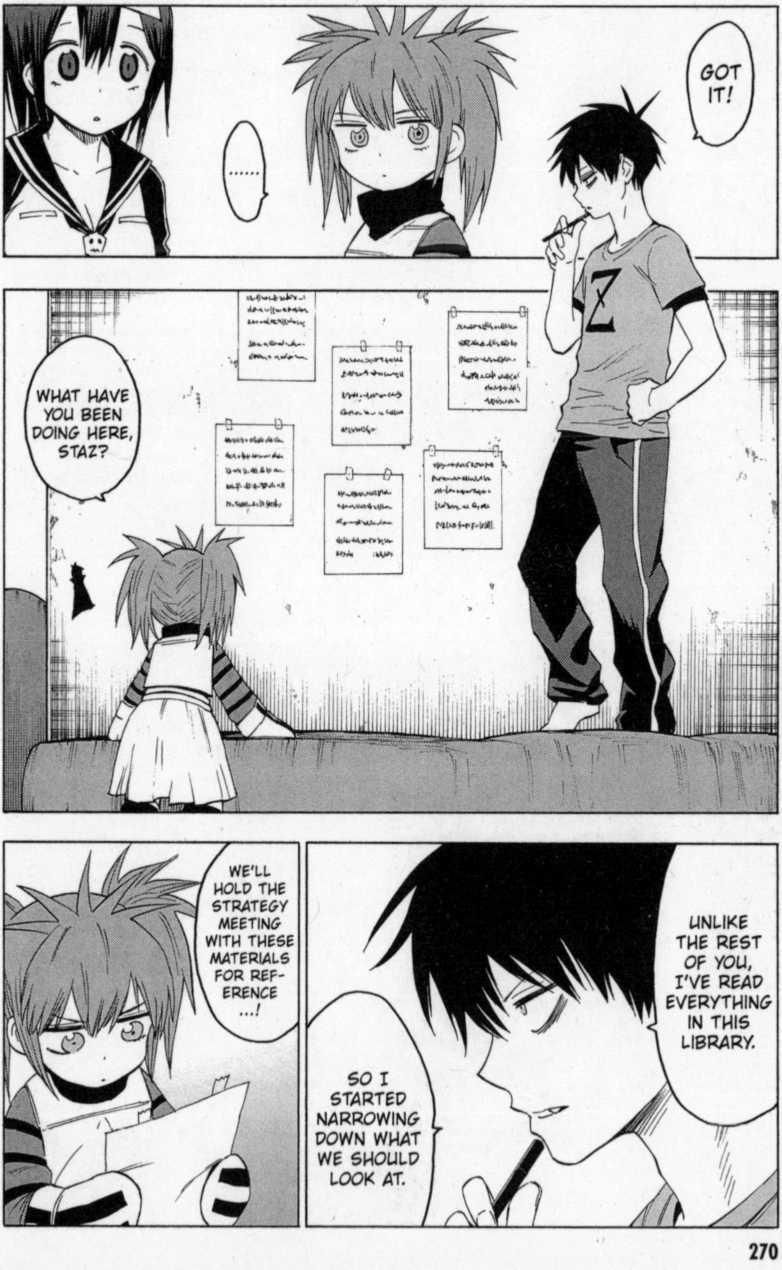
GOT IT!
......
WHAT HAVE YOU BEEN DOING HERE, STAZ?
UNLIKE THE REST OF YOU, I'VE READ EVERYTHING IN THIS LIBRARY.
SO I STARTED NARROWING DOWN WHAT WE SHOULD LOOK AT.
WE'LL HOLD THE STRATEGY MEETING WITH THESE MATERIALS FOR REFER-ENCE...!

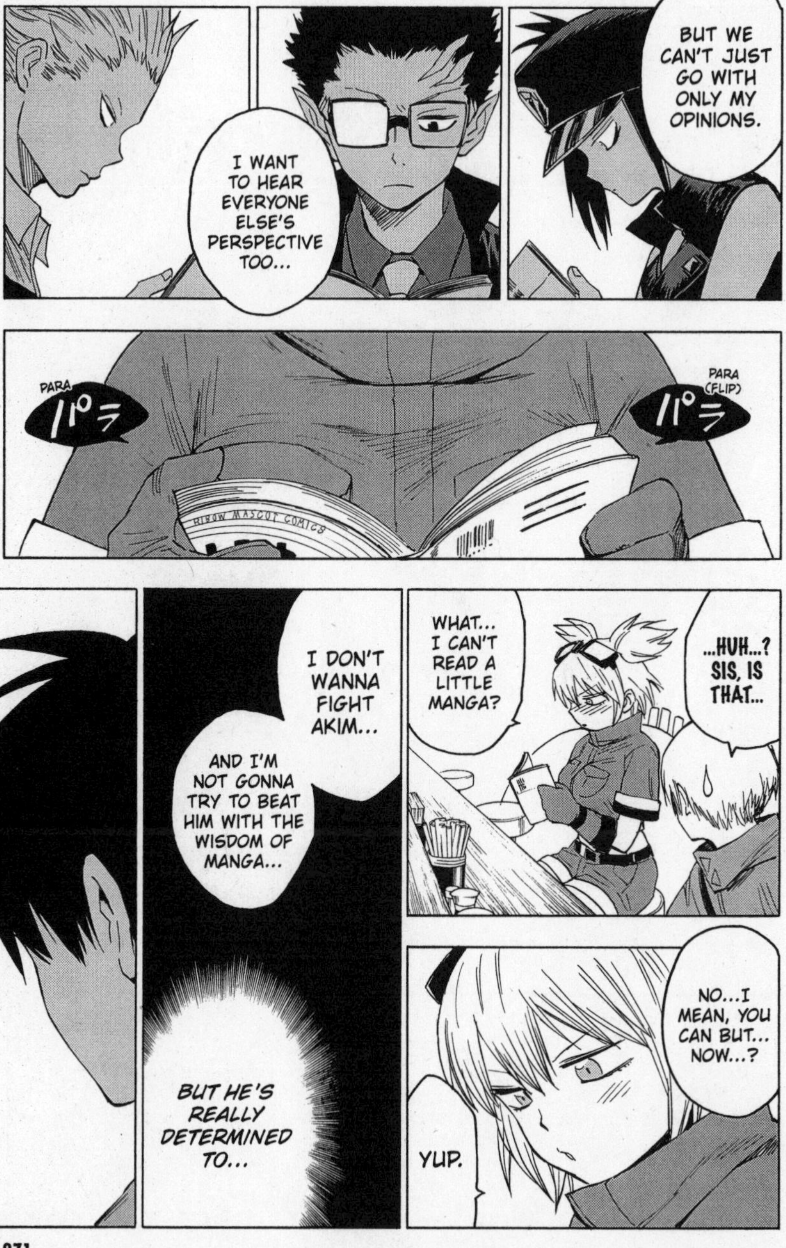
BUT WE CAN'T JUST GO WITH ONLY MY OPINIONS.
I WANT TO HEAR EVERYONE ELSE'S PERSPECTIVE TOO...
PARA (FLIP)
パラ
PARA
パラ
...HUH...? SIS, IS THAT...
WHAT... I CAN'T READ A LITTLE MANGA?
NO...I MEAN, YOU CAN BUT... NOW...?
YUP.
I DON'T WANNA FIGHT AKIM...
AND I'M NOT GONNA TRY TO BEAT HIM WITH THE WISDOM OF MANGA...
BUT HE'S REALLY DETERMINED TO...

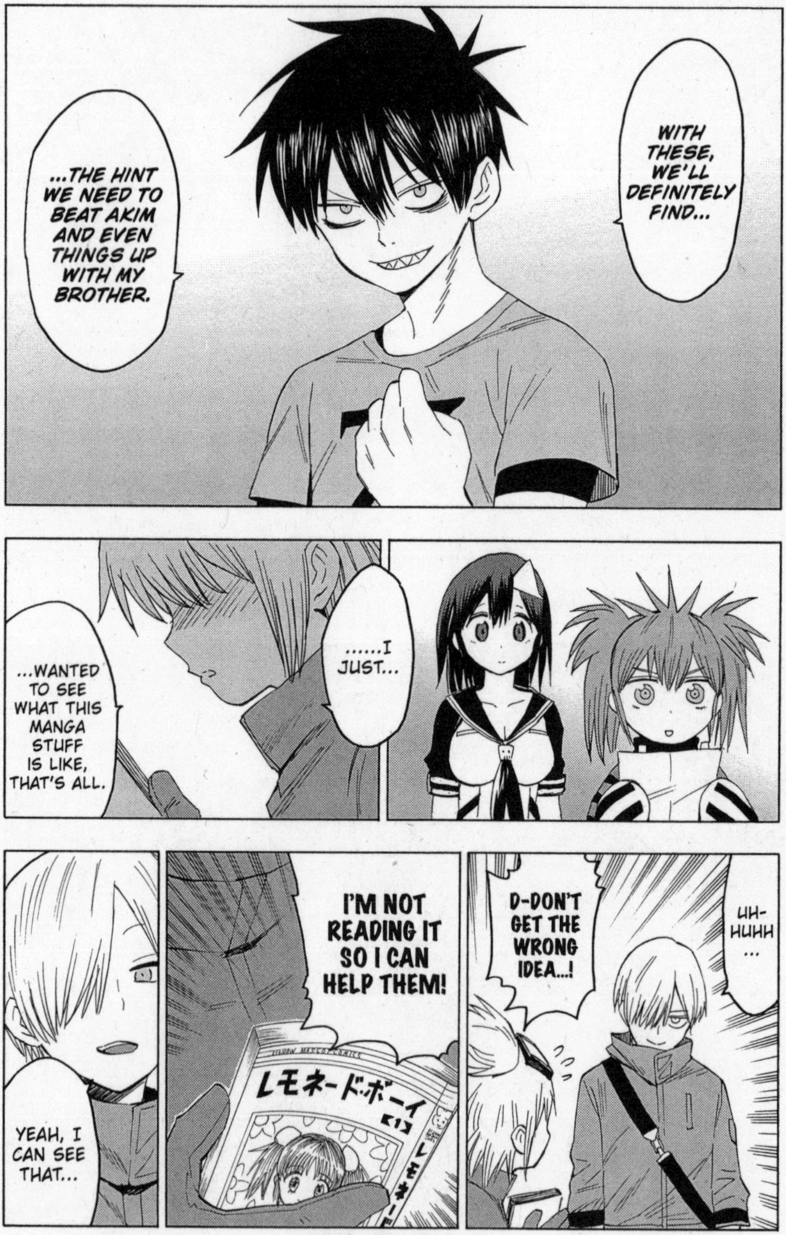
WITH THESE, WE'LL DEFINITELY FIND...
...THE HINT WE NEED TO BEAT AKIM AND EVEN THINGS UP WITH MY BROTHER.
......I JUST...
...WANTED TO SEE WHAT THIS MANGA STUFF IS LIKE, THAT'S ALL.
UH-HUHH...
D-DON'T GET THE WRONG IDEA...!
I'M NOT READING IT SO I CAN HELP THEM!
レモネード・ボーイ
【1】
YEAH, I CAN SEE THAT...

MANGA: LEMONADE BOY

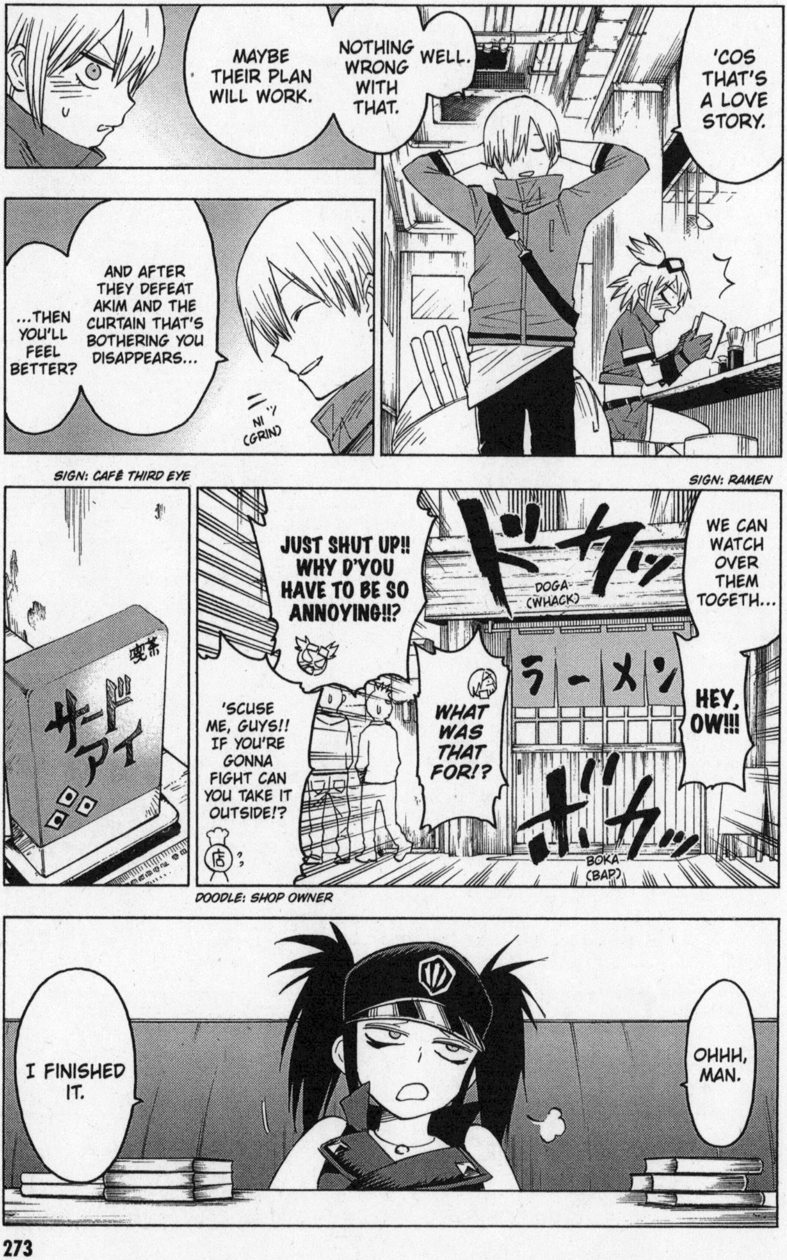
'COS THAT'S A LOVE STORY.
WELL.
NOTHING WRONG WITH THAT.
MAYBE THEIR PLAN WILL WORK.
AND AFTER THEY DEFEAT AKIM AND THE CURTAIN THAT'S BOTHERING YOU DISAPPEARS...
...THEN YOU'LL FEEL BETTER?
ニッ
NI (GRIN)
SIGN: RAMEN
WE CAN WATCH OVER THEM TOGETH...
ドカッ
DOGA (WHACK)
HEY, OW!!!
ボカッ
BOKA (BAP)
ラーメン
WHAT WAS THAT FOR!?
JUST SHUT UP!! WHY D'YOU HAVE TO BE SO ANNOYING!!?
'SCUSE ME, GUYS!! IF YOU'RE GONNA FIGHT CAN YOU TAKE IT OUTSIDE!?
店
DOODLE: SHOP OWNER
SIGN: CAFÉ THIRD EYE
喫茶
サードアイ
OHHH, MAN.
I FINISHED IT.

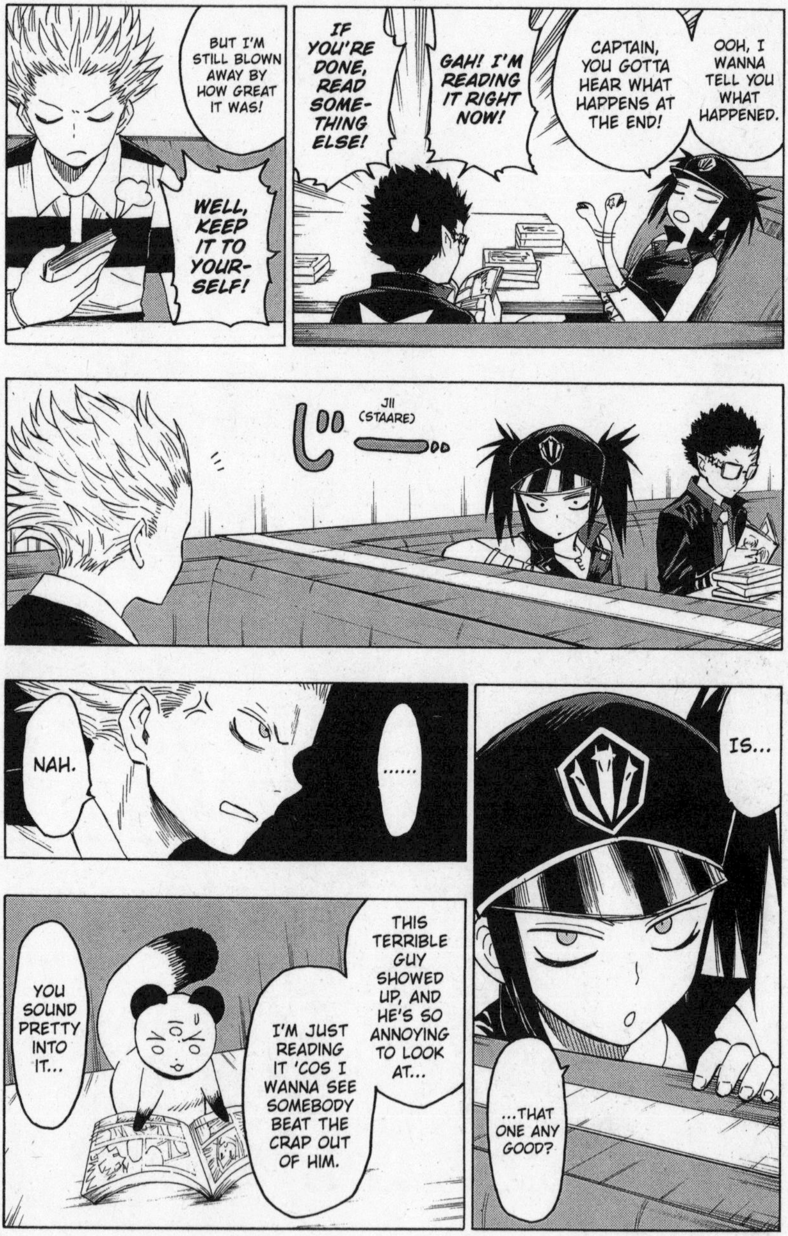
OOH, I WANNA TELL YOU WHAT HAPPENED.
CAPTAIN, YOU GOTTA HEAR WHAT HAPPENS AT THE END!
GAH! I'M READING IT RIGHT NOW!
IF YOU'RE DONE, READ SOMETHING ELSE!
BUT I'M STILL BLOWN AWAY BY HOW GREAT IT WAS!
WELL, KEEP IT TO YOURSELF!
JII (STAARE)
IS...
...THAT ONE ANY GOOD?
......
NAH.
THIS TERRIBLE GUY SHOWED UP, AND HE'S SO ANNOYING TO LOOK AT...
I'M JUST READING IT 'COS I WANNA SEE SOMEBODY BEAT THE CRAP OUT OF HIM.
YOU SOUND PRETTY INTO IT...

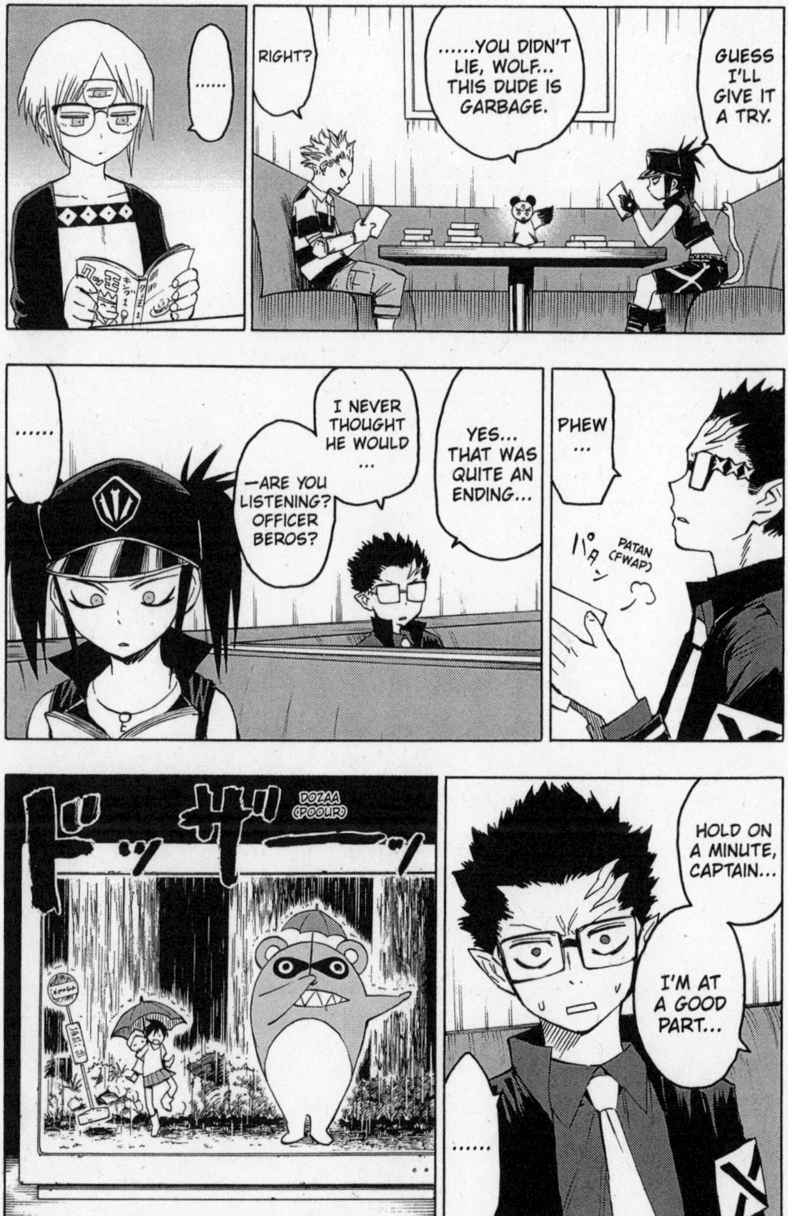
GUESS I'LL GIVE IT A TRY.
......YOU DIDN'T LIE, WOLF... THIS DUDE IS GARBAGE.
RIGHT?
......
PHEW ...
パタン
PATAN (FWAP)
YES... THAT WAS QUITE AN ENDING...
I NEVER THOUGHT HE WOULD ...
—ARE YOU LISTENING? OFFICER BEROS?
......
HOLD ON A MINUTE, CAPTAIN...
I'M AT A GOOD PART...
......
ドッザーッ
DOZAA (POOUR)

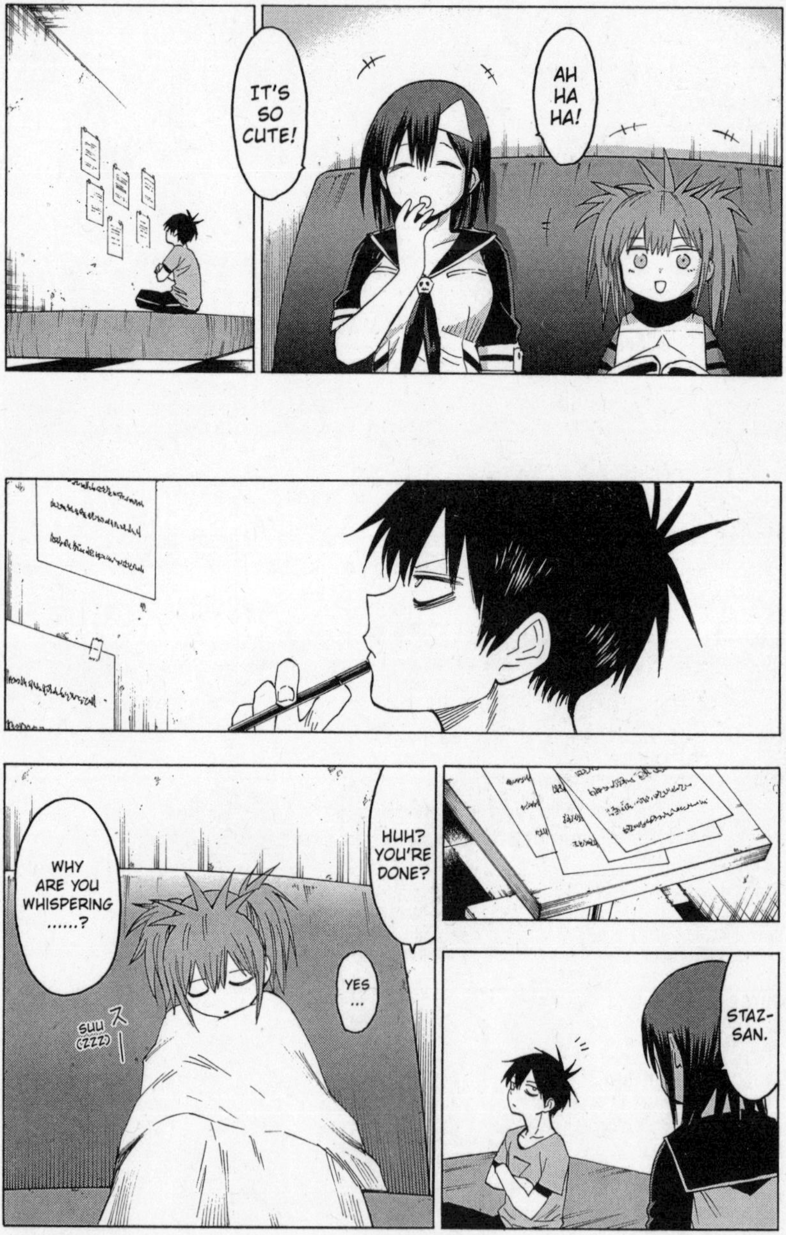
AH HA HA!
IT'S SO CUTE!
STAZ-SAN.
HUH? YOU'RE DONE?
WHY ARE YOU WHISPERING ......?
YES ...
スー
SUU (ZZZ)

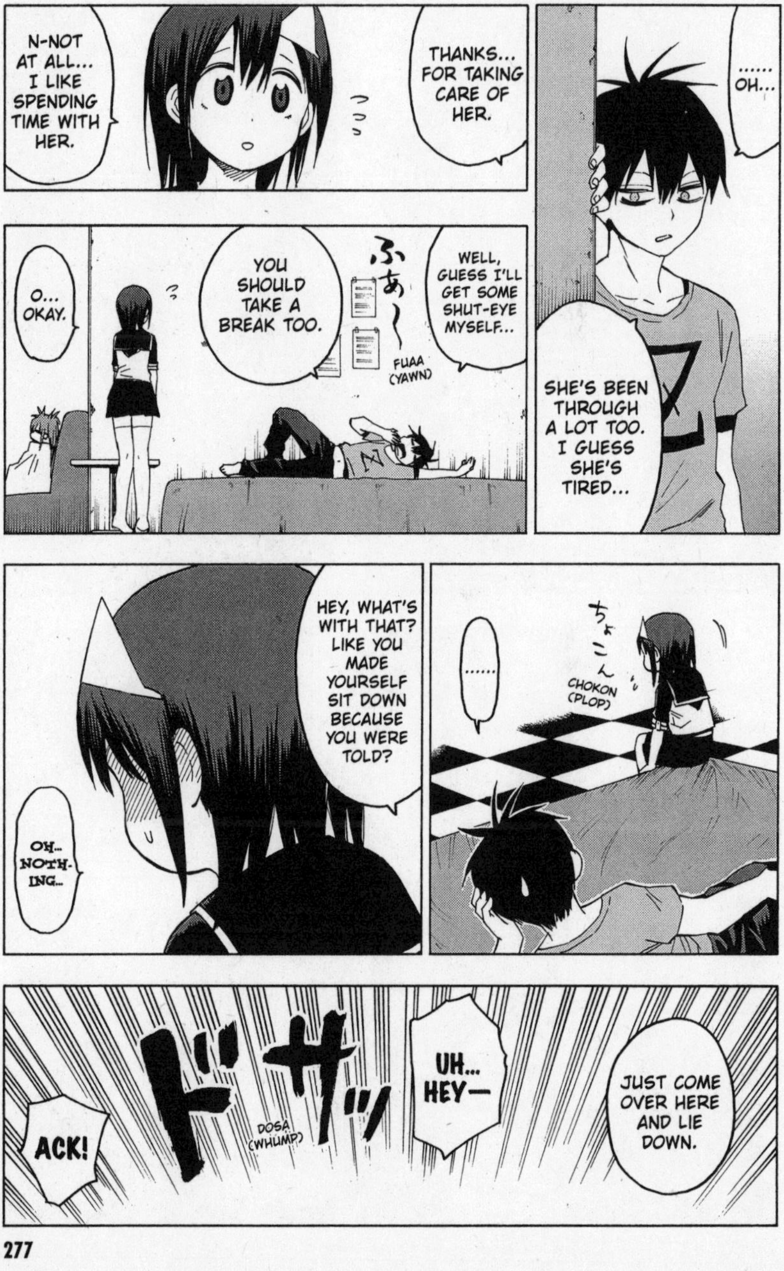
......OH...
SHE'S BEEN THROUGH A LOT TOO. I GUESS SHE'S TIRED...
THANKS... FOR TAKING CARE OF HER.
N-NOT AT ALL... I LIKE SPENDING TIME WITH HER.
WELL, GUESS I'LL GET SOME SHUT-EYE MYSELF...
ふあ～
FUAA (YAWN)
YOU SHOULD TAKE A BREAK TOO.
O... OKAY.
ちょこん
CHOKON (PLOP)
......
HEY, WHAT'S WITH THAT? LIKE YOU MADE YOURSELF SIT DOWN BECAUSE YOU WERE TOLD?
OH... NOTHING...
JUST COME OVER HERE AND LIE DOWN.
UH... HEY—
ドサッ
DOSA (WHUMP)
ACK!

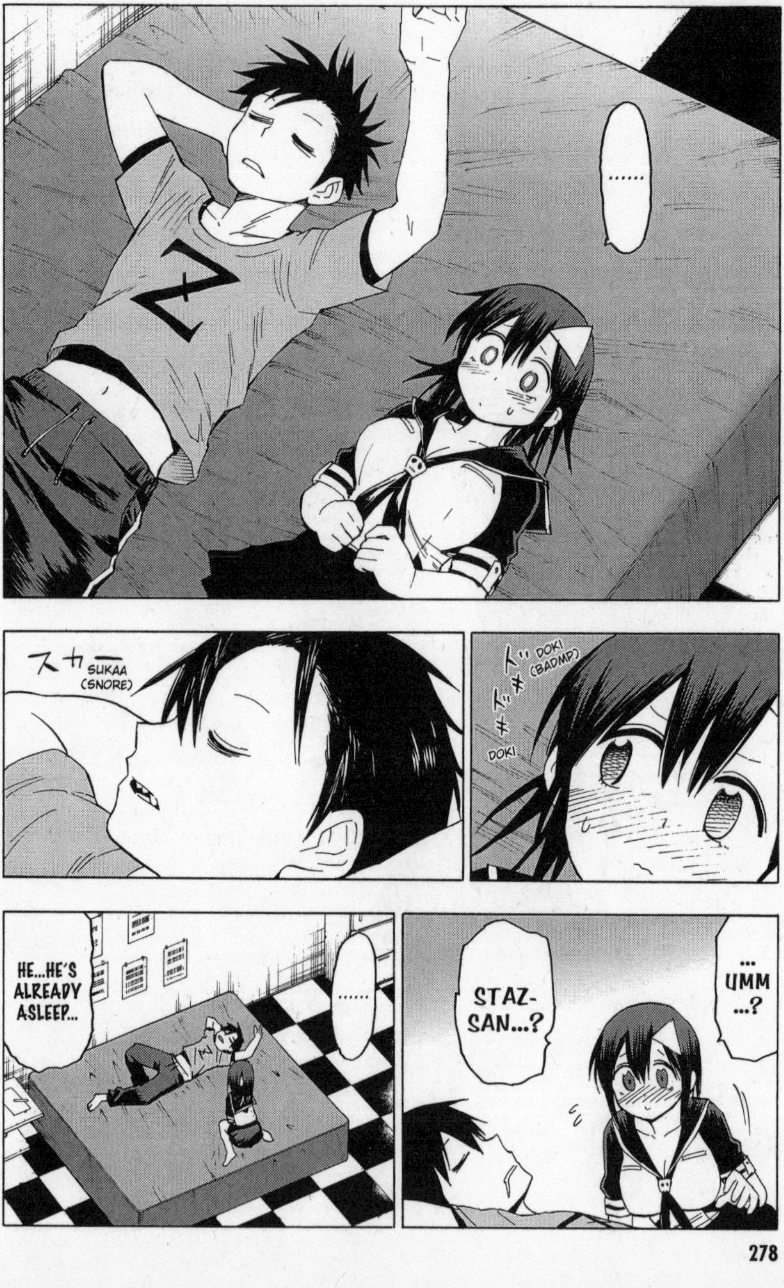
......
ドキ DOKI (BADMP)
ドキ DOKI
スカー SUKAA (SNORE)
... UMM ...?
STAZ-SAN...?
......
HE...HE'S ALREADY ASLEEP...

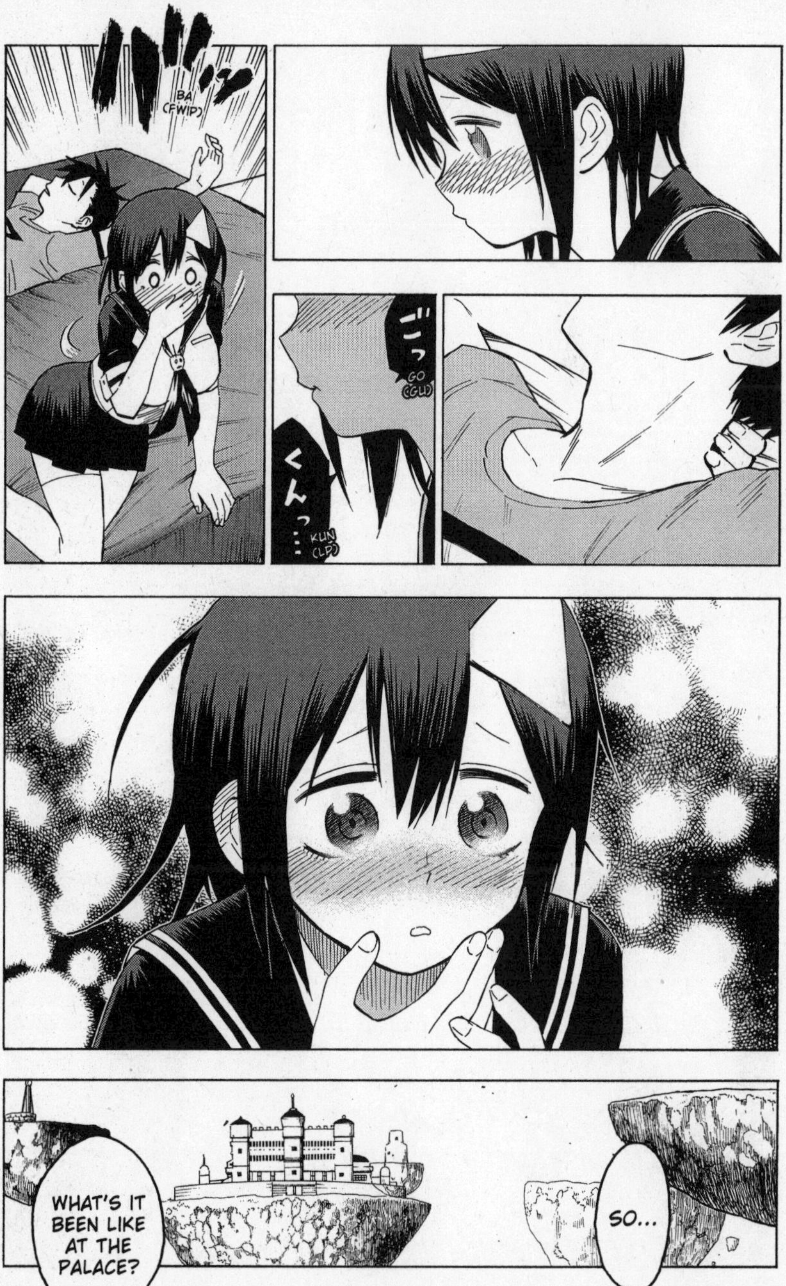

ごっ
GO (GU)
くんっ…
KUN (LP)
BA (FWIP)
SO...
WHAT'S IT BEEN LIKE AT THE PALACE?

SHIRT: NEYN ♡

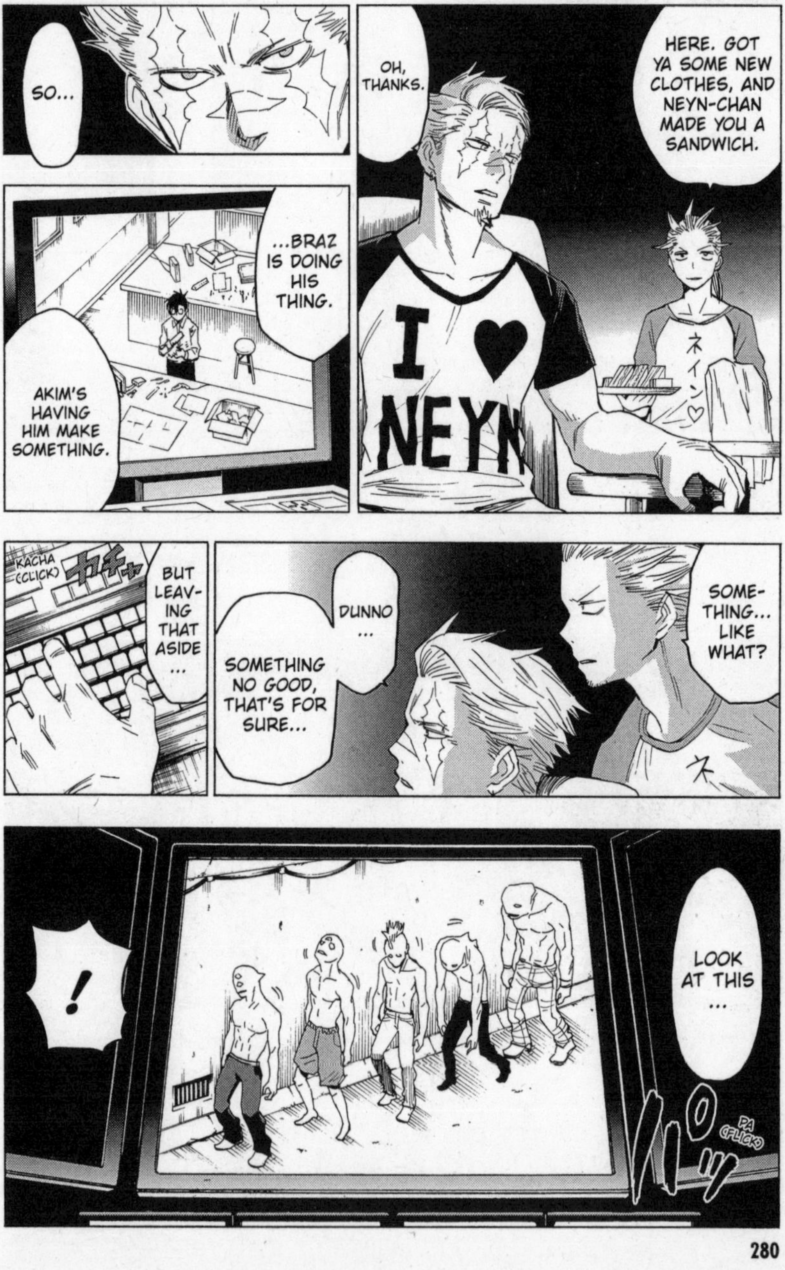

HERE. GOT YA SOME NEW CLOTHES, AND NEYN-CHAN MADE YOU A SANDWICH.
OH, THANKS.
I ♥ NEYN
ネイン♡
SO...
...BRAZ IS DOING HIS THING.
AKIM'S HAVING HIM MAKE SOMETHING.
SOME-THING... LIKE WHAT?
DUNNO...
SOMETHING NO GOOD, THAT'S FOR SURE...
KACHA (CLICK)
BUT LEAV-ING THAT ASIDE...
LOOK AT THIS...
PA (FLICK)
!

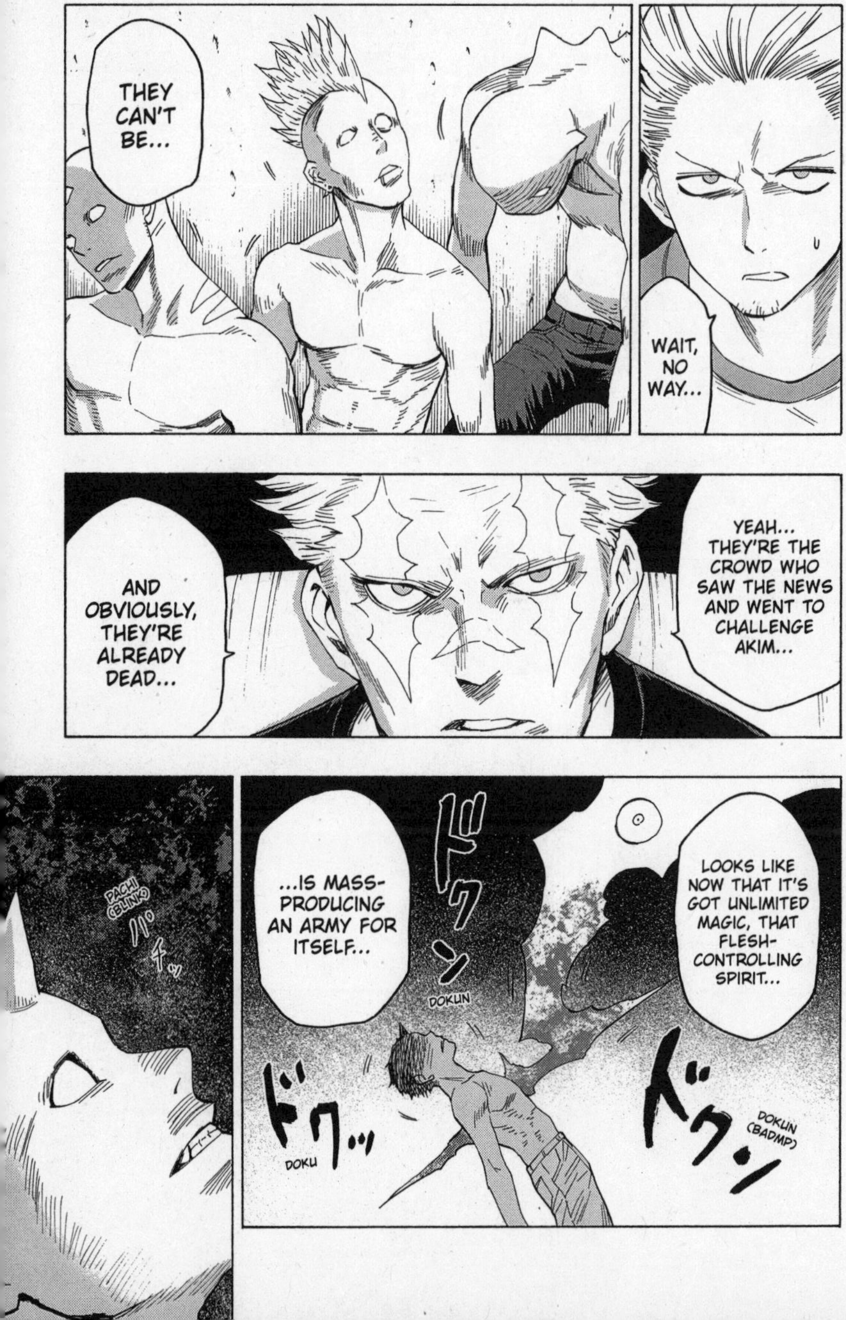
WAIT, NO WAY...
THEY CAN'T BE...
YEAH... THEY'RE THE CROWD WHO SAW THE NEWS AND WENT TO CHALLENGE AKIM...
AND OBVIOUSLY, THEY'RE ALREADY DEAD...
LOOKS LIKE NOW THAT IT'S GOT UNLIMITED MAGIC, THAT FLESH-CONTROLLING SPIRIT...
ドクン
DOKUN (BADMP)
...IS MASS-PRODUCING AN ARMY FOR ITSELF...
ドクン
DOKUN
ドクッ
DOKU
パチッ
PACHI (BLINK)

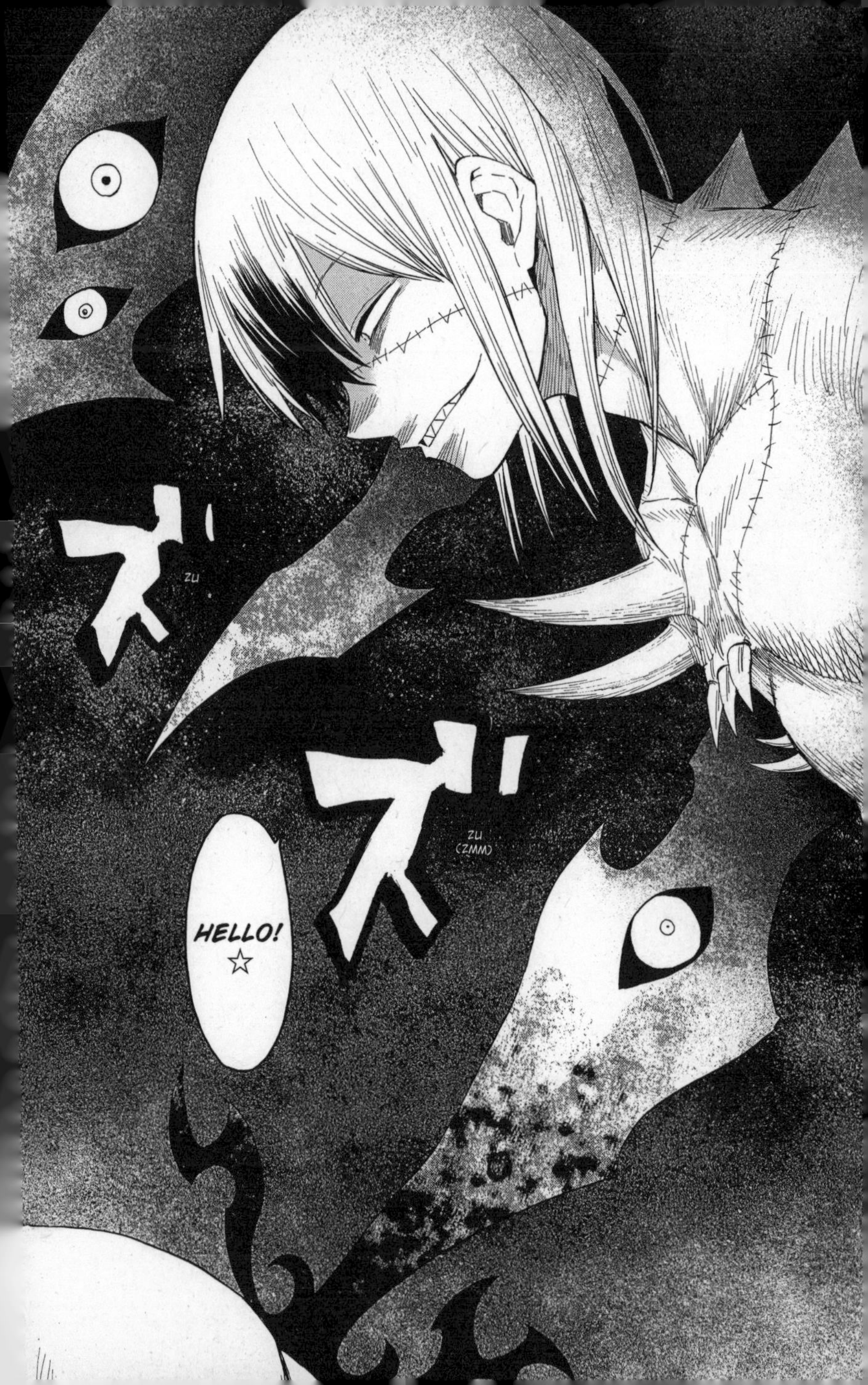
ズ
ZU
ズ
ZU
(ZMM)
HELLO! ☆

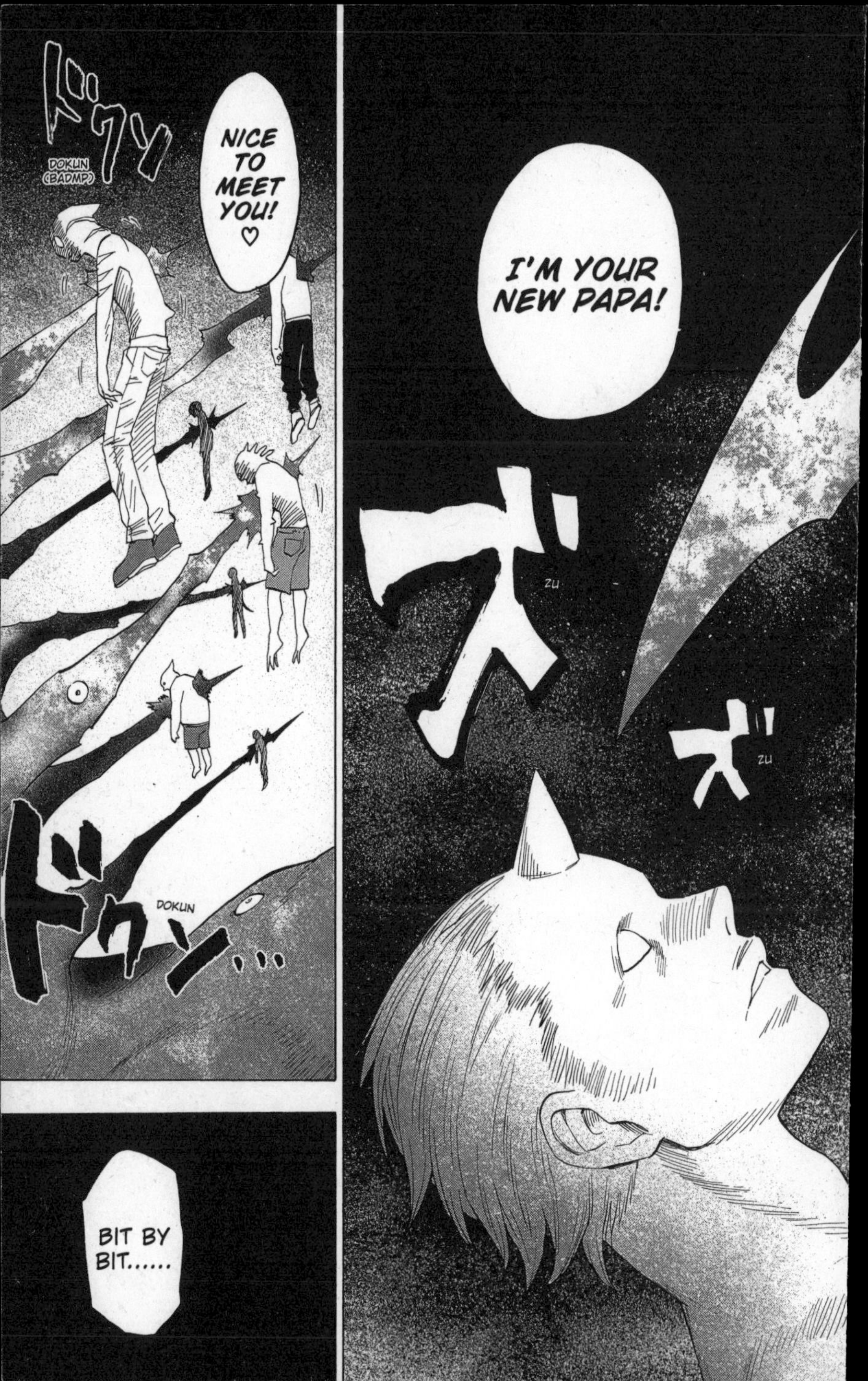
I'M YOUR NEW PAPA!
ズ
ZU
ズ
ZU
NICE TO MEET YOU! ♡
ドクン
DOKUN (BADMP)
ドクン
DOKUN
BIT BY BIT......

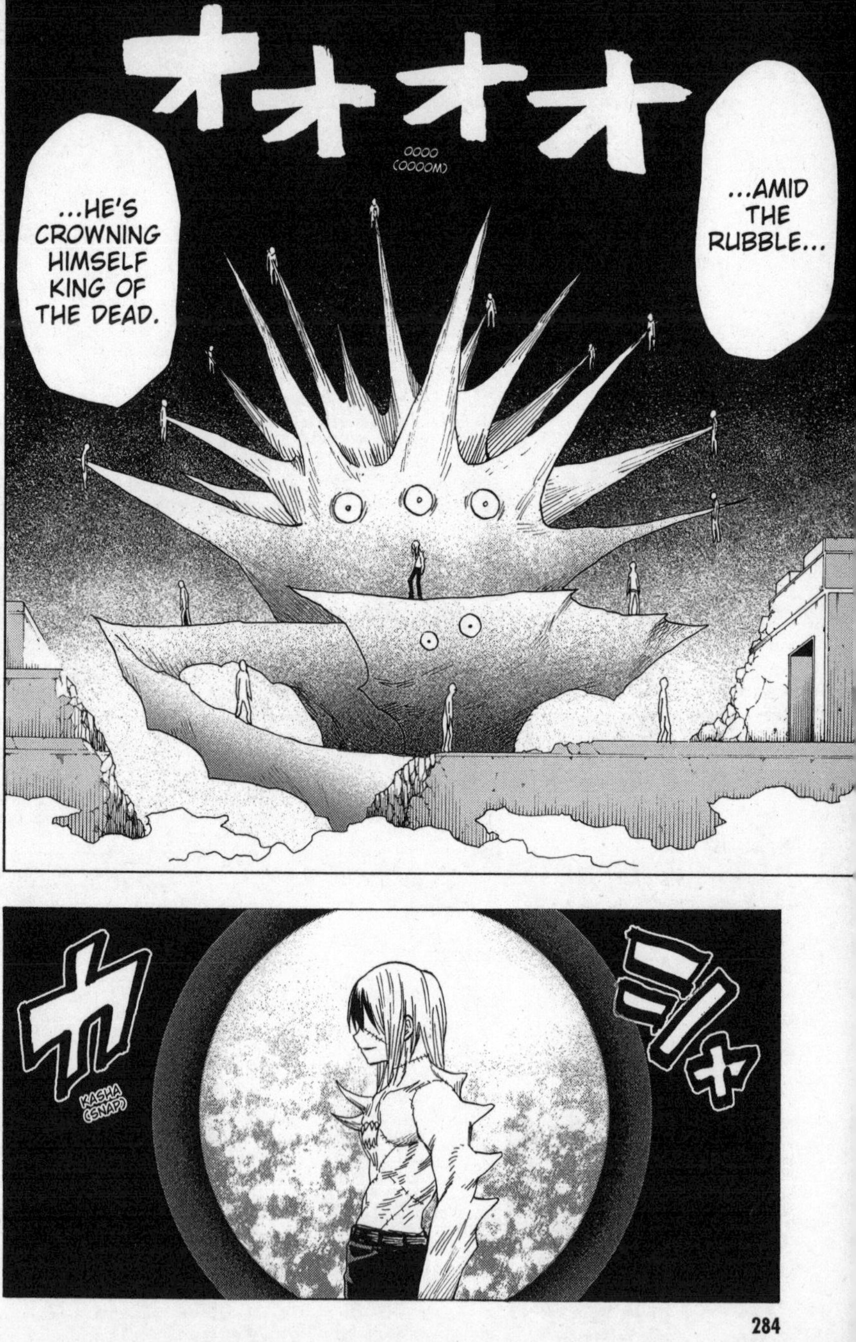
オオオオ
OOOO (OOOOM)
...AMID THE RUBBLE...
...HE'S CROWNING HIMSELF KING OF THE DEAD.
カシャ
KASHA (SNAP)

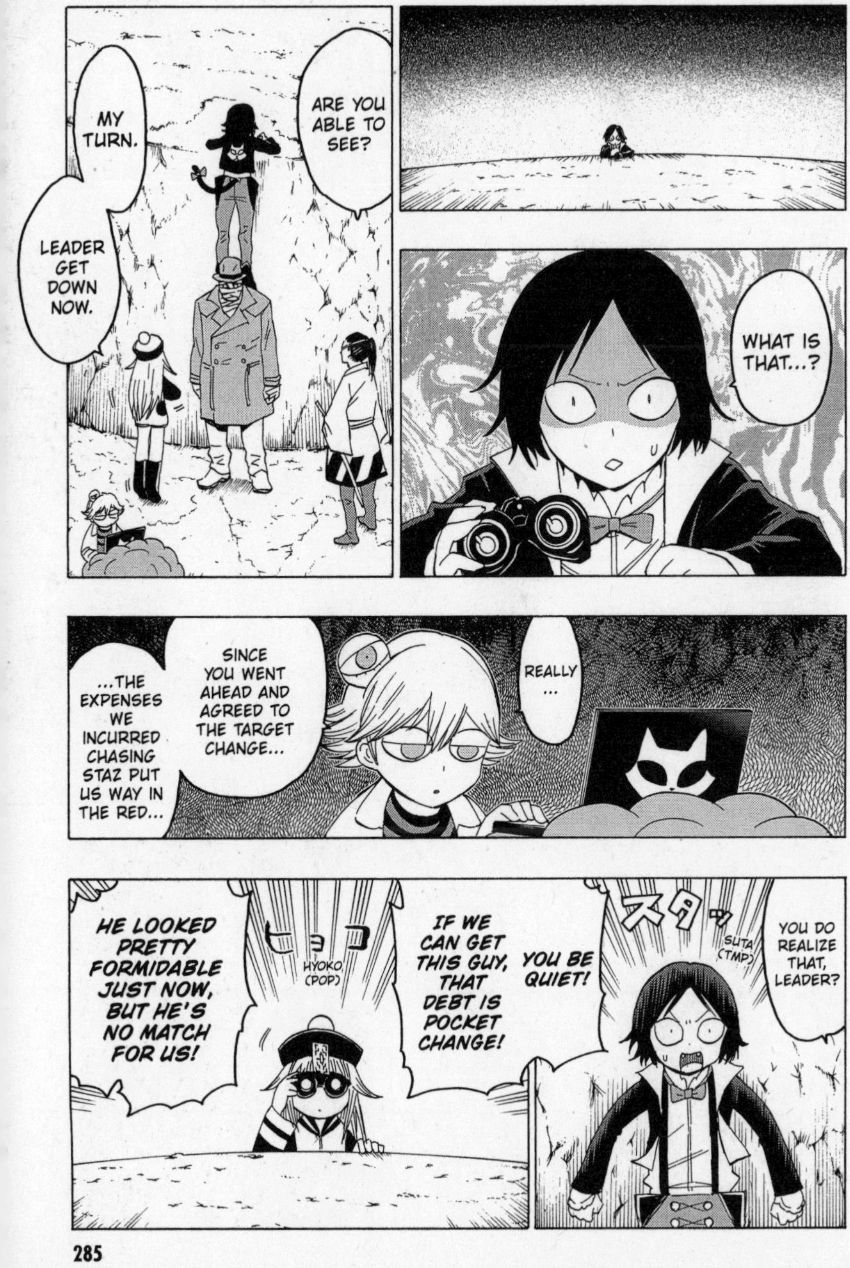
WHAT IS THAT...?
ARE YOU ABLE TO SEE?
MY TURN.
LEADER GET DOWN NOW.
REALLY...
SINCE YOU WENT AHEAD AND AGREED TO THE TARGET CHANGE...
...THE EXPENSES WE INCURRED CHASING STAZ PUT US WAY IN THE RED...
YOU DO REALIZE THAT, LEADER?
スタッ
SUTA (TMP)
YOU BE QUIET!
IF WE CAN GET THIS GUY, THAT DEBT IS POCKET CHANGE!
ヒョコ
HYOKO (POP)
HE LOOKED PRETTY FORMIDABLE JUST NOW, BUT HE'S NO MATCH FOR US!

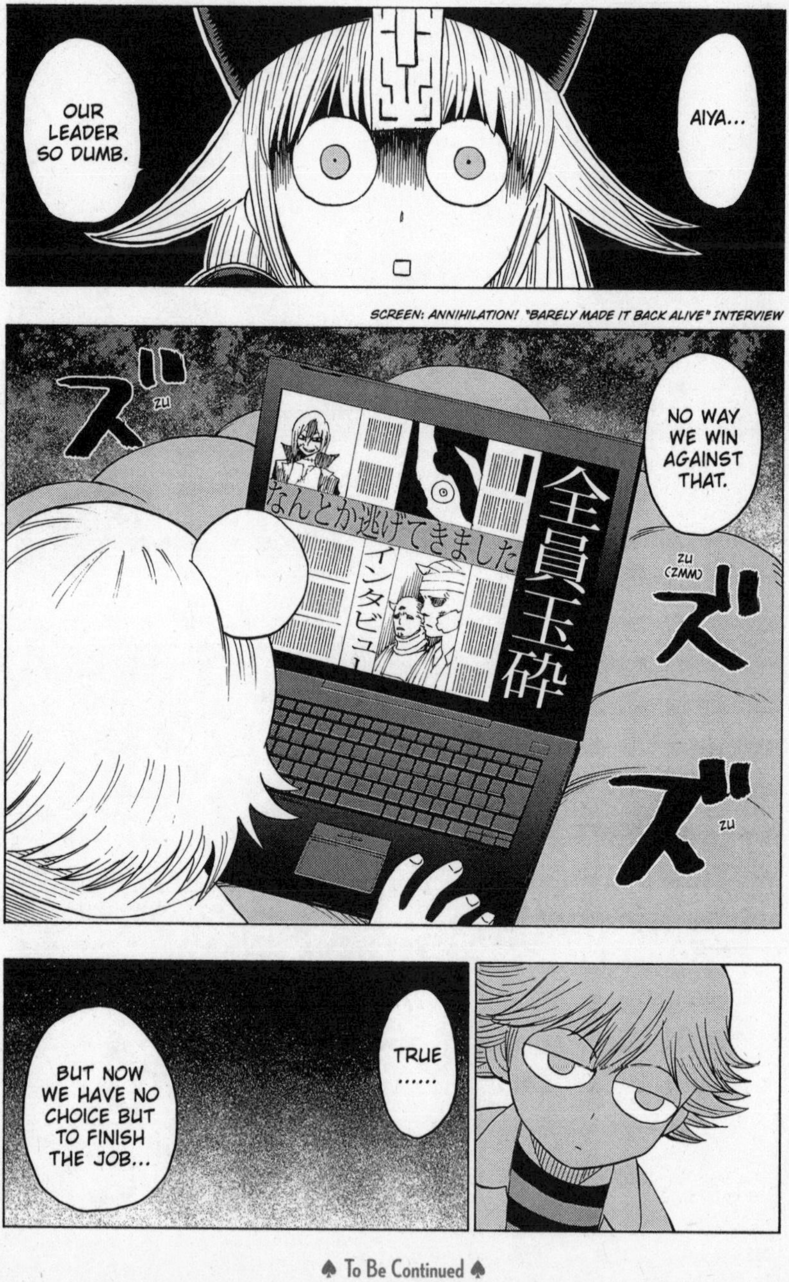
AIYA...
OUR LEADER SO DUMB.
SCREEN: ANNIHILATION! "BARELY MADE IT BACK ALIVE" INTERVIEW
NO WAY WE WIN AGAINST THAT.
ズ
ZU (ZMM)
ズ
ZU
全員玉砕
なんとか逃げてきました
インタビュ
ズ
ZU
TRUE ......
BUT NOW WE HAVE NO CHOICE BUT TO FINISH THE JOB...

♠ To Be Continued ♠

TELE-PORT

Hydrabell

MP ▲ 26900 organ

BLOOD LAD

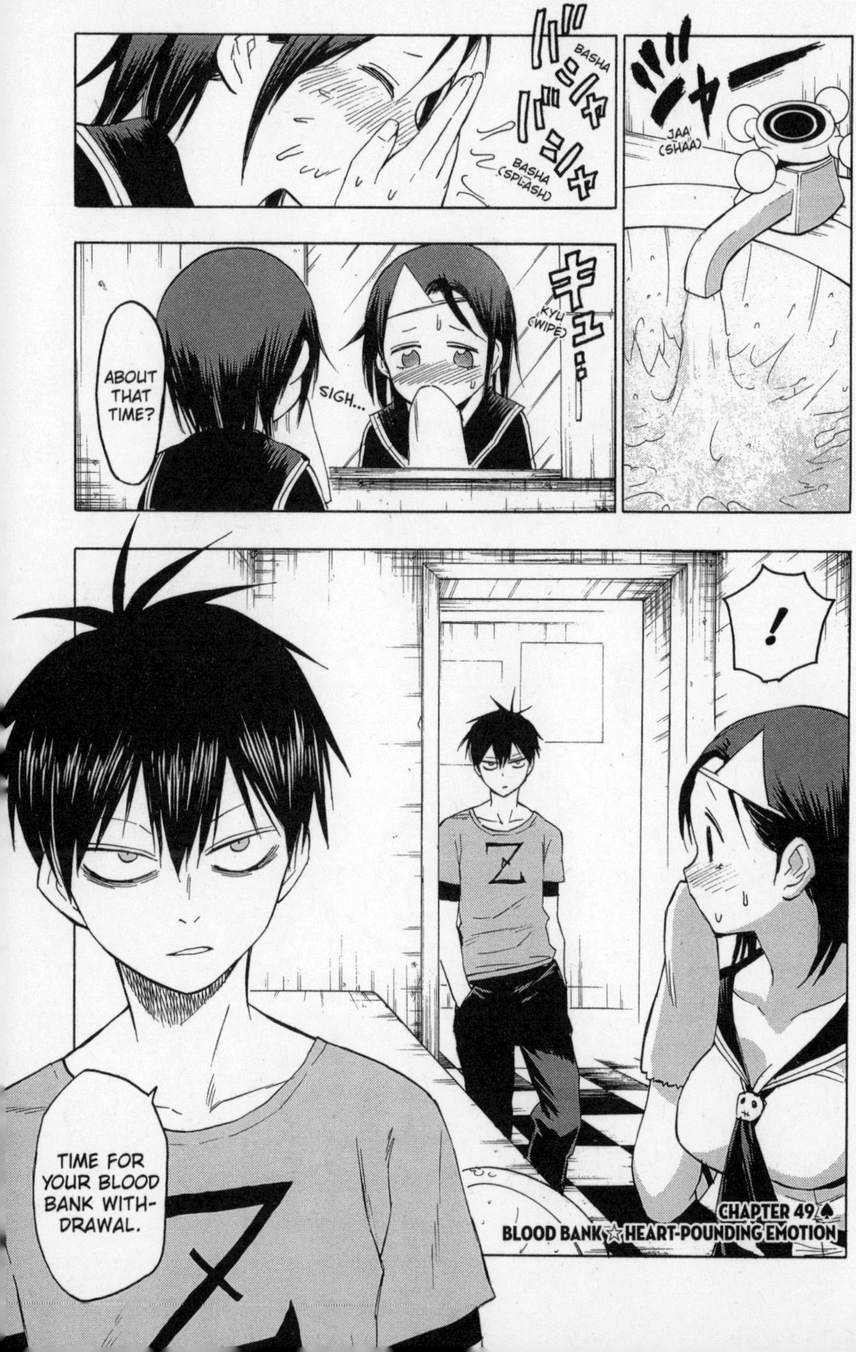
ジャー
JAA (SHAA)
バシャバシャ
BASHA BASHA (SPLASH)
キュ
KYU (WIPE)
SIGH...
ABOUT THAT TIME?
!
TIME FOR YOUR BLOOD BANK WITH-DRAWAL.
CHAPTER 49
BLOOD BANK☆HEART-POUNDING EMOTION

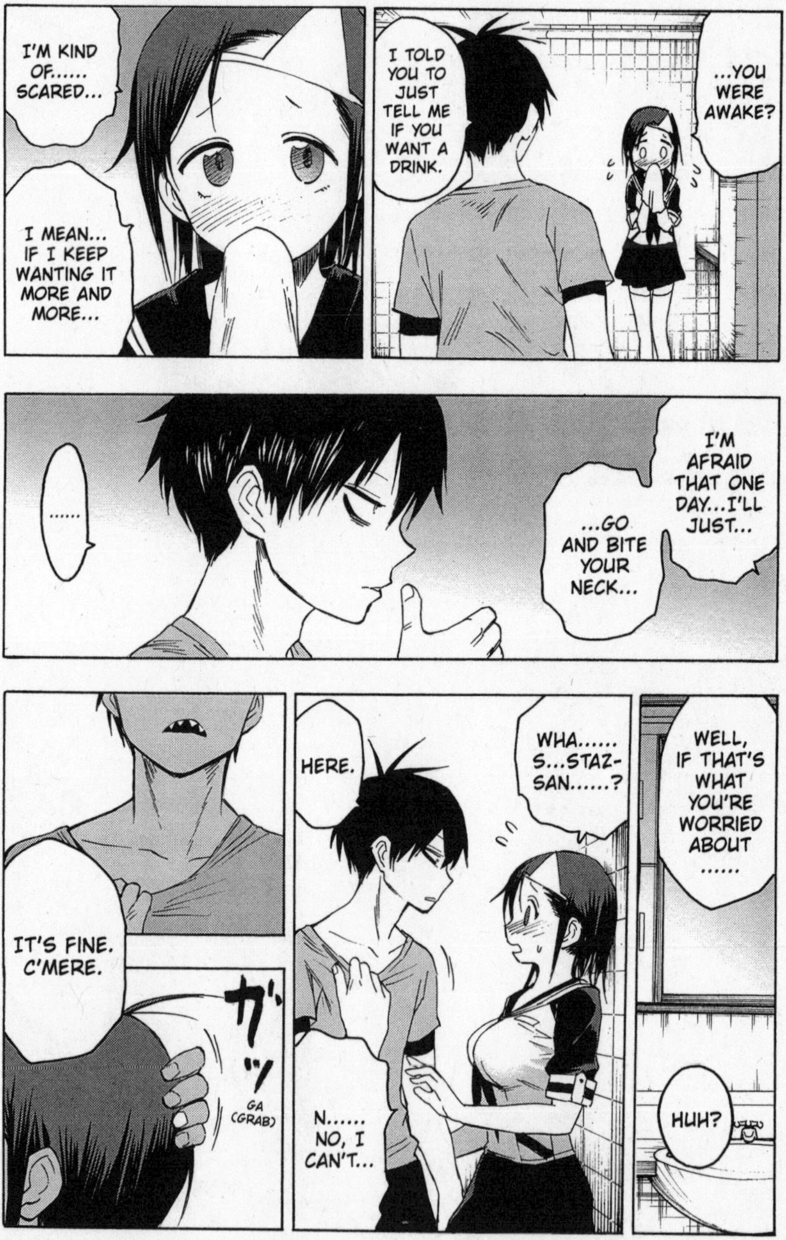
...YOU WERE AWAKE?
I TOLD YOU TO JUST TELL ME IF YOU WANT A DRINK.
I'M KIND OF...... SCARED...
I MEAN... IF I KEEP WANTING IT MORE AND MORE...
I'M AFRAID THAT ONE DAY...I'LL JUST...
...GO AND BITE YOUR NECK...
......
WELL, IF THAT'S WHAT YOU'RE WORRIED ABOUT ......
HUH?
WHA...... S...STAZ-SAN......?
HERE.
N...... NO, I CAN'T...
IT'S FINE. C'MERE.
ガッ
GA (GRAB)

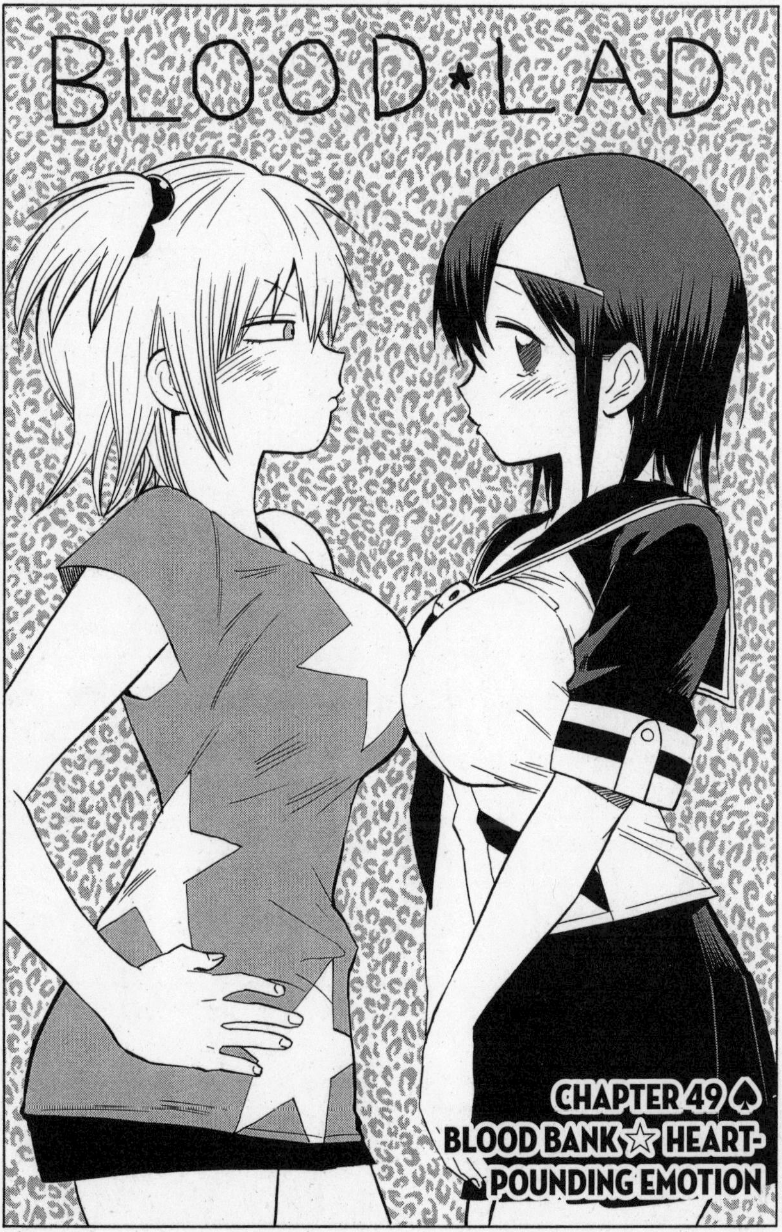
BLOOD★LAD
CHAPTER 49 ♠
BLOOD BANK☆HEART-
POUNDING EMOTION

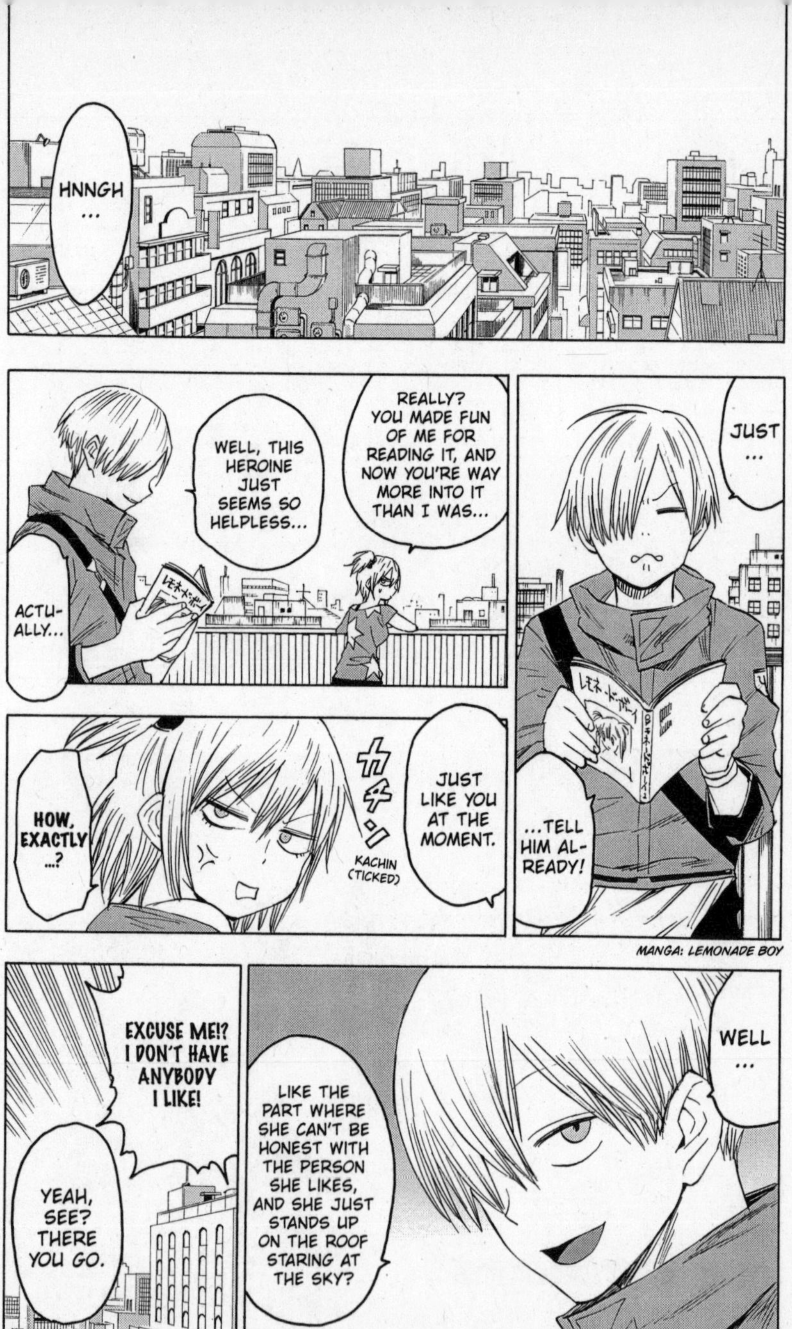
HNNGH ...
JUST ...
...TELL HIM AL-READY!
REALLY? YOU MADE FUN OF ME FOR READING IT, AND NOW YOU'RE WAY MORE INTO IT THAN I WAS...
WELL, THIS HEROINE JUST SEEMS SO HELPLESS...
ACTU-ALLY...
JUST LIKE YOU AT THE MOMENT.
カチン
KACHIN (TICKED)
HOW, EXACTLY ...?
MANGA: LEMONADE BOY
WELL ...
LIKE THE PART WHERE SHE CAN'T BE HONEST WITH THE PERSON SHE LIKES, AND SHE JUST STANDS UP ON THE ROOF STARING AT THE SKY?
EXCUSE ME!? I DON'T HAVE ANYBODY I LIKE!
YEAH, SEE? THERE YOU GO.

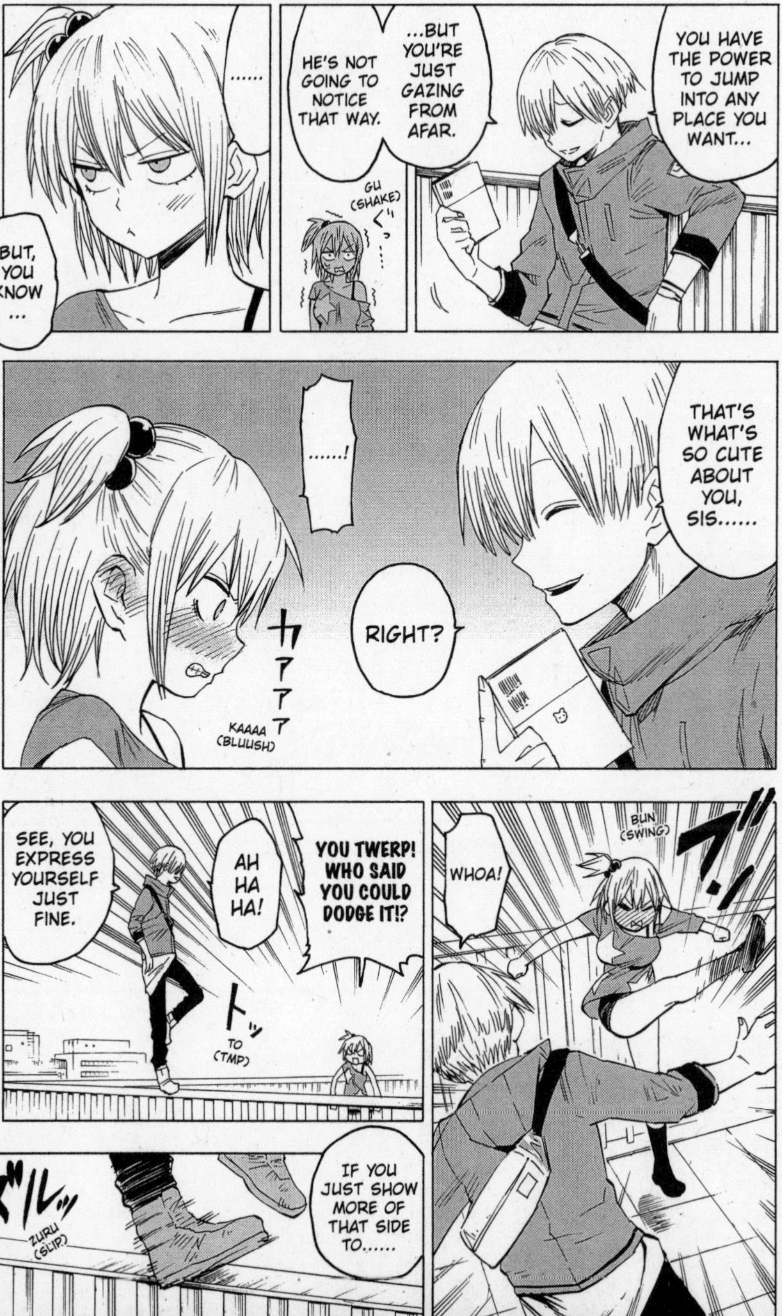
YOU HAVE THE POWER TO JUMP INTO ANY PLACE YOU WANT...
...BUT YOU'RE JUST GAZING FROM AFAR.
HE'S NOT GOING TO NOTICE THAT WAY.
GU (SHAKE)
......
BUT, YOU KNOW ...
THAT'S WHAT'S SO CUTE ABOUT YOU, SIS......
RIGHT?
......!
KAAAA (BLUUSH)
BUN (SWING)
WHOA!
YOU TWERP! WHO SAID YOU COULD DODGE IT!?
AH HA HA!
SEE, YOU EXPRESS YOURSELF JUST FINE.
TO (TMP)
IF YOU JUST SHOW MORE OF THAT SIDE TO......
ZURU (SLIP)

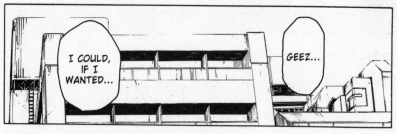

I COULD, IF I WANTED...

GEEZ...

GU
(GRAB)

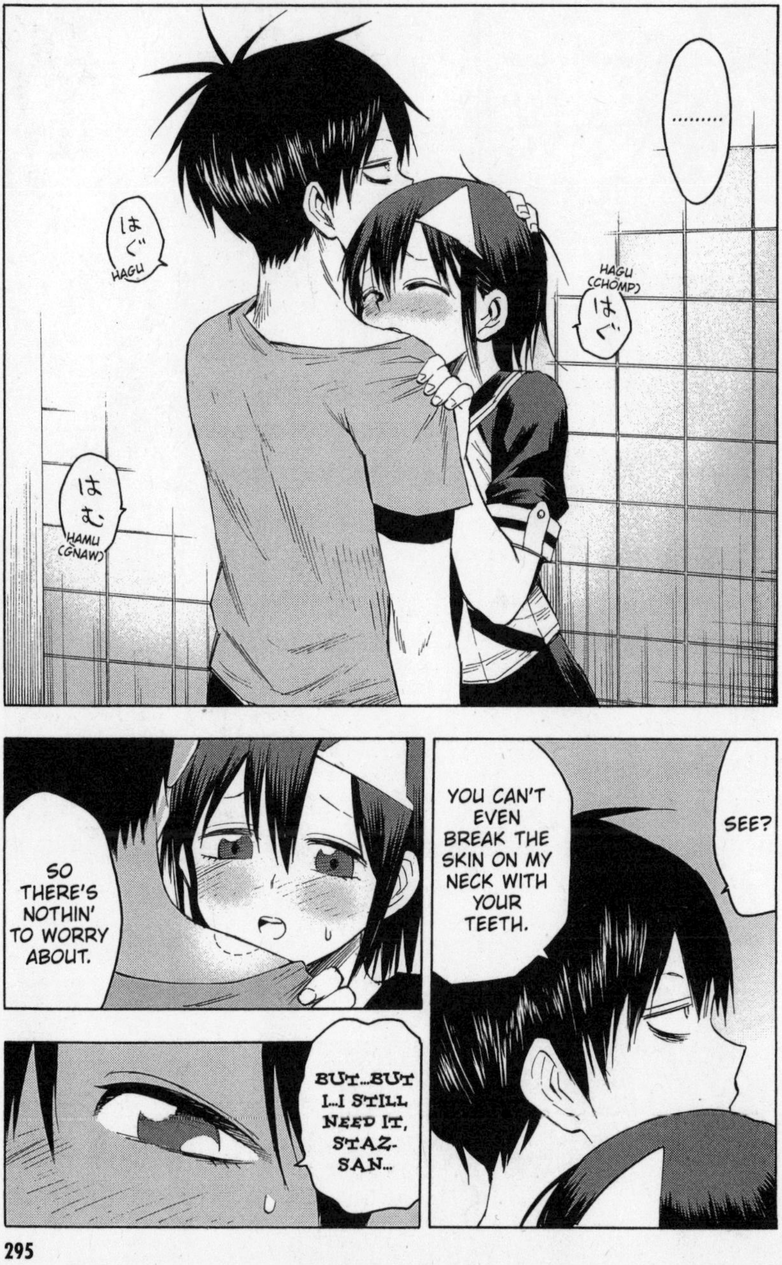
....
HAGU (CHOMP) はぐ
はぐ HAGU
はむ HAMU (GNAW)
SEE?
YOU CAN'T EVEN BREAK THE SKIN ON MY NECK WITH YOUR TEETH.
SO THERE'S NOTHIN' TO WORRY ABOUT.
BUT...BUT I...I STILL NEED IT, STAZ-SAN...

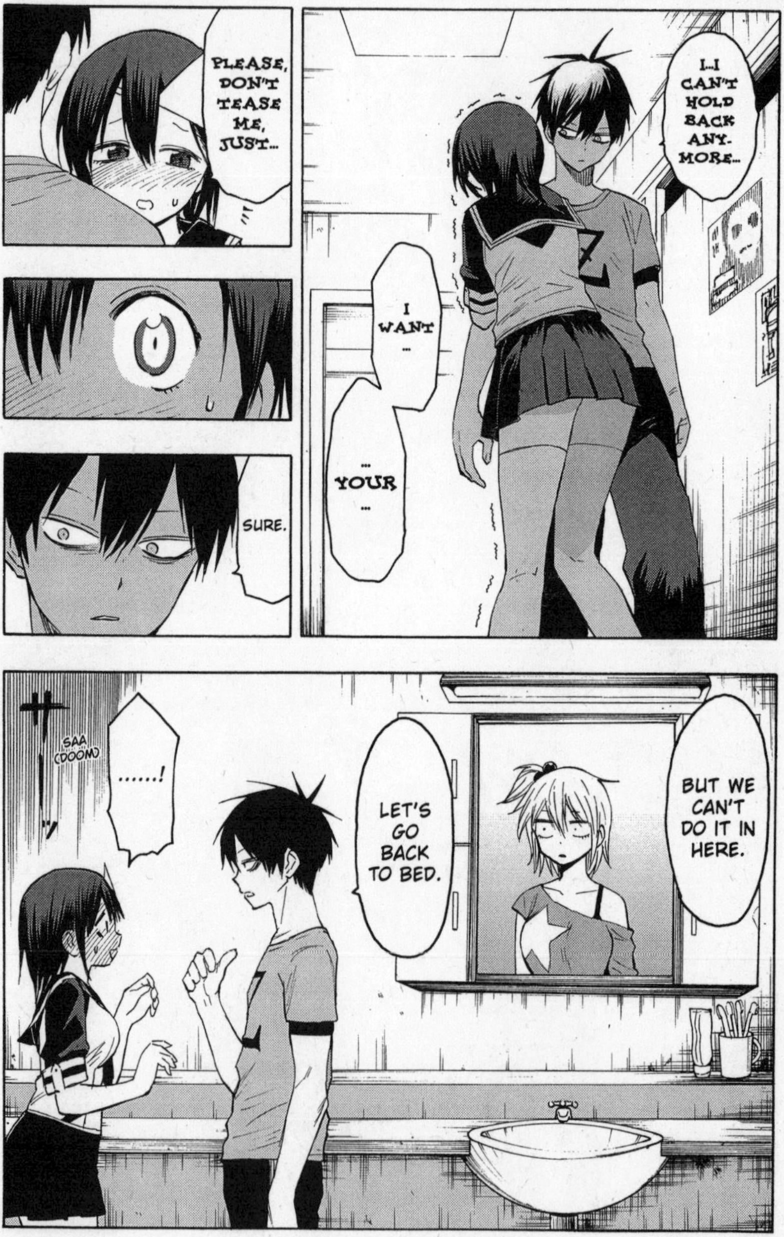
I..I CAN'T HOLD BACK ANY-MORE...
I WANT ...
... YOUR ...
PLEASE, DON'T TEASE ME, JUST...
SURE.
BUT WE CAN'T DO IT IN HERE.
LET'S GO BACK TO BED.
......!
SAA (DOOM)

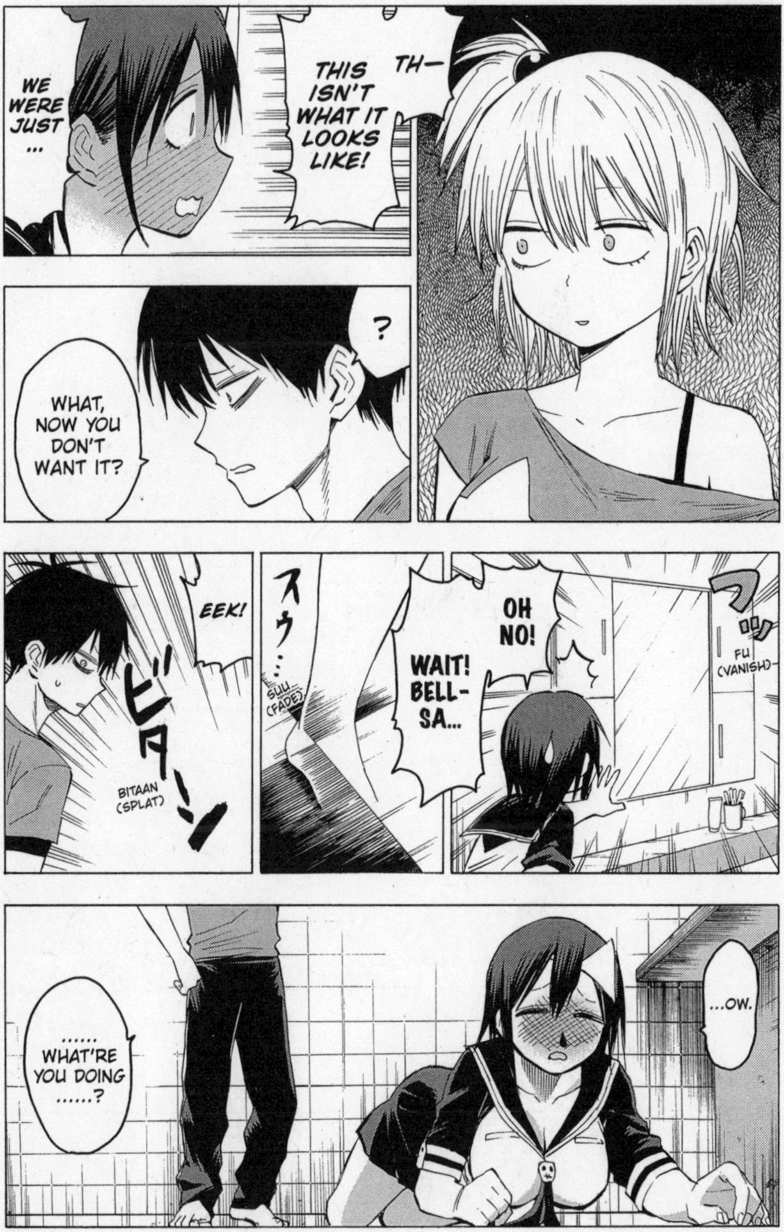
TH—
THIS ISN'T WHAT IT LOOKS LIKE!
WE WERE JUST ...
?
WHAT, NOW YOU DON'T WANT IT?
FU (VANISH)
OH NO!
WAIT! BELL-SA...
SUU (FADE)
EEK!
BITAAN (SPLAT)
...OW.
...... WHAT'RE YOU DOING ......?

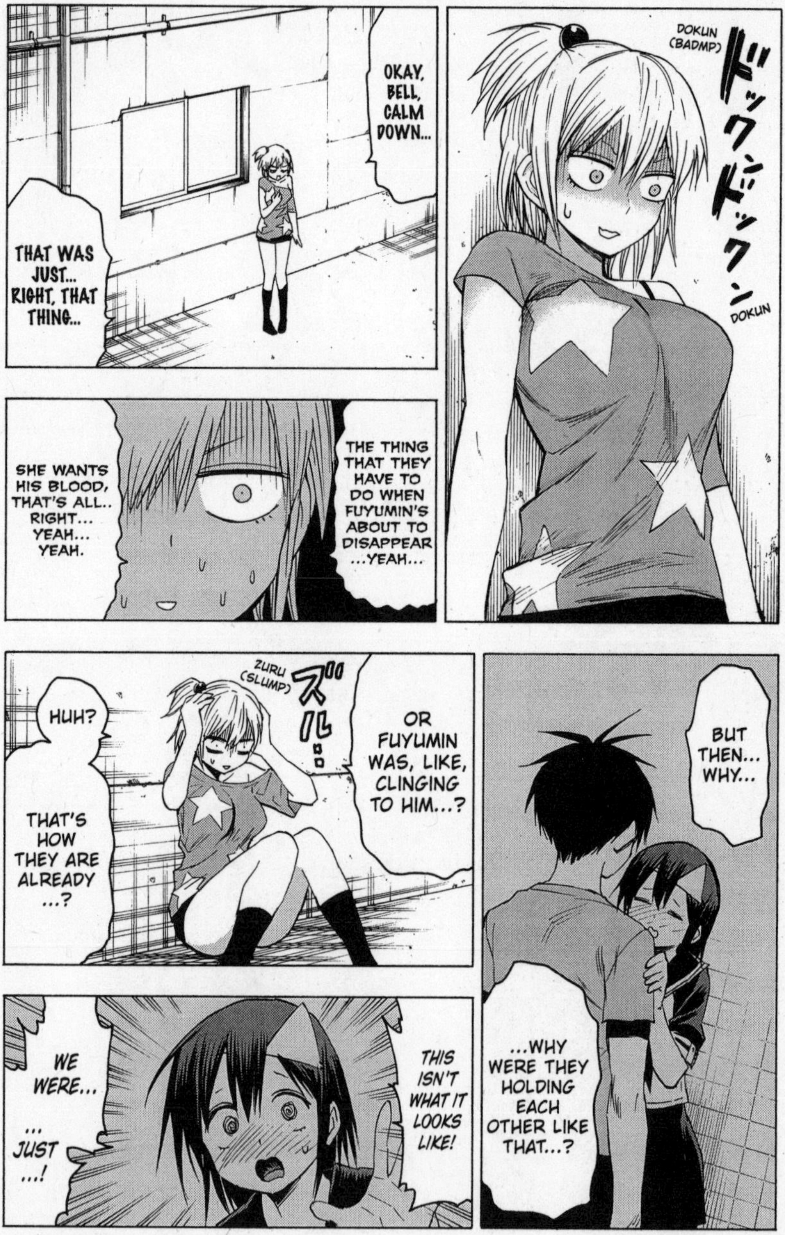
DOKUN (BADMP)
ドックンドックン
DOKUN
OKAY, BELL, CALM DOWN...
THAT WAS JUST... RIGHT, THAT THING...
THE THING THAT THEY HAVE TO DO WHEN FUYUMIN'S ABOUT TO DISAPPEAR ...YEAH...
SHE WANTS HIS BLOOD, THAT'S ALL.. RIGHT... YEAH... YEAH.
BUT THEN... WHY...
...WHY WERE THEY HOLDING EACH OTHER LIKE THAT...?
ZURU (SLUMP)
ズル
OR FUYUMIN WAS, LIKE, CLINGING TO HIM...?
HUH?
THAT'S HOW THEY ARE ALREADY ...?
THIS ISN'T WHAT IT LOOKS LIKE!
WE WERE...
... JUST ...!

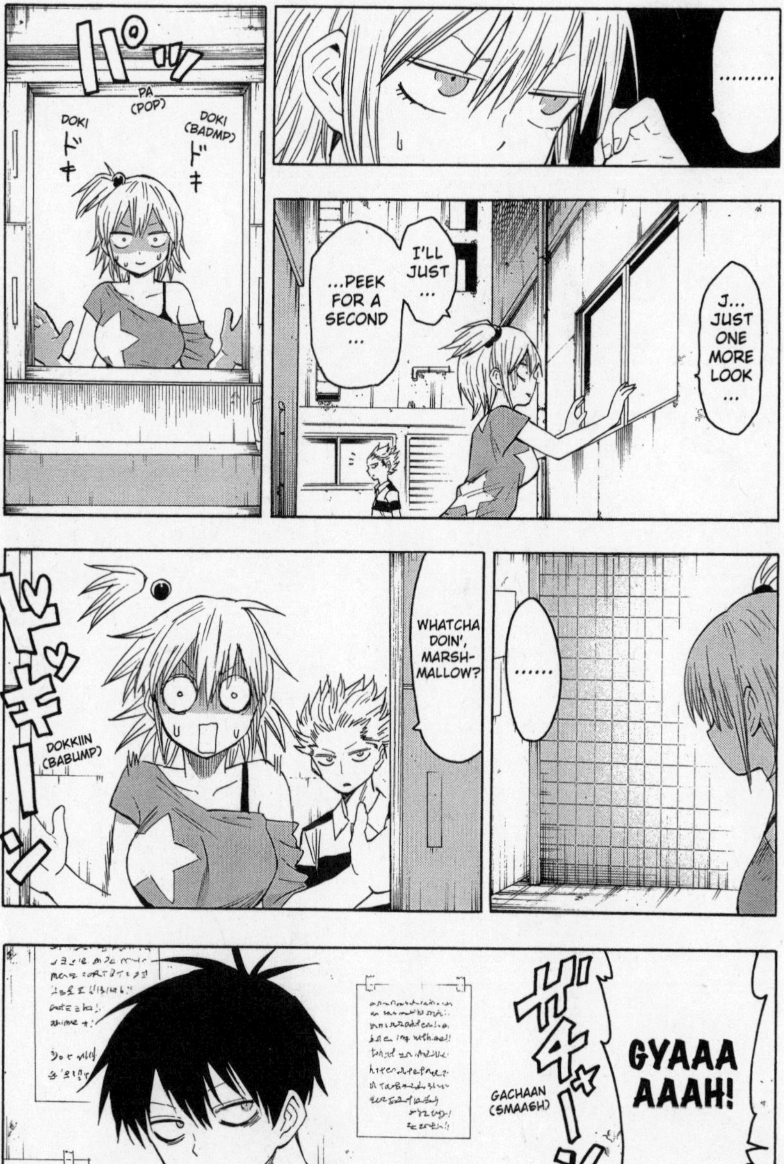

....
J... JUST ONE MORE LOOK ...
I'LL JUST ...
...PEEK FOR A SECOND ...
パッ
PA (POP)
ドキ
DOKI (BADMP)
ドキ
DOKI
......
WHATCHA DOIN', MARSHMALLOW?
ドッキーン
DOKKIIN (BABUMP)
GYAAA AAAH!
ガチャーン
GACHAAN (SMAASH)

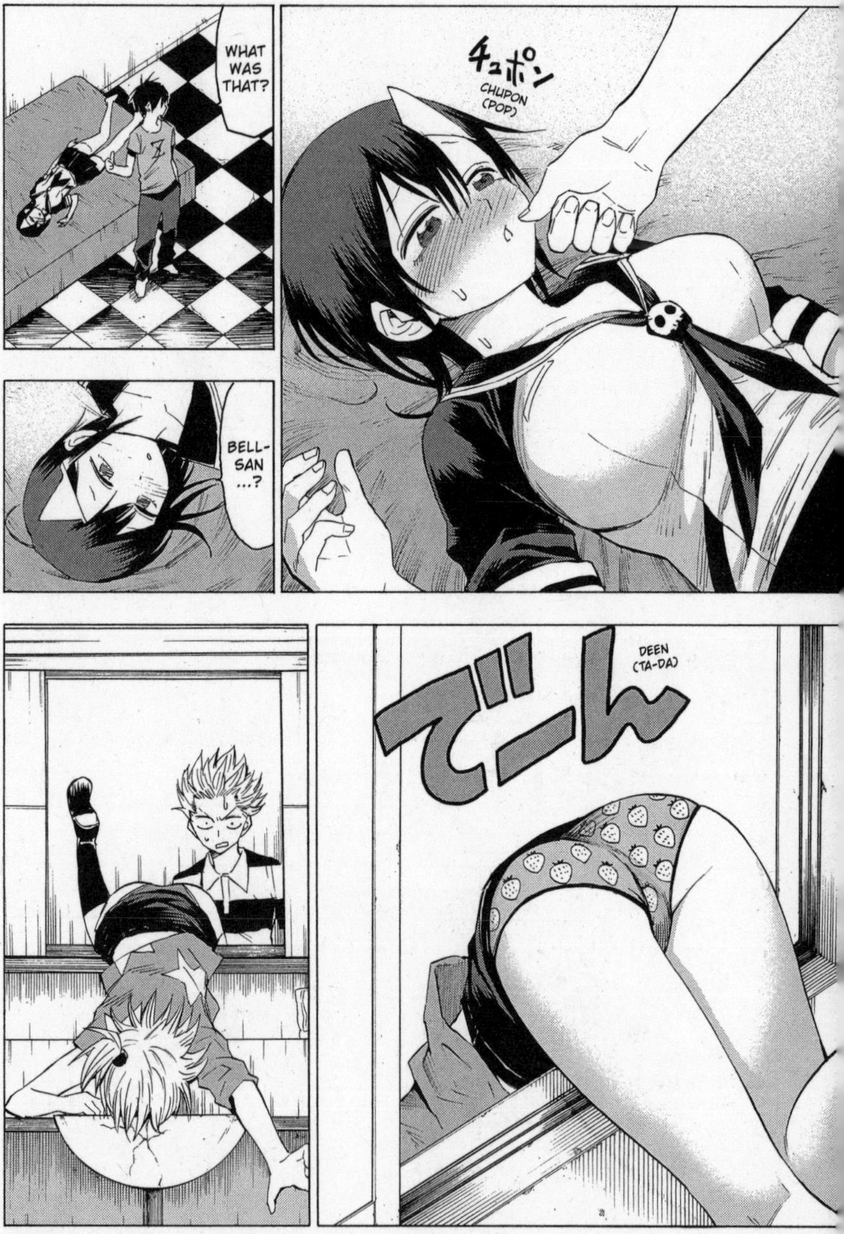
チュポン
CHUPON (POP)
WHAT WAS THAT?
BELL-SAN ...?
でーん
DEEN (TA-DA)

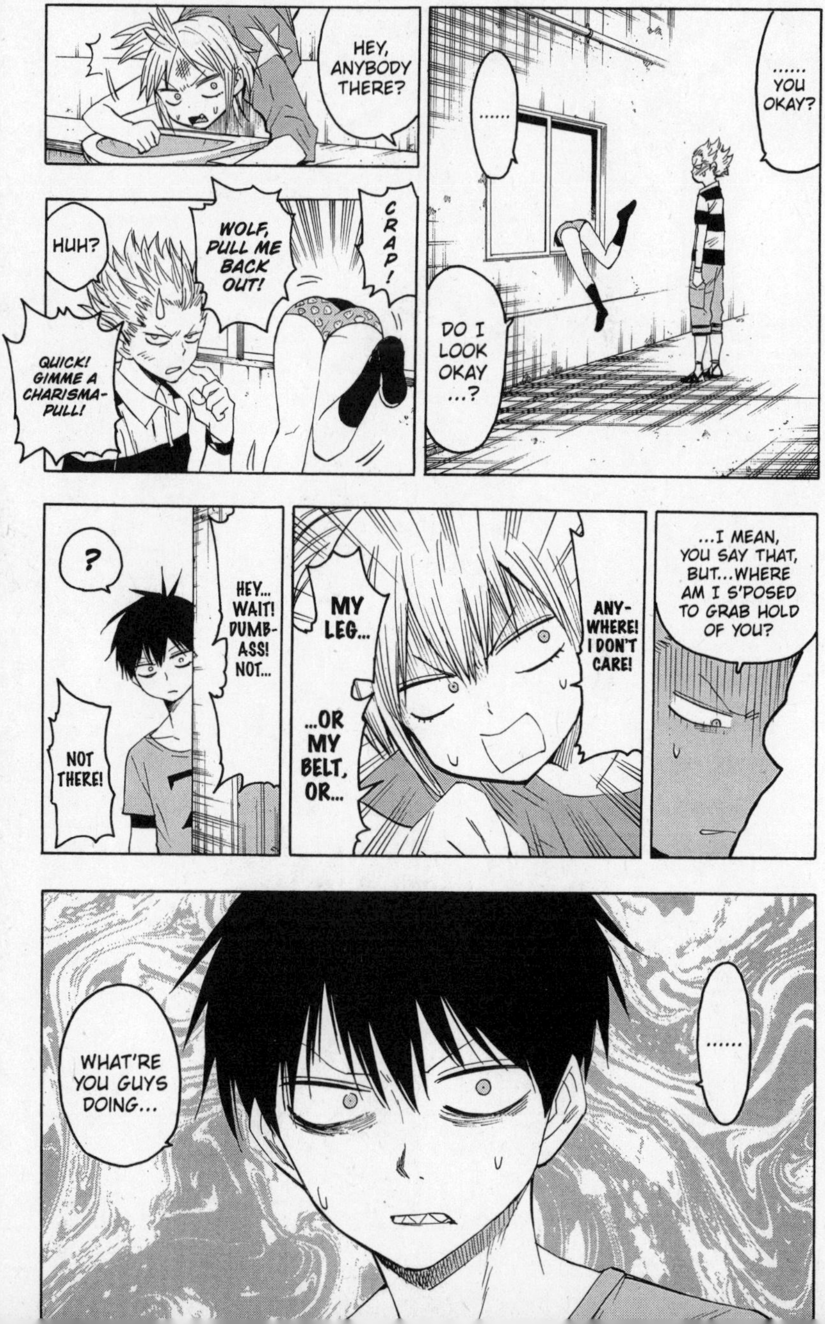
......
YOU OKAY?
......
DO I LOOK OKAY ...?
HEY, ANYBODY THERE?
CRAP!
WOLF, PULL ME BACK OUT!
HUH?
QUICK! GIMME A CHARISMA-PULL!
...I MEAN, YOU SAY THAT, BUT...WHERE AM I S'POSED TO GRAB HOLD OF YOU?
ANY-WHERE! I DON'T CARE!
MY LEG...
...OR MY BELT, OR...
HEY... WAIT! DUMB-ASS! NOT...
?
NOT THERE!
......
WHAT'RE YOU GUYS DOING...

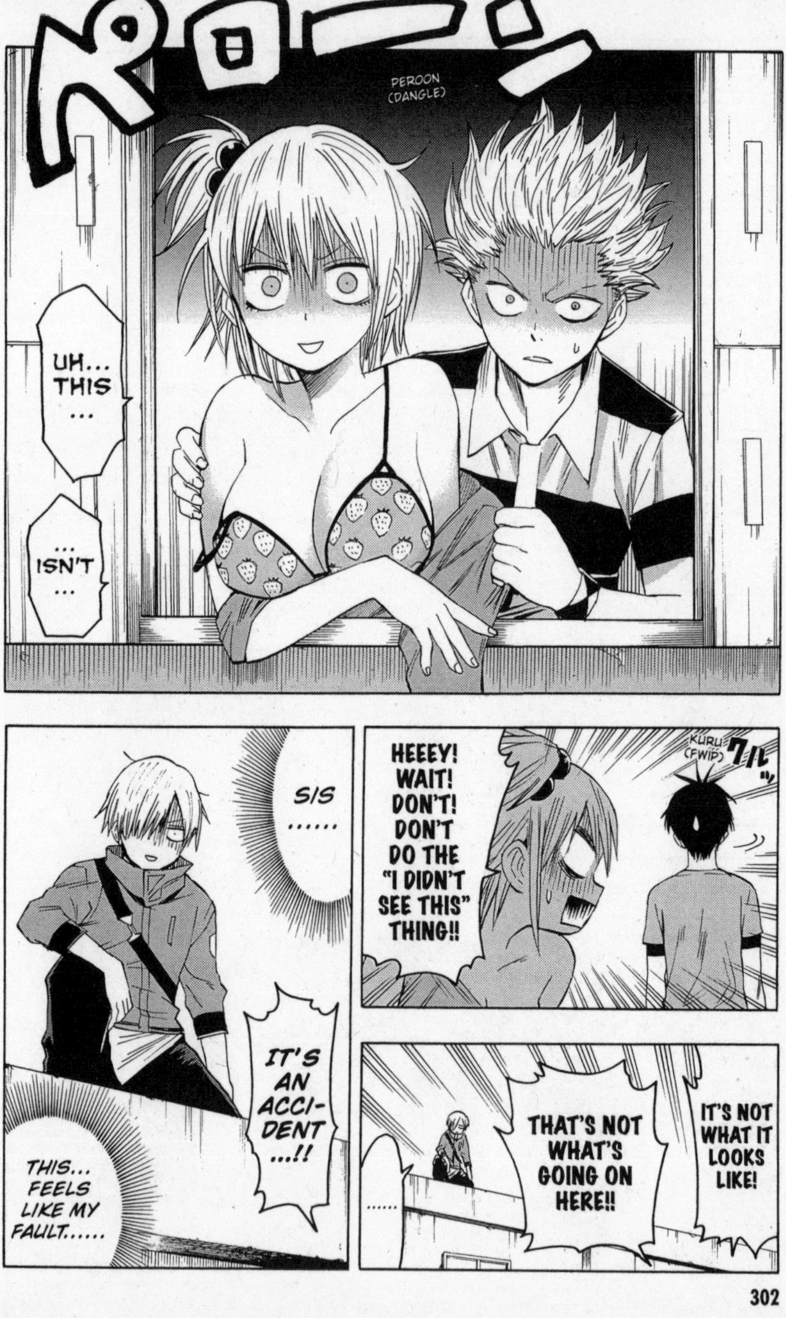
ペローン
PEROON (DANGLE)
UH... THIS ...
... ISN'T ...
クル
KURU (FWIP)
HEEEY! WAIT! DON'T! DON'T DO THE "I DIDN'T SEE THIS" THING!!
IT'S NOT WHAT IT LOOKS LIKE!
THAT'S NOT WHAT'S GOING ON HERE!!
......
SIS ......
IT'S AN ACCI-DENT ...!!
THIS... FEELS LIKE MY FAULT......

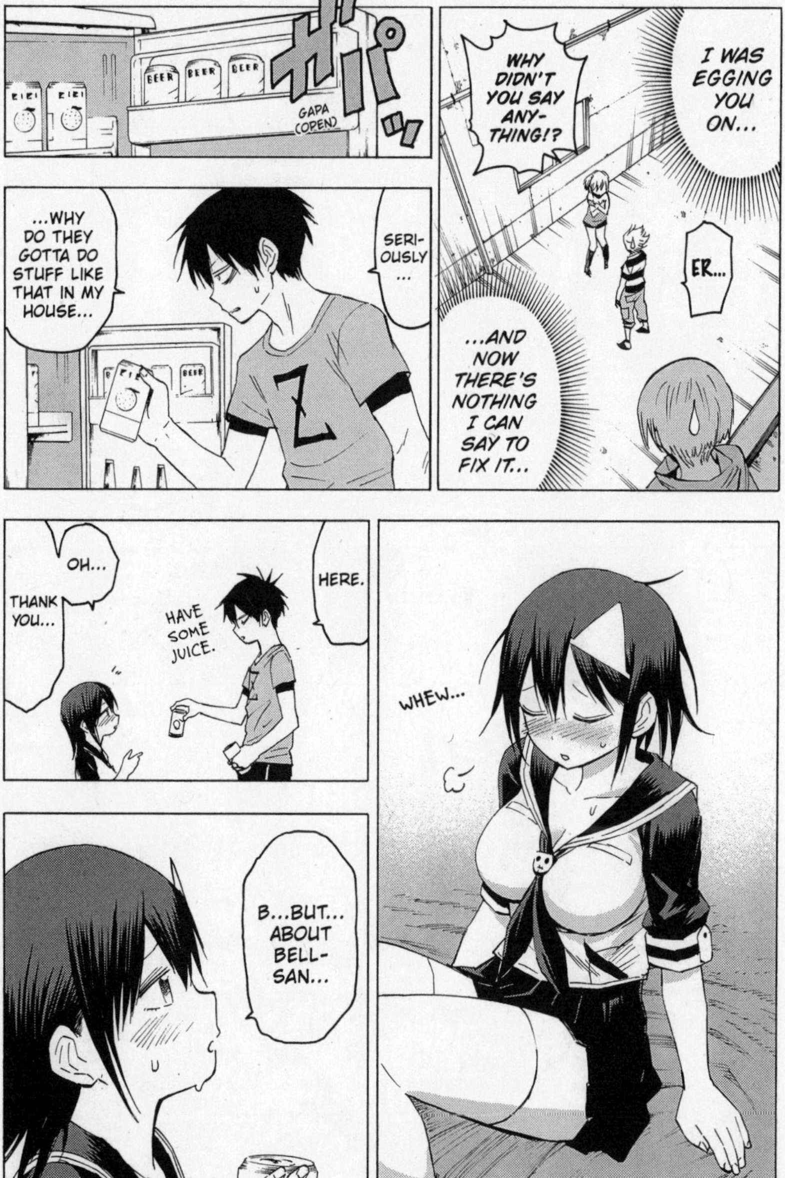
I WAS EGGING YOU ON...
WHY DIDN'T YOU SAY ANY-THING!?
ER...
...AND NOW THERE'S NOTHING I CAN SAY TO FIX IT...
GAPA (OPEN)
SERI-OUSLY...
...WHY DO THEY GOTTA DO STUFF LIKE THAT IN MY HOUSE...
WHEW...
HERE.
HAVE SOME JUICE.
OH...
THANK YOU...
B...BUT... ABOUT BELL-SAN...

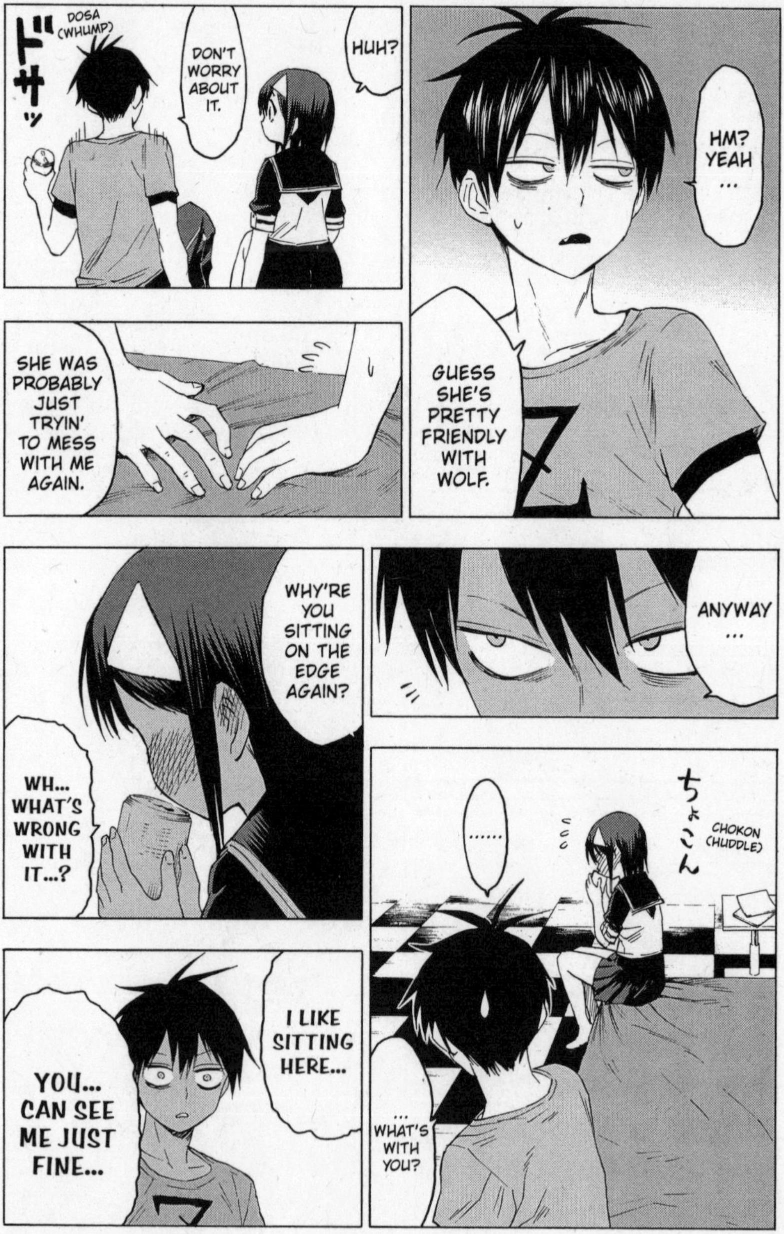
HM? YEAH ...
GUESS SHE'S PRETTY FRIENDLY WITH WOLF.
HUH?
DON'T WORRY ABOUT IT.
ドサッ
DOSA (WHUMP)
SHE WAS PROBABLY JUST TRYIN' TO MESS WITH ME AGAIN.
ANYWAY ...
WHY'RE YOU SITTING ON THE EDGE AGAIN?
WH... WHAT'S WRONG WITH IT...?
ちょこん
CHOKON (HUDDLE)
......
... WHAT'S WITH YOU?
I LIKE SITTING HERE...
YOU... CAN SEE ME JUST FINE...

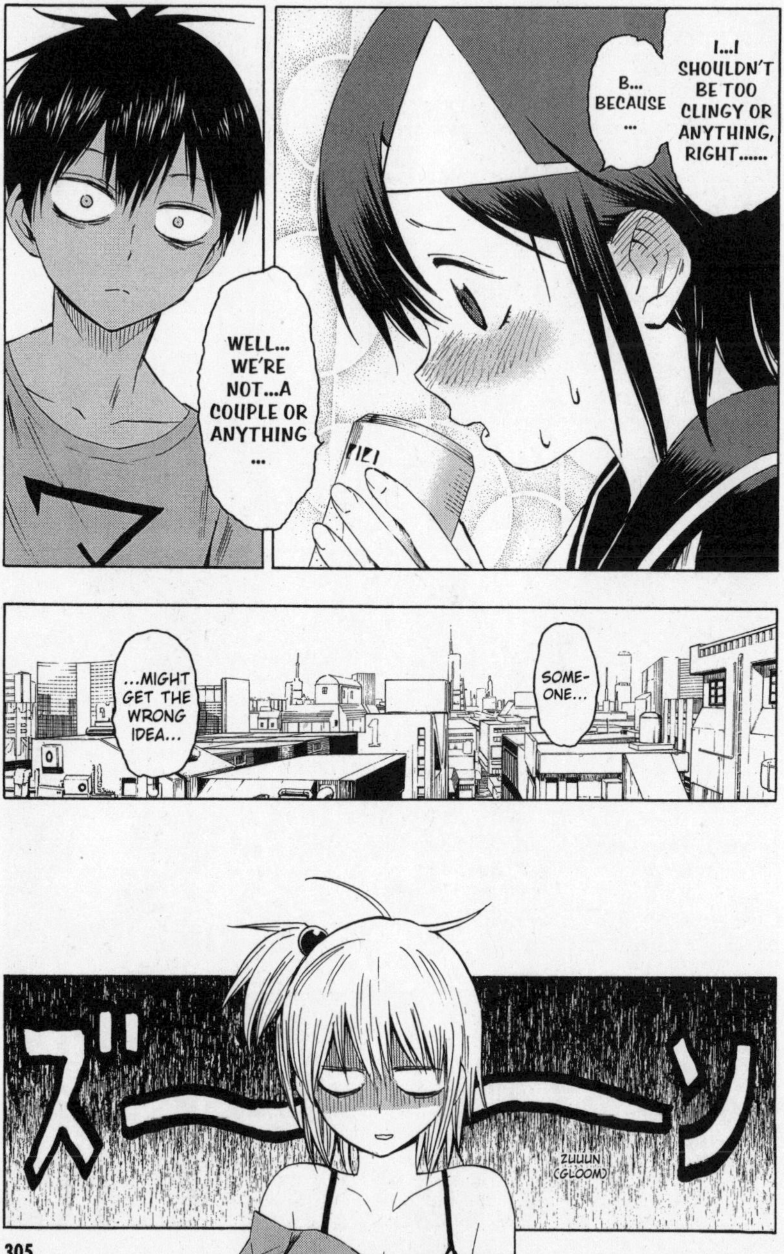
I...I SHOULDN'T BE TOO CLINGY OR ANYTHING, RIGHT......
B... BECAUSE ...
WELL... WE'RE NOT...A COUPLE OR ANYTHING ...
SOME-ONE...
...MIGHT GET THE WRONG IDEA...
ズーン
ZUUUN (GLOOM)

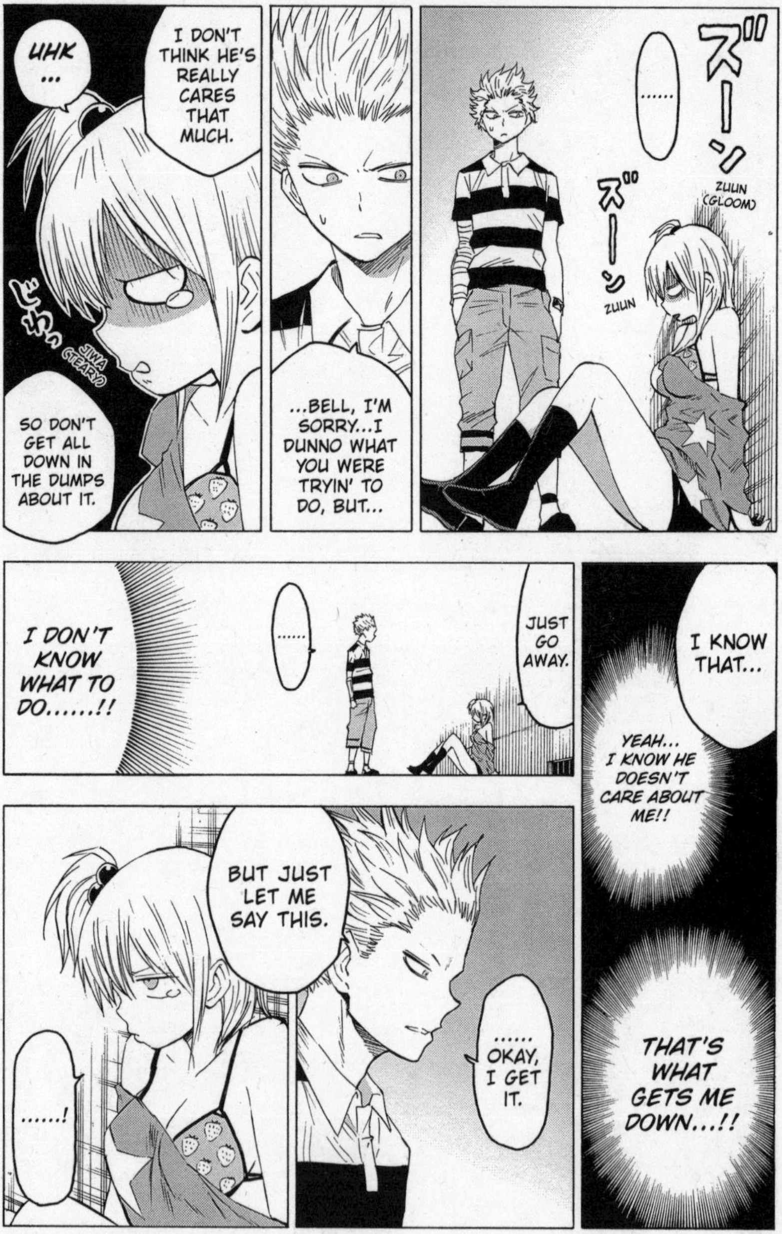

......
ズーン
ZUUN (GLOOM)
ズーン
ZUUN
...BELL, I'M SORRY...I DUNNO WHAT YOU WERE TRYIN' TO DO, BUT...
I DON'T THINK HE'S REALLY CARES THAT MUCH.
UHK ...
じわっ
JIWA (TEARY)
SO DON'T GET ALL DOWN IN THE DUMPS ABOUT IT.
I KNOW THAT...
YEAH... I KNOW HE DOESN'T CARE ABOUT ME!!
THAT'S WHAT GETS ME DOWN...!!
JUST GO AWAY.
......
I DON'T KNOW WHAT TO DO......!!
BUT JUST LET ME SAY THIS.
...... OKAY, I GET IT.
......!

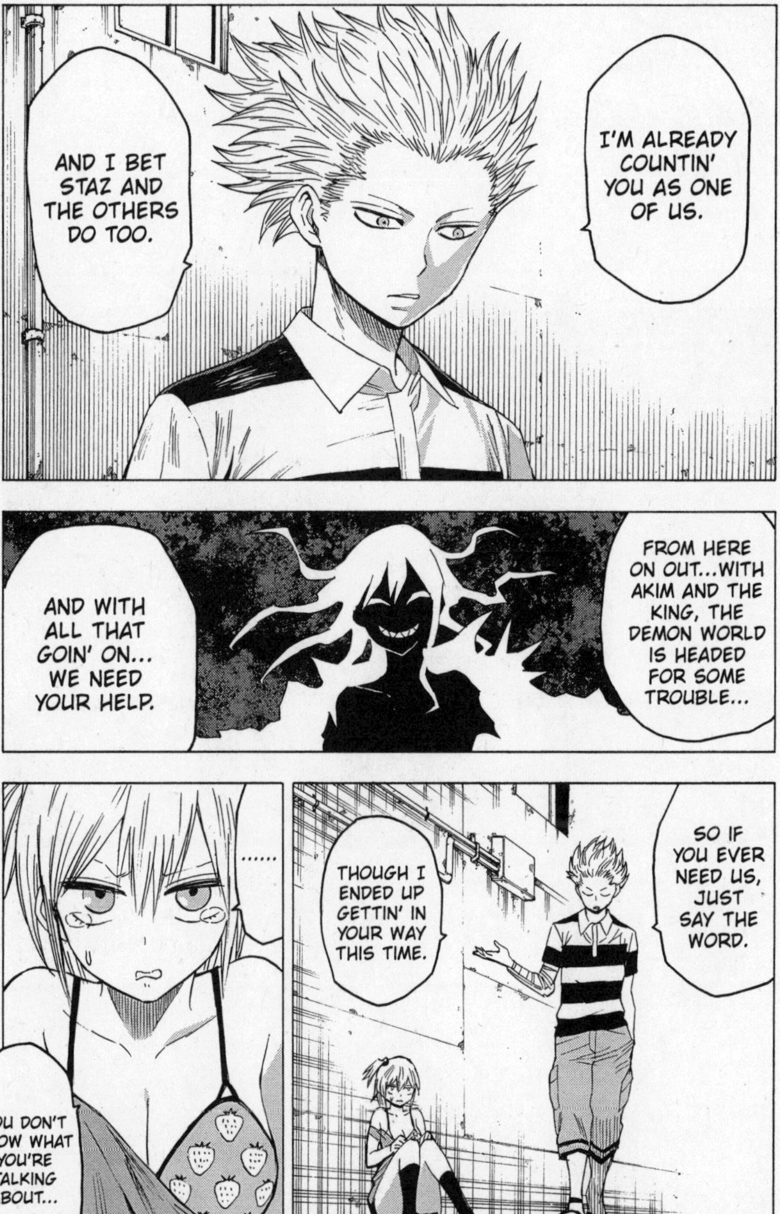
I'M ALREADY COUNTIN' YOU AS ONE OF US.
AND I BET STAZ AND THE OTHERS DO TOO.
FROM HERE ON OUT...WITH AKIM AND THE KING, THE DEMON WORLD IS HEADED FOR SOME TROUBLE...
AND WITH ALL THAT GOIN' ON... WE NEED YOUR HELP.
SO IF YOU EVER NEED US, JUST SAY THE WORD.
THOUGH I ENDED UP GETTIN' IN YOUR WAY THIS TIME.
......
YOU DON'T KNOW WHAT YOU'RE TALKING ABOUT...

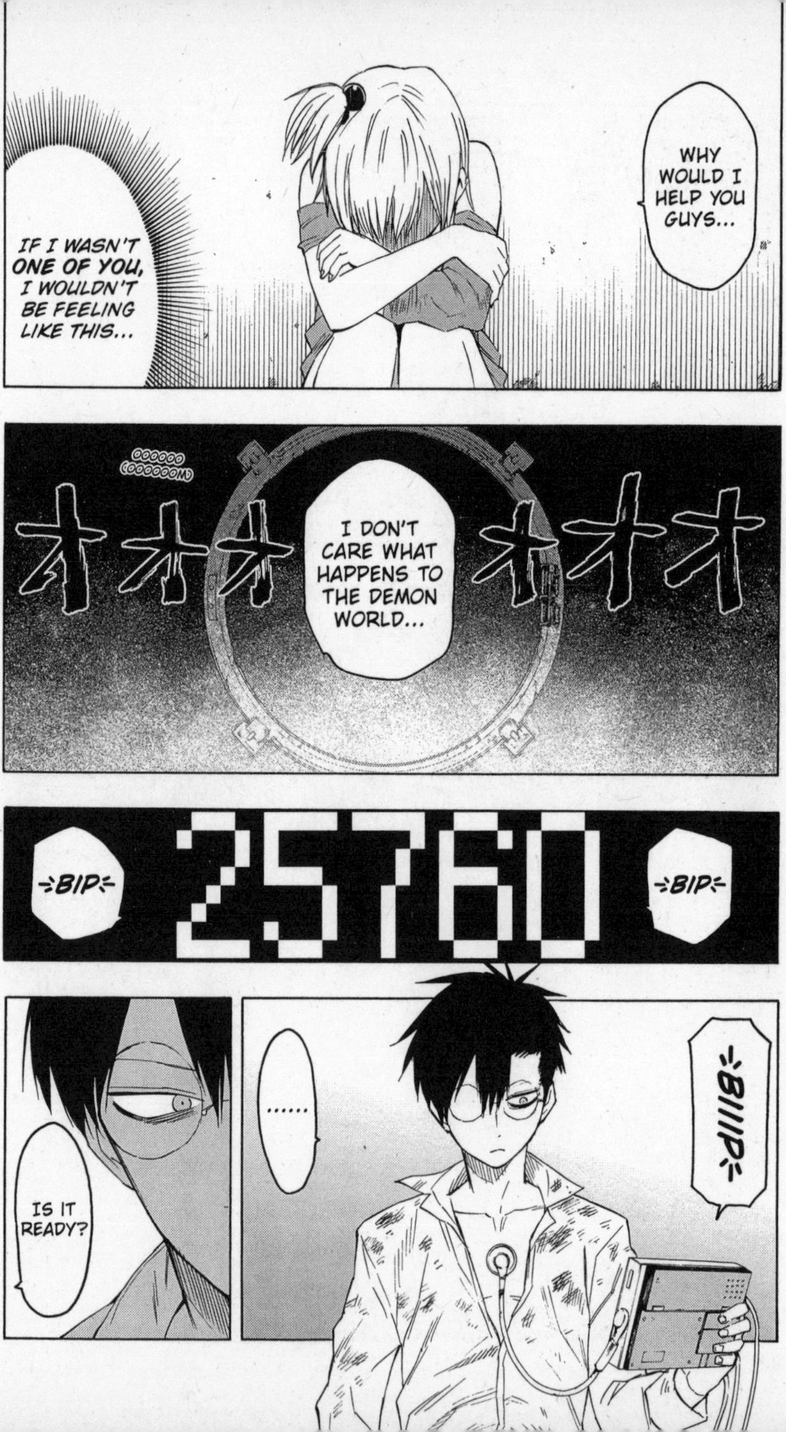
WHY WOULD I HELP YOU GUYS...
IF I WASN'T ONE OF YOU, I WOULDN'T BE FEELING LIKE THIS...
I DON'T CARE WHAT HAPPENS TO THE DEMON WORLD...
オオオオオオ
OOOOOO (OOOOOOM)
BIP
25760
BIP
BIIIP
......
IS IT READY?

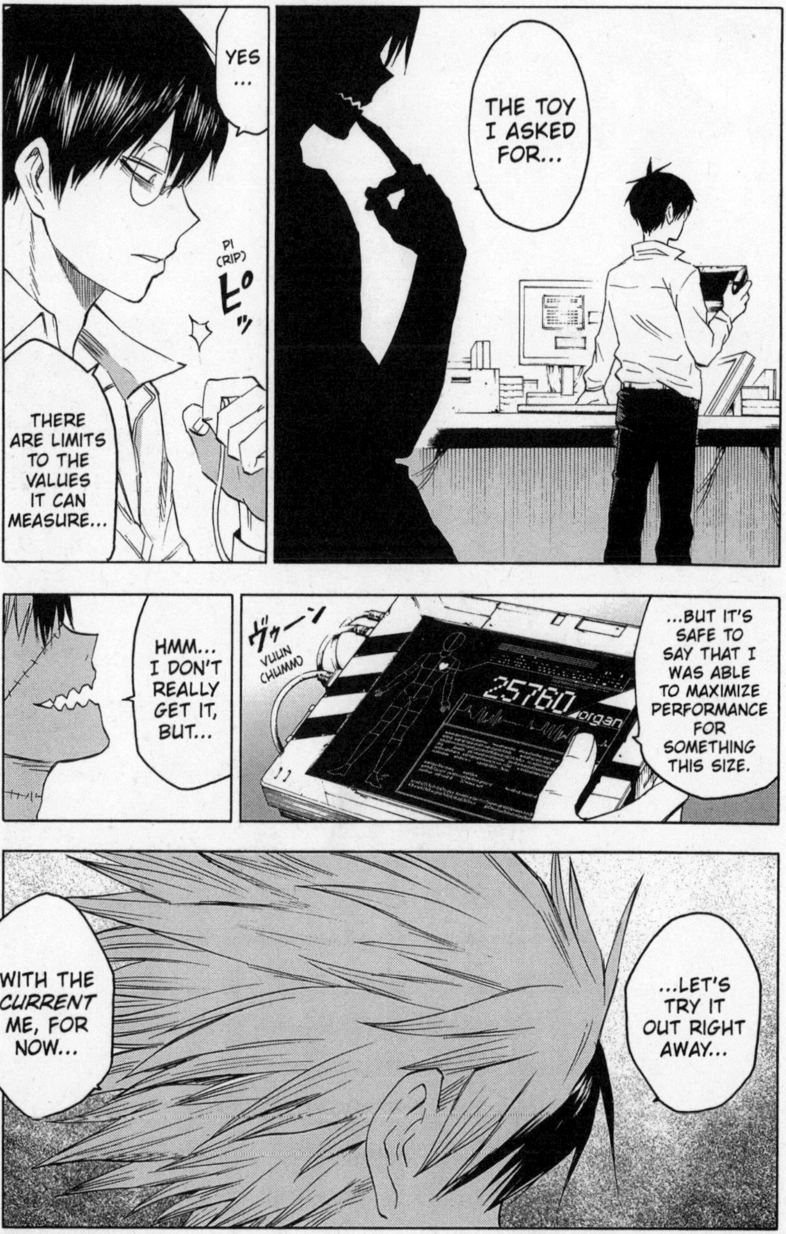
THE TOY I ASKED FOR...
YES ...
ピッ
PI (RIP)
THERE ARE LIMITS TO THE VALUES IT CAN MEASURE...
...BUT IT'S SAFE TO SAY THAT I WAS ABLE TO MAXIMIZE PERFORMANCE FOR SOMETHING THIS SIZE.
ヴゥーン
VUUN (HUMM)
25760
organ
HMM... I DON'T REALLY GET IT, BUT...
...LET'S TRY IT OUT RIGHT AWAY...
WITH THE *CURRENT* ME, FOR NOW...

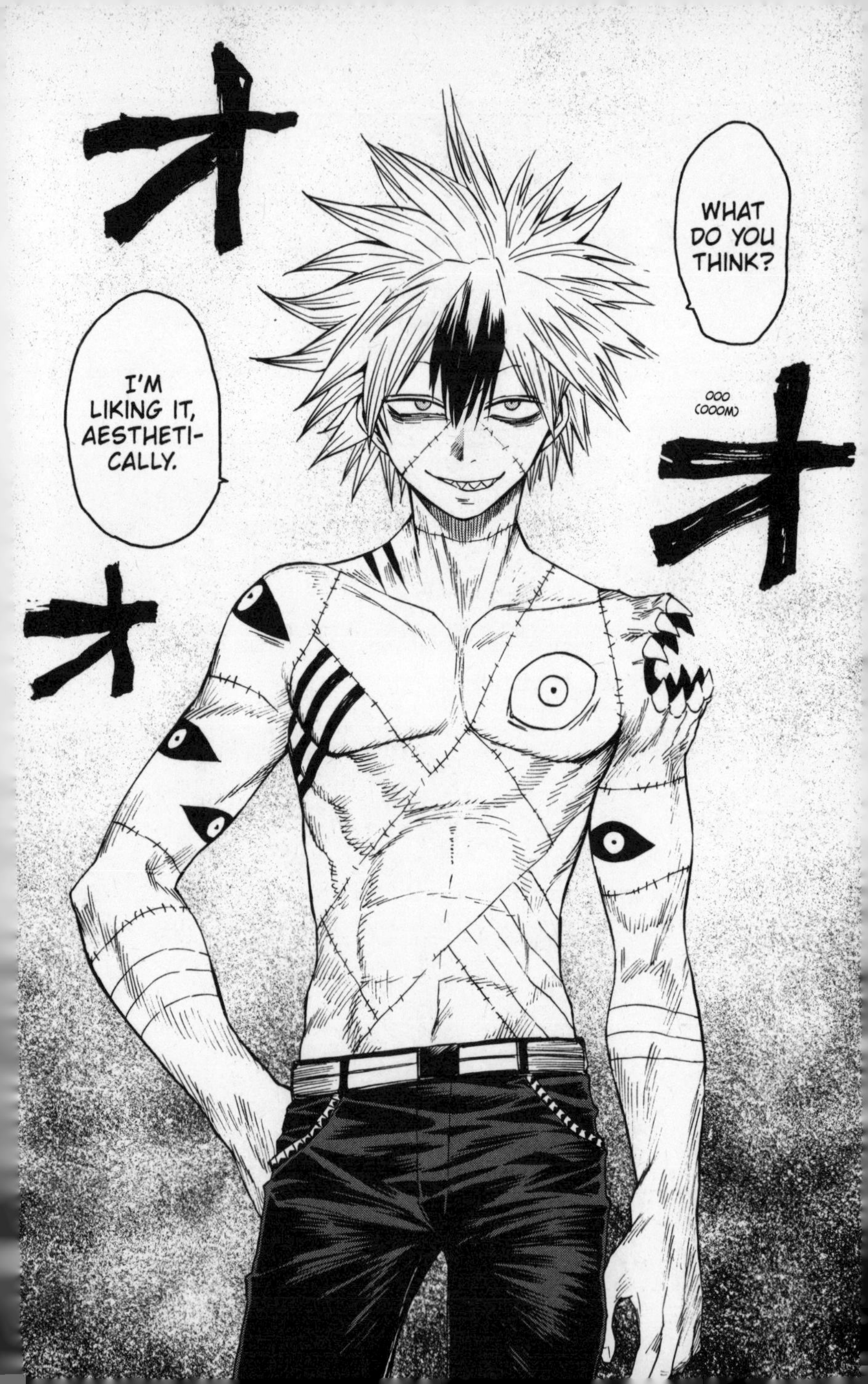
WHAT DO YOU THINK?
オオオ
OOO (OOOM)
I'M LIKING IT, AESTHETICALLY.

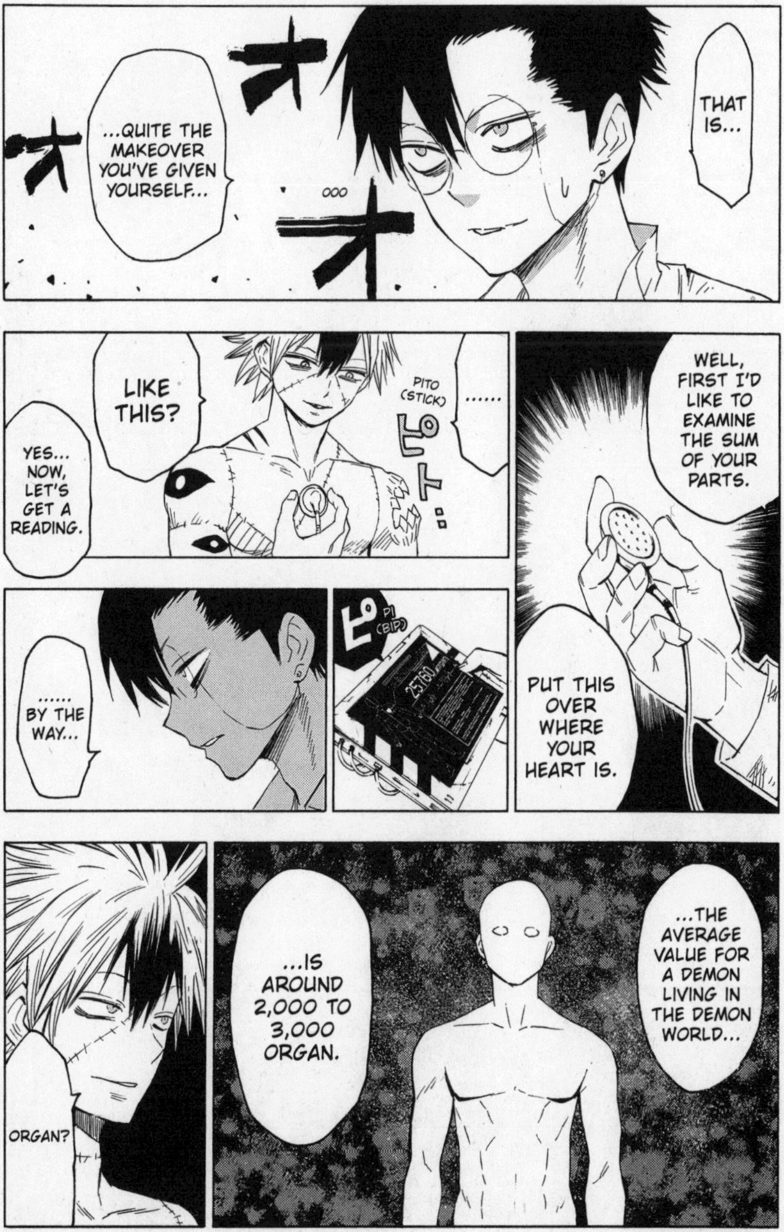
THAT IS...
オ オ オ
...QUITE THE MAKEOVER YOU'VE GIVEN YOURSELF...
OOO
WELL, FIRST I'D LIKE TO EXAMINE THE SUM OF YOUR PARTS.
PUT THIS OVER WHERE YOUR HEART IS.
......
ピト
PITO (STICK)
LIKE THIS?
YES... NOW, LET'S GET A READING.
ピ
PI (BIP)
25760
...... BY THE WAY...
...THE AVERAGE VALUE FOR A DEMON LIVING IN THE DEMON WORLD...
...IS AROUND 2,000 TO 3,000 ORGAN.
ORGAN?

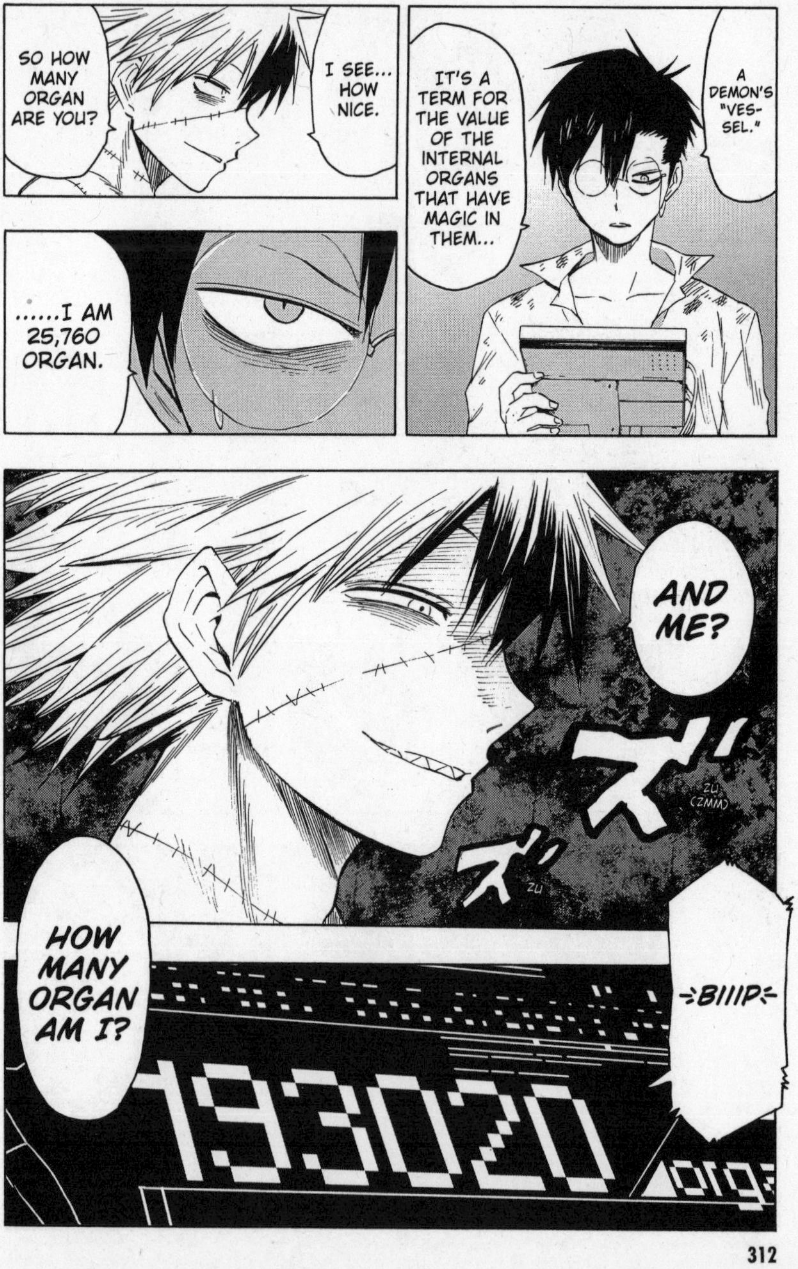
A DEMON'S "VES-SEL."
IT'S A TERM FOR THE VALUE OF THE INTERNAL ORGANS THAT HAVE MAGIC IN THEM...
I SEE... HOW NICE.
SO HOW MANY ORGAN ARE YOU?
......I AM 25,760 ORGAN.
AND ME?
ズ
ZU (ZMM)
ズ
ZU
HOW MANY ORGAN AM I?
BIIIP

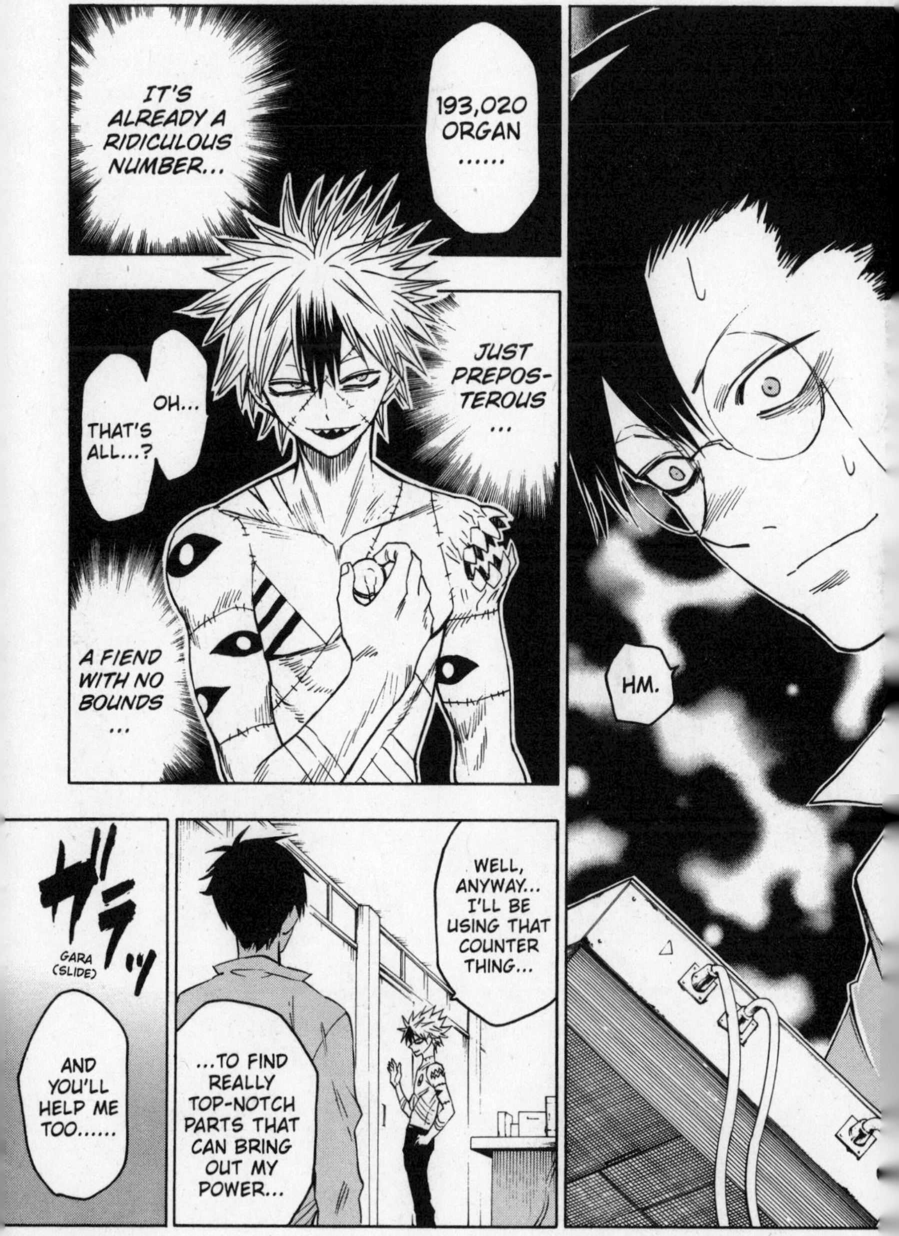
HM.
193,020 ORGAN ......
IT'S ALREADY A RIDICULOUS NUMBER...
JUST PREPOSTEROUS ...
OH... THAT'S ALL...?
A FIEND WITH NO BOUNDS ...
WELL, ANYWAY... I'LL BE USING THAT COUNTER THING...
...TO FIND REALLY TOP-NOTCH PARTS THAT CAN BRING OUT MY POWER...
ガラッ
GARA (SLIDE)
AND YOU'LL HELP ME TOO......

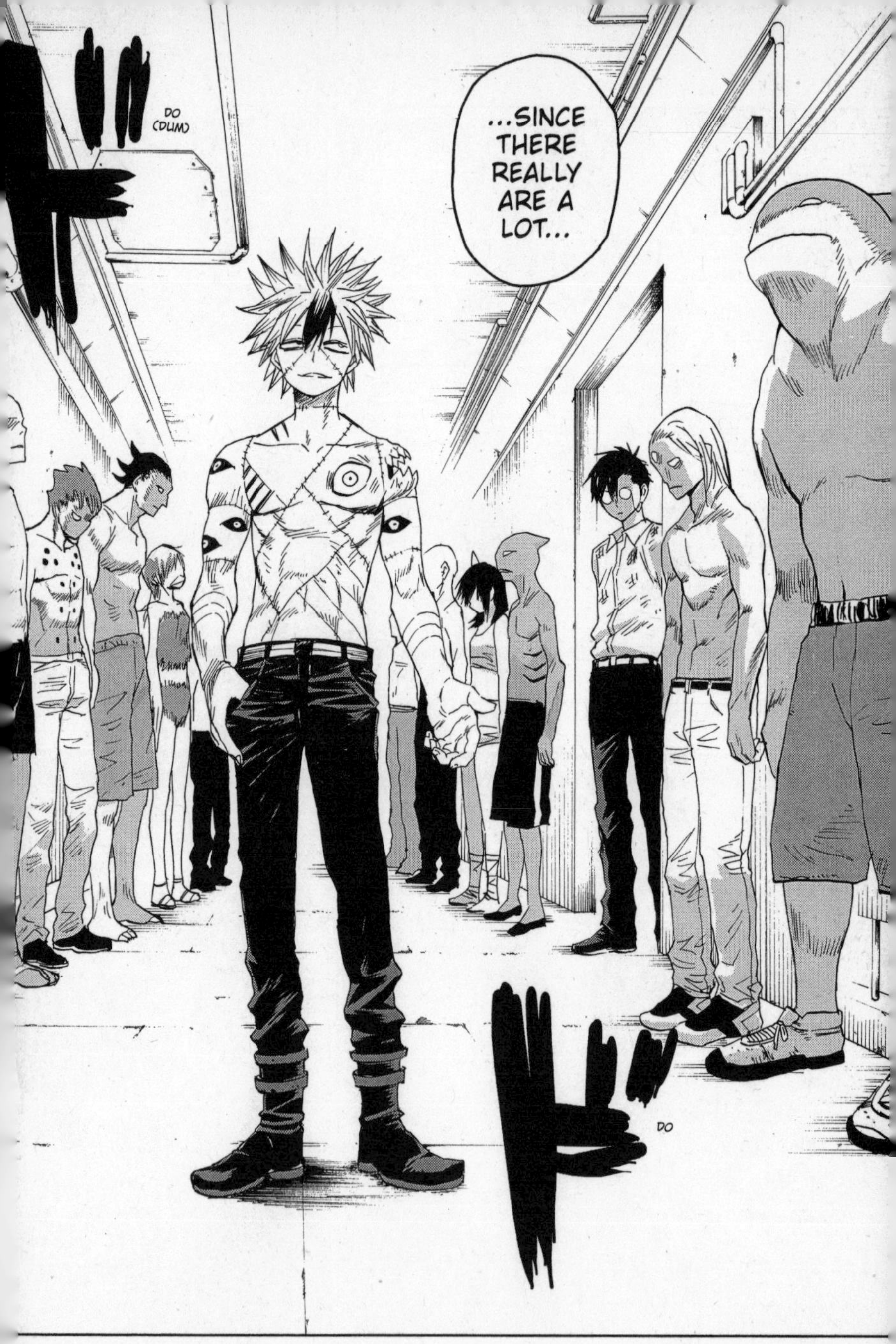
DO (DUM)
...SINCE THERE REALLY ARE A LOT...
DO

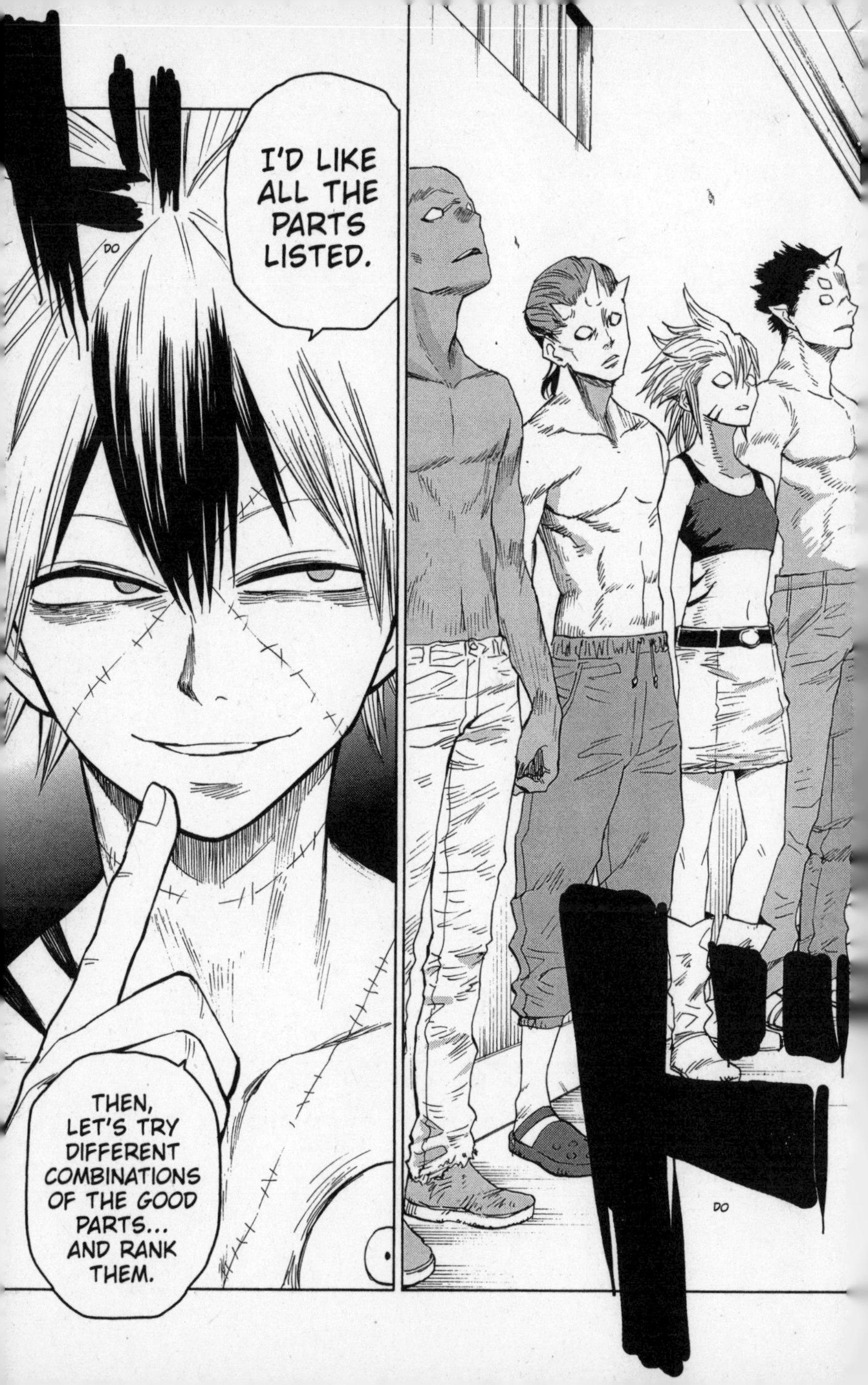
DO
I'D LIKE ALL THE PARTS LISTED.
DO
THEN, LET'S TRY DIFFERENT COMBINATIONS OF THE GOOD PARTS... AND RANK THEM.

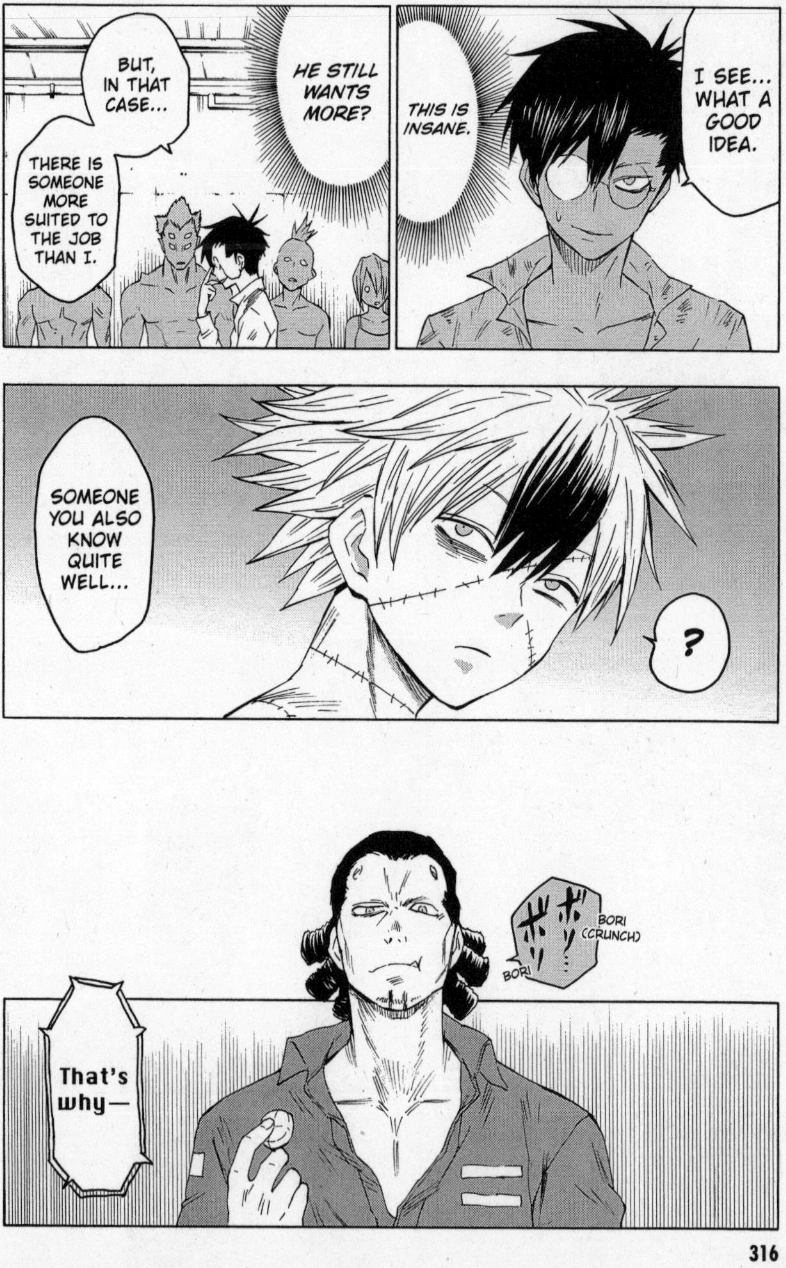
I SEE... WHAT A GOOD IDEA.
THIS IS INSANE.
HE STILL WANTS MORE?
BUT, IN THAT CASE...
THERE IS SOMEONE MORE SUITED TO THE JOB THAN I.
SOMEONE YOU ALSO KNOW QUITE WELL...
?
ボリボリ…
BORI (CRUNCH)
BORI
That's why—

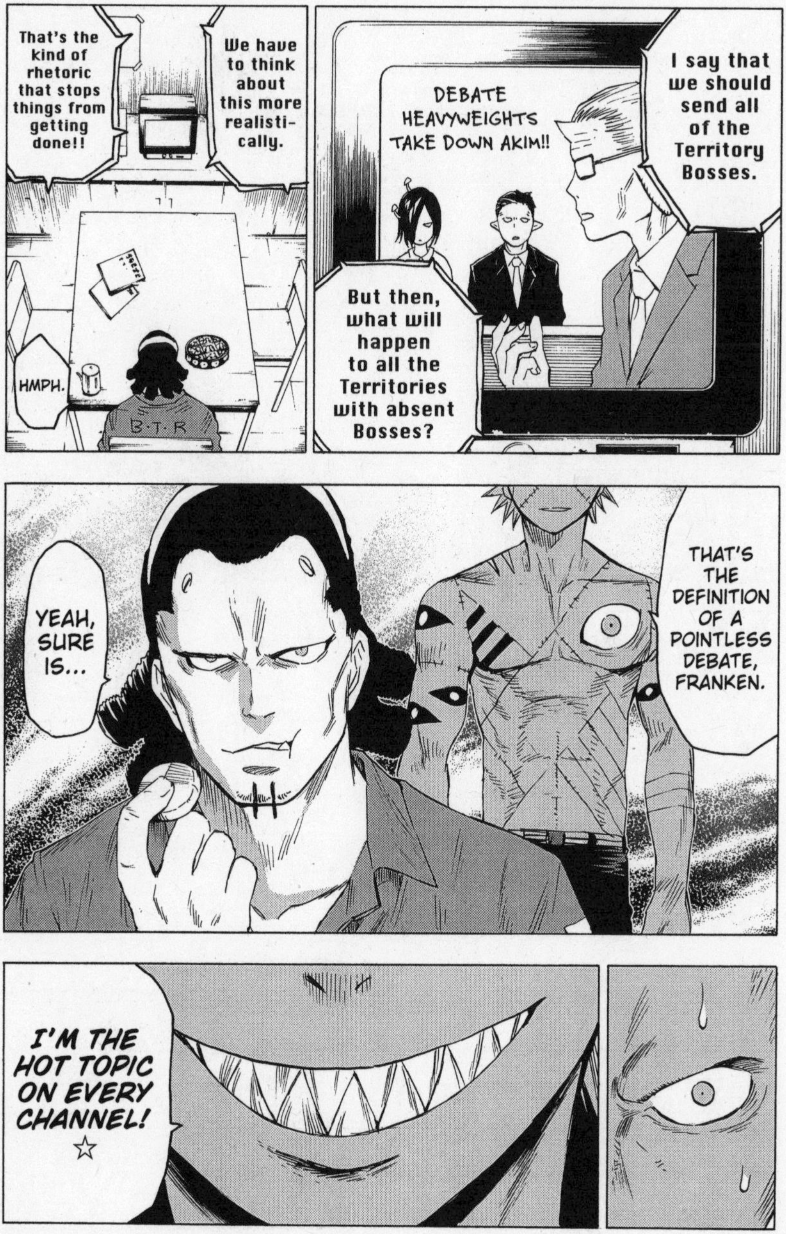
I say that we should send all of the Territory Bosses.
DEBATE HEAVYWEIGHTS TAKE DOWN AKIM!!
But then, what will happen to all the Territories with absent Bosses?
We have to think about this more realistically.
That's the kind of rhetoric that stops things from getting done!!
HMPH.
THAT'S THE DEFINITION OF A POINTLESS DEBATE, FRANKEN.
YEAH, SURE IS...
I'M THE HOT TOPIC ON EVERY CHANNEL! ☆

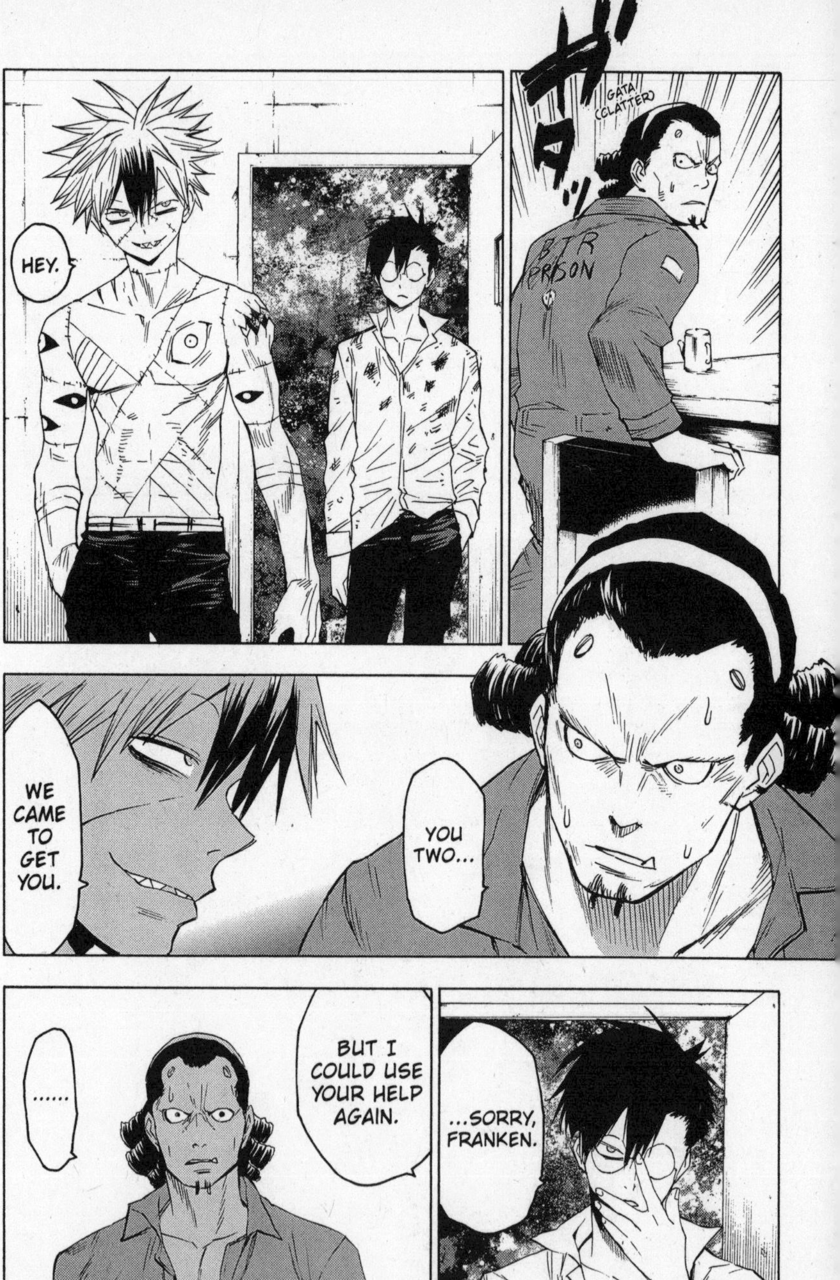
GATA (CLATTER)
HEY.
YOU TWO...
WE CAME TO GET YOU.
...SORRY, FRANKEN.
BUT I COULD USE YOUR HELP AGAIN.
......

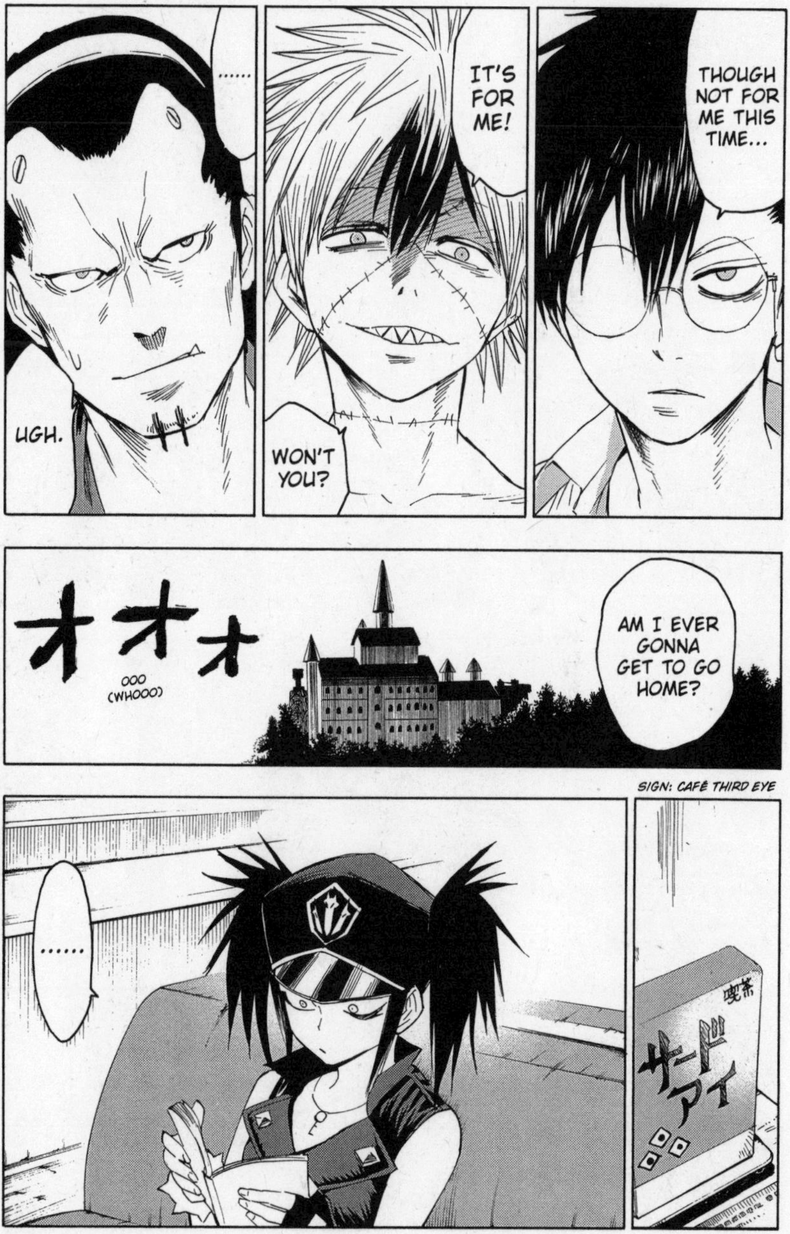
THOUGH NOT FOR ME THIS TIME...
IT'S FOR ME!
WON'T YOU?
......
UGH.
AM I EVER GONNA GET TO GO HOME?
オオオ
OOO (WHOOO)
SIGN: CAFÉ THIRD EYE
喫茶
サードアイ
......

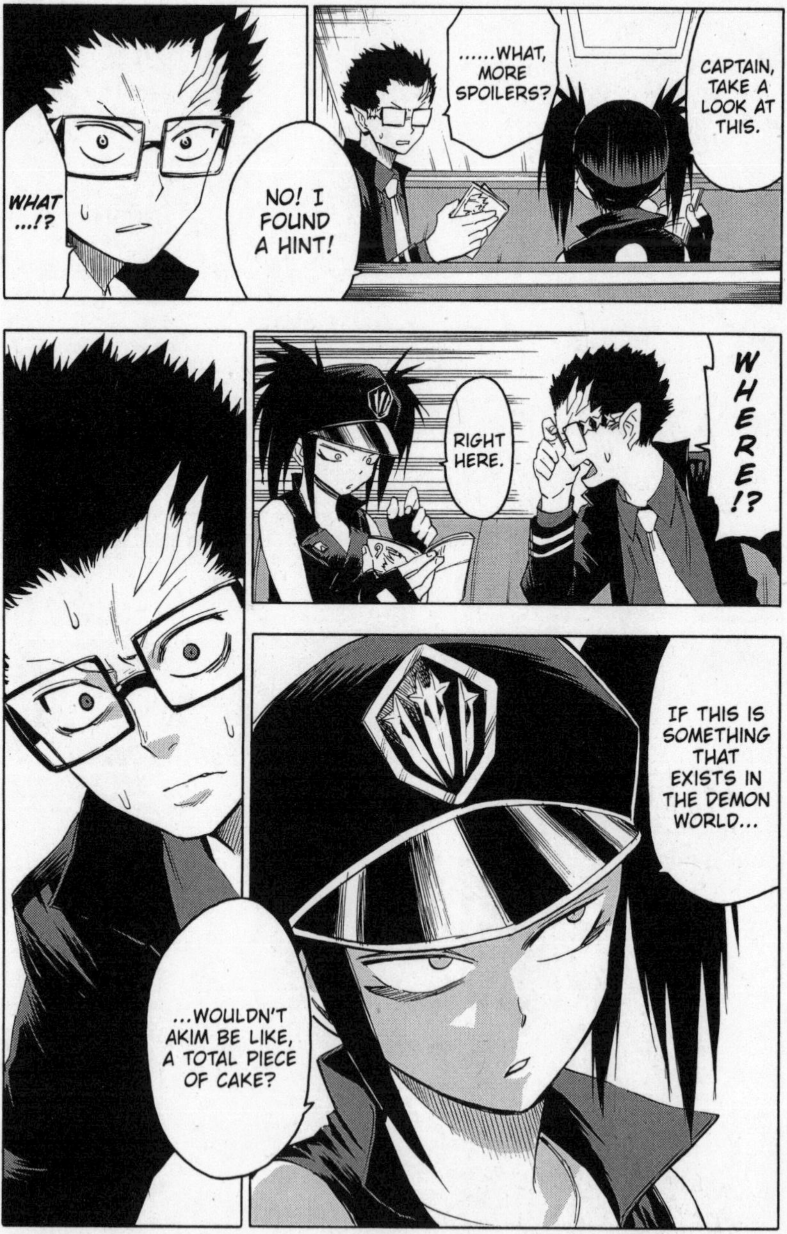
CAPTAIN, TAKE A LOOK AT THIS.
......WHAT, MORE SPOILERS?
NO! I FOUND A HINT!
WHAT ...!?
WHERE!?
RIGHT HERE.
IF THIS IS SOMETHING THAT EXISTS IN THE DEMON WORLD...
...WOULDN'T AKIM BE LIKE, A TOTAL PIECE OF CAKE?

♠ To Be Continued ♠

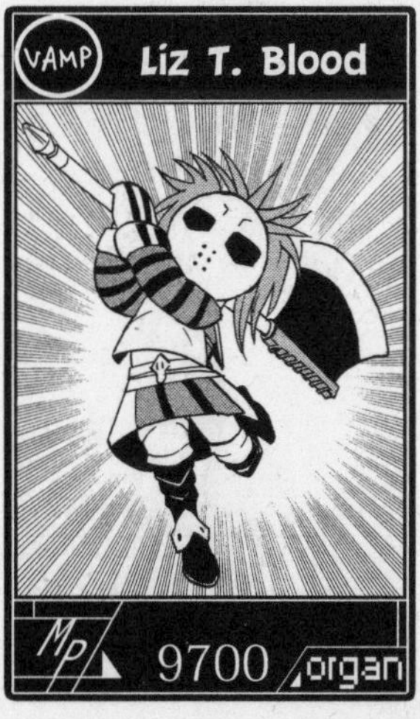
VAMP
Liz T. Blood
9700
organ

BLOOD LAD

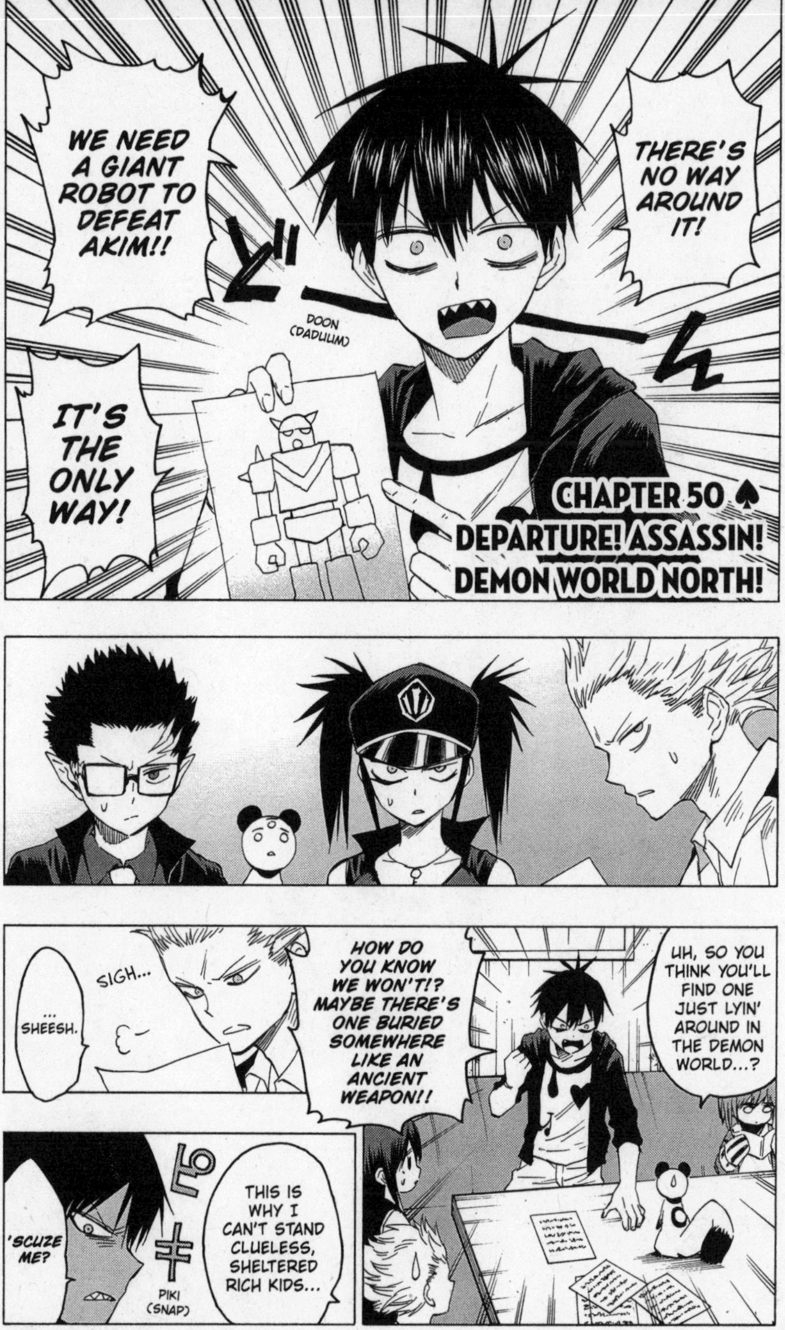
THERE'S NO WAY AROUND IT!
WE NEED A GIANT ROBOT TO DEFEAT AKIM!!
DOON (DADUUM)
IT'S THE ONLY WAY!
CHAPTER 50 ♠ DEPARTURE! ASSASSIN! DEMON WORLD NORTH!
UH, SO YOU THINK YOU'LL FIND ONE JUST LYIN' AROUND IN THE DEMON WORLD...?
HOW DO YOU KNOW WE WON'T!? MAYBE THERE'S ONE BURIED SOMEWHERE LIKE AN ANCIENT WEAPON!!
SIGH...
... SHEESH.
THIS IS WHY I CAN'T STAND CLUELESS, SHELTERED RICH KIDS...
PIKI (SNAP)
'SCUZE ME?

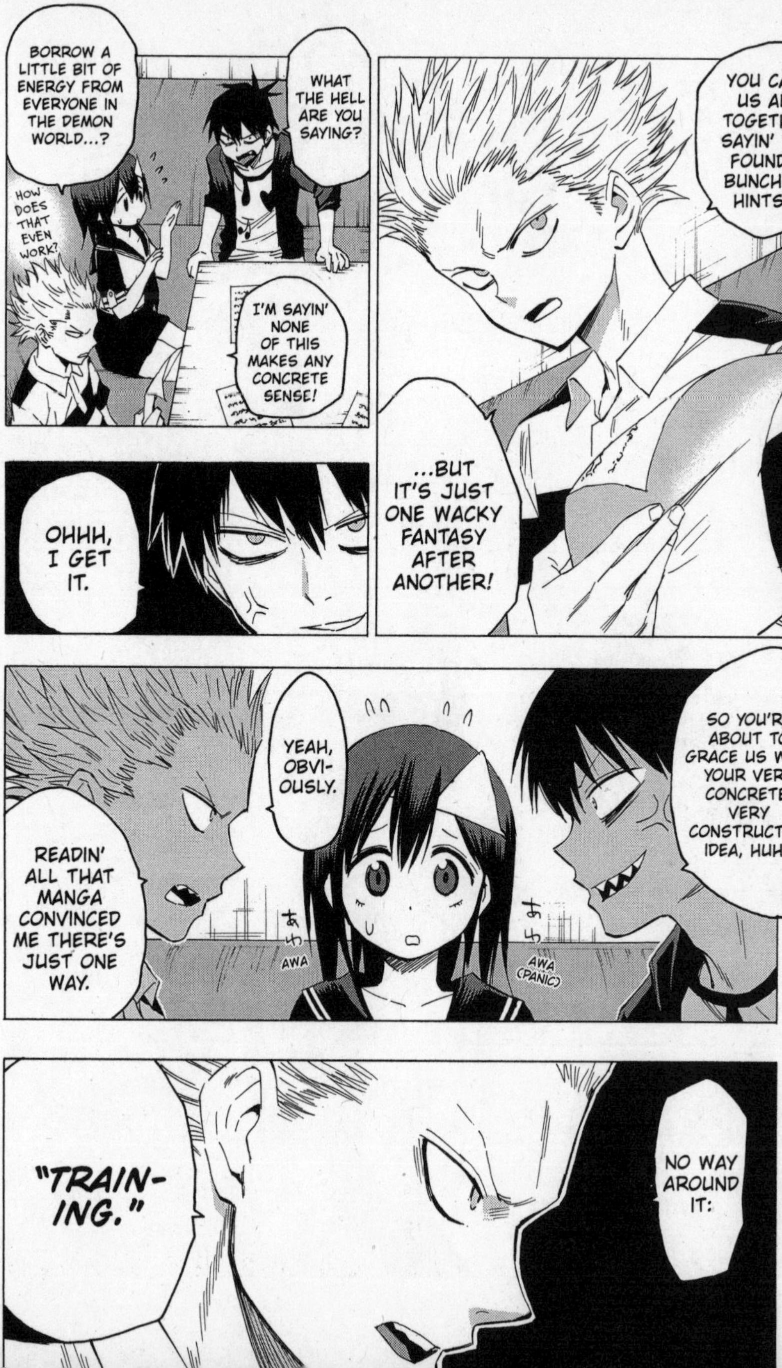
YOU CALL US ALL TOGETHER SAYIN' YOU FOUND A BUNCH OF HINTS...
...BUT IT'S JUST ONE WACKY FANTASY AFTER ANOTHER!
BORROW A LITTLE BIT OF ENERGY FROM EVERYONE IN THE DEMON WORLD...?
HOW DOES THAT EVEN WORK?
WHAT THE HELL ARE YOU SAYING?
I'M SAYIN' NONE OF THIS MAKES ANY CONCRETE SENSE!
OHHH, I GET IT.
SO YOU'RE ABOUT TO GRACE US WITH YOUR VERY CONCRETE, VERY CONSTRUCTIVE IDEA, HUH?
あわ
AWA (PANIC)
YEAH, OBVI-OUSLY.
あわ
AWA
READIN' ALL THAT MANGA CONVINCED ME THERE'S JUST ONE WAY.
NO WAY AROUND IT:
"TRAIN-ING."

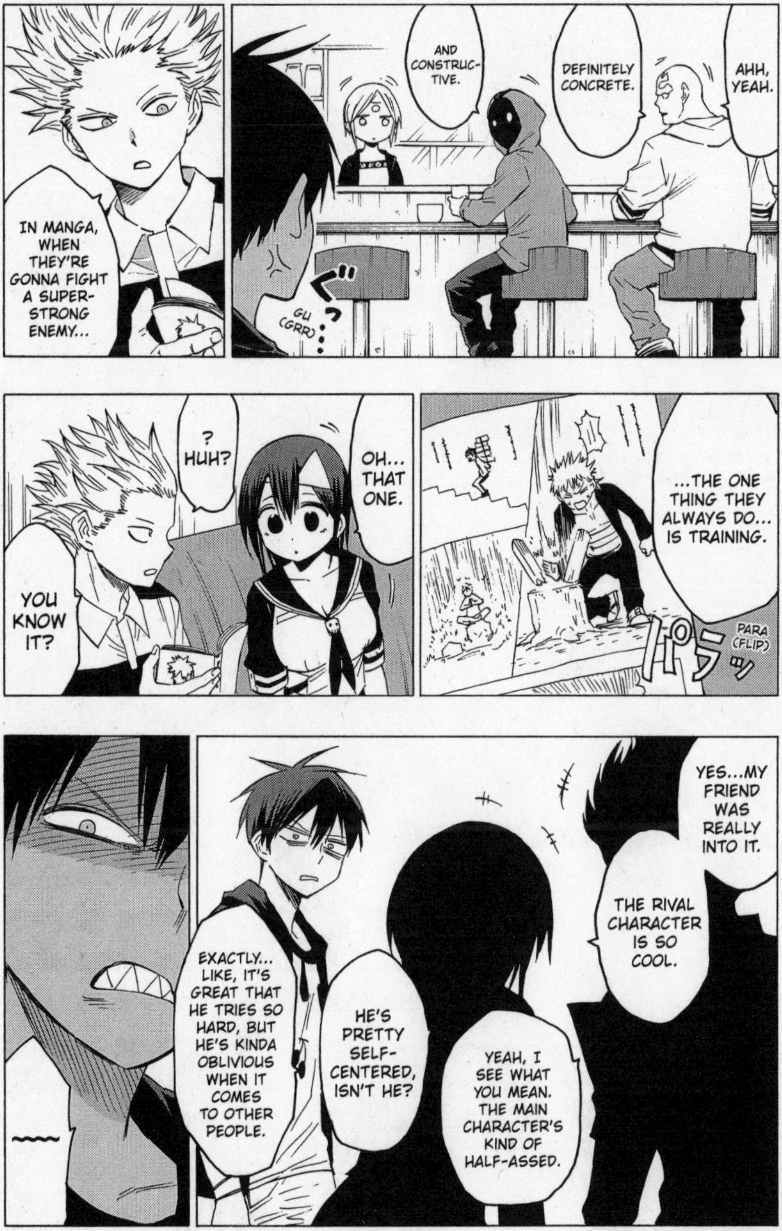
AHH, YEAH.
DEFINITELY CONCRETE.
AND CONSTRUCTIVE.
GU (GRR)...
IN MANGA, WHEN THEY'RE GONNA FIGHT A SUPER-STRONG ENEMY...
...THE ONE THING THEY ALWAYS DO... IS TRAINING.
PARA (FLIP)
OH... THAT ONE.
? HUH?
YOU KNOW IT?
YES...MY FRIEND WAS REALLY INTO IT.
THE RIVAL CHARACTER IS SO COOL.
YEAH, I SEE WHAT YOU MEAN. THE MAIN CHARACTER'S KIND OF HALF-ASSED.
HE'S PRETTY SELF-CENTERED, ISN'T HE?
EXACTLY... LIKE, IT'S GREAT THAT HE TRIES SO HARD, BUT HE'S KINDA OBLIVIOUS WHEN IT COMES TO OTHER PEOPLE.

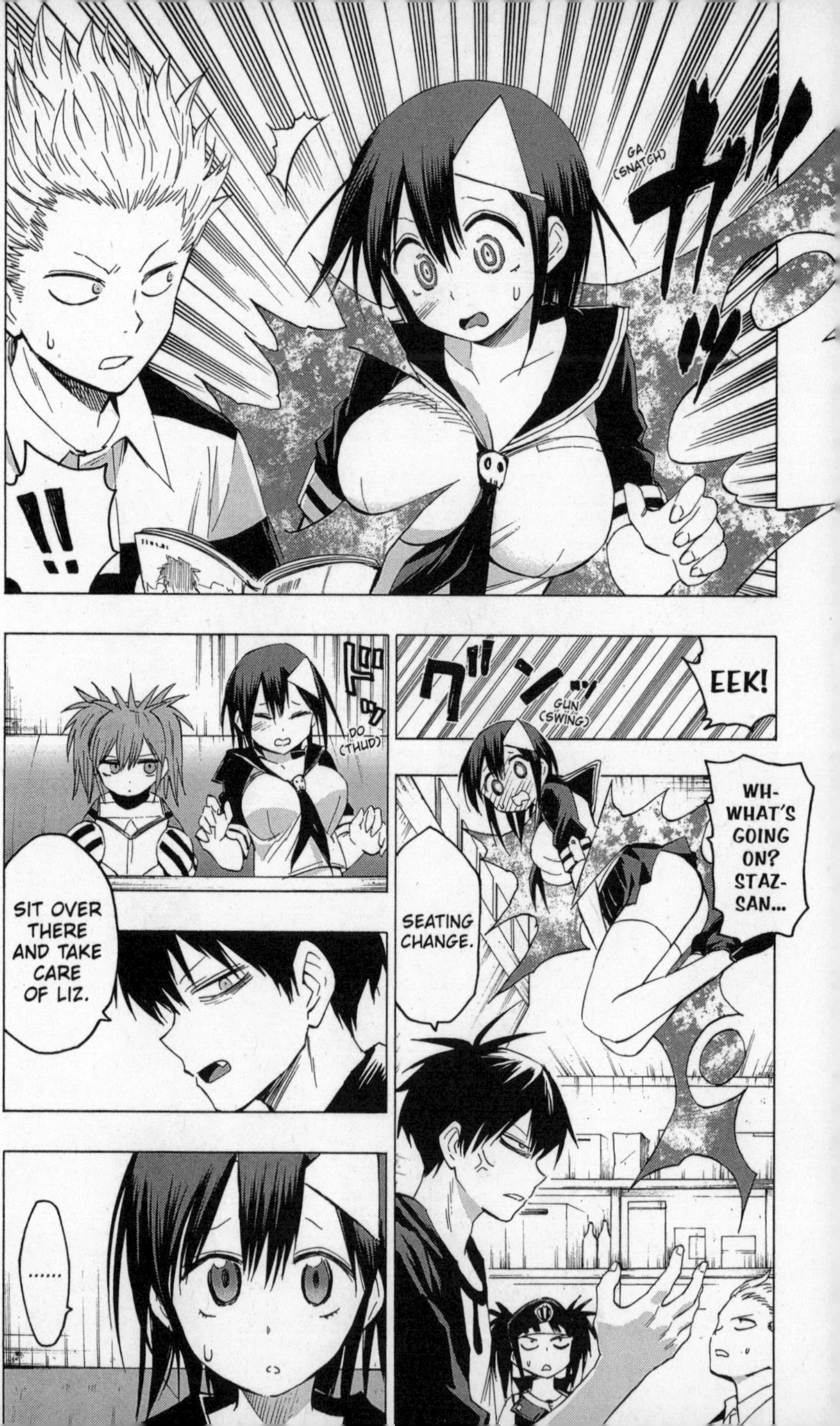
GA (SNATCH)
!!
GUN (SWING)
EEK!
WH- WHAT'S GOING ON? STAZ-SAN...
SEATING CHANGE.
DO (THUD)
SIT OVER THERE AND TAKE CARE OF LIZ.
......

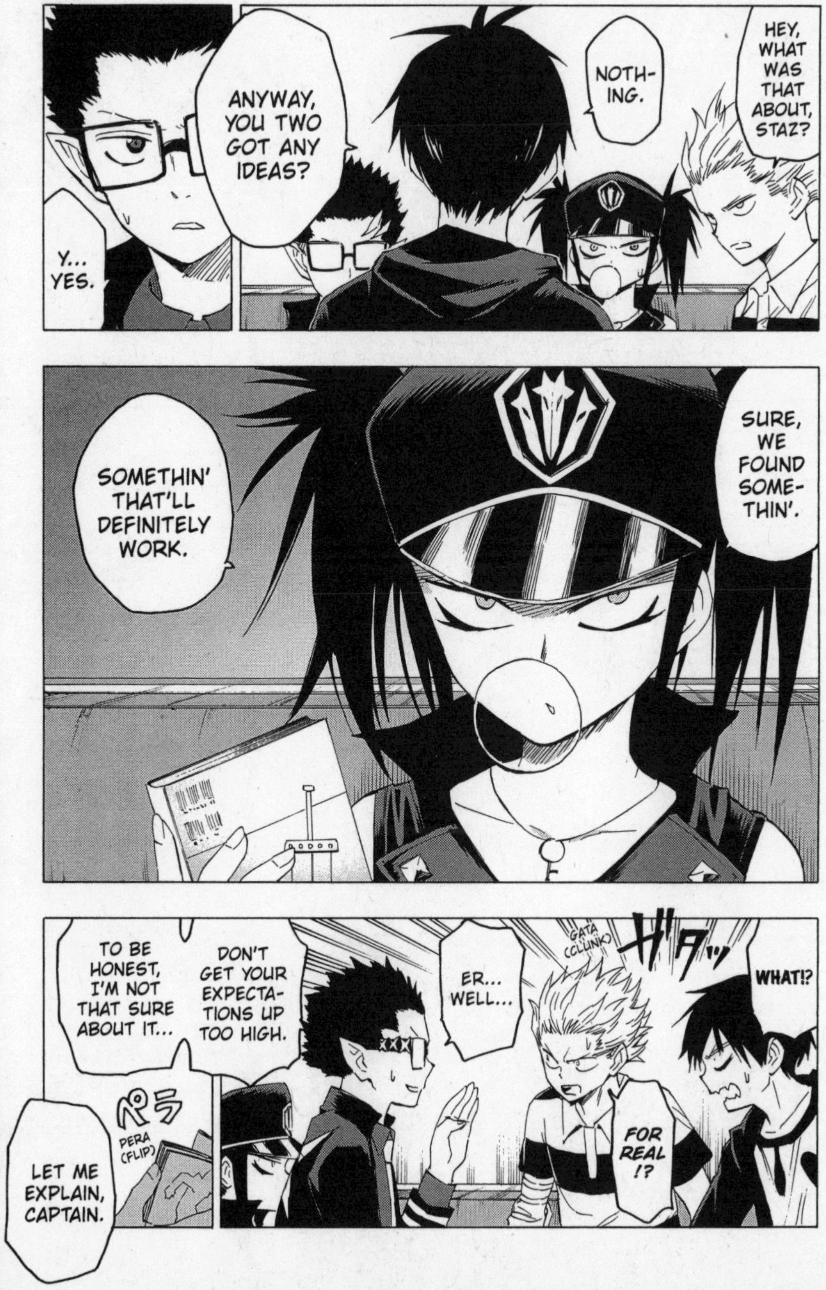
HEY, WHAT WAS THAT ABOUT, STAZ?
NOTH-ING.
ANYWAY, YOU TWO GOT ANY IDEAS?
Y... YES.
SURE, WE FOUND SOME-THIN'.
SOMETHIN' THAT'LL DEFINITELY WORK.
WHAT!?
ガタッ
GATA (CLUNK)
FOR REAL!?
ER... WELL...
DON'T GET YOUR EXPECTA-TIONS UP TOO HIGH.
TO BE HONEST, I'M NOT THAT SURE ABOUT IT...
ペラ
PERA (FLIP)
LET ME EXPLAIN, CAPTAIN.

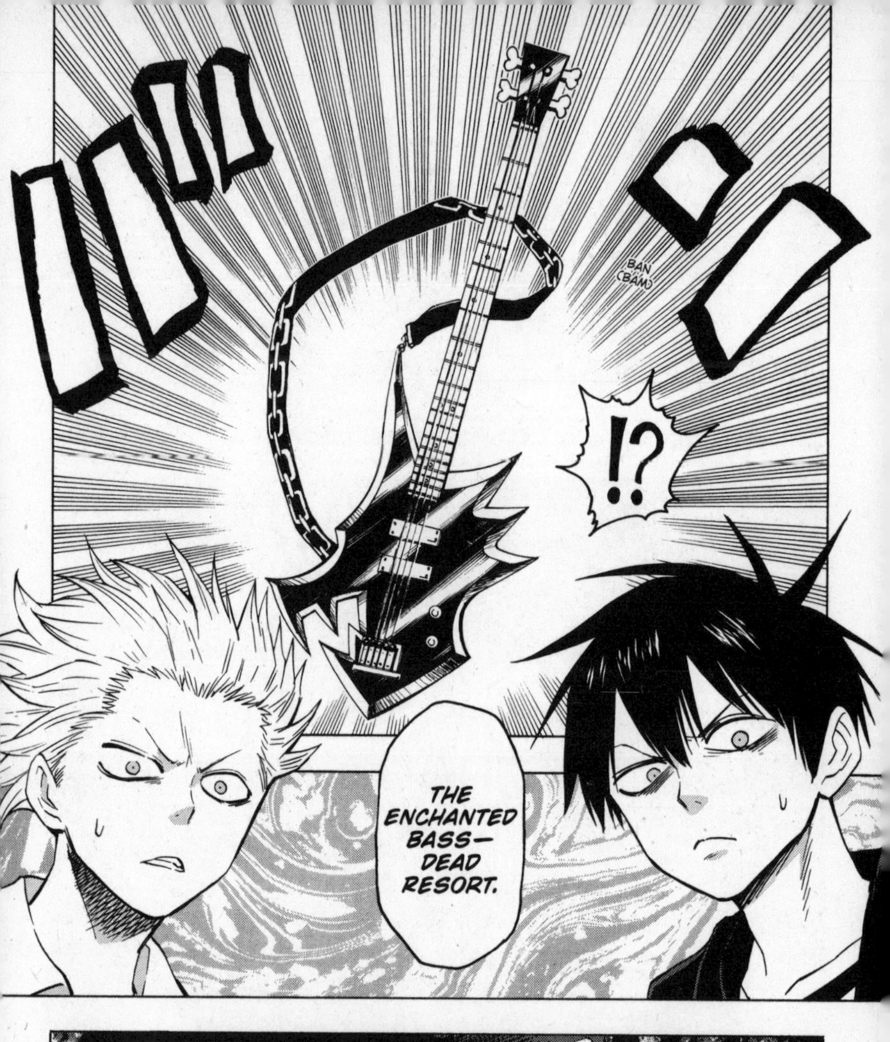
BAN (BAM)
!?
THE ENCHANTED BASS—DEAD RESORT.
WHEN IT'S PLAYED, THE NOTES... THAT IS, THE VIBRATIONS...
...HAVE THE POWER TO BREAK DOWN MAGIC...

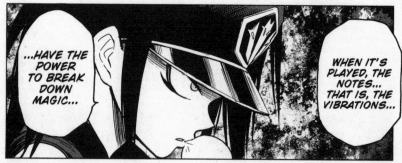

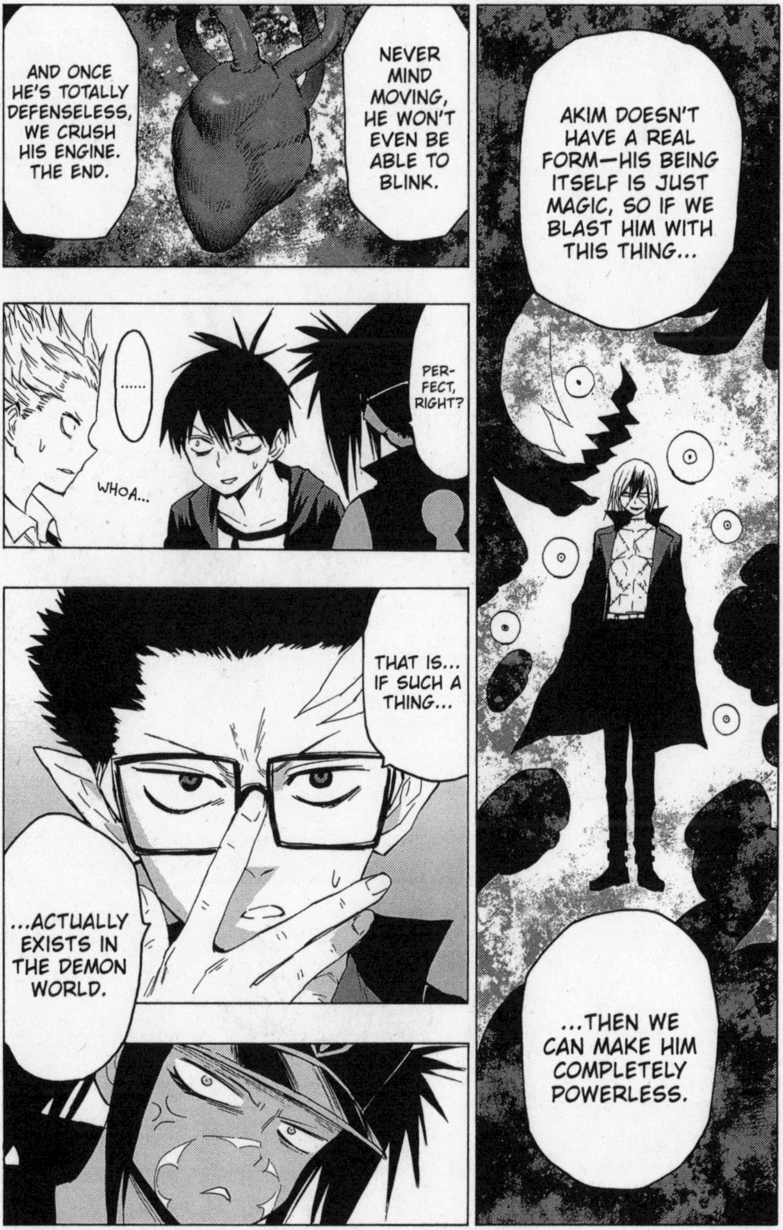
AKIM DOESN'T HAVE A REAL FORM—HIS BEING ITSELF IS JUST MAGIC, SO IF WE BLAST HIM WITH THIS THING...
...THEN WE CAN MAKE HIM COMPLETELY POWERLESS.
NEVER MIND MOVING, HE WON'T EVEN BE ABLE TO BLINK.
AND ONCE HE'S TOTALLY DEFENSELESS, WE CRUSH HIS ENGINE. THE END.
PER-FECT, RIGHT?
......
WHOA...
THAT IS... IF SUCH A THING...
...ACTUALLY EXISTS IN THE DEMON WORLD.

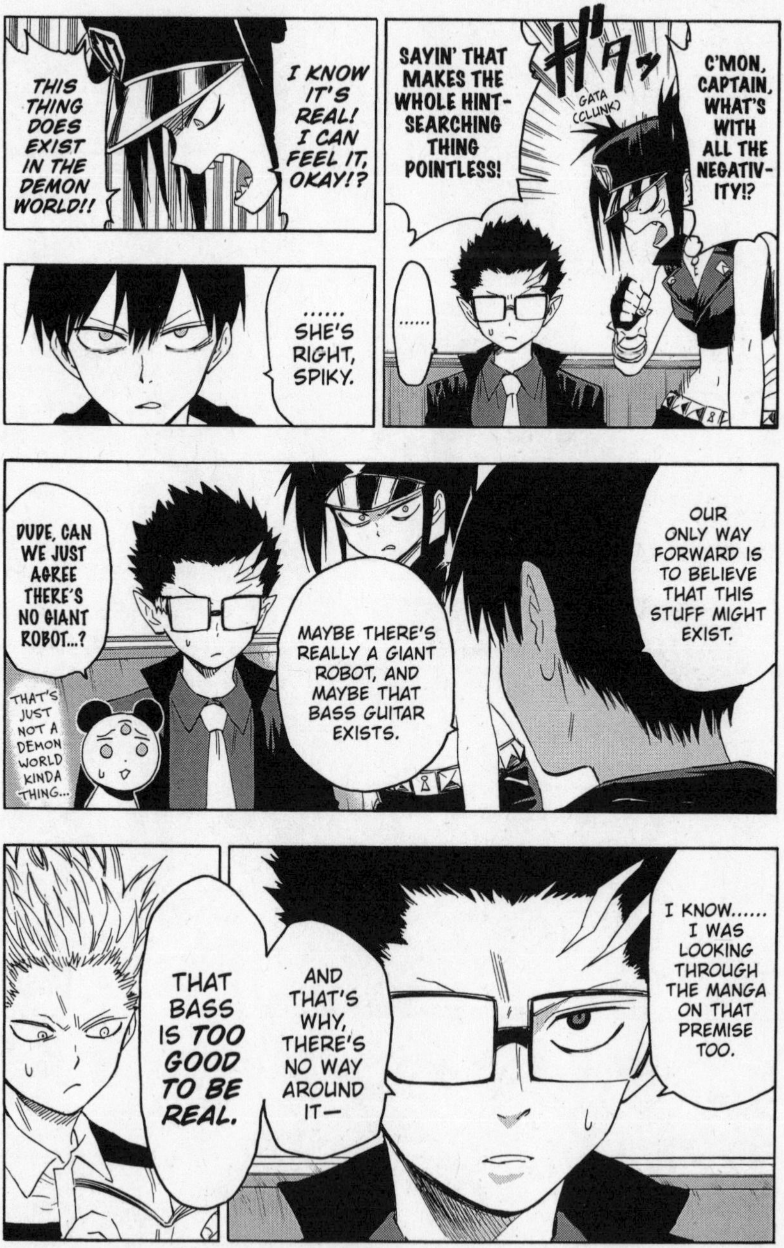

C'MON, CAPTAIN, WHAT'S WITH ALL THE NEGATIVITY!?
ガタッ
GATA (CLUNK)
SAYIN' THAT MAKES THE WHOLE HINT-SEARCHING THING POINTLESS!
......
I KNOW IT'S REAL! I CAN FEEL IT, OKAY!?
THIS THING DOES EXIST IN THE DEMON WORLD!!
...... SHE'S RIGHT, SPIKY.
OUR ONLY WAY FORWARD IS TO BELIEVE THAT THIS STUFF MIGHT EXIST.
MAYBE THERE'S REALLY A GIANT ROBOT, AND MAYBE THAT BASS GUITAR EXISTS.
DUDE, CAN WE JUST AGREE THERE'S NO GIANT ROBOT...?
THAT'S JUST NOT A DEMON WORLD KINDA THING...
I KNOW...... I WAS LOOKING THROUGH THE MANGA ON THAT PREMISE TOO.
AND THAT'S WHY, THERE'S NO WAY AROUND IT—
THAT BASS IS *TOO GOOD TO BE REAL.*

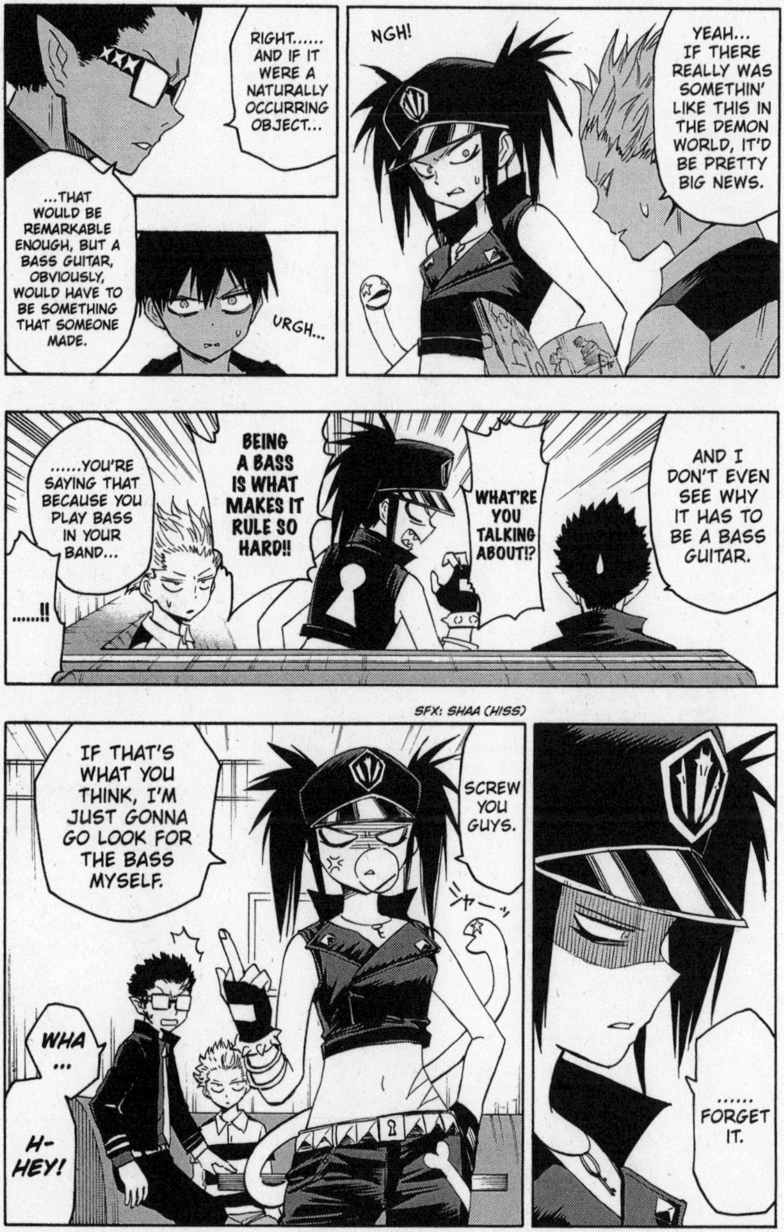
YEAH... IF THERE REALLY WAS SOMETHIN' LIKE THIS IN THE DEMON WORLD, IT'D BE PRETTY BIG NEWS.
NGH!
RIGHT...... AND IF IT WERE A NATURALLY OCCURRING OBJECT...
...THAT WOULD BE REMARKABLE ENOUGH, BUT A BASS GUITAR, OBVIOUSLY, WOULD HAVE TO BE SOMETHING THAT SOMEONE MADE.
URGH...
AND I DON'T EVEN SEE WHY IT HAS TO BE A BASS GUITAR.
WHAT'RE YOU TALKING ABOUT!?
BEING A BASS IS WHAT MAKES IT RULE SO HARD!!
......YOU'RE SAYING THAT BECAUSE YOU PLAY BASS IN YOUR BAND...
......!!
SFX: SHAA (HISS)
...... FORGET IT.
SCREW YOU GUYS.
IF THAT'S WHAT YOU THINK, I'M JUST GONNA GO LOOK FOR THE BASS MYSELF.
シャーッ
WHA ...
H-HEY!

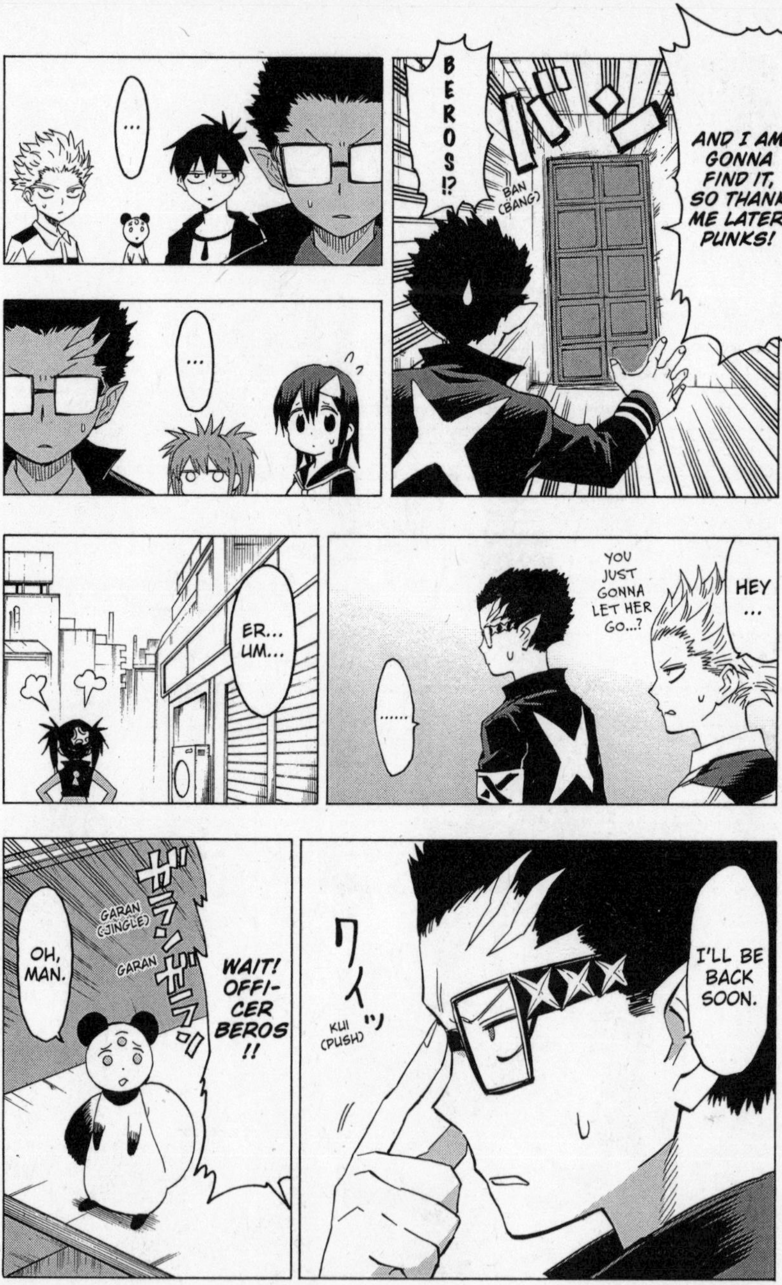
AND I AM GONNA FIND IT, SO THANK ME LATER, PUNKS!
BEROS!?
BAN (BANG)
...
...
HEY ...
YOU JUST GONNA LET HER GO...?
......
ER... UM...
I'LL BE BACK SOON.
KUI (PUSH)
WAIT! OFFI-CER BEROS!!
GARAN (JINGLE)
GARAN
OH, MAN.

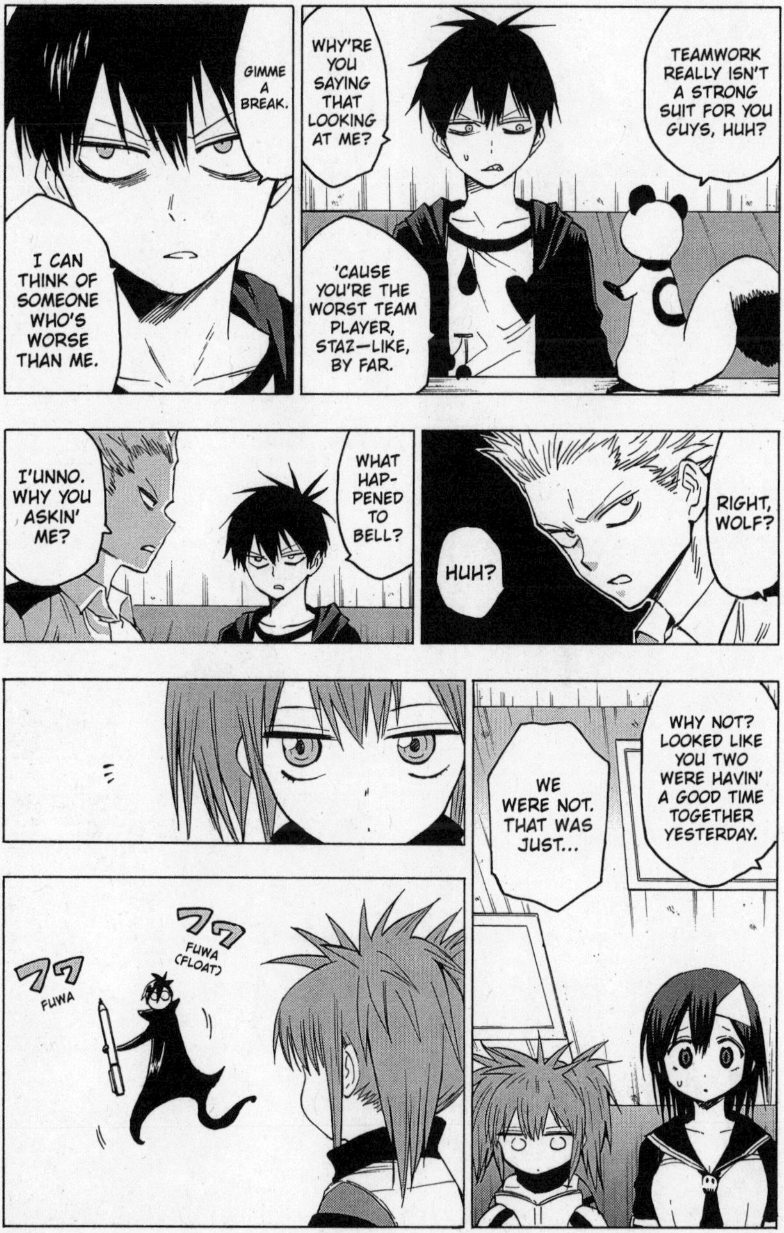
TEAMWORK REALLY ISN'T A STRONG SUIT FOR YOU GUYS, HUH?
WHY'RE YOU SAYING THAT LOOKING AT ME?
'CAUSE YOU'RE THE WORST TEAM PLAYER, STAZ—LIKE, BY FAR.
GIMME A BREAK.
I CAN THINK OF SOMEONE WHO'S WORSE THAN ME.
RIGHT, WOLF?
HUH?
WHAT HAP-PENED TO BELL?
I'UNNO. WHY YOU ASKIN' ME?
WHY NOT? LOOKED LIKE YOU TWO WERE HAVIN' A GOOD TIME TOGETHER YESTERDAY.
WE WERE NOT. THAT WAS JUST...
フワ
FUWA (FLOAT)
フワ
FUWA

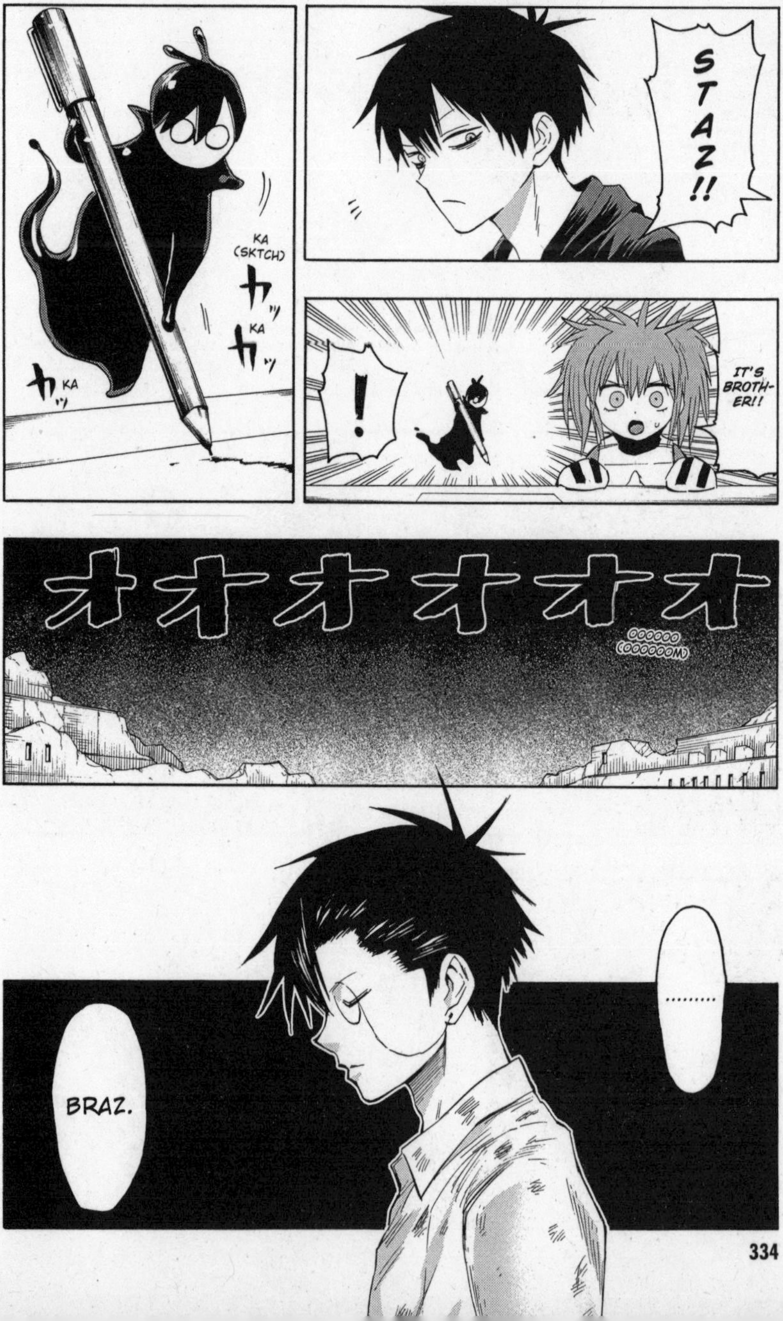
STAZ!!
!
IT'S BROTHER!!
KA (SKTCH)
カッ
KA
ガッ
カッ
KA
オオオオオオ
OOOOOO (OOOOOOM)
....
BRAZ.

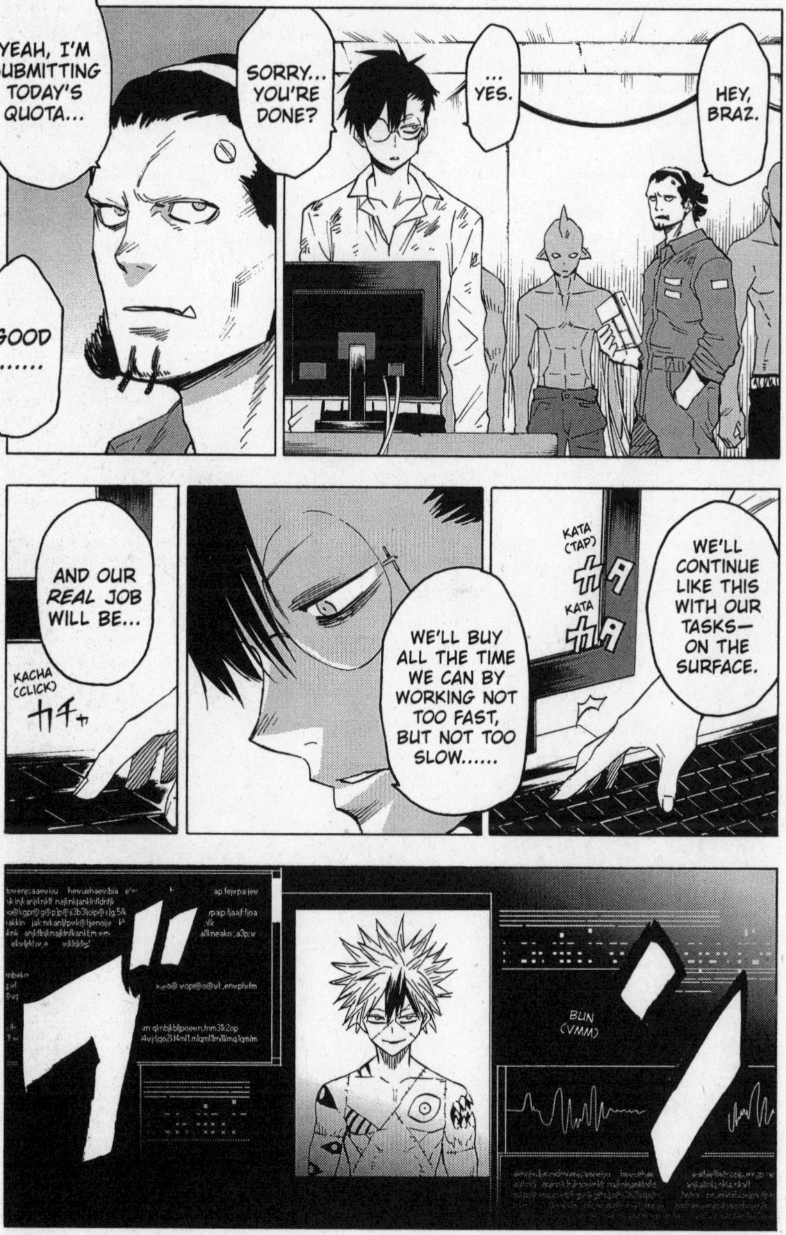
HEY, BRAZ.
... YES.
SORRY... YOU'RE DONE?
YEAH, I'M SUBMITTING TODAY'S QUOTA...
GOOD ......
KATA (TAP)
カタ
KATA
カタ
WE'LL CONTINUE LIKE THIS WITH OUR TASKS— ON THE SURFACE.
WE'LL BUY ALL THE TIME WE CAN BY WORKING NOT TOO FAST, BUT NOT TOO SLOW......
AND OUR *REAL* JOB WILL BE...
KACHA (CLICK)
カチャ
BUN (VMM)

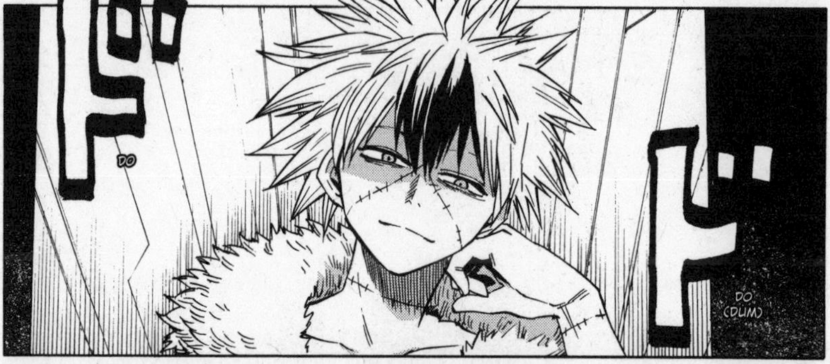
ド
DO
ド
DO (DUM)
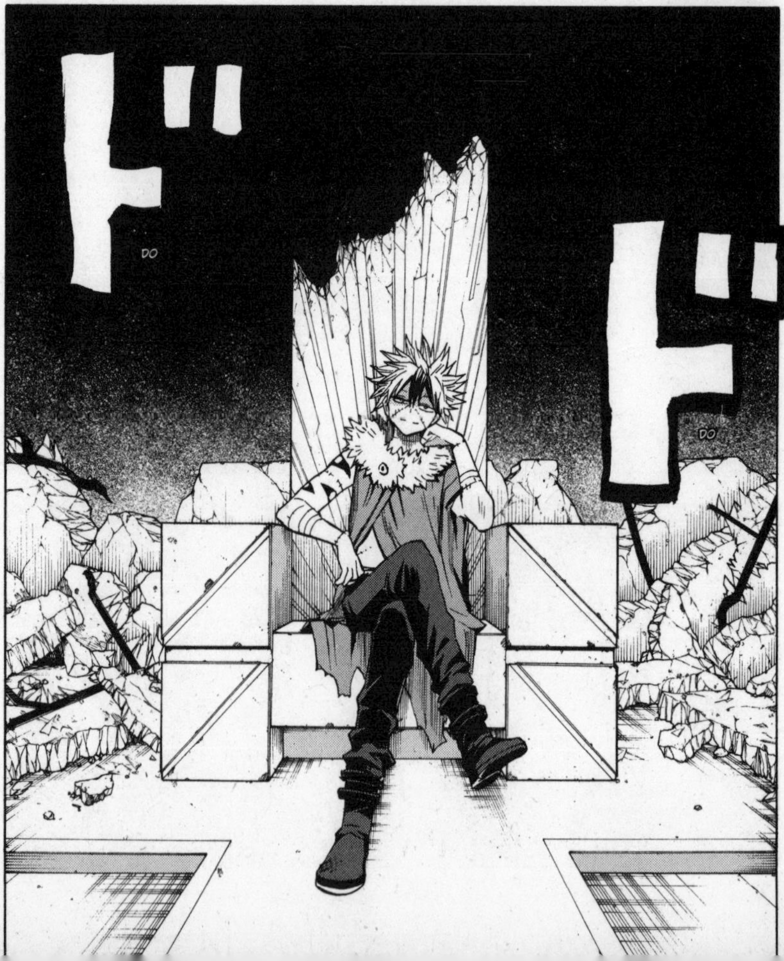
ド
DO
ド
DO

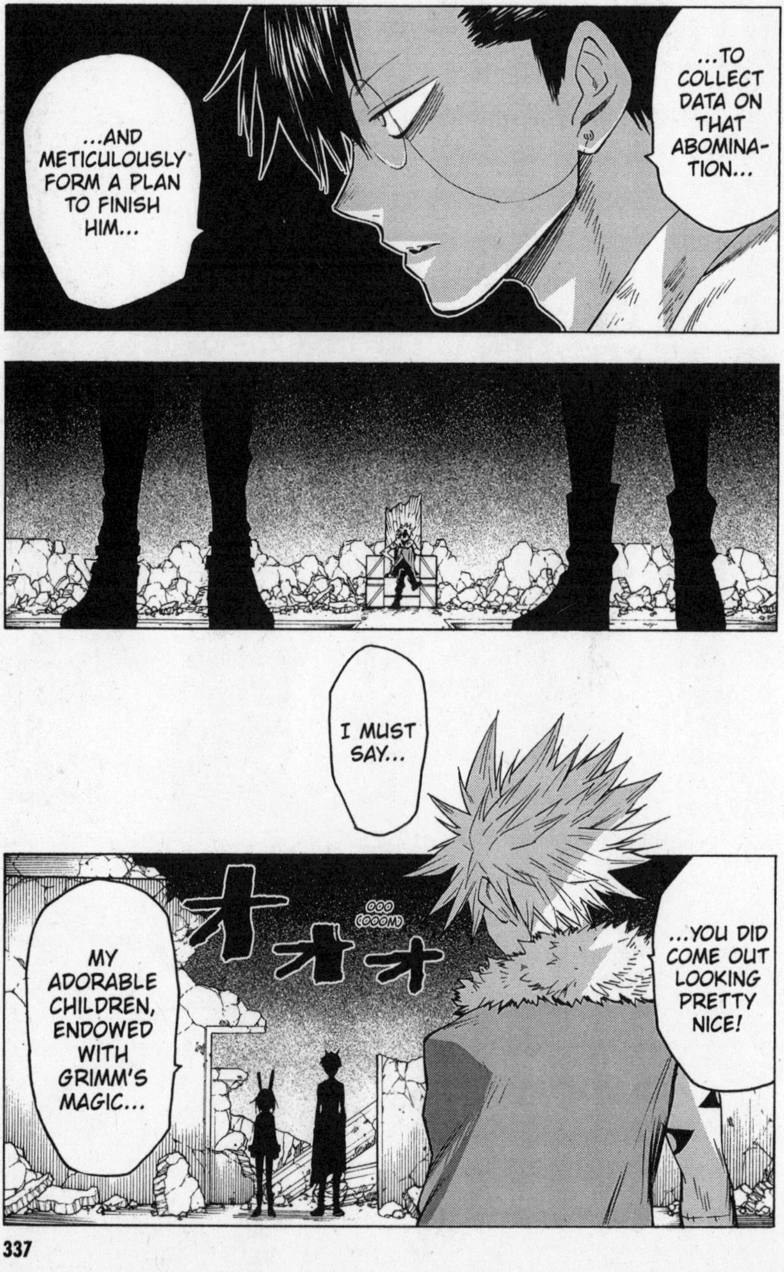
...TO COLLECT DATA ON THAT ABOMINATION...
...AND METICULOUSLY FORM A PLAN TO FINISH HIM...
I MUST SAY...
...YOU DID COME OUT LOOKING PRETTY NICE!
OOO (OOOM)
MY ADORABLE CHILDREN, ENDOWED WITH GRIMM'S MAGIC...

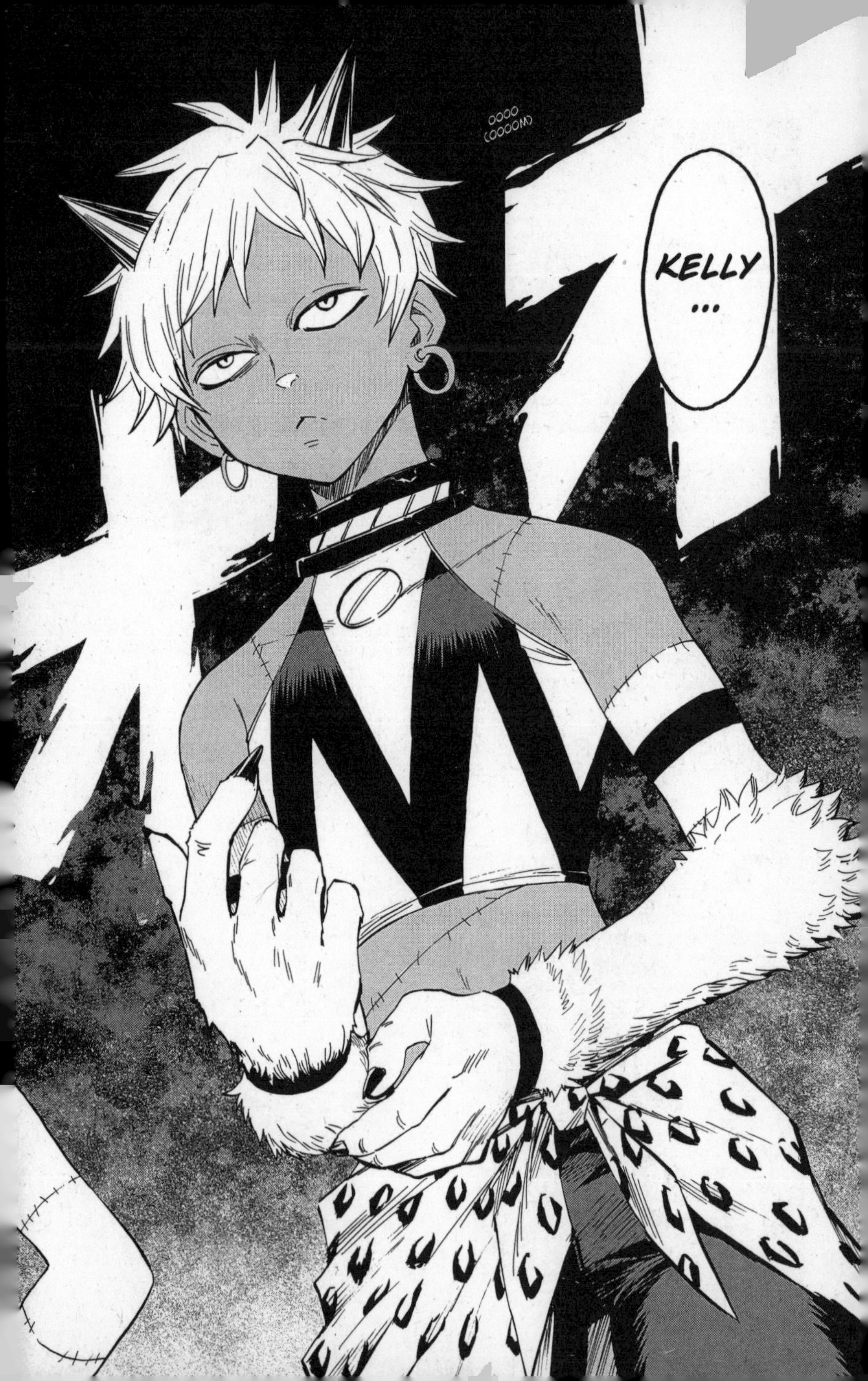
OOOO (OOOOM)
KELLY ...

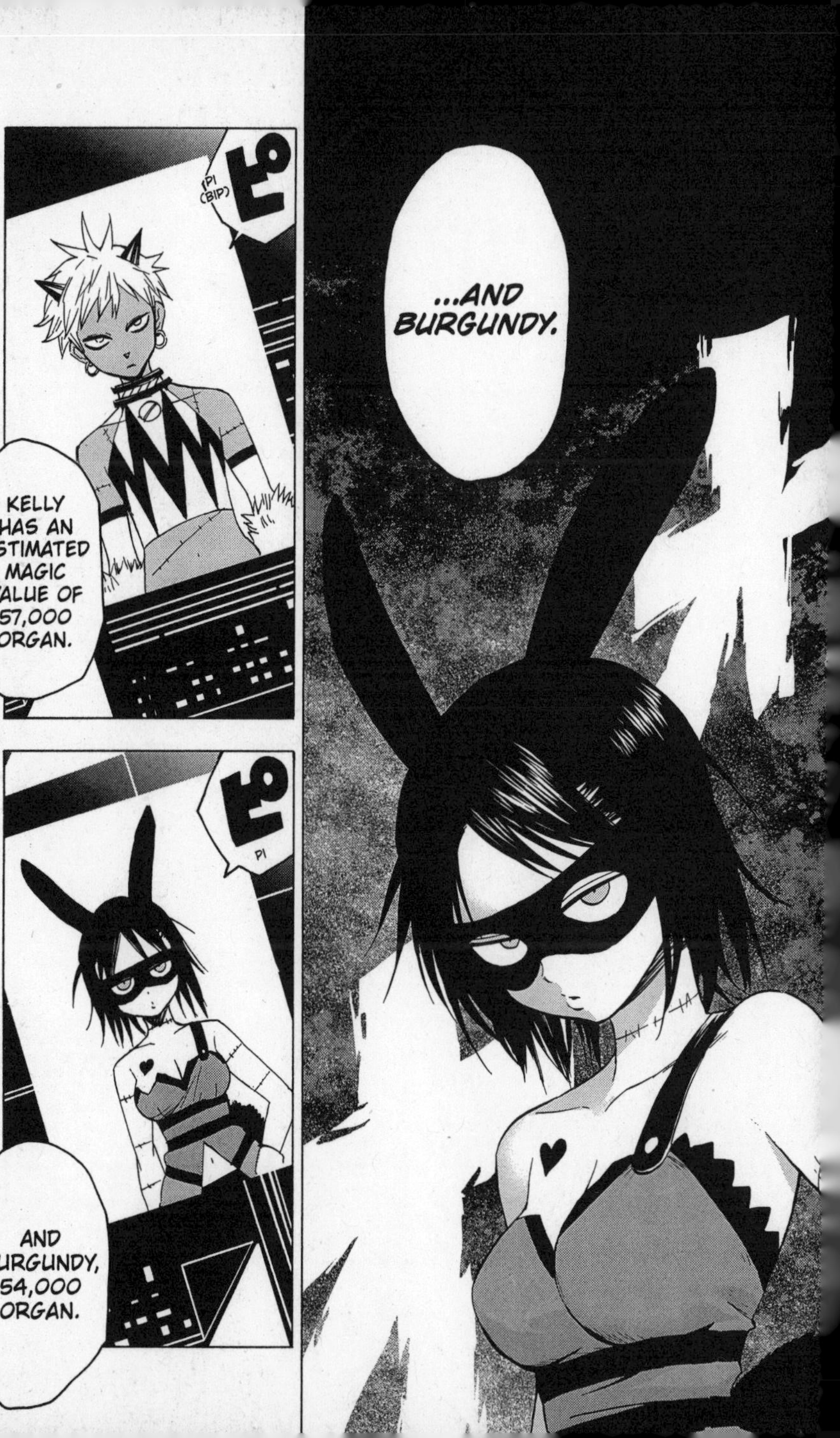
...AND BURGUNDY.
PI (BIP)
KELLY HAS AN ESTIMATED MAGIC VALUE OF 57,000 ORGAN.
PI
AND BURGUNDY, 54,000 ORGAN.

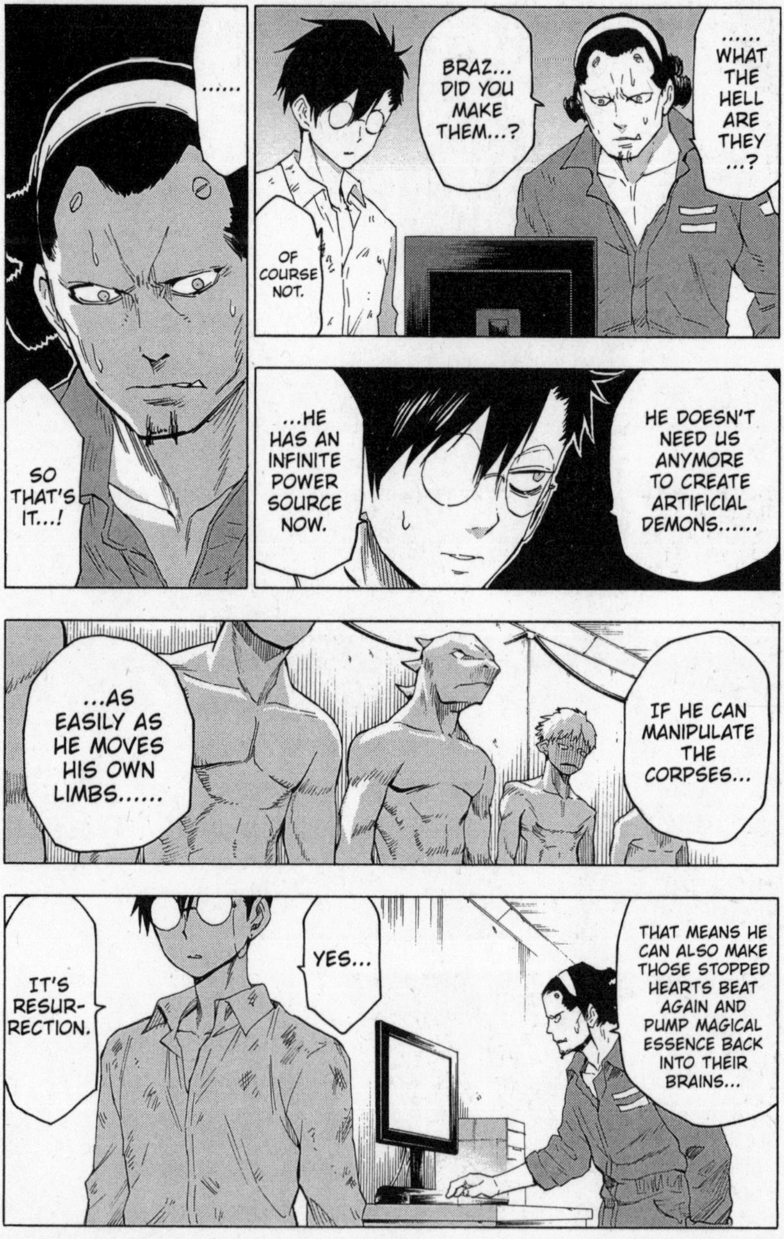

...... WHAT THE HELL ARE THEY ...?
BRAZ... DID YOU MAKE THEM...?
OF COURSE NOT.
HE DOESN'T NEED US ANYMORE TO CREATE ARTIFICIAL DEMONS......
...HE HAS AN INFINITE POWER SOURCE NOW.
......
SO THAT'S IT...!
IF HE CAN MANIPULATE THE CORPSES...
...AS EASILY AS HE MOVES HIS OWN LIMBS......
THAT MEANS HE CAN ALSO MAKE THOSE STOPPED HEARTS BEAT AGAIN AND PUMP MAGICAL ESSENCE BACK INTO THEIR BRAINS...
YES...
IT'S RESURRECTION.

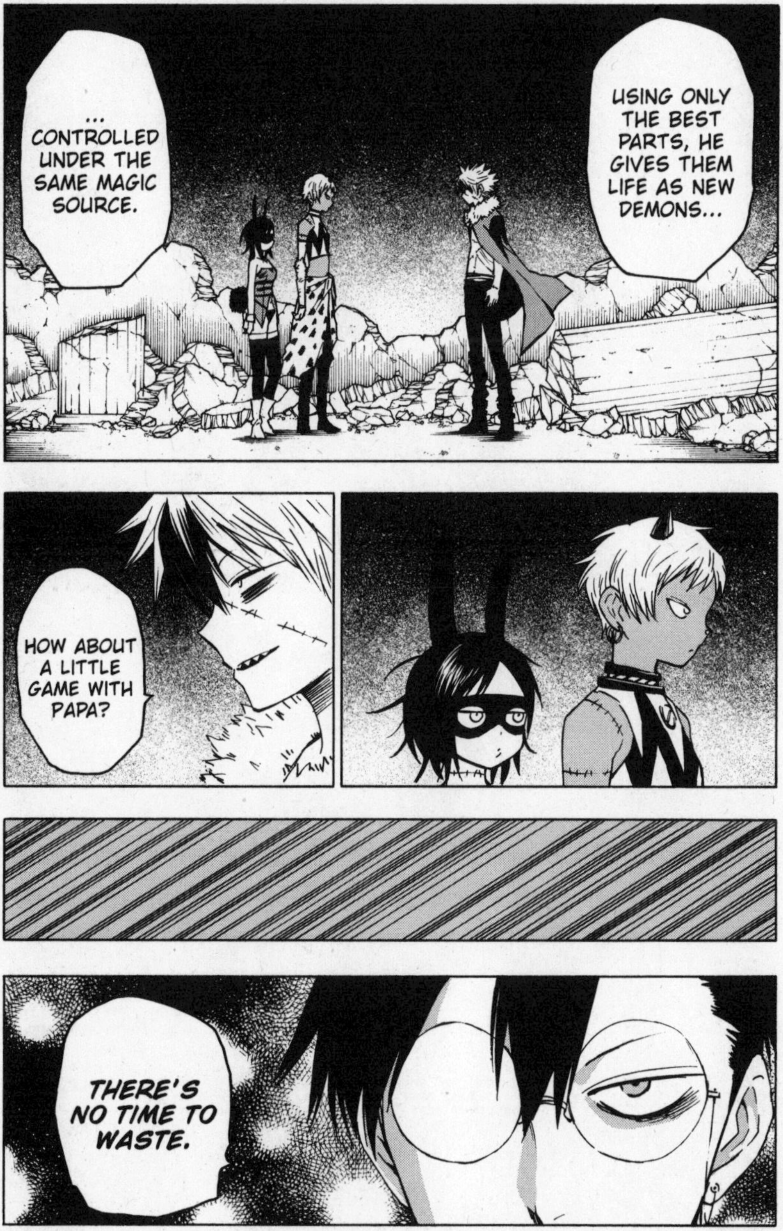
USING ONLY THE BEST PARTS, HE GIVES THEM LIFE AS NEW DEMONS...
... CONTROLLED UNDER THE SAME MAGIC SOURCE.
HOW ABOUT A LITTLE GAME WITH PAPA?
THERE'S NO TIME TO WASTE.

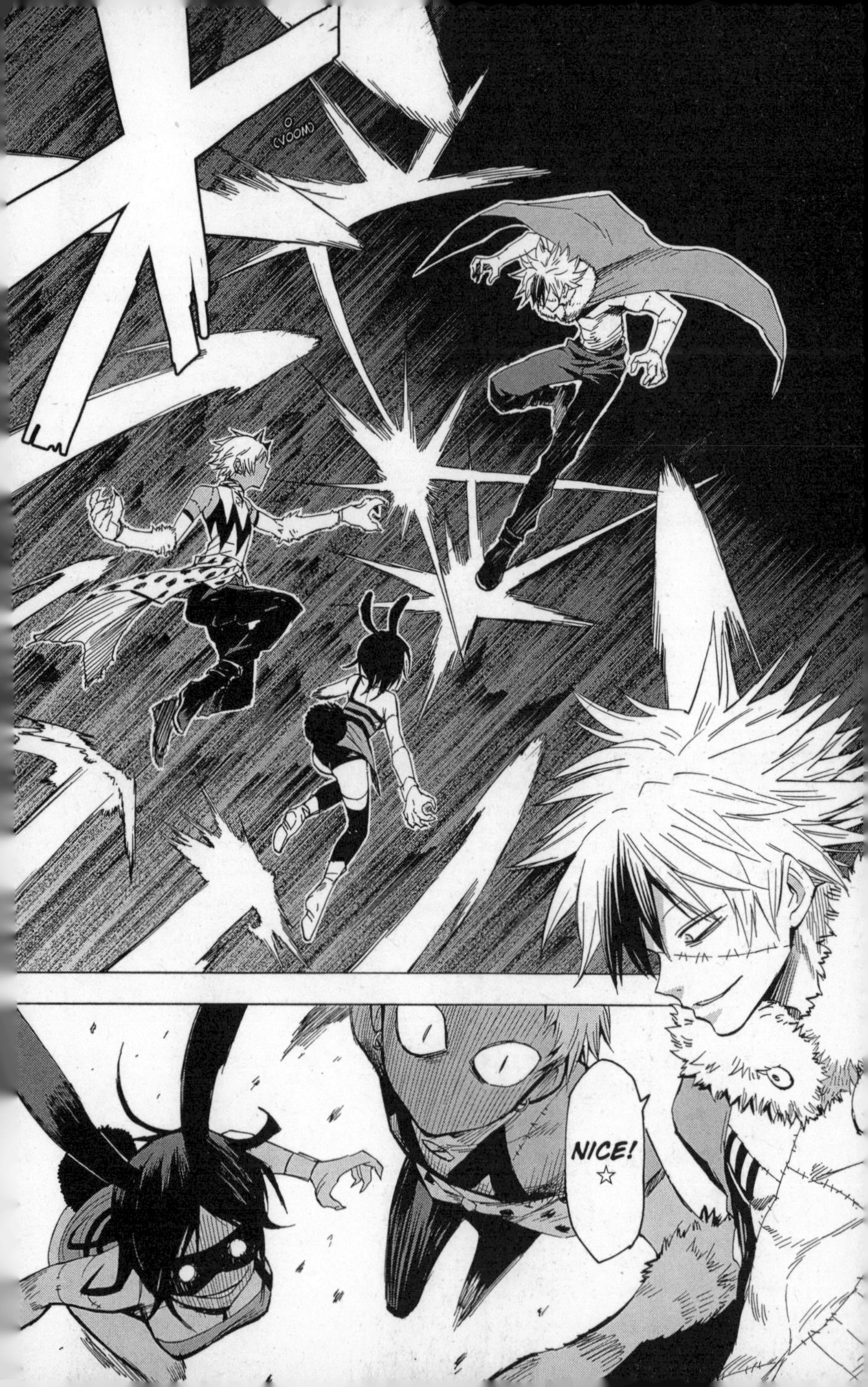
O
(VOOM)
NICE! ☆

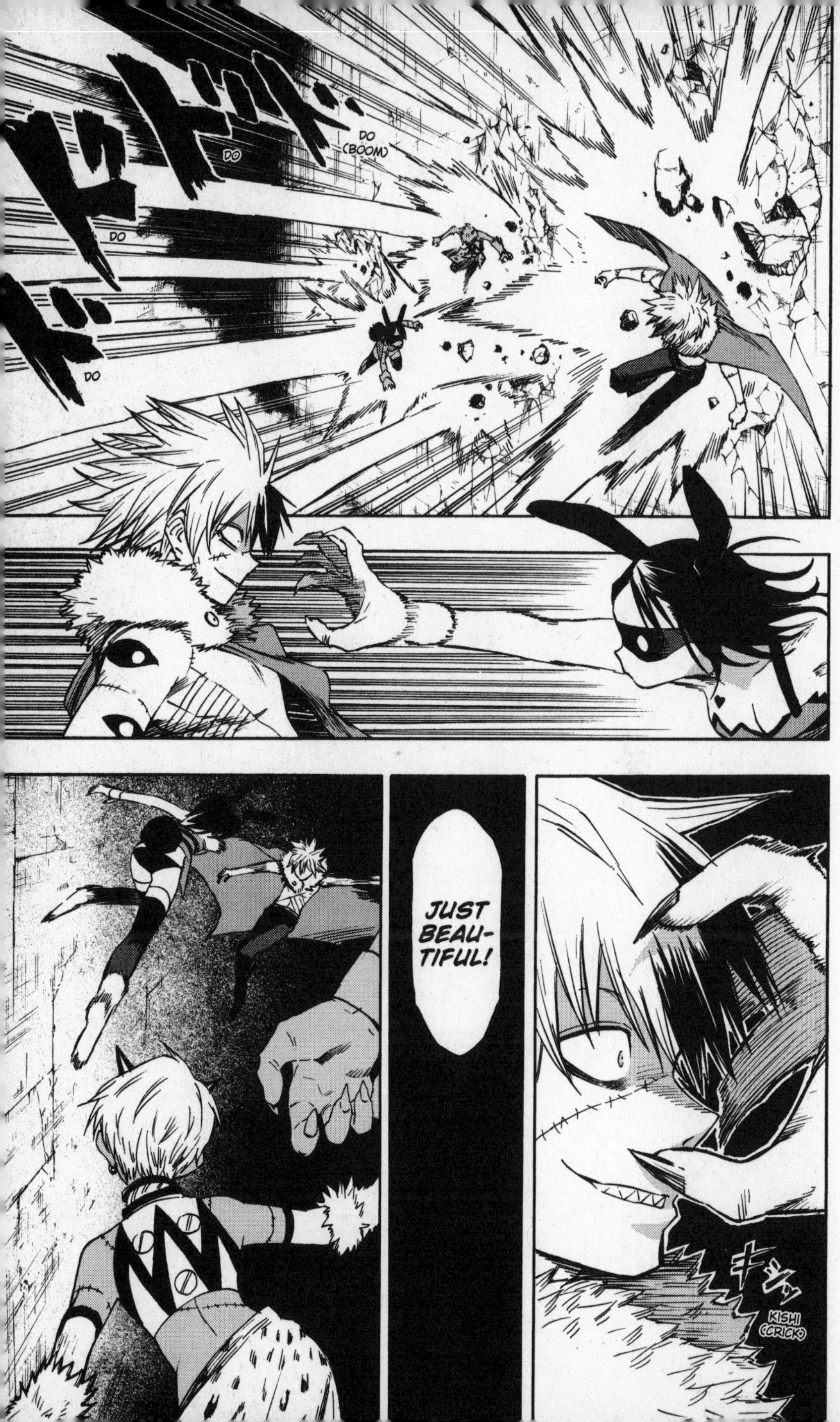
DO (BOOM)
DO
DO
DO
KISHI (CRICK)
JUST BEAU-TIFUL!

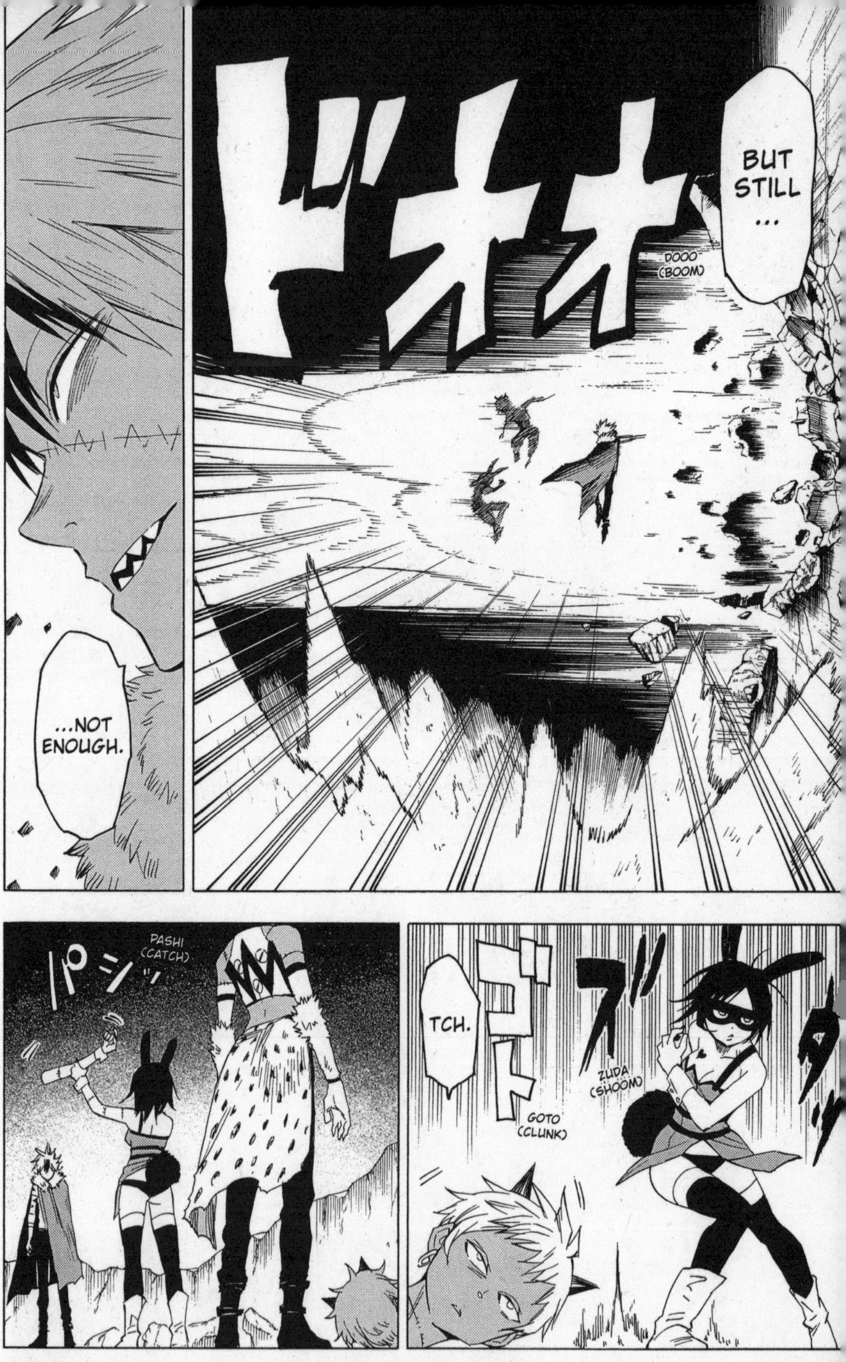

BUT STILL ...
DOOO (BOOM)
...NOT ENOUGH.
ZUDA (SHOOM)
TCH.
GOTO (CLUNK)
PASHI (CATCH)

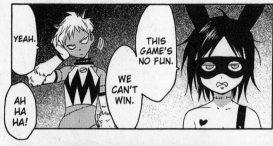

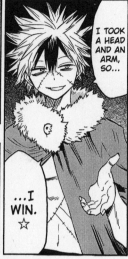

I TOOK A HEAD AND AN ARM, SO...
...I WIN. ☆
THIS GAME'S NO FUN.
YEAH.
WE CAN'T WIN.
AH HA HA!
THEN WHY DON'T WE PLAY SOMETHING ELSE?
EHH...
DON'T WORRY... THIS ONE WILL DEFINITELY BE FUN.
THE GAME'S CALLED TERRITORY BREACH!
NII (GRIN)
TERRITORY...? WHAT'S THAT MEAN?
SOUNDS LIKE FUN.
THE RULES ARE SIMPLE...
...YOU TWO GO DOWN TO THE DEMON WORLD AND FIND THE ONE IN EACH AREA CALLED THE TERRITORY BOSS...

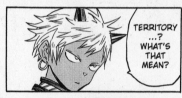

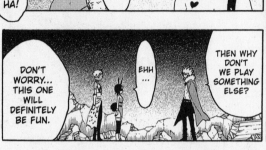

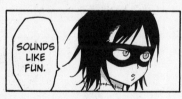

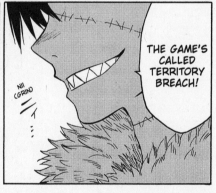

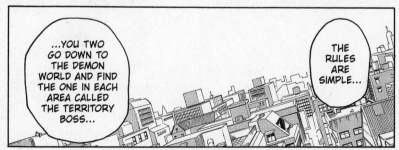

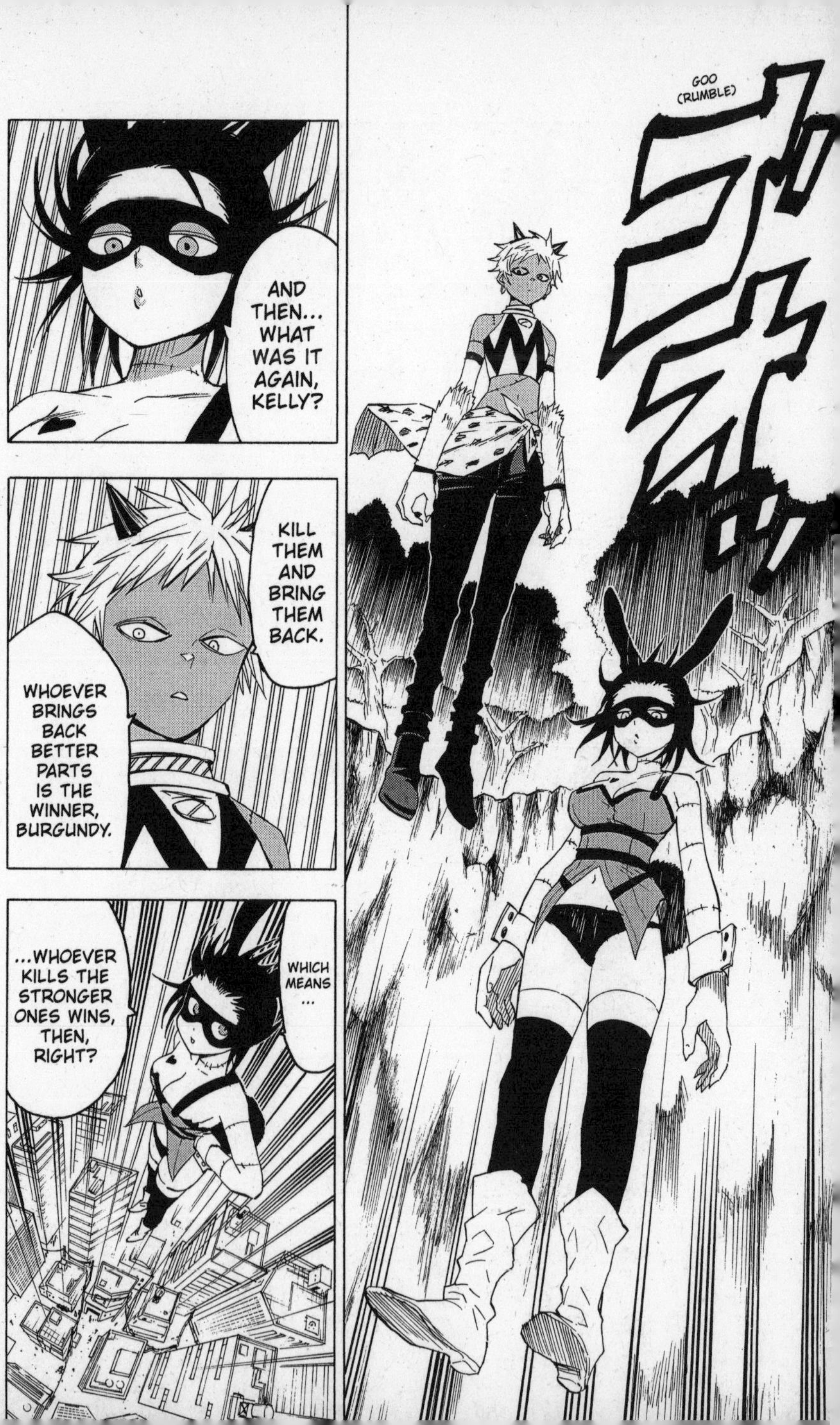
GOO (RUMBLE)
AND THEN... WHAT WAS IT AGAIN, KELLY?
KILL THEM AND BRING THEM BACK.
WHOEVER BRINGS BACK BETTER PARTS IS THE WINNER, BURGUNDY.
WHICH MEANS...
...WHOEVER KILLS THE STRONGER ONES WINS, THEN, RIGHT?

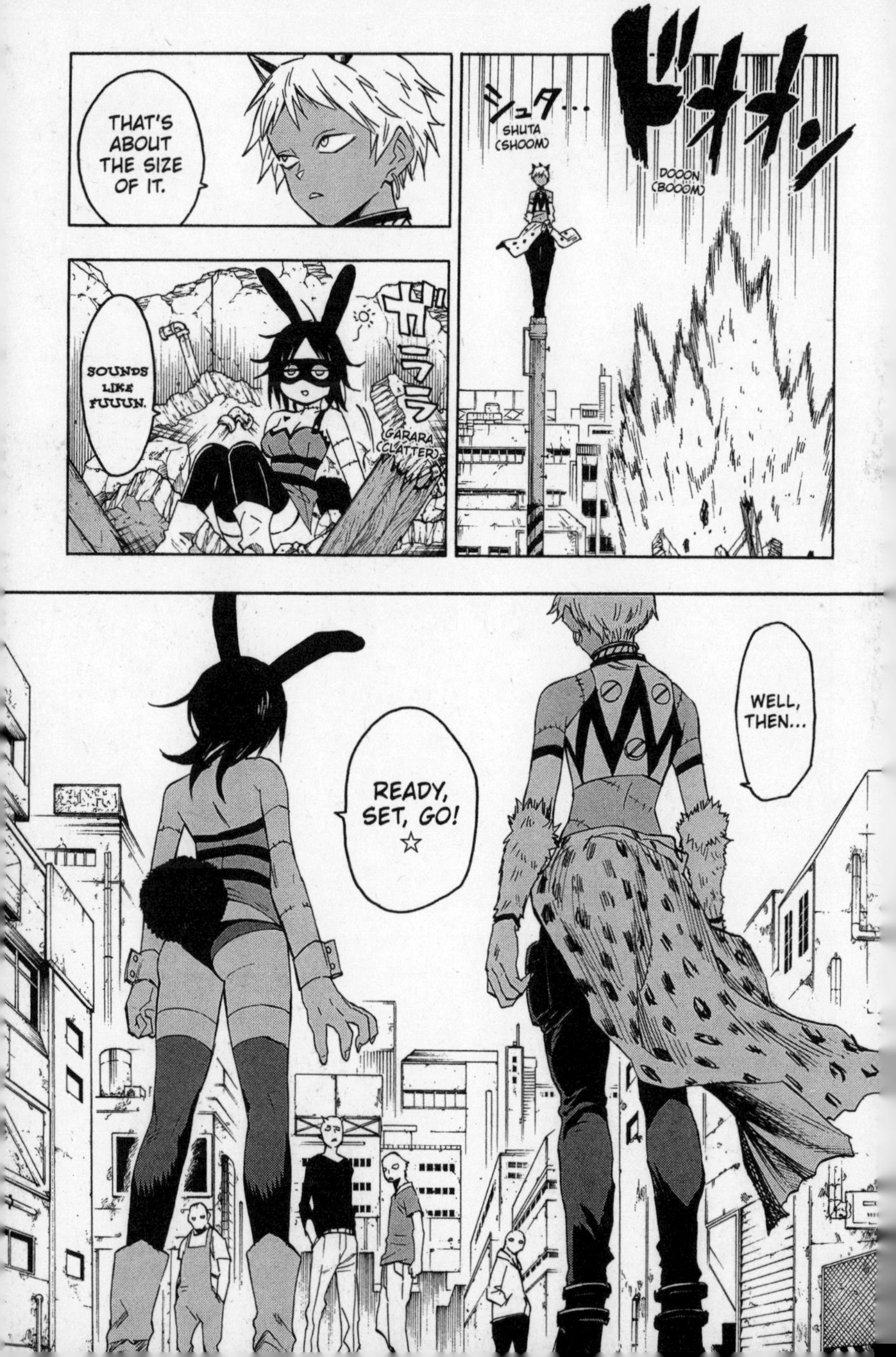
ドオオン
DOOON (BOOOM)
シュタ…
SHUTA (SHOOM)
THAT'S ABOUT THE SIZE OF IT.
ガララ
GARARA (CLATTER)
SOUNDS LIKE FUUUN.
WELL, THEN...
READY, SET, GO! ☆

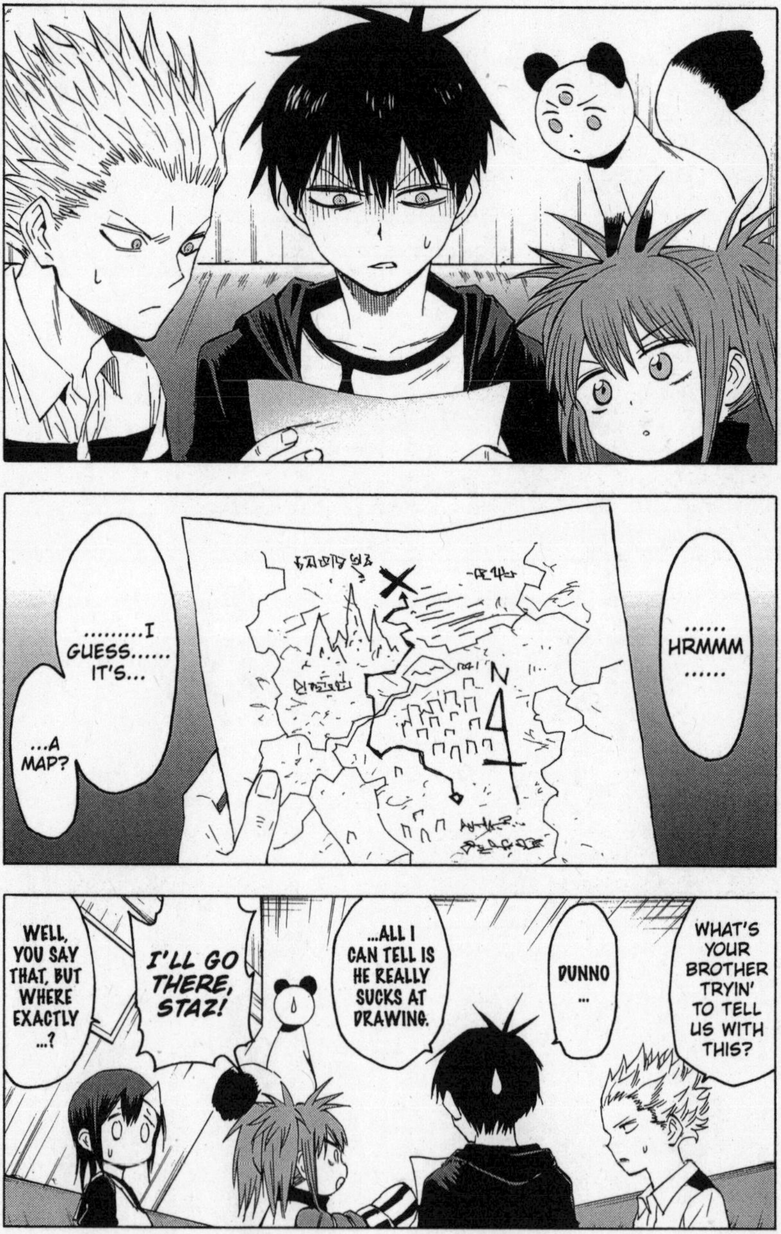
......HRMMM......
.........I GUESS...... IT'S...
...A MAP?
WHAT'S YOUR BROTHER TRYIN' TO TELL US WITH THIS?
DUNNO...
...ALL I CAN TELL IS HE REALLY SUCKS AT DRAWING.
I'LL GO THERE, STAZ!
WELL, YOU SAY THAT, BUT WHERE EXACTLY...?

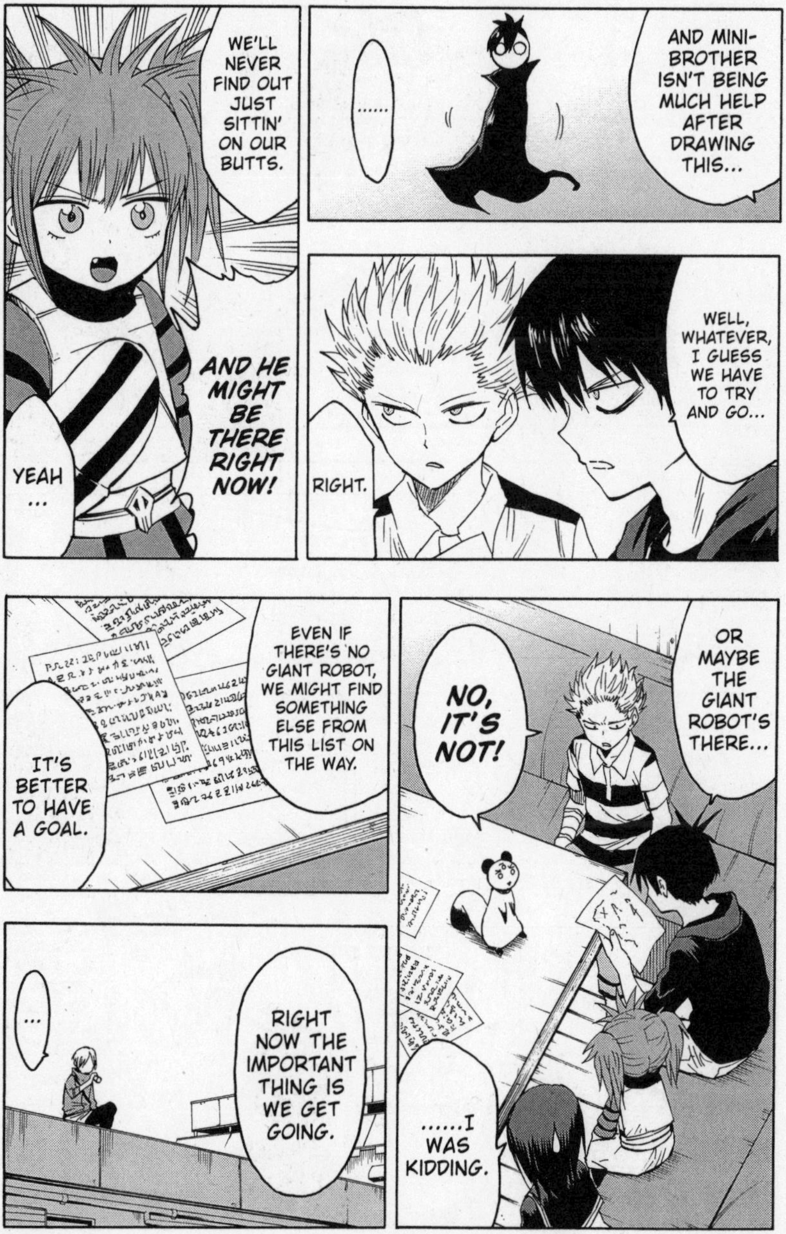
AND MINI-BROTHER ISN'T BEING MUCH HELP AFTER DRAWING THIS...
......
WELL, WHATEVER, I GUESS WE HAVE TO TRY AND GO...
RIGHT.
WE'LL NEVER FIND OUT JUST SITTIN' ON OUR BUTTS.
AND HE MIGHT BE THERE RIGHT NOW!
YEAH...
OR MAYBE THE GIANT ROBOT'S THERE...
NO, IT'S NOT!
......I WAS KIDDING.
EVEN IF THERE'S NO GIANT ROBOT, WE MIGHT FIND SOMETHING ELSE FROM THIS LIST ON THE WAY.
IT'S BETTER TO HAVE A GOAL.
RIGHT NOW THE IMPORTANT THING IS WE GET GOING.
...

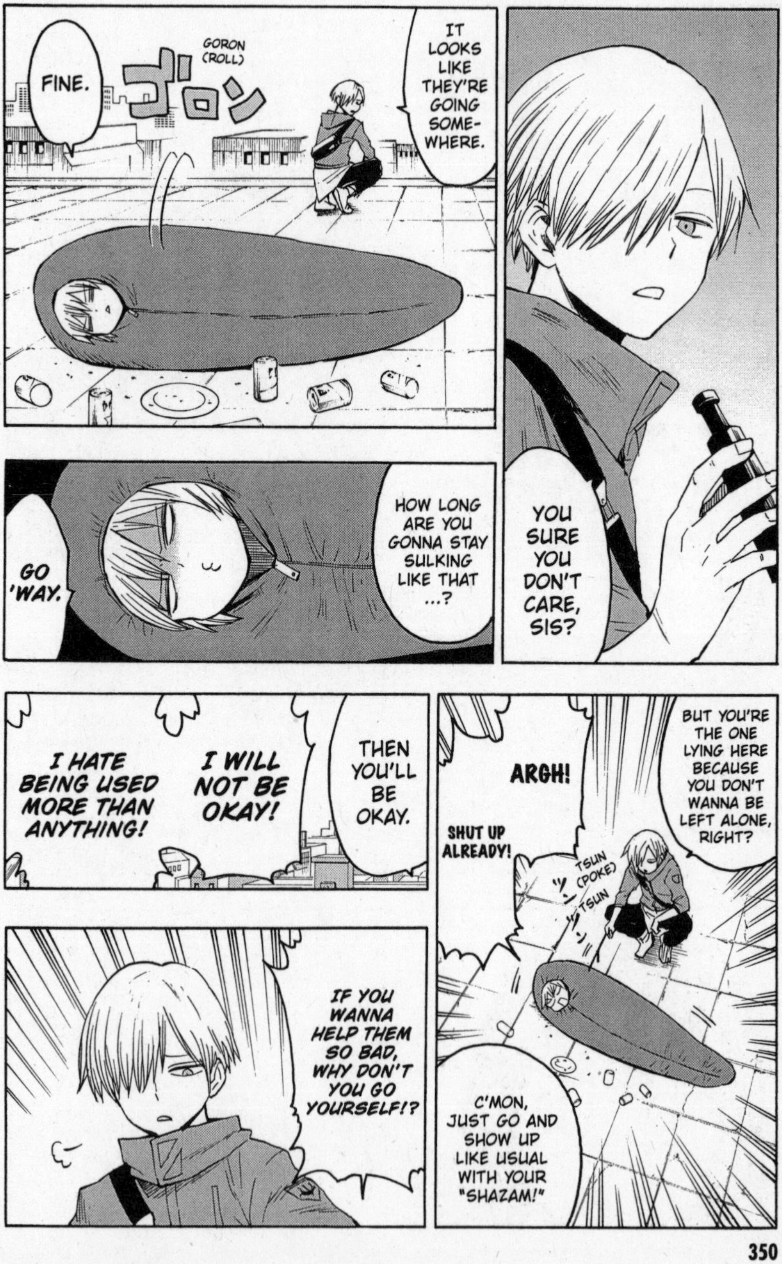
YOU SURE YOU DON'T CARE, SIS?
IT LOOKS LIKE THEY'RE GOING SOME-WHERE.
GORON (ROLL)
FINE.
HOW LONG ARE YOU GONNA STAY SULKING LIKE THAT ...?
GO 'WAY.
BUT YOU'RE THE ONE LYING HERE BECAUSE YOU DON'T WANNA BE LEFT ALONE, RIGHT?
ARGH!
SHUT UP ALREADY!
TSUN (POKE)
TSUN
C'MON, JUST GO AND SHOW UP LIKE USUAL WITH YOUR "SHAZAM!"
THEN YOU'LL BE OKAY.
I WILL NOT BE OKAY!
I HATE BEING USED MORE THAN ANYTHING!
IF YOU WANNA HELP THEM SO BAD, WHY DON'T YOU GO YOURSELF!?

SIGN: CAFÉ THIRD EYE

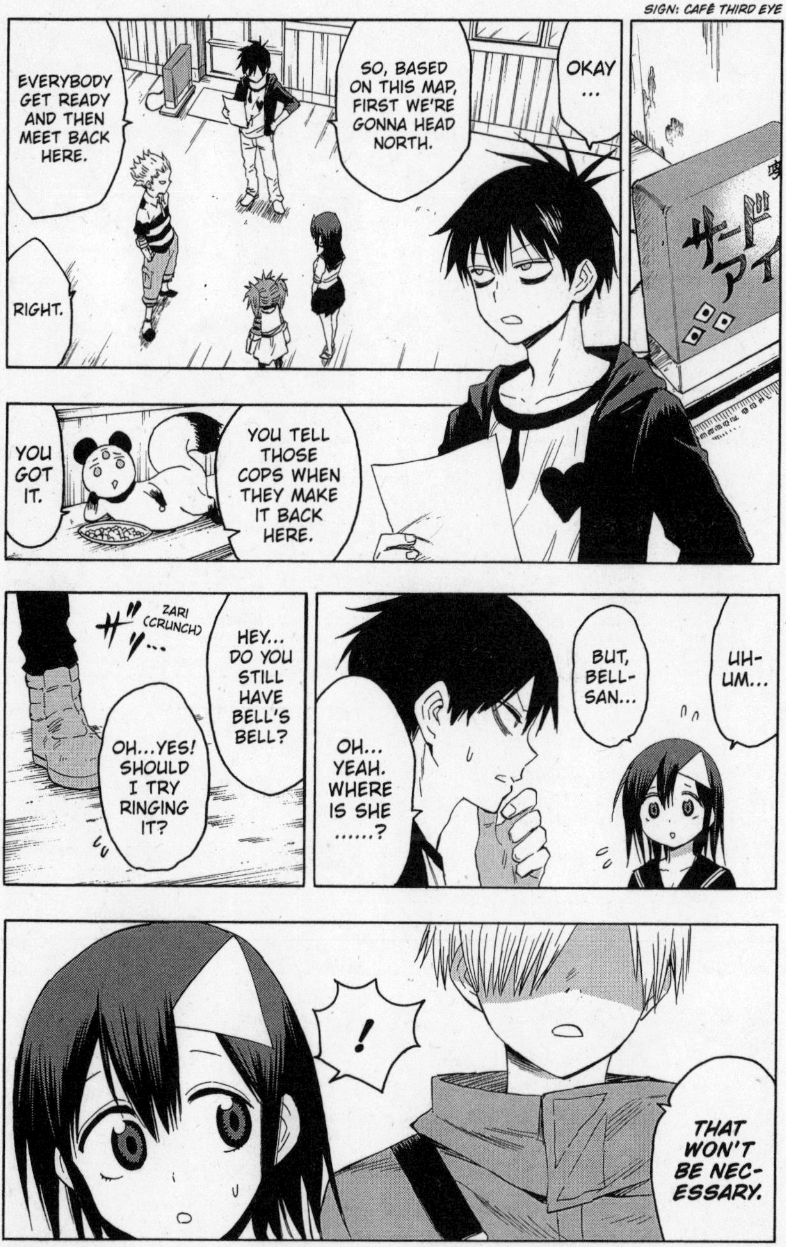
OKAY ...
SO, BASED ON THIS MAP, FIRST WE'RE GONNA HEAD NORTH.
EVERYBODY GET READY AND THEN MEET BACK HERE.
RIGHT.
YOU TELL THOSE COPS WHEN THEY MAKE IT BACK HERE.
YOU GOT IT.
UH-UM...
BUT, BELL-SAN...
OH... YEAH. WHERE IS SHE ......?
HEY... DO YOU STILL HAVE BELL'S BELL?
ZARI (CRUNCH)
OH...YES! SHOULD I TRY RINGING IT?
THAT WON'T BE NECESSARY.
!

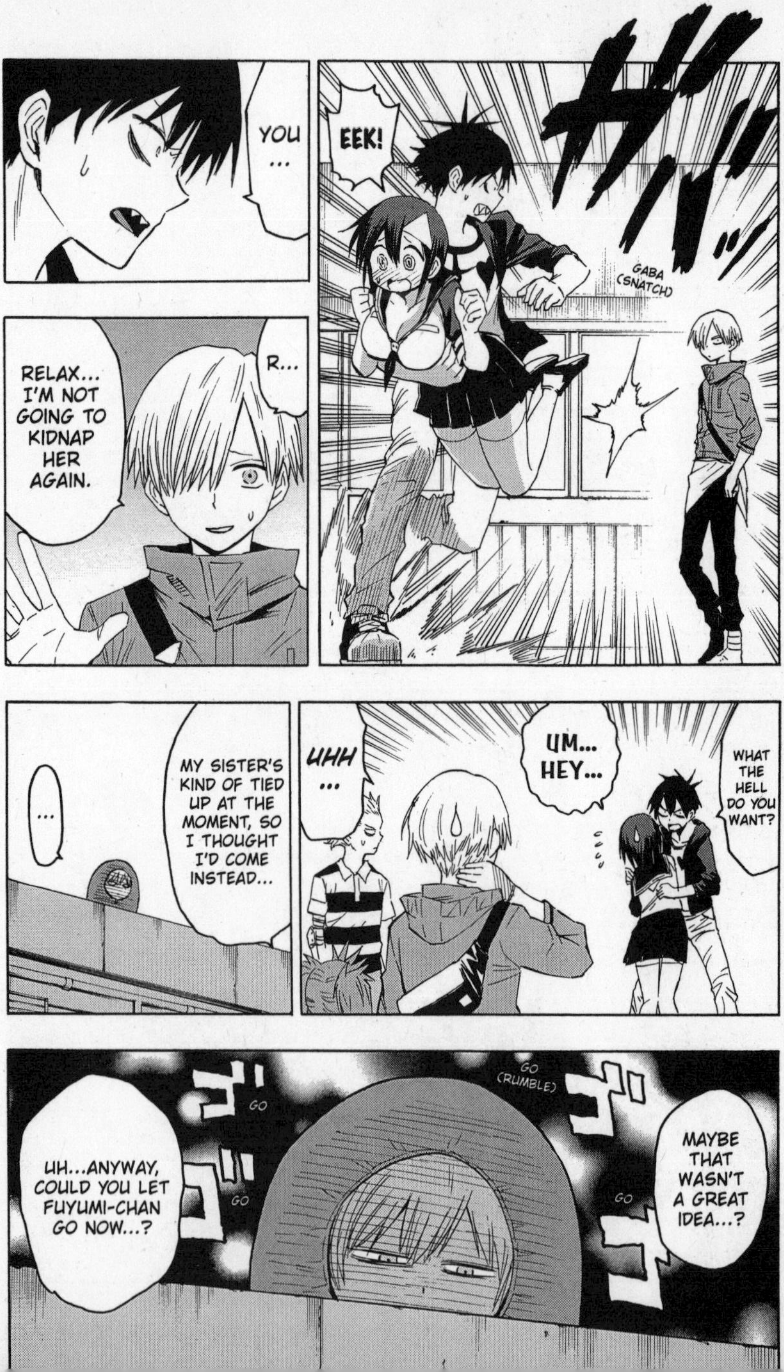
GABA (SNATCH)
EEK!
YOU ...
R...
RELAX... I'M NOT GOING TO KIDNAP HER AGAIN.
WHAT THE HELL DO YOU WANT?
UM... HEY...
UHH ...
MY SISTER'S KIND OF TIED UP AT THE MOMENT, SO I THOUGHT I'D COME INSTEAD...
...
MAYBE THAT WASN'T A GREAT IDEA...?
GO (RUMBLE)
GO
GO
GO
UH...ANYWAY, COULD YOU LET FUYUMI-CHAN GO NOW...?

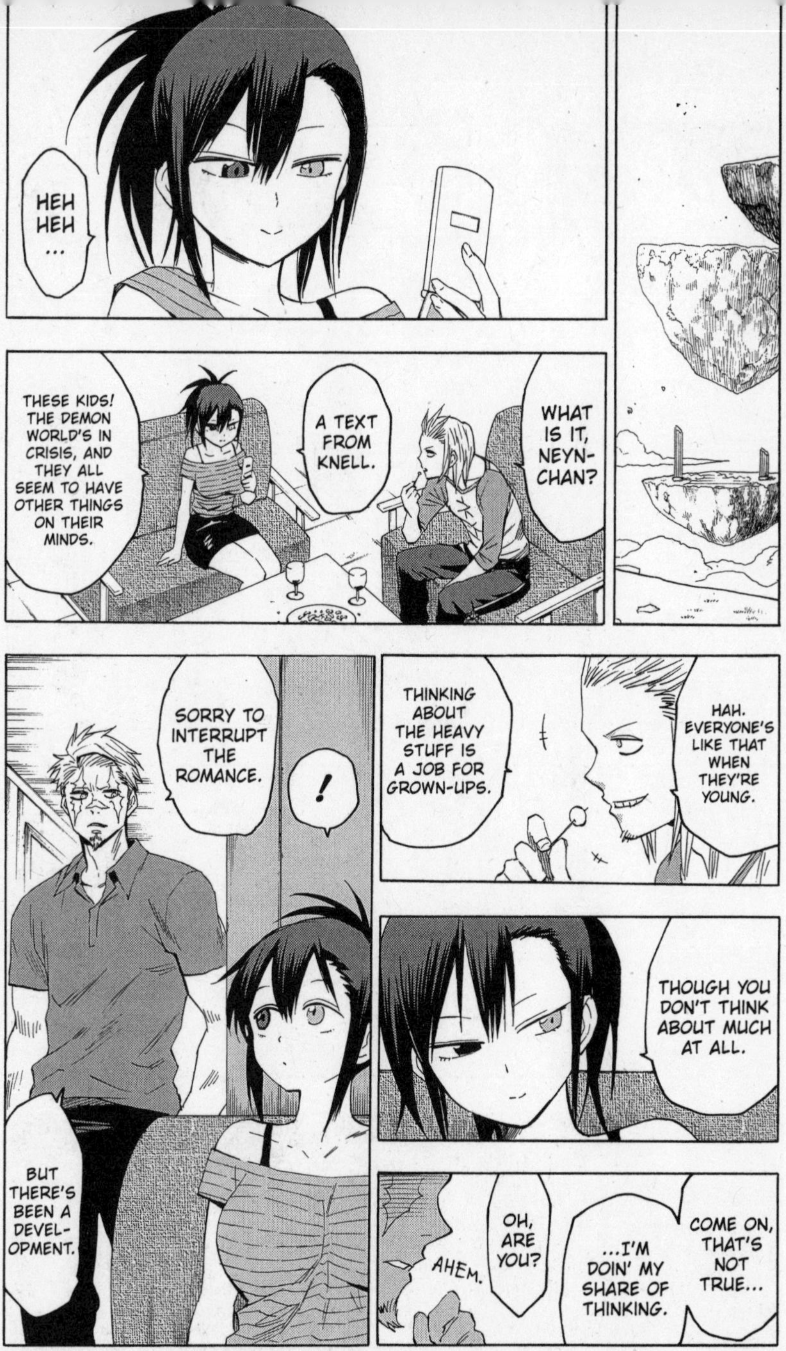
HEH HEH ...
WHAT IS IT, NEYN-CHAN?
A TEXT FROM KNELL.
THESE KIDS! THE DEMON WORLD'S IN CRISIS, AND THEY ALL SEEM TO HAVE OTHER THINGS ON THEIR MINDS.
HAH. EVERYONE'S LIKE THAT WHEN THEY'RE YOUNG.
THINKING ABOUT THE HEAVY STUFF IS A JOB FOR GROWN-UPS.
THOUGH YOU DON'T THINK ABOUT MUCH AT ALL.
COME ON, THAT'S NOT TRUE...
...I'M DOIN' MY SHARE OF THINKING.
OH, ARE YOU?
AHEM.
SORRY TO INTERRUPT THE ROMANCE.
!
BUT THERE'S BEEN A DEVELOPMENT.

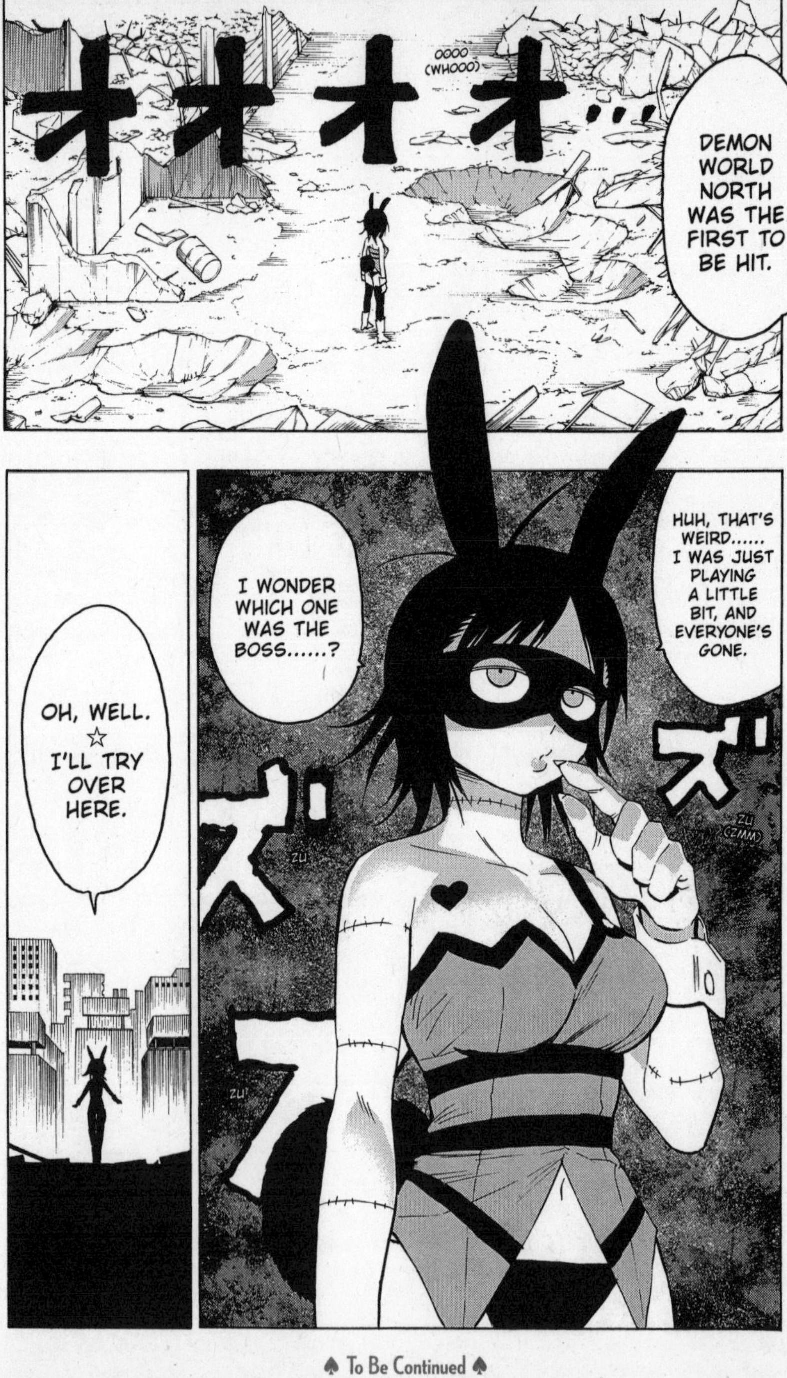
オオオオ…
OOOO (WHOOO)
DEMON WORLD NORTH WAS THE FIRST TO BE HIT.
HUH, THAT'S WEIRD...... I WAS JUST PLAYING A LITTLE BIT, AND EVERYONE'S GONE.
I WONDER WHICH ONE WAS THE BOSS......?
ズ
ZU (ZMM)
ズ
ZU
ズ
ZU
OH, WELL. ☆ I'LL TRY OVER HERE.

♠ To Be Continued ♠

GHOST **Fuyumi Yanagi**

Mp   50 /organ

BLOOD LAD

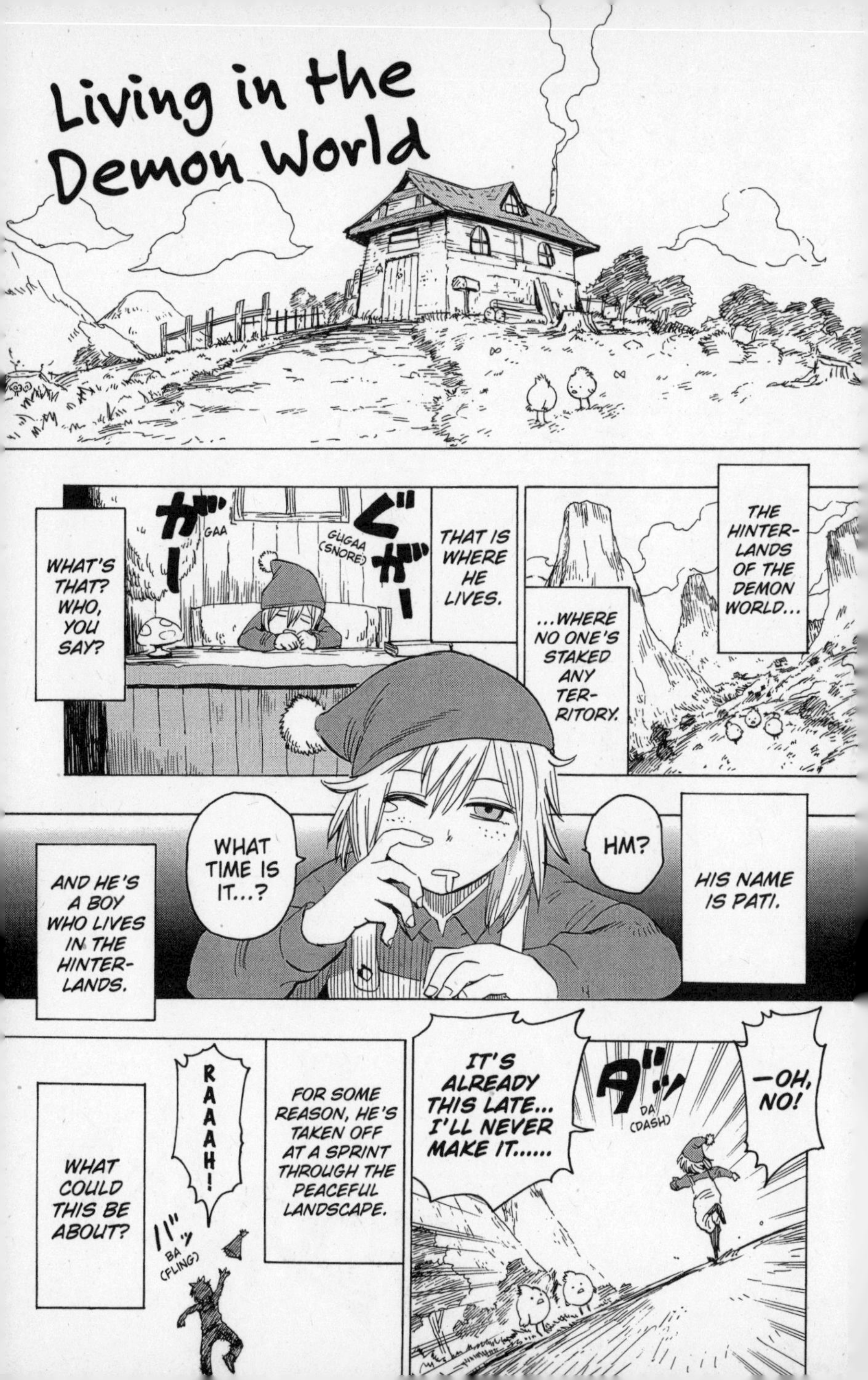
Living in the Demon World
THE HINTER-LANDS OF THE DEMON WORLD...
...WHERE NO ONE'S STAKED ANY TER-RITORY.
THAT IS WHERE HE LIVES.
GUGAA (SNORE)
GAA
WHAT'S THAT? WHO, YOU SAY?
HIS NAME IS PATI.
HM?
WHAT TIME IS IT...?
AND HE'S A BOY WHO LIVES IN THE HINTER-LANDS.
—OH, NO!
DA (DASH)
IT'S ALREADY THIS LATE... I'LL NEVER MAKE IT......
FOR SOME REASON, HE'S TAKEN OFF AT A SPRINT THROUGH THE PEACEFUL LANDSCAPE.
RAAAAH!
BA (FLING)
WHAT COULD THIS BE ABOUT?

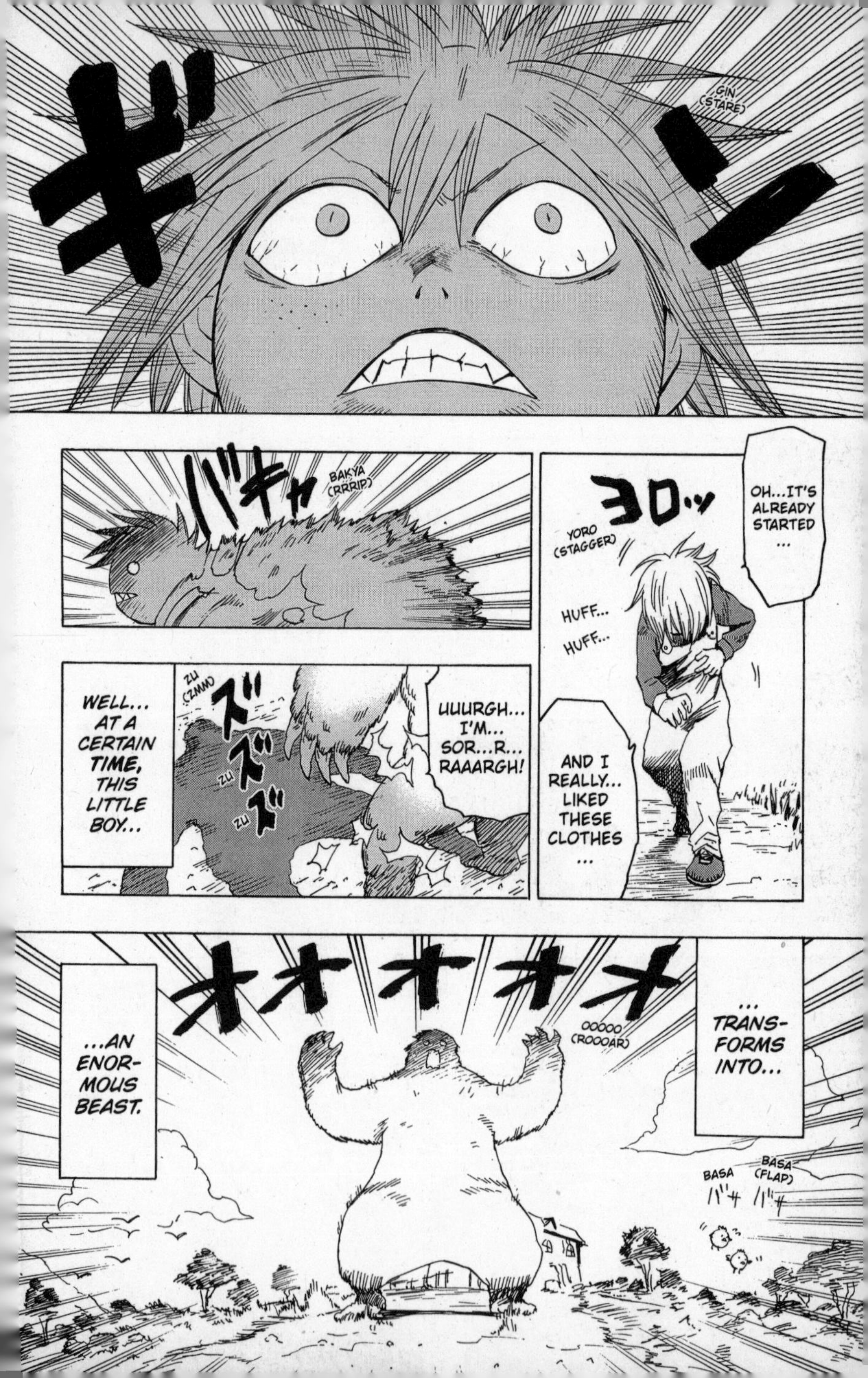
GIN (STARE)
OH...IT'S ALREADY STARTED ...
YORO (STAGGER)
HUFF... HUFF...
AND I REALLY... LIKED THESE CLOTHES ...
BAKYA (RRRIP)
UUURGH... I'M... SOR...R... RAAARGH!
ZU (ZMMM)
ZU
ZU
WELL... AT A CERTAIN TIME, THIS LITTLE BOY...
... TRANS-FORMS INTO...
OOOOO (ROOOAR)
BASA
BASA (FLAP)
...AN ENOR-MOUS BEAST.

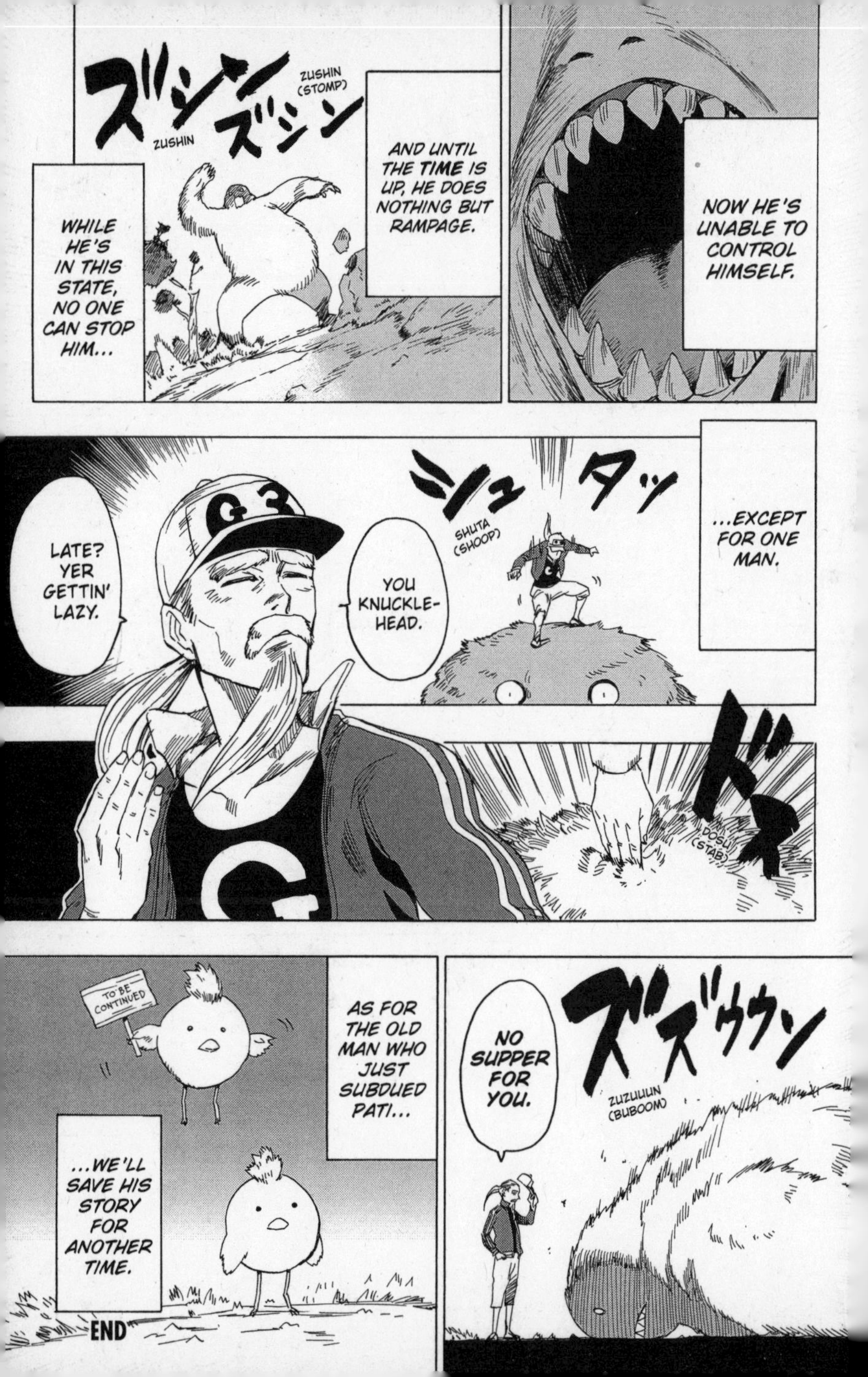
NOW HE'S UNABLE TO CONTROL HIMSELF.
AND UNTIL THE TIME IS UP, HE DOES NOTHING BUT RAMPAGE.
ZUSHIN (STOMP)
ZUSHIN
WHILE HE'S IN THIS STATE, NO ONE CAN STOP HIM...
...EXCEPT FOR ONE MAN.
SHUTA (SHOOP)
YOU KNUCKLE-HEAD.
LATE? YER GETTIN' LAZY.
DOSU (STAB)
ZUZUUUN (BUBOOM)
NO SUPPER FOR YOU.
AS FOR THE OLD MAN WHO JUST SUBDUED PATI...
TO BE CONTINUED
...WE'LL SAVE HIS STORY FOR ANOTHER TIME.
END

BLOOD LAD 10

These images appeared under the jacket of the original edition of *Blood Lad*!

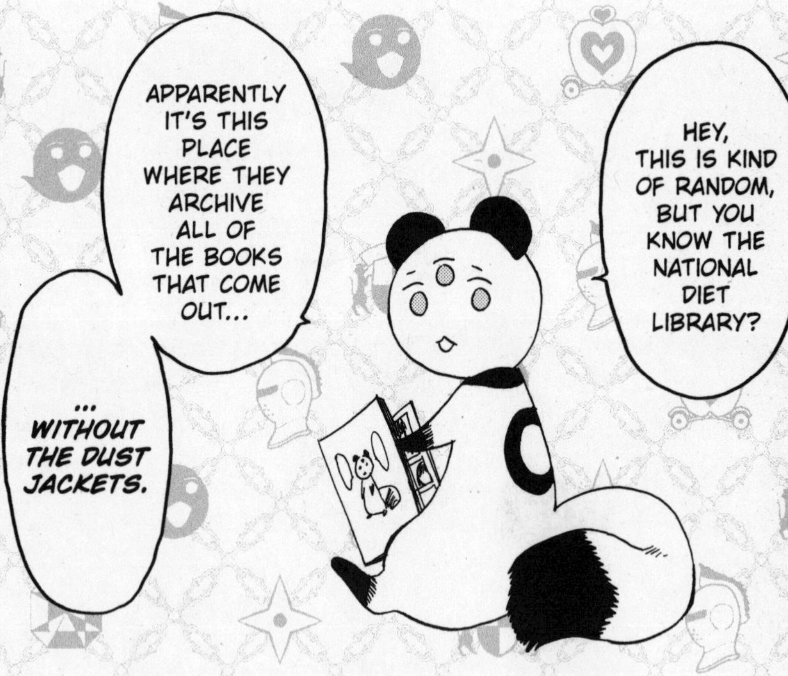
HEY, THIS IS KIND OF RANDOM, BUT YOU KNOW THE NATIONAL DIET LIBRARY?
APPARENTLY IT'S THIS PLACE WHERE THEY ARCHIVE ALL OF THE BOOKS THAT COME OUT...
...WITHOUT THE DUST JACKETS.

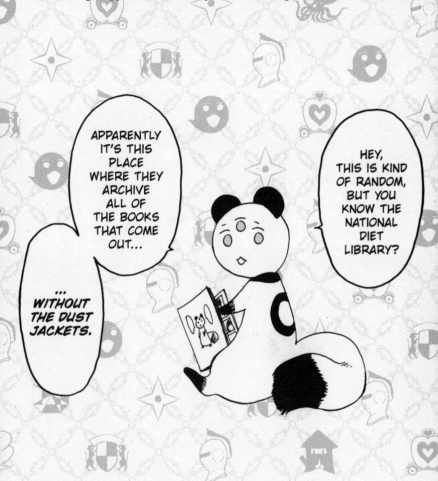

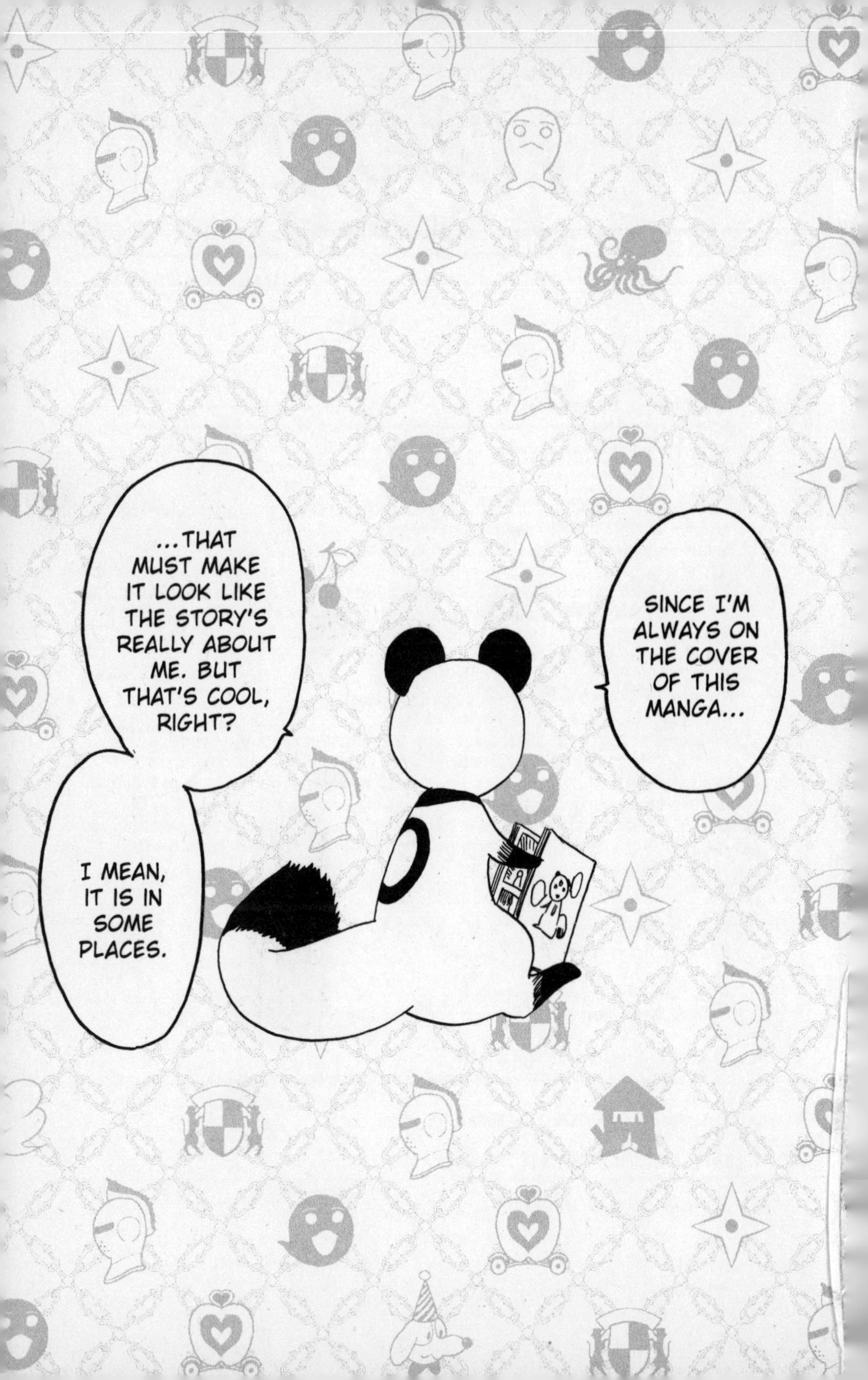
SINCE I'M ALWAYS ON THE COVER OF THIS MANGA...
...THAT MUST MAKE IT LOOK LIKE THE STORY'S REALLY ABOUT ME. BUT THAT'S COOL, RIGHT?
I MEAN, IT IS IN SOME PLACES.

BLOOD LAD ⑤

YUUKI KODAMA

Translation: Melissa Tanaka

Lettering: Alexis Eckerman

BLOOD LAD Volumes 9 and 10 © Yuuki KODAMA 2013. Edited by KADOKAWA SHOTEN. First published in Japan in 2013 by KADOKAWA CORPORATION, Tokyo. English translation rights arranged with KADOKAWA CORPORATION, Tokyo, through TUTTLE-MORI AGENCY, INC., Tokyo.

Translation © 2014 by Hachette Book Group, Inc.

Yen Press
Hachette Book Group
237 Park Avenue, New York, NY 10017

www.HachetteBookGroup.com
www.YenPress.com

Yen Press is an imprint of Hachette Book Group, Inc.
The Yen Press name and logo are trademarks of Hachette Book Group, Inc.

First Yen Press Edition: July 2014

ISBN: 978-0-316-37672-3

10 9 8 7 6 5 4 3 2 1

BVG

Printed in the United States of America